Medium High

A Novel

Bernard Buckley

ISBN: 978-0-9997875-1-9
LCCN: 2018900733

Bisonic Press
Highlands Ranch, Colorado

Visit www.BernardBuckley.US

*Dedicated to my family and friends here,
there, and everywhere.*

*Especially dedicated to
Terre, the love of my lives.*

CHAPTERS

IN THE OUT DOOR

"Your story should build your dreams. Don't let your dreams build your story."

Henry had been having the same dream so often that he decided to write these instructions on his wall directly in front of his bed. It would be the first thing he saw every morning.

Serene. Purifying. Blue sky and green grass, but without the threat of sunburn, bug bites, or allergies. There were rustic, charming buildings in which to live, fun, casual buildings in which to play, restaurants that were endlessly inviting, both in their aromas and allure, and an endless array of distractions, both inside and out, in which to play. It was like a more carnal, rewarding Disneyland.

On the outside, people awoke to the mundane: their families, their jobs, their loneliness. In this place people awoke to do precisely what they wanted. If they wanted to read a great book, they would have the finest available instantly. If they wanted to fish, a fresh pond or stream was only a short walk away. If they wanted to play music, they could perform flawlessly. If they wanted more physical pleasures, the ideal partner or partners would be eagerly available.

But for all of his satisfaction and enjoyment in prior visits, he was still a visitor. He would be expected to leave. The emptiness of this reality was the fuel that made the vision return, even more often recently. This place was where he wanted to be. Not now of course, but when the time came. For now it was out of reach because he had not earned the right. His impatience was bursting through again, and here he was, starting another day with this dream as his first waking thought.

He attempted an entry through a supernatural servant's entrance. Just as he managed to pry the door open wide enough to think about sliding through, he felt a sharp, loud palm slap to the forehead from a figure, vague and stern, its message clear.

He tried to enter by climbing a large stone wall, but the other side showed a drop into vast, unending nothingness.

He finally approached someone to ask about gaining entry. When he tapped the figure on the shoulder, it turned. He gazed into an endless void, but the figure was looking past his eyes, directly into his soul. Henry's familiarity with this entity was immediate, as he was looked upon with great affection.

His attempt this time, like all times, was futile. However, rather than a message of guilt or shame for making the attempt yet again, the message received from this mysterious, powerful figure was one of compassion and encouragement, with impatience that matched Henry's.

Despite the positive energy, he could only mumble, "Have a nice rest of your day."

It was morning again. Henry Stark sat on the edge of his bed, awake again before the alarm. This recurring process of stepping into the mundane usually started with daily questions about how to interpret his dreams which, he reminded himself in large angry letters, were not supposed to build his story.

Despite the advice, Henry Stark stalked the earth as a restless man. During his early years in foster homes and orphanages, his restive nature blossomed. He moved around from place to place so often because as he grew from a child into a teenager, he became more difficult to keep in a single place. Grades and his focus in school were not the issue as much as continually questioning where his effort was leading. He wanted a better place now, and his dreams were still a constant reminder, after all this time.

And so it would be a slog through another day as a software engineer at Blasmos, a job and company with no discernible magnetic attraction, particularly on this morning.

In northeastern Massachusetts in November, the morning light suggested a new day but invited doubt whether the sun would fully rise at all. This particular Tuesday began cloudy and cold, but the clouds were moving. Henry gazed out his window to see the trees gently bending and swaying.

One of Henry's first actions each morning was to look out the window at the unpredictable New England weather. He played the daily game of transferring the view outside his window into the makings of the day ahead. It appeared he was in for a gloomy day, breezy but dry.

He pulled running clothes from his dresser drawer and tightened his running shoes. He ran with a small pack, in which he packed three things: water, his cell phone, and a snack of some kind. Perhaps a run would allow him to sort out today's unusual combination of detachment and restlessness.

His first steps into the cool air were an instant rush, and he started with a brisk pace to generate body heat and to get his juices flowing. Almost immediately, his mind moved into reassembly mode, fitting his dreams in with the real experiences of his life to this point in an attempt to understand what was ahead. Considering the clarity and consistency of his dreams, and the truth that they seemed to be moving in the same direction, varying less with each night, some change was surely ahead.

His run through Jonathan Belcher Park, named after a colonial governor, was perfect for a morning run with one exception. The firm path that curved along small ponds and lightly wooded areas provided perfect cover for all sorts of outdoor creatures; squirrels, rabbits, and many types of birds that were hunkering down in preparation for the coming winter.

The park also provided cover for homeless people who were able to take advantage of its proximity to prosperous Boston suburbs. By day these nomads could easily walk to one of the towns, or they could even travel to Boston if they found their way onto a train. By night the park offered an assortment of shelter options.

On Henry's early morning runs, his only concern was in avoiding frightening one of the park's human inhabitants into a defensive action that might be dangerous for either of them. He kept his eyes and ears open, but let his mind decipher his uncertain place in the world.

During this run he thought back on one of his few pleasant childhood memories, a family he remembered above all the others, the Starks. They had three children of their own, two boys older than Henry and one younger girl. He longed for their companionship but learned to accept, eventually with some relief, that he would never be a part of the pecking order. Their biological sons, Carl and Max, picked on Henry in creative ways, which distracted the boys from bothering their vulnerable younger sister, Delilah. She was the only bright spot in an otherwise gloomy home life for Henry.

As an adult Henry enjoyed thinking back on Delilah's warm smile and shaggy blond curls. She was less than a year younger, and the two grew close in their brief time together. They enjoyed escaping to the basement or other hiding places to pretend they belonged to a normal family. Because the rest of the family had darker hair, Henry would try to convince Delilah that she was, like him, adopted. She played along because it made him happy. He was a bright part of her world as well.

As Henry sliced along the trails of Belcher Park, he pieced together the possibility that his attempts to find a permanent home in the cherished city of his dreams was just the result of his inability to find a permanent family. Now, after thirty-four years on the planet, not being part of something bigger was part of who he truly was. It showed in the way he moved through each day, and now as he sliced his way along the familiar trails.

The snack that he would tuck in his pack before each run depended on what his kitchen could offer. Sometimes it was unopened, directly from the grocer. Sometimes it was leftovers that he had meticulously packed to looked untouched for presentation to one of these lost, ghostly souls.

His homeless companions in the park were starting to stir in the cool, damp morning. Their mental state could not always be predicted, so he was careful to approach them in a calm, non-threatening way. He approached a younger man, probably about his age but who appeared many years older. To his relief, the man eagerly accepted his gift.

Lately the ritual left him feeling that no matter how his day would go, he had done at least one worthwhile thing. Soon it would be back to the job that he repelled more with each day.

Your story should build your dreams. Don't let your dreams build your story. His restive nature was evolving into a simmering need to change his world.

After showering he started the kettle. With his cleansing cup of morning tea in hand, he pulled up his favorite news web sites, a mix of local news and sports. He absorbed toast with almond butter, tea with lemon, political vitriol with international violence, and American football and hockey. He lurched into the twenty minute commute to his office.

His company was called Blasmos, and it created custom software for the banking industry. Henry and some coworkers had decided long ago that Blasmos, a name without root or provenance, must have been the Greek God of Apathy. A respectable office bet hung in the balance that would likely never be won.

As a few other employees meandered into the building ahead of him, he noticed the distinctive form of a fellow Programmer Analyst walking in the opposite direction toward him.

Lenny Carsher was a heavy man a few years older than Henry. Colleagues considered him a very talented developer, but from their conversations he had no social life and no family that he spoke of. He spent most of his time outside Blasmos in online gaming. His demeanor alternated between too playful and too serious, with an occasional burst of laughter over things others did not find as funny.

Apart from the odd sight of Lenny, or any employee, walking out of the building at 8:15 am, there was something very different about him, a lightness in his heavy frame as he walked, a carefree attitude that made Henry smile as he approached his colleague.

"Lenny, what's up? I think you're headed in the wrong direction."

Lenny paused. His cherubic, bearded face turned serious as he locked Henry's eyes. "Oh trust me, Henry, I'm headed in the right direction. You're the one who should think about turning around."

Henry looked at him curiously, smiling, expecting more. Instead his friend whistled past. He turned back with one last comment. "There's nothing for you in there, Henry."

Henry shrugged and continued on his way into Blasmos.

The front desk was vacant, another abnormality that slightly alarmed Henry. Normally there was someone from the security agency watching the front desk during the busy hours in the morning as employees badged into the building.

He moved through the security area and down a corridor to the vast space occupied by row after row of cubicles.

On a normal day he would hear the buzz of employees chattering and keyboards clacking, but today it was nearly silent, except for a few voices rising above a hush. The sound of an ambulance was heard in the distance.

Henry saw a crowd gathered, including many of his closest acquaintances. He moved quickly toward the crowd, his concern growing as no one noticed his approach. The normal occupants of the cubicles and offices were consumed with something urgent. He approached a woman he knew He tapped her on the shoulder.

"What's happening?"

"Someone collapsed. It must be serious because he's not getting up. Paramedics are on the way."

He considered moving through the crowd to find out if it was someone close to him, but instead moved around to his desk to drop off his bag. From there he kept moving to the outside of the throng to where he saw a gap, which might allow him to see what was happening. A familiar coworker was nearby. Elaine Santangelo was a woman a few years older than Henry with a dry wit and a long-time smoking habit. She always had something to say.

"Elaine, good morning. What's happening?"

"Hi Henry. Not off to a good start this morning. Man down."

"I heard. Who is it?"

"Lenny. He was coming back from the break room and staggered, grabbed his chest and just sort of fell over. It has to be a heart attack. They're trying CPR."

"What? I just saw him out front!"

"Yeah," she said, "it happens fast."

Henry went through a lightheaded moment, grounded in something surreal. There had to be a mistake.

A young man named Devin Hogan was leaning over the large person lying prone on the floor. While he rhythmically moved the palms of both hands into the chest of the man, the look on his face was one of terror. Each person in the crowd leaned anxiously over, waiting for some response from the large man on the floor.

Henry moved a few feet closer to see who Elaine had mistaken for their friend Lenny. It was indeed Lenny Carsher, wearing the same clothes Henry saw him walking in three minutes before.

How could it be? Was he still partially in a dream?

Henry moved back next to Elaine. "That's impossible. I just saw him."

Elaine said nothing, instead raising a hand to rub Henry's shoulder.

Paramedics split the crowd, telling the group to disperse. Henry, Elaine and the others moved away from the scene, most staying in smaller groups and mumbling quietly.

Henry walked unsteadily back toward his desk, wanting no contact with anyone. He was not one to spend time chattering about typical office gossip, and now he was questioning his own perceptions. He needed time to think.

He flipped on his monitor, logged in to his account, and clicked the icon for email. His inbox showed a mass of new messages that would pull him deeply into a normal work day. But this was far from a regular work day. He could not imagine what would make it so. He continued to glance toward the paramedics and the small group of work colleagues that remained. Nothing in their gestures indicated that Lenny would return.

During those few minutes, he was not grieving his friend Lenny. He was soberly considering the direction of his life.

Could he even trust his senses, what he saw and heard just a few minutes earlier? Was Lenny's apparition in front of the building something he had concocted?

With his monitor off and his eyes staring at a blank space in his cubicle wall, he decided that it was really Lenny, and moment had great meaning for him personally. Further, he felt some relief that he came to work at the exact time he did. If not, he may have missed a valuable message.

He walked toward his boss's office. Brad Clifton's chair was empty, and Henry glanced over and saw him standing among the smaller crowd near the paramedics. He walked over just as the last attempts at CPR were complete.

The paramedics mumbled, scribbling onto a clipboard, then began the process of moving Lenny's body onto a stretcher. Their pace and demeanor was considerably more relaxed than just a few seconds earlier.

Brad's expression was blank. As Henry approached him, he did not respond to his presence. Now was not the time to bother his boss.

He walked back to his cubicle, turned on the computer, and typed a message.

"Brad, I'd like to go home for the day. I'll call tomorrow if I won't make it in."

He gathered his things and headed back out to the parking lot. Along the way, he could not resist looking for Lenny hiding in the bushes or behind cars. There was no reappearance.

Henry spent the day at home, alternating between restlessness and mental exhaustion. When the weariness took over, he lounged on his couch watching old movies. When restless he would raid snacks in the kitchen, or find internet porn that distracted him, if even for a short time. He would scan through the turbulent global news, only to find it too disturbing and violent to keep his attention.

He spent the evening alone in his apartment with just a bottle of wine and his thoughts.

He dissected the meaning from Lenny again and again. Was there more to it than what his friend had succinctly said?

"There's nothing for you in there, Henry."

The message was that a change was needed in Henry's life. He needed to put Blasmos behind him as quickly as possible. Lenny's voice was as clear in his mind as when he had heard it hours before.

He picked up the phone and dialed the main line for Blasmos, and routed his call to Brad Clifton. He hoped that Brad was not still in the office at this late hour, and he was relieved when the call went to voicemail.

"Brad, this is Henry. Today was tough on everyone, probably especially for you. Listen, I've been thinking all day about the direction of my life, and this is not it. I won't be in tomorrow, or the day after that. I just need a fresh start. I'll prepare a letter of resignation in the morning, but I wanted to have you hear this first. Just so you know, my decision isn't being made out of grief or shock. It's something I have to do. Thanks, and call me if you need to."

As the evening wore on and the bottle wore down, he explored the sense of detachment before that he felt but didn't really understand. After making the phone call to Brad, it began to solidify. It really meant that he was attached to something that he should not have been; a conventional life, a regular job, a good paycheck, but with no one to share it with. Hence there was no satisfaction, so why maintain the attachment to such a life?

Now that he had decided on a new direction for his life, the detachment just *felt right*.

As his interest in the last movie of the day waned and he was able to form what was probably his last odd thoughts in this very, very odd day, he intentionally wondered about what was ahead. Better days were surely ahead, but it would not be without a struggle.

He took a long look around his apartment, with the reality that he had nowhere else to go the next morning.

His last waking thought was that he would look back on the events of the last few days with confidence that things turned out exactly the way they were meant to.

For the second night in a row Henry had a dream that was very vivid and much longer than most. The sky was bluer than any he could remember. The smell of fresh grass permeated his senses. A soft breeze blew through him and around him, absorbing him as a welcome guest. But this time there was difference: he had company. Not discernible as a male or female, this companion was clearly there to support and guide. It was a graceful, familiar presence that he welcomed as he explored and observed things that were new to him.

As with the prior night's visit, he watched from a distance as people played together, stared into each other's eyes, talked quietly, and enjoyed whatever activity urged them on. Scattered across the countryside, in the small shops, on benches, in playgrounds, picnicking on the grass, clusters of people were all around in a cohesive community. Some of the groups were together for what appeared to be the first time, while others had been reunited after long absences. The common thread with all here was peace, and an appreciation for being with the ones they wanted to be with in the place they wanted to be.

Occasionally there were only two people together. The couples were evidently lovers or spouses, but he did not understand variations from the norm. When three were together, could they be siblings? Was it some unusual romantic attachment, such as spouses from different marriages?

His confusion reinforced that he was only an observer, not entitled to any deep kind of understanding just yet. He felt a mild frustration brewing with his thin depth of knowledge of how things operated here, to the point where his guide noticed the change and reminded him to slow down and enjoy the chance to be here. He followed the advice, and turned it into a determination that someday he would have a deep and profound understanding of all of this place.

Henry glided for what seemed like an hour or more, but was surely just a few minutes. Everywhere he traveled he sensed peaceful feelings from people who were settled and happily a part of this place. These people were attached.

Henry wanted desperately to stay, but his companion convinced him without speaking that he had worn out his welcome.

The dream faded.

Henry awoke the next morning out of habit at the time his alarm clock usually sounded, this morning a little groggy from the wine. It took him a few moments to realize why his alarm did not go off, that the events of the prior day were not some strange dream.

Staring out an another gloomy, drippy Northeastern day, he decided that one night was enough to exhaust his supply of self-pity. There was no need for regrets or nostalgia. It was time to move on to more productive pursuits.

With great care and in no rush, he measured out the ideal amount of coffee and just a hint of nutmeg and cinnamon to produce a thick, spiced pot of coffee, one of the best he had made in a long time. He smiled with satisfaction at his success, even reminding himself that taking the extra time could make all the difference in the end product. It was an approach he would try more often.

He pulled up the Boston Globe online and moved toward the kitchen nook in his apartment with deliberateness and ease. After reading through the day's grimness for close to an hour, he glanced through the Employment section.

He read methodically through the advertisements, scanning through a few that resembled his prior job. Thinking he would find order and purpose in sticking closer to his routine, he made the executive decision to shower and dress in the normal way. In that way, inspiration for this new challenge would surely come. Even at Blasmos, productivity followed procrastination, and it was all part of his routine.

After showering and dressing the same as normal, jeans and a dress shirt, but this time accentuated with his favorite slippers, Spider Man in size eleven, he decided to try some of the employment-only sites. He skimmed through many, finding a few that were nearly a perfect match for his technical skills. But with each of these job descriptions he found himself basing its appeal on how different it would be from Blasmos.

Finally the truth came to him. He would not go back to a similar situation. He could not erase the visual image of Lenny Carsher reaching the end of his journey, lifeless on the office floor.

Henry looked deep into his own eyes in the bathroom mirror. In a dizzying moment, he remembered his dream from the past two nights in vivid detail. It was paradise. The weather was perfect, there was no conflict, people sincerely wanted to be there, and the place welcomed each and every one of them. He was being pulled in a specific direction, but where it would lead was impossible to know.

He knew that people build up defenses during the waking hours to conceal the things they worry about. The dreams they conjure up in a sleep state probably represent the individual in its truest form. The insecurities reappear, but often they are disguised or softened to allow the psyche to contend with them properly.

Trudging through life as a programmer created a numbing effect, a sort of anesthetic that his brain had devised to conceal the dream, but it was like plywood over a broken window. Eventually his future would have to emerge.

His had to leave Blasmos.

But what specifically was he to make of the dream? He saw people together in couples are larger groups but happy, depending on each other while in a state of refreshment and reinvigoration. Perhaps the end state he was meant to achieve was helping people achieve this level of bliss.

There was no way to know what position could possibly fulfill that goal, but as his thick coffee kicked in on this dreary November morning in New England, life was a wide-open book and he was the author. Finding the right job would be the challenge. With his passion for starting something exciting and incredible, landing the job would be the easy part.

In a caffeine-fueled hurry, he tried the most popular of the Boston career sites. He entered a few search terms around the idea of partnership, collaboration, team building, and matching. There were a few positions that mostly were consulting and sales in the IT world, not too different from his old life. He skimmed past each, uninspired.

As he scoured page after page, all were professionally done, slick with the most current buzzwords that were meant to put life into jobs that were inanimate, no more alive than a mannequin. He continually imagined the person writing it, a recruiter or staff manager trying to write a job description more clever and appealing than all the rest.

Near the bottom of the listings one stood out. It was less polished, with no graphics and no attempt to sound trendy. This hiring manager was looking for a different candidate.

DATING SERVICE TECHNICAL PROFESSIONAL. Use your online skills to help those looking for companionship. People need people and you can help them find each other. Kind heart required, great people skills helpful. Complete your life with one call. 617-555-0897.

He clicked through to the full entry and there was not much more, other than a salary that was a little more than half what he was making at Blasmos, plus incentives.

Henry read the ad twice, then a third time. *"Use your online skills to help those looking for companionship. People need people and you can help them find each other."*

The words burned into his brain. This appeared to be the one, a perfect bridge opportunity from his old life that relied on technical skill but little else, to a new life that required humanity. This could be the perfect next step. He called the number

"Finders Keepers," the woman's voice proclaimed. "How may I help you?"

"Yes," Henry said. "I'd like to inquire about the ad for a Dating Service Professional."

After a short hold, a man named Ryan came on the line. "Hello, how can I help you today?"

Henry began, "Yes, my name is Henry Stark. I was calling about the want ad for 'Dating Service Technical Professional.' Is the position still open?"

"It is indeed. What makes you interested in this kind of job?"

"Well I worked for few years as a software developer, which was challenging, but the personal interactions were somewhat … lacking. The only part of the job I enjoyed was connecting people who needed something they needed. It might not sound like there's much in common, but this job seems to give me just what I was missing before.

"I see," Ryan said without displaying any excitement in the candidate. "Do you have any experience in the dating business?"

"None. Except for dates I've had on my own. I've had lots and lots of them, so I have some perspective of the dating mentality."

Ryan hesitated before asking, "So you've dated a lot. Have any of your dates ended up happily?"

"Oh a few," Henry answered. "It's hit or miss. Usually it's me that misses, not 'the miss.'"

"You don't sound like you're very good at this dating thing," Ryan said dryly.

"Well that depends on your perspective. From my point of view, I haven't been ready to settle down with anyone. I haven't wasted anyone's time, any more than absolutely necessary, so to that extent I've been pretty effective. Then again I'm not a great candidate for settling down, so I don't think I should have done anything differently.

"I'm not doing a very good job of selling myself," Henry said. "Do you think we're talking about the same skill set?"

"Maybe," Ryan paused. "It sounds like you're calling for the right reasons.

Ryan invited Henry in for an in-person interview the next morning.

The office was sparsely furnished, with just enough amenities to allow employees to enjoy modest comfort, but not enough to distract them from their only purpose: to be on the phones for every possible second. The newer, more stylish areas were reserved for the entertainment of clients, and these rooms were unambiguously - but discreetly - divided from the outbound phone calling areas.

Henry's first impression walking through the door was that he would be depressed if he were not offered this position. The job rewarded communication skills, persistence, and at least a modest hunger to earn money. Henry felt more than adequate on all counts.

Near the end of the interview, Ryan was clearly struggling with a question that needed to be asked. Henry gently coaxed it out of him.

"Am I right to assume your experience in technology means that you're pretty good with trouble-shooting computer systems?"

Henry was relieved. "Yeah, I picked up a lot along the way. Why do you ask?"

"Because our computer setup makes me want to burn my eyeballs out with a soldering iron."

"I think I can help you with that too," Henry said with a smile.

As expected, Ryan offered him the position at the close of the interview. Henry agreed, and promised to be ready to go in the morning.

Henry was excited for the official start of his new career. He learned all about the company's web site, including how to set up individual postings for his clients and tips on searching for just the right companion. He also learned how to operate the equipment, especially videotaping and uploading the movies, which were typically only about two minutes long. Along the way he took notes of technical problems that needed correcting, and little programs he could create to automate some of their manual tasks.

At its core, Henry's job involved calling candidates who had expressed interest in the service to try to persuade them to sign up. It was explained that leads came in two forms: through the company's marketing efforts, in which customers responded online to their ads by providing enough information to be contacted or through "cold call" efforts using phone numbers that interested customers provided, or which were provided by database listing services. The phone lists were slightly better than taking numbers from the phone book because they were purchased based on what they believed to be their target demographic, single people between 28 and 54.

After receiving a few pointers from Ryan on phone technique, Henry was ready to begin making calls. Ryan provided a script, strongly suggested that Henry stick with it as closely as possible.

Henry nervously picked up the phone and dialed the first number. Disconnected. He crossed that off the list and moved on to the next. It rang and rang and rang. He marked that lead 'NA' in the margin for 'no answer' and moved on. He tried again. It rang twice before someone answered.

"Szervusz," the faint female voice said.

"Uh, hello my name is Henry and I'm calling from Finders Keepers, a local company providing matchmaking services to Boston-area singles. Am I speaking with … Kata Pantichin…?"

"En vagyok Kata Pantichin," the woman replied.

"Do you speak English?" Henry spoke slowly.

"Te ezt nem érted," the woman sounded forlorn.

"I'm sorry I can't speak your language, Mrs. Pantichin. Good bye."

"Végtelenül sajnálom. Búcsú."

Henry had no idea what language the woman was speaking, and he moved on to the next number, quietly hoping Kata Pantichin would not show up the next day expecting to move in.

Of his next five calls, one was disconnected, one rang and rang, and three went to a voice mailbox. Finally there was a human response in English.

"Hello," a man's voice answered, deep and gravelly.

"Hello sir, my name is Henry and I'm calling from Finders Keepers. We're a service that provides all the necessary resources that have helped many, many single people find the perfect companion. Am I speaking with Mr. Thomas Simmons?"

"Yeah, this is him. So you guys are matchmakers?"

"Uh, yes sir, I suppose you could call it that. In fact we use all the latest technological tools to help get your story told to help you find that perfect someone. This assumes, of course, that you're single and interested in finding a significant other. Is that true in your case, Mr. Simmons?"

"Yeah, I'm single. I guess I'm interested in finding the right person but it depends on what it costs, and whether it works."

"Well, sir, we can't guarantee that we'll find someone perfect for every one of our customers, but we have over forty-thousand people in our database in this area, and we try to make it easy for our customers to sign up. We charge a fee up front to get your image and your story onto our listings, then we charge you when a date is agreed upon mutually."

Henry was encouraged, determined to make the most of the call.

"Well I'm not so sure I can find the right person on your listings, or that they'll find me. How much is the up-front fee?"

"Mr. Simmons, the standard fee is 299 dollars, and that buys you a two minute video listing for up to one year. We also offer lower-priced packages if you're not interested in a video, or in no picture at all. Then we charge 49.99 for each contact that is successfully made, usually in the form of a date that we arrange. As for your concern about not finding the right person, Mr. Simmons, I can assure you that we've created matches for hundreds of people."

There was a pause before the prospect continued. "Yeah but I'm looking for something very specific in a companion. I'd prefer it to be a woman that's financially independent. Maybe somebody that own a business of her own."

"Okay, I think I understand," Henry wrote while he talked. "You'd like a professional woman, maybe an entrepreneur."

"Yeah, an entrepreneur. But it's best if she owns something like a liquor store or a cigar shop or betting parlor, or something like that. A liquor store would be the best."

The motivations of Thomas Simmons were becoming clear. "Can you give me your age and occupation?"

"I'm 38 and unemployed. Before I spent some time away taking care of a sick friend I was, um, away for a couple years. Before that I worked in a liquor store, so I know them really well. So I guess you could say I'm between positions at the present time."

Henry's hopes for this call resulting in anything productive were now completely dry. "Well, there's always a chance you'll find the right match. Can we interest you in signing up for some level of our services?"

Gravel guy answered with a question. "Can you get me on your service for under twenty bucks?"

"No I'm sorry sir, the lowest priced package we have is a three month commitment at $17.99 per month, but that would need to be paid in advance."

"Nah, I'm not interested." Click.

The rest of his afternoon produced more of the same. As he began to lose energy, he summoned energy for the coming days by considering this one a pure learning experience.

Over the next few days, Henry's phone technique became efficient and effective. He learned to see quickly through customers who were not worth investing time, and in having the intuition to say just the right thing to customers who were on the fence.

Although he was unsure where this road would take him or how long he would travel it, it seemed to offer a promising bridge to the future.

Alice Martinez sat in the same waiting area that Henry saw for the first time only a couple months before. An older dark-haired man was the only other person in the small room, sitting patiently to the right of Alice and looking contentedly around the room.

Henry heard the door open from his cubicle down the hall. He was expecting her. He finished his notes and came to greet her.

"Hi, I'm Henry. Are you Alice?"

She blinked and blushed and held out her hand awkwardly. "Yes. Nice to meet you."

"Alice, thanks so much for coming in. Why don't you come this way and we'll get you set up." Alice moved timidly toward the back offices.

Henry followed her through the inner door but first looked back toward the man waiting. "Someone will be with you shortly, sir." The man looked up and nodded and smiled. She craned her neck back toward the waiting area curiously, then kept walking toward the conference room.

When they were both seated Henry began the interview process. "Alice, I understand this isn't something you've done before and I really appreciate that you came in. I plan to have you walk out of here feeling really good about this decision. Can I get you some coffee?"

"Yes, thanks. A little sugar please, no cream." Alice was short with dark features, a full build, pale complexion and dark hair. She looked to Henry to be in her late twenties, with an attractive face that was wise beyond her years. She was guarded, as if she had been through some difficult times.

Henry opened the shades to give his client a view of a beautiful late winter day in Massachusetts and left the room. When he passed the waiting area he noticed that the older man was no longer there. Henry never heard the front door open or close.

He returned breezily into the room with a cup of coffee for Alice in one hand, his briefcase in the other. He learned that the way he carried himself, showing some urgency with a new client, along with efficiency of time and motion, were great assets in making customers feel comfortable with their decision to work with Finders Keepers. When meeting new clients he tried to avoid leaving them alone for more than just a few seconds, because given extra time to think, some would lose their courage and decide to leave. He packed his briefcase meticulously so that it contained everything he would need to get through an interview.

"So Alice," Henry began, "we start this process by going through a questionnaire that takes about fifteen minutes or so. When I ask the questions, your honest answers will provide a really good personal profile of you and what kind of person you might be compatible with. The key word is 'essence.' If we've captured your essence for potential matches, then it's a lot more likely you'll find someone to create a future together."

Alice smiled. "So far so good. I'll give you honest answers. When will I get to see my video? What if I hate the way I look?"

"You'll see it before you leave. We work fast. If you hate it we'll re-shoot until you're happy."

Henry was confident Alice would draw interest from at least a few sincere men in their database.

He next began the most important phase of the process, asking questions.

"Okay Alice, question one. Could you please describe yourself and your current personal status?"

"Well," Alice began, "I'm single, 27 years old and I've never been married. I've dated a little but nothing too serious. I graduated from Boston College with a degree in Classical Literature. It was a great major but the job offers didn't exactly pour in after graduation so I worked in local libraries for a while, with some retail work just to keep the bills paid. Then I got a job about three years ago with the state as a Clerk in their Zoning Department. That's turned out to be really enjoyable, so I'm kind of in a good place as far as my job goes. I think I do a good job and my bosses agree, so I like that part of my life very much."

"Are you close to your family?"

"Emotionally yes, physically no. My parents came up here to New England after they met in a Cuban restaurant in Miami, but my dad died in a car accident when I was 14. Somebody broad-sided his car, killing him instantly, then drove away. We never found out who did that to us. It was very hard for Mom and me. I have no brothers or sisters and mom just loved Dad with all her heart. I thought Dad was Superman and Batman rolled into one. He was funny, affectionate, and always kind. I don't ever remember him saying a mean word to me. His name was Carlos. I had my friends but my mom and me became closer after that. I don't know how we both survived that."

"Anyway, after I got out of high school I decided to go to BC. Mom was so cute. After a while she asked if I felt secure, if everything felt good for me. She was obviously building up to something, and she wanted to go back to Florida to be with family. She did and all is good."

"So to answer your question, here I am. I don't have family here but it feels like home to me. I love New England. Go Sox! Mom and I used to go to as many games as we could, but since she moved away I never get to Fenway any more."

"What is your idea of the perfect companion, not just for yourself but in general?"

Alice thought about this for a few seconds before answering. "Someone who takes care of the people close to him before he takes care of himself, even if he really needs it. Someone who cares about the past and the future more than he does the present. Someone who knows what's right for his partner before his partner does."

"Great answer." Henry continued, "Why do you think that more than half of all marriages in this country end up in divorce?"

Alice did not hesitate this time. "I think it's because people get married to an image of the person instead of to the actual person, flaws and all. Then when they're further into their relationship, they continue to avoid those flaws. When they're finally forced to see their partner for who he or she really is, they're disappointed. These mental images we create are perfect, but real people are far from perfect. Instead of resetting their course, they hold on to the perfect image until disappointment gets the best of them. Most people simply don't appreciate what they have."

Henry felt he was very close to an accurate profile of Alice Martinez. For good or for bad, she was honest about his questions and she gave answers that reflected her essence. He felt a momentary wave of satisfaction with his decision to leave Blasmos.

As Henry's client base continued to grow and he learned and grew in the role of matchmaker, Henry began to understand more about the course his life was on. He remained certain that his calling was to bring people together, but he maintained a persistent feeling that this journey would be a rough one, and probably temporary.

One day he connected with a client who was unlike any of the others. There was just a feeling about her.

"You must be Aisling," Henry announced as he greeted her with his customary warm smile and handshake.

"Aye, that's me. And you're Henry." She had an Irish dialect that Henry found charming. She was probably in her fifties, Henry guessed, and she had piercing green eyes, pale, smooth skin, and reddish-white hair. Henry suspected that in younger days her hair was likely a stunning color of red, and he wished he had a chance to see it. She was gaunt, Henry noticed, but had a radiance that he had never seen.

"Aisling, it's a pleasure to meet you," Henry began. "I appreciate that you came in to speak with me and learn more about the services we offer. I plan to make your visit worth your time."

He originally contacted her through a cold call, but this one went far easier than most. It was as if she was expecting him. She barely asked about the normal things that bothered clients, such as cost, insecurity, and the time commitment. She was ready to try something new, and Henry's call came at the perfect time.

Something seemed too right, and he made notes about his concerns. "This went too easily. Is she gullible? Does she know what she's getting into?" He was concerned with the possibility that she might be prone to scammers and crooks, perhaps due to excess trust or some social disorder, so he wanted to be sure he was guarding her personal interests.

In the waiting area he took a few minutes to recap the services offered by Finders Keepers. She understood his explanation perfectly, smiling and nodding at the right queues.

"So I gather you would like to go ahead and have us collect your profile?"

"Yes, that sounds lovely," Aisling replied brightly. "You'll take a personal check?"

"Of course." Henry said. "We'll take care of that business later. Shall we get started?" With her nod he led her into the conference room.

When they were settled Henry began his usual questions. "Can I ask your occupation please?"

"Yes indeed," Aisling began. "It's a little unusual. I'm a Medium."

"A Medium?" Henry was intrigued. "Meaning, you see into the future, speak with spirits, that kind of thing?"

"That's partly true," Aisling replied in her soft Irish tone. "I communicate with spirits, and I pass along messages they might deliver about what will happen in the future, although they're careful not to do that very often. But I don't see future events before they happen. That's the business of others, I suppose."

Henry was captivated by the matter-of-fact way that Aisling explained her business.

"I've read a few things about Mediums and seances and spirits, and I've always wondered, can you people read other people's minds?"

"Some can indeed, but those are psychics. I'm not a psychic." Aisling was gracious and patient about answering all of his questions. "I wouldn't want to know others thoughts anyway. I can barely figure out my own. It's not mind-reading, but sometimes I pick things up that others might not. I wonder myself whether it's clairvoyance or just an enhanced perception of subtle things. For example I can't tell what you're thinking right now, other than your curiosity with my occupation. I sense that you're an honest man, Henry, and that your intentions are honorable in your occupation. So whether that's clairvoyance, my super intellect, or some spirits guiding me, I've not a clue. I don't spend much time thinking about it."

"Thanks for the compliment. I'm new at this job, but I like to believe I'm here for the right reasons. By the way, I should probably start doing that." Henry laughed softly and looked down at his interview sheet. "What else can you tell me about yourself, besides your occupation?"

"Well, I was born in the Republic of Ireland, in County Sligo, which is in the north and west, along the coast. The town I was born is called Cooldrumman, in Carney, neither of which anyone here has heard of. I came over here to America about forty years ago now, when I was barely out of school. My brother, who was just a few years older than I, had been living here in the States with an uncle since he was very young. Unfortunately our uncle died some years ago so my brother – who was called Niall – was left alone as a young man just out of school. Over time he developed a nice career as an automobile mechanic, and was even close to opening his own business when he became ill. With no family nearby, your country was kind enough to allow me to come take care of him during his illness. It turned out to be incurable, sadly, and once he died I was able to gain citizenship. The opportunities in America are boundless. I just fell in love with your country, and thankfully I was able to stay. Niall left the money he had saved to me, and I was able to get by on my own for quite some time."

Henry's expression was sympathetic. "That's a sad story with a happy ending, I suppose."

He paused before posing a question he could not resist. "As a medium, have you been in communication with your brother since his passing?"

Aisling did not hesitate in her reply. "Oh yes, very often. He visited me yesterday in fact, just to check in on me. He's much better about that sort of thing now that he's in the spirit world. When he was alive and I was still in

Ireland you'd hardly think there was paper here in America, much less ink. Staying in touch was never one of his strengths. But now that he's passed beyond this world he appreciates how much people loved him, and how much others meant to him. He tells me often how much he appreciated the kindness I showed during his illness, even though it's far from necessary. He would have done the same for me. I'm certain of that."

"But he's happy now?" Henry pressed on. "He has no regrets? Is he in heaven?"

"Happy?" Aisling smiled. "You have no idea. His happiness makes me envious, which he is quick to remind me. As for regrets, of course. Everyone dies with some regrets, some things in their life they wish they could change. Niall's regret was the family he left behind in Ireland. He was never able to fulfill his wish to rejoin the family. As he and other spirits have pointed out, the soul's journey is a series of mistakes and corrections. You learn, adjust, try not to repeat the same errors, and move onward and upward. Niall was a good man that usually put others' needs before his own. He never tried to hurt anyone. His path is a good one, but he hasn't earned his way to heaven yet either. I think someday he'll be in heaven but he's not there yet."

"Mind you," Aisling leaned forward in her chair, "I wasn't a medium when Niall died. I didn't have the vision that I have now. It was a very sad and lonely time for me. It was only later that I was brought to recognize my gift. Once I came to recognize what I had, of course the first person I contacted was my brother. But it took some time to develop the courage to contact him."

"I see." Henry looked down at his interview sheet, which was almost completely blank. He had been intrigued by the answers he was hearing but had not gathered much that would justify the money Aisling had agreed to pay. Henry was enjoying hearing Aisling speak. He had always enjoyed listening to the Irish dialect and Aisling rendered it beautifully.

"So Aisling, I should really try to help you spend your money with us wisely. You've decided that you'd like to use our services to find a partner for yourself. In this life at least." Henry paused and smiled at his pun.

Aisling smiled back. "Soul mates, as some people call them, often stay with each other through multiple lives. In my years I have yet to rediscover mine, so when you called I considered it a curious twist, one of those odd junctures in the great tapestry of life. I figured why not give myself a chance to meet someone new? Father Time waits for no one. Why not try it?"

"I'm honored that you chose to try us out." Henry felt there was nothing false about Aisling, and that someone with her charm would have many options for finding a companion. Yet she chose Finders Keepers. Henry believed it unlikely to be random chance that brought them together.

"We have many people around your age looking for a companion," he said, straightening his notebook and gathering his pen. "Aisling, I'd like you to take a 'third person' approach to this. If you had to draw the perfect person, what kind of partner would be considered ideal?"

"For a starter, I'd look for a farter." Aisling cackled at her rhyme. "If there's one thing I've never been able to run from, it's the IAB's."

"IAB's?" Henry couldn't leave this one untouched.

"Irish Air Biscuits. I can't help it. I maintain a good healthy diet, but there's no gas shortage when I'm around. Or at least where I've recently been. There's an old Irish saying that I just made up: Men don't make passes when girls emit gasses.

"Anyway, that's part of my 'profile' as you call it, so whoever is watching this might as well understand. I suspect it might have something to do with my attraction to a glass of Jameson every night at half nine. If so, that's a mystery better left unsolved. I'd rather keep my whiskey than settle for a man with a persnickety sense of smell."

Henry loved that every day brought new challenges, but this was one that he had not confronted in his short time in the profession. He decided on a diplomatic tack.

"I think information like that is vital to be out in the open in for a good relationship, but I really think it might be better for conversations during a date. The fourth or fifth date, in my opinion."

Aisling laughed quietly. "Aye, you're probably right. No sense scaring off the poor sod before I have the chance to do it on my own. Besides, who's to say? The right man might well think my biscuits smell like roses!" Again Aisling laughed, and this time Henry joined her.

She continued. "The right mate for me likes to laugh and look at the scenery. Someone that can enjoy the simple things in life and let go of the past, no matter how much pain was involved or whether that pain happened in this life or another. Someone that understands that keeping steady kindness, a generous heart, and respect for every living thing is a sure path to heaven. Someone who understands that love isn't something you find. Love finds you, as long as you're not hiding. That's why I'm here, Henry."

He had never met anyone like this, let alone as a dating service client, yet here she was, a medium with a great attitude, a sense of humor, and an open mind.

Henry finished the interview portion of the process and moved on to the videotape session. He wondered how she would come across on camera. Aisling hid nothing, which would scare some away. He considered downplaying or even concealing her occupation, but instead chose to alter nothing about this woman's portrait.

The two laughed the entire way through the video session. She was a sparkling diamond on camera. He felt her personality came through beautifully, and he confidently predicted there would certainly be men that appreciated her unique approach to life and the afterlife.

After he put together a brief video presentation of which Aisling approved enthusiastically, he was ready to move her into the "Active" cycle, which meant that potential suitors could access limited information about her to decide if they were interested. If a person expressed an interest in meeting her, he would ask the service to forward along his profile for her review. If her interest was mutual, Henry would arrange a contact. Going through the initial process could take several days or even weeks, so they had accomplished all they could for the day.

While escorting her out he casually asked, "Aside from legitimacy, what separates a good medium from a great medium?"

She paused thoughtfully before answering. "I suspect it's no different from this dating business, Henry. If you put the needs of your client before your own, the goodwill snowballs. To really succeed and achieve satisfaction at the same time, you need to stick to the path you know is right. I knew when you first called me that you haven't been doing this very long, but your sincerity and passion was evident."

He had a new perspective on why the process had gone so well.

"When people come to you with a request to contact their relatives or friends, they have to trust in you completely to take the first step. That's a very courageous step. You must repay that trust with honesty, otherwise you're in the business for the wrong reasons. It will come back to haunt you, if you'll forgive the expression."

"So to answer your question Henry, I charge minimum wage times six for a one hour session. If it has to go beyond an hour I let the client know, but I'm very liberal on what constitutes a one hour session. I've had three hour sessions that were officially an hour. I don't worry too much about money, and my customers reward me by continued business, and by spreading the word about my service."

"When did you learn you were psychic," Henry, asked, "and how in the world did you decide to make it your profession?"

Aisling smiled at Henry and paused, as if considering many different places to begin.

"I had my first visions of this gift when I was a young girl, maybe 6 or 7. As a child in Sligo I listened to elders and generally believed what they said, which is what children generally should do, I think. But I could always tell when someone was spinning a crooked yarn. It just seemed easy, and it made me unpopular with my young friends, because they often interpreted my honesty something it wasn't, jealousy and the like. My honesty cost me friendships, and when some of my childhood friends decided I was a little too honest for their tastes, I became a bit of a loner. This awareness was something I felt all through my school years, but it was never something I spoke much of."

"When the call came to help Niall, the decision to break away was easy. I was nearly out of school anyway. I never regretted my decision, but I do miss it there. After Niall died I knew I needed to work. I started in the usual jobs that immigrants do when they come to the US. I started out as a chamber maid in hotels around Boston, but I left that because it scared me. There are too many unhappy spirits that frequent hotels, especially some of the older ones. Sad spirits stuck in unhappy places, and at the time I just didn't know how to help them. Later I went on to be a rental car agent, plus a few other low-paying positions.

"I found that as I learned my way in the US my job prospects became better. I eventually found an office job with a big company here in Boston. They paid me a much better wage, plus I developed some great friendships working there over time. In that situation things began to change for me.

"My ability to communicate with spirits became more pronounced once I overcame my fear of it. It became more and more difficult to hide once I tried a few readings with friends. People talked, and the word spread. After a while it consumed so much of my time that people suggested I start charging money for it. I did charge modestly for the readings I did over evenings and weekends, but it became a little too demanding on my time. After a while the company ran into some lean times and they offered what was called a 'voluntary separation' package, which was a cowardly way of bribing me to leave on my own before they would fire me.

"That's another curiosity about your country, by the way. There's so much money here that if they want you out, they'll pay you to stop taking up the space they owned from the start!" She cackled.

"Anyway, I decided that option was better than waiting a while and having them fire me or someone else. Since then I've devoted all my time and energy to being a medium."

Henry was captivated. "When you decided to be a medium full time, did you have to find other ways to bring customers in, or were the contacts you made at the insurance company enough to keep you busy?"

"Why Henry," it was Aisling's turn to be surprised. "I didn't say it was an insurance company I worked for! How did you know that?"

Henry blinked and paused. "Aisling, I think you told me that."

"No, in fact I did not. I make it a point to not mention 'the I word' because people like insurance companies about as much as they like kidney stones."

"Henry, you clearly read my thoughts. There are hundreds of large companies in Boston and you knew it was an insurance company I worked for. I can't 'plant information' in your head from mine, so either you've been researching my background or perhaps you have some special talents of your own. Some of us are just tuned in at a higher frequency, and you seemed that way when I met you."

"I never really thought of it," he replied, "but sometimes right after I've been thinking about someone the phone rings and it's that person. Or I just have this feeling when something odd is about to happen, then it does. I've come to believe it's something other than coincidence."

"Well," Aisling looked intently into Henry's eyes, "most people do have some extra-sensory abilities, but rarely do they explore them or try to understand more about them. Most people just pass them off as coincidence or worse, something to be feared or concealed. It's as if they think they'll see something they shouldn't, like parents having sex or an attractive other on the toilet. The fear is usually puritanical."

Henry enjoyed laughter with this customer who was, before his eyes, becoming more than a customer. "I don't want to take your valuable time but it feels like I have a thousand questions I'd like to ask you. Maybe I'll schedule a meeting with you some time."

"I'd like that very much, Henry. You'd be surprised what you can learn about yourself and the spirits around you. Was there something in particular that you'd like me to try to help with?"

"Actually yes, there is." Henry replied. "I never asked anyone this in my life."

She nodded and smiled patiently.

"My parents died when I was a small child. I've never been able to find out anything about them, and it's been one of the great mysteries of my life. Also one of the most frustrating. Can you tell me anything about them?"

"Henry, I don't see parents with you, but I do pick up on a male presence nearby, someone not far from you in age. A brother perhaps?"

Henry was stunned. He turned to look back but saw nothing. He looked at Aisling doubtfully. "I don't have any brothers or sisters. I was told it was just me and my parents. Are you sure it couldn't be my father?"

"No, this is definitely not your father, Henry. This is someone that cares a great deal for you, but he's coming through to me with the kind of love that a sibling has. Are you sure you never had a brother?"

"No, I'm not sure. My parents died when I was very young. My memories of my life at that age have faded."

Henry stood and walked an anxious circle around the room.

"I can't believe this! Even stranger, if I did have a brother, now you're saying he's dead?"

"Well to be clear, 'dead' is not the expression I use, nor should you. Souls don't die, bodies do. It does appear that someone close in age and sharing many common traits, including family bonds, has passed on to a higher level. Perhaps it's a cousin. I'm glad to explore this further if you'd like. Here's my card. I'm very sorry if I've upset you. I really try not to hold back information from my friends, even if it might prove painful or troublesome."

"I appreciate your honesty," Henry said. "I can't wait to talk to you more."

As he closed the door behind her, he felt a surging mix of excitement and confusion. He would plan to set up an appointment for a full reading.

Almost as important to Henry was the feeling that he had found a friendship that would open doors that did not exist before today. It was a journey that would change the world he thought he knew.

THE TWISTED JOURNEY

In the few months since Henry Stark joined Finders Keepers, he developed a reputation among his bosses and peers as the person to speak with for truthful, unvarnished advice. He would ask the uncomfortable questions that others would avoid, but with humor and kindness toward their clients. He had a way of looking at certain situations in a way that no one else could. Some of his clients liked and trusted him more than they trusted their attorneys or other family members.

Surprisingly to Henry, and almost before he expected it, money began to come in. Within three months of starting with Finders Keepers he was making nearly what he was making with Blasmos. Macaroni and cheese became more the exception than the rule.

Yet something was still missing. While it was true he was bringing people together and this still felt like his calling, there was so much he was not truly knowing about his customers. He enlisted customers, then they signed up for his service. They deeply admired what he did for them. Henry was a "Godsend" for them, many had told him. He was flattered by remarks like that, but he felt that their sense of perspective was usually skewed by years of bad luck with the opposite sex. If there was some divine reason for him being in this position, he was frustrated by the emerging reality that this job was not his destination.

The word "essence" was something he preached to his clients as what he intended on capturing, yet it was so elusive. As he looked at his clients in person and watched their responses, he couldn't help but notice the difference between what he saw with his eyes and what he saw on video. Seeing their video delivery was like watching a computer animated rendering of a human. "Existence" was something any camera could capture, but "essence" was something different, the difference between first hand observation and a second hand account.

Aisling had the vision to capture the essence of the people around her. Henry longed for that ability. As the weeks went by, he grew to increasingly believe he was giving his customers only a fraction of the insight he was capable of delivering.

One afternoon he was treated with a surprise visit from his first customer. He was in the back office working on some paperwork and he heard the door open. When he came to the front, Alice Martinez looked radiant.

"Hi Henry, it's great to see you! I just came in to thank you for helping me."

"Alice, it's wonderful to see you too. I'm so glad I was able to help you out. Are you two still seeing each other?"

Alice spoke excitedly. "More than seeing each other Henry, we've gotten really close over the last few weeks. Dennis is a great guy – he and I have so much in common. We just enjoy spending time together. I don't want to curse myself but this seems like we're two people made for each other."

"That's fantastic to hear!" Henry was beaming with pride. "Happy outcomes make me glad I came into the business. It's a beautiful thing when it all works out."

As he was talking to Alice, Henry noticed a man standing outside the front window of the office looking in toward them. The man, vaguely familiar, did not seem to be inclined to come inside, instead he just stood looking in with a contented smile. It took Henry a moment before he recognized the man from a few weeks before.

He turned to Alice, "Do you happen to know that man standing outside?"

Alice looked out the window. "Who? I don't see anyone."

Henry began to point at the man that was no more than twenty feet away, but just as suddenly he was gone. "That was really strange. There was a man standing outside looking in, as if he had some business here." Henry walked toward the window for a closer look. "That's odd."

Alice also peered out the window again and asked Henry, "What did he look like?"

Well," Henry said, "he was probably in his fifties. He had dark hair with a touch of white. He looked approachable I guess. Not threatening at all. Big forehead, great hair. He looked like he might have been from a Latin background. He was wearing one of those Southwestern ties - a Bolero, I think they're called - with a cross in the center."

Alice smiled awkwardly, glancing out again. "It sounds like you just described my father." She reached into her purse and pulled out a wallet thick with pictures. She pointed to one and said, "I miss this guy."

Henry gasped. His face turned pale white as he looked intently at the picture, then out the window and back at the picture again. "Oh my God, this looks identical to the man I saw standing outside."

Alice stared at Henry with a mix of surprise and disbelief. "Henry, are you playing some kind of cruel joke on me? I'm not sure how you could know what my father looked like, but this isn't something I appreciate." She began to turn red, her lips curling.

"Alice, no." Henry's tone was reassuring and sincere. "I'm absolutely not trying to pull anything over on you. You know I wouldn't do that. It's just that I saw him, just as plain as day. And it's not the first time I saw him, either. When you first came in to the office I saw the same man sitting in the waiting area near you. Later on I went to check on him and he wasn't there, just like this time.

"I have to confide in you, Alice. A few weeks ago a client came in and she was a medium. We talked at length about her profession. It really interested me, and she was just a lovely person. Anyway she told me some things about my family that no one had ever said to me before. I'm adopted so I knew nothing about my birth family. It was really amazing. Something I said made her think that I might have some psychic abilities too. I'm starting to think she's right because it seems like I just saw an apparition of your father.

"Alice, it's really obvious to me how much you loved your Dad, and clearly he loved you with all his heart and soul. If that was your dad, I can tell you that he looked very happy and content both times I saw him. I think he's really proud of you, Alice."

By now Alice was speechless and fully in tears. Her momentary anger had turned to an emotional mix. All she could do was cry, and Henry gave her a shoulder to cry on.

"Alice, I don't mean to upset you. I get the feeling he's there when you need him, and he wants you to know that. Please don't be upset with me."

"I'm not. Just a little confused and overwhelmed, I guess. I'm sorry Henry, I didn't mean to attack you."

"This is all pretty confusing to me too," Henry said.

When Alice left, Henry made up his mind. He dug in his drawer for Aisling's card.

In the days since his first meeting with Aisling, the conversations from their first visit rarely strayed too far from his thoughts.

The possibility that he once had a brother was still so difficult to believe. Surely he would remember an older brother, even if the two parted ways when he was barely a year old. But he had no recollection of a brother, nor his parents.

Aisling detected no hint of his dead parents. Why? Could it mean they were simply not concerned with him, or not able to because of their current state? If there was indeed a hell, maybe they were in it and Aisling had no way of knowing it.

If they were still alive, was there any possibility of finding them?

Henry thought of someone afraid to be tested for HIV. Finding out what happened to them could be worse than not knowing. If his worst fears were true, that they had died and that in the afterlife they chose not to be near him, perhaps Aisling could help him discover why. If they were still alive, they had apparently never sought to find him.

Either way, the decision on whether to do anything about finding his parents was his alone, one that would come when it came.

Since speaking with Aisling, he gradually came to terms with her opinion that he too might have psychic abilities. Through his life he always felt the existence of an extra gear that helped him navigate through troubled times, so this new understanding was not a complete surprise to him.

Still the question remained: Is it something he should pursue? Her world of sensing and seeing things beyond the normal was captivating, but what was the point in exploring it further?

The easy path would be to avoid this whim and continue on his current direction. However his current situation as a matchmaker seemed to be falling short of his needs, whatever they were. He knew that his past life as a programmer was not one he cared to resume.

He dialed Aisling's number. She picked up on the third ring.

"Well," she answered in a lyrical voice, "it's good to hear from you, Henry. I was beginning to think I scared you away. How has life been treating you, dear boy? Like the hammer or the nail?"

"Life's been great. More like a rusty screw, I think. Have you been on the site looking for prospects, Aisling? There's no shortage of men in their middle years looking for women who are acceptably crazy. I looked at the number of hits on your profile, and you've gotten a lot of interest. You should take a look at your inbox."

"I did look through a few of those, Henry. As the old saying goes, the odds are good but the goods are odd. There are some colorful characters in there."

"Try to keep your mind open. If any of them seem like they're worth a lunch, let me know and I'll set it up."

"Duly noted, my dear, as long as you agree to chaperone. I wouldn't want any of these dirty old men raiding my booty, looking for a treasure chest without a chaperone nearby to assure them it's worth the effort."

They laughed together.

"Aisling, ever since the last time we talked I've been thinking about all the things you told me. What an eye opener! The idea of having a brother is something I never even considered. And no hint of my parents. I don't know what to think about that. On top of it all, you thought that I might have some gifts of my own. It turns out you might be right. It seems I might have seen a ghost."

Henry told her the whole story, which she absorbed with no hint of surprise.

"An experience like that will certainly get your attention. It does indeed sound like you were seeing an apparition of the girl's father. The thing to remember about apparitions, Henry, is that if you have the gift of seeing them, then it's possible that you've had the gift for quite some time, maybe even your whole life. Some people you see on the street and barely pay attention to may not be what they seem. Having this gift teaches you to pay closer attention to all the things around you.

"You might be surprised to know that during my career I've met many, many people who had the gift without realizing it. Some are open to learning about it, most are not. Not only is it a rare gift, but it's a precious one too. Some who have it are better off avoiding it. Those who have the wisdom and maturity to master it should embrace it. You could be one of the lucky ones, Henry."

"Donkey balls" was all Henry could muster.

"Nicely articulated, Henry. Another small victory for the US educational system."

"Oh sorry," Henry said. "I just wonder what I'm getting into here. It's a lot to process, that some of the people I see on the street may not be alive at all."

"Oh, they're alive," Aisling corrected. "They're as alive as you or I, in spirit. It's just that you're seeing them in a different dimension. Their soul is there and they see you. They might even talk to you, but they could be spirits of people who have not been here physically for quite some time."

"How would I know?"

"Without training and experience, there's no simple way to tell. Remember that this gift is rare, and the way these messages are received can vary greatly. However, once you come to terms with what you see in front of you in each passing moment, then it becomes easier to discern those things that are obscured from normal vision. At this point, Henry, you're only seeing a small bit of what's really around you."

"Aisling, I need to know more. Would a reading be the best place to start?"

"It would," Aisling spoke patiently, trying not to scare Henry from what could be his destiny. "For one thing you'll see how a reading works. You'll also learn more about your life, which it sounds is full of unanswered questions. Can you make it in tomorrow at four in the afternoon? It's a light day for readings, so that would be the last of the day. I can take some extra time over tea, and I can try to answer as many of your questions as I can."

"Four o'clock sounds perfect," Henry said. "but in the meantime, where can you see some of these spirits? They have to have some places they prefer."

"Do you know where Racquette Park is, near the bus station?"

"Sure, I'm only a few miles from there. Why?"

"Well, there are many spirits that frequent the place, from what I've seen. Wander down there and converse with some of the locals. You're more than likely to meet a spirit or two."

"I go running there a lot. Mostly I just see drifters, homeless people. How will I be able to recognize a spirit from all the other lost souls who are still in their actual bodies?"

"It sounds like you've seen plenty of them, Henry. Maybe you should pay closer attention. See you tomorrow afternoon."

On the next afternoon, Henry hurried through traffic and arrived at Aisling's address early. Her home was one block from the main thoroughfare in Revere. It was a smaller, older wood frame home with impeccable landscaping and a fresh coat of emerald green paint - in true Irish spirit,

Henry thought - with pale yellow trim. While the traffic was busy, it was not loud and provided easy access to Aisling's business.

Aisling had selected a perfect location for this kind of business. It was walking distance to many nearby homes, very close to an important thoroughfare in the town, yet the building had more the look of a comfortable home than an impersonal business.

Her sign was modest yet distinct: "See and Understand with Aisling. 19 Washington Street." Henry noticed that the street was filled with parked cars but that oddly, two or three spaces in front of her property were clear. It was as if people were avoiding being seen near her business.

Just before four, Henry knocked on the wooden door and waited. Aisling came to the door soon with her usual bright smile. "Henry, I'm so glad you're here. I've been looking forward to your visit."

Henry offered his hand. "I'm excited about it too. Frankly I've been nervous all day."

"Your first reading can be nerve-wracking," she replied. "We'll get through it at your own pace. You'll be glad you came. Please make yourself at home."

The inside of Aisling's home matched its outer appearance. A small parlor area contained stuffed chairs that surrounded a classical coffee table, upon which were several books with large color photographs of the Irish coast and countryside. Her dining area contained an elegant walnut dining room set with classic photographs and Irish memorabilia on the walls, including an Irish cross.

Henry sat in the parlor area in one of the comfortable stuffed chairs. Aisling came in with a tray of tea and poured him a cup.

"So Aisling, what do ghosts sound like?" Henry was clearly ready to dive right in.

"You need to get your terms straight, dear boy. We don't refer to them as 'ghosts'. That's for people who watch too many scary movies. We call them 'spirits' because that's what they are, in totality. You and I are spirits, but we happen to have a body to occupy. These are just disembodied spirits.

"And they don't 'sound' like anything, really. They communicate in other ways, through thoughts mainly. It's in a high vibratory wavelength that's out of the range of a normal person's perceptions."

Henry was determined to understand completely. "But does it feel like you're conversing with a regular living, breathing person like me? At least, I assume I'm living and breathing. Aren't I?"

"Yes, Henry, you're very much alive in this time and place, just as you think you are. So am I. My aches and pains are as real as can be.

"Normal communications with those in the spirit realm are fairly similar to communication with the present living, but emotions are conveyed foremost. In nearly all the readings of which I've been a part, the primary emotions are love and appreciation. Most spirits express love for the living, and an appreciation for things the living have done in the past or are doing now. After a while you hardly notice that the soul communicating with you doesn't possess the same physical presence as you and I. It never becomes routine exactly, but the means for communication with spirits are just as varied as if you selected ten people in a crowded bus station. Each experience would be substantially different from the others. Mediums are able to read them because they *allow* us to, mainly."

"Are they always around?" Henry was leaning forward, eager for information. "Or is it like a big Ouija Board or a séance, where you conjure up spirits and they come when called?"

"No, it's not like that at all." Aisling's tone was firm. "Each of those represent ways to communicate with spirits, but each is forced communication. I would never recommend using a Ouija board. More often than not they've been used to frighten and titillate interest in the occult. 'Séances' were popular in the early twentieth century, sort of a party trick.

"Spirits appear when they want to appear, unless they've been given little choice in the matter. Forcing a séance or forcing an apparition through Ouija is like waking someone up when they're in the midst of a wonderful dream. In some instances they'll appear, but often they won't appreciate the imposition. If they sense that the requestors' intentions are less than honorable, they'll do their utmost to stay away. In rare cases they can be downright hostile or menacing. That's why these matters are best left to those who respect the tranquility of those in the spirit world, and who are willing to work within their comfort zone rather than on the terms of some living, breathing soul in search of a thrill."

"I guess that's the way I'd prefer it if I went to 'eternal rest,' as the headstones say. Do they spend most of their time somewhere else, then just appear when they know a medium is in the general vicinity?"

"It sounds like you've thought a lot about this. You should first change the way you think of time. Time in the spirit world is different. I suspect that spirits need to adjust to our notion of time when their attention is requested, because it's less of a consideration in theirs.

"Any spirits that might want to communicate with you need only to pick this moment along the great timeline. If they contact us today, it is because they chosen the moment just after you and I met for our first reading. There's probably no waiting involved for them, just a choice of when to visit."

Henry moved forward in his seat. "Wait a second. That seems to suggest that people in the spirit realm can see not only what's happening now and what's happened before, but also what will happen later. Is that what you're saying?"

Aisling paused, with a knowing smile that she tried to contain. Clearly Henry was a pupil with profound curiosity that was well ahead of his other undiscovered senses.

"Again Henry, that's partially true. Don't think of all spirits as being equal. Some spirits are relatively 'wet behind the ears,' and don't have the wisdom of some others. What I've found is that some spirits have a better sense of the entire timeline of living spirits than some others. So yes, in that sense it's true that spirits can see into the future. Other spirits don't have the wisdom or experience to understand what lies ahead of the living in their life journey.

"The important thing to know is that life has a natural order and sequence that is to be respected above all else. This order is what separates purposeful lives from lives without direction. Humans, with our keen senses and boundless imperfections, use our lifelines to track our progress through milestones within a life. Disruption of that natural order may bring profoundly negative consequences.

"The disruptions I think you're hinting about – telling the future – is a spirit telling the living what lies ahead in their life journey. This simply cannot be done. Any spirit who is willing to provide that information is clearly not committed to obtaining higher ground in their spiritual journey. They're encouraging cheating, and any spiritualist who doesn't understand that is the most profound sort of fool. If a spirit were to come along and warn you of the dangers of a path you've chosen or certain decisions you must make, that spirit is placing itself between you and destiny, which is between you and God. People need to make their own choices without intervention, and that includes spirits. If a person ignores certain advice or chooses to live in a certain way, that will need to be answered for, good or bad.

"This", she continued "is why fortune tellers have been relegated to second tier citizens among the living," she explained. "I'm not sure if you're a religious person, but even in the Old Testament, in the book of Kings I think, there are references to 'seers' and how God directly warned them to 'turn from their evil ways.' Originally prophets were tolerated, sometimes warmly embraced, until they turned away from the ways of God. That's one curiosity that makes the Bible such a necessary book, and just adds to its mystery. There are other disruptions of the natural order that you'll learn for yourself in due time.

"Is all of this making sense, Henry, or am I just blathering on?"

"It makes sense, but I've never looked at things this way. It takes some getting used to."

Aisling nodded. "If it makes you feel better, I have so many things that I want to understand better as well. As you encounter spirits, you're bound to develop questions. I have so many that I've accumulated over the years that I am still awaiting answers for! When I've asked directly, the message back, in quite certain terms, is that I need to wait. I'm not the most patient person, so I continue to ask the questions. In time they'll all be answered."

Henry was deep in thought, hands folded to his mouth.

Aisling broke his introspection. "So Henry, how do you feel about getting on with your reading?"

"I guess I'm as ready as I'll ever be."

Aisling led Henry into a room in her home that was probably for a servant when the home was first built. It was small with no windows, two doors and high ceilings. Henry was particularly fixated on the two exit doors, not especially comfortable with what might happen.

In the center was a simple place-setting with a candle in the center. On the walls were serene watercolors of mountains and shores and airborne birds.

"Well," Henry mused, "this isn't exactly what I expected."

Aisling had helped acclimate first-timers many times before. "You were expecting a crystal ball. Would it make you feel better if I put on a turban and started speaking with an Eastern European accent?"

He laughed. "No, none of that. Just something less pleasant and homey, I guess."

"Most of my customers don't have much idea at all of what to expect," she answered. "The truth is that every legitimate medium has their own approach. It's a matter of creating a peaceful, loving, accepting mood."

The two sat across from each other. Aisling appeared to be attempting to gain some sort of balance. She was relaxed and peaceful.

"Henry, I have to explain briefly what we're doing here. You must realize that in essence we're opening a door to a realm that is not ours. As such we must pay respect to everyone who recognizes our visit, and especially for any who may choose to approach the door.

"I like to start my sessions with a prayer and a wish. Either may be answered if the spirits decide the request is valid or they might not, but being demanding is just bad form. So I'd suggest that if you want to take that next step, you initiate yourself into this way of communicating by tuning up your own spirit. Put away your fears, and open your mind to spirits who communicate in different ways than you're accustomed to."

Henry appeared nervous but focused. "Are you asking me to pray?"

"It's not really a prayer in the normal sense, where you say, 'God please help me and my loved ones, and dissuade my enemies.' It's more a message to all under God, a declaration if you will, that we respect one another and that our intentions are honorable. We will both behave ourselves. You'd be surprised at how many communications are initiated that are reckless, not respectful. The most important thing we're doing is connecting you with your spiritual self, which is a necessity in connecting you with other spirits. If what I suspect is true, we'll find that at least some in other realms are eager to speak to you too. Your situation, as an orphan with no familial contact, would seem to make the possibilities most interesting. Spirits know the situation you've been in your whole life, and you might be surprised at the the love and support that's always been around you. Are you ready to start?"

"Yes," Henry was more relaxed. "I'm all set."

Aisling looked at Henry as she bowed her head, closed her eyes softly, and clasped her hands in front. Henry followed her lead.

"Dear Lord, thank you for all the blessings you've bestowed upon me, your child Aisling, and my brother Henry. Please accept our thanks for the gifts you've given us in the way of life, health, happiness, and the window to the next world we have been so blessed to see."

"We wish the permission of you and your Guardian Protectors to speak with those that are near to my brother, Henry Stark. Please consider our request to be respectful, honorable and true, devoid of all the influences of false gods and evil spirits."

"Thank you for your blessing." With that Aisling opened her eyes and expanded her hands outward. She looked straight ahead into space for close to a minute.

Henry stared down uncomfortably, then closed his eyes to wait until she had finished doing whatever it was she was doing. The serene prayer made him briefly forget that this was as nervous as he had felt in a long, long time.

Finally she smiled and looked at Henry. "Henry, how are you feeling?" Her peaceful gaze suggested that she knew something he did not.

"I'm feeling okay. Anxious I guess. Are you sensing anyone nearby?"

"The lines of communication are open. Keep your mind clear. You might sense some presence on your own."

"Okay, I'll try." Henry closed his eyes softly and opened them slowly.

"Henry, there are some people nearby who would like to say hello to you."

Henry was startled. "Who do you see?"

"There is much love directed your way. They regret that you've never been able to connect with family in your life. They would like very much to see that corrected. They tell me that you've undergone a great deal of uncertainty in your life because of events with your family.

"There's one person that seems especially eager to speak with you. This is a spirit that says his name is Freddy. He says you two were borne of the same parents, and that he's so disappointed you two never had a chance to grow up together. You two were together too briefly, and he loved having you as his younger brother. He's profoundly sad that you two were torn apart the way you were.

"So it's true! I have an older brother!" Henry's was astounded. His voice rose loudly. "I couldn't be be more thrilled. Tell Freddy it's nice to meet him, or I guess to meet him again after so much time. But our parents! What became of them?"

Aisling's demeanor was anxious and studious. Clearly she was struggling to deliver a message.

"He's explaining that your parents are not with them, Henry. He's not explaining why. He's just saying that they're not with us now. However he is showing me that your grandparents are looking on, shining brightly upon the life you're living now. They're very proud of you, and the life you're living. Freddy is pointing to aunts and uncles and a whole extended family that has one unified message: you were dealt a really bad hand, Henry, but keep up the great work. We're all proud of you! Don't worry about your parents for right now. It will all turn out fine."

"Don't worry about them?" Henry leaned forward with desperation. "He says they're not there now, but does that mean they're in hell?"

"Your parents are not in hell. We're not getting much detail because I suppose we are not meant to. These issues can be complicated." Aisling was looking directly at Henry now but looking through him, past him. She was the messenger, and he was beginning to adjust to the idea.

"Henry, most spirits are on a spiritual journey and their goal is to ultimately reach heaven, but it doesn't happen automatically." She was speaking directly to him now, just the two of them.

"The soul needs to go through a great deal to advance beyond this world. As I explained, spirits must not interfere with the path of the living. What Freddy is telling me quite clearly is that if he were to disclose everything to you about your parents, it would be a serious wrong. He knows you're anxious to learn more, but these are things you must learn for yourself."

Henry was frustrated. "Can he at least tell me how he died? How I lost my brother that I never knew I had?"

Aisling gazed beyond Henry's shoulder and began to smile. Henry looked behind his back and thought he saw a blur but was not nearly certain. He did not see forms of people, but clearly the wall behind him was not in focus. He felt warmth as he turned, and turned back to Aisling.

"He was hoping you would ask. He said that your family lived in a small town. He died at age five. He says it was a tragedy in that it changed many lives, not just his own. He's feels sorry about that, although he knows there is nothing a small child could have done about that. He just feels great sadness about the way things turned out, and he's hoping you forgive him for not being there for you."

"Please tell him," Henry said with conviction, "that I forgive him completely. My life has been okay. I haven't missed meals, I was never abused, and I'm doing fine now. Tell him that there's nothing he should be asking forgiveness for, and that I'm so thankful that he decided to communicate with me.

"Please ask him, Aisling, if he felt any pain. Ask him where he's buried. Do I have any living relatives?" Henry's emotions were overwhelming. He felt like a deaf man who was just hearing for the first time.

"He can't give you details on relatives but yes, you have living relatives. He says he's buried in the town where he died and no, he felt no pain when he died. Only confusion at first but that did not last long. Loving spirits were there to help him.

"Henry, Freddy is encouraging you to go and find his burial place. He says you'll find some peace there, and who knows, maybe you'll find some connections with your past."

"I'll do that. Tell him I'll do that." Henry considered that his promise was based on information that was bleak, but he knew he would oblige.

"He's heard you, Henry. There are some other people who would like to say hello to you. They're your grandparents, and they just want to tell you they love you and that they're proud of the life you've lived. Their names are Gerald and Evelyn. Gerald seems to be communicating that you need to stop chasing your tail and go with your greatest gifts. He says you're headed in the right direction, but be careful of detours that will take you from your path. Evelyn is showing me a clock and a baby's face. It might be your face. I'm not sure. I think she's saying that time is wasting and there are babies to be had. They're both full of love for you Henry, and they said to tell you that they love your parents very much as well, just in case there's any doubt in your mind."

Henry was looking down now. Tears were in his eyes and words would not come, but his message was delivered. There were many other questions he wanted to ask, but he was overcome with the weight of the experience. Aisling waited patiently. Finally he formed a question.

"Aisling, ask them where they lived and when they died. Please?"

"Both died of natural causes, but both died near the time you were born. It appears Gerald has a black area near his lungs. It could be lung cancer. Evelyn's heart is drawing my attention, as if she had a weak heart and something or someone broke it while she was in the natural world."

The evening was surreal. He reminded himself this was not a dream but rather a moment he had waited for his whole life.

When the reading was complete, he folded his arms in front of him on the table and dropped his head over his arms.

In exasperation he said, "I don't even know where to begin."

Aisling was quiet, not knowing what to say to help him.

Then warm air surrounded him, very different from just a few seconds before. A soft male voice whispered, "Go and find out, brother."

Henry's head jerked up and he looked around, then stared at Aisling. "Did you hear that?"

"I'm sorry dear. No, I didn't hear anything. If you received a message, it wasn't meant for my ears."

Henry just stared, unsure what to do or say next.

LEAP OF FAITH

Henry scarcely remembered his drive home that evening. His mind moved in many directions, none moving him close to satisfaction.

Later, in front of the TV's glow and hum, he picked up a blank notepad and began writing. He needed to get some thoughts from his head onto the paper.

> *A brother? WTF? My BROTHER talked to me!*
>
> *I have a past?*
>
> *Find where Freddy was buried.*
>
> *Is Aisling even sane? Is this some kind of scam?*
>
> *AAAAARGGGGHH!*

Henry's thoughts were outpacing his writing. He put down his pen and tried to focus.

As his mind slowed and he tried to slowly replay the evening, he picked up the pen again to transcribe his final thoughts for the day.

> *If I ever had a brother, THAT was my brother. He was glad to be in my ear. He has more to tell me! I need to know where he died. It wasn't Boston. Where? What was our family name? When did he die? HOW did he die? Why wasn't I with my parents after he died? NEED TO KNOW WHERE.*

He finally nodded to sleep with the pad and pencil on his lap.

When he awoke, Henry's only thought was to arrange the next meeting with Aisling, but it was a workday. He braced himself for the challenge of focusing on his work.

He showered and munched on toast while headed out the door, his notebook by his side.

After checking his emails and voicemails, his first phone call of the day was to Aisling. He expected only to leave a voice message, and was delighted to hear her living voice.

"Aisling," she answered, simple and direct.

"Good morning. It's Henry. Sorry to bug you so soon but I'd really like to continue our discussions. How is your calendar?"

"Mine suggests a lot of living days ahead, but trains have been known to jump the track without warning. Would you like me to tell you about YOUR calendar?" Aisling's voice smiled with the question.

"Okay, now you're getting creepy. You know what I meant."

Aisling's laugh was a welcome break from the weighty thoughts of his last twelve hours.

"My day is full but we can meet at 5:00 today, at the end of my afternoon appointments and before I break for supper. Can you make that?"

Henry confirmed the time, and immediately began looking forward to it.

To get through the day, he took several walks around the office park, dwelling near a pond to remind himself of his real surroundings in the real world. Water, air, and sky. Everything was exactly as it appeared.

When four-thirty finally came, Henry hurried out with a fast goodbye to his co-workers. They were amazed that he would ever leave the office before five.

In Aisling's home the greetings were pleasant but brief. The two barely spoke but felt an immediate sense of purpose.

"Aisling, I'm still having a hard time with the notion that I even had a brother, not to mention that he contacted me directly. But I'm nearly certain that happened. So I guess the next question is, what do I do next? My brother encouraged me to find him, but I have no idea where to begin. I want to ask him directly. Otherwise I'll be sitting around waiting for some kind of sign that might never come."

"Henry, it's important to understand," Aisling said slowly, "your brother is taking a risk by suggesting that you take any sort of action at all. Your actions are supposed to be up to you. When spirits interfere in the actions of earth-bound people, they risk upsetting a natural order. When they do it, it's usually because they're hopelessly alone and not sure where to turn. We often see this in spirits who haven't come to face that this life is over, and that they need to move on. On top of that, you're asking me to interpret that which wasn't meant for my ears. Why would I interfere with family business?"

"You really didn't hear what he said to me?"

"Conversations with spirits are not in the same range of hearing as conversations that occur between us in this living world. No, I didn't hear it. The truth is, if I were to hear every conversation that went on between spirits in this world and in other realms, can you imagine how deaf I'd wish I were?"

"I think I get it. It's just hard to imagine that communications can be so precise that even people close by have no idea of what's being said."

"Spirits can direct their communications the way they choose, just like I can. Someday maybe you'll be able to. Maybe very soon. Your brother holds some secrets that he seems eager to share with you. I have not for a moment detected that he's trying to mislead you in any way. While I only caught a passing sense of him, his intentions seemed honest and true to me."

"I feel the same way," Henry said.

"Still, there are a few things you must remember." Aisling gave him the 'stop and listen' look. "People die in their human form, but spirits persist, usually through many lives. So our connection to another spirit might extend much further than you can possibly imagine. This spirit that says he was your brother in your current life might have known you in other ways in other lives."

"I had completely forgotten about that, but why is it important?"

"It may not be, but it's hard to know for sure. The point is, you should understand as much as you can about the spirit world before you make a decision to take action based on what one spirit says to you. I think Freddy is on the level, but that you two probably go way back, even though you're not aware of it. Even though the experience in this life has left you desperately curious about your past and his past, that could be only part of the story."

"So you're suggesting," Henry tried, "that while his intention might be honorable in the present tense, there could be baggage from long ago."

"Possibly. It's something to be aware of. Past life regression is not one of my areas of specialization. However many civilizations believed that souls go through many tests before they earn their way into a pure existence. Those tests are the lives they live. In between those lives they learn from all of their experiences - their failures and their successes - and they do it all again until they've learned all they can possibly learn."

Henry appeared skeptical. "It sounds like you're talking about Nirvana."

"I suppose I am, although different religions have different terms for the notion of a pure existence."

When she mentioned "religion," her distasteful look caught Henry by surprise.

"Whether you believe in this notion of souls getting another chance or not, there were several early scholars in just about every one of the major faiths that talked about it. Most had it handed down to them, so they assumed it a much more gradual path than simply living a good life and going straight to heaven.

"For example, Plato was a big believer in reincarnation, and he developed that belief by studying the Greeks that lived long before he was born. That includes Pythagoras, who lived a couple hundred years before and claimed to remember past lives."

Henry just stared.

"Most of the contemporary religions only accept the notion of reincarnation in passing, but the Hindus and most of the other Indian religions embrace it without question. Buddhism doesn't embrace the idea directly because, well Buddhism is more of a discipline for living, and their beliefs discourage the notion of a spirit's continuation of any kind. But the Buddha himself referred to past lives! So there seems to be some basis in their faith.

"Some religions reject the whole idea outright as against the interests they're trying to support. The Catholic notion is that the 'Patron Saint of the Do-Over,' Saint Mulligan, might encourage immorality. After all, what's the penalty for doing wrong if you know you'll have another chance to get it right? In Christianity there was a fellow named Origen who espoused the notion of souls having lived before they found their current life on this earth. Today's Catholic Church doesn't support that belief, but most available research indicates that he was a firm believer in the 'The Holy Mulligan,' reincarnation. The church came together a couple centuries after his death to seal that notion away forever, but some artifacts survived which suggest the church made a rather radical departure from their history, which Origen and others took for granted."

"What about Islam and their idea of seventy-two virgins, and all of that?" Henry was trying to keep up with Aisling's monologue.

"I've read about some quotes from Muhammad about 72 wives and hundreds of servants, but in the Koran there is a fairly direct reference to life, death, and life again. There was a well-respected Muslim author from Egypt called Al-Suyuti who believed that heaven and hell are part of the present world. He wrote his belief that spirits not in this world can move about, visiting the living through dreams and visions. There are even references to reincarnation in the Zohar, which is the authoritative source for Jewish mysticism. That's fairly significant, Henry, because the Jewish faith is especially vague about the afterlife in all forms."

"Aisling, how did you learn all this?" Henry was astounded by Aisling's casual approach to such a weighty topic.

"From reading about it, dear boy, how else? It came about from natural curiosity, spending day after day communicating with spirits, in the flesh and not, learning how these souls came to their beliefs. The history of religion is available for anyone who wants to read about it, including how each of them dealt with the notion of souls being recycled over time. Some denied it completely, others embraced it completely. Witnessing it here in our time is quite fascinating. It's like the game we played as children, when a sentence was whispered from one child to another, then another, then another. By the time it reached the final child, and the first and the last would compare sentences, the two didn't resemble each other at all. I think that's what happened to the message of what really happens to souls. Most religions have so changed the original idea of achieving soul perfection, that the message now is nothing like it was centuries ago. If anyone were to look closely at their origins, they'd realize their notions of the fate of souls are not very different at all. It's time and time alone that changed what they currently believe."

"What I don't understand," Henry asked, "is why are certain spirits are even willing to be contacted. Don't they have other things they should be doing, like moving onto the next life? Or if they're done living lives, moving on to heaven or Nirvana, or whatever you want to call it."

"It's an important question," Aisling began. "When you mention the term 'reincarnation' people think of famous people they might have been in past lives. Well, get real people, we can't all have been Joan of Arc or George Washington. The simple fact is there have been millions of humans walking this earth, and not so many of them are well known. That doesn't mean that in a past life you weren't an extremely good and noble soul, or a bad one, or maybe just dumb as a stump. Who's to say their soul wasn't headed in a noble direction, but their mother ate dirt and liked the dizzy feeling from running into rocks while pregnant? Sometimes we're just dealt a bad hand. We meant well, but events conspired against us."

"The important thing to remember is that all souls who seek goodness are in search of the same thing, to get better at this. Perhaps a soul can even reach a state of perfection, or if not perfection, true wisdom. The idea is, if you go through the process and make the very most of the soul you've been given, the brass ring is yours.

"As the saying goes, 'Life is short.' The unfortunate truth is that one life is nearly always too short to achieve the kind of wisdom we hope to achieve. Many people go to their death bed full of regret for the things they didn't accomplish. In my opinion, they're being too hard on themselves. Half your life is spent figuring out how you'll survive for the next half.

"So most souls, when their human incarnation has expired, are placed into a waiting pattern until they get another chance to start over to try to cover all that ground they didn't have time for in the last life. Many of the spirits I contact are in this place."

"Purgatory, right?" Henry felt confident about this guess.

"That's what the Catholics used to call it. I take it you've met priests or nuns, Henry?"

Henry nodded with a smile.

"Considering the end product I see before me, they must have been very kind to you. The Catholics have gotten a terrible rendering in the last few years compared to the immeasurable charity they've performed over the centuries. Much of the recent bad news was their fault, of course, but historically they've been a pillar in building families and helping the less fortunate. A church family can't simply ignore its problems, but that's exactly what they did. Still, I'm proud to count myself as a product of the Catholic faith, although not quite proud enough to call myself a practicing Catholic. I'm afraid they wouldn't have me, with the kind of hoodlums I associate myself with these days."

Aisling let out only a quiet laugh this time.

"Other faiths are vague about that in between place. Most of them couldn't get past the simple notion that time doesn't really matter, so they dismissed the notion entirely. It's more convenient to assume that when one soul dies it immediately goes to heaven or hell. In the movies when they bring up reincarnation, death means that a souls jumps like a flea into another body, an awful, impractical concept that audiences love. Fortunately, that doesn't occur. Time is a factor, but it's not an important one.

"What's been fun for me is that some spirits I've come across have different terms for this place where they now find themselves. I've heard it called the Dog Pound, the God Pound - for dyslexic spirits - the Electoral College, Taint - as in, 'tain't heaven, 'tain't hell' - Limbo, Nebraska, and quite a few others. The spirits I'm in contact with – and the one you've been in contact with, so it seems – are not typically residents of heaven, as we think of it. Nearly all of them plan to get to heaven, but understand they are not of heaven now. The distance between heaven and earth is beyond our comprehension. It's not measured in distance, or in time. It's measured in the progression of the soul, which often spans many lifetimes – perhaps a hundred or more – and is the difference between a walking, cussing lug like you or me, and perfection."

Henry added, "That's like in baseball. You're saying that a spirit that enters heaven is a perfect hitter who gets a hit every time it comes to bat. Nobody achieves that level of perfection."

"Yes, good comparison. A baseball star can be invited to the All Star game by getting a hit every third time at bat. In the realm of souls, that might get you an invitation to be the janitor in a third world brothel. The perfection we're talking about is more difficult than batting a thousand. After a few dozen lives to practice, you should be much better than the greatest hitter of all, Ted Williams."

"You know Henry, Ted Williams of the Red Sox was the last player to hit more than four hundred, and ..."

"You don't need to tell me about that, Aisling. In my early years I believed Yankees fans were spawns of hell. To this day, when a strong wind blows at Fenway and some Yankee hats go flying, I still look for their horns." Henry smiled quietly. Aisling cackled.

"Aisling, do you enjoy being a medium? Is it a satisfying way to make a living?"

"That's such a complicated question, Henry. For me yes, it's very satisfying. I can't imagine spending my life differently. Living in only this dimension would be like being in a jail cell with a small window, seeing only the same view day after day.

"For you? I have no way to predict whether you could enjoy this vocation. What you soon discover when you become a medium is that when a person decides to have you read for them, there must be a very high degree of trust in place. If not, there's a very strong chance that things will end up badly. You'll learn things about people that is deeply personal, and you'd better be prepared. Still, a gift is a gift, and you have an opportunity to make their lives more fulfilled."

Henry was taking in this information in wonder, an eager student riveted on a fascinating subject.

"When deaths occur suddenly, with no warning, the adverse effects ripple very far. The wounds from these very sad events are not limited to those you can see in this world. Can you imagine the trauma and confusion of a young car crash victim as she suddenly is expected to leave this realm? It's an incredible transition that results in confusion and fear for a person who has barely become comfortable in her current skin.

"Often the transition is unexpected on the other side too. So for a very brief period, this spirit is simply in a state of disorientation because her spirit guide and other close spirits may not be entirely ready for such an abrupt transition. These events may cause chaos and confusion on the ground, but it's not too unlike what is happening in the spirit world either. Young, unexpected deaths are very sad for all involved."

Henry was wrapped in the conversation, and finally summoned a question. "Aisling what about fate? I've heard it discussed in movies and books, but have you any insight there?"

"People talk about fate, as if our lives are preordained. If you believe nothing else I tell you today Henry, believe this: Purer shit has never been shat. Events occur and people make decisions in response, none which could have foreseen. Events affect other events in ways that no one, except perhaps God, can understand entirely. The decisions we make many times per day affect those around us. For example, if you bring a child into this world then ignore him, that decision will likely create negative consequences, perhaps tragic. The damage that child caused were put in motion by you, and that becomes part of your legacy.

"People say 'it was meant to happen,' as if God decided that a car accident or mass shooting would in some way be helpful. Natural disasters maybe, but I doubt it. They happen, and many unfortunate souls are affected. Man-made disasters? Hogwash. From what I see, the pain of every single life affected by that killer is compounded onto the soul of the offender. Think about that, Henry. If you were to walk into a crowded market and explode a bomb that killed twenty people, are only twenty people irrevocably changed by your terrible action? Of course not. When twenty people die suddenly, their many friends and family are tortured by the pain. Hundreds – if not thousands – of people are affected. If their lives aren't torn apart, then their faith in the goodness of humanity has been eroded. The action may be done to justify a religious or a political point, or some point rooted in insanity, but the effects go far, far beyond the original intention.

"So you ask me if it's a satisfying job? Incredibly satisfying, Henry, but incredibly weighty too. I've learned things about humanity that I never knew I could handle. I enjoy it immensely most of the time. In those other times, I wish I were doing anything else. There is little enjoyment in serving up news that people don't want to hear, but which they must."

"Oh my," Henry said. "I didn't consider that."

"There was a recent customer who came in asking to contact a spouse who had committed suicide. These are always difficult situations, so I was prepared. In this case the spirit did respond to our summoning, but I wish he hadn't. He was angry, very bitter. I barely asked why he took his own life, and he told me he had no choice. He could not bear another moment with the person sitting across the table from me. He was going to take her life or his own, and he chose the latter.

"The worst of all is when your customer is there for the wrong reasons. Usually you don't know that for sure, but you have a feeling. Your customer is trying to learn something that will help him in this world, and if you agree to take your fee from them, you're bound to honor their request to the best of your ability. These are difficult decisions, but we realize this and bear the weight of our responsibility accordingly."

Henry took all this in with a steady stare off in the distance. "How can you have such confidence that you're qualified for all this? How can you know your judgement will be good enough all the time?"

"You can't, but getting good at this just takes time. I would never suggest taking money from someone unless you're certain you'll provide something of even higher value in return. If a customer pays for the truth, they should get the truth. More than once I've had customers walk out the door when I explained that I will not lie to them no matter what."

Henry sat before her, slowly nodding his head as if to comprehend all he was hearing. Then he looked at his watch. "Wow, I've taken up almost half an hour already. I did come here for some specific reasons."

"My goodness, you're right, Henry, I'm so sorry for going on like this. We can take all the time you need from here. I have no other appointments."

"Thanks," he said. "I still have so many questions."

Aisling inhaled. "I can't promise you'll have answers to them all today, but perhaps we can make progress. You're most interested in your family background, I assume."

"I need to know all I can about Freddy," he began. "Beyond him, I still don't have any idea who my family was. You told me they were nearby last time, but who are they? Where are they from? Do I have any living relatives?"

She nodded. "Let's begin."

Aisling gave a sincere, respectful praise to God and all the angels and other spirits who would be there on his behalf. This time Henry was able to flow easily into the necessary mood. When he closed his eyes, they did not feel entirely closed. He had heard the term "mind's eye," and felt his was completely open.

Within seconds they each had achieved the right balance between the tangible and spirit worlds.

Aisling smiled contentedly and said, "Henry, are you feeling open to communication with family tonight?"

"I am indeed." His focus was strong. "Are you sensing spirits nearby?"

"Aye, that I am."

"I feel it too. Can you help me understand who's with us today?"

"Your grandparents are nearby, bursting with pride as they were yesterday. Your brother is here. It seems he's glad you've returned, and that you're staying open to communication."

"Thank God," Henry said. "Me too."

Then Henry felt a more real physical presence, just to his left. He glanced toward the warmth and could see only a glow, like the faint image of an aura. But there was another combination of sensations too, the same sensation he felt the night before. This was familiar, a feeling from long ago. This was the closest he had ever come to a memory of someone in his actual family.

"Aisling, I think I feel his presence too. It's amazing, but I think I remember him!"

She smiled at Henry, eyes open this time. "He's relieved to know that, Henry. He certainly remembers you."

Aisling focused her attention above and to Henry's side. After a few seconds, she looked back at Henry.

"Your brother has some things to tell you but he's finding the communication difficult, or maybe frustrating. I can't tell whether he's frustrated that he can't speak directly with you, or if he's not certain he should."

"I'm just glad he's here," Henry said. "I hope to get better at communicating with him on my own. Until then," Henry said, "can you ask him how he died? Where he died? What his last name was, even?"

She paused only briefly before answering. "Your brother is not sure how much he should disclose, but he very much would like to encourage you to learn these things."

She appeared to be listening to something Freddy was telling her, then chose her words carefully.

"He's telling me something about a leap, Henry, but to look beyond the obvious. This has to do with his death, but he's not comfortable disclosing much more than that."

"Where did he die, and where did we live? I have no idea where to even start." Henry continually looked over his shoulder, as if to find reassurance in his brother's presence.

"I'm getting a forest of some kind. It looks very green. I don't get the whole thing." Aisling looked apologetically at Henry.

"A forest? Isn't there anything more? A state or a year, or anything? Maybe Forest is my last name?"

"That's not it. I can tell from his reaction. And I can also tell that he's not comfortable telling you even this much."

Henry understood the limits of the information Aisling could provide, and Freddy's dilemma in communicating anything at all. To ease tension, he directed his full energy on the room rather than through only Aisling. He immediately gained more focus, as if waking from a nap.

Eyes closed, he sensed a being above and to the left of Aisling. The aura he had seen before was morphing into a more clear spirit form. Henry was able to recognize the unique characteristics of his brother. He was kind and masculine, forgiving and nonjudgmental, anxious to communicate but close to a precipice. Henry sensed what Aisling was feeling, that he was there on his own volition but taking a chance in doing so.

"I'm Henry. Thanks for visiting me."

"You're welcome. I'm Freddy. Do you remember me?"

"I guess I do, but it was so long ago."

"You were little. I was there and then I was gone. It would be very painful to remember."

"I remember sadness, but it just never ended. After that it seems like I just sort of did what I was told for years."

"None of that was your fault. You must understand that."

"I do, and I trust you, but there's so much more I need to understand."

"Of course there is. Stay focused, and listen to your friend's advice. She is very highly regarded."

"Can you help me understand where to begin?"

"Not easily. I'm not permitted to interfere very much with your life, but instead show you loving support. Black Forest was where we were together. Until the leap."

"What about our parents?"

His brother paused, as if hearing from higher spirits. "I cannot say any more. As with everything, you need to open your eyes wide."

"Are our parents alive?"

"It's time for me to go. Follow where your heart and mind lead you, but watch for warning signs. I love you and I can't tell you what it means to talk with you. I won't be far from you, but I cannot guide you either. This journey is yours."

"I love you too."

The sensation was gone. Henry looked at Aisling in front of him, as if she had just entered the room.

"Henry, you're back. You made a strong connection, I see. Are you okay?"

"I'm blown away, Aisling. I was speaking with my brother. The feeling was incredible. He loves me and misses me. He's my brother!" Henry permitted himself a broad grin that Aisling returned.

"That's wonderful. I trust your connection was an important one."

Henry paused. "Important. Very important, but it feels like I have so much work to do. At least now I have a place to start."

For the second evening in a row, Henry again found himself in a haze in his apartment after the overwhelming events of the day. He was invigorated by the intense connection with his brother, but felt the full weight of the mysteries that he was drawn to confront.

His whole life he had felt disconnected from anything resembling a family, now he was compelled to somehow pull together his legacy. His brother died at a young age, a tragedy with its own mysterious circumstances. From what Henry could only guess, the circumstances that ended Freddy's life meant the end of their small young family. If his parents died in the same event that took his brother's life, why were they unavailable in the spirit world?

If they were not dead, why was he forced to live in foster homes? Perhaps there were some reasons they were unable to care for him. If they were incarcerated, that would explain their absence, as would some sort of permanently disability that both suffered. If the two had been in prison or in a care facility for the last few decades, he would be incensed. All this time he could have been in touch with them, were it not for the fumbling of the state of Massachusetts and their inability to handle children who were wards of the state. He had been trying for years to find information from them, but each attempt ran into a wall. Those state employees who were sympathetic and willing to help him would soon become frustrated with the lack of information available.

A more troubling possibility was that his parents had chosen to abandon him. After Freddy's death, perhaps they decided that being parents was not something they could handle. It would be easier to give their younger son a new start under new circumstances than risk failing again. That would be the cruelest of all outcomes he could imagine, so he put the possibility furthest from his mind.

He decided to research the one tangible shred of information that came from his contact with Freddy: he could learn more about Black Forest.

Several years earlier Henry performed some similar research on Jacksonville, where his earliest adoptive family, the Starks, had moved when he was seven. His trip was mainly an attempt to contacts the Starks to learn about how he had come into their family. His attempts to track them down proved fruitless. He tried calling all the combinations of names he remembered – the sons Carl and Max, the daughter Delilah who was his earliest friend in life, the parents William and Claudine – but none were to be found. If he had managed to reach them, they were not willing to admit their identity. He felt certain that Delilah would welcome his contact, but there was no Delilah Stark in any phone book, possibly meaning she was married, or more likely had decided to move on from this cold family.

After his many phone calls to Florida, Henry shifted his attention to the local area. He contacted every adoption agency in the Boston area that he was able to find. None had a record of adopting him to the Stark family. It was as if neither the Stark family nor Henry had ever existed. He began to wonder if he truly did exist, even now.

A simple internet search on Black Forest turned up the most hits on a rectangular, wooded area in Southwest Germany consisting of about 4500 square miles and a smattering of small towns. It was known for its natural beauty and history of mining and agriculture, but otherwise unremarkable to an American with no real understanding of Europe.

He meticulously combed through information about many of the towns and few cities in Black Forest. Baden-Baden, Freiburg, Gengenbach, Gütenbach, Bad Herrenalb, Wolfach, Staufen, Freudenstadt, and several others. He was awake until well past midnight trying to understand more about the region and the culture.

He began to contemplate his strategy for a trip across the ocean. The language barrier would be difficult, but performing a meaningful search over a week or two with so little additional information seemed to hold little chance for success.

Following an exhausting sleep, with tangled, chaotic dreams that imagined a host of strange lineages, from a traveling circus background to a father who was a Nobel Prize winner, to parents who were war heroes, Henry awoke to the reality that the search into his beginnings was starting from very meager beginnings.

With tired eyes and a whirling mind, Henry started into his workday trying to focus on the task at hand, his current occupation. He logged into his computer to be sure of his appointments for the day. It was a light schedule. He launched right back into his work from the night before. He started a list of things he needed to think about, including checking the status of his passport, finding reasonable plane fares, figuring out transportation once he got there, conversing with local government officials in German, and so much more.

He was nearly an hour into all these details when the weight of the challenge caught up with him. He decided to take a short walk outside to clear his mind. Ingesting the cool, clean air, his mind was able to understand the challenge, then to pose a basic question. The thought of going to a strange land, fighting through a language he did not understand, was imposing. What if there was another Black Forest?

In front of his computer, he searched on Black Forest again. He looked further down the list and found a news story about a drilling dispute in Colorado in a town called Black Forest. He learned that it was a small, charming-looking town north of the US Air Force Academy on the Palmer Divide that separated the nearby Colorado Springs metro area from the high plains south of the Denver metro area.

Henry dove into his internet research with renewed enthusiasm. After only a few minutes he learned there were a few other areas called Black Forest around the country, but most were named for commercial ventures like campgrounds, bakeries, and restaurants. Except for an uninhabited wild lands area east of Flagstaff, Arizona, he couldn't find a single town in the US or Canada with the same name.

There were only two possibilities – Germany or Colorado. Henry reasoned that transporting a two year old – or younger – across the ocean would have been very difficult to orchestrate, highly unlikely for German parents to even consider. There would have been many parents within the country willing to adopt a healthy toddler. Black Forest, Colorado was far more likely. From viewing available pictures of real estate and satellite images of the streets, he became more convinced that this should be the focus of his search.

For the next few days he did all he could to learn about the town. Located in El Paso County, there were about 15,000 inhabitants. The terrain was wooded, expansive, and interesting. It was an expensive place to live, with large lots and rustic homes. It was over 7,000 feet above sea level, close to a rise called Monument Hill on Interstate 25 that was the bane of travelers during the hard weather months.

From a few well-placed phone calls, he determined that official records were available through the El Paso County Clerk and Recorder's office in downtown Colorado Springs. Its employees were very willing to make their resources available to visitors, but were not willing to conduct searches on request. The kind of search Henry had in mind, one that was lacking in specific dates and names, would require a personal visit.

The Colorado Springs Gazette would be his best source for any birth or death announcements dating back years, and their online archives were limited to the past ten years. Historical records before that time were available on microfiche, on premises only. Henry's quest for his past finally had some direction.

That evening he found affordable tickets on a direct flight from Boston to Denver leaving early the next morning. He phoned Aisling to tell her of his plans.

"Henry, this is something you must do. I applaud you for following your instincts."

"Funny," Henry said, "that sounds a lot like something my brother said to me."

"Henry, something tells me your trip won't be a vain. I think it's appropriate to give you a blessing that my brother gave me before my first trip to the states.

May you have warm words on a cold evening,

A full moon on a dark night,
And the road downhill all the way to your door."

"Aisling, that's wonderful."

"Sláinte Mhaith, Henry. Be well. I'll look forward to hearing all about your discoveries when you return."

His plane landed at Denver International Airport on a bright blue, cold Colorado morning.

As he drove his rental car south on Interstate 25 south of Castle Rock, he marveled at the miles of high rolling plains, framed by Pikes Peak in the distance to the Southwest. The experience was surreal. Just a day before he was pondering the logistics of a trip to the Black Forest in Southern Germany. Now here he was, just a few miles from where he very possibly may have spent his early years.

By noon he was approaching the town of Monument, which offered the most direct route to Black Forest. As he drove over the Palmer Divide and down Monument Hill, his heart began to flutter. He exited on Baptist Road as his mind moved in a thousand directions. He was not certain whether this intense rush of emotions was the result of jet lag, the altitude, or something else, but he had never experienced this feeling before. After being on the high plains for miles since the airport, the notion of suddenly being in a thick forest was disorienting.

He turned east then south again on Black Forest Road. The roads in this small but private, wooded town all seemed familiar. As he drove along these long straight roads, past large rustic properties that concealed tasteful, private homes, the familiarity was pervasive. Fragments of memories were etched in the trees, the snow on the ground, the shadows, and the sky barely visible through the tall trees.

There is no question, Henry thought, *I used to live here.*

He knew from his inquiries at home that there were no local records to be searched in town, so his research would need to happen in Colorado Springs. He drove back toward the interstate and continued south. His first stop was the Colorado Springs Gazette, which had been the primary newspaper for the area since the 1940s. When he found the Archives area, he approached the older man at the desk. His name tag said simply "Martin Francis, Archivist."

Henry explained to the man his intent to look through obituaries from the late 1970s or early 80s, that he was adopted, and that he came upon information suggesting he might have had a brother who died as a child. He also admitted that he was uncertain if he spent his young years in Colorado, Massachusetts, or somewhere in between.

"That sounds like quite a puzzle. Let's get you started." He brought Henry into a secure area, where he gave instruction on how the microfiche archives were organized, how to use the machine, and how to print out specific pages of interest. "We close at five," the man mumbled as he shuffled away.

Henry spent most of the time that afternoon becoming acquainted with the layout of the newspaper, understanding how things were reported so many years before. He glanced through articles at various times during the year and always tried to view the obituaries for children that had passed. In his short time looking through archives that afternoon, it was rare to find a reference to a child that had passed away unexpectedly.

When five o'clock approached, Henry packed up his notes. Walking past the Archivist, he thanked him and said, "See you tomorrow. Lots more work to do."

"Very good," the man replied. "Welcome to Colorado, or maybe I should say welcome back."

By the time he arrived in the Gazette office the next morning, he had already formulated his strategy.

Henry had long felt that he was born sometime around 1980. From his contact with Freddy, he guessed Freddy was probably two or three years older, and that Freddy died at about age four or five. That would put his birth somewhere in 1977 or 1978, and his death in 1981 or 1982. It was probable but not guaranteed that either of them was born in Colorado, and that neither of their first names were completely reliable for tracking down official records. His original name might not have been Henry at all. A conclusion that he deemed to be odd was that Freddy's name, heard from an unseen spirit just a couple days before, seemed more reliable than his own.

Finding a child about three or four who had died in a fall in 1981 or 82 would most likely pinpoint his brother. If he found a record that was a match for these tragic series of events, the pieces might finally fall into place. However any death of a small boy would be something to study closely. El Paso County was home to no more than two or three hundred thousand people at the time, so the death of a five year old would have been a rarity.

The approach he took to his research was tedious, but he wanted to be thorough. He went through each obituary from the beginning of 1980 through the end of 1982, which meant scrolling down roll after roll of microfiche. Although he read the details of every child's death, for each death of a child ages four to six during the period, he wrote down on his pad all the details about their life and death that might help in his quest.

During the three year period he found seven children that met his criteria in all of El Paso County. Of those children, he found two girls who he ruled out immediately. Despite Aisling's explanations about reincarnation and how spirits stay together through various lives, the voice speaking to them was clearly a male.

His search lasted beyond the morning. By one-thirty he had a list of five boys near age five that had died unexpectedly in El Paso County in the years around 1980 and 1981.

Gerald McCullum, Age 4, Born October 16, 1975, Died May 29, 1980. Died from an accidental gunshot in his home in Monument.

Christopher Chernoff, Age 5, Born February 13, 1975, Died July 4, 1980. Died from an accidental fireworks incident in front of his home near Montebello and Flintridge, in the Northeast part of the city.

Renaldo Wilk, Age 5, Born January 2, 1975, Died December 10, 1980. Hit by a passing motorist while near his home at E. Costilla and South Cedar, east of the downtown area. (Driver stopped.)

Marcus Chimera, Age 5, Born June 4, 1974, Died February 29, 1980. Hit by a passing motorist while near his home in Monument. (Hit and run, driver not found.)

Rory Shook, Age 4, Born November 26, 1977, Died April 20, 1982. Died of complications from appendicitis at Penrose Hospital in Colorado Springs.

When he had finished the list, he believed he had come up empty, that this was a wasted trip. He saw no deaths that appeared to come from a fall.

Henry stood up, shook his head, stretched, and walked near the old caretaker.

"How's the research coming along?"

"Slow progress, but I'm getting there. My name is Henry." He extended his hand.

"Call me Marty. While you're doing your work, don't hesitate to check in with me now and then. I've worked here since 1968, and I've read each paper cover to cover in all that time."

"Thanks Marty, I'll do that." Henry stepped out into the brisk Colorado afternoon. In a matter of seconds he realized that in this thin, cool air, the difference between standing in the sun and in the shade was about 25 degrees. After a brisk walk around the block he stood in the sun for a few minutes with his eyes closed. When he headed back in for work, he was energized.

Henry went back to rolls from 1980 to learn about the death of these children. He hoped their deaths at such young ages would have justified a newspaper story regardless of circumstances, and he was right. Some details were more available than others, due in part, Henry assumed, to how well the family was known locally.

Henry printed each of the stories and analyzed them closely. He was deflated to see that none of the children died from any kind of fall.

One boy's story caught his attention because of the location of death.

Marcus Chimera was also hit by a passing motorist, one who apparently did not stop to find out his condition. The accident occurred on Burgess Road in South Monument, which was not an especially busy thoroughfare. The article explained that some roads in this part of El Paso County tended to attract vehicles that were in a hurry because Monument was along two popular north-south roads, Interstate 25 and Highway 83. Officers believed Marcus was trying to chase down his pet dog when he was struck. A black sedan was being sought, but no license number was reported. Unlike nearly all reports of accidental deaths that Henry read, there was no mention of a surviving family.

His thoughts were interrupted by Marty's approach.

"Henry, I hate to do this do you but it's time to close up. It's five fifteen already, and I have an appointment with my wife over gourmet hot dogs and baked beans. She's a gourmet cook, at least she tells me, but I suspect it must've been on a cattle drive."

Henry laughed wearily. Marty steadied his gaze on Henry. "May I ask where your research brought you today?"

"I found five boys that died from 1980 through 1982, which is about the right time frame. One of them died up near Black Forest, in Monument, so at the moment I'm focused on that boy. The problem is, I see no mention of a family."

"Maybe I can suggest something you hadn't thought of," Marty said
"What's that?"

"Maybe you should talk to somebody that was here during that time. Like me, maybe." Marty was stone faced.

Henry laughed. "Oh God, you're right. I should have stopped by to see you. Analysis paralysis, I guess."

"It happens," Marty said. "Can I see the names on your list?"

Henry shuffled through his paper and pulled out the articles.

Marty pulled his specs over his long nose and skimmed through each. "Oh yeah, I remember that case. That was awful. Oh dang, that was a bad one too." Marty looked up at Henry with a thoughtful glance. "These are some sad memories, Henry. A lot of families had a hard time recovering."

Henry nodded. "These stories really touched me too. Even after all these years, I can almost imagine their pain."

Marty was silent for several seconds as he read the last article. "I remember this one too well, the Chimera boy. The reporter had a bear of a time getting any information out of the cops on the case. We'll talk in the morning. I might be able to find some other notes that will jog my memory."

Henry was ready for an uninspired evening of melting in front of his hotel room television with some pizza and a bottle of red wine. As he turned north on Cascade toward his hotel, he decided he was not ready to retire to his hotel room quite yet. With almost an hour of twilight left, he decided to drive to north to Black Forest. The urge to go there again was hard to explain to himself, but with little else drawing him back to the hotel, he did not fight it.

It was a twenty minute ride in heavy rush hour traffic, and soon he was driving on the same wooded country roads that looked so familiar a few hours before.

He drove slowly, looking at each property for some sign of recognition. The roads were long and straight, tree lined with few intersections. The speed limit was 45 and when a car or truck came along it indeed appeared to be in a hurry, just as he had read. He moved to the shoulder to let cars pass, the drivers barely noticing him.

The sun was drawing down, the shadows long, and the streaks of sunlight through the trees were growing longer. As he drove north on Black Forest Road he noticed a street sign for Burgess Road. He recognized the name from his research earlier in the day and turned right.

Within seconds a strange feeling began to overtake him. He immediately felt the presence of a force he could not control. He pulled his car to the side of the road and looked all around. The immediate area was more familiar than anything he had experienced since landing in Colorado. The foliage was larger and thicker, but the driveways, mailboxes, and homes were a familiar sight from many years before. To the right he saw a modest blue house tucked away, barely visible from the road. To his left was a driveway, thick trees blocking the far end.

The relief of familiarity soon gave way to nausea and dizziness. He wanted to survey the area for signs of recognition, but it brought only a throbbing pain.

It subsided only when he closed his eyes, replaced by a nearly perfect image of the area around him. Rather than a mid-spring evening with just traces of snow around, he saw a bright winter day. An inch or two of new-fallen snow was all around. He opened his eyes to try to understand the conflict brought on by his heightened senses, but the sick feeling returned. He closed his eyes to focus on the image coming from somewhere within.

From the distance there appeared the headlights of an oncoming car moving rapidly toward him. Just then a dog, which had the markings of perhaps a Shepherd or Doberman mix, came bounding through the snow from the wooded area on the left. He was momentarily alarmed that the dog was in danger, but the dog easily crossed before the car passed. His eyes followed the dog as it continued, then he turned back to the oncoming car. His relief turned to horror. A small boy was sprinting from the woods toward the street after the dog. In a fraction of a second his thoughts raced. "Surely the kid will see the car. SURELY the car will see the kid coming from the woods. *He doesn't see it!*"

The boy and the car met in the road. The car braked at the last possible moment, but it was too late. The boy never appeared to see the car, and the result was horrific. A dark red cloud appeared in the air in front of the car, and the child flew back and to Henry's left as the car finally slowed.

The car did not come to a full stop until it was behind and to Henry's left. As it passed him, he was certain that it was an unmarked police car. A spotlight was mounted in the driver's side door, and extra warning lights in the rear window. He glanced at the driver but could not discern features beyond what appeared to be a tall man with very short hair.

The car stopped about two hundred feet from the point of impact, pulling halfway onto the shoulder. Henry was still stunned by the scene. He braced for the bright lights of the cruiser, but the lights never came on and the car door never opened. Henry found himself trying to intervene, to yell at the officer. The opportunity never came and the cruiser sped away.

His next image was of a slender woman with brown hair running through the woods. A small child was toddling behind her. She stopped at the road and fell to her knees at the bloody sight before her on the side of the road. She sobbed, horrified. The small child soon caught up to her. She turned to the small boy, covered his face, and carried him back to the house, her body convulsing as she walked.

Henry opened his eyes. The evening was darker, full twilight. The sick feeling was gone, but shock and horror remained. He held his face in his hands to try to get a grip on reality, to understand what he just witnessed. After a few moments he got out of his car. His instincts told him that he had to go try to find the boy. As he turned back to the point of impact then scanned the long distance to where the boy would have landed, there was no blood, and in fact no snow on the ground. He realized that what he had seen was a vision of something that happened here years before, the death of Marcus Chimera.

Still, he struggled to find anything to link this death to his quest. Then he remembered the words his brother spoke to him: *"Black Forest was where we were together. Until the leap."* He pulled out his notes and the article from Marcus's death. The death occurred "on Burgess Road in South Monument," but the two towns were so close that it was likely a misprint He was clearly ON Burgess Road, but it was in the town of Black Forest, not in South Monument.

Then he looked at his notes from earlier in the day for something else that might help.

Marcus Chimera, Age 5, Born June 4, 1974, Died February 29, 1980. Hit by a passing motorist while near his home in Monument. (Hit and run incident, driver not found.)

There it was! Marcus died on February 29, Leap Day! All this time he had assumed the term "leap" referred to a fall, that Marcus had jumped to his death. Marcus, his brother, died on Leap Day in 1980.

Henry laid his head back on his headrest, feeling a small sense of accomplishment. He smiled as a mystery was solved, that of his last name. It was *Chimera.*

There were still many more pieces of this puzzle remaining, including the fate of his parents and what happened to them after Marcus's death. Or was it Freddy? Was one of them just a nickname? There were still missing puzzle pieces, but he felt a deep satisfaction with his progress.

He closed his eyes for a few seconds, then opened them to see the final orange glow of sunset over Pike's Peak.

A Boy and His Dog

Henry awoke in his hotel room in a haze. The travel of the prior day combined with his research and discoveries put him in a place of half dream, half reality. When he knew he was awake he took stock in what he knew to be real, contemplating how he could make the most of his remaining time in Colorado. The sheriff's department? Cemeteries? Black Forest again? Certainly the Gazette for starters to align his thinking with Marty, who was glad to help.

As he opened the curtains in his hotel room, a cold but glorious Colorado day welcomed him. After a light breakfast with plenty of coffee, he headed directly to Colorado Springs Gazette.

Marty the archivist was expecting him. "Good to see you back, Henry. You look ready for a new round of sleuthing."

"Good morning, Marty. I'm not sure what's next but I'm ready for it."

The older man looked down at his desk, scattered with freshly printed articles from long ago. "I dug around for some of the follow up articles on the Chimera boy from what you showed me yesterday. There's some good reading to start your day."

"You're the best. Since I left, I'm even more sure I have the right boy."

Marty looked up quickly. "What happened since you left here yesterday?"

"Call it a hunch. I drove up to Black Forest last night and I think I have some real memories of that place. I know it sounds loopy, but I just have a really strong feeling that's where my past is."

"Well if you lived there," Marty said, "even as a toddler, you might have some lingering memories."

"Thanks again for digging these out. You saved me valuable time. What's your take on the Chimera case from reading these articles after all these years?"

Marty's expression did not allow Henry much optimism. "I remember this case, and the reporter that covered it. He had a really hard time getting to the bottom of what happened but it wasn't all his fault. He dug in pretty hard but the case was never solved. The person that hit the boy was never brought to justice."

Henry thought back yet again to his vision from the previous night of an unmarked police car running down his brother.

"That's frustrating," he replied, trying to appear objective. "Obviously forensics weren't as advanced back then, but a violent accident like that, you would think there'd be something to build on."

"Well, as you'll see from the articles I pulled out, the investigation was sidetracked, to put it mildly."

"Sidetracked? What could possibly sidetrack a case like this? I'm guessing fatal hit and runs didn't happen very often near Colorado Springs back then."

"Have a look for yourself."

Henry brought the articles into the next room. He read carefully through each of the four articles that spanned two weeks following the child's death. As he read, a heaviness crept over his mood.

The first article was the same one he had found from the previous day, but the events took on a new meaning. After reading through it again, he walked over to Marty's desk.

"This article talks about the accident happening on Burgess Road in South Monument, but I drove through there last night and I thought I was in Black Forest. Can you help me understand that?"

"I don't know what to tell you about that," Marty answered. "There's really no such thing as 'South Monument,' and Black Forest was definitely its own area back then. The reporter wasn't originally from here and wasn't too familiar with that area. There wasn't much development all the way up from the city back then. It was really separated from Colorado Springs proper. Anyway yeah, I found that odd too. Jimmy Shell, the reporter, hasn't worked here in years. I have no idea where he'd be today, or even if he's still writing."

Henry drifted into the next room.

The second article explained that Marcus was probably chasing his dog Scooby through the woods after it left their yard. The boy probably never realized he was crossing into the street. It went on to describe how an "unidentified motorist, probably passing through" hit him, killing him instantly.

The article quoted Sheriff W. T. Mahon. "We're not entirely certain whether the motorist knew what he or she collided with. I encourage anyone who has any information about this terrible accident to contact us immediately."

The sheriff was quick to assume that a passing motorist was responsible, Henry noted, discouraging any suspicion directed toward locals.

Then Henry read something that he had been waiting a lifetime to learn.

"Marcus Chimera leaves behind his grieving parents, Roland and Jenny Chimera."

He finally knew his parents names! Instead of a faded image of loving parents with no identity, he now had something to call them. Roland and Jenny. They began to gather features in his mind. He closed his eyes and began to allow the images to form in his mind. He allowed the new information to wash over and through him eyes closed.

Next he focused on their last names. He had heard the word "chimera" before, and decided to perform a search on the meaning.

"1. In Greek mythology, a fire-breathing she-monster usually represented as a composite of a lion, a goat, and a serpent. 2. A creation of the imagination; an impossible and foolish fantasy. 3. In Biology, an organism, especially a plant, containing tissues from at least two genetically distinct parents."

At that moment he made the decision to have his name legally changed from Stark to Chimera. He still had no idea of what became of them after his brother's death, but this would bring him closer to his past in a small way.

Then he noticed another oddity. There was no mention of a younger sibling in the article. It was as though he never existed! Yet the sight of this horrified mother caring for her surviving child in the seconds following the accident would never leave him.

The next article was from several days later. Henry immediately understood Marty's comment about how the investigation was sidetracked. It explained that when the El Paso County Sheriff's Department came to the Chimera home to interview the grieving parents, they had reason to suspect the presence of drugs. Upon further examination, they came upon a large quantity of marijuana in the home and placed the couple under arrest.

Could that be? Could Henry's parents have been pot dealers in the 1970s? Black Forest, just east of the Air Force Academy and in one of the most conservative counties in Colorado, was an unlikely place to deal illegal drugs.

The final article was printed in a Sunday edition of the Gazette, and offered no information that was not already revealed. However the tone of the last article changed completely even though Jimmy Shell was the reporter throughout.

The story focus shifted completely away from the death of a five year old boy, and to the shock that a local couple was allegedly dealing drugs. This abomination was happening within a mile of a local school. The writer managed to remind his readers that a child was killed by an unknown hit and run driver, but only as added background for the story about drug-dealing parents. This had to mean only one thing, Henry reasoned. The sheriff was unwilling to give Jimmy Shell any information on the accident, and the writer had no choice but to write a story about what facts he could pull from the police.

None of the articles mentioned another child in the home. Henry was convinced this was not a simple omission. He decided it was time to talk with his new friend Marty.

"Marty, how far forward did you look on this case? Were there other articles after these?"

"I had a feeling you'd ask that. We have a system for indexing and cross-referencing articles that have the same primary story line. Henry, it's the damnedest thing. I can't find another article on the Chimeras after mid-March."

"Any idea why?"

"Jimmy left the paper at about that time, and maybe nobody picked up the story. The strange thing is that if your parents were busted for dealing pot, that case would be in the news as it went through the county court system. It would've been impossible to miss in this town, and honestly I just don't remember what became of them. Maybe their case ended up in the

Federal court up in Denver. I would have thought some reporter would have stayed with the story, even if Jimmy left. But I haven't seen anything."

Marty took off his glasses. "As you probably noticed, this county and this town are very conservative today. Not only do we have the Air Force Academy next door, but also Fort Carson and Peterson Air Force base. There are lots of military folks here now, and there were then too. Not to mention the standard conservatism that was here before any of the defense money. So a case like this would've been big news back then. I suppose the story would've faded away if there were no clues and little hope for solving the case. The paper didn't have a lot of reporters back then."

"That may be the case, but wouldn't it be worth the Sheriffs investigating, putting out the word to watch cars for damage of some kind? Sure, it could've been somebody coming through, but it just as easily could've been a neighbor coming home from work." Henry's agitation was apparent to Marty.

"Definitely, but Black Forest didn't have their own police department back then, so it would've been the El Paso Sheriffs that investigated. I can only guess that once they found the pot and the parents were behind bars, there was nobody left to push them into making it a higher priority. I'm not defending them, Henry. I'm just guessing about why nothing came of the case."

"I understand," Henry brooded. "but there are at least two loose ends that I can think of."

Marty interrupted him. "I'm with you. One of those 'loose ends' is standing in front of me. Am I right?"

"Yeah, and the other is, what happened to my parents? Marcus's parents."

"Those are questions worth pursuing. Maybe I can go back and look through birth announcements, wedding announcements, that sort of thing. Why don't you leave that to me, and you focus on public records, since you're only here for a few days."

Henry brightened up a bit. "Are you sure? That's asking a lot, Marty. I wouldn't feel right taking you away from your other work."

"It's part of my job to help customers with their searches. Plus I can do this faster than you. Spend your time today digging for public records. Come on back this afternoon and I'll let you know what I found. The County Records Office is at 210 South Tejon Street. That's about seven or eight blocks west of here. See you this afternoon."

Henry thanked him and hurried to the Public Records section of the El Paso County Sheriff's Department. He approached a uniformed deputy, clean-shaven and muscular. Henry explained his challenge concisely but with urgency.

The deputy explained that searches through Sheriff records needed to be performed by employees, and that a separate form was needed for each individual being searched. He was cautioned that some information might be blacked out on reports. Henry filled out a form for his brother and his mother, showed his driver's license, paid a small fee, and handed them to the deputy.

"Things are looking quiet this morning so far, so we can probably pull this together this morning. Come back after lunch and we'll try to pull together what we can for you."

One minor but nagging mystery was that he had never known his actual birthdate. Perhaps he would finally find that out today. His adopted parents usually decided to celebrate his birthday on some other holiday, usually Christmas. That always had the effect on Henry that he could not own even the most basic right of a child, a date to call his own special day.

In the El Paso County Department of Health and Environment, he first went for the easy search, however the clerk seemed determined to ensure there was no such thing. She seemed to Henry to believe her job responsibility was to ensure that only people with vested interest in vital records could have access to them. When he explained that he was adopted and was searching out his birth records, she gave him a grudging look to signal that he gave her the only possible correct answer. She presented him with a brief form, photocopied his driver's license, and gave him the green light to roam the county's database of vital records.

Within minutes he had found the birth record for his brother in a computerized index. He scribbled the reference number and birth date, and brought it to the counter. In no more than two minutes the clerk handed him the record.

Marcus Gerald Chimera, born to Jennifer Brown Chimera and Roland Frederick Chimera, May 4, 1977, at 4:26 p.m. in Penrose Hospital, Colorado Springs. Denomination: Catholic.

"That's it?" He was disappointed at how little there was.

Henry launched into his next search with doubt, etched in his mind over decades, that he would find any record of his own birth. All his hope was pinned on some recent visions that could easily have been the product of an overactive imagination.

Henry had gone through his timeline more times than he could remember, but he did once more. He began Kindergarten in the fall of 1985 and considered himself about the same age developmentally as most of his classmates, so he focused on 1980 but began a year earlier. He now had a last name to work with, so he hoped his search had a fighting chance.

There was nothing. It was as if he had never been born.

After several minutes of wondering why, including the possibility that he might have been born elsewhere, he could have predicted this outcome. His life had one big mystery, and the details always managed to remain hidden from view. He would learn and move on, as he had always done.

Despite the setback, he still believed he had a good chance of finding a death certificate for his brother and a marriage certificate of his parents. He was correct in the first assumption but would be disappointed on the second.

The death certificate for Marcus, dated February 29, 1980, described his cause of death as "Impact trauma to the middle torso region, resulting in organ damage to the liver, one kidney, heart, and one lung, which resulted in the child's immediate death."

Henry's only thought was that his brother's death was swift and devoid of suffering, a blessing.

He spent over an hour looking for a record of his parents' marriage, spanning the years 1964 to 1972. It came up empty. He finally gave up the search.

In thinking through what other searches he could possibly perform while here, he decided that the only one left was to try to find death certificates for his parents. This too came up empty. He looked through all records up through the most recent using the name Chimera, which was somewhat unusual. Of those few who had died in El Paso County in the years since 1981, no first names were near to a match with his mother or father. He even tried his mother's apparent maiden name, Brown, and found no deaths of a Jennifer or a Roland.

By the time he finished his searches it was after two o'clock. He barely noticed his hunger pains. He paid the clerk for extra copies of the birth certificates. After consuming but barely tasting a burger and fries from a corner fast food restaurant, he headed back to the Sheriff's Department. The deputy at the desk was the same man that helped him that morning.

"Yes sir, Mister Chimera, we have a couple reports for you here. Two reports, each less than ten pages. That'll be twelve dollars."

Henry reached for his cash while the deputy retrieved two manila folders.

"Some text on the report about the Chimera couple was deleted. There must have been some information that couldn't be released to the public."

"These were my parents," Henry protested. "and whatever they did happened over thirty years ago. Don't you have an original of the report? What's the point of hiding information now?"

"Yes sir, I understand your point." The deputy was probably no more than in his mid-thirties and didn't appear to be hiding anything, but he seemed to have no inclination to go outside any rules for this out of state visitor either.

"The way things have always been handled here in El Paso County, is that every record is kept in two places when they're made public, which usually happens within forty-five days of final disposition. The Sheriff's Department keeps the original copy in a file vault that isn't accessible to the public. The other copy is made available to the public. Some, like this one, has parts that have been redacted because the D. A. and Sheriff at the time decided that information should never be released to the public. That decision is not revisited unless a case is reopened and things change, then they'll always tear up the old public copy and start over. Sometimes they delete nothing, sometimes a lot. On cases that are still open, there's almost always text that's redacted from public view."

Henry moved closer to the deputy. "So you're saying this case might still be open?"

The deputy was deliberate in his reply. "Extradited cases are always considered open. They never close unless the extradition fails and the legal process continues. I'd suggest you read the report, then maybe I can help."

"Extradited? To where?" Henry was amazed at the turns this search was taking.

"Mexico, sir. Read the report. We're open for another ninety minutes."

Henry took the report to a public area with tables and chairs. The report contained more deleted text than legible. The only descriptions available included the basics of the case: the people involved, the circumstances for their search, and that the couple were defiant in protest while they were arrested. It also described the couple as "distraught, wailing through the whole process."

He read through the legible text several times, trying to imagine how he would react as a parent as his life, everything he and his partner had worked for, was being shattered in a single evening. From what he could discern, the deputies arrived after a frantic phone call from the mother. They arrived on the scene and found the father weeping over the boy's crushed body. They went into the house with the consent of the parents and found the mother weeping in the kitchen. There was a smell of marijuana smoke, and a small red water pipe was visible in the living room. Based on the standard of probable cause, they searched the premises. They found fourteen ounces of a green leafy substance in plastic bags in the freezer, later confirmed as marijuana. The deputies cuffed the father and mother for the remainder of the interview, then transported them to the county jail for booking. No mention of another child was legible in the police report, but there were vast sections of text that could contain great detail on the presence of another child.

On the final page of the report, Henry was able to read several paragraphs that gave him the only clue what may have become of his parents.

"A routine computer search of Mr. Chimera revealed there was a warrant for his arrest in the Mexican State of Sinaloa, in the city of Los Mochis. The warrant indicated he is wanted for questioning in the murder of a police officer in a case related to marijuana trafficking. The warrant also named Mrs. Chimera as a suspect. The Chimeras were extradited to Sinaloa on 19 March 1981. Sheriff Mahon and Deputy Brighton accompanied the couple to Culiacán, the state capital."

Henry was shaken by what he was reading. Despite his odds of pulling anything more from the Deputy, he had nothing more to lose.

"Deputy, why would the El Paso District Attorney's office agree to transport two people that were suspected of being pot dealers down to Sinaloa? I don't know much about that state, but I've read that drug cartels are fairly active there these days. Why would the D. A. do that instead of charging them here in the states?"

"Sir," the deputy sincerely replied. "I have no information about that but I can tell you – and I checked with my supervisor – that this could not have been done without the recommendation of the D. A. and the confirmation of the court. So the decision could not have been an arbitrary decision by the D. A. A judge had to be involved, and he would have based his decision on whatever he thought was appropriate for the circumstances."

"Okay, fair enough," Henry continued calmly, "but I'm here because these were my parents. I believe I was there in the house when they were arrested but there's no mention of another child in the house, at least that I'm allowed to read. How could I get access to the original report?"

"Well, sir, I could have you speak with my supervisor, but he and I talked already. It will take a motion in court to unseal these records. Given the nature of your request, that there isn't any kind of open investigation, that it's just to settle an old mystery, the courts would not get to it anytime soon. It would be a long process."

"What's become of Sheriff Mahon and Deputy Brighton?"

"I know that Deputy Brighton died of natural causes – cancer I think – back in the late 1980s. He left the department a few years before that, my boss tells me. I know that Sheriff Mahon retired around the same time. That's about all I know. I can see if Sergeant Adams is available. Would you like to speak with him?"

"Yes, please."

Henry sat in the waiting area, and the deputy disappeared into the back. Within a few minutes, a middle aged African American man came into the waiting area. In his earlier years he was probably a large, intimidating man. Now he looked weathered and nearly ready to retire.

"I'm Sergeant Andre Adams. You're Mister Stark?" Adams held out his hand.

The two officers invited Henry into a conference room. Henry wasted no time. "Sergeant, you read my report?" The older man nodded.

"If there was another child in the home at the time, what would have happened to him?"

"If that were the case, the child would have been given up to the County Health Services folks. If the child was adopted out, which is what usually happens in cases where the parents are unavailable for a long stretch and no relatives are willing to step up, I can tell you that you won't get any info out of them. They don't even hold onto information any longer than ten years."

"You're kidding me!"

"No sir, that policy's been in place for years. They avoid situations where they're forced to give up information they wouldn't want to reveal, so they decided ten years then destroy. I have to say, in the years I've been here, it's kept them out of trouble."

"Did you at least know the Sheriff and the Deputy that brought them down to Mexico?"

"I knew both of them. They were old guys when I started. Brighton died of cancer just a few years after he retired. Mahon was the Sheriff when I got here, but he retired shortly after I started, about '87. He went back east somewhere, near Boston I think. We haven't heard from him since."

Henry was startled. "Boston? Any idea why he moved to Boston from way out here?"

"I heard he had family out there. Everybody I spoke with about it was glad he had a place to retire that wasn't nearby."

"So what did you think of these guys when you worked with them?"

Adams looked closely at Henry for a few seconds before answering, as if deciding whether to allow a higher degree of candor. "I didn't like either of 'em. Brighton was a difficult guy to be around. I've always felt there are two reasons that guys become cops. It's either because they really want to get bad guys and make the world a safer place to live, or they just want to be a prick. Brighton wanted to be a prick. I suspect he was determined to make life miserable for people for as long as he possibly could. Then when he retired, he didn't have that anymore. So he shriveled up and died."

"And Mahon?"

"Mahon ran a tidy operation here. It's a tough job to be Sheriff in this county, but this department functioned very well. With so many military guys, there are always situations that come along that push the bounds of jurisdiction and authority. Mahon set the table for how that's handled and I can tell you, he wasn't an easy act to follow. He had relations with everyone – Army, Air Force, DA, the State, you name it."

"Good relations?"

Adams laughed. "He had relations with all of them, for good or for bad. He wasn't the warmest man I've ever known, and he seemed to be in it for himself. He let you know your boundaries, but you knew where you stood with him. If you were doing your job and a problem came up with somebody outside the department, you were working for the right guy."

Henry wanted to keep the Sergeant talking.

"There's something that doesn't add up, Sergeant." Adams looked at Henry but said nothing. "You say the Sheriff ran a clean department, but this case – from what I'm allowed to read of it – is messy. Some things seem very 'untidy' to me about this case, starting with what happened to my parents, followed by what happened to me."

Adams paused before replying. "What I said was that he ran a tidy department. I didn't say clean. Mahon controlled everything. He was a detail guy. I didn't work much with him directly – I was a young deputy at the time – but I'm told he had things in motion that were not anyone's business but his. There were never any scandals, which might just mean that he kept everything close to the vest. Mr. Stark, I don't say what I'm about to say lightly, and I'd like your assurance that our conversation stays between us."

Henry nodded sternly.

"The Sheriff was one to take care of himself first. If an opportunity arose that would benefit him personally while not endangering his reputation, there's little doubt in my mind that he would've jumped on it. However as I read through the case this morning, I didn't see any indication that this was one of those opportunities. If he profited personally from this situation, I don't see how he did it. From what I gather, your parents faced serious charges down in Mexico. The case was unusual, heart-breaking really, but not criminal in the way it was handled. Now you showing up and saying you were part of the family, it doesn't make sense to me that you would not be in the report. Who knows, maybe your parents had a say in that to ensure you of a better outcome than becoming a ward of the state of Colorado."

Henry suppressed a sense of anger as he considered a reply. "If the plan was that I'd have a great upbringing, then somebody miscalculated. You're saying that maybe it was my parents that orchestrated my move East?"

"Possibly," Adams replied. "I don't know of a way to tell for sure. But when you become of a ward of this state or any state, there's no way to predict what situation you'll end up in. Your parents, or the Sheriff's Department, may have been trying to do you a favor. The fact is, Mister Stark, from what I read of this report they probably didn't have any great options for you."

At that moment Henry decided to put an end to the search for his parents. He thanked the men, left his contact information, and decide to move on with his life. But before leaving Colorado, there were a few small ends to tie.

When he arrived at the Gazette, Marty was waiting for him. Henry filled him in on what he had learned while careful not to disclose the Sergeant's suspicions about Sheriff Mahon. He also filled him in on his small victory, finding a birth certificate for Marcus.

"Well," Marty said, "that spoils that surprise. And what about your birth certificate?"

"No luck," Henry said with a frown.

"Well, then," Marty said. "it looks like I'm able to help you after all!"

"Excuse me?" All of Henry's senses were at full attention.

"I found you! Here you go." Marty handed him a paper copy that was printed from microfiche.

"Henry Darrell Chimera, born to Jennifer Brown Chimera and Roland Frederick Chimera, March 21, 1980, at 6:20 a.m. in Penrose Hospital, Colorado Springs. Denomination: Catholic."

Henry stared, reading the text over and over. Marty finally wandered back to his desk, allowing Henry to absorb his past. After a few minutes Henry followed.

"I can't tell you how much this means to me," Henry said through soggy eyes.

The old archivist just nodded.

"I did some more reading on Sheriff Mahon. In their notes, the reporters gave him a well-deserved nickname, 'The Wall,' because it was impossible get information out of him. Mahon retired in 1988 at age 62 with full commendations. The paper had all these quotes from local big shots about how great the Sheriff was. I remember the coverage – it was too much. Nobody seemed to like the guy, but it was like a big celebration when it was time for him to retire. Anyway, about the only thing I noticed is that he retired up in your neck of the woods. Here's the article. Have a look."

Henry read through the article and found nothing too consequential, until he came to the last paragraph.

"Sheriff Walter T. Mahon retires in good health and is expected to move to the Boston, Massachusetts area with his wife of 39 years, Constance Stark Mahon. Mrs. Mahon has family in the Boston area, and is looking forward to returning home."

Henry's eyes bulged as he stared at the wife's name. Constance Stark Mahon.

Could it be a coincidence that his first adopted family was also in Boston shared his last name, Stark? And then there was the first name. He vaguely remembered a woman from his childhood that he was asked to call "Aunt Connie."

Marty noticed his surprised expression. "Do you see something you can use?"

"I think I know why I ended up in Boston. Evidently I was meant to be a Stark, and it was the Sheriff who made it happen. I think I remember an older woman named Aunt Connie. She was always interested in how I was doing, more than she cared about the Stark kids who weren't adopted."

"Well, I'll be damned!"

Henry gathered his papers and profoundly thanked Marty Francis. He left the Gazette Building with some questions answered, and a few new mysteries from the Centennial State.

There were still a few hours of daylight left. Before leaving town he had one important piece of business remaining.

Henry knew there were just a few cemeteries in the immediate area of Black Forest that existed in the 1980s, before the area experienced its recent population boom. Eastonville, Monument, Table Rock, and Bluff.

Table Rock appeared to only have occupants that passed in the late nineteenth century. Bluff was not far from town but did not appear to be active in the 1970s. Monument was the largest in the area, and the fastest growing. Eastonville was the closest to Black Forest. It was small, but people were buried there at least until the 1990s.

He decided to try Eastonville. If that proved fruitless, he would go through as much of Monument as he could manage with the limited time remaining before he made the drive to Denver for a late flight.

The iron sign above the cemetery announced "EASTONVILLE. Est. 1865." It was a scenic cemetery on the cusp of the Black Forest area and the high plains, a perfect place to lay a body down eternally and a perfect place to wander, even if he found nothing else that tied him to his family.

The cemetery was well maintained. There were no more than about one hundred headstones, which made it easy to spot the newer additions. He went through each family plot and individual headstone with interest.

He wandered through the scenic grounds, stopping to pay respects and try to imagine the people who were laid to rest during the past century in this remote burial ground.

As he was about to circle back toward his rental car he nearly tripped over a small headstone, barely a foot tall.

He turned to read it. The message was simple.

Marcus Gerald Chimera
B. 1975 D. 1981
Beloved Son and Brother

He was overcome with emotion. His final stop in Colorado was his only sibling's place of rest.

The word "brother" jumped out at Henry. Could there be any doubt now that he and Marcus were brothers?

High grass covered the base of the headstone. He cleared it away and discovered a picture beneath the inscription.

As he looked closer, and began laughing. One of his earliest and happiest memories from childhood stared into his eyes.

Henry's flight left Denver International Airport's Terminal B just a few minutes before midnight. He had left the departure back to Boston open, and had no trouble finding an empty seat for a redeye flight.

As the plane sailed through the darkness, seven miles above the surface of the earth, Henry felt a tremendous sense of satisfaction. As he looked down over the dark landscape, highlighted on occasion by the lights of small towns from more than seven miles above the ground, he began to feel something resembling attachment for the very first time in his memory. He believed his life was crossing through a gateway, and on the other side was certainty and purpose, an existence he would need to learn all about.

In Henry's terrifying vision on his first day in Black Forest he saw a large dog with floppy ears bounding across the highway. Soon after the dog came a young boy, met tragically by an unmarked police cruiser.

The image sickened Henry, so he tried to focus on the moments before the collision. There was great happiness in the revelation that his brother "Freddy" was chasing after his own dog.

He thought of the image on his brother's headstone and smiled. Scooby Doo, the popular canine character from the 1970's cartoon, smiled at him in stone. In the TV series, the dog's human sidekick was named Freddy.

It was another piece out of a thousand in the jigsaw puzzle of his life. After so much wondering, he was finally finding a few pieces that fit. It was a small victory, but a good start.

As the plane descended toward Boston it was nearing six in the morning. Daylight was just beginning to show over the Atlantic. Henry emerged from three hours of sound sleep, surprisingly energized. He had an important task this morning, before returning to work.

Henry took his time in the airport, buying a Herald and planting himself down at the best breakfast establishment he could find. He was taking his time until eight o'clock, when the Suffolk County Family and Probate Court would open for business.

He deliberately finished his breakfast and took the moving walkway to where his rental car awaited. Traffic was heavy as he moved through the Sumner Tunnel into downtown. He navigated through the clutter with an uncommonly peaceful demeanor, refusing to allow dive-bombing Boston drivers to ruin the important mission he was on.

He had no trouble finding parking at such an early hour, close to the court near the intersection of Merrimac and New Chardon. He entered the building at ten minutes past eight, moved through a light security line, and took the stairs to the third floor.

After a short wait, his number was called.

"I'd like to file paperwork for a last name change, please."

He would finally cast aside the name Stark. To the world at large and the world within, his name would again be Henry Chimera.

Once home, Henry was determined to try his best to get back into the swing with Finders Keepers, but he knew the temptations would be great to continue unraveling the mysteries of his past.

His first morning back in the office, Henry answered his phone calls and handled all pressing business, but found himself drifting toward matters on hold in the back of his mind. His income depended on reaching out for new customers, but little by little his priorities were beginning to shift. His sense of loyalty trumped his urges for the moment, urges he hoped would pass within a few days. Still, he needed to solve the one mystery he had some control over.

He began with a Boston area phone book. As he suspected, there were hundreds of Mahons, including dozens of people named Walter Mahon, W. Mahon, and even a few W. T. Mahons.

He called each reasonable possibility, making notes about each outcome of each response. Trying to sound more personable than a telemarketer, he explained that he might be a distant relative of the Mahon family – not a complete lie – who was trying to reach long lost relatives. Most people were skeptical of his motives, but he finished with the same question: Have you ever lived in the Colorado Springs area?

Call after call, the answer was "no, sorry I can't help you."

When he reached the end of the possibilities it was nearly six o'clock. He had missed lunch and was growing light headed. Ryan and Shelly had left for the day with a quick good night, fully aware that Henry was still on his personal mission. He ordered Chinese food to be delivered and kept working.

He decided to go back through the list of people who did not answer their phone, or to try to find his former Aunt Connie on the possibility that the sheriff had passed away. He looked through the phone for anyone with a similar name, but found no one named Constance or Connie. He found several people named C. Mahon, so he began with this short list.

The first person he reached was an elderly woman, and he introduced himself in the normal way. When he asked about Colorado Springs, he had to process the response a second time before responding.

She answered, "Yes, we moved from Colorado Springs many years ago. Who did you say you are again?"

His voice lifted from the weariness. "My name is Henry. Henry Stark."

"Oh my goodness." The woman's voice trailed off. There was little doubt she knew who he was. "You were so small the last time I saw you. I certainly didn't expect to hear from you after all this time."

"I suppose not," Henry said. "I was trying to reach Sheriff Mahon, and I've tried every combination of names in the phone book I could think of."

"He passed away some years ago." Her voice was emotionless.

"I'm very sorry to hear that. I wondered if I might meet with you, Mrs. Mahon."

"I don't think that's such a good idea. I've been in poor health lately."

"Well, Mrs. Mahon, I've been on quite a journey to uncover my past. I was very young when I left Colorado, and I have little memory of the place, so I just traveled there. I spoke with an old newspaperman who remembers my case, and helped me dig out all those old stories. I even visited the Sheriff's Department. There wasn't much recollection of those events from so long ago, but I learned that I was there."

He waited for the woman to respond, but there was only silence.

"If I understand correctly, my adoptive family was your brother and his wife. My memory of those years is more clear. It wasn't a happy home. In looking back, I wonder why they wanted to take me in at all. They had children of their own, so there isn't always room for an adopted child."

"That's one way to say it," the woman replied. "Another is that we hoped they would be in it for the goodness in their heart, but that didn't turn out to be the case. I think they did you wrong."

It was Henry's turn to be silent.

"You deserved better than what you got from them. After they left here, they moved to Florida. I assumed they took you with them. It was years later when I found out they gave you up. I was furious! I tried to get information from the adoption agencies but they wouldn't tell me anything. I never spoke with them again after that. Any family that would abandon a child, especially one they agreed to take in after your early troubles, didn't deserve another second of my attention."

"It changed my life, that much is sure. Mrs. Mahon, the main reason I contacted you was not to reconnect with the family that ran away from me, but to try to find out what happened to my birth family. You said I was orphaned. Do you know for sure they're dead? Can you tell me anything at all about them?"

"No, I don't know for sure they're dead." The woman did not elaborate.

"An article I found said that my parents committed some crimes and somehow ended up in Mexico. Do you know anything about that?"

"Only what my husband told me, and it wasn't much more than what I read in the paper. The Sheriff and I had an understanding over certain things, including when it was and wasn't okay to discuss business affairs. The situation with your family was definitely one where I was not encouraged to pry. There was probably more to it than what was in the newspaper stories you read, but exactly what, I'm not sure."

"Mrs. Mahon, do you remember Deputy Brighton?"

"How could I forget him? That one was nothing but trouble. He made my husband's job difficult, more so as time went on."

"How so?"

"He didn't share details," she said, "but after your brother was killed in that terrible accident, both your parents and Deputy Brighton were soon gone. I told my husband that I thought it was terrible what they did to your parents after they lost a son. He insisted that I keep my nose out of it and to stop asking questions. He assured me that your parents deserved what they were getting."

"And what was that?"

"He wouldn't tell me. That left you as the odd one out. Out of decency we tried to place you with a family that would take you in, treat you like one of their own. I was in close touch with my brother at the time, and I told him what I knew about your circumstances. He convinced us that having you live with them would be the best option. We could have left it to the authorities in

Colorado to find you a home, but my husband didn't have much confidence in how that would turn out. Nobody questioned what became of you, and it all seemed to work out for the best at the time. If we had it to do over, I guess we would have turned you over to the state to be adopted."

"Mrs. Mahon, do you have any idea what became of the Starks' daughter Delilah?"

"I heard through other relatives that she left her family as soon as she was old enough to strike out on her own. The last I heard, she had no interest in staying in touch with her family. The two of us have that in common."

"She was the only one in that family that I was close to," Henry said.

"Sorry I can't tell you more. In spite of the difficult hand you were dealt, it seems you've been a very brave man through it all. I'm guessing great things are ahead for you, Henry."

"Well, I've taken enough of your time. Thank you so much, Mrs. Mahon."

Only in the few days following his talk with the Sheriff's widow did Henry reflect on his obsession with his family search and how it had changed his view of the world. In less than a week he went from an apparition by a dead brother that he did not remember, to finding his grave almost two thousand miles away. He even had a vision of the way his brother died, which led him back to the Sheriff and his widow from years before.

Initially he considered it possible that his brother's visit in Aisling's parlor was an illusion, the result of something he wanted to believe. Aisling suggested that he might have psychic abilities. He nervously laughed it off at the time, but what he uncovered in Colorado was no illusion. For a man who had wandered for years with no real grounding, he finally felt close to some connections that would be permanent. He decided to fall to his best source for all recent advice.

PICKING THROUGH THE WRECKAGE

Henry settled in at Aisling's table with a glass of Jameson's on ice. He rambled through his his trip to Colorado, sparing no details.

"Henry, I'm impressed. For someone so new to communicating with other realms, you're showing great promise as a seer. I can only imagine how you'll progress with more practice and focus."

Henry was agitated by her comment. "Aisling, please slow down. I'm not sure this is a direction I really want to go. Frankly it's all a little intimidating to me, and I'm not sure how it really applies to my life, other than solving the remaining mysteries about my family."

"I understand your trepidation, my dear," Aisling's tone was firm, her demeanor purposeful. "but you must understand that these things are not voluntary in this life. It's often said that everyone possesses extra-sensory abilities, but few choose to develop the skill. The truth is that it is rare gift indeed. When it appears to be effortless in some people, it nearly always means the gift was very strong for them early on. To deny the gift would be one of the biggest wastes of your life."

"But what practical good does it offer, Aisling? Assuming I can develop this so-called 'gift,', where's the guarantee that my life will be better off as a result?"

"Well, is the human race better off for understanding how our own bodies work? Only a few generations ago, very brilliant humans had no idea of how the human nervous system functioned, the importance of sterilization, what DNA was, and on and on. We still don't fully understand the function of the human brain or our immune systems, yet no one doubts that further understanding will help our species. To understand perception beyond this realm is to understand how this layer of humans – the people alive and breathing today – fits into the much larger scheme of humankind before us and after us. You may not believe this, Henry, but I feel very confident about what awaits me after this heart stops beating."

"That's not so uncommon." His whiskey was a catalyst. "There are millions of people walking this earth who are certain of their future. Christians, Jews, Muslims, Hindus, Buddhists. Each of the major religions is founded on the premise that your actions will lead you toward an expected outcome."

"Yes, Henry, but they're basing their beliefs on faith that was inherited from prior generations. Only a select few within those groups have the gift of seeing for themselves what lies beyond. Also, those religions have developed surprisingly different versions of what happens to the faithful after they die, even though there sacred texts show so many things in common. Do you really think they can all be right?"

"Well, I don't see why not. Why can't they all be right?" Henry suspected he was beginning to walk into Aisling's trap.

"Do you consider yourself a pagan or an infidel? Are you comfortable with those labels?"

"Excuse me? Of course I'm not comfortable with those terms."

"Well, that is exactly the view of some of those religions towards some others. You ask, why can't they all be right? Because most of the so-called 'major religions' preach that theirs is the only way. As an example, Hindus believe in polytheism, the belief that many gods exist, but Christians talk about One True God, or monotheism. Jews and Muslims agree, although they obviously have fairly profound differences about what that means, as we've seen for a thousand years or more.

"My dear boy, do you think they can all be right?"

Henry shook his head, as if to shake bugs from his hair. "I don't know the answer to that question, but it seems to me that what's important is that they believe they're right, and they each follow what they believe. As long as their faith doesn't include the destruction of any other, then I see no harm in it all. Besides, how in the hell did we go from my extrasensory perception to questioning whether I'm a heathen? How are the two connected?"

"I'm attempting to you get you to understand that there are threads running through our existence that connect all of these fervent belief systems. Now, I don't often have devout Hindus, Christians, Jews, Muslims, or Buddhists come in for psychic readings. However it's very rare when one of my customers does not have at least the foundation of his or her faith deeply rooted into them. As I probe into their past and the spirits they are connected with, an understanding of the foundations of their faith is essential to being a valued spiritual advisor. It's just like a physician who specializes in the kidneys and the renal system. He must know how the liver is supposed to function, and he better have a very thorough understanding of the body's immune system. It's all connected. Understanding only a portion of our existence – where our soul is as of this moment – is incredibly shortsighted. Most people have no understanding of that. They're completely focused on the here and now. You can't do this with one foot in, one foot out."

"I do see your point, but exactly what are you suggesting?"

"So glad you asked, Henry." She winked, smiled, and gulped from her whiskey glass. "I suggest you become my unofficial apprentice."

"Your apprentice? How would that work?"

"I call it 'unofficial' because you wouldn't really earn much money until you start working with your own clients, but you can help me with at least some of my readings. Eventually you'll have the confidence and skill to do your own. You would learn a great deal, especially the many reasons people have for coming. That can be the most rewarding part."

"Whoa there, Aisling! I'm not ready to take this on as a new profession. It's all new to me. I'm just observing, taking all of this in. I'm nowhere near ready to think about it as an occupation."

"You can proceed at your own pace, and if you find that you're not interested, then you back off completely. I'm not suggesting you compromise anything about your current job. You owe it to your employers to continue working in earnest. Call it a hobby for now, if that's easier."

"Won't your clients be wary of some guy showing up out of the blue?"

"Some might, but my best customers trust me implicitly. They know I would never do anything to make them feel uncomfortable in such a personal setting, plus many of my customers have become used to the idea of spirits that are present unexpectedly. You're just another one."

Aisling and Henry continued talking until after eleven about what lay ahead. Over time Henry became more convinced there was no harm in a trial situation. They agreed on Tuesday and Thursday evenings, and Saturday daytime appointments.

At the end of the evening they toasted their new partnership. "Well, here's to a new adventure," Henry said. "I'm not sure I know what I'm in for, but I'm also not sure I have much to lose."

"There's always something to lose, Henry, but a life without risk is no life at all."

"Sláinte."

Henry's first day as an apprentice was a Saturday. They decided their first day together as collaborators should be one which they had the whole day to sort through the particulars of their sessions.

For scheduling purposes, Aisling allowed ninety minutes for each appointment, which included a full sixty minutes for the reading and thirty minutes afterward to allow time to prepare for the next client, and to inscribe notes into her log book.

Henry noticed that she retreated to another room to retrieve the log book, and when she was done inscribing her notes, she promptly returned it. She explained to Henry that she shared the contents of the log book with no one, that the privacy of the book was as important to her as were the notes of a physician or psychiatrist about their customers. "It's my oath to protect their privacy. In this vocation, if you don't have your client's complete faith, things will fall apart eventually."

He was relieved. For now he just wanted to open his senses and observe, avoiding nuances about the intimate details about other people's lives.

Aisling prepared Henry for what to expect when clients arrived for readings.

"I'll explain to my customers that you're here as a reader that is just beginning to understand his gifts. During the readings I would like you to keep your observations and opinions to yourself. We'll have time to discuss things later. If your vision is clear, you will most certainly notice that there are some things I don't share with my clients about their friends and relatives on the other side. I have a history that goes back years with some, and I've gained a sense for what they can handle and what they can't. Sometimes it's necessary to hide information from them that might lessen their opinion of the people they're in contact with. I'm not trying to be dishonest, but I do have some latitude in how I describe the communication. I'm not here to change their fond memories of loved ones."

"Are there ever situations where the spirit you're contacting is just nasty?"

"Sadly, yes. If a client is trying to contact a dark spirit, I'll normally realize that very quickly. I sense love because I'm most open to that emotion, but I sense others as well. If I don't believe the customer can benefit from the situation in any way, I'll tell them the spirit is in no mood to communicate, or the spirit has nothing helpful to share, that kind of thing. I'm here to help my customers find what they're looking for, and none of them are looking to have their optimism dashed by some relative who was drunk and surly in life, and just as surly after life, no longer drunk. Does that seem dishonest to you?"

"A little bit," he replied. "If someone has made the hard decision to come in and put down their money to find answers, in nearly all cases I think they deserve the truth. That probably sounds naive."

"I would ask you to suspend judgment on that until you view a few situations. I do try to prepare for these possibilities when I'm first getting to know the customer. I ask them hypothetical questions to test their limits, for example if we learned that your late father had been having a secret affair during his life, would you wish to know this? Those kinds of questions in the early going can give them an early dose of reality. That's one of the reasons I keep a log, to help me remember these important details."

Their first client of the day rang the bell a few minutes before 10:30. Aisling swept to the door with enthusiasm.

"Dolores, it is lovely to see you! Please come in."

Into the foyer stepped a woman who appeared to be in her fifties. She was heavy set, wearing modest makeup and a simple overcoat. She wore a knee-length flowered cotton dress and simple but attractive jewelry.

Aisling introduced Henry as her assistant. She offered a soft hand in Henry's direction while never looking at him directly. They retreated to Aisling's designated reading room, and the three found their places around the table. Aisling turned down the lights and sat. She bowed, closed her eyes, clasped her hands, and began to give thanks.

"Dear Lord, thank you for bringing us to this place today, where we can count our blessings to be among your loving children. Please guide us in what we do. We ask of you and your Guardian Protectors the permission to speak with those that are near to our sister, Dolores Little. We enter this place with love and respect in our hearts."

Aisling looked at Dolores and smiled kindly. "It wasn't a wasted trip, Dolores. Your mother and father are here to express their love."

Dolores beamed. "Tell Mommy and Daddy I love them and miss them!"

Aisling nodded and kept her gaze on Dolores. "Your mother says she's very proud of the commitment you've shown on your diet, Dolores. She wants to remind you that life is a precious thing, and protecting your health is the most important gift you can give back to yourself."

"Tell Mommy I'm trying, I'm really trying."

"She says she knows," Aisling says kindly. "She says a little less of the peach ice cream might be a good idea."

"I'll try. Ask Daddy how they're treating him up there!"

"He says he's doing wonderfully, Dolores, and that he loves you very much." Aisling smiled widely. "He says the chowder is to die for." They giggled.

During the reading Henry avoided any attempt to connect with the spirits that Aisling was seeing. Without trying he sensed a vague blur behind Dolores, but focused more on Aisling's demeanor with her client. The notion of intruding on someone else's conversation was not yet something he was comfortable with.

After saying their good byes, Aisling retreated to the rear room for the log book. She wrote a few notes and Henry patiently waited to ask his questions.

When she closed the book he pounced. "That was great! Was it as smooth as it seemed?"

"Yes, she's one of my easier customers. Her parents love her very much but they want her to stop being so clingy. We'll see if they become more direct about telling her to live her own life."

Henry nodded as an eager student, absorbing and analyzing.

"As you can see, Henry, people have different reasons for connecting with those on the other side. In Dolores' case, I guess it's a continuation of her progress as an adult. And of course the Big L."

Henry looked at her without a guess at what that might mean.

"Loneliness. There's so much loneliness out there. Some of my customers have very little in their lives, so the loss of a loved one on this side can be devastating. Some depend on these sessions to fill that void."

After a few minutes, Aisling was ready for the next session. "My next session is one I don't look forward to. There are some uncomfortable moments when I read for Mr. Schoenfeld."

"Why is that?"

"The spirits that appear for his readings aren't always those he requests. I've described their physical appearance to him and he doesn't seem to recognize them. So either he has a terrible memory, which I doubt, or his wife is carrying around some unwanted baggage. I've prodded him a little on who they might be, and he hasn't given me much. I don't think he's lying to me or to himself, so I've left it alone."

Within minutes, Amos Schoenfeld was in Aisling's foyer, removing his hat and coat. He was a very old man, likely into his nineties, and had a peaceful, kind appearance. Henry sensed immediately he was not a man to hide anything, and that he was looking forward to his reading.

"Please come into the reading room, Amos." Aisling was eager to get on with the session. He thought she might delay their session for as long as she could, but it seemed the opposite. The man politely followed her fast pace into the parlor.

After giving their customary prayers of thanks and settling in through breathing, concentration, and peaceful thoughts, they began. Soon Aisling looked at her client. "Your wife is here to tell you she loves you, Amos."

Mr. Schoenfeld's eyes welled with tears. "Tell her I miss her every day."

"She knows. She says she's near you always, that in due time you'll be with her."

The old man smiled softly. "Tell her my bridge game is getting better every day. Tell her I'm much better than I was when we played."

Aisling nodded. "She seems to be proud of you for that, Mr. Schoenfeld, and wants to remind you that you couldn't possibly be worse than when you played together."

The old man allowed himself a subdued laugh.

"Irena has some people with her. Two men and a woman. They've been here before with her. Would you like to say hello to them, Mr. Schoenfeld?"

"I'm afraid I don't know who they could be." The old man was impassive, not appearing especially curious or anxious. He was here only for his wife.

"I'm sensing from your wife that these are people that are especially important to her, but I'm not getting a very strong connection either. There is great emotion there, a very strong bond."

The old man appeared curious but content with this mystery he would not solve. Aisling paused, giving him one last chance to explore their presence. He folded hands in front, saying nothing.

As the reading progressed and Aisling facilitated a touching reunion between these two loving partners, Henry felt himself being drawn in closely to the spirits in the room. He sensed the two women and two men who were with them. Images began racing to him quickly, much too fast to see or comprehend. It was like a movie being played in fast motion. It was as though he was catching up to the fast moving treadmill. Then, with very little effort, he felt the force of the story unfolding before him.

"Treblinka," he said.

Both Aisling and Amos stopped their conversation and looked at Henry. Their eyes were wide open. "Excuse me Henry?" Aisling was sincerely puzzled.

Henry's interruption surprised even himself. He hesitated, wondering if this was one of those moments when Aisling would normally hold information back from her client for their own protection. Her look indicated that was not the case. She clearly wanted him to explain.

"Treblinka. They died in the prison camp in Poland. They're her brothers and sister. She was the youngest, and she was spared. She's finally met her siblings."

"But," Amos said slowly, "she always said she was an only child. She never told me of siblings. All she knew was that she was taken away from a camp at a very young age, but she barely remembered it."

"I don't think she knew about them until after death, Mr. Schoenfeld. She's very happy to be with them, but as Aisling says, she's glad be with you too. She thinks you'll love them. She says her brother Jozef reminds her of you."

Aisling was astonished. "Henry, what else can you tell Mr. Schoenfeld?"

"That her parents are not here now because they're in another place, a better place. These are people that have found real happiness with each other."

Mr. Schoenfeld was smiling widely through tears as he looked at Henry with appreciation.

Aisling continued with the reading. Introductions were made, and the whole group enjoyed the absence of a wall that Henry helped to bring down.

After Amos Schoenfeld left, Aisling turned to Henry.

"Henry, that was quite something. I had no idea your gift was as advanced as it is. Have you been so acute in your sensitivities all this time?"

"Not at all. Other than the times with my brother here and in Colorado, this is really the first time I've ever made such a strong connection with spirits."

He paused. "Well, now that I think of it, there was one other time in my office at *Finders Keepers* when I saw the spirit of a client's departed father. At first I didn't even know he was a spirit. So I suppose it's been there a long time, but I've been ignoring it."

"Denying yourself a gift like this would be like a person with sight walking around wearing a blindfold. Henry, you have so much to see and so much to offer. You need to continue developing this gift. During our sessions I want you to continue focusing and connecting, and speaking when you feel it's important. As I said before, you always want to be cautious. However the spirits generally provide guidance by what they reveal. At this point in your development, I believe the most important thing is for you to practice, open up the channel."

"I guess I just need to confront this gift, as you call it," Henry said, "and figure out how to work with it. As I think about it, this isn't too different from my current job of being a matchmaker. I get satisfaction from bringing people together, only in the ethereal sense."

Aisling brightened at Henry's openness. "Very true, but I would raise the stakes a bit. Not only are you bringing people together, but in some cases you're answering questions and resolving issues they could never do on their own. Sometimes they're desperate, paralyzed even, because they're missing something or someone that they've been with for decades, centuries even."

"You're saying some of your clients are looking for spirits they've been with through multiple lives?"

"In some cases, most definitely. Fate may have intervened to separate our customer from a spirit they have always been with. In other cases, they're just looking for a missing piece in their life. They're alone, and it's not satisfying. They need someone to care for. That's what the path to the top is all about, Henry. Surrounding yourself with good souls, and advancing beyond mortal living until you've grabbed the Golden Ring. Heaven, Nirvana, Righteousness, whatever you want to call it."

"Reincarnation." Henry's tone was steady. He was beginning to grasp the larger picture.

"Yes, that's the underlying reality of this occupation. Some religions believe that this life is a ladder directly to heaven if you remain virtuous. Others believe that the spirit comes back, is reborn into new bodies, and grows through new challenges and experiences."

Aisling stood. "Well, Henry, it's been lovely chatting with you about all this but we have one more client for the day. He's a new one. I haven't really gotten much of a feel for what he's after. We talked briefly on the phone and he was fine. So let me catch my notes up in the next few minutes before he arrives." She disappeared into the back.

Henry rose to stretch, moved to the kitchen to pour some water, and within moments the doorbell rang. Aisling's voice rose from the back of the house.

"Could you get that, Henry? That's probably Mister Donnelly, a little early."

Henry opened the door to find a well dressed man near Henry's age, somewhere in his thirties, with a bit of a swagger and a winning smile. His dress was casual but tasteful. The man did not appear to Henry to be a likely candidate for a spiritual reading. Inviting him in, Henry introduced himself as Aisling's assistant, just beginning to learn the skills of the profession.

"So what is it that draws someone to this occupation, Mr. Chimera?"

"As I'm finding, it's more that the occupation draws you in. I had no intention of picking this up as even a part time hobby, but it seems I have a knack for this kind of work."

"What type of knack is that?" Donnelly smiled as he asked.

"After thirty-four years on the planet, it turns out that I'm able to see spirits. Aisling believes I'm a late bloomer."

"Fascinating," he said, with no trace of sincerity. "Thanks for sharing."

Aisling entered the front room. "Mister Donnelly, thank you for coming in. It's a pleasure to meet you."

"Please, call me John." He held out a manicured hand, a perfect complement to his winning smile.

"I will. Henry, please take John's coat. Would you like a refreshment before we get comfortable?"

"No thanks, I'm fine. I'm just looking forward to seeing how this works."

When the three were settled at the table, it was back to business for Aisling. The pleasantries subsided.

"Well, John, there is always a degree of exploration when a new client comes in. There's never guarantee that I'll be able to give you want you want, and either of us can choose to discontinue this or future sessions any time we like, preferably with no hard feelings. So to build a collaborative relationship in this endeavor, we'll both need to be on the same page. So far so good?"

"Very good." The smile.

"Excellent," Aisling continued. "Unfortunately we didn't have much time to discuss on the phone what you're hoping for. Can you explain that, for our benefit? You mentioned something about an illness in your family."

It was Donnelly's turn to be all business as the smile dissolved.

"Actually, this really is an exploratory mission for me too. It's kind of a strange story. We're thinking of having a child and we have some concerns. You see, my wife's father is in the late stages of Parkinson's disease, so obviously there's a genetic link to the disease on her side. I'm interested in learning more about my family. I'm an only child and I'm not close to my parents at all. When I decided not to get into my father's business, he didn't take it well. That was about five years ago and we haven't been able to reconcile. The subject of family illness isn't one that I ever discussed with them in great detail, but I remember my mother talking about some mental illness on her side. They were each only children like me, so there's really nobody available or willing to give details on what it might've been. I'm hopeful it was just some sort of anomaly that never happened before and might never again.

"The mental illness in my family probably happened long before they had an understanding of these conditions, so even the treatable ones were lumped in with the more severe. All I know is that there was some 'lunacy' in my mother's family, but who knows what that really was. With those cards stacked against us, I'm wondering if it's fair to bring a child into the world with a chance of Parkinson's or some kind of mental illness that's almost as serious. From what I've found out through info available online, some of these conditions seem to be handed down genetically, and I find that rather ominous.

"So we have some difficult decisions to make. If we feel the odds are high that our child will grow into a very challenging set of circumstances, we might choose another direction, like adoption."

"I see," Aisling said. She remained quiet for several seconds, considering the challenge. "This is somewhat of an unusual situation for a reading, at least in my experience. Usually the reasons are more emotional."

One of things that Henry appreciated about Aisling was her directness.

"Well," Donnelly was quick to point out, "for my wife and I this is a very emotional decision. We've really agonized over what to do for almost a year. Then a few weeks ago we were watching a psychic on TV, and my wife had the idea to go this route. I thought it was worth a try. It was better than any ideas I had. We weren't really making any progress in our decision."

"Yes, I suppose," Aisling said. "I just wonder whether the spirits will come through who can provide guidance the way you expect it. Most of the spirits I come across in readings make themselves apparent straight away. So far I'm not picking up any spirits at all. So as long as you understand that there are no guarantees, then we can try."

Donnelly nodded. "It's fine. You're obviously an honest person, so I don't mind paying for the session if there's a chance. We're just trying to cover all the bases we can, and I couldn't think of anything to lose by giving this a try."

"Fine then, let's get started." She carefully explained her approach to Donnelly, including the prayer for thanks and her standard ways to try to reach spirits.

The experience was new to Henry as well. He had never experienced a reading in which the spirits weren't readily available to be contacted. He was eager to see how this one progressed.

With some hesitation, she asked, "Mr. Donnelly, I don't think we've discussed the spirit or spirits we'll be trying to contact. I'll let you know if any spirits in particular emerge, but can you give me some inkling of who it is that will be most helpful to you?"

"Oh yes, sorry." His smile also hinted at embarrassment.

"Well, it really could be anyone along my mother's family line. Her parents both died years ago. Their family name was Livingston. My grandfather was Bert – Bertram – and my grandmother was named Annabelle. His parents were named Walter and Abigail Livingston, and my grandmother's parents were John and Victoria Schultz. If you contact any of them I'll be eager to hear anything they suggest."

"Very well, John, I'm hopeful that information will prove useful. Let's begin by giving thanks."

In the next few minutes, Aisling's eyes were mostly closed, her attentions totally focused. She spoke little. Donnelly watched her intently, anxiously. Finally Aisling began to speak.

"The souls in this room request the honor of communication with the family of Mr. John Donnelly, who seeks information that will help extend the health and happiness of the Livingston, Schultz, and Donnelly bloodlines. Our request is made in sincerity, in the spirit of peace and goodwill."

While Aisling continued, Henry's senses began to percolate. He felt a fullness in his lungs and heart and brain, and a sense of warm energy surrounded him. In the moments that followed, the sensation became sharper and more focused. In a sign of his growing maturation as a psychic, he was able to contend with this emerging vibration without changing his outward appearance. He kept his eyes closed, his focus steady and open. Gradually he felt a distinct spirit with its gaze on him directly. As he returned the gaze, he felt it similar to someone adjusting his eyes to sunlight after hours in a cave. It was the spirit of a woman who was not pleased to be present. There was no room for misinterpretation, and he expected that Aisling sensed the same mood.

This was Annabelle Livingston. Henry expressed appreciation for her presence, reinforcing that their intentions were honorable. She acknowledged this message, making it clear that she was comfortable speaking with him directly. Henry was relieved. He opened his eyes to look at Aisling. She was deep in a meditative state, still trying to make a connection. Momentary panic set in as Henry came to understand that Annabelle Livingston was only communicating with him. The next message from Annabelle was given with the understanding that Henry was to convey it precisely. No diplomacy was necessary.

"Let him know that he has no business being here. His reasons given are deceitful, and he is taking influence from the wrong places. He needs to go back to the path that he knows is correct."

Henry felt the full weight of the message, along with an urgency to deliver it quickly. He was pleased with his easy ability to shift his focus from Annabelle Livingston back to the two people at the table with him. He saw that Aisling had detected nothing of his conversation with Annabelle. He was unsure of what to do next. Aisling had been trying to come up with something for her customer for probably close to five minutes with no evident success. He was probably helping her by jumping in.

"Aisling, may I?" He asked softly. "I think I'm picking up on something."

The question surprised her. She smiled subtly. "Yes, of course, my dear."

He looked directly at Donnelly and spoke directly. "Mr. Donnelly, Annabelle Livingston spoke to me, and her welcome was not a warm one."

Both Donnelly and Aisling were at full attention as they looked at Henry. Aisling was the first to speak.

"Henry, are you quite sure? Dear boy, please don't intervene unless you're completely certain the message was meant in the way you think it was."

In the weeks he had known Aisling he had never come close to an uncomfortable moment, but this was most definitely one. She was clearly very concerned about what he would say next, but her eyes displayed trust. Henry looked back at her with confidence. She was right to encourage him to think carefully, and he was.

"I do understand," he replied. "but I'm being told to deliver this message without trying to massage it."

He turned to Donnelly. "Your grandmother says that you shouldn't be here. She said you came under false pretenses, and she's not pleased that you've gone off the path. She believes you're taking influence from the wrong places. She thinks you know the right path, but you're just choosing not to take it at the moment."

Donnelly looked at him with an icy stare, saying nothing.

Aisling stiffened. "Henry, are you quite certain that was the message?"

"It's not my message, Aisling. Mister Donnelly, I'm sorry if the message is unpleasant, but it was not ambiguous. And there is no doubt in my mind that it was Annabelle Livingston speaking to me."

Donnelly rose from the table, picked up his coat and began to leave the room. As he reached the doorway he turned back to Aisling. "Please send me a bill for your time."

His heavy footsteps across her foyer ended with a slam.

"Oh my dear, I suppose we won't be seeing him again."

In the coming months, such a reduction would have been called wishful thinking.

Into the Thick

"The truth of the matter, Aisling, is that I don't really know what I've done. I was just delivering a message that I felt compelled to deliver." The stress showed on his face. "If she was playing me for a fool, then I fit the part perfectly."

"Are you quite sure that was her message?"

"Absolutely," he answered. "and she was clear that she didn't want me to sugarcoat it."

"Then don't be too hard on yourself. I've been in the same position myself. So I suppose I would have reacted the same way."

Henry took some comfort in Aisling's words. "She was definitely Annabelle Livingston. I feel very certain about that."

"Well, then," Aisling pondered, "considering Mr. Donnelly's departure, he was probably just embarrassed that his deception was revealed. He didn't offer a denial, nor accuse you of deception. So Henry, I suppose the only thing we've lost is a client, and that kind of client I think we can do without."

"Thanks Aisling, that means a lot to me."

"Did he really think he could come here and pull one over on a spirit? The guy must have stones the size of grapefruits. Oops, sorry Aisling." Henry smiled weakly toward his older friend.

"It's quite all right, Henry. I was thinking just the same thing. I've had devious clients before, but generally they're fooling themselves and don't even realize they're attempting to fool a spirit. In this case, the man seemed to know exactly what he was doing. Big stones indeed."

"The other piece of this that I'm stuck on," he continued, "was her comment that he's taking influence from the wrong places. Do you think she's talking about the devil?"

"Well, I certainly take the comment to mean that he's been influenced by people or spirits that are negative, but whether they're THAT evil I can't say. I rather doubt we're talking about the hand of Satan here."

"I had the impression that she knew exactly who was influencing him, and so did he. It's as if she was trying to relay the message to whoever put him up to this."

Aisling stared into the distance before replying. "If we are talking about the devil, that would indeed be a troublesome thought. In all the years I've been doing this, that would be a first. I've never been concerned there might be 'devilish' factors in play. I've certainly seen fear, contempt, superstition, and some very complex problems rooted in some of the absurdities that come from conventional religions, but I've never seen anything that resembles – or even suggests – the devil, hell, and those kinds of notions. Quite frankly, Henry, I'm not at all convinced we've seen anything very evil in this reading. Mister Donnelly wanted something we couldn't provide, and all the charm and money the man has at his disposal couldn't make it so. We did our jobs, thanks to you." Aisling rose from her chair to make notes in her log.

"I didn't sense anything sinister either," he said. "I'm not certain I would have recognized it, but it just wasn't something I picked up on. There was something else going on."

Aisling stopped in the doorway to listen to her pupil. "Please continue, dear boy."

"I'm trying to understand what he was really expecting. Is there really a pregnancy at the center of this, or did he come for some completely different reason? I guess he figured that if he could get you to go 'in a trance' to contact his deceased relatives, you'd be so preoccupied that you wouldn't notice why he was really here. Arrogance!"

"Welcome to the wild world of mystery, Henry. I'm no mind reader. Once I've explained the ground rules, and the severity of what we're about to do, it's between the customer, the spirits they came to find, and God what they choose to make of the situation. It was quite clear that Mr. Donnelly wasn't being perfectly honest with us, and through your talents you made that evident. You can wonder away about the man's motivations, but I think you did your job very well today. A plus!"

She passed by the television on her way out of the room, and flipped it on. Henry had never noticed the television in his visits. A man on CNN was talking about record high temperatures in the Rockies, where he had been the week before. Aisling turned down the sound, not losing her train of thought.

"I mentioned reincarnation to you, Henry, my belief that you and I have likely lived many lives before. Since you're advancing so quickly as a medium, I think it's probably timely to share a little more with you."

"I'd like that," he answered. "I really never thought much about reincarnation beyond those stupid movies where people come back as talking animals"

"Yes, those are dreadful. To start with, very few cultures believe that reincarnation applies to any species other than human. It's never appeared in any past life regression studies I've heard of, and I've certainly never met any spirits who mentioned it. There have been some literary references where it was used as a threat of punishment, like if some human didn't behave he would come back as a Dung Beetle, but nothing to suggest it's possible. This concept isn't too much more of a stretch than the Christian notion that bad people go to hell. I think the idea was conjured up by St. Augustine, the creator of 'the original sin.' Many early theologians didn't subscribe to the notion of hellfire and brimstone, and in fact the Old Testament provides only indirect references to the afterlife at all. Those books provide SO much detail about so many things, but isn't it strange that afterlife is not one of them?"

"I thought the idea of hell and damnation had been handed down from many centuries before," he said.

"Well, the early Christians probably did receive their ideas about it from the Egyptians, but it was far from a universally accepted notion. In fact, some of the spirits I have been in communication with expressed to me that among their incarnations on this earth they were vicious, self-serving people, sometimes murderers with no regret. Yet these souls, rather than being cast into a pit of burning fire, were restored and reassigned to new lives here on earth, after they reflected and restored their inner good, of course."

Henry raised his hand, shaking his head. "You have got to be kidding me! Souls don't pay for barbaric actions after they're dead? They're just put back into circulation after a period of reflection?"

"Not exactly. 'Rebuilt' is more like it, but after some serious rehabilitation. In this modern era, horrific crimes and criminals gain great attention and some killers even gain notoriety for their callousness, but in centuries past being especially vicious could help ensure survival. Today we call it evil. A thousand years ago it might have been called resourceful. As surely as you and I are sitting here today, we communicate with souls like this on a regular basis. Not as evil spirits, but as reformed spirits that are making amends for their past transgressions. Who knows? It could be you or me.

"There's an entire field devoted to Past Life Regression where people, usually psychologists, use hypnosis to bring their patients through their past incarnations. What they report is that some people may have lived evil lives, but they found a way to move past it and become better. The important point is that there is evil in the world, but almost without fail, souls committing that evil will eventually try to improve the direction of their path."

Henry deliberated on Aisling's outpouring of theory. "When I think about it, we've all heard about the tunnel to the white light and all that, but you never hear about the opposite. Somebody has a near death experience, but instead of moving toward a white light, they're plummeting toward the depths of hell. Why do you think that is? Does it have anything to do with ghosts and hauntings and all that?"

"Excellent questions, my dear. It's apparent to me that there are not competing circles 'above and below' who are fighting for your soul. There is a correct path and many wrong ones. It's the soul's choice whether to follow the correct path or not. If the choice is to deny the correct path and stay entrenched in this world, then the spirit will be left to wander in an in-between state. Most souls are very eager to be unbound by the constraints of these bodies, so they move straight to the next plane. Other spirits are confused, damaged, or troubled, and they may not ascend right away. Their spirits may remain in our plane for quite some time. Gradually they are encouraged along, but it can take a very long time in some cases. The most difficult are the sudden deaths, suicides, accidents and the like, and random acts of violence against people just going on about their business, living their lives. These are not only the saddest of the spirits I meet, but also the most in need of assistance. Hollywood movies have made so much money on the idea of ghosts and hauntings over the years. The reality is far more sad and lonely than it is horrifying. Spirits who are now what we consider ghosts are lonely and lost. They have not come to realize they need to move onward and upward."

Henry was still struggling to accept some of this. "How in the world can a spirit, or a soul, or whatever you call them, be repaired? That still makes no sense to me."

"Well, you yourself mentioned the white light, the tunnel, and all of that. After a spirit ascends above this dimension, they return to a familiar place of healing and regeneration until they're ready to try again. What happens there is not entirely clear to me, but I know it is not a fast process, nor is it necessarily easy. If a soul badly fails the test in this life, the restoration process will be difficult. The spirit will not just be recycled as a damaged unit. It's a healing place, where the learning restarts. Still, the souls who have referenced the place are very eager to return to it after their lives on earth."

"So that's not heaven?" Henry eyed her uncertainly.

"No, it's definitely not heaven. Heaven, nirvana, paradise, or whatever you wish to call it, that's our desired destination. I have never met a soul who has been there, however it seems clear that the long term goal of every soul is to find their way to heaven, and our lives on earth are the means to achieve that. I hear this very often from the spirits I contact. However, the place the spirits ascend to directly after their life on earth is most definitely not what they consider their final resting place."

"It sounds like what the Catholics used to call Purgatory," Henry said. "Not good, not bad. The dog pound I guess, or a halfway house. Or Nebraska. Does that sound about right?"

Aisling laughed softly at his examples. "I suppose, however my impression is that it's far lovelier than those places you mention. Most of the spirits I've heard from are very pleased to be there. Some actually regret that they'll need to incarnate, go back into a physical body, anytime soon. They describe it as a place of great beauty, where they can relax and repair from their lives on earth, learn from their mistakes, and just be around other souls they care about, and who care about them."

Henry considered this notion with a wry smile. "So in a sense, when souls die, they're going back to school to learn about how to be good people. It seems strange that they'd ever forget that."

"Life changes people, Henry. They start out with great optimism over the things they'll accomplish in life. As years go on and they realize how difficult those accomplishments are, that optimism can easily turn to defeat, cynicism even. However, when they're back with the ones they love, restoring their sense of purpose, they find their path again. I think you'll notice, many of the people who come in for readings need a reminder about their path. They've lost their connection to their past and they're trying to regain it. Modern medicine means people are living longer, therefore are more likely to grow old and become forgetful, like when you walk into a room and forget why you're there. They forget the details of their past, so they come in here to try to connect. It's great for business!" The cackling laugh.

Henry smiled uncomfortably, trying to process all of this new information while also trying to make the most of his limited time with Aisling. "So Aisling, here's a brainteaser for you. How can a spirit be in two places at once? What I mean is, you say spirits are always available for the people that want to see them. Yet surely some of these spirits have been reincarnated. How can that be? If you've taken on a new life, you can't be available to support the ones you left behind, can you? It doesn't seem possible that a spirit could be occupying the body of some newborn in Fresno while his soul is also comforting his daughter Peggy in West Roxbury."

"You're asking all the right questions, Henry. You really must read some of these books." She pointed to a large bookcase in the main room. "I'll give you a couple to look through that will answer your questions in much more satisfying detail. But the short answer is that even though you, in this world, are bound by the notion of time, souls are not. There's no such thing as 'at the same time' in the spirit world. How does a waitress in a busy breakfast diner take care of ten tables at once? If she's good, each of the customers believes her to be ever-present. She takes care of all their dining needs, yet she can only be in one place at a time, can't she?"

"Okay fine. Let's talk about clueless people. How can a person – a soul – that's been reincarnated, that's lived before through a bunch of lives, show up so oblivious about anyone's needs but their own? If they're a wise soul born into a bad situation, maybe where there's little education or social structure, will they forget everything they learned? I'm talking about people that probably live within ten minutes of here who think the world was created for them alone. I see them every day. People who get to the top of an escalator and STOP, as if that might not cause a slight problem if people are behind them! Or men who throw paper towels on the floor in bathrooms, as if there aren't other people that need to clean up after them. Or people who have never used a turn signal in their LIFE, for crying out loud!"

Aisling gave a hearty laugh. "Henry, it sounds like your problems with other people have more to do with your impatience than their blissful stupidity. Obviously, it's true that people can be very unaware of the world around them and completely oblivious to their place in the world, but there are many explanations for the kinds of people you mention. Maybe they're just new souls, very early in their development. Everyone starts somewhere. Besides, why is it so hard for you to fathom that when you get to the top of an escalator and racks and racks of women's shoes are on display a few feet away, that the proper reaction is to stop and marvel at the wonders before you? New souls might never have seen such a fabulous array of styles and sizes!"

"Well, I wasn't going to target women, but since you brought it up, ..."

"I was defending women, Henry, so perhaps we should leave it at that. Besides, does it occur to men that even when I'm driving in the slow lane, maybe it's not very helpful to drive your enormous pickup truck, which belongs on a farm to begin with, 18 inches from my back bumper? Or that if their aim is bad, perhaps sitting down to pee is the considerate thing to do, somewhat relaxing, and one reason we have locks on bathroom doors?"

Henry smiled and nodded. "Touché, point well taken. I guess idiocy doesn't know gender boundaries."

"Indeed it doesn't. Not surprisingly, new souls are the least able to deal with life's challenges, and usually the most likely to fail in challenging circumstances. Even after four or five, or even ten lifetimes, a soul is still considered comparatively new. New souls may partly explain the behavior you're complaining about, but not completely. Sometimes the soul may be experienced, but the body it's working with is, um, sub-par."

"Okay, you've lost me again. We're talking about a soul here. The essence of being. You're telling me that a superior soul can't overcome bad genes?"

"Certainly not in all situations, but you must realize that a soul will often select life situations that will challenge it. Imagine the the opportunities for growth if a veteran soul is borne into a life where abuse, ignorance, and fear are rampant. To overcome those challenges would be very, very fulfilling. These are the stories of inspiration we read about as children."

Henry objected. "But you said yourself, it's a veteran soul. It's seen all kinds of situations and probably already overcome some very difficult ones. What's to be gained by choosing a really unfortunate situation? Couldn't you make more of an impact with a bit of a head start?"

"Well, it isn't only the social situation. It could also be that the body itself presents extreme obstacles. Perhaps it's someone borne into a situation of intolerance AND who has a very low IQ or perhaps some kind of impairment. Imagine how difficult that would be to overcome! The other thing you're forgetting, Henry, is that souls don't necessarily make use of all the lessons they learned in past lives. Experiences is one thing, but learning and acting on those experiences is really the essence of life, isn't it? This understanding should give everyone an important perspective, which is why we share it. In your case the life you've lived hasn't exactly been easy, Henry, but the way you've handled it – the man you've turned into – is a great testament to the wisdom of your soul."

"It's kind of you to say that, Aisling, but are you saying I chose this situation? That I looked at all the other life options out there and picked the one where my whole family was taken from me?"

"I don't know the answer to that, but I would guess that's entirely possible."

The mere thought was almost too much for Henry to comprehend. He stared into space for a few seconds saying nothing, then his gaze wandered to the television, which was muted and the furthest thing from all of their thoughts.

CNN was showing a close-up still picture of the face of the Dalai Lama. The graphic text that appeared on the screen stunned them.

Dalai Lama apparent kidnapping victim while on Washington visit.

"Oh my God!" Aisling held her hand to her mouth in disbelief.

"That's incredible," Henry said. "Why in the world would anyone kidnap the Dalai Lama? I know things have been a little dicey between Tibet and China for years, but this makes no sense."

"No sense indeed," Aisling replied slowly. "and somewhat of a coincidence when you consider our conversation. Reincarnation is at the very core of the Tibetan Buddhist belief system. With all the other problems happening in the world around religious conflict, this one makes the least sense of all."

She turned up the television. An Asian man, seemingly very familiar with the Dalai Lama, was speaking into the camera.

"The Dalai Lama is considered to be a 'Buddhist Master' whose soul has moved beyond the normal cycle of birth and rebirth – reincarnation – and is incarnate to provide enlightenment for other Tibetan Buddhists."

A female announcer appeared onscreen to provide background.

"The Dalai Lama was on his way to bless a temple that was opening in Virginia. His visit was heavily guarded, however his abduction was obviously a meticulously planned operation. The FBI is releasing few details, other than to say that four or five black SUV's were involved and that the other three people in his traveling party were left behind, unharmed but tied up.

"He has become somewhat of an icon for Tibet's struggle to achieve independence from China, although police are not saying whether political motivations were behind the abduction. They're only providing descriptions of the vehicles involved. Descriptions of the assailants that were released are only that they were wearing black clothes with masks, and that they were bearing firearms."

"This seems completely senseless," Aisling said. "What's to be gained by stealing a man who preaches love and goodness? Whatever they're after, they won't find it."

"I didn't realize he was considered a master of reincarnation," Henry said. "I knew he was considered the most revered Buddhist, but I didn't realize he had the choice to ascend but instead continued the cycle. His abduction has to be about money. That's the only reason they would overlook the sheer irony of the situation."

"I suppose they might get money," Aisling replied. "but Tibetan Buddhists aren't exactly the people to hoard material possessions. Whoever it is, they must be very desperate people."

"Well, Aisling, on that note, I think I need to say goodnight." Henry rose to leave. "I can't thank you enough. What an amazing day it's been. My head is spinning. I feel like I need to sit on my couch and stare at the wall for like four hours."

Aisling's smile returned. "You're welcome, my dear. This was an important day for both of us."

Before he was out the door, she stopped. "Oh, I need to assign you some homework. Let me get you a few books to read."

In the coming days Henry took Aisling's advice and read through the books she chose for him. What he read opened his eyes even wider.

He learned that people under hypnosis, brought through past lives, gave remarkably similar accounts of their experience after death. It sounded very similar to what Aisling described. There were also many detailed, compelling stories of their past lives, including how they lived, how they died, what they gained from each life, their relationship with their personal spirit guide, and the choices they made about lives to come. He found the discussions of spirit guides were particularly interesting because the authors pointed out that many religions have a similar entity assigned to souls. The Catholics call it a Guardian Angel, which was what Henry was taught.

The questions and subjects to discuss with Aisling began to pile up, so he decided to buy a stack of blank index cards and began inscribing different ideas on each. On the cards he unloaded all his ideas from all the scary movies he grew up watching and books read about ghosts, hauntings, poltergeists, possessions, exorcisms, and more. He wrote down comments and questions about things like abortion, miscarriages, suicides, and murderous acts of terror. He was eager to learn Aisling's views on all of these things, and do some research on his own. Having this new perspective on reincarnation made him view old notions on spiritualism with a whole different perspective.

The phone rang before noon on a Sunday morning following a late night of such reading. He had been awake for a short while and answered on the second ring. It was Aisling.

"Henry, there's something important I need to speak with you about. Would you have time for a visit today? I'm terribly sorry to ask you to travel all this way again, but something important came up."

"What is it? Is everything okay? This sounds serious."

"I'm afraid I'd rather discuss it in person Henry. I hope you can understand. Can you be here some time after lunch?"

"Sure, I'll see you at two. I have a few things I'd like to talk with you about as well."

He glanced at the thick stack of index cards on his bedside table, each with detailed notes.

When he arrived, Aisling's mood was somber. This situation, whatever it was, was weighing very heavily on her. She appeared frail this afternoon.

"Henry, I have something quite serious to speak with you about." They settled in for tea in her living room, which was small but offered an angled view of the sun finally peaking through after countless overcast days.

"What's going on, Aisling?"

"I need to leave for Ireland. There's a family matter that requires my presence, and it isn't a small matter. I have no idea when I might return."

"Oh my God, Aisling. I'm so sorry to hear that. I hope everything is okay. You have so much going on here, so many people who depend on you. This must be really serious. Are you sure you can't be back soon?"

"Unfortunately, this is something that can't be resolved easily."

They stared around the room, each unsure what to say next. Aisling finally broke the silence. "Henry, I need you to take over the business here. You've met just a small fraction of my clients, but I feel very confident that you can succeed at this. You have the gift, the integrity, and the personality to make this a winning situation for you and for my customers. You know how important they are to me"

"Aisling, I have no idea what to say, or what to think. I have no money to buy your business, and I've been a medium for like twelve minutes. Plus I have no idea what it takes to run a business, let alone a business like this."

Aisling considered Henry's words. "These are weighty matters, Henry, but the suddenness of this situation has left me with very few options. Under a perfect situation I would screen through other mediums before I would consider handing over my client list to them. If you were the best candidate of all those I interviewed, which I have no doubt you would be, I would have given you months more work and practice. Believe me, Henry, if I could delay this until we had more training time, I would do that. I will understand if you decide this is not something you wish to do. However I've never seen someone with the instincts and talents you have, more prepared for the challenges of handling this responsibility. I know that your other job is quite important to you. However if you can't take over the practice, then given the urgency of the situation I'm facing, my only choice will be to close the doors until I return, whenever that will be."

Henry shook his head slowly, still numb from the news. "But how could I pay for all this? I have no money saved. I'd have to apply for some kind of business loan."

"Money is not the point. I've saved money over the years, so being reimbursed for the business seems silly anyway. The business is worth the earning potential of the person running it. If you fail, it will be worthless. If I close the doors for now, it will still be worthless. I would like you to keep up the payments on the house, but they're reasonably small since I've been here for years. So you would need to keep the mortgage current, pay the utilities, and maintain the house. The money you make beyond those expenses is yours to keep."

"I'm not even sure what to say, Aisling." Henry felt the full weight of her predicament. "Whatever it is I'll say a prayer for you and your family. Let me give it some thought for a day or two and I'll let you know. "

"Whatever you decide about the business is fine," she said, looking down. "It's your life and you need to do what's right for you. I wouldn't turn my customers over to someone I don't trust."

"Your faith in me means the world. Speaking of life decisions," Henry said, lightening the mood, "I spent a lot of time reading through the books you gave me. You were right, there's great information in there. They really got my juices flowing."

For the first time on that day, Aisling smiled. "That's wonderful, Henry. I knew you'd appreciate them. The more you think about these matters, the more questions you're driven to find answers for."

"That reminds me, I wanted to be sure to ask about your experience with 'spirit guides.' According to these authors, that seems like a fairly consistent theme across many of these religions."

Aisling smiled and spoke softly. "Yes indeed, that appears to be consistently true."

"Surely with all your experience with the spirit world you've come across them, right?"

Aisling paused before replying. "Yes, of course, Henry. I see these companions on quite a regular basis. My communications with them are quite limited because they're nearby for one reason only, and that is to lend support to the souls that are under their watch. Typically they have no reason to communicate with me, nor me with them, so I don't have much to tell you on the subject."

"How can you tell one of these guides from a regular spirit that's come to visit?"

"They're sort of comforting connection to goodness and light. They're a completely different form of energy. I've noticed that their presence seems to be far more noticeable when something significant is happening in the lives of their subjects. It tends to be around the time when a transition is happening, like a death of someone close, for example, or even if the death of my client is drawing near. It's hard to know all the time, but their 'heavier' presence usually means they're especially needed. You'll see what I mean."

Henry sighed and scratched his head. "It's like I've been swimming at the top of the ocean and never looked down. Then when I do, the place is just teeming with life.

"Aisling, I appreciate what you're doing for me. You've paid me an incredible compliment by asking me to take over the business, but it's overwhelming right now. Right now I think I just need to think through all this."

"Not at all, my dear. Thank you for coming by on such short notice."

As he arose, Aisling stood up too. Spontaneously he hugged her. The two embraced tightly for several seconds.

"I can let myself out. Thanks for everything, Aisling." He turned to leave.

At the door he looked back at Aisling, staring at him warmly.

Barely visible above and to the right of Aisling was an image, hovering in a sort of bluish and yellow light. It was faint and shimmering, very difficult to make out detail. Aisling did not seem to notice what he was looking at, and the spirit did not seem to care whether Henry noticed it or not. It was obviously there for Aisling and nothing else.

He waved to her again and left.

Henry took the long way home. He drove through areas that gave him the most comfort, places he would stop often to enjoy his solitude. At a clearing overlooking Cambridge Reservoir he left his car and laid on the hood, enjoying the light breeze and the songbirds.

For the first time since he could remember, his career path was in a good place. Yet this 'gift' came along – with Aisling as the catalyst – and everything was changing direction yet again. He balanced the good he was doing for so many people in the dating business versus a world that he did not completely understand; one that was mysterious, frightening, and alluring.

Finders Keepers had the potential to be a very successful business, particularly considering how he had grown his client base and income in just a short time. In the future, he was confident his role would become even more critical to their growth and success. However what Aisling had built and what she meant to her clients was inspiring. She filled in missing pieces in their lives, and all seemed grateful.

Even those clients like Donnelly, who were somehow trying to take advantage of things beyond their reach, needed her. For the well guided and the misguided, the responsibility of being a medium was a weighty one. The idea that there were practicing mediums who took the profession lightly, as Aisling had suggested, presented an even more compelling reason for pursuing the occupation.

Through this contemplation, scanning the reservoir and the green trees budding on this cool spring day, Henry decided that being a medium was a far more rare and important occupation than working for a dating service. Finders Keepers would continue with or without him.

Once the decision was made, he considered all that lay ahead. There was the perpetually recurring sense of uncertainty, disconnectedness. He was turning yet another corner, going down yet another dark alley that was riskier but more impactful than any decision he had ever made.

His inner voice rose to the surface. *This is the right decision. You are needed here.*

While his decision was made, there was another clear and unambiguous sense: he would be tested in ways he could never imagine.

On Monday morning Henry felt a great weight had been removed. He settled in with his coffee, his oatmeal, and the Boston Globe. Most of the stories were about international turmoil instead of the usual local tales of political corruption and violent crime. Further, he noticed, all were all centered on religion.

Tibetan Buddhists Speak Out Against Chinese Imperialism
Militant Party Claims Election Victory in Israel
Al Qaida Resurgence Fuels Concerns in Europe Following Train Attack
Hostilities Escalate on Indian-Pakistani Border Following Nuclear Declaration
Pontiff's Silence on Holocaust Memorial Draws Criticism

The increasing number of stories about religion-based conflicts in recent months forced him to consider whether his recent discussions with Aisling on religion raised his awareness about religious conflict, or whether there were simply more stories to report in recent days.

As his coffee grew cold he determined that world conflicts had little bearing on the conflict raging inside, so he prepared for his last commute to *Finders Keepers*.

During his career transition, Henry was in nearly constant communication with Aisling. In his last weeks with the dating service, he would usually stop in during the evening and on weekends to become acquainted with her clientele. Nearly all the clients felt immediately comfortable with Henry, and Aisling was confident that the few who were wary of the change would either come around or move on. She believed any client attrition would be easily offset by his energy and passion for the role.

Aisling was consistently vague about her reasons for going back to Ireland, and Henry respected her silence on the matter. Gradually her disinterest and low energy became apparent, but he attributed this to stress over the difficulties that awaited her at home. When he asked what she would do once she returned to Ireland, she replied vaguely about taking care of a few others for a brief time before she could finally take care of herself. As her days in the states wound down, his questions persisted but her replies became repetitive. "You'll figure it out, my dear" was becoming the common answer.

Among the details that Henry labored to get her to consider was what was to be done about Aisling's home from a legal sense. The two worked out an arrangement whereby Henry would take over payments on her mortgage, and Aisling would retain a legal stake in the value of the property and the business. She gave him the contact information for her attorney, assuring him that her will was up to date.

Despite his repeated offers to seek a bank loan to repay her, she reiterated that the future value of the business would be solely up to what Henry chose to put into it. She explained that the business had given her more than she ever expected, which Henry took to mean that she had managed to put away some money. He came to realize that his care of her clients was all the thanks she needed.

On the morning of the day when Aisling was to leave, a small moving truck showed up in the morning. Aisling had prepared quietly but efficiently. The moving men loaded the few belongings she wished to bring across the ocean onto a wooden palate. He was surprised at how little she wished to bring.

"The rest of it belongs to the house, my dear. Guard it with your life, unless of course your life is in danger. Then run like hell!"

Her flight was to depart at nine at night, a redeye across the ocean. Henry insisted on driving her to the airport, although she fought the imposition. When it was time to leave she barely glanced back at the home she built to help so many. Her work here was complete, Henry thought. It was time for a new start for his dear friend and mentor.

After checking in for the flight, they headed for the security queue, which would be their farewell. They both paused uncomfortably. Henry was the first to speak.

"Aisling, I just want to tell you now much you've meant to me. You've changed everything, including the way I view every event, every person, and I can't thank you enough." He was struggling against a full waterfall.

"Henry, if you haven't figured it out by now, you've been nothing short of a blessing to me. Your showing up on my doorstep was no coincidence at all. You were meant to be in this position, Henry. Now it's up to you to make the most of it. Great things await you if you keep your heart and mind open."

"I won't let you down."

"That's the spirit, young man."

"Aisling, will you ever come back for a visit?"

"Probably not, to be honest, but I feel confident that we'll cross paths again."

"That's comforting to know, but how can I reach you? You didn't give me a phone number or address."

"I won't be settled for a little while, my dear, and when I do, I'm not exactly sure where it will be. I can only promise that you will hear from me again. Will that suffice for now?"

Henry felt foolish, like an insecure boy being dropped off for his first day of school. "Yes, Aisling, that will suffice."

"My boy, you'll do just fine. Challenge yourself, and trust yourself. It will all be fine. You'll make a world of difference, I just know it."

He embraced her and they offered each other a simple goodbye as he realized that he was on his own again.

The next time he would see her it would be under very different circumstances.

It was a Sunday evening after dark, but Henry could not bring himself to go back to Aisling's house. As anxious as he was to get things started in his new life, he needed the security of his old apartment on this evening. At home he found himself in a familiar position during times of transition, with a glass of wine in hand and his thoughts going in a thousand directions.

As sleep began to envelop him, odd images began to enter his mind, at first slowly then much faster. A Hebrew star. A crucifix and crown of thorns. The crescent moon and star, symbol of Islam. The Buddha. A bindi on the head of a Hindu woman. A swastika. Some were unnerving, some grounded in love. Some came from the basest of human emotions, some from curiosity and awakening, others from spiritual discovery that came from experimentation. Some images displayed the burden of strong faith and the persecution and horror that often followed.

He saw images that he could not identify, but the emotions behind each became clear as more passed. As an image of terror went rushing by Henry, it was quickly followed by a feeling that glowed with forgiveness. An image of greed for money and power was quickly followed by a glimpse of pure selflessness. An image of intense nakedness and loneliness moved past, trailed immediately by warm comfort, the product of a mother's love.

The disparity and contrast of these images and emotions were exhausting, even in his light sleep state.

Finally the images blended, and he was left with a consortium, a tapestry of images. As his mind's eye moved away from all the images and emotions, he was still able to discern each of the hundreds of images, even from a distance. Back and back he moved, away from the discrete images and emotions until they grew so small they looked like cells of a larger organism.

The final image he saw was a single, red, long stemmed rose. It hung before him. The aroma and voluptuous beauty were as clear in his senses as the sharpness of the thorns.

On Monday morning it was time to start his new life. He was at Aisling's home, key in hand, at seven twenty in the morning. His first order of business was to check the day's schedule, the second was to pull out Aisling's client log to study up on the clients he would be viewing for the day.

For the day, Henry had a total of five clients scheduled. For each customer he found that Aisling kept detailed, descriptive notes in lovely handwriting. Her descriptions focused on the emotions of her clients, what they were going through when they came in to see her, and only secondarily on the spirits they came to see and what transpired. Typically, the only detailed mention of spirits was when customers did not receive the reaction they expected from spirits.

Vivian came to visit with her brother Earl, but was dismayed when Earl's spirit barely gave her a passing nod. He was respectful of the contact and understanding of her need for support, but made it clear there was nothing the two needed to discuss. Earl indicated it wouldn't be long before she was next to him, so she should cling to humankind instead of his memory. His message is clear – she isn't helping herself in this life as much as she could. She needs to be around other people. Next time try to help Earl and Vivian come up with ideas, else it will be more of the same.

Many of her passages contained similar themes: live life while you have it. Your circumstance in the next life might make that much more difficult. Aisling usually tried to stay positive in her transcriptions, but staying true to their messages as well. She rarely wrote anything negative, and Henry promised himself to try hard to continue the positivity.

Janice Reynolds was his first appointment, at ten o'clock. She was a widow in her late seventies. Aisling's notes explained that her needs were simple, to visit with her father, mother, and husband, in that precise order. In prior sessions she had left disappointed that there was too little contact from her father.

"Hello Mrs. Reynolds, my name is Henry. As Aisling told you, I'll be assisting you in your readings. Can I offer you a cup of tea or coffee?"

She was not the warmest of customers, but she was respectful and almost reverent toward Aisling. She seemed doubtful that someone else could have similar insights as Aisling. Henry inhaled, full aware that most of his early sessions would be just like this one.

"Will that be charged to me?" She seemed anxious.

"The coffee? Oh, of course not. Never. I'll always have complimentary coffee or tea for you, Mrs. Reynolds." Henry was his most assuring. "Drinks, on the other hand, are available by credit card only on this flight. No cash accepted."

Mrs. Reynolds cast an odd look upon him.

"I'm sorry, Mrs. Reynolds. I just flew to Colorado. That was a little joke. Anyway, whatever you want is on the house."

"Nothing for me, thank you." She brushed past him toward the room she knew well.

They sat. Out of habit Henry waited for someone else in the room to take charge, then he quickly came to his senses as Mrs. Reynolds stared at him, waiting for his lead.

"Well, let's begin, Mrs. Reynolds. Shall we say a prayer?"

He recited a prayer of thanks, during which she bowed her head and folded her hands. When it was finished, the woman seemed satisfied, unfolded her hands and stared at Henry in silence.

Henry returned her gaze. "Mrs. Reynolds, I was able to go through some notes from previous readings with Aisling, and I'd like to continue the progress you've made in these meetings with minimal interruption. Could you explain to me briefly your expectations for these readings?" As he spoke the feelings of spirit presence were becoming powerful and tangible. He smelled a male musky scent, and the faint whiff of cigars and perfume.

"Well, yes, of course." Her tone lightened "I come here to visit with the people that I've spent most of my living days, my parents and my husband. It's important that I pay my respects to my father and mother first since they brought me into this world."

Henry sensed the father coming across the strongest but most reluctant. The spiritual message being given by the father was ambiguous, almost as if he was reluctant to receive any form of adoration. Still, his message was clearly one of unfiltered love, and he made it clear to Henry that he wanted her to know it. He remembered his deep conversations with Aisling, so it occurred to him that these two souls – father and daughter in the most recent life – had a long history together, probably in other lifetimes.

"He's here with you, Mrs. Reynolds. He sends his profound love, and wants you to know that it means a great deal to him that his daughter shows such love and dedication. He indicates that he's happy, and that his life on the other side is very rich and rewarding."

Mrs. Reynolds showed emotion for the first time. Through her wet eyes she said unevenly, "Tell father that I miss him terribly, every day."

"He knows that, Mrs. Reynolds, and he wants you to be happy during this time while you two are apart."

The old woman said nothing, tears through a soft smile.

"Was your father a somewhat gruff man, Mrs. Reynolds?"

"Yes, I suppose," she said, smile fading away.

"Because it sounds like he wants you to stop missing him so much. He loves that you come to visit him, but it doesn't sound as though he's comfortable being the object of affection. Was that how he was in life too?"

The woman did not expect such directness. "I suppose he did tend to avoid too much sappiness, as he called it."

"Well, it doesn't sound like that's changed." Henry brightened his tone. "Your mother sends her love as well. She wants to be sure you're eating right, that you're feeding your mind and your body with the right things."

"Oh," Mrs. Reynolds laughed softly, "tell her she doesn't need to worry about that."

Henry could read from the message being passed along that her parents worried that the woman spent much of her time in front of the television listening to evangelists, that she used their view of the world as her reservoir for opinions and ideas. Henry explained delicately that there was concern that the personal agendas of some, including politics and their version of morality, was clouding the messages she was hearing. She seemed open to the suggestion, and Henry decided that she had probably heard this message before through Aisling.

Mrs. Reynolds left the house apparently satisfied with the session because she asked Henry to put her in the book for the same time next month.

The remainder of his first day went smoothly. A woman came in to connect with family, who promptly scolded her for pretending she was a nun. A young man connected with a cousin that had passed. An older man that missed his wife terribly. A former truck driver that connected with two former wives, neither of whom seemed to mind the other's presence. In each case Henry was able to help his clients gain some comfort and focus on the things that would help them move forward. It was an excellent first day.

As he was getting ready to leave, jacket and keys in hand, the phone rang. On the other end was a man's voice, tentative and a bit shaky.

"May I speak with Aisling please?"

"I'm very sorry but Aisling has left the country for an indefinite period. In her absence I'm helping out. My name is Henry Chimera. Can I help you?"

"Oh." The voice trailed off.

"I'd be happy to help you, sir. Would you like to set some time to come in?"

"This is John Donnelly. I met you the last time I was in to see Aisling."

Henry was stunned. Donnelly, who had tried to deceive he and Aisling, was the last person he expected to hear from.

"Mr. Chimera," he said with a trace of fear in his voice, "I think I've done something terrible. Can you make time for me tomorrow?"

He agreed to see Donnelly at the very end of the next day, as the last of his appointments.

SOUL MATH

The prospect of Henry's second day as a full time medium provoked nearly as much anxiety as the first. He had the confidence of a solid day of readings behind him, however the phone call from Donnelly threw him. His concern was around the possibility that Donnelly might be a lot more savvy about the afterlife than he let on. Henry had the confidence that his first and best experience directly with a spirit was with Annabelle Livingston, Donnelly's grandmother. This was even the experience that convinced Aisling that he had a special gift, but was the gift ready for whatever trick Donnelly had planned next? This man that had been deceitful once could certainly try something even more clever and damaging.

Before considering that hurdle, there was first the matter of his other clients. It was a full slate of readings, and some of these customers offered what seemed to be odd challenges. Aisling's notes on each were complete as usual, but each was a work in progress, and Aisling's notes did not reveal where that work might take him.

His first appointment was with a middle aged man called Raja Abdullah. Henry could only discern from Aisling's notes that he was on a spiritual journey, and that he was troubled by his current direction in life. He had previously connected with a spirit named Qismah, and that the connection gave him some comfort.

When the man arrived, Henry went through the formalities of explaining his philosophy and approach, which was greatly influenced his mentor. Raja seemed satisfied with this introduction. He was in his late thirties or early forties, but very quiet. Henry could scarcely get the man to return his gaze and respond to his questions.

Finally Henry asked him directly, "Mr. Abdullah, you seem reluctant to be here. I hope I'm not making you uncomfortable from anything I'm doing."

The man was slow to reply. "No, Mister Chimera, it isn't anything you're doing. It's just that in my faith, this kind of encounter is strictly forbidden. It is considered heresy to try to find meaning in anything other than the Quran, or in one's own talks with God. Each time I come in I go through severe doubts about whether I should be here."

"Please call me Henry." His tone was calming. "I don't possess a detailed understanding of your Islamic faith, Mr. Abdullah, as I wish I could, however I do believe we're all on a personal journey. I doubt you'll hurt anyone else by being here, and I don't for a moment believe you're hurting yourself."

That seemed to ease the man's anxiety slightly. "Thank you. I suppose that is true, however I am quite certain that others would be greatly irritated by the mere fact that I am here."

The man hesitated. "Nonetheless, I've made the decision and I am here now. We can get started any time you like." At this, the man focused inwardly. After a few awkward moments, he spoke. "Most people call me Raj."

They moved to the reading room and began the standard preparations. During their prayer, Henry watched his words to be sure his message was non-denominational. Aisling had led him down a religiously neutral path, a sound business decision. At least Henry believed that to be true. He noticed the man's head bowed deeply in prayer while he was giving thanks.

When he was done he felt obliged to ask, "Raj, is there anything else you would like to add that is specific to your faith?"

Raj looked up peacefully. "No, your prayer was lovely, and I prayed in my own way along with you."

Henry began the process of clearing his mind of all outside thoughts. When he acquired some mental clarity he saw his customer in a different light, which required adjustment. The man sitting before him was no longer a lonely man with a curious religious background, but rather a complex spirit with a much-traveled journey in his past. He was an old soul. While Henry recognized the long roads that led into this man's mind, it took some time to calibrate. After a few moments of looking, thinking, then looking again, he carefully considered his words.

"Mr. Abdullah, you have quite a remarkable history."

Abdullah looked at him with curiosity. "I'm not sure what you mean, Mr. Chimera."

"Well, Raj, I see that you have many experiences behind you, not necessarily in this life, although I suppose this one hasn't been an easy one for you either. It appears that your soul has been through a great many experiences, which has probably given you rare wisdom."

The man began to show impatience. "I'm not sure what you mean. I'm here to reinforce my peace with my family because I miss them terribly. I don't know what else there is."

Henry delicately moved on, not bothering to press on the man's self-awareness.

The reading went quickly into deep water. Henry quickly connected with Quismah, the only other spirit available, and a formidable one.

"Raj, have you spoken to Quismah before?"

"Yes, of course. She's been a great comfort to me, overseeing my family."

"Does she oversee your family, or your connection with your family?"

"I suppose it's the latter, but there has been great comfort from Quismah. She first appeared in my prior visits with Aisling, and I'm pleased that she's here now."

"She's definitely here now," Henry encouraged, "and she's very comfortable in your presence. She's proud that you're reaching toward important things. I get the message that you are an important source of pride for those in a position to watch your progress. Quismah extends you a message of encouragement, and of love. Quismah hopes you take great comfort in the message."

"I do not." Abdullah was quick to respond.

"How so?"

"I don't know who I'm speaking with. When I met with Aisling, I received the same assurances. However, I am very interested in knowing who I'm speaking with. I'm anxious to speak with my father and mother."

"I see. Well, please give me a few moments to communicate with Quismah. I'll see what I can learn."

Henry concentrated on the female spirit within his range. Quismah came across as a loving but protective spirit. He perceived a smile, but one that might be reluctant to give up information that was not immediately important to Raj. The man was a customer to Henry, but something more than this to the spirit.

In his gestures to the spirit, Henry extended respect and pure intentions. Quismah in turn expressed that Raj was more than a loved one, that he was her responsibility. Henry noted the bond between the two, and that this spirit was also an older spirit who emitted a deep energy, filled with wisdom.

The message of trust Henry received back took him by surprise. "As kindred spirits, I similarly recognize your hard-earned wisdom. Together we will certainly do justice for those we care for."

Henry was taken by surprise. "Why do you believe I'm so experienced? I'm new at this, and learning with each experience. I barely know what I'm doing!"

Quismah replied without hesitation. "You're more experienced than you know. In this life you're learning so much so fast, but much of your wisdom was learned before. You are following a very strong path. You are prepared for the work before you now."

The personal attention was not something Henry expected, nor felt especially comfortable with. He opened his eyes to glance at his client, who seemed content that progress of some kind was being made. Henry remembered what he was being paid for, and turned his attention back to the case before him.

"Quismah, my client has great faith in you but doesn't understand your role. Can you explain that please?"

"I can explain it, but you must exercise caution in what you disclose to Raj. We are not to cause any form of doubt in his faith, nor are we to alter the path he has chosen."

"Understood, and I will be discreet, however this man seems desperate for some information about his parents. He trusts you, but I am not sure what to make of your role."

"I am his spirit guide, and his soul is my responsibility."

"I see. My experience is limited with spirit guides, by I am familiar with your purpose."

"Yes," the spirit seemed most interested in continuing this dialogue. "We normally stay in the background because we have other responsibilities, but when we are needed, we are there."

"But why are you needed here and now for Mr. Abdullah? Why are his parents unavailable?"

"The reason for my presence in Mr. Abdullah's life at this time is that his parents, while passed beyond that life, cannot be contacted."

"Why?"

"They do not wish to be bothered. They have not ascended to their sanctuary. They remain earthbound."

"Excuse me?" Henry was flabbergasted. His surprise was noticed by Raj.

"What is it?" Raj Abdullah leaned forward, eager to understand what Henry was learning.

Henry looked at him with some embarrassment. His inexperience showed. He should not have displayed such an emotion to his customer before fully understanding the implications.

"I'm making progress, Mr. Abdullah. Please bear with me while I interpret the messages I'm receiving. I'll be back to you very soon, I promise."

Abdullah seemed to accept this explanation easily. Henry turned back to his communication with Quismah, which was reliably in place.

Quismah continued. "When spirits depart life on earth, they need to be ready to ascend to a place of healing and learning. A soul goes through many lives and experiences, and each life brings forth a new understanding of the development of the soul. When a soul leaves earth, it is critical that the experiences – good and bad – learned from that life are studied, understood, and absorbed. How else can a soul develop but from learning from mistakes and successes?"

"Yes," Henry said, "I've heard the 'sanctuary' you are speaking of, a destination for recently departed souls to reflect and to heal. Are you saying that his parents have not ascended? Are they earthbound ghosts, inhabiting their prior home or some other place?"

"Nothing so dramatic," the Quismah replied. "His parents have remained in the earthly realm out of choice. In their later years, while still in their most recent lives, they became wary of change. Yet they've been through the ultimate change, the end of their mortal lives, and they are, sadly, unaware of their current condition."

"Isn't it your job to make them aware?"

"They've kept their focus on this realm, and have chosen to keep it there. The invitation has been open for some time. Help is always available to those who look for it. I do not envy your position, but you must somehow explain to Raj that they cannot be reached through you and me."

"I certainly respect that you can't intervene, but is there nothing he can do?"

"Yes, of course. He can pray. He can pray for his parents to seek a better place. There are many useless messages conveyed by the major religions, but they are very right about one thing: prayer is powerful. Perhaps you can get that across to your friend."

"Thank you, I will do that."

Henry turned his attention to his client. "Mr. Abdullah, Quismah informs me that your parents are unavailable because they wish to remain unavailable. I am told that they're not open to communication from above, but it's possible they may be open to communication from you."

Abdullah looked at Henry blankly. "I don't understand. What does this mean?'"

"You can pray, and direct your prayers to your parents. Pray that they recognize that the light that is available to them."

From Abdullah's expression, the man was satisfied with the message he received. Henry made himself available for future readings, but he cautioned that there was a strong chance he would not hear a different result for some time. Abdullah thanked Henry politely and left quietly.

As Henry scribbled notes on the session, his comments drifted into the mysterious circumstances of his own parents. "Is this what's happening with my parents? Is it only a matter of prayer to get them out of whatever ditch they're in?"

Henry's readings during the middle of the day were relatively routine, particularly compared to the uneasy conversation with Raja Abdullah, and what was likely coming at the end of the day with John Donnelly. A couple came to speak to the woman's sister and parents. An older man wished to contact his wife. Each was a happy experience with a few tears and satisfied customers. Finally, his last scheduled appointment left the house at 5:30, leaving just a few minutes before Donnelly was to arrive.

As exhausted as he was from a full day of work, Henry looked forward to reviewing the session notes from Donnelly's visit a few weeks earlier. His memory of the session came back easily, including the vision of Annabelle Livingston, Donnelly's grandmother, and her stern instructions. She was clearly perturbed about his first visit here, so any attempt at further trickery by Donnelly would be dicey.

Finally the doorbell rang. Henry greeted the man coolly.

"Listen Henry, I want to apologize right off the bat. I know I have some explaining to do."

"Fair enough." Henry looked impassively away from the man. "Shall we sit?"

Henry offered Donnelly a beer, which he readily accepted, and which precluded the possibility that any reading would take place on this evening. The two men sat facing each other in the living room, which was designed around Aisling's tastes rather than two younger men savoring a truce beer. As they settled into the stiff furniture, both men knew it would be Donnelly doing most of the talking, at least to start.

Donnelly asked about Aisling. Henry provided only minimal details about her departure. He emphasized that she was quick to entrust her business and all her clients to him.

"You don't need to convince me of how good you are at this, Henry. Your connection with my grandmother taught me all I needed to know about you and your skill. I didn't doubt for a second that she was in that room scolding me, just like when I was a kid. She was a great lady, but when she was angry everyone knew it. There's no doubt that was Annabelle Livingston."

"Mr. Donnelly, your grandmother was pissed. What were you trying to do?"

Donnelly looked down as he began to speak. "First off, please call me John. What I was doing was based on a real need, but it was absolutely the wrong way to approach it. I just presented our situation in a way that was dishonest. That's all my fault."

"What were you hiding? And you can call me Henry."

"We really are interested in having a child, but we're not really worried about insanity or Parkinson's or any of that. We have as good a chance of having a healthy child as anyone does. My wife and I both come from an advantaged background. We had wealthy relatives and were always expected to go to good schools and make great things of our lives. We've been married for just over eleven years, and we've been talking about having a family all that time but never found the time right. It finally seems right, but the thought of what our child might become worries us."

"How come? Thousands and thousands of parents roll the dice every year, and the chances of success are overwhelming. I don't get it."

"What we've noticed, in comparing our families to the people we knew growing up, is that while we have really healthy stock, we have a really high incidence of people in both our families turning out to be assholes. I guess it's just part of being advantaged, growing up not having to fight and scrap for every little gain. It just makes for arrogant people, unless you have the combination of a strong upbringing, which we're fully committed to providing, and a strong soul to start with. Both Janice and I noticed that we each have cousins that had great parents – and I mean GREAT parents – but at least some of their kids still ended up as annoying little turds. Then they grew up to be annoying big turds. We simply don't want that to happen to us."

Henry replied quickly. "I'm not a parent, but what parent doesn't worry that their kid will have some kind of character flaw? I suspect people who really worry about that will take extra measures to make sure it happen, like giving their child a spiritual upbringing, or making them perform humbling volunteer work, that kind of thing. Also, you really thought you'd get help from a relative that's passed beyond this life?"

"Well, that's part of it. There's a little more to it than that. I think I mentioned the last time we talked that we saw a psychic on TV that got us really interested in reincarnation."

"I do remember that."

"Well, I lied. It wasn't really a psychic. It was a guy that we read about online, a theologian or historian, I guess. It turns out that his group is Christian, but based on some different ideas. Evidently the VERY early Christian Church was fine with reincarnation, so these guys are kind of going back to that original message. Their literature says it goes back to within two or three hundred years of Christ's death. The message we picked up was that souls waiting for their next 'assignment' in this life would tend to pick a life circumstance that would be challenging, to help them grow and acquire wisdom. I guess that's not always the case, but it tends to be fairly common."

Henry thought about some of the books Aisling had him read. "That's the way I understood it too, but I didn't get the impression these things are predictable in any way."

"Perhaps not," Donnelly continued, "but what would a really advanced, wise soul have to gain from being born into a privileged position? Janice and I began to believe that we're far more likely to have a younger, raw soul as a child than the next Abraham Lincoln or Mahatma Gandhi, great men borne of humble beginnings."

Henry shook his head at this and smiled, but avoided judgement for the moment.

"From what I read, it sounds as though there's a strong possibility we'll have a newer, unpolished soul. That might explain why there are so many people in our families who just aren't pleasant to be around, because they're young souls that need grooming, more experience through lifetimes. I don't want a son or daughter like that. We just did not want to take that chance.

"So anyway, we decided to dig into reincarnation, and I mean DIG IN. We learned a lot. Some of the things we read just blew us away. The theologian I mentioned was from a group calling themselves 'Origenists'. They're a lot like a traditional church, but they follow an early church teacher named Origen, who just sort've took reincarnation for granted. Evidently his views conflicted with the early church's ideas on how they'd survive as a church if the people didn't see this life as a make or break deal. Basically, they believed reincarnation was not a notion that would prompt their followers to reliably behave themselves, so it didn't last. 1500 years ago, the church felt that if they embraced reincarnation it would make people lazy. If 'heaven' wasn't a reward that came right after this life, people would consider a failed life as not that big a deal. A do-over would be bound to happen, so why try too hard?"

Henry perked up. "Aisling's been talking to me about some of this exact stuff. The more I've read about it, the more sense it makes, specifically when you consider the beliefs the conventional religions have thrown out there over the centuries."

"I couldn't agree more." Donnelly seemed relieved. "So based on that, we dug in even deeper. We got around to pure logistics, numbers. The thing we couldn't get away from was the net effect of two counteracting forces that are undeniable: the life spans of humans are increasing, which has partly led to the earth's population explosion over the past century. On the one hand, people are living longer thanks to better medicine and improved access to all forms of health care, even in poorer countries. So on a grand scale, people are dying less often, which means there are fewer souls available for the 'reincarnation pool.' On top of that, SO many more people are being born."

Donnelly pulled a scrap of paper from his jacket. "Henry, did you know that soon there will over EIGHT BILLION people in the world, whereas a century ago there were less than two billion? My wife Janice and I had some fun with this one night. What we found was that around the first century BC, world population was increasing at a rate of about 100,000 souls each year. Since then there have been some periods where growth was slow or negative, like plagues or large wars, but by the eighteenth century that number was increasing to about one million new souls per year.

"Now think about reincarnation again. The soul production machine REALLY needed to kick into overdrive to match that growth to keep up with all those new humans."

"I see your point," Henry said, squinting his eyes.

"It gets even more amazing. When we looked at population increases through the twentieth and into the twenty-first centuries, we couldn't believe it. In the most recent years, the number of new souls is approaching 90 million per year!"

"Can that be right?"

"It's accurate. I rechecked the math a bunch of times. So Henry, where do those new souls come from? However new souls are created or distributed, doesn't it place a tremendous strain on the need to make each of them unique? I figure that some souls will ascend into heaven, leaving the reincarnation cycle, but it stands to reason that the vast majority of deaths are followed by rebirth. Perhaps not right away, but before very long. They need to come from somewhere. Assuming there's no limit to the number of new and unique souls that can be created – which, when you think about it, is a staggering thought in itself – doesn't that mean there are an extraordinarily high number of new souls bumbling all around us?"

Henry let out a chuckle. "No wonder it seems like the world is full of people who don't have a clue. They don't! They're all newbies!"

"Exactly. We call it 'Soul Math.'"

Henry smiled.

"I was misguided to come in here the way I did, I'll admit. Janice went along with it, but it was mostly my idea to find an unsuspecting psychic and try to contact a relative that might be willing to help. That's when we called Aisling. I thought that maybe my grandmother would be sympathetic to what we were trying to do, in the interest of our family. Obviously I was wrong about that. Like I said, I'm really sorry for the deception."

Henry was fascinated by the story. "Well, apology accepted. I guess I can't blame you for trying, but I would like to learn more about these Origenists."

"Well, they were really helpful, but a little on the secretive side," Donnelly continued. "It was almost as if they wanted to be sure I was who I said I was. When I asked them why they care who I am, they just said something to the effect that some people aren't very fond of their ideas."

"Anyway, about a week later I got a call from someone asking if we had gotten materials from that web site. The person at first said they were with some fraud division of the state of Massachusetts. They wanted information on the people that ran the web site, but I didn't have much to tell them, other than the basic info. Besides, I figured if they were investigating them, they knew a lot more about them than I know, which isn't much. They were actually pretty obnoxious about it, considering it was a phone call out of the blue. I really had no sure way of knowing who I was speaking with. I pressed the guy on the phone to prove who he was. Then his tone completely changed. He started getting nasty, threatening me. His message was basically that I needed to cease contact with these guys or trouble would come my way."

"Whoa, that's bizarre, and kind of frightening," Henry said. "Do you have any idea who it might've been?"

"No idea. The guy said something like, 'If you don't, it'll be my pleasure to send you off to hell, where people like you belong.' I didn't tell Janice that last part – I thought it would freak her out just a little too much."

"You're kidding me!" Henry was stunned. "Did you ID the number from your phone?"

"Nah it just said, 'Restricted Number.' That's when I decided to call you. So Henry, I have a question to ask you, and I'd like you to be honest."

"What is it?"

"Did you or Aisling tell anybody about this? I know I probably offended both of you by coming here, but you two were the only people that knew my wife and I were thinking about this."

"Absolutely not," Henry answered. "Sure, we both felt like you tried to manipulate us, but we felt as though the message from your grandmother was clear. Whatever you were trying to do – which I didn't understand at the time – was wrong. I figured I'd never see you again."

Henry paused before continuing. "I wonder if somebody's out there trying to get these Origenists to stop what they're doing."

"It sure seems that way," Donnelly said, "but I really think the Origenists are just small timers who are trying to grow their base of supporters. We didn't spend a lot for their materials, so they don't seem to be trying to get rich, but their web site was compelling. These guys are passionate about what they believe, that life is all about doing better the next time around."

"A mulligan," Henry said, referring to a golf term in which a wayward shot is quickly replaced as if it never happened.

Donnelly laughed. "Yeah, a Mulligan. Today's Christian Church isn't down with Mulligans."

They both swigged the last of their beer. Henry asked, "Care for another?"

"No thanks, I have a long drive home. I was going to ask you if you think it would be wise idea to be back in touch with my grandmother. I feel terrible for trying to manipulate her like that. Do you have an opinion?"

At that moment Henry felt a strong sense that Annabelle Livingston was nearby. He did not see her presence, but felt her distinct vibration. The sense he was receiving from the grandmother was that her love for him was unwavering.

"As a matter of fact, I do," Henry answered. "I don't think it's necessary. Spirits don't typically hold grudges like we do. I wouldn't say that your grandmother was angry when she spoke to me. It was more of a forceful message to you to stop it. I got the impression from her that the message was delivered and that was the end of it."

"Seriously? Wow, I can't tell you how relieved that makes me feel."

"People make mistakes. I can tell you that she definitely cares about you. Most spirits don't hang with their living relatives all the time, but usually departed souls care about our progress."

"That's very reassuring. I think I'll get going, but thanks so much for being cool about this."

"I never thought I'd say this after our first meeting," Henry said, "but I enjoyed hanging out. Stay in touch."

The two men shook hands and exchanged cell phone numbers, and Donnelly was off. Henry finished his notes on the day's sessions, taking special care to include detail on his unexpected, frank discussion with Donnelly.

About fifteen minutes after Donnelly left, Henry realized he had left his sunglasses. He would call Donnelly in the morning.

Henry gathered his things and paused in the front hallway before the night time drive to his apartment. He glanced back into the main rooms. The house was all about Aisling. She had built its foundation as a sacred place, where so many had entrusted her with their closest secrets. Her spirit was all around. Henry was proud to be maintaining her legacy.

As he locked the door in the cool but dry Massachusetts evening, his responsibilities felt like a heavy weight. His thoughts consumed him as he headed for his car. What if Aisling had casually mentioned their experience with Donnelly. Or worse, what if Aisling somehow decided that harm could come to Donnelly? He wrestled with the idea of Aisling as conspirator, and decided it was not something he could take seriously, especially not tonight, after a long day of working with the people that had trusted her with their most important secrets.

The street was completely still and quiet, without even wind through the trees. He unlocked his car, and instinctively glanced to his right, behind his car. A dark car was sitting only fifty feet away. He couldn't see clearly inside, but it appeared to be a male figure in the driver's seat. He stared for a few moments and the figure did not move.

He climbed slowly into his car and started it, shifting his gaze to his side mirror. There was no movement behind him. He considered wheeling his car around to flash his lights on the car, but decided he was letting paranoia affect him. Instead he shifted around in his car to pretend to look for something in the back seat. He glanced back at the suspicious car. The male figure in the driver's seat was no longer there. The seat appeared empty.

What a curious world he had entered.

PASSING SHIPS

During the coming weeks Henry developed strength and confidence as a medium. He continued to nurture clients that needed nurturing, and reassuring clients that weren't accustomed to his style of reading. His goal was to keep steady the customer base that Aisling handed him, which included nearly a hundred clients. He knew there would be turnover, but hoped he would add clients too as his reputation became established.

He also decided to learn more about reincarnation. He was embarrassed that until he met Aisling and his life moved toward its current course, his understanding of reincarnation was constrained by the belief that people could come back in another life as animals or even insects. The more he read, the more he came to understand how much he was missing. Through simple internet research, he decided to immerse himself in all available literature about reincarnation. He read books from Brian Weiss, Michael Newton, Elizabeth Clare Prophet, and others, who had developed their insights through their own gifts or the gifts possessed by those they studied. In some cases it was past life regression, which depended on hypnotism. Other books he read relayed detailed stories of visions and visitations by psychics, but the themes were consistent throughout. There was a vast, complex afterlife that provided the entire basis for human existence. Henry pored through the readings voraciously.

The authors opened his eyes to how reincarnation was not nearly as removed from conventional religion as he believed. Nearly all major religions have elements of reincarnation threaded throughout their belief systems. As Donnelly mentioned, the early Christian church had strategic reasons for eliminating it as part of the soul's formula. The foundations of each of the three major monotheistic religions – Islam, Christianity, and Judaism – contained references to reincarnation in their earliest writings. In some cases the references were veiled, in other cases quite obvious.

He discovered that transmigration among different species – reincarnation between humans and non-humans – was something that very few dogmas supported. None of the authors he read suggested it was likely, but rather that the soul's path to heaven often extended over many centuries and sometimes hundreds of lifetimes.

He discovered with some surprise that reincarnation scholars rarely cited proof of pure evil, or the presence of Satan. The evil they identified was the kind that originated from humans and their tendency toward fear, greed, and insecurity. He found that his lifelong notion that evil people went to hell was a difficult one to prove. His reading indicated that lives lived in pure evil, such as Hitler or other merciless mass murderers, presented no exceptions to the cycle of reincarnation, although their path would be more indirect and difficult. The authors suggested consistently that souls who led this kind of evil life were given other chances at rebirth, but that it would always follow a period of intensive rehabilitation and mending, and their progress would be watched closely by kindred spirits.

Some, like the author Prophet – as curious a name for a spiritual writer as he could think of – made the case that Jesus may have openly preached about achieving perfection and grace through multiple lives. She felt that Jesus probably believed that developing a soul in a single lifetime was nearly an impossible endeavor; multiple lifetimes were an absolute necessity.

Some of the founders of the early Christian church were likely staunch believers in reincarnation, most notably Origen, the Christian scholar and theologian that Donnelly mentioned. Origen lived only 300 years after Christ, yet by most accounts was a believer in the inevitability of rebirth. Even before Origen there was Philo, a Jewish spiritual leader who lived during the time of Christ and based many of his teachings on reincarnation.

The notion of reincarnation was gradually eliminated from church doctrine by the Romans, specifically during the time of the Emperor Constantine in the late third and early fourth century. There are many theories on the reason for reincarnation being removed from Church doctrine, but the prevailing opinion seemed to be that the idea of the soul's returning to earthly incarnations was simply incompatible with the notions of the Christian trinity, and that it might compromise some of the most fundamental beliefs in the Church about the Jesus Christ and his ascension into heaven.

In short, Henry decided, the Church chose to promote a path of salvation through a single life. If we knew we would be given multiple chances to perfect our souls, we might be less inclined to live this life as flawlessly as we could. Mulligans were removed from the playbook.

For the first time in his life, Henry bought a Bible. He spent hours focused on the book, with particular attention on the New Testament and the stories and quotes attributed to Jesus. His interest drew him mainly to specific passages from the four Gospels, but in the other books in which Jesus was active as well. He was drawn heavily to the conflicting portraits of Jesus presented in the traditional Bible as compared to nontraditional texts such as the Gnostic Gospels, some of which were discovered in a remote region of Egypt called Nag Hammadi in 1945. The discovery amounted to a watershed event in the research of the early days of the Christian church, and Henry consumed all he could on the subject.

Through his studies, Henry reinforced his understanding of what happens just after a life is lived. The Sanctuary, as he chose to think of it, was not heaven, not a place where the soul spent eternity. Instead it was a place where the soul was to rest, repair, and learn lessons from the life just lived. In the Sanctuary the soul was given every chance to grow from the most recent life experience, but it was also given the choice to forget it ever happened. Because it is the soul's responsibility to choose its next assignment, souls were encouraged to choose their next earthly incarnation based on the improvement needed in the soul's long path toward wholeness.

If a soul needed work on compassion for the disabled, it might choose a life in which a birth defect caused a disability of some kind. If it had shown disregard for human life in one incarnation, it might choose a life that experienced profound, stinging loss in the next.

He came to understand the importance of the notion that souls are often closely aligned with others across multiple lifetimes. Often they will reincarnate in a variety of roles close to each other, but that these roles often change. One's father in this lifetime might be a son in the next, or a sibling. Naturally people would never be aware of this during their lives.

He began to appreciate, in an odd way, John Donnelly's attempt to subvert the process. Donnelly's idea about trying to wrangle an older, more experienced soul made sense at a basic level, but it was bound to fail because this complex system was founded entirely on a soul's ability to choose. The more Henry read, the more absurdity he found in the attempt.

He gained a new perspective on the notions of ghosts, hauntings, and so-called paranormal phenomena. He had always been fascinated by these concepts, and obviously the last few months of his life had brought this to a more personal level than he ever expected to confront. He read that ghosts are deceased spirits that, for whatever reason, have chosen not to ascend to the place of healing and learning. It could be because the soul is confused, not entirely aware that its mortal life has ended. Violent deaths, for example, nearly always take a life before it is meant to leave the body, its earthly host. After a very violent incident, the vessel is often no longer inhabitable.

It was during this intensive period of reading and research that Henry also came to the realization that the three monotheistic faiths have a few important things in common. First, each chose to ignore reincarnation in the modern eras. Secondly, "spirit guides" seemed to be present in many stories from years past, and even depicted unambiguously in some sacred texts.

The notion of spirit guides being assigned to souls originated with the ancient Greeks, and many faiths have continued supporting the idea. Most faiths believe the link between the spirit and the soul cannot be broken. In some, these spirits play an important role in assisting the soul in the transitions to and from this life. The soul is understandably disoriented at these and other times, and the spirit guide provides comfort and guidance when it is most needed.

Through his readings Henry consistently kept one notion at the back of his mind, the notion of Soul Math that Donnelly described. He saw nothing in his writings to explain how 90 million new souls per year could be "integrated" into life on earth without important ramifications. He concluded that Donnelly's hunch was probably right, that most of these souls had to be newbies, first-timers to this life. He also figured that most would be born into place that produced the most new lives each year, China, India, and in African countries.

The long term implication for these societies was profound. The idea was overwhelming, but so was the whole idea of birth and rebirth.

There was so much to learn, and such a narrow window in which to view it.

Some of Henry's clients came in for readings every week, some every month or two, and it varied widely. He maintained meticulous notes, in keeping with Aisling's habits, and was always prepared for his sessions. The referral pipeline was showing strong results after only a few short months.

As a pleasant surprise, the money was good, even better than he expected. For the first time in his life he was regularly saving money. As time went on, he was easily able to pay the mortgage for Aisling's home and the rent for his apartment. He considered letting the apartment go, but decided he needed a place to be away from this very personal work. There was also the chance that Aisling could return someday.

On a sunny May morning, he woke to a normal day of work, grabbed the paper as he usually did, and turned on the television. Good Morning America was the entertainment while he made his morning coffee. With his paper in front of him, waiting for the coffee to percolate, he was riveted on the guest, the Reverend Ernest B. Grandby. A dapper sixty-something man with a shock of white hair, great teeth and a sincere, confident smile, Grandby was the head of a church that had gained enormous popularity in recent years.

Based in Atlanta, the Church of the Tortured Christ was hard to ignore. It was not only a force on television and the internet, it had increasingly become of a strong voice of the religious right in America. Their message was unwavering in their stances in favor of evangelical Christianity, in support of conservative political and social causes, and opposed to any lifestyles they deemed to be outside what God prescribed.

Under normal circumstances Henry would not have listened closely to the Reverend Grandby, but with all the reading and research he had been consuming in recent weeks, he was riveted. With their massive following came huge contributions, and of course political might. Their involvement in the political process was focused and sharp. From what Henry had read, they had been careful to avoid the potholes that had relegated past Christian organizations to the fringes of American politics. They managed to stay relevant while not seeming politically manipulative. This had served the Reverend well during the past decade, as the sheer number within his flock increased massively.

Henry went online to learn more about the vast organization. Behind the scenes, the Church of the Tortured Christ exerted as much influence over its flock as any religious organization in the United States. When Grandby spoke his flock listened, and when he needed action, his flock acted. Whether it was financial donations toward sympathetic causes or tidal waves of email or US mail, his followers were ready to show their determination to uphold the traditional values he so eloquently set forth. Politicians were wise to stay on the good side of the Reverend. It was apparent that many politicians benefited substantially from his support.

"We're all free to do as we choose," the Reverend said, speaking into the camera, "but we must understand there are consequences to our actions. The Bible is replete with stories of decisions and implications. Nothing has changed in that regard. Our church teaches that decisions add up to a final summation. The result is heaven or hell. We believe that a spirit can repent until its last dying breath, but every action matters, and the words of our Lord and Savior Jesus Christ as written in the Holy Bible provides the training manual for salvation."

"Reverend, when you talk about a 'final summation,' what is it you believe that a spirit goes through at the end of mortal life?" The TV interviewer clearly had done her homework.

"Well, just as you hear or read about, there is a final reckoning. Your 'goods' are measured against your 'bads'. Unlike some of the other religions, we don't believe there's a 'gray area' awaiting people who are not especially bad, nor especially good. Your life is what you make it. Our decisions today will factor into our long term salvation. If the balance is on the good side, you go to heaven. If it's bad you go to hell. However one bad can be far worse than many small goods."

"Can someone who repents with his last dying breath be saved, even after a lifetime of questionable actions?"

"Repentance on its own is no guarantee of salvation, but there are many souls living good and righteous lives who have never allowed Jesus into their souls. These are the people I'm speaking of. For everyone else, we believe you can overcome bad decisions with good decisions. We're quite strong in our conviction that the end game is a simple one. Did you leave the world in a better condition than you found it? Were your contributions a net gain or a net loss? Did you accept Jesus as your personal Lord and savior? Live each day like it's your last.' We feel that's great advice because your actions today could dictate whether your soul burns in hell or enjoys the peace of heaven." With this, Granby flashed his great smile at the host.

The smiling TV host shifted his tone. "So if you would, please allow me to create a hypothetical situation. Suppose one of the World Trade Center killers in 2001 had survived. If he served out the rest of his life undoing his evil, you're saying he might find some redemption? This person wouldn't go straight down to burn in the pit of despair?"

"Well, it's unlikely but yes, that's exactly what I'm saying. As awful as those actions were, is it possible one of those men might have done greater good in the long run? For those killers, their big mistake – aside, of course, from the atrocity of killing so many innocent people – was killing themselves. They deprived themselves of the chance to make amends for their awful actions. Now they'll certainly burn in hell for eternity. One bad decision followed by another. End of story."

"They could have made amends for killing hundreds of innocent people? How in the world could they have made amends for that horrific morning in a single lifetime?"

"Well, suppose if one of them prevented the deaths of many more? What if each turned into the next Billy Graham or Mother Teresa? I'm not saying it's a simple matter. I'm only saying that it's possible. However, they decided that issue once and for all by ending their lives."

"So you're quite certain those men are burning in hell."

"Quite certain, yes. They deprived themselves of the chance to be saved." Grandby looked at the interviewer with a steady smile.

"And what of the innocent people that died on September 11? Do you believe their souls received some recompense for having their lives ended so abruptly at the hands of these killers?"

"No, not at all. Sadly, the victims of those attacks received their judgement on that day. That's one of the great tragedies of these types of events. Besides ending so many lives and all the pain associated with those deaths, the victims are driven to their final judgement before they've lived a complete life."

"That seems rather … incomplete." The interviewer seemed unconvinced.

"It's very incomplete, but how many people exit this life believing they're really ready for their Final Judgement? As the saying goes, live each day like it's your last!"

Henry was captivated by the starkness of this man's positions, especially considering what he recently learned about the beliefs of Origen and other early Christians. Obviously the Bible he preached did not openly support reincarnation, but he had to know that his views were not completely aligned with the thinking in the years that closely followed Christ's life.

Henry cleared his mind to focus on other events of the day. His workday was a full one, with three familiar customers, two others that had been infrequent clients of Aisling, and one new client.

In the early afternoon a tall man came in, graying but obviously still in his working years. His demeanor was serious, his movements purposeful. His visit did not seem based on the need for comfort or reassurance. The man carried himself into the appointment as if he was going to a funeral, or perhaps returning to one. From reading the notes Aisling left him, it was clear why.

"I assume you're Mr. Gilkyson?" Henry extended his hand with a businesslike but welcoming smile.

"Yes, please call me Will."

Henry judged that the man wished to go directly to work. He led him into the reading room.

"Will, I read some of your history from Aisling's notes. I understand the last few years have been incredibly challenging for you and your family, and I have to say that I admire your courage for pursuing this."

"Well, I don't really see it as courageous so much as an act of love." The man's blue eyes looked directly at Henry, unflinching. He seemed to be well practiced at keeping all of his emotions in check.

"Do you have children, Henry?"

"No sir, I'm single with no children."

"Well, a parent who loves and cares about their children – as most of us do – doesn't stop caring about them when bad things happen to them, even if it's the result of their own carelessness."

Henry nodded silently.

"Even if their mistakes result in their death. Once you get over the immediate pain of the loss, it's impossible to just stop caring about how they're doing. You raise them from nothing. You know everything about them. What they're excited about, their insecurities, what scares them, everything. Then suddenly they're lifeless in front of you, on sterile white sheets under fluorescent lights."

"I can't even imagine what that must feel like." Henry had his own challenge keeping his emotions steady.

"As you raise your child, you try to steer them through the good and the bad choices. You celebrate and encourage the positive things they do, and you try to be there with guidance when they make the bad choices. At times while they're growing up they resent you for that, but it's still your role as a parent. Well, in Rayna's case, she didn't make too many mistakes. Sure, she had her moments as any teenager did. She'd act out and we'd discipline her as needed, but she generally never made the same mistake twice. She would get mad then go into solitude for a few days or a week, but over time she seemed to come around to what we were trying to get across to her."

For the moment, Henry needed to be a good listener and nothing more.

"My point in all this, Henry, is that when she made the biggest mistake in her life, I couldn't do a damn thing about it. There was no opportunity for coaching any more. It was a very real test, and unfortunately it resulted in her death. Each time I've contacted her in this setting, she's not very responsive to my reasons for being here. It's been very frustrating for me, but I can't give up on her now."

"Why do you think that is? Does she think she's in trouble, that you're angry with her?"

"I don't know, but I wish I did. Maybe you can help me with that. All I'm getting is hostility. She's not happy right now, and I have a hard time living with that."

Henry hesitated before finding the right words. "Aisling's notes were a little sketchy on her death. I'm sorry for bringing up such a terrible memory, but how did she pass away?"

"She was driving by herself and only had her license for about eight months. It was just a single car accident. She was wearing her seatbelt as we always insisted, but it just wasn't enough. She somehow became distracted, the car veered onto the median and she lost control and hit a bridge support head on. She died instantly. We're not sure how she became distracted. Perhaps the cell phone, which we always told her meant trouble. Nobody really saw the accident. She was coming home from her job at the restaurant, so it was dark."

"Is her mother alive?"

"Alive yes, but shattered. She hasn't worked. She's just not herself, and I'm not sure if that will ever change."

"I'm very sorry for your loss, but it helps to understand what happened."

Henry began the session through using customary rituals, intending to extend some special words to Rayna, who may or may not have been listening. Henry had not yet picked up her presence. He focused his attention fully on the wavelengths that usually were helpful in attracting the attention of spirits.

"Rayna Gilkyson, your father is here to visit you. He extends his love, and he is here to let you know that no matter what, he's your father and he loves you."

Henry found no indication of her presence. He continued to speak in the hope the girl would eventually have to respond. "He wants to be sure you know that whatever happened in the past is less important than how you are today, this very minute. He needs to know that you're safe and happy."

Within a few seconds Henry began to feel pressure in his head, in his conscience. It was mounting and building. Before long it was pulsating, like a headache that would have immobilized him under normal circumstances. He kept his focus on this father and daughter, building a channel between them. The pain enveloped him, took him over, and he felt himself sweating and gasping. There were very powerful emotions entering the room.

"Henry, are you okay?"

Henry could not open his eyes to respond. Through the suffocating sensations he did not feel in immediate danger. He knew it was important to allow these sensations to take over for the benefit of this union he was trying to facilitate. He acquiesced fully.

A voice. "He has nothing to say to me, and I have nothing to say to him."

Henry gathered strength to speak back. "I believe you're mistaken. There is so much that needs to be said."

The pain subsided enough so that Henry could open his eyes to see Gilkyson staring at him in alarm. He lifted a hand and nodded his head to indicate that he was okay, that necessary progress was being made.

The voice again. "He's decided I'm reckless and stupid. Nothing I say or do can change that."

This time Henry spoke aloud. "Your father is here to tell you that he's not angry. His only concern is that you're happy and safe."

"If only I could believe that." The voice Henry was hearing was an emotional one. Scared, angry, defiant. Her emotions were a tangle that Henry was having a difficult time hearing through.

"What are you hearing? What's she saying?" Will Gilkyson was anxiously leaning toward Henry, hoping for anything positive.

Henry's intense discomfort lessened. His nervous system seemed to be adjusting to an unfamiliar wavelength, one that was far more volatile than any he had experienced. It was like stepping into a club with the music cranked to pounding levels. The first few seconds were tortuous, but then his senses adjusted and it became bearable.

Through a wince, he looked at her father. "She sounds convinced you've made up your mind that she was reckless, and nothing will change your mind on that."

Gilkyson showed his concern. "Can't you explain that none of that is important? I only care that she finds peace."

If it was possible for a spirit to scoff telepathically, Henry was hearing it now. She believed nothing her father was saying.

"Will, she doesn't believe you, but I'll keep talking with her."

Gilkyson took this as a queue to remain quiet while Henry communicated with the girl. He tried to send a message of calming conciliation before asking, "His first question to me was whether you're okay. So are you okay?"

The message back from the girl was intense and angry. "No, I'm not okay and it's his fault."

Henry calmly replied, "The issue here isn't who's at fault. He's here for one reason, and that's because he's worried about you, how you are and where you are."

The girl replied, "Well he should be worried about me. I'm here! I haven't gone anywhere! And wherever this place is, it SUCKS. And there's nothing I can do about it. If he wants to help me, then why is he just sitting there doing nothing? And where is Mommy?"

Henry understood that the girl was a stuck spirit. She probably had no idea that she was no longer among the living, and that her extreme emotions were perhaps the only lifeline she had. He also recognized that her existence must have been terrifying for someone so young.

Henry spoke aloud. "Rayna, I'm certain your father would do anything he could to help you out of the situation you're in right now, but it's not something he can control. It's up to you to sort through this and get a handle on the situation you're in."

The intensity was rising again in Henry's senses. His brain's translation was a sharp physical pain that again made him clench and sweat.

Finally she spoke again, this time quietly. "Fuck you, you're just like him."

Then it was gone - the intense emotion, the vibration, the voice, and the pain. He spent the next few minutes explaining to Gilkyson what he sensed, a toxic mix of anger and confusion.

"Will, she doesn't realize that she's passed from this life. That's why she's confused. She's probably angry because she thinks you're doing this to her to punish her."

"But I would never do that!"

"Of course you wouldn't," Henry reassured him. "but the shock of this transition is still very much there. I won't lie to you, Mister Gilkyson, I haven't encountered too many spirits who can't remove themselves from this state, especially not one with this level of hostility and fear. She's built kind of a wall, and we need to keep chipping at it. I don't know if her anger will subside, but maybe I can take a different approach next time."

"Can you try again right now?"

"I don't think she'd return," Henry said, "and if she did she might be even angrier than before. Let's give this a little time."

Gilkyson seemed to appreciate the predicament, and vowed to return.

As he left, Henry guessed this family's position was probably no different from their last visit with Aisling. Henry probably had not hurt the situation, but he did not help it either.

He was relieved that he had nearly thirty minutes until his next appointment. He needed the time to collect his thoughts and regain his confidence. The intense emotion of the young woman was draining, and it would be challenging to recover in time for his next visit. A ten minute walk through the neighborhood was exactly what he needed.

He had little in the way of background notes for his next appointment, as the woman had never been in for a reading. When he took the call the week before, the woman was vague about how she had heard of the business, only saying that she had heard the sessions can provide a great deal of comfort.

"You must be Mrs. Swenson." Henry offered his hand with a warm smile.

"Yes, please call me Joan."

Henry led the woman through the house as he tried to make her feel at ease. She was clearly out of her element, nervous in this surrounding. She was conservatively dressed, an attractive, middle-aged woman with long dark hair. Henry noticed a crucifix on a chain around her neck.

When they were settled, with a cup a tea in the reading room and the afternoon sun providing a comforting light, Henry smiled softly to begin the proceedings. "So what brings you in, Joan?"

"Well, this is not something I've ever done before, and quite honestly, I'm not certain it's a very wise idea for me to be here. I really don't know if my being here is consistent with my faith."

In situations where religion was a factor, Henry was careful to allow his clients the chance to decide for themselves whether a reading was appropriate, applying no unnecessary pressure on their decision to stay or to leave.

"Well, I certainly can respect your reluctance. If it's any help, I don't believe anything we do here is consistent with biblical teaching. The scriptures refer to 'false prophets', but I certainly don't consider this prophecy of any kind. My service here involves providing comfort to people in a way that's hard to achieve through any other means. Sometimes it works, sometimes it doesn't. So Joan, if you feel uncomfortable with what's happening at any point, please speak up and we can end things at any time. I won't charge for my time if you see no value in the time you spent here. I extend that offer to all my new clients."

She seemed content with the approach, and Henry decided to move the process forward. "So is there someone in particular you're interested in connecting with?"

"Well, my father died of a sudden heart attack years ago when I was away at college. He meant the world to me, and I've always been heartbroken that I never had the chance to say goodbye."

"I see. Trying to say goodbye hardly seems like an 'un-Christian' thing to do."

"I suppose not. I confided to a friend in my church once, and she suggested this approach. I just don't know if I'm interfering with his peace, or with some things that I really don't understand."

Henry was hesitant to mention too soon the presence of several spirits in the room with the woman. The sense he was receiving was one of love and support, making it easier to encourage her to continue.

"Well, if your father doesn't wish to be disturbed for whatever reason, he probably won't make an appearance." Henry paused to consider his wording before continuing. "Joan, in your situation I feel pretty confident there won't be any hostility involved if your father chooses to communicate with you."

"How can you tell that?"

Henry smiled gently. "Let's just say I have a sense for these things sometimes. Before we get started I have a process I like to go through."

The two enjoyed a productive, emotional reading. Joan Swenson's father appeared to explain to her that he was very proud of the life she was living and that he knew she loved him and missed him. He expressed his own remorse at leaving her so soon.

As they neared the end of the reading, her father passed a message through Henry that caught him by surprise.

"You've lived your life quietly, even afraid sometimes, but in the coming months you will need to be brave. It may be hard to know this right now, but you're on a very important mission. Do not run from it. I love you, Joan. Be brave."

Her eyes opened wide in surprise, almost embarrassment, that Henry heard the personal message.

"Tell him I heard him, and I love him too."

"He knows," Henry said.

He expected her to ask him about the message from her father and what it might mean, but she had no interest in pursuing the subject. It was as if she knew exactly what her father meant. Henry resisted the urge to inquire.

When they were finished with the reading and she paid him for the service, she lingered before leaving.

Henry asked, "Is there something else on your mind, Joan?"

"Well, yes actually. How do you think reincarnation fits into all of this? I guess my father isn't reincarnated if he's here speaking with me, right?"

"Not necessarily." Henry summarized his views on the subject, including the difficult concept that a spirit might be reincarnated while simultaneously being available to support their loved ones. It turned into a long discussion, with the woman asking question after question. Henry was surprised at her curiosity, but answered each as directly as he could. She seemed to take in all of his answers seriously and thoughtfully.

"Obviously it's something you've thought about a lot. I can refer some good books to you if you'd like."

"Maybe. To be honest, it's something that someone in my church brought up. I thought you might have an opinion on the subject so I thought I'd ask. Thanks for helping me understand it all better."

"Really? Someone in your church? Conventional religions, especially Christian, don't typically have much room for reincarnation in their order of priorities."

"Yes, I suppose that's true." She abruptly started for the door, pulling her coat off a hook.

Henry did not expect Joan to return for another visit, but thought it important to extend a welcome if she ever felt the need to return.

"Well, Joan, if you ever decide to come back for another reading, I'd be happy to help you."

"Perhaps but probably not right away," Joan answered. "I guess I worried needlessly."

"I hope I didn't get you in any trouble with your church." Henry smiled and winked. "What's it called?"

"It's in Wellesley. Perhaps you've heard of it, The Church of the Tortured Christ."

Henry was startled. It was the national brand, supported by the Reverent Ernest Grandby himself.

"It sounds familiar. Maybe I'll check it out."

CURIOSITY'S OTHER SIDE

Henry's career as a medium was now in full stride. Satisfied that he succeeded in his transition from matchmaker to medium, only in recent weeks had he finally felt that the training wheels were off. It had been nearly three months since he had any contact with Aisling. He considered trying to reach her, but her choice to leave was obviously a very personal one, therefore it needed to be her decision when she chose to contact him.

One morning as he was going through the morning ritual of reading through the news and sipping coffee before work, his phone rang. It was Donnelly.

"How's the ghost hassling business treating you, Henry?"

"It's going fine. I don't really hassle them, but they get all over me sometimes."

"How are things with you? Any more threatening phone calls lately?"

Donnelly's tone turned serious. "No, not phone calls, but things have been tense lately."

"How so?"

"Just the occasional feeling that someone's watching me. A car following me for a while that turns away when I slow down, that kind of thing. That phone call from a few weeks ago scared the hell out of me, so now I'm looking over my shoulder all the time."

"I'd be on edge too. You never know who you're dealing with. It's probably nothing, but better to be on the safe side, at least for a while."

"I will, thanks. Hey, I think I left a part of prescription sunglasses at your place. Did you come across a pair?"

"Yeah, I have them. Aviators, right? I meant to call you. I stuck them in a drawer and totally forgot. Sorry about that."

"I've got some business on your side of town this afternoon. Will you still be there around five?"

"Yeah, past five for sure. It's a full day of appointments."

"If I don't make it, be afraid. Be very afraid." Donnelly hesitated then laughed.

"Very funny," Henry said. "See you later on."

Henry turned his attention back to the news. He never felt particularly attuned to international events, but nearly every major news story he read about conflict had religion at the core. Even the lingering drama around the disappearance of the Dalai Lama seemed to be based more on the man's religious status than his political views. The accepted spiritual leader of Tibetan Buddhism had been missing for weeks with little indication he would ever reappear. The only communication received by authorities about his disappearance said that his kidnapping was the result of his lingering support for the independence of Tibet from China. However international authorities, including some proficient with the Chinese language, were doubtful the message was legitimate. The communication, believed to be from his captors, contained some fairly basic errors in their use of written Chinese. The mystery lingered.

Conditions in the Middle East were deteriorating rapidly. Leaders from Syria and Jordan had recently been hostile toward Israel, and political experts seemed caught off guard that the Lebanese seemed to be joining in the anti-Israeli hostility, in part because Lebanon had a sizable Christian population, with nearly as many Christians as Muslims. Lebanese leaders were vocal in their criticism of Israel's increasingly aggressive policies in their handling of Palestinians in the West Bank and the Gaza Strip, which also worried international analysts.

In response, the tone from Israeli leadership was increasingly threatening about the retaliation that would follow rapidly from any anti-Israeli aggression. Border skirmishes seemed to be happening more frequently with all Israeli neighbors. The cycle was a familiar one, but it seemed to be building to unusually tense levels.

His recent experiences in the spirit world made him view these worldly conflicts differently. Before he would try to find fault with one party or another, or both. Now he wondered what all the fuss was about. The more he read about these local skirmishes over religion, the more pointless he found it all. He doubted there were major differences between the path of souls in one religion or the next, so all these flaring tempers over religion struck him as an enormous waste of energy. Most had some form of reincarnation as part of their original dogma, so why not get back on the same page and save all the misery?

Dream on, he told himself.

After a productive with clients, he cleaned up his notes and reviewed notes for the next day's readings while waiting for Donnelly to arrive. After six, he began to wonder why there was no call or visit. He was tired and growing hungry. He dialed Donnelly's cell and it rang several times before going to voicemail. He waited a few minutes and tried again. This time it rang three times before he heard a click and a pause. Then an unfamiliar voice.

"Hello, who's calling please?"

"This is Henry Chimera. I'm trying call John Donnelly on his cell. Did I dial the wrong number?"

"Mister Chimera, this is Officer Abrams with the Waltham Police Department. Mister Donnelly isn't available right now. Can I ask what your call is regarding?"

Henry was alarmed. "Is Donnelly okay? What's happening?"

"I'm afraid I can't discuss that in detail right now. Can you tell me why you need to speak with him?"

"He was supposed to come by my place of work to pick up some glasses an hour ago and never showed. Why can't you tell me what's going on?"

"There's been a crime committed, and I'm not at liberty to answer your questions right now, but I would like to speak with you in person. Can someone stop by this evening?"

His concerns for Donnelly's safety were surging through his mind, as his fears about his own safety finally felt justified. The officer asked Henry for his address and other personal information. They agreed that Henry would meet them at the police station on his way home.

Henry finished his work, picked up an unhealthy volume of fast food, and at it on the way to the Waltham Police Department. After a short wait he was approached by a man in his fifties, rumpled with a full head of hair that badly needed grooming, if not sheering. He had a tired, impatient demeanor.

"Mister Chimera, I'm Detective Lacey. Can you follow me please?"

Henry was led into a small windowless office with little more than a table, three chairs, and a large mirror on one wall. He assumed the mirror was two-way, and that someone could be watching their conversation.

"Can you tell me what's going on with John? Is he okay?"

The detective deflected Henry's questions. "We'll get to that in a moment. Can you tell me about your relationship with Mr. Donnelly?"

Henry explained all about the unusual circumstances for their friendship, and that while he had met him weeks before, he had only gotten to know him for a short time. He was quick to explain about the threats Donnelly was feeling, and how he thought it came from their early reading and his inquiries into reincarnation.

The detective was scribbling into a theme notebook, looking down as Henry responded to his general questions, explaining little more than the fact that Donnelly was a customer. Finally the detective posed the question that he had only heard on television, and which he dreaded.

"Do you know of anyone that would want to hurt Mister Donnelly?"

He had a sunken feeling as he answered. "Nobody in particular, but like I told you, he felt threatened by a phone call after the first time we met. Can you please tell me if my friend is okay, Detective?"

The Detective looked closely at Henry, expressionless while pausing for a few moments before answering. "I'm afraid I have some bad news, Mister Chimera. Mister Donnelly passed away this evening."

"WHAT? How?" Henry was halfway out of his seat. A feeling of nausea came over him as he waited for the man's reply.

"It appears to be a homicide. His car sustained a flat tire on Totten Pond Road. Evidently he pulled over to fix it and someone assaulted him. Robbery may have been a motive, but obviously the investigation is just getting started. We don't have a suspect, and right now we don't have any witnesses. A couple teenagers found him in a pull-off area a few feet from the road. We believe he died very quickly."

Henry was numb. He sat motionless, staring into space. Finally he thought of Donnelly's family. "Have you told his wife yet?"

"Yes sir, she was the first person we contacted, in person of course. She's extremely upset, obviously. We have some officers with her now."

When they were nearly done exchanging questions, some answered and some avoided, Lacey shifted his questioning.

"So you're a psychic, Mr. Chimera?"

"I'm a medium. There are some important differences. I can't read your mind, and I can't see the future. I just can speak with spirits that have passed beyond this living world."

"What was it Donnelly was looking for when he set up his appointment with you?"

"He came to me with some concerns about having a family. He thought that perhaps my skills would be useful if he and his wife decided to have a baby."

"How could you help him with that?"

Henry was reluctant to reveal too much about Donnelly's interest in reincarnation, believing that was a private matter between he and his client. On the other hand, the last thing he wanted was to stand in the way of the investigation.

"He came to me asking if I knew ways to provide certain … assurances about the character of his unborn child. It was a misguided direction he was headed in, and when our first and only session was over, he understood it was a bad idea. Once we straightened that out, we enjoyed a nice chat over a beer. All was cool between us."

"Tell me about this phone call."

"After he got some information from this group called Origenists, he got a phone call telling him to back off from his inquiries into reincarnation. He told me it put a scare into him."

"Who else knew about his visit to you, Mr. Chimera?"

Henry looked at the Detective and asked earnestly, "You mean living people, right?"

The Detective glared back. "Is that some kind of joke? Of course I mean living people."

"Well, I think his wife knew about it. I gather she wasn't thrilled about his idea to come see me. I really don't know who else, if anyone."

Lacey scribbled into his book. "How did he learn about this group?"

"He found them on the web and just requested info. I don't think he spoke with anyone directly."

The detective added more notes.

"Can you prove your whereabouts this afternoon?"

"I had appointments until five. I told Donnelly to come by then. If you'd like to stop by to see my log book, be my guest. It has notes on all my appointments for the day."

"That would be helpful, yes," Lacey said.

After they traded business cards, Henry left the building in a fog. He had never met Donnelly's wife, but considered contacting her to offer sympathy. After a few minutes he decided against it. For now his grief and shock was his alone.

He sat in his car in the dark for several minutes, tired and stunned by the developments of the past few hours. Finally he started the car because he knew that eventually he would have to, but still he sat, alone in his thoughts.

He thought carefully about his contact with Rayna Gilkyson and her father, remembering that sometimes when a soul experiences a sudden and unexpected death, it is often confused about its current condition. The spirit can be unaware of its own death and remain close to its physical location near the time of death. The spirit can remain in this condition for some time before it eventually gives in to the advice and encouragement from kindred spirits and ascends to Sanctuary. There was no way to predict how long Rayna would remain in this condition, and it was possible that Donnelly was in the same state.

He decided to drive past the scene of the crime. He was familiar with the road where the murder took place, only a few minutes' drive from the police station. As he drove on Totten Pond Road, in an otherwise dark stretch of the road he saw bright lights that were oddly out of place. As he neared the lights he saw police still at the crime scene. He stopped his car on the other side of the road, far enough from the scene that no police would think he was a morbidly curious passerby or worse, the murderer that decided to see for himself the aftereffects of his work. He turned off his car and closed his eyes, alone in the dark with just his thoughts.

Out of habit he began with a prayer, similar to his readings. He asked for blessings, and created a mental blanket of protective energy around his own spirit. With the violent nature of Donnelly's death and his own tired state, he was concerned about vulnerability from any negative spirit energies that might be nearby. He directed his thought energy toward Donnelly. He envisioned the man's essence, his somewhat careless but charming mannerism, and his willingness to come forward to make amends with Henry over his poor judgment. Within seconds Henry began to feel a connection with what seemed to be the essence of John Donnelly, and it was not pleasant. Donnelly's soul did not appear to be in pain, but rather confused and agitated. There was a pause as Henry brought him into mental focus.

Henry extended a cautious greeting. "John, is that you?"

"Henry, what are you doing here?"

Henry had never communicated with a spirit that had so recently passed. He was not completely sure of the right or wrong messages to send, so he decided to keep his communication simple.

"I'm just here to check on you, John. Are you okay?"

"Definitely not okay."

"Would you like to talk about it?"

"Did you bring me my glasses? I really need those glasses. I'm having a hard time seeing anything."

"Sorry but I don't have your glasses with me right now." Henry was unsure where to take the conversation. Clearly Donnelly was disoriented, probably with no idea he had passed to the next dimension.

"John, what do you see where you are?"

"I told you, Henry, I can't see much of anything. Just darkness. I really need those glasses." Donnelly expressed annoyance, but Henry interpreted a message of confusion and fear.

"John, I'm not sure the glasses will help you. Something awful happened to you that wasn't your fault. I want you to know that you're not alone."

The spirit was unmoved, distracted by his unfamiliar surroundings. Henry recalled how newly departed spirits can be almost compulsive in their habits until they find some form of orientation. He knew that some gifted mediums, much more experienced than he, were sometimes able to break the spirits from the deadlock. It was possible to persuade spirits to accept the help that was available to them by moving closer to the light.

The reasons for avoiding the transition varied widely. Some were afraid of what awaited them on the other side, often due to notions about the afterlife that they harbored while living. Some worried about the possibility of going to hell. Most simply refused to accept the possibility that their life was over. Their surroundings would often appear nearly identical to what they were accustomed to while living, and it was only their consciousness that was altered. In such a confused state it could be difficult for a spirit to unlock itself from the most recent set of perceptions. Henry knew that his lack of experience would make the challenge with John Donnelly very difficult. His priority was to avoid making matters worse in any way.

Henry reminded himself that a killer was still on the loose. The police told him that no witnesses had come forward yet, which probably meant there were no witnesses at all. The person in the best position to identify the killer was Donnelly himself. The question was, did Donnelly have any recollection of what happened? It was first important to stabilize Donnelly's perceptions, and to have Donnelly's spirit understand the crime that occurred.

"You need to understand, John, that there's a very important change that's occurred. It will take some time to get used to it, but you must accept it."

"I have no idea what you're talking about, Henry. You're not helping me."

"I am helping you, John. That's exactly why I'm here. There was an incident and you're not fine, at least not fine in the way you used to be."

"You're talking in circles, Henry. No one could understand what you're saying right now."

"John, you're in the spirit world." He aimed to keep the message brief and to the point.

"Is this some kind of joke? We're all in the spirit world. We've talked about this before. Don't play games with me."

"It's no game, John, trust me. You're no longer in the physical world. Your spirit has left your body."

There was only silence from Donnelly, but rapidly intensifying emotions. Henry sensed a whirl of emotions, including confusion, anger, denial, and more confusion. Through it all there was silence. Henry wished the man would communicate. The void went for several seconds before Henry decided to give Donnelly a new direction for his thoughts.

"John, this is a terribly sad day for your wife, your friends, and your family, but you must not waste this opportunity. You have extremely important work ahead of you."

He remained silent, but there was a curiosity. He was listening.

Henry continued. "You came to Aisling and me to talk about reincarnation, and the progression of souls. I know that you've studied the subject, and I know I don't need to explain to you how real and incredibly important that is."

"This feels like a joke," Donnelly finally said. "Some shitty joke that's being played on me that has no punch line."

"It's not a joke, John. It's very serious indeed, but you need to understand that everything is going to be okay. Things are confusing now, but it will all make sense in time."

The message seemed to calm him. His anger was beginning to subside, and he was thinking more about what had happened, trying to begin to understand how and why he may have died. Then the intense emotions took over once again, and Donnelly seemed to fall back.

"What's the matter, John? Please talk to me."

"I don't understand. one minute I was in my car, the next I'm above my car, looking down at my bleeding body. Hatred. Venom. Why? This makes no sense!"

Donnelly's spirit was in agony. "Calm down, John. It's over. That person can't hurt you any more. Your future is entirely up to you now. Try to focus on what exactly happened. Maybe we can make some sense out of this, and you can help someone else."

"I can't even help myself!"

Henry replied calmly. "Well, we can slow down and try to understand some of the details. Perhaps we can help the police find this person so this doesn't happen to anyone again. Do you remember anything about who did this?"

Donnelly's attentions were diverted from his confusing circumstance, and his uncertainty with what was ahead.

"Dark. It was dark and I was in the car. I needed to stop to check out something that was wrong with the tire. There didn't seem to be anyone around. I didn't even know anyone was around. Suddenly my body was on the ground. I recognized it and it was the strangest feeling. There wasn't any pain, just a … detachment. I knew it was my body, but it seemed like an old coat that I wouldn't need any more, just laying there on the ground, useless."

"Did you see the person that attacked you?"

"No. Just the sense of hatred, but hatred that was based on a sense of … justification. This man felt justified in killing me, and he knew me. I was the one he wanted to kill, but I don't even know him. He thinks he was on a mission from God. Do you think he was on a mission from God, Henry?"

"Absolutely not. It was a misguided, deranged person, John, and we need to find him. Can you think of any other details?"

"A dark wool hat, the kind that young people wear. A long sharp knife with blood. My blood. And a long dark coat. He runs fast, like a deer in the night."

Henry spent a few more minutes trying to conjure details from Donnelly, but details were sparse. When it was clear Donnelly told him all he could, Henry focused on stabilizing the emotions of this disjointed spirit, helping him gain his emotional balance. He patiently helped Donnelly recount his accomplishments in life, and of the people that loved him from his earliest years. The approach seemed bring Donnelly some peace and satisfaction, and a sense of balance. Henry used the shift to prompt his spirit into action.

"I know this is all very new to you," Henry started slowly, "but it's important that you give some thought to what it will take to bring you peace with your life. It's important that you find a way to move on from where you are now. Your wife is in great pain, but she will find a way to move on."

Abruptly Donnelly's mood changed from stability to a deep, intense sadness. "Janice. Oh my God, Janice."

Then he was gone.

A memorial service for Donnelly was to be conducted on the following Thursday afternoon, with a traditional wake the evening before. His obituary did not mention a burial.

Henry decided to avoid the wake and made no other attempt to contact Janice Donnelly before the service. He preferred to look for a chance to delicately offer his condolences personally, providing her emotional state allowed it. For all Henry knew, she might hold him somehow accountable for her husband's ideas, or even his demise. The obituary listed the location: the Light of the World Worship Center in Newton. The service was to begin at two o'clock.

On the day of the service, Henry finished his morning appointments and decided to take a few moments to open up communications with Donnelly if he chose to make himself available. He did not summon Donnelly, but rather opened the channels to his conscious state. Praying for his soul would allow Donnelly to contact him if he so desired.

Henry picked up Donnelly's presence, but with an emotion that he did not easily recognize. It seemed like anger, but laced with profound regret. Donnelly seemed upset with himself, as though some of his actions while living might have contributed in some way to the sadness that his death caused. They were weighed heavily on his spirit. Henry tried to get Donnelly to open up to him as a therapist might, but the had no interest. Henry assured him that he was in his thoughts and prayers, and Donnelly returned a quiet acknowledgment.

Henry arrived at the service on a warm spring afternoon. The church seemed to be a warm, tranquil venue for the sendoff of his departed friend. The parking lot was nearly full. He was glad to have arrived a few minutes early. He hurried through the vestibule, unaware of what kind of church it was or who belonged. The space was designed in a round configuration, large enough to seat two or three hundred people. A podium was at the center with a large cross behind it, well lit and majestic. The room was filling fast, and he found a seat toward the left side that gave him a view of the service while allowing him to remain as much in the background as possible. He uneasily caught his first look at the widow, Janice Donnelly.

She was a dark-haired beauty, dignified and lovely in her grief, composed in handling her circumstances but visibly, deeply in mourning. Henry took a few moments to pray for the spirit of his departed friend, and for all those closest to Donnelly who were traumatized by his abrupt death. As was so often the case, their spirits were badly scarred by his passing.

Within a few moments, Henry's attention was fixated on a woman walking to the podium. She was attractive and smartly dressed, with amber hair and complementary makeup that perfectly matched the dignity and solemnity of the service. The woman seemed very comfortable with the gathering, waving and gently smiling, entirely in her element. She paused meaningfully before speaking.

"Welcome to our house, God's house," she started gently. "There are few words in these times of sorrow that can ease the pain we're feeling. Only over time do we come to understand that while there are no easy answers for the loss we are asked by God to endure, we learn where comfort can be found. God knows that it can seem impossible to find peace during these hours, but he is always there, carrying us through the darkness."

She stepped slightly away from the microphone. Her delivery and tone provided assurance and warmth. Janice Donnelly struggled to maintain her focus as the woman spoke, distracted by her pain. Henry noticed a lightness hovering near Janice, slightly behind her, close to her ear. It was John Donnelly, there to support her wounded spirit.

After a respectful pause, the woman looked down at the lectern and spoke again.

"A passage from Job 38:

"Hast thou commanded the morning since thy days began, And caused the dayspring to know its place;

That it might take hold of the ends of the earth, And the wicked be shaken out of it?

It is changed as clay under the seal; And all things stand forth as a garment:

And from the wicked their light is witholden, And the high arm is broken.

Hast thou entered into the springs of the sea? Or hast thou walked in the recesses of the deep?

Have the gates of death been revealed unto thee? Or hast thou seen the gates of the shadow of death?

Hast thou comprehended the earth in its breadth? Declare, if thou knowest it all.

Where is the way to the dwelling of light? And as for darkness, where is the place thereof,

That thou shouldest take it to the bound thereof, And that thou shouldest discern the paths to the house thereof?

Doubtless, thou knowest, for thou wast then born, And the number of thy days is great!

"From this passage we are reminded by God of the wonders of life and of death, and given a taste of the futility of trying to understand all that lies behind each. Brothers and sisters, life is mystery. Death is mystery. The only thing we can be sure of from the experience of death is that we are left to pick up the pieces of what remains from our grief. We're expected to move on, regardless of our grief, our confusion, even our anger.

"John Donnelly was a fine man that passed on before we feel he should have. We don't know the reasons behind his senseless death. Perhaps he diverted from the Word in only ways that John and our Lord and Savior Jesus Christ can understand. Perhaps the Lord may not want us to know the reasons behind this heartbreaking event. But he does want us to move on with our lives so that we may join him in heaven. Whatever the reasons, it is our obligation to the memory of John Donnelly and his Lord and Savior to learn from life and from death the things that will help guide us to the right hand of the Father."

These comments struck Henry as curious. Was the woman implying that Donnelly's exploration into reincarnation may have directly or indirectly contributed to his death? Or was he reading too much into her words, which were only meant to comfort a very sad group of people?

He remembered their contact with the grandmother, who warned him of the foolishness of his actions. Could this somehow have hastened Donnelly's death, or did it instead place him in a more positive place in the days leading up to his death? Henry considered Donnelly's inquiry into Soul Math as a harmless expedition that left no lasting effect on anyone, positive or negative, but perhaps there was someone so deeply offended by his curiosity that they decided he needed to die.

Attendees were invited to the microphone to share their reminiscences. Some were funny, some touching, some only meaningful to the person telling the story. The affection for the man was real, as was the intense sorrow over his sudden passing. His widow seemed to take all the stories with the perfect mix of grace, humor, and sadness.

During the service Henry noticed a woman next to Janice Donnelly, whispering and attending to her needs. It was difficult for Henry to see her features behind her sweeping dark hat. Something about her was familiar.

After about an hour, the woman leading the service closed with a passage from the Book of Isaiah.

Yet it pleased the Lord to bruise him; he hath put him to grief: when thou shalt make his soul an offering for sin, he shall see his seed, he shall prolong his days, and the pleasure of the Lord shall prosper in his hand.

He shall see of the travail of his soul, and shall be satisfied: by his knowledge shall my righteous servant justify many; for he shall bear their iniquities.

Therefore will I divide him a portion with the great, and he shall divide the spoil with the strong; because he hath poured out his soul unto death: and he was numbered with the transgressors; and he bare the sin of many, and made intercession for the transgressors.

The front row was the first to exit, beginning with the widow and her closest family and friends. As they turned toward the vestibule, Henry was able to catch his first clear view of the woman comforting the widow. He stared in disbelief.

It was Joan Swenson, his new client from just a few days earlier. As he was deciding whether to approach the woman, he felt a tap on his shoulder.

"Mr. Chimera, may I have a word?"

Henry turned, surprised that someone here would know his name. It was Detective Lacey.

"Detective Lacey. Of course, we can talk." The two retreated to a quiet hallway. "What brings you here?"

"It's customary to attend funerals while there's an open investigation into why the person died. Wouldn't you want to know who showed up?"

"I hadn't really thought about it. What can I do for you, Detective?"

"Have you had any other revelations since we talked? You never know if something that seems small might be important to the investigation. Anything at all?"

"I can't stop thinking about it, but there's nothing I forgot to tell you. Why are you asking? Am I a suspect?"

"Why are you worried? You said you had an alibi, that you had appointments. It should check out, right?"

"It will check out. I emailed you the name and contact info of my afternoon appointments that day, but it would be a waste of your time to include me as a suspect."

"I would call you a person of interest but not a suspect. If you have information about the crime, regardless of how it came to you, you have an obligation to share it."

"That doesn't give me much comfort, Detective. Do 'persons of interest' usually need legal representation?"

"It's your choice, Henry. A lawyer will tell you to keep your mouth shut, but I'd prefer you share with us that might help."

"I'll keep that in mind, Detective."

He walked into the vestibule of the Worship Hall and saw that Janice Donnelly was busy with a group of people, some older than her, probably relatives. Joan Swenson was off by herself, waiting on the periphery.

"Hi Joan. I'm surprised to see you here."

The woman turned curiously toward Henry, not recognizing him at first.

"Henry! I didn't expect to see you here either." She was nervous, unsure whether she should speak with him. "Are you an acquaintance of the Donnelly's?"

"I got to know John in recent weeks. He was a client of mine. His death was quite a shock. How about you? How do you know Janice?"

"We've become quite close through our church. John didn't really attend too much, but the church is a really important part of Janice's life."

"But I thought you said you were a part of that large church in Arlington, the one I've seen commercials for on TV."

"I am. That's our church, and it's part of the larger network of Tortured Christ churches around the country."

"Then why did they have the service here?"

"This is the newest in our network of churches. It's a little smaller and closer to where the Donnelly's live, so I guess it made sense to have it here."

Henry noticed that Joan was anxiously looking past Janice Donnelly, toward the front door. Subtly Henry shifted his position to try to see who she was avoiding. It was the woman that performed the service.

"Well, it was a touching ceremony. It all came from the heart, although the choice of Scripture was interesting."

"How do you mean?"

"It seemed to suggest that John was punished for his behavior. Did you interpret it that way?"

"I suppose," Joan Swenson was considering her words carefully, "but doesn't that apply to all of us? Aren't we all judged by our actions? I guess I didn't see that the passage applied more to John than it applies to you and me."

"I suppose. I hope Mrs. Donnelly gets through this okay."

Joan nodded, gazing downward.

"Who was the woman that conducted the service? She was remarkable."

She hesitated, glancing toward the woman's commanding presence. "That was the Reverend Ellen Grandby Sullivan. We're very blessed to have her here in the Northeast, at least for the time being."

"Meaning what? She's moving onto another area sometime soon?"

"She's the daughter of the church founder, Ernest Grandby, so she tends to go where the church needs her the most. She's been an incredibly important part of the growth of the church. We're just blessed that the church feels she's needed here now. I have amazing respect for the Reverend. She's taught me so much in the short time she's been here."

"I guess it's fortunate timing for the Donnelly's," Henry said casually, looking across the room.

"How do you mean?"

"It's just quite a coincidence that such an important person is here to offer support during Mrs. Donnelly's darkest time."

Joan did not respond, but instead moved her attention away from Henry as the Reverend scanned the room, aware of their conversation. Henry caught the Reverend's eye, held her gaze and smiled. She returned his smile, then abruptly shifted her attention to the widow, still speaking with her relatives.

"Joan, when you came in for your reading you mentioned that someone from your church brought up the whole idea of readings, spirits and such. Was that the Reverend Sullivan that brought that up?"

She looked at him with some sense of alarm. "Of course not! Why would someone of her stature care about that kind of thing? Henry, I came to you in confidence. I hope you'll respect that and keep our conversation to yourself."

"Absolutely, Joan, I wouldn't share that with anyone. I just thought it odd that someone from this church would come see someone in my ... line of work. If you wish, this can be the last we speak of it."

She seemed relieved. "Yes, I'd like that. Thank you for understanding. Now if you'll excuse me."

Henry decided there was nothing to be gained from speaking directly with Janice Donnelly in this setting. He would allow emotions to settle, then find a better opportunity. He left the church discreetly.

Walking toward his car in the parking lot, he noticed a man in dark sunglasses and a dark suit walking behind him. The man looked directly at Henry, not bothering to look away, then he stared down at the back of Henry's car. He paused a moment, pulled a small notepad from his pocket, wrote something, then turned back toward the church.

As Henry drove back toward home, he asked himself, what have I gotten myself into this time?

REBIRTH RIPPLES

Several weeks later, on a misty, early summer morning in the Boston suburbs, Henry was met with a pale gray sky as he went for a morning jog. It was warm and humid. Spring was turning to summer.

He ran through the same park that had ignited his change in direction months before, and which he often chose for frequent cold weather jogs. He was reminded of how far he had come as a medium in just a few short months.

Before he met Aisling, he was unaware that disembodied spirits even existed. Soon after he had a difficult time seeing the difference between a living and a nonliving spirit. Now that his gifts were out in the open, growing with each passing day, he was able to easily assess the state of a spirit at a single glance.

After he discovered the gift, he began the habit of stopping during his runs to strike up conversations with both living and nonliving spirits, although many in each category resisted any kind of conversation. He began to realize there was not much difference between living and nonliving spirits who were largely detached from their surroundings. All tended to be confused and diffused, and Henry tried to make some connection with them whether they were still breathing or not. Nearly all in this condition were homeless with little idea of what to do about it.

Some disembodied spirits were bound to places, some to people. The spirits bound to other people might have an endless variety of reasons for staying earth bound. In some cases it was a surviving child the deceased parent could not bear to leave. In other cases, spirits were consumed with regret over some wrong that was done to them, or which they had done to another. In these circumstances the soul possessed an intense need to make things right, but no realistic ability to do so. This powerlessness often left them frustrated and confused, so they lingered.

The spirits bound to places were sad and predictable, but in limbo nonetheless. They usually occupied places that had left a significant imprint on their lives. Often, Henry noticed, their deaths happened while they were going through transitional periods – childhood to adolescence, adolescence to adulthood, and so on. The events that led to these transitions often left a profound mark on the souls which they could not get past, and death offered little relief.

Rayna Gilkyson was a perfect example. She was a girl just beginning the transition to womanhood, and the anger from her tragic death, placed upon her father, was magnified because of her inability to transition.

Some spirits were bound to nothing, really. These were the saddest that Henry came across, as they tended to have the most loose ends, hence the greatest number of worries that consumed them. Many lacked the "soul maturity" to escape their living limitations, hence were not fortunate enough to be in a position where support from others could lift them from their difficult circumstances. These souls were often stuck in neutral in life and remained that way in death.

There were occasions when spirits would approach him, anxious for his intervention with the living over some matter they considered pressing. He was always hesitant to intervene, in part because he was too new to the spirit world to judge whether he was aiding a spirit in interfering when it should not. He only seriously considered these requests when a living person's health or life was in peril.

On those rare situations when he decided his intervention was justified, he was careful to approach his target cautiously. Most people were skeptical of his intentions – or even his sanity – as he warned them of impending danger.

Usually when he took action, he would try to appear sane, calm, and reassuring in his warnings. When his advice was ignored, there were only a few times that he tried to contact someone a second time. If the first contact did not yield results, second and later visits were likely to draw a visit from the police. For good or for bad, people had one chance to listen to his advice.

As he thought about the unusual contacts between departed and living spirits, Henry dwelled far too long on the circumstances of Donnelly's death. He wondered if there was something more he could do to intervene in finding his killer.

As much as he thought, night after night, about the circumstances of his communications with Donnelly and what he knew about the man and his wanderings into reincarnation, his wife Janice, her friends and her church, he could come up with no motivation for why anyone would want Donnelly dead.

Henry pressed the Contacts button on his phone to find a number that he had stored weeks before, but had never dialed. He pressed the Call button.

It rang twice before a woman's voice answered softly. "Hello."

"Hello, this is Henry Chimera. Am I speaking with Mrs. Donnelly?"

"Yes, this is she. I wondered if I'd hear from you, Mr. Chimera."

"Yes, well, I guess I wasn't sure if you wanted to hear from me. I'm very sorry for your loss, Mrs. Donnelly. I didn't know John long, but we became friends despite our awkward introduction."

"That's nice to hear."

"Mrs. Donnelly," Henry continued, "I'm calling you to offer my condolences, but also to let you know that I can't get John's death out of my mind. I still can't understand why someone would have wanted him dead."

"That makes two of us, but but in my case it may be a frame of mind that will be with me for a long, long time, perhaps my whole life."

"Could we meet personally, Mrs. Donnelly? I'd like to get a chance to understand a few things."

The woman did not hesitate. "I think not. It may help you, but I rather doubt it would help me."

"I understand," Henry answered. "I'm sorry you feel that way, but I understand. Can I ask you just one thing?"

"You may ask."

"Well," Henry explained, "John came to me and my mentor with a rather confusing request about reincarnation. It was a question that I had never had heard before, and my partner, who was a lot more experienced than me, was caught off guard as well."

"Yes, John told me about that."

"It didn't turn into much. We laughed about it later, and the absurdity of it sort of became the foundation of our friendship."

Her reply was noticeably lighter. "John told me that as well. I can't say I was pleased with his reason for contacting you, but I only learned about it after the fact. He was justifiably embarrassed, but relieved that you managed to get past it so easily."

"We weren't too pleased about it either. It put us in a very uncomfortable situation. It might even have been dangerous."

Janice Donnelly paused before softly replying, "I didn't know that."

"Our friendship would've been a good one. It was too brief. I keep wondering if our experience had anything to do with his death."

"I kind of doubt that. John had some eccentric ideas. At times he seemed to go through life thinking he could manipulate his way through all sorts of challenges. He didn't seem to be afraid of anything. That's what drew me to him when we first met.

Henry heard faint sobbing on the other end of the connection. Finally she collected her thoughts. "After all the things he's tried over the years, if THIS was the one thing that angered somebody enough to kill him, I'd be amazed. I didn't really care about John's interest in reincarnation. That was his thing, a passing obsession, I guess, that I knew wouldn't last. I didn't really see any harm in the whole thing. It just seemed like his way of making sure no stone was left unturned when it came to having a child. But when he told me that he was in contact with his grandmother, that's when it didn't seem harmless anymore."

Henry interrupted. "For all of us."

"Yes, I suppose so."

"For my own piece of mind, Mrs. Donnelly, was there anybody else who might have been upset by our experience in that reading?"

"Who else would be upset by it except each of you, me and my husband? I'm not sure who else you could mean."

"I'm just searching for answers. I'm just trying to fill in the missing pieces."

"Maybe his death had something to do with some of his business dealings, or maybe somebody held a grudge from years ago, his school years even. Maybe it was just a random, senseless act of violence by somebody that had no idea of the real harm they were causing. The police have been hard at work trying to figure all of that out. In any case, he won't be coming back to me in this life, so I'm not sure I can help you find any answers. Once they find who was responsible for his death, I plan to move on with my life. I suggest you do the same, but only after you've cooperated with the police."

"That is my plan. Thanks for your time, Mrs. Donnelly.

"I'm glad you called, Henry. Oh, before you hang up, there's something you should know. It turns out I'm pregnant."

Henry paused. "Oh my goodness! I'm not sure what to say. Congratulations … I guess?"

Janice Donnelly laughed softly. "That's the right thing to say. Thanks. This gives me something positive in my life to focus on."

"Well, in that case," Henry continued, "I'm really happy for you. I know that John would be thrilled."

Henry ended the call relieved there was no bitterness toward him, at least none evident.

The only people that could have known about Donnelly's visit were he, Aisling, Janice Donnelly, the deceased relatives, and perhaps Joan Swenson. Would any of them have a reason to wish harm on the man? As unlikely as that was, it was far more likely that Henry's own curious nature was getting the best of him in trying to apply sense to the senseless.

Over the coming days Henry chose to focus his energy on his work, and on the things he could learn from the Donnelly experience. Another lingering question from the events of the last few weeks was the mystery surrounding the Origenists. They seemed to be a shadowy group whose intentions were wholly unclear. While Henry was determined to stop dwelling on Donnelly's murder, there were the ominous signs that centered on Donnelly's contact with the group.

On a dreary Saturday morning he decided to find out what he could about the Origenists. He went online and entered Origen's name to learn more about the man. There was plenty of information available that described his lofty standing as one of the pillars of what would become the Roman Catholic Church.

Origen was born in 185 AD in Alexandria, which also happened to be the birthplace of the renowned Jewish philosopher Philo, himself an early proponent of the recurrence of the soul in living humans. Origen became a great teacher and promoter of the Christian faith, even castrating himself to allow the freedom to teach both women and men the worthiness of a life devoted to Christ's teachings. He placed himself in harm's way many times during his nearly seventy years, which was a very long life for the times. Eventually he was labeled a heretic for his belief in reincarnation, and was tortured in his elderly years for these and other beliefs.

Next he decided to search for the Origenists. He found only two links under the key word "Origenist," and each ended with a page error. If a web site once existed at the address, it existed no more. He searched thoroughly for anything that might lead him to the Origenists, but there was nothing to be found. There was not a single mention from anyone that had any opinion about the congregation, good, bad or indifferent. It was as if someone had intentionally removed every trace of the group, or the group never existed at all.

After several hours of futility, he finally decided to fall back on his days as a technologist. It was an unlikely path, he knew, but perhaps worth the effort.

The only proof he had of the group's existence was the two orphaned web pages. He noted the IP addresses of the two sites and found a utility site that promoted its ability to find information about a web site from just the IP address. When he entered the first site, it revealed only the geographic source of the address, in Toronto, Canada. The second showed Albany, New York. Neither gave any additional information. He tried a number of free services that offered information about the IP addresses, but each time they returned only the two locations.

Finally he entered the Albany IP address in a service that was far down the list of IP lookup services. To his amazement, the site provided him with more than just the city. It gave him an actual phone number and a name: David Herbrit, Albany, New York. He jumped to his phone.

He dialed. The phone rang and rang. Finally it went to a phone message, a man's humorless, deep voice. "This is David. I'm not available to take your call. Leave your message at the beep." Before the beep, Henry hung up. He did not want to reveal his reasons for calling in a recorded message, believing that his first contact with this man should be a live contact, even if by phone. If the man's phone featured Caller ID, he would think it a simple wrong number. His priority was to avoid unnecessarily frightening the man, as his intentions and state of mind were completely unknown.

His plan for Sunday was to drive to Albany to find David Herbrit. First he needed to find anything he could about the man, starting with an address. He tried several White Pages directory web sites that might provide a listing, but nothing came up. Finally he tried the simplest of all internet searches. He entered "david herbrit" and "albany" into a search engine. It returned several results.

One was from an online newsletter generated by a bowling alley. When he clicked the link, he saw that it listed a David Herbrit as being among the top bowlers in a league that operated almost seven years before.

The next was from a church bulletin. He clicked the link and saw that it was a Sunday bulletin in PDF form from a Catholic Church, Saint James the Apostle. He searched the bulletin and found Herbrit's name as the subject of a Novena, or prayer devotion. It did not explain why he was to receive prayers, but it was usually because of illness or the death of a loved one. Not much help, Henry decided. If Herbrit was ill, he had likely recovered because his phone number still seemed active. That provided some encouragement.

The last link seemed to offer the least promise. It was from a genealogy web site, and each site post mentioned a few people in the Herbrit family. This site was obviously for people trying to fill holes in their genealogical research, and the thread about the Herbrit family contained a total of four posts. The first was from a woman with a different last name. Henry opened it.

"Am looking for a link to Westport, Cty. Mayo family Moran, father Cornelius mother Honora married approx. 1863 children Mary, Lawrence, Thomas, Robert and perhaps some later."

The reply came later from a man only identified as "David Herbrit, NY."

"Possible link. My grandfather on my mother's side was Lawrence Moran. I know he was born in Westport, County Mayo in 1890. Does this sound like a match?"

Several weeks later the woman replied excitedly.

"This sounds like a match! How wonderful! I have quite a lot of research I've been gathering that I'm very willing to share. Can you send along contact info?"

It was two months before the man replied again.

"Yes, I'd be very interested in seeing that. In the meantime I'll pull together the information I have about my grandfather and mail it to you. Please send via US mail, David Herbrit, 1204 N. Troy Ave, Apt E, Albany NY 11231."

An address! Henry's plans for Sunday were set.

In preparation for the three hour trip to Albany, Henry packed as if he was a character from a John le Carré spy novel. Binoculars. Camera (135 MM Zoom lens). High protein snacks. Rain gear. Sleeping bag. Containers for water, both incoming and outgoing. He was ready for whatever would come his way. At least he hoped.

He timed the trip to be at the man's home by noon, on the chance he would be coming home from church. He easily found 1204 North Troy Avenue, and was relieved that unit E faced the street. He discreetly drove around the immediate area, believing it might be helpful to understand traffic flows. Given the distance from the front door to the nearest available parking, he guessed the man came and went through the front door.

His strategy was to first take a picture of the man, then later approach him. He hoped the picture might prove useful later for others in identifying him. If a terrible fate befell Henry, it would help the police identify the person who killed him.

Henry knew his imagination was probably getting the best of him, but he chose to take no chances with a group that preferred to remain in the shadows.

The area included mostly upscale apartments and condominiums that probably belonged to working professionals without families. Entry doors were mostly visible from other units, but the neighbors seemed to be younger people who were more in a hurry to get to their destination than worry about who or what they saw on the way.

There was a fair amount of activity for a Sunday. Henry was accustomed to trying to be intentionally discreet, as discretion was thrust upon him from an early age. When someone walked by his car from either direction, he took great care to pretend not to notice him or her.

Much of the parking in the area was on the street, so Henry intended to gradually move his car closer to Herbrit's front door as people came and went. His zoom lens would be able to get a reasonably clear shot of the man from about a block away, but of course the closer the better.

He waited and waited. To pass the time he listened to his music player and read magazines, with an eye constantly shifting to the front door of unit E. By three in the afternoon he was exhausted from the stillness. He was not accustomed to this level of inactivity, and began to appreciate police on stakeouts, whose job, it appeared, consisted of many hours of boredom punctuated by moments of excitement.

At almost five there was finally some activity. The window shades directly to the left of the door opened. A figure peered out, as if looking for someone, or perhaps checking the weather. He readied his camera. A couple with a baby walked by and noticed his camera and zoom lens. He was completely unprepared, so he smiled and waved. He felt as though he had been caught naked in his car. They eyed him suspiciously and kept walking.

Finally the front door opened. Henry zoomed in as a man stepped from the home. He appeared very tall, thin, and gray, likely in his sixties. Henry snapped several photos of the man as he fumbled with his keys to lock the door. His clothes were drab but neat and clean. A newspaper was under his arm.

Henry hurriedly put his camera on the floor of the car, piling clothes over the top to conceal it. He grabbed his wallet, phone and keys as he opened the door, watching the man as he walked slowly toward the parking lot on the side of the building. Henry tucked in his shirt and readied himself for a "chance" encounter with the man. He took an angle toward the parking lot rather than toward him. The last thing he wanted was for the man to mistake his approach as threatening. Timing their intersection, Henry looked up at the man as if in surprise.

"Oh hello. Are you Mister Herbrit?"

The man clearly had noticed Henry's approach and stopped immediately when Henry spoke, glaring at him instantly, suspiciously.

"Who the hell are you and why are you asking me that?"

"My name is Henry Chimera, and I'm a great admirer of the life work of Origen. I'm a practicing medium – actually fairly new as a full-timer – and the notion of reincarnation is just threaded throughout my work. I've been doing some research, and there are only a few people who have been out in front as far as really understanding what reincarnation means in traditional religions."

Henry smiled as he spoke, trying to sound cheery while maintaining eye contact

"Well, that's definitely not me, and any decent Christian man should stay away from that crap anyway. It's blasphemous. There's no place for it in God's world."

"I see." Henry tried to maintain a positive tone. "Well, the reason for my interest is that some of these ideas go all the way back to the very beginning of the Church, many centuries. From what I've been able to tell, Church doctrine changed over the centuries because it had to. Political and practical necessity, I've read, although I'm nowhere near an expert on the subject."

The man continued his icy stare at Henry, pausing for a few uncomfortable seconds before he spoke. "Well, the church I follow is the church of today. That church tells me that it's not really our concern what was happening hundreds of years ago, is it?"

"No, I suppose not."

"There are plenty of problems in this world, son, and it doesn't sound to me that there's a single thing in what you just said that will solve any of them."

"Well, I'm not so sure of that, sir."

The man's glare turned to a sneer. "Oh no? How would the things you describe help us through any important world problems?"

"Well, sir, I've come to believe that so many of the problems of today are related – at least indirectly – to the massive population explosion we've had over the last hundred years or so."

The man stood defiantly, saying nothing but making no attempt to move away.

"By the way, you are David Herbrit, correct?" He smiled and waited for a reply, but the man's expression did not change.

"Well, anyway, when so many millions and millions of people are born each year and the number continues to massively outnumber the ones who die, whether you believe in rebirth or not, there's going to be a strain on heaven's capacity to create new souls. We're pushing out tens of millions of new souls each year. How can they all be wise? They can't! That's a pretty big problem. A friend of mine called it 'Soul Math.'"

"It's an interesting theory, but what's the use in trying to imagine what the abilities in heaven are to generate souls?" Henry had broken through. "That's not something we could possibly ever have a grasp of. Even if overpopulation is creating some excess demand of souls over available supply, why not focus your energy on the things the Church has always supported, like providing aid and assistance to the people that need it?"

"I understand your point," Henry replied, "but I'm more interested in knowing the effects of the phenomenon because that could help explain many, if not most of the troubles we see today, and who knows, perhaps correct some of the wrongs in the world. I can't say what or how, but the more I think about Soul Math, the more I believe the impacts must be profound, and probably right in front of our noses."

"How so?" The man still maintained a distance from Henry, but clearly was not as eager to end the conversation.

"At some point you have to address the basic question of where all those souls are coming from. If you have any belief in reincarnation at all, you can't deny that the increase in new souls in the last couple centuries has been staggering. The number of new humans each year has gone from something like one million per year about two centuries ago to almost ninety-million per year now. I don't pretend to understand what goes into producing new souls, but surely there has to be some downside to that, don't you think?"

These comments from Henry seemed to surprise and anger the man. His face reddened noticeably as he glared more intensely at Henry.

"Mister Chimera, I believe you're getting into subjects that you have no business getting into, and for which you're completely unqualified to deal with."

Henry was startled by the man's sudden change. "I admit that, but is any living human really qualified in these matters? I'm more interested in the impacts of this … phenomenon. There's inhumanity everywhere. Greed, suffering, savagery, you name it. There's more political instability around the globe today than there was just a few years ago, and really at any point in my lifetime. It's very alarming."

The reply was fast and loud. "The subjects you're talking about are heretical, possibly even dangerous. You do understand that, don't you, Mister Chimera? Are you so naïve as to think there wouldn't be powerful interests motivated to maintain Church doctrine that has been in place for many centuries?"

"Actually Mr. Herbrit, that occurred to me recently in a very personal way."

The man stared at him impassively before answering. "Trust me, Mister Chimera. You need to back off from this line of inquiry or you might very well end up meeting the same fate as your friend, Mister Donnelly."

The man's threatening stare chilled Henry to the bone. He paused before speaking. "I'm sorry to have troubled you, sir."

"It's not my trouble, young man. Watch yourself." David Herbrit turned and walked toward his car.

During the three-hour ride home, Henry drove in stunned silence as his thoughts whirled. Recounting their brief conversation over and over, he focused on a few important details.

Henry gambled by calling him out as Herbrit instead of asking directly, and the man offered no denial. Henry was certain he had not brought up Donnelly's name, so Herbrit was keenly aware of his recent murder. The man did not renounce reincarnation, although he spoke of heresy. Was his talk of reincarnation the only cause, or was there something more?

Whatever it all meant, the man's warnings were clearly not to be dismissed.

Finally, he settled on one certainty: He was passing through a key threshold yet again. This one would be bigger than all the others combined.

Sword and Stone

While Henry was attempting to unravel the mystery around his friend's death, tensions around the world were gathering attention from American media because of their unprecedented levels. In nearly every corner of the globe there were conflicts that were reaching frightening levels. There was a common theme that Henry noticed but was not played up heavily in the news, that each conflict had religion at the center.

In the Middle East, hostilities between Israel and the Muslim world were steadily escalating. Israeli leadership had recently embraced a zero tolerance policy toward any person or group that opposed its policies, particularly those that involved the contested territories of the West Bank and Gaza Strip. Israelis believed that the lands were rightfully theirs, and in recent months their concern about the opinion of the international community was lessening. They only tolerated the Palestinians because of international pressures, looking for any reason to eject Palestinians from the country for even the most minor offenses.

In one circumstance, a story spread about a teenage Palestinian boy who was arrested for being on the streets past ten at night. The rumor circulated that Israeli authorities put him in jail for days without notifying his family. Several weeks after the boy's disappearance, his body was found far from the last place he had been seen, in a remote area across the Jordanian border. Despite persistent Israeli denials about having any role in the boy's arrest or death, the Arab world was outraged. Whoever murdered the boy had inflicted serious damage on any prospects for peace in the region, at least for the near future.

Palestinians living in these areas grew increasingly hostile over the lack of basic services available to them and of the denial by Israeli authorities of conveniences that Jewish citizens came to expect, such as reliable utilities, trash pickup, and timely responses to emergencies. In a subtle show of protest, Palestinians looked for any opportunity to vandalize Israeli property, or increasingly, to exact violence on Israeli citizens. Crude but devastating homemade bombs began to explode in a unpredictable gathering places for Israelis citizens. Some Palestinians celebrated excessively when the bombs were effective, which was highlighted on news programs and further served to heighten hostilities.

One such event especially outraged Jews around the world. A suicide bomber posing as a caterer interrupted a wedding party in Tel Aviv. Thirty-seven people were killed and dozens more injured. Among the victims were three Holocaust survivors, including the grandmother of the bride.

Each action from either side seemed to be met with an angrier reaction from the other in a cycle that continued for months. Some Middle East experts guessed that an open civil war was inevitable.

The US State Department was on high alert, doing what it could to keep Israel from proactively launching missile strikes in areas believed to be the sources of the attacks. More daunting was the challenge of trying to reassure the Arab world, with its dispersed groups in various countries, that Israeli reactions were borne of self-preservation.

Off the coast of North Korea, a South Korean shipping vessel mysteriously disappeared in the middle of the night, presumably to the bottom of the Yellow Sea. The South Korean government accused North Korea of sinking the vessel, while North Korea steadfastly denied involvement. All 27 sailors aboard were missing without a trace, and there were no radio signals to suggest their fate. Military analysts believed this indicated a fast, efficient sinking that was unlikely to be the result of natural events. Following the disappearance, satellite imagery captured by US surveillance showed a buildup of troops along both borders.

Bombings in civilian settings throughout India were on the increase. It was commonly believed the bombings were at the hands of Pakistanis. Whether the Pakistani government supported the attacks was unknown; no one took credit for the murders. The rhetoric of Indian leadership was increasingly shrill while treatment of Pakistani citizens within India was becoming hostile, when not overtly violent. In the meantime the Indian government beefed up its troop presence all along the border of Pakistan.

In Northern Ireland, years of peace went quickly by the wayside from a series of bombings in high profile, high impact locations around the province. The IRA in its new form decried the violence, swearing it had no part. The British were skeptical but avoided directly accusing the Catholic group of lying. Cryptic messages received by the authorities did not mention the IRA, but instead blamed the oppression of the "Fascist Royal Occupants" for the violence. The Loyalist parades that were the source of so much conflict and pride were just a few weeks ahead. It was barely summertime.

While the fate of the Dalai Lama was still unknown, the High Lamas of the Gelug sect of Tibetan Buddhism were making no plans to identify his successor. Under even normal circumstances the process of selection could take several years, but they were content to wait until his fate was known before making plans of any kind to move forward.

Believing his disappearance to be no random act, some of the High Lamas were increasingly speaking out against those that opposed their political positions. The Tibetan government, which was in exile since the Chinese "Invasion of Tibet" in 1950, expressed outrage that the Chinese now may have had some role in taking away their spiritual leader as well. Even though the original invasion took place many decades earlier, resentment among the Tibetan people toward the Chinese remained profound.

Chinese leadership vigorously denied any involvement in the abduction of the Dalai Lama. Their public comments were firm but careful to avoid language that a nervous world might view as confrontational. Their official releases suggested they had more important things to worry about than the Dalai Lama.

The Tibetans had always objected to condescending treatment by the Chinese, so the dismissive tone of the Chinese remarks generated even more suspicion. Tibetans were becoming restless, and those Tibetans in exile in various countries were being uncharacteristically vocal about the threat posed by the Chinese. Analysts noted that the Tibetans had never before been this agitated or vocal toward the Chinese.

China's substantial might allowed them to choose whatever approach and causes served their interests best. History suggested the Chinese would not tolerate impertinence from the inhabitants of even one of its remotest regions, but pragmatism – based on their recent commercial success in financial dealings with the West – suggested they had nothing to gain by inflaming the situation with Tibet. Still, human rights organizations around the world were on high alert about how China would deal with the wild accusations coming their way.

Henry awoke in the same mental condition he was in when he fell asleep on the couch, with half a glass of wine on the table next to him and a sense of impending harm vaguely nearby. After making some coffee and stumbling around the kitchen trying to make sense of what to do next, he found himself staring at the television, mostly in a fog. During one of the commercial breaks on the morning news program, a familiar face appeared.

Ernest B. Grandby smiled, comparing exercise and eating right with caring for one's soul. Henry took the message to heart as a sign. He needed to visit Ellen Grandby Sullivan – today.

His workday started routinely enough, with an elderly widow checking in with her husband that had passed four years before. Henry passed along the messages between the lovely couple, and the woman left his office content.

The next client was a man that had only been in for a reading once before. Roy Dexter was an introverted man in his mid-fifties who explained during his last visit with Henry that he had never been married, but that he was especially close with his mother, who passed away five years before. From Henry's notes, he recalled that the woman was very particular about Roy's grooming, eating, and sleeping habits, and almost smothering him even after her death.

Following the standard warming up routines, Henry and Roy moved easily into a connective frame of mind. He felt the oncoming presence of the woman and before he could exchange any greetings, her spirit filled the room. Henry felt the equivalent of hard breeze. His senses froze. He was like a cat that had been hoisted by its neck; he could do nothing but limply stare into space. It was indeed Roy's mother, and she was not interested in a three-way conversation. She was here to speak to her son and her son alone. Henry was the microphone, nothing more.

"Hello Roy." It was Henry's voice, but the woman had taken control of the speech portion of his brain. Henry did not fight the dialogue, and it might have been futile if he had. "Are you eating right? Sleeping on a firm mattress? Living your life the way I always taught you?"

"Yes, mother, I'm doing well. I've never been happier."

The two conversed for several minutes about Roy's lifestyle, whether there was a chance he would find a mate, the status of their earthly possessions, and other topics that any parent and child would discuss after an absence. Henry shifted his presence into the background, not intervening in their discussion. Eventually they either forgot he was present, or ceased to care. Then the conversation changed.

"Roy, you need to watch this one."

"Your medium friend. He has some troubled waters ahead, and I don't want to see you get in the middle of something you might not be able to get out of."

"You're suggesting that I stop coming to speak with you?"

"That's what I suggest, at least until this storm passes."

Henry remained silent, allowing them to say their goodbyes. When they were finished and the woman left the room, Henry knew it and emerged, as if from a deep sleep.

"Did you both have a good visit?" Henry rubbed his eyes and straightened in his chair.

Roy was clearly unsure what Henry had heard, and clearly uncomfortable not knowing. "I hope that wasn't too difficult for you."

"Not at all," Henry replied. "It was probably harder on you than me."

Roy Dexter nodded. "At least neither of us got the toilet treatment."

Henry laughed. "I guess it's better that neither of us know what that is. Would you like to schedule your next appointment?"

Roy stood from his chair. "I'll call you when I'm ready for the next one."

After the man left, Henry sank into the nearest chair. What the hell was that? Why would she be the one to know about anything that hasn't happened yet? He had no answers, other than something was ahead of him that demanded his full attention.

He made up his mind to visit Ellen Grandby Sullivan.He looked at the clock. There were nearly two hours until his next appointment, so plenty of time for a round trip to the Church of the Tortured Christ. Life was short with or without chances taken, he told himself. May as well plunge in.

The ride was easy and traffic was light. Henry kept looking at the road ahead and in the mirror behind, expecting something ominous. Finally he was in the driveway of the church.

He walked through the modern, warm vestibule of the building, decorated with tasteful Christian images. As he entered the Administrative Office, a woman was picking and pecking at her computer. When Henry entered she looked up and smiled brightly.

"May I help you?"

"Yes, hi. I was hoping to get a chance to visit with Ellen Grandby Sullivan." Henry smiled humbly. "Please forgive me for showing up unannounced."

The middle-aged, plumpish woman looked at him with a mix of surprise and sympathy. "Oh, I'm terribly sorry sir, but Mrs. Sullivan is so verrrrrrrry busy. She sets her appointments well in advance. Can we set an appointment for sometime in the very near future?"

"Well, perhaps, but I have a feeling she might wish to see me. Before we set an appointment and I drive all the way back to my office, is there any way you get a message to her? Could you perhaps just tell her that Henry Chimera is here and I'd like just five minutes with her? I was a good friend of John Donnelly, who just passed away recently."

The woman looked at him uncertainly, with no idea why his message would make a difference to her boss. "I guess I can check, but she does have a super important meeting in her office."

Henry looked at her appreciatively. "Thanks so much. I'll just have a seat here and wait," smiling as he turned toward a group of seats before a splendid view of downtown Boston.

After a few moments the woman returned, looked passively at Henry and said, "Well Mister Chimera she is in some important meetings today, but she said she could try to squeeze a few minutes in with you if you can wait."

"I can wait for a while. Thank you again."

It was more than fifteen minutes before her office door opened. The woman came through the door, walking toward him at a brisk pace. She wore a flowing, full-length burgundy dress that was stylish, yet with a fabric that was light enough for an early summer day. Henry noticed that no one exited the room as she emerged.

"Mister Chimera? Hello, I'm Ellen Grandby Sullivan. Won't you come in?" She offered a firm handshake and a winning smile as she led him into her office. Henry did a fast scan of the room and estimated the number of cross symbols that were placed on every wall. He guessed there had to be at least forty, from big to large, made of everything from wood to stone to what looked like Play Doh. The crosses were punctuated with pictures of herself at various ages, an undergraduate degree from Georgia Tech, a Master of Divinity degree from a college in Tennessee, and other photos of her father next to US presidents and a few foreign leaders.

"Reverend Sullivan, I'm very sorry to impose on you. I had a break in my schedule, and I've been eager to meet you since the Donnelly service. It was so impressive. I'm not really sure what motivated me to try my luck. I know you're extremely busy and your time is in great demand, but I really wanted to meet you."

"Well, I'm flattered that you made the effort, Mister Chimera. It's unusual that you caught me at a reasonably calm time. Please call me Ellen."

"And please call me Henry."

They both smiled. "So what brings you here, Henry?"

"Well, John's death affected me very personally. We had only gotten to know one another over the last few weeks, but I felt we were building a lasting friendship. I guess I'm wondering how well you knew John, and where he went wrong. There were some things in common between his life and mine, and I was hoping you can offer some insight into what this all means."

"I only knew John in passing. His wife is a very loyal member of our flock, very active in this branch of the church. I've seen John at a few events during the short time I've been here. So no, I didn't know him well. I can't imagine what Mister Donnelly might have done to provoke that kind of violence, yet violence was invoked."

She rose from her chair and walked to a window. "Are you a Christian man, Henry?"

"I've gained great inspiration from Christ's words and message, but I'd categorize myself as someone open to the positive messages from all faiths."

"I see." She smiled and kept her gaze.

Henry cut off whatever thoughts she was forming. "Whether his death was invoked or provoked, it wasn't justified." He paused, wondering how far he should go in explaining how he and John came to become friends.

"I'm not sure if Janice told you, but I'm a psychic," Henry said. "That's why John came to see me. I hope that isn't too much at odds with your faith."

Ellen showed no trace of surprise. "I don't think so. Like everyone else, I've heard the stories about so-called 'psychics' that tell people only what they want to hear just to get to their money. From my understanding of psychics, the really good ones bring great comfort to people. There are some traditional religions that have a problem with what you do, but I guess I have yet to see the harm in it when it's done correctly and with the right intentions. The Bible provides some guidance over the influence of 'seers' and 'prophets,' but it doesn't universally condemn people with your gifts, so I don't feel it's my place to judge. Plus Janice told me she felt comfortable with you when you two spoke."

"Oh, she told you we spoke. Did she tell you that John came to see me for a reading?"

"Yes. She was probably more upset about it than she should have been, I think because John did it on his own, without consulting her."

The Reverend Sullivan had a way of speaking authoritatively but with kind eyes. Henry found her steady, slow manner to be soothing.

"His reasons for coming in were not completely honest, but we got past that and became friends soon enough."

"Really? I hadn't heard that. What reasons did he give?"

Henry responded quickly. "I don't think that's something I should talk about, especially considering that his murderer is still out there somewhere."

The Reverend looked at him apologetically. "Oh, I'm so sorry. My curiosity got the best of me. Have you spoken with the police about your experiences with John?"

"Yes, but I'm not sure how much help it was."

"Well, that's all we can do," Sullivan replied. "Detective Lacey came to see me as well."

Henry perked up. "Oh he did? Wow, he's a thorough guy. No stone unturned."

"Yes, I definitely get that impression. John's murder has everyone nervous and upset, so I found the Detective's visit to be reassuring. There are a few other odd things that have people on edge around here as well."

"Oh really? What else?"

She measured Henry again before deciding how to respond, then moved easily past caution.

"Well, I suppose there's no harm in saying that we've noticed some people around here that seem, shall we say, somewhat out of place. I thought they might be police, but when I asked Detective Lacey if he was aware of anyone that could be keeping an eye on us he was surprised, hopeful to get descriptions of who they were. We didn't have much to tell him, really. They were just nondescript men who seemed to be lurking around during the past few weeks. I would never have noticed it being new here, but some of the staffers brought it to my attention."

Henry nearly barked out to the woman that he had had the same experience, but held himself back. Instead he offered, "I can see how that would be nerve-wracking, especially with John's death so close to home. That's something I should also watch for."

The two parted company warmly. Henry apologized again for his unannounced appearance, but the Reverent Sullivan assured him that she was glad he decided to visit. Henry left the church pleased that he made the trip.

Several days later Lacey phoned asking for chance to stop by to ask a few questions to follow up from their prior conversation. Henry agreed to see him that evening, following the last of his readings for the day. The detective showed up on time, pad and pencil in hand.

"So what brings you here, Detective?" Henry was tired from a long day of readings, ready to get down to business.

Lacey was happy to oblige. "Have you thought of any other conversations you had with Donnelly that you didn't mention before?"

"I'm sorry to disappoint you, Detective, but I can't really think of anything new to add to what I already told you. But I should mention that I went to see Ellen Grandby Sullivan."

Lacey perked up. "Is that so? Why did you decide to visit her?"

"I guess it was just to commiserate, or maybe just to see if she had any insight into the murder that I didn't."

"I see." Lacey looked down. "Is this some sort of private investigation that you're taking on, Mister Chimera? Because I strongly advise against that."

"Not at all. I'm just having a hard time with this and I don't really have anyone to speak with about it."

"Did she have any new insight to offer?"

"Not especially, but I guess it was reassuring that she has some of the same worries I have. She also mentioned something that's bothered me too."

"What's that?"

"She said that some of her staff noticed that there were some odd characters hanging around, that seemed to be watching her. She said she mentioned that to you. Detective, I think I've noticed that too."

Lacey shifted in his seat. "Okay for starters, it would be best if our conversations stay private. What you tell me is in confidence, and what Ms. Sullivan tells me should be private too. Got it?"

"Yes, sorry about that."

"So now tell me what you saw."

"Well, at Donnelly's service there was a guy in a dark suit who wrote down my license plate number. I thought he was a cop or some kind of church security detail. It's probably nothing. I'm probably just on edge."

"Well, that would be understandable," Lacey said, "considering that your friend was killed. If it happens again, I'd appreciate a phone call. Okay?"

"Definitely. I'll call. Detective, should I be worried?"

"At this point I have no way of knowing that, but it never hurts to watch your back. Be aware of where you are, keep your phone handy, and don't get yourself into situations you can't easily get out of."

"In that parking lot," Henry said, "if it was a cop writing down license plates, would you tell me?"

Lacey stared directly at Henry. "Probably not, but if someone's shadowing you, then you should go to a public place with people all around, like a grocery store or mall. When you're safe, you call me."

Henry began to stand, believing the questioning to be over. Lacey stayed in his seat.

"Henry I really wanted to talk with you about this special skill you have."

"You mean as a medium?"

"Exactly. I watch those TV shows about murder mysteries," Lacey said, "the ones where evidence is sparse and they're open to anything. If you can offer me some tips to point me in the right direction, I won't ignore them. I don't suppose you've been in contact with Mister Donnelly's spirit?"

Henry was stunned at the question, but was impassive as he returned a question. "I bet that's not a question you're used to asking people, Detective. Am I right?"

"That's for sure, but we don't have any suspects at this point so here I am." Lacey looked at him dryly.

"I've watched some of those shows too, and I know that if a psychic learns certain things that no one else could know except someone at the crime scene, that makes THAT person a suspect. I didn't kill Donnelly and I wasn't at the crime scene, so what assurance do I have that you won't arrest me?"

"I'm not going to arrest you today if you give me information that you swear you heard from Donnelly's spirit or some other spirit. I promise. And it's unlikely I'd arrest you in the future if your story doesn't change and your alibi checks out okay. Do we have a deal?"

Henry paused and exhaled.

"I drove past the crime scene after you called me that night. I sat there by the roadside and tried to pick up on Donnelly's spirit, just in case it was still hanging around."

"And?"

"And there was a connection. It wasn't a pleasant conversation, as you can imagine. Recently passed spirits sometimes barely know they're dead. They're disoriented, almost in a fog. The current condition sometimes hasn't sunk in all the way. It can be really difficult."

"Did you hear any details about the attack?"

"I don't think he told me much that would be helpful to your investigation."

"That isn't really for you to judge, Henry. We have a deal. Just tell me what you know."

"Donnelly communicated to me that he got a flat and pulled off. Before he knew it he was lying there. He didn't really know what hit him. He described his attacker as wearing a knit hat, the kind that kids wear, and he described a long coat. He said the guy ran fast, like 'a deer in the night' is how he put it."

Lacey deliberately wrote into his notepad, only glancing back up to Henry when he was done. "Anything else? Anything at all?"

"And he described a knife. With his blood on it."

Lacey looked closely at Henry. "Are you sure you didn't hear that somewhere else, Henry? Maybe from one of the cops on the scene?"

"I didn't speak with anyone at the scene except Donnelly's spirit hours after the attack. I'm quite sure it was him."

"It's good that you told me, Henry. This might help us. What else?"

"Just that there was hatred and some sort of justification hanging with the killer. It doesn't sound like a random thing. It sounds like Donnelly was targeted to die. I have no idea why that is, but it really sounds that way from what Donnelly said, the emotions he picked up from the killer. There is one other thing that I should probably mention to you. I told you that Donnelly was looking into reincarnation to sort of circumvent the uncertainty about having a child."

"Yup, I noted that, and you also told me he was worried about his safety. What else?"

"Well, I did a little digging into the Origenists, who Donnelly evidently contacted in the first place."

Henry explained how he came across David Herbrit through his own investigative work.

"Really. It sounds like you're back to trying to be a detective. Go on."

"Well, I tried calling the man. When I couldn't reach him I drove to Albany."

"You drove all the way to Albany to see this Herbrit fellow?" Lacey was not pleased.

"Well, yeah, it's something that interests me too."

Lacey moved forward in his chair. "Do you realize, Mr. Chimera, that your actions can easily be interpreted as interfering in a murder investigation, and that it's illegal to interfere in ANY police investigation, let alone a murder?"

Henry was not sure which he regretted more, his actions or telling Lacey about his actions.

"I had no intention of interfering in anything, Detective. I merely wanted to meet a man who, from what I can tell, has experience related to my field that nobody else has. That's all, nothing more."

Lacey was not convinced. "For starters, you might be putting yourself in danger. You have no idea who these people are or what their motivations are, and yet you go sticking your nose into their business. You should consider yourself fortunate that he didn't find a nice, secluded place to slash your throat."

Henry said nothing, avoiding looking at the detective.

"On top of that, you should have told me about this information when you found out about it instead of trying to do my job for me. Is that clear?"

"Yes, it's clear. I'm sorry about that, Detective."

Lacey looked at Henry with a mixture of disappointment and pity. "Yeah me too. God only knows what you're digging yourself into here."

After a pause in which both men remained silent, Lacey continued. "Look, Henry, I don't care if you go on the web searching for information about these guys. Be my guest, but before you contact anyone, and this includes email, you need to talk to me. That isn't a request. Now tell me every single thing you know about this Herbrit fellow and your visit. Leave nothing out. If I find out later that you're hiding anything from me, I'll arrest you. Then we can talk whenever I feel like it instead of whenever you do."

Henry assured him that he would be completely truthful. He spent the next hour explaining all the details of how he found Herbrit, the visit, the man's appearance, his interpretation of the man's warning, and everything in between. When they were finished, Henry was exhausted, hungry, and still contrite.

At home, Henry ate supper and watched the end of a baseball game on television. The Red Sox were putting the finishing touches on a 10-8 victory over the Orioles. Before the game was over he drifted to sleep.

He dreamed of a familiar face. It was Aisling. She was talking to him. He was delighted to hear from her, but she had no interest in pleasantries. Her message was delivered with love and impatience.

Be very careful about what you're doing. You're in a situation with no easy exit. Mind who you're speaking with and what you say. Trust no one. There are powerful forces who will wish to move you from your path. There are others depending on you to succeed, but be vigilant.

TRUE SOLDIERS OF CHRIST

On the surface Henry had no reason to be drawn in by the circumstances around Donnelly's death. People were murdered every day in this country, often for nothing more than wallet cash or a shiny watch. Why was Donnelly's death any different?

Yet he was drawn in. He spent days trying to decide why. Perhaps it was because he had never been close to someone murdered, or perhaps it was the shock of the event, which affected him more than he expected. And there was the strange circumstances around the death and the lingering question of why. All factors created a strange concoction of intrigue that he found impossible to ignore.

Lacey contacted Henry at least once every week following the murder, verifying specific details in Henry's contacts with Donnelly, usually to the point of repetition. During their discussions he heard nothing to indicate the police were close to finding the killer. The lack of progress by the police only added to his obsession with the lingering mystery. The nature of his new occupation which involved seeing and hearing from spirits that he never knew existed, compounded the obsession. His tendency to construct intricate explanations for Donnelly's death and the many possible roles of characters, some he knew of and some he imagined, began to overtake his waking and sleeping hours.

David Herbrit was an added contour of mystery that acted as a lubricant in the gears of his imagination. The fact that Herbrit knew about he and Donnelly, and that he warned of encroaching danger, drew Henry to want to know all he could about the man. His obsession was taking on a new facet, and he welcomed it. He considered what could be gained from another contact with Herbrit given that the man would likely be less cooperative than last time, and perhaps downright hostile. There was no way to know whether the man was a harbinger of danger, or danger itself.

Detective Lacey, on the other hand, offered an undeniable threat to Henry, although only because the man's phone calls would not cease. Henry was clearly still a suspect, which paralyzed him into inaction. Despite his desire to mount a personal crusade to find Donnelly's killer, he decided it was time for a self-imposed time out until the police showed some progress.

That seemed like a perfect plan until the phone rang one evening. It was a deep voice, speaking with some hesitation. "Mister Chimera?"

"This is he. Who's calling please?"

"This is David Herbrit."

Initially he did not believe the call was legitimate. "Really? Why would David Herbrit be calling me?"

"Well, why would Henry Chimera come to visit me unannounced, starting a ridiculous conversation about reincarnation in a parking lot?"

"Duly noted, Mister Herbrit. What can I do for you?"

"I think it's best that we meet in person. I can make the drive this time. Is tomorrow too soon?" They made plans to meet the following afternoon about an hour west of Revere, allowing Herbrit to avoid Boston area traffic.

In preparation for his meeting, Henry worried for his safety. Buying a gun was out of the question, for one because Henry had never fired a gun and did not trust himself. The Commonwealth of Massachusetts did not require a waiting period for the purchase of firearms but it did require a state license. His desire to stay under the radar, a tendency he was increasingly learning, convinced him that a simply hunting knife would be easier. He chose a lightweight model at a local sports store.

They met in a diner near the Massachusetts turnpike at four o'clock. Henry was ten minutes early and Herbrit was already in a booth waiting for him over of a cup of green tea.

"Thank you for reaching out to me, Mister Herbrit."

"It's David."

"So why did you contact me, David? I figured you'd avoid me permanently. Our last contact didn't exactly seem to be the beginnings of a warm friendship."

"Well, my intention was to completely avoid any future contact with you. Your introduction was clumsy and frightening. Some of the things you were talking about are incredibly powerful. Plus it was very evident that you had no idea of what you were getting into. Maybe you still don't."

"Well, I might not," Henry started, "but I needed to get your attention."

"You certainly did. This 'Soul Math' concept, as you call it, is something that in theory anyone could have figured out, but very few have. That's mainly because people have ridiculous notions of reincarnation, believing it only applies to Eastern religions or that in our next life we'll be an animal or an insect. However, the implications are ... more substantial than that, as you pointed out. The mere fact that a novice like yourself is thinking through it at a fairly high level is perhaps a little alarming because you were so quick to come speak with a stranger about something so controversial. A little caution is the least you could have managed."

"Lesson learned. I'm new at this, Mister Herbrit."

Herbrit sipped his tea and said nothing.

"You haven't told me why you called," Henry said. "Did you contact me just to tell me not to shoot off my mouth?"

"It was one important reason, but not the only one."

"I'm listening." It was Henry's turn to be smug. Herbrit did not seem to notice.

"I gather from your speech that you've done some studying on the origins of reincarnation, and that you understand that the teachings we support are far from radical. We believe them to be among the most fundamental and traditional of all Christian precepts. The notion of reincarnation was what Jesus believed. Its purging from the tenets of the Church, we believe, would have deeply saddened him."

"My understanding," Henry began cautiously, "was that there were some pragmatic reasons for early Church leaders believing reincarnation was not sustainable. Times were tough for them, with political forces exerting a heavy influence on all religion. If one Christian notion had to go, is it so preposterous that reincarnation would be the one?"

Herbrit's eyes blazed. "Yes, it's preposterous! The reasons for casting the notion of rebirth from their body of beliefs were more about expedience than love. Instead of choosing the right course, they chose this ridiculous and misleading campaign to teach schoolchildren that if they lived a pure life, avoiding 'dirty thoughts,' whatever the hell they are, that they'd be on the expressway to heaven. It's BULLSHIT. Even Jesus was not perfect. How could anyone else be? It makes no sense now to any thinking adult, and didn't make sense at the time. Back then anyone who argued with their 'new enlightened reasoning' was persecuted, which would have appalled Christ."

Henry glanced around the diner to see if Herbrit's outburst attracted any attention. A few patrons looked briefly at them but went back to their meals and conversations.

"I'm with you so far. The idea of reincarnation makes a lot more sense to me than a 'one and done' situation, where you go to either heaven or hell. That always seemed harsh, not to mention very unchristian."

"Precisely." Herbrit sipped his tea.

"It's still not clear to me why you made the long drive. Why did you want to speak with me?"

Herbrit inhaled, taking a long moment before answering Henry's question.

"I've been on this mission for over thirty years now. Others were on the mission before me. There have been times where we felt we were gaining momentum, even convincing powerful people that our version of Christianity is far more in line with what Christ had in mind than what's been adopted and promoted for centuries. Yet we've never turned the corner. There was always too much opposition to overcome.

"Some opponents have had their beliefs in place for centuries, notably the Roman Catholic church, but even non-Catholics consistently rejected the idea of reincarnation for the very same reasons the Catholics did: they felt it discouraged a virtuous life. The reasons haven't changed. Neo-Christians are frightened by the implications, and too lazy to consider anything other than the New Testament to understand the WHOLE message of Christ. The books of the New Testament were written many years after Christ's death by people who never knew him. Those books were changed and filtered by human hands to fit the expedience of the day, and some other candidates for inclusion in the New Testament were rejected that offered great insight into the life of Christ. The notion of rebirth is a casualty of history. Reincarnation was not a notion the writers of the Bible wanted to promote, and so they didn't. But does that change the future of souls? Of course not. The forces that kept reincarnation in the dark for all these centuries have been powerful, without question. They were never hostile, but things are changing, Henry. Something is different. A newer, more potent set of forces is in play now to suppress our message. In the decades that I've been involved in promoting the Origenist movement, I've never felt this level of resistance."

"How so? How do you even know it's happening?"

"There's never been intimidation before. We've been labeled blasphemers and worse through the years, but never with this level of spite and calculation. There have been attacks on our web sites that have been very well coordinated and very effective. The tone of the attacks is even different. In the past, aggressors would show their face when they attacked our message. We knew who we were dealing with. Now they're in the shadows. They're more potent than ever, and more secretive. One of the things I find most troubling is that their message doesn't come from the same place, that we're subverting the message of the Bible. Their threats are pinpointed and very, very personal. It's almost like they know that what they're doing isn't compatible with a Christian message, so the threats have reached a new level. When you know who you're dealing with, at least you have a chance to defend yourself. But when your attackers don't identify themselves and their message is simply 'go away or else,' the game has changed."

"How can you even be sure they're Christians?"

"They may not be, honestly, and it's hard to know how serious their threats are. They're just insisting that we need to go away. I can't imagine who else they could be, or why they care what we have to say. In truth we have no idea."

As Herbrit spoke, Henry noticed an attractive blond woman in a booth across the room. Her soft beauty would have been enough to catch Henry's attention, but he noticed she was glancing over toward them every so often. She was alone, which was somewhat unusual for a young attractive woman in a diner. There was only a cup of coffee and magazine in front of her.

"So you're telling me, David, that the reason you wanted to speak with me is that the stakes have gone up lately, and that I should be careful?"

"Well, yes, it's essential that you understand that we don't know who we're up against here. If we're feeling that more caution is needed than ever before, you should feel the same way."

"Thanks for the warning, but couldn't you have gotten this message across to me over the phone?"

"I suppose so, but who knows what these people are capable of? They're sophisticated, so I have to assume that they're able to hear my phone conversations. If you're someone I'm contacting, they'd likely be interested in hearing your conversations too. I'm doing this to protect you. Of course, they may have already begun listening to you."

Henry smiled at him, disbelieving. "That can't be true. I'd know if they were listening to my phone conversations."

"You might or you might not," Herbrit was quick to reply. "Again, we don't know how good these people are. I can tell you from the attacks we've experienced, they aren't amateurs and they are determined."

Henry processed this information uneasily. "Thanks for the warning and the visit. I'll be on guard."

"Indeed." Herbrit was not finished. "We also wanted to get your reaction about trying to perhaps align some of our efforts."

"Excuse me?"

"Well, it seems that you're motivated to get to the bottom of the death of your friend Donnelly. Otherwise you wouldn't have driven to see me. I'd feel the same. It also seems that you have a sincere interest in reincarnation and what it means to your professional practice, and to your clients."

"So far I'd say all that's true. In our first conversation you brought Donnelly's name up completely out of the blue. How in the world did you connect me to him?"

"Putting two and two together wasn't difficult. Donnelly contacted us through our web site in his initial inquiries into reincarnation. It was apparent that his reasons for researching the subject were not well thought out, to say the least. Then when I heard from some detective from Boston investigating Donnelly's death, it was easy to connect your clumsy research with his clumsy research. Your friend's death was a terrible thing, and we can't let the same thing happen to you."

"Thanks for your concern, but what's the point of aligning our efforts? Would that somehow make all your troubles go away? I don't mind helping you stay safe, but there's just one problem. Detective Lacey told me to drop my amateur sleuthing. He sounded serious about it too."

Herbrit gazed out the window before replying. "Lacey is the one that contacted me too. That's something to consider, but there's nothing illegal about you and I working on research together that forms a kind of common ground between your profession and mine. Our work together doesn't necessarily need to be intended to investigate Mister Donnelly's death, but if that's an outcome from our cooperation, then surely there's nothing wrong with that."

"I suppose you're right," Henry replied, "but some discretion is probably wise just in case."

For the next few minutes the men discussed the best way to communicate between Albany and Boston. They agreed on a method that involved veiled messages that were initiated in various ways, including phone cards, internet calls, pay phones, and other means. When one of them initiated a call, the message would include the time that a phone call was to occur, and the target phone number. When they were wrapping up their conversation, Herbrit motioned to the blond woman sitting across the diner who had caught Henry's eye. She saw his gesture, gathered her things at the table, and started toward Herbrit.

As she approached, Henry first noticed her sheer, radiant beauty. The closer she came toward their table, the more he became transfixed. Her hair was luminescent. Her light skin accentuated dark blue eyes, thin, lush lips, and a slender, graceful way of moving. Then he felt a kind of fond familiarity. He was not sure if she reminded him of a TV or movie star or someone he knew personally. Whatever the source, Henry was captivated.

Herbrit seemed to anticipate Henry's interest in this sudden beauty that had been lurking across the diner for the past hour or so. "Henry, I'd like you to meet my associate. Her name is Dee. Dee, this is Henry Chimera."

She glanced only briefly at Henry, nodding without a smile. "David, are you ready to head back?"

"Yes," Herbrit replied, "I think we're done. Henry, I'm glad we had this opportunity to speak in person after the difficulty of the last few weeks. I believe we have a number of ways to help each other out, and perhaps keep each other from trouble."

They shook hands and exchanged a brief goodbye. Henry tried to catch Dee's attention, but she was headed toward the door.

After the short drive home, Henry settled into his place of refuge for the evening, his couch with a glass of wine. He turned on CNN with the sound down, listening to soft music. He needed quiet time to sort out his conflicting thoughts. They alternated between Herbrit and the Origenist cause he represented, Dee the mystery woman, and the Church of the Tortured Christ. There was also the murder of a friend.

After his second experience with Herbrit, Henry began to warm up to the man's sincerity and sense of purpose. He seemed to speak from principles and self-preservation rather than aggression. He felt his belief system was under attack, and he was unapologetic about trying to defend them. Whether the attacks were a product of his imagination was difficult to determine. If he was delusional, why would a rare beauty like Dee hang around? She seemed to have a sincere admiration for him. Clearly Herbrit was more to her than some doddering old man that she was following around to keep from hurting himself. She was more like an apprentice with an intense focus on some unknown mission. Clearly Herbrit was someone to facilitate her mission, and judging by the utter lack of regard she paid to Henry, it was unlikely she viewed him as anything other than a potential obstacle, a distraction from their important business.

Until that afternoon Henry never considered his attraction to unattainable women. He invested several healthy gulps of wine trying to decide whether it was her lack of interest in him that drew him in, the mysterious, possibly evil work she was involved in, or perhaps just her intense beauty. He amused himself by contemplating their connection in some past life.

Inevitably his thoughts moved back to Donnelly's death, the event at the center of his unrelenting anxiety. His trust had shifted in the direction of the Origenists, which meant, in his simple way of thinking, that the Church of the Tortured Christ should be the focus of his suspicions. But what had they really done to warrant his distrust? The only reason he carried a whit of suspicion about them was that Donnelly's widow was a member of the church, and that they were very popular due to the high profile of their leader. On the other hand, wasn't their high profile about survival and growth, like any church? Ernest Grandby acquired his prominence because many thousands of followers believed in the message he delivered and reinforced. It was a message of faith, tolerance, and understanding.

Henry tasted distinct remorse along with his red wine as he admitted that it was nothing more than their success that attracted his suspicions. The stark reality was that perhaps Donnelly's death was that it was a random event after all. After all his suspicion and conspiracy-building over the Origenists, the Church of the Tortured Christ and other unseen, sinister groups, perhaps Donnelly's death was one of thousands of senseless deaths that occurred in the US every year.

A freshly uncorked bottle of wine was nearly empty. Henry's eyes were getting heavy as he focused briefly on the TV images in front of him. While a CNN meteorologist pointed to a radar image of a tropical storm that was moving threateningly toward the Carolina coasts and Georgia, he lazily read the "crawlers" that rolled across the bottom of the screen.

Escalations mount between the US and China over accusations by US Congressman about the disappearance of Dalai Lama. Still no leads into the disappearance. World Buddhist leaders putting international pressure on China to find the Tibetan leader.

Henry drifted off. He fell deeper into slumber, his dreams a hodgepodge of thoughts and images and dull emotions. Before long a stark image came into focus. It was of the Tibetan leader himself, the Dalai Lama. He was in an unusual setting, at a sparse dining room table with bright lights. Two figures were in front of him, facing him, their attentions directed at him alone. He was being questioned. It was a vivid image. He could understand the basic idea behind their discussions, although he was not sure of the language being spoken.

"Since you and your people left China so many years ago, you insist on telling us there are no 'Yellow Hats' still in China, trying to disrupt things?"

His Holiness wearily but patiently tried to explain. "If there are, they are working on their own. We have no interest in covert politics. Our politics are based on the law of the eternal soul."

"Perhaps, but enforcing the 'law of the eternal soul' would most certainly be made easier by lessening some of the political factors that you Gelug believe have been imposed on you, would it not?"

The vision became more focused, more crisp. The men were Caucasian. Both carried a distinctive cross on a chain around their neck, etched silver with a garnet in the center.

The questioners were trying to maintain their patience with the Holy man, but their impatience was increasing.

The Dalai Lama explained, "I will not conceal that our existence has been difficult since we were forced to flee to India so many years ago."

"I see. You were FORCED to flee the country. You had no choice in the matter."

"I believe that to be quite evident, not only from the circumstances at the time that made practicing our faith impossible, but also as evidenced by the truth that you are detaining me now, against my will."

At this the questioner became instantly furious. He reached back and with his full force delivered an openhanded slap to the face of the Dalai Lama. The teacher's glasses flew from his face as a stream of blood gush from his nose. The Buddhist teacher and his chair lurched backward, momentarily air bound before his head hit the floor with a sickening thump. He was motionless on the floor.

The other questioner viewed the scene with a sudden look of horror. "What have you done?"

In the days that followed his last contact with Herbrit, Henry grew weary of his state of uncertainty, fear, and paranoia. Living souls burdened with challenges too great to overcome tend to let their defenses down, sometimes attracting mis-guided spirits who are drawn to easy living targets. Especially vulnerable people can draw multiple spirits. This accumulation can be a heavy weight to carry, a burden of which they may be completely unaware.

Henry felt his defenses were down, and he had learned from his customers that this was no condition to live one's life for any extended period. Those who came into his readings in this condition, he noticed, tended to attract the most harmful spirits and make his job and their lives much more difficult. He made up his mind to think less about the recent difficult events and to enhance the positive developments that were happening under his nose, in particular the growth of his business.

His client base was beginning to evolve toward a loyal group who were very comfortable with his particular style. Their trust in him grew, and his familiarity was growing in regard to their individual paths through life. His journal entries were maintained to ensure that progress would be continued through ongoing sessions. Even the spirits he contacted on a regular basis grew more comfortable with him as the sessions progressed.

Within this welcome routine, Henry could not shake the image of one of the holiest men on the planet being assaulted by thugs wearing a cross who had forgotten what Christianity means. His experience with visions was limited, and he certainly had never experienced one that was so far removed from his daily existence. The disappearance of the Dalai Lama was perplexing and very troublesome, but he was lost in understanding what it had to do with Henry Chimera.

Donnelly's death was becoming old, sad news. From the dwindling news accounts of his friend's heinous death, there were no developments being reported. He had not heard from Lacey in weeks. It might be a wound that would fester for months, years, or forever. While the rationalist in him accepted that likelihood, the fighter in him refused to accept it.

The tenuous string that held the two events together in Henry's mind was Christianity, and Henry found that he was wasting mental energy in trying to forge a connection.

How the Origenists fit into anything remained a mystery, but one that consumed less of his attention. From all Henry had been able to determine, the Origenists were a secret organization that did not really have any valuable secrets to keep. In all things that mattered, they had a lot less to hide than they seemed to think. So what if they believed in the notion of reincarnation, a notion that traditional Christians abandoned fifteen hundred years before?

As for the Church of the Tortured Christ, the Christian target that was closest to home, Henry's discomfort amounted to a general distrust for any religion that needed to use television to attract worshipers. He saw them as little more than a growing ministry that showed no signs of abusing the faith that others had placed in them. They did not seem to spend lavishly, and they seemed to avoid negative publicity. While he was nowhere close to joining their flock, he felt very comfortable with his one contact with Ellen Grandby Sullivan. The only reason she was in Massachusetts and accessible to his approach was that the local parish needed her. They were a fundamentalist Christian church in a traditionally Catholic part of the country, and local Catholics were notoriously reluctant to accept ideas from outsiders in personal matters like religion. The fact that she was succeeding in her mission in the land of the Irish Catholics was a testament to her message and her method of delivering it.

Henry found himself at a decision point, whether to walk away from the whole mystery in favor of some new hobby, like bowling or skydiving, or to pursue the mystery with abandon. Each would likely involve more alcohol and at least some falling down, so the arguments were compelling on both sides.

A third option would be to become a member of the Church of the Tortured Christ. While there were surely lovely, kindhearted people at the center of the church's local branch, he was not confident in their long term acceptance of his occupation. Ellen Grandby Sullivan seemed, in their first and only meeting, to completely avoid judgement of his profession, but his commitment in this direction would require a complete abandonment of his occupation.

Ultimately he decided on the most difficult path, toward the Origenists. He had only met two so far, and one of them was a stunner.

✧ ✧ ✧ ✧ ✧ ✧ ✧ ✧ ✧ ✧ ✧ ✧ ✧

The following Tuesday morning, a desk phone rang in the home office of David Herbrit.

"Hello?"

"Greetings, this is Sam calling from Halston Auto."

A pause. "Hello, how can I help you?"

"You had scheduled an appointment to bring your car in for the oil change and tire rotation. Sorry we couldn't take your call. Busy this week. Will noon work for you?"

"Yes, that will be fine. See you then."

Two days later at twelve sharp, Henry approached a couple sitting at a booth in the Halston Diner in Latham, New York.

"You know Henry, it wasn't exactly easy to find a Halston Diner in the Albany area. This place changed ownership and its name late last year."

"Well, sorry, David, but if I found it you should have too. See, there's this thing called the internet ..."

"Yes, I get that, Henry, but there's also this book called Yellow Pages. Perhaps you're old enough to have heard of it."

"Yeah, they used to make us sit on them at the orphanage to boost us up to the table. Anyway, I guess our code worked out okay since you're here. You didn't show up yesterday, did you?"

"No, it was very clear. 'Sam' for Saturday and 'Halston' for the diner to be named later. It worked out well. I just hope this place serves edible food."

"Me too. They almost turned this into a pet store, so at least our food will be cooked."

"Let's not make rash assumptions quite yet."

Henry chuckled. "Dee, how are you?"

This time she was able to answer Henry without distraction. "Fine. Good to see you again." There was no hint of affection, but at least she looked him in the eyes before returning to looking out the window. Henry looked in the direction she was looking, saw nothing of remote interest, and turned attention back to Herbrit.

"You both know what my occupation is. I'm a medium. I connect living people with people from their past who are no longer living. It's something I never gave a single thought to doing until I met a medium."

Herbrit nodded nonchalantly. Dee glance his way then resumed her vigil. The image that came to Henry was that of an alluring guard dog looking for trouble.

Both looked at Henry. Dee surprised Henry by asking, "What kind of skill?"

"Visions. I've had them before, some small, some bigger, more vivid. The first big one I had was when I was on a trip to Colorado to try to learn about my family. I saw the death of my brother from more than thirty years ago, in amazing detail. Through some basic research I confirmed that my vision was accurate."

There was no reaction from the other two, but they were listening closely.

"Last week I had a similar vision, and this one was almost as disturbing. The vision was of the Dalai Lama in captivity. A couple of guys were questioning him about some of the details of reincarnation. The questioning got a little heated, and one of them smacked him hard. He went over and out. This is 'His Holiness', the Dalai Lama! His glasses went flying, there was blood. It was terrible."

"Where were you when you saw this?"

"At home, on my couch. Okay, it was late and you'll wonder whether it was a dream. I admit, that's a possibility but I examine many of my dreams, and I've never had a dream like this. My dreams are never that violent and never present me with the color, the sound, the smells ... This was no dream. The two guys were questioning his reasons for leaving China, whether he had people causing problems for the Chinese now. 'Yellow Hats', they called them. Each of these guys had a necklace with a silver cross and a red stone in the middle. It looked like a garnet to me."

Herbrit paused, glanced at Dee, then down to his coffee as he stirred. Dee kept her stare on Henry.

Finally Herbrit spoke. "What do you expect us to do with this information?"

"How would I know? That's why I came all this way. Reincarnation is YOUR world. I don't know myself what to do with what I know."

Herbrit straightened in his chair. "I appreciate that you did, Henry. It's a horrifying image, and it doesn't surprise me in the least."

"It doesn't surprise you?" Henry's voice rose above the murmur in the diner. "How could it not surprise you? Why would Christians suddenly care enough about reincarnation to abduct the spiritual leader of Tibetan Buddhism?"

"I don't know the answer to that question," Herbrit began, "but I do know there's been quite a lingering discomfort between some Christians and any group that includes reincarnation as part of their belief system. Some traditional Christians might feel threatened by that, but I can't imagine why they would abduct the Buddhist leader now.

Dee finally spoke up, nearly startling Henry. "Did you go online to see if you could find any references to a silver cross with garnet in the center?"

"No, I didn't think of that. I think I'd recognize it if I saw it. The etching was distinctive, and I know it was a red stone in the middle, pretty sure a garnet." He pulled out his phone.

"Well, since you've driven all this way, would you like to join us at my house to see what we can learn about it? It might be easier than on your phone."

Henry was surprised at the offer. "Yeah, that sounds great. I won't stay long. I do have to get back tonight. Thanks for the offer."

They finished their lunch and Herbrit insisted on paying. Because the drive to Herbrit's house usually took about twenty minutes and was not direct, Herbrit suggested that Dee ride with Henry. She was clearly not comfortable with the idea, but Herbrit agreed that it made sense. She quietly directed Henry to the most direct road to Albany, Route 9. Their trip started in silence while Henry considered a way to get Dee to open up.

"How long have you been a part of the Origenist movement?"

She bristled before replying. "Let's get something straight. Our belief system has been in place longer than most of today's Christian churches were even dreamed up. We don't consider this a 'movement' any more than Catholicism is a movement."

"Sorry, no offense," he said quickly.

"I know I sound defensive. It's just that whenever this subject comes up, I have to explain that this is the real traditionalism. The reaction sometimes is that we're blasphemous, which is infuriating but only true if you buy into the notion that the winners make the rules. That might be historically accurate, but it doesn't make those rules right. Origen wrote a lot about the true meaning of Christianity, and a big part of that was the rebirth of the soul. There was so much more to his life, but that's what sets us apart from traditional Christian religions."

Henry looked at her and smiled. "It's good to hear your passion over this. I don't think I've heard more than five words from you since we met. What else is it about Origen that caused so much division, apart from reincarnation, that is."

"Most of his beliefs were about the essence of God, whether God is a real being that can be seen and touched, or an invisible force. He was a prolific writer and a man deeply committed to the teachings of Christ. In his writings he explored everything around the ideas that were left behind by Jesus. Many of his teachings were so fundamental to the thinking of the time over what to make of Christ's life, that the early church was not able to make progress without his innovative ideas and writings. It was only his teaching on the continuity of the human soul that separated him from the church. During his life they managed to use his brilliant ideas while somehow excising the ideas they didn't care to endorse. That could not have been an easy trick, if you think about it.

"Then in two or three hundred years following his death, he was completely marginalized, condemned from the church. So they stole his brilliant ideas but cast him off because of the ideas that weren't self-serving enough for them, the ones around reincarnation."

Henry glanced at Dee as she spoke. "The church controlled the message that much, that they could erase virtually him from history?"

"Momentum was gaining toward a strong Christian church, thanks in large part to his lifetime of work, so it probably wasn't all that difficult to control the outbound message as more power and influence came their way. Their basis for erasing him, was either directly or indirectly around the notion of reincarnation. The idea conflicted with their plans for promoting salvation of the human spirit. If you knew you'd have another shot at life, would you be fully motivated to sacrifice your life, if needed, to the church? They needed soldiers in Christ, and what better way to go straight to heaven than to die in his name on the battlefield?

"Also, there was the matter of Christ's resurrection. The Christian church back then was very interested in tying the body to the soul, as they preached, by Christ's resurrection after three days. After all, how could they claim he was still alive if we couldn't see him walking among us? The more you read Origen's writings, the more you realize he had beautifully reconciled Christ's life with the continuation of the human soul. But the early church probably just didn't feel they could get such advanced ideas across to a largely uneducated population."

Henry was captivated by this beautiful woman talking so passionately about a subject so important to her. As she spoke, she gradually turned in the passenger seat to speak directly to him. She was becoming far more comfortable with Henry, to his great relief.

"I think I've been here before," Henry said, looking at street signs.

"You mean in this life?" She showed a smug smile.

"No, I mean a few weeks ago."

"Yes, David told me you could probably find your way here after the first time you stalked him."

"Yeah well, I felt kinda creepy doing that, but he's not an easy man to reach by phone."

Her tone turned serious. "There's a reason for that, Henry. Unfortunately, these days our discretion is more important than ever. It's just frustrating that we don't know why."

Herbrit was waiting to let them in. As Henry finally entered the apartment, he found it much larger inside than it appeared from the outside. There was a large dining area that appeared to double as a meeting space, with a doorway that connected to a large, elegant library. Hundreds of volumes lined the bookshelves on every wall.

As he was showing them around the large apartment, the mood was light. Herbrit was talkative as he showed Henry various knickknacks, books, and artifacts he had collected in a lifetime of travel and study. Dee and Henry walked together as Herbrit reminisced. If Dee had been through the tour before or heard Herbrit's stories, she did not give it away.

Herbrit directed them to a conference table in the library, set up with a large flat-screen monitor that could be seen easily by all at the table. Once three were situated, Herbrit performed an image search using the keywords "silver cross garnet," which produced several results. Herbrit allowed Henry a chance to view an enlarged image of each. One by one Henry ruled the pictures out. Herbrit tried several combinations of key words that generated a number of cross designs with red gemstones at the center, including ruby, sapphire, beryl, spinel, tourmaline, and several others that none had heard of. None returned a perfect match with what Henry remembered.

Finally Dee asked, "Are you sure your memory of the cross was that exact? It couldn't be any of these?"

"I know what I saw. The cross around each of their necks was the same as the other's and it was very distinctive. The engraving in the crosses made them unique, something I'll never forget."

"How can you be sure the metal was silver?"

Henry hesitated. "I guess I assumed it was silver. Maybe it wasn't. I'm not so sure about that part."

"It could be white gold," Dee offered. Herbrit tried several combinations of white gold with crosses. Some generated images worth a review, but Henry recognized none.

"What else could it be?"

"Platinum," Herbrit spoke as he began typing into the search bar. *Platinum cross red stone.*

There were three images that appeared on the screen that matched the description, several others below that were not close.

"THAT'S IT!" Henry nearly screamed as he pointed at the screen.

Herbrit clicked the link beneath the first image that appeared. When the screen refreshed, it wasn't of only the image of the platinum cross. It was of the cross around a man's neck, on top of his necktie.

This time it was Dee's turn to speak.

"Holy shit, it's him."

A Passing

Henry, Herbrit, and Dee stared at the image in disbelief.

Herbrit was the first to speak. "Ernest B. Grandby, the head of the Church of the Tortured Christ himself."

Henry quickly followed. "Why the hell would that church have any interest the Dalai Lama, or in reincarnation for that matter?"

Herbrit replied sharply. "Because it's something out of their control, and that makes them uncomfortable."

Henry squinted toward him. "I have a really hard time believing that Grandby himself is involved in this. The guy has everything going for him. What's to gain? I think the kidnapping is probably an isolated effort by some people outside the power structure of the church. "

"Well, power is addictive." Herbrit was somber in his reply. "However, I'm not really sure what the church would have to gain by digging into the 'inner secrets' of reincarnation, other than perhaps they see it as a threat, just as Christians did sixteen centuries ago. Maybe by learning what reincarnation is all about, they feel they can wipe the notion from the face of the earth for good."

"I have to believe," Henry said, "that the church has bigger fish to fry than Buddhists' belief in reincarnation. Buddhism has been around since before some of the books in the Old Testament, and it's the most passive religion in the game. If they were looking for threats, I would think they'd have their sights set on higher priorities like the pro-choice movement, or other religions they've had problems with in the past, like Islam or Judaism. Look, maybe it was just a dream after all. Maybe I saw Grandby on TV with that cross before and it sunk into my unconscious. This could all be a silly exercise."

"You seemed determined that it was a vision, not a dream," Dee said. "You were convinced. Now not so much?"

Henry looked down at his hands, folded on his lap, then back to Dee. "It didn't seem like a dream. This thing took hold of me. I know the difference."

Herbrit nodded. "I don't think we should go too far off the deep end over this, but we shouldn't ignore the possibilities either. The history books tell us is that the most rigorous defenders of the New Testament have seen reincarnation as at least blasphemy, if not a direct threat. Grandby's flock is the fastest-growing Christian group in the world and the staunchest defenders of the Holy Bible. So perhaps in their eyes they see it as their duty to maintain the traditional notions of heaven and hell."

"So you think this might be some kind of preemptive strike on their part?"

"Perhaps," Herbrit said. "That makes more sense than anything I can think of."

"But why now? Why the Dalai Lama?" Henry elevated himself in his chair. "He's been in exile for more than half a century, and the only power the Tibetan Buddhists seem to hold is spiritual. The Church of the Tortured Christ doesn't seem to be lacking in spiritual power right now. It just doesn't add up."

"These are good questions, Henry. I'm just throwing out possibilities, and so far none of them are very compelling. We can only hope the answers don't involve any further harm coming to the man."

"All I know for sure," Dee offered, "is that we need to watch every step we take. All I've read and heard about this church is that they have huge influence and huge piles of money. I don't think we want to be on their list of enemies."

The two men nodded in agreement.

"You in particular Henry," Dee continued. "You've been in direct contact with Grandby's daughter. That's a little too close for comfort. They know who you are, and they may even know you've been in touch with us. That might put you on their list of people to watch."

"Thanks but you don't need to remind me."

Herbrit turned toward Henry. "Be vigilant. Take nothing for granted, and watch everything around you. I'd strongly advise that you avoid contact with us unless absolutely necessary. If anyone from the church contacts you, don't give them anything about you to be suspicious of. Just keep yourself above the mess."

"Lay low. Got it. I wish it was easier to stay in touch with you two, but I don't see any other options. I'll just go on about my business, but I'd like to keep our protocol in place for contacting each other."

The three agreed to continue their clandestine means of communication. Henry asked to use the toilet before leaving, and paused in the hallway to look at a Herbrit family photo on the wall. He thought he was out of ear shot of Herbrit's library, but he overheard Herbrit speaking to Dee.

"You'll let the others know of our ... newfound information?"

"Yes," Dee replied.

"We'll discuss any strategic adjustments in our next gathering."

"Sounds good."

During the return trip to Revere and through the evening, Henry's mind whirled with questions, and not all around the mystery of the Dalai Lama. Who was in 'the group' that Herbrit mentioned to Dee? There had to be other Origenists, but David and Dee never mentioned any others during their visit. Evidently they were not ready to trust him completely.

As he considered the general paranoia between and among them, he concluded he was not entirely ready to trust them either. John Donnelly's death was still an unsolved murder, and anyone near the recent events had to be under suspicion. This included anyone within the church and any of the Origenists, and of course Henry himself. As much as Henry had come to respect both Herbrit and Dee for their sturdy convictions, they were still an underground group. They had no public presence, and he was troubled that while their beliefs were passionate, their objectives were still unclear. Neither Herbrit nor Dee had ever explained to him their long term mission, nor the lengths they were willing to go through to achieve their unstated goals.

He also contemplated the extent to which he should protect himself. To sustain his business he needed to continue to operate in the light of day. Any lowering of his profile might not only hurt his business, but also would signal that he was on guard, which in itself might be dangerous. He considered various approaches, included changing his route to work and his other routines. In the end he decided on peak vigilance, but to maintain his basic routines and lifestyle. His instincts had always served him well, and would continue relying on them.

During the ride home Henry heard details about the escalating tensions between the US and China on National Public Radio. Discussions between leaders of the two countries were achieving little in the way of progress. While relations had been deteriorating for several years because of commerce, human rights, and accusations over state-sponsored spying, the root cause of the tension was the lingering mystery around the disappearance of the Dalai Lama. The Chinese disavowed any knowledge of his disappearance, and cautioned against suspicion in their direction.

Henry was convinced his vision was accurate, and that China had nothing to do with the holy man's disappearance. He briefly considered contacting someone in the US State Department to let them know of his vision, but he dismissed the idea. His vision would be discounted as delusional, and he would probably end up on one or more government lists of 'crazy people to watch.' Even if he were to offer the information anonymously, there was no solid proof that his vision was reality, and it could not provide a specific location of the man or his captors. There was nothing he could realistically do to help, which he used as grim proof of his sanity.

In his apartment, he lowered the lights with soft, spiritual music setting the mood for inner exploration. He sat comfortably, both feet on the floor, hands gently folded in front, eyes closed. He said a brief prayer to affirm his good intentions, and to discourage any spirits or energies that might be disruptive or harmful.

He focused on the Dalai Lama, including every detail he could conjure about the man, his life, and his beliefs. During this meditative state he felt safe, unthreatened by any invasive spirits or energies. Within the positive glow that enveloped him, he looked for any sign of what was happening with the holy man. The process was a challenge, but he persisted.

Finally a voice came to him. It was a familiar voice with an Irish lilt. "That's not for you to know right now."

A PASSING

Over the coming days Henry resumed his routine, putting recent events in the past. He regained a sense of security by settling back into the now comfortable pattern of providing a full schedule of readings for his customers. The healthy business was a testament both to the loyalty Aisling had created and to the way he managed to nourish it. His customers were thankful, and his financial security was never better.

During his sessions he was careful to silence his office and cell phones to avoid distractions during readings. During one break between sessions he noticed a call that he had missed.

"Mister Chimera this is Detective Lacey from the Waltham Police Department. I'd like to speak with you please, at your earliest convenience. It's important. Please phone me back."

Henry felt momentary panic. Lacey had to be calling because of his recent trip to Albany to visit Herbrit, but how could he possibly have known about that? Had he been watching Henry, tailing him without his knowledge? He recalled their earlier conversation, when Lacey had warned him to stay away from Herbrit, that his activities could be considered interference in a police investigation. When he reached him, the detective revealed nothing over the phone, insisting on visiting Henry in person. They agreed to meet that evening, just following Henry's final reading of the day. He reasoned that if Lacey planned to arrest him, he would not have phoned first.

Arriving on time Lacey banged loudly on the front door, rattling windows and avoiding the lit doorbell. He introduced another man wearing a drab suit and tie as Detective Carpenter, a black man of about the same age and disposition as Lacey. The two men shook hands coldly with Henry as he led them in.

Lacey wasted no time. "Henry, where were you this past weekend?"

"I spent some time with friends."

"Where did you meet these friends?"

Henry steeled himself with the conviction that he had done nothing wrong or illegal, and truly had nothing to hide. He was prepared to defend his relationship with Herbrit and Dee as that of professional colleagues.

"That's really my business, Detective."

"You need to trust me on this, Henry. Things will be easier for all of us if you answer my questions, and answer them honestly."

Henry stared at the two dour policemen. "Fine. I drove to Albany last weekend."

Both detectives visibly perked up from their hunched poses. Carpenter glanced at Lacey with a look of amazement.

"You went to Albany last week." A statement, not a question. "And why would you have gone to Albany?"

"To visit with David Herbrit. He's a professional acquaintance and there's a lot in common between our professions."

"How did the meeting go?"

"What do you mean, how did the meeting go? It went fine. David Herbrit has become a friend of mine. Like I said, we have a lot in common."

"Like what, Henry? Where's the common ground between your work and Herbrit?" Lacey's tone was sharp.

"You're really interested in this, Detective?"

"I am, very much so."

Henry patiently explained his interest in reincarnation and how he was drawn to Herbrit as an expert on the subject. He made the case that he had a great deal to learn from Herbrit's knowledge and research. Lacey and Carpenter took in Henry's explanation with no emotion.

"When did you come back home?"

"On Saturday afternoon. I beat it out of there just before rush hour, which in hindsight I probably didn't need to worry about since it's Albany."

"Was anyone else there?" The questions were becoming methodical.

"Yeah a younger woman named Dee. Kind of his associate, I guess."

"What's her last name?"

"I have no idea. He just introduced me to her as Dee."

"Did Herbrit say anything about what he was doing, people he was meeting, that kind of thing?"

Henry remembered that the last time he had such a conversation with Lacey, it was about the death of John Donnelly. Henry was on edge.

"No. What are you not telling me, Detective? Did something happen to Herbrit?"

"Can you just answer the question please?" Lacey was intent on controlling every aspect of their conversation.

"I'm not really sure I should. If something bad happened to Herbrit, you're probably here because you consider me a suspect. Can you please cut the bullshit and tell me why you're here, Detective?"

Lacey exhaled and leaned back in his chair. "Yes, Henry, something happened to Herbrit."

Carpenter finally spoke. "Mister Chimera, I'm with the Albany Police Department. Mister Herbrit has passed away and we'd like to know what you know about that."

"WHAT? I know NOTHING about that! What happened? How did he ... pass away?"

The two detectives glanced at each other briefly before Carpenter spoke again. "Unnatural causes. We're still investigating."

"Oh my God." Henry's face sunk into his hands. "Not again."

Next to his mild shock over the death of a man that knew he was in danger, his next thought was what he could possibly say to these detectives that would not be twisted into something sinister.

"I'm sorry to hear that," he tried. "I don't know what else to say. I'm sure you can't give me any details about how he died or who you think killed him, so I don't know what help I can be."

"You could tell us anything you know about what he was involved in," Lacey started. "For example, we'd like to know about this Dee woman."

"I know she's an Origenist, like Herbrit, and she's ... beautiful. She was with Herbrit both times I met with him. Both times Dee was in the background, sort of his assistant. They didn't seem to be lovers, but they were both fierce about their cause. I imagine she's afraid for her life right now."

"We'd like to speak with her. How can we reach her? Maybe she'd like to know there are people who'd like to keep her from being the next victim."

From Lacey's choice of words, Henry was convinced that Herbrit was murdered. "I have no way to contact her. I had an arrangement with Herbrit, but I don't have her number and I never exchanged numbers with her, or ever planned to be in touch with her directly. My business was with Herbrit."

The two officers looked at each other with frustration, saying nothing.

"If you think of a way to contact her, we'd appreciate it."

He thought of mentioning his Dalai Lama vision, but decided against it. At best they would think he was delusional, at worse it could lead to a line of questioning for which he could provide no answers.

The detectives asked him a few more questions about his discussions with Herbrit, digging for any morsel of information that might help their investigation. He answered their questions directly but was on guard against drawing unwanted suspicion.

Just as Lacey was getting up to leave, he settled back into his seat for one more question. "Henry do you think that perhaps your friend Donnelly was a lot closer to these Origenists than you've been telling us?"

"What exactly do you mean, Detective?"

"I mean, do you think he was one of them? On the inside of the group. Because that would kind of change the direction of the investigation."

If Donnelly was an insider, then that would mean two of the three known Origenists were dead. Either the lone survivor, Dee, would be a top suspect in their murder, or Henry himself.

"I seriously doubt that," Henry answered, shaking his head. "Unless Donnelly was a great liar, which I doubt, he stumbled onto these Origenists randomly. He had a dumb idea, and thought they could help him. From what I can tell, they told him to get lost. That was that. Why do you ask? Do you think the same people that killed Donnelly also killed Herbrit?"

"It's our job to look at all possibilities. You know that."

"I don't know why either man would be killed. It makes no sense."

"Unless," Lacey pointedly said, "Herbrit's death was retribution for Donnelly's death."

"By whom?"

"Well, we were hoping you could help us with that. You have to admit, it's an unbelievable coincidence that you know both these guys that died barely a month apart."

Now the spotlight of suspicion was shining brightly. Lacey was theorizing that Henry believed Herbrit was responsible for Donnelly's death, and that Henry went to Albany on a mission of retribution.

"I don't claim anything coincidental, but I had nothing to do with either of these deaths. And it makes no sense for Dee to want to harm Herbrit."

"If that's true, I'd be concerned if I were you." Lacey's tone was flat.

"That doesn't provide me much comfort, Detective."

"I don't have any comfort to offer you, but telling us everything you know gives us the best chance to unravel this whole thing. And to keep you from harm."

They finished their questioning by confirming that Henry had no more planned trips, and that he would be immediately available if the detectives needed him for further questions. Both detectives left him a business card.

Henry melted into the nearest couch. He stared into space for close to thirty minutes, lost in thought, before finally locking up Aisling's house and heading home. On the ride back to his apartment, he spent nearly as much time looking in his rear view mirror as he did at the road ahead.

He spent the evening mashing through the implications of Herbrit's death. He went online to learn what he could about his murder, but there was nothing on the Albany Times Union's web site. He briefly entertained the notion that the detectives were bluffing, that Herbrit had not been killed at all, but he dismissed the idea. In a smaller city like Albany it was probably not too difficult to suppress the news.

Above all he was concerned about Dee, who must have been in shock after losing the man that was not only her mentor but the closest she had to a father. She had to be devastated. Was she on the run? Did she have anyone to retreat to for safety?

He forced himself to consider whether Dee might have had any possible reason for causing the death of Herbrit. If she was the killer, his world was a crazy one.

Was Henry's life in danger? Clearly his proximity to these two victims was beyond coincidence, as they agreed. Henry knew he would be a fool to ignore the very real danger that surrounded him. Since Donnelly's death he had learned to be vigilant, but now there was no possibility that either death was random.

Henry considered buying a gun, even though he never in his life thought he needed one and did not especially trust himself around them. While he did not dismiss the possibility entirely, he felt sure that if someone wanted him dead, he would be dead before he could ever draw his gun in defense.

As a small matter of insurance, he entered the phone numbers of Lacey and Carpenter into his cell phone, along with 911 under Speed Dial.

He endured a restless night of sleep, asking himself questions that he had no way to answer, scared about his own future. His dreams on this night were fragmented, probably due to the emotionally difficult day he had been through and all the mental energy he invested trying to make sense of the mess around him.

He sensed someone trying to a reach him, a visit from an old friend. He felt warmth and comfort that she was looking in on him.

"You've been through a great deal of trouble lately."

"Aisling, it's you. I've missed you."

"I've missed you as well. I see that you're managing things just fine, keeping my customers and friends satisfied."

"Thanks to you. It's been challenging but very rewarding."

In the comfort of deep sleep Henry did not think to ask basic questions about Aisling's visit. He was only pleased that she was there to talk with him. It was as if she had never left.

After a pause for affection, a sort of telepathic hug, Aisling's tone turned serious. "I'm here with an important message for you, Henry."

"You're going to tell me that I need to be careful, aren't you? That won't exactly surprise me."

"Yes, and for more reasons than you can know."

"I already feel like my life is in danger."

"The same ones that might harm you could cause harm to many, many more souls. You are carrying more weight than you can know. There is no one in the position of being ... in the balance ... as you are now, in the position to change the course of events."

"In the balance? What do you mean? How can I even make a difference if I don't even know who I'm up against?"

"The signs will be there. Trust your instincts, and read them. Keep all of your senses open. When the time comes for action, you will know what to do. I have faith in you, Henry."

He eased from the dream, still reaching for her to return, to clarify her message, but she was out of reach. The message was delivered and she was gone. It had been several months since Aisling left his world, but today it seemed the distance was lessened.

His searching mind would not leave the basic questions unasked. If it was more vision than dream, how could Aisling have come to see him? She was a living mortal just like he was. Unless she had found an unknown gift, traveling through a vast distance into his mind as if she were a spirit from another dimension, then it was likely just an illusion, something created by his subconscious to provide him comfort during a time of worry.

He dwelled on her curious statement about the ones that would harm him also harming many others, There was no escaping the fact that two people he was close to were now dead, only days or weeks after he had first met them. If the same person or people were responsible for both murders, as he was now coming strongly to believe, was it leading to a much broader path of violence?

He remembered his vision, that the people tormenting the Dalai Lama wore the cross of the Church of the Tortured Christ. They had substantial power and influence; perhaps they wanted it all, or at least as much as they could acquire.

When Henry, Herbrit and Dee met the week before, they spent time hashing through theories of the church's interest in the Dalai Lama and whether reincarnation could possibly be involved. None had a single viable theory about why the church would be threatened by a small group of people interested in reincarnation and the teachings of Origen. While the three had stretched their imaginations to think of links between Donnelly's death and their activities, they failed to come up with anything. Now, with the death of Herbrit, there was still nothing to tie all of these events together.

It was almost eight in the evening. There was little he could do to answer his own questions, or calm himself down. He tried television. He tried a few of his favorite web sites, but there was no use. His mind kept coming back to the conundrum that was his life, and back to so many questions with no answers.

Finally he stood up, sure of nothing except that he no longer wished to sit. It was a week night, but he wanted out. He checked online and found an interesting-sounding band in a bar nearby. That usually meant acoustics, something mellow and not too invasive. It was a comfortable place, and probably would allow him a chance to sip some whiskey and get away from his thoughts.

But what of his commitment to vigilance? Leaving the apartment at this time of night would be the exact opposite of his decision be cautious, to watch his every step. After contemplating this dilemma, he concluded that sitting alone in his apartment was only slightly safer than moving around outside. A cautious trip might ease his stress, as long as he stayed in the shadows.

Henry never believed that he would end up being a victim of murder, as Herbrit and Donnelly had been. He recognized that danger was likely nearby, and that the men were killed because somebody wanted them dead more than they could have expected. Donnelly probably did not expect that someone would want him dead, but Herbrit surely did. If someone killed Herbrit despite his awareness, then Henry was a fool to think he was immune.

As a measure of protection he slipped a sheathed knife into one pocket and his cell phone into the other. He chose the back door of his apartment, which led into a well lit alley that offered no place to hide for a would-be attacker. The night was warm and wet, but quiet. He felt he could hear everything.

Henry's first steps into the evening were invigorating. Still, he paced himself. As he came into sight of any shadows or cars, he ducked quietly into shadows, slowly scanning the area ahead. After a slow block of walking and ducking, he gained confidence about walking at a regular clip. Cars drove back and forth on quiet Clarkson Street, but no one looked at him. He saw nothing that drew his suspicion, but he was vigilant.

He walked into the small bar, *Hogan's Hello,* and saw a dozen people and a guitar on a stand in a corner. He found a seat on the corner that was away from the front door with an easy view of everything in the room. He ordered a top-shelf label of whiskey, knowing he would not overdo it this evening. A man and woman slightly older came into the bar and sat near him. They talked and looked around. To his disappointment, they seemed to want to strike up a conversation with him. They were likely a long-married couple that wanted to drink tonight, but not alone with each other on this particular night.

He sipped his drink and engaged with them politely. He was enjoying himself. It felt good to be away from his seclusion. He glanced at replays from the earlier Red Sox game, but avoided showing too much interest because as much as he loved the game, he did not follow the team and could not offer much insight or even a strong opinion, each of which was greatly valued in these parts.

As he relaxed he naturally thought about what a predator might be thinking, which was probably that because of all the stress around him, a man like Henry Chimera would naturally dive toward a drunken escape. He was determined not to be the lamb in that sacrifice, so he sipped his drink slowly, watched what was around him, and enjoyed his time away from his normal routine until it was time to leave.

He ordered a second. He drank the second in about the same time as the first, close to an hour. He ordered ice water. He made eye contact with everyone that entered.

When he decided to leave, he looked all around as he left, inside the bar and out. He walked toward his apartment, and it was easy.

With no warning he felt a fast, intense pain on the back right side of his skull, which went away quickly.

It was a long wait, even boring. He waited for the head pain to subside to allow his eyes to open, to hear, touch, feel, think, and see. It was nothing Henry could rush or control.

He awoke gradually, at first for only a few seconds before he drifted off again. When awake he was aware of the empty room, but sometimes there would be a few sets of eyes away from him that were most definitely riveted on him.

There were times during his 'time out' that his natural curiosity pulled him into what was happening in his life. Over time as he shook off the effects of his thump on the head, he realized his arms and legs were bound. He glanced generally in the direction of a man with dark features, dressed in drab hospital linen.

"Where am I?"

"In our world. Right here and right now. Can you swallow some water?"

He sipped the water and stared at the ceiling. His head ached badly, but he was alive. If these people wanted him dead it would have been so.

"Do you think you could eat something?"

"Fuck no."

He noticed a camera bubble on the ceiling as he faded back into sleep. There were some normal dreams, and he felt himself stirring. Sleep was more difficult, and he saw light behind a covered window.

He had not quite gotten his bearings when he felt two pistons bearing down on his chest. They gripped and lifted, then threw.

His weakened body went flying toward the corner of the room. He rolled once, banged against the wall then landed face-down. His arms and legs were still bound. He felt blood run down his face into his eyes. A knee went into his back as an unseen hand grabbed his hair and pulled his hair back.

"Are you ready for a conversation?"

MASQUERADE

The windows were covered, either to prevent him from seeing where he was being held or to prevent neighbors from seeing inside. He could see a glimpse of bright light around the edge of the dark curtain. It was daytime, probably early morning. He was upright in a chair. His hands and feet were bound. His back and neck combined to form a long, dull ache. He was mildly dehydrated and had some semblance of hunger, although he had no idea how long it had been since he last ate. He felt mostly dazed, not entirely awake.

After several minutes in a haze between sleep and confusion, a man came into the room. He was tall and imposing with a cloth that entirely covered his face. He wore jeans and a flannel shirt pulled partway up his arms. On his muscular forearm Henry could make out a tattoo, but he could not discern the image. He pulled a stool from behind Henry and planted it a few feet before him. He sat and straddled the stool, then folded his arms.

"Talk about what you've been doing lately and why you've been doing it."

Henry stared briefly at the man, unsure what to make of his questioning. "I don't know how long I've been here, but I suspect I've been spending most of my time with you."

"Don't be a smart ass. Try again."

"I've been spending time with my clients, doing readings. I work for nobody but them."

"Continue."

"I'm a medium. People come to me to connect with family and friends. Those are my clients, and those are the people I spend time with."

"Who else besides your clients?"

"Nobody. I don't have much of a social life."

"Lying to me is not in your best interest, Mr. Chimera. You can make this go quickly and easily, or slowly and painfully. It's entirely up to you. Who else have you been talking with lately?"

"Nobody that I care to share with you. I've done nothing illegal, and I've done nothing to harm anyone."

The man whipped a slap across Henry's face that made him rock back in his chair, nearly falling backward. His ears rang and his face and nose stung. He felt a trickle of blood fall slowly from one nostril.

"This isn't amateur shit, son. We'll get out of you what we want to get out of you. It's only a matter of how much of my time you waste, and how energetic I need to be to get it from you. I had a long sleep and a good breakfast, so I feel like I have the energy to stay with this for quite a long while. If I don't get what I want today, I'll try again tomorrow, but today will be a long one."

After lifting his shoulder to his bleeding nose, Henry shook off the bad start. "Everything I've been doing has come from my work, which is new to me. I go for runs, then I go back to work. I go to the grocery store, then I sleep, then I go to work. That's the truth. Now who would like to know?"

"You'll know that when I want you to know. Now I want to hear about every person, aside from your pathetic customers, who you've spent time with over the past few weeks."

"Why the hell should I? If you're going to kill me anyway, why should I tell you anything?"

The man looked at him with a half smile. "Did I say I was going to kill you?"

"No, but a few people around me have been dying lately. I'm guessing my number is up next."

"Why do you think that is?"

He used the word 'we'. The last time he had a vision of an abduction, it turned out to be members of the Church of the Tortured Christ. He identified them by their distinctive medals, a white gold cross with a red gemstone in the center. Henry discreetly glanced at the man's neck. His neck was bare.

"I was trying to figure that out when you guys kidnapped me."

"How did you plan to find that out?"

"I didn't exactly have a great plan. I'm no detective, and lately it's been a matter of trying to keep myself from harm. Obviously that didn't work out well."

He was trying to steal time while trying to gain any sense of who the man was. Was he from the Church of the Tortured Christ? If so, he had a twisted way of exercising his faith. Were they Origenists? He would not have expected the bully treatment from people that were aligned with Herbrit. Were they cops? This seemed the most plausible, that to pull information from him about the recent murders, the police would have him detained in this discreet location, where no rules applied. Or was there yet another group that somehow had an interest in his business?

"So it seems that harm follows you."

"I'm not very good at harming others. If you're suggesting that I had anything to do with these murders, you're mistaken."

"Of course you would say that. But what you're not saying is that you've recently spent time with both men who were killed. You're lying and we know it. There's still time to tell the truth."

Henry's challenge was to keep his contact with Dee and Herbrit from this man. Herbrit was already dead, and the last thing Henry wanted to do was disclose his contact with Dee. Henry was prepared to protect her in any way he could, even if meant sacrificing his own life.

"You know what I know."

The man's face grew red. Henry braced for whatever might come his way, but instead of hitting Henry again, the man stood and turned toward the door. He exited, slamming the door behind him.

Henry heard muffled, angry words between men, probably about what was next for him. The man who had been with him seemed to be the louder of the two voices.

He prayed. He closed his eyes and asked for his death, if it had to come, to be as fast and as painless as possible. It was impossible to keep track of the time in his weakened state as he waited.

Finally the man came bursting back into the room. Another man was with him this time, also wearing a full-face mask, smaller than the first man.

"You're moving." The large man grabbed Henry's shirt and pulled him backward to the floor, the chair tipping to the ground. With Henry on the floor, the man untied his ankles from the chair. With his hands still bound, the man lifted Henry by the shirt to his feet. He swayed and wobbled. He had not stood on his feet for hours.

"Start walking." The larger man had his hand on the back of Henry's shirt as he forced him out the door, to the left, then into another room. The door closed behind them. Straight ahead was his fate.

In one corner of the room a thick rope hung from a metal hook on the ceiling. On the end of the rope was a noose. On the floor directly below the noose was a wooden box.

The two men allowed the scene to sink in before the larger one spoke. "Are you ready to do a little more talking, Mister Chimera?"

"I'd prefer that my remaining acquaintances stay alive, thank you. My business is my business."

"It won't be your business much longer if you don't start talking."

Henry said nothing.

"Fine, have it your way." The larger man shoved Henry toward the corner. The second man pulled a dark linen hood from his back pocket and approached Henry. He separated the cloth and pulled it over Henry's head. He could see nothing, but was able to breathe.

"Step up."

Henry thought about head-butting one of the men and making a run for it, but abandoned that idea when he tested the strength of the rope around his wrists. If death was to come, he would accept it with dignity.

The man guided him closer to the box and he stepped up. The noose went around the hood and his neck and tightened.

"A word to the wise," the man growled, "you might want to stay on the box."

He heard the two walk out, slamming the door behind them. Henry was able to breathe but there was little slack. Clearly if he weakened and fell, he would hang. If the box was to fall away because of his diminishing strength, he was in trouble.

He found small encouragement that he was still alive at all. Perhaps they did not want him dead at all. Even so, what if he were to pass out and fall off the box? Would the men even notice that he was strangling? He needed to put all of his effort into not finding out those answers.

Minutes seemed to drip into hours. His legs and ankles and feet throbbed in pain as time went on. He would begin to doze off, but before very long the wobble of the box and the noose around his neck startled him back to a rigid position.

He forced himself to think of things other than his predicament, such as how long he had been gone. His clients would be showing up for readings, only to find the doors to Aisling's house locked with no one in sight. The more time that passed by, more clients would assume that he gave up the business without notice. Each day meant an increasing erosion of the client base that Aisling had worked so hard to build up, which was obviously very important to her when she chose him as her successor. The longer he was in the hands of these captors, the more difficult it would be to recover what she had built over years.

Perhaps a client would call the police, knowing that Henry's absence was completely out of character. If that were to happen, the police would likely have no idea of where to begin their investigation.

If he were to die after this disappearance, would anyone even care? He had no wife, no children, not even any extended family that he knew of. His death would be like his life, nearly inconsequential. Growing up as an orphan he thought he knew what true loneliness felt like, but he never truly considered the absence of a difference, the void created from growing up lonely and remaining lonely. This was true despair, and he had no choice but to face it.

He turned his thoughts to more productive uses, thinking through other possible scenarios and causes for recent tragic events. For his captors to come after him so angrily, there were only two possibilities. Either they believed he was behind the two deaths, or they were the killers and he would die next.

Dee and Herbrit had mentioned 'others,' presumably other Origenists, but could they possibly be aligned with such thugs? If they were police, would they resort to these tactics, and even think they could get away with them? If they were from the church, how could they possibly believe him to be a threat?

If they were indeed from the Church of the Tortured Christ, what were they after? Could they really be behind the deaths of his two friends? From his visions he was convinced that they were not above seriously illegal activities, such as kidnapping one of the most prominent religious figures in the world, but they had not shown the willingness to murder. An organization of their might and power surely needed to go into the trenches to get what they wanted, he reasoned. If they were capable of kidnapping such a high profile person as the Dalai Lama, his abduction would be a mere blip.

Henry's ankles felt like they were about to explode. He continued to keep his thoughts and ideas flowing now as a matter of self-preservation, to stay alert. Allowing the fog to take over would be suicide. The struggle to avoid dropping his weight began to steal his energy, and having the hood over his head made the challenge more difficult. His senses were slowly depleting. His legs wobbled more often. The pain in his lower legs felt like dozens of razor blades pressed against his muscles and tendons. Strength was slowly slipping away. No visions came to him this time, no visits from Aisling, no voices. He began to face the real possibility of death. When it came it would be a relief.

Darkness, then a sharp noise. Footsteps coming his way. The same firm hand on the back of his shirt. The noose came off his neck. He crumbled off the box as he let out a groan that sounded like a wounded dog. The firm hand allowed him to fall to the floor with something less than the full force of his body.

The sense of relief in his legs was immediate. The sharp pain was replaced by a dull but still profound ache. This pain was manageable, even welcome. The hood was left on his head as the man spoke to him

"This is just the beginning, Henry. There are so many ways to make your life unbearable. Now tell me what I need to know."

"I have nothing of interest to you."

"Then what's the harm in telling us who you've been with?"

"Because sometimes I spend time with people I care about. I'd rather die than have you anywhere near them."

"That's very noble of you. We have no interest in harming anyone else. Our reasons for this unpleasant treatment are all about protecting our interests. This is war that we didn't start and didn't ask for. But we're in it, and we will fight back."

"Who are you?"

"You'll learn that in time, providing you cooperate."

"I'm not giving up my friends to you."

"Has it occurred to you that the 'friends' you're protecting may be beyond your protection, beyond help even?"

Henry assumed they were talking about Herbrit, not realizing he already knew Herbrit had been murdered. His strongest, fiercest hope was that they were not referring to Dee.

"Yes, that has occurred to me. I've done no harm to anyone."

"Yes, well, not everyone is so convinced of that. That, my friend, is the reason you're here."

"Since you already think I"m guilty, there's not much more to talk about is there?"

The man let out an impatient sigh. The conversation was not going the way he intended.

Henry could hear the man stand up. "Perhaps it's time to take our conversation in a different direction."

Henry said nothing. The man made no attempt to stand Henry up again, to his great relief. Instead he pushed Henry down to the floor. He reached down and pulled a rope tightly around Henry's ankles. The intense pain returned.

"It looks somebody has some swelling. It doesn't look like you'll be making a break for it."

The man tied the other end of the rope to the restraints around Henry's wrists, then left the room.

Henry was nearly unable to move in any direction without pain. Despite his frustration and exhaustion, he drew strength from the knowledge that if they really wanted him dead it probably would have already happened. The only piece of information he had that could be remotely valuable to them was Dee's identity. Herbrit was already dead, and they probably knew it. If they were the ones that killed him, then perhaps he and Dee were the two remaining pieces to exterminate. This would mean that Dee was still on the loose, which gave him all the reason he needed to keep from talking.

Lying on the floor gave him the first chance in hours to fade into sleep. He went quickly into unconsciousness.

The familiar Irish lilt came to him.

"How are you holding up, Henry?"

"Fine, Aisling, fine. The pain was unlike anything I've ever felt, but pain is temporary. I'm managing."

"Do you realize the troubles you're involved with?"

"I suppose I do, but there isn't much I can do to change the situation."

"The real trouble is deeper than what you're experiencing now. It goes deeper, much deeper."

"How do you mean?"

"I cannot reveal that to you, son. It is for you to learn. Keep your eyes and ears open. Things are not as they appear. There is a Judas in the house."

She faded.

Some time later, Henry heard the familiar clunking of the big man's footsteps coming his way. This roused him before the door opened.

The man reached down and untied the rope from Henry's ankles.

"Up you go. I have someone I'd like you to see."

He kept the hood on Henry's head while he led him down the hall to another room. He opened the door and pushed Henry inside.

The man removed the hood. In front of Henry's eyes was the one sight he dreaded seeing.

AWAKENING

Sitting in a chair, tied up with a gag over her mouth, was Dee. Henry stared at her, frozen. He had already come to terms with the possibility that he might not ever leave this place, but the idea of Dee meeting the same fate filled him with despair.

For the first time Henry was able to see the face of his captor. The man had light hair and a piercing gaze. His face did not seem accustomed to smiling, but now it showed a smirk. He seemed to enjoy watching Henry simmer.

"Now then, does this change what you'd like to tell us?"

Dee looked at Henry with pain in her eyes. Henry was unsure what he could possibly say or not say that would keep Dee from harm. He tried to weigh whether there was anything to be gained by revealing that he had indeed been spending time with Dee and Herbrit. She was already a captive; would his revelation about the time they spent together put her in more danger?

"It does, and it's something important."

"What's that?"

"Before I only suspected but now I know. You are indeed the piece of shit I suspected you were."

The smirk left the man's face.

"You already know everything you've been trying to pull out of me, just as I figured. So you've been making my life miserable for the last few days for absolutely no reason."

"Oh, we're quite certain you still have things you're hiding things from us."

"You're wrong again. You've been right about nothing. *Nothing!*"

The smirk was back. "Well, we'll find out, won't we?"

"Look, you already have the one person I was trying to keep away from you and you have me. Herbrit, the only other person I'd want to protect, is already dead. The cops have me under suspicion. It's you who's hiding something."

"That's not the case, I assure you, but it does serve as a clever distraction for you. Two people you've been in touch with in recent weeks are now dead and you accuse US of killing them? You chose to contact these people for unknown reasons. Who put you up to it? Did you do it on your own? I hope you were at least paid well, even if you never can spend the money."

"I told you, I'm a medium." Henry glared at the man. "I'm interested in everything having to do with the afterlife, especially after events of the last few weeks. These people obviously know a lot about it; things I don't know."

"Go on." The man sat in a chair in front of the door while Henry continued standing.

"Obviously I met with Herbrit and ... this woman, one of your other victims, over the last few weeks." Henry avoided giving up Dee's name in case it was worth anything to him.

"We've just been getting to know each other over the past month or so. Each time I was with her I was also with Herbrit. That's it. That's all I was keeping from you. Is that so important that you would treat us like animals?"

"We did know that already, which proves that you're lying."

Henry was unable to conceal his contempt. "I suppose protecting people who are important to you is a notion that vermin wouldn't understand."

The man glared back at Henry. Dee looked at Henry too, surprised.

The man's smug smile returned. "You've demonstrated that you're very good at holding back information, even if it means it results in some personal discomfort to you."

"Discomfort? What you put me through for God knows how many hours is called 'forced standing.' It's a torture technique that's SO effective because the pain increases by the minute. Oh, and it doesn't really leave marks, so when I'm dead no one could prove what you did to me. You propped me up on a flimsy box with a noose around my neck. 'Discomfort' my ass."

Dee snapped her head in the direction of her captor, eyes glaring.

"Fine, call it what you like." The man looked at Dee. His smirk was replaced by an earnest expression, the first time Henry remembered seeing anything other than scorn.

"Your suffering is duly noted. If it turns out you're really no harm to us then we'll make things right, but I doubt that. You're a crafty one. Who knows what you're keeping up your sleeve."

Henry looked impassively at him. "We all know who's in control of this situation."

"Yes, well, this has been a nice little chat but I think our time is up."

He arose toward Henry, grabbed the back of his shirt and roughly led him out the door toward the same room he was in before. He tied Henry's wrists tightly to the back of the chair. Henry winced, trying to allow blood to flow. The man walked slowly to a seat across the room. Henry noticed for the first time a mirror embedded on a side wall, behind where he was previously positioned.

"Here's the deal, Henry. I'm not going to fuck around with you any more. If you don't tell us the truth, we will kill your friend Dee. She'll be dead inside the hour. I will personally put a knife to her throat and watch as the life drains from her. Oh, and you will watch every drop of blood pour out of her. I'll prop your eyes open if I need to. Are we clear?"

"Clear. Still clear. What's it matter what I say to you? You've already decided to kill us both."

"That is simply not true, Henry." The man crossed his legs and leaned back in his chair. "Your words can save her life and save your life. If you know anything at all about noble causes, you understand that extreme measures are sometimes necessary. If you can convince me that you've told me everything, then both you and Dee will walk out of here on your own. So talk. If you have nothing to hide, it shouldn't be difficult."

He was not sure how long he had been in this house but it had been days with only the minimum amount of food and water. Knowing that Dee was in the other room, with her life perhaps in the balance, provided all the energy Henry needed.

"Fine, I'll take you at your word. I don't believe a word you say, but I'll do what I can to save Dee.

So Henry talked. He held nothing back about his activities with this man that he despised. He talked, thorough and descriptive, about his contacts with Aisling, with Donnelly, with Herbrit, with the church, with Lacey, even with his customers, the more interesting ones and those not as much. The man occasionally interrupted with a question, but otherwise allowed Henry to roam freely between his experiences of the past several months. Henry spoke for nearly half an hour, hiding nothing. When he finished his oratory, he melted into his chair. Any remaining energy was now gone

The man sighed and leaned back. "Very impressive performance, Henry. Now of all that fine storytelling, I heard nothing of who might be trying to exterminate us."

Something about the comment seemed odd to Henry, even in his reduced mental state.

"If someone is trying to exterminate you, then I suppose I'm expendable too." Henry's voice was weak. He had little fight left.

The man rose and grabbed Henry from behind, hoisting him to his feet. Henry was powerless to resist. He was able to stand, but was able to do little else with his hands tied behind. The man pushed him toward the box.

"If you have any desire left to live, you'll get up on the box." The man pulled a black hood from his back pocket and yanked it down over Henry's head.

Henry straightened his back, turning slowly to the man. "What do you mean by 'us'? You said, 'someone is looking to exterminate us. Are you with the Origenists?"

The door burst open. He heard multiple footsteps rushing into the room.

"Enough, Lars!" A woman's voice shrieking, familiar. "This ends now!"

Dee's voice! Through the fog of exhaustion, Henry's first thought was that she had somehow escaped and come to rescue him. But she called him Lars! His suspicion was correct. This was a ploy, and Dee was a participant.

"How dare you interrupt the process! This cannot be undone! You've ruined days of hard work!"

"He gave in and told you everything I told you. This is absurd." Dee and his captor were on the same side. Henry felt nauseous.

Lars spoke firmly to Dee. "Let's discuss this privately." He pulled Henry roughly back to the chair, tying his hands in back while keeping the hood in place. There was the intense discomfort again, but he was too exhausted to care.

After they left the room, he heard muffled voices speaking at a high volume, but he could not hear what they were saying. It went on for several minutes as he drifted in and out of consciousness.

When he roused, it was as though he was coming out of anesthesia. Every sense was distorted. He opened his eyes to see a soft light and an image sitting, nondescript. There was soft jazz playing. He instinctively moved his arms to the side in a stretching motion and they moved, freely but with difficulty. Every muscle that moved was in some form of pain from exertion, restraint, or atrophy. He ran his hands around his head and neck, stretched his legs out. There was tremendous relief in simply moving his torso and limbs in any direction he chose.

"Take it slowly, Henry. You've been through a lot."

Her voice. Its presence brought him comfort.

"Thanks for noticing."

As he gained focus, he noticed her soft smile. "It would've been hard not to notice."

Slowly Henry was gaining back his senses and even his short term memory. He was groggy, but beginning to piece together the sequence of his waking moments during the last few days.

"It just feels good to move."

She poured him cold ice water from a pitcher, and placed a bowl of fresh, sliced fruit in front of him. "Drink water please, and eat, but take it slow. Build your strength back."

After a few quiet minutes rehydrating and allowing his blood sugar to rise, he silently thought through the many questions he had. He silently considered the two likely possibilities, that she was a true Origenist, fighting for survival alongside others that included this man Lars, or that they were working to bring the group down. If the latter were true, Dee was not to be trusted. She was the good cop to Lars' bad cop. Sweet and lovely, but every bit as evil.

As he replenished, she waited patiently by his side. Surely she knew what was coming.

"So do you want to tell me why we're both sitting here?"

"We're under attack. We're in a battle that we didn't ask for, and we don't even know who the enemy is."

"Rewind," Henry answered quickly. "First of all, who is 'we.' Who are you with?"

"You know very well who I'm with, Henry. David and I explained in great detail about who we are."

"I know what you told me, Dee. Your name is Dee, by the way, correct?"

She laughed softly. "Yes, it's Dee. I haven't lied to you, but I'm guilty of misleading you that I was a captive too. I'm not proud about the way you were treated, nor the deception I was a part of yesterday, but I didn't lie to you about our group and our goals. Neither did David."

"You and David convinced me your movement is peaceful, that it plans to change minds through education and outreach, nothing controversial. So what's changed?"

"What's changed?" Her tone sharpened. "David was murdered, that's what changed. That raised the stakes by a lot. I'm sorry you've been pulled into this, especially in this way, but we're all in this whether we like it or not."

"That makes two of us," Henry said with a snarl. "There's been nothing but death and pain since Donnelly called. I was warned about negative energies. This is it. You guys are it."

Henry's words caught Dee between the eyes. She hesitated, hurt and unsure how to respond. She spoke slowly. "I guess I didn't see you as much a victim of this whole thing as we are, but Jesus, you are."

Her hand came to her eyes, and there were tears. If she was acting again, Henry thought, this is convincing.

"We didn't mean for any of this to happen," she said. "We asked for none of it. This may be hard to believe, but you found us at the worst possible time, just as we're struggling for our lives, struggling to survive."

She straightened in her chair as a teary, light smile appeared.

"In spite of all this, I'm glad we met you. I convinced David that he should hear what you had to say, and neither of us regretted the decision. The second time we met you was David's idea. Your perspective was just what we needed. It was like you showed up at just the right time, when we were starting to wonder if it was even worth it. You asked some of the fundamental questions that reminded us of where we started."

Henry listened warily. "Well, I'm glad I was able to keep things interesting, but if David trusted me and you trusted me, why wasn't that enough for the evil prick who's been terrorizing me for the last week, or however long it's been?"

"I don't agree with the way you were treated," Dee said. "I tried everything I could to talk them out of it, short of quitting the group, but the others convinced me that we had no choice but to guard against our enemies. Obviously we have some very serious enemies, although we're not sure what we've done to deserve them."

"I'm not your enemy," Henry said

"I know that," Dee replied, "but at least some of my colleagues think your presence puts us at risk."

"Meaning what, exactly?"

"Whether you agree or not, it is possible that you might have drawn our enemies to us. We don't know how, but it's possible. Self preservation is our top priority right now, and you're a link to the outside that makes people uncomfortable. Because of that, you've gotten the full force of our attention."

"I hope you realize," Henry said sharply, "that cuts both ways."

"Excuse me?" Dee's olive eyes flared.

"Think about what I've seen," Henry said. "Before this little vacation with your thug, one of my clients was murdered with absolutely no warning. Then a few weeks later, I learned from a cop that David was murdered. Obviously somebody is after you guys, and of course I'm a suspect. The next thing I know, I've been kidnapped and I'm being brutalized, and what do you know? It turns out that it's the Origenists! So the cops think I'm out to get you guys for some unexplained reason, you guys think I'm out to get you, and I'm taken away from my life against my will! So while you're busy being suspicious of me, from where I sit, you guys are the ones who seem intent on destroying MY life. It sounds like the cops should be here talking to *you*."

Henry leaned forward in his chair toward Dee. "Who's to say an Origenist didn't kill Donnelly? And if that person killed John, why not Herbrit? Maybe somebody in your group thought David needed to be killed because an amateur like me was able to find him!"

"Don't be ridiculous," she said, rising and walking toward the kitchen. "David was our leader, our inspiration. I'm not even sure we can continue without him. Look Henry, I'm sorry for what you've been through, really I am. Lars' tactics went way overboard, and I'm not sure if you'll ever get over that, or if I will, but he and others felt we had little choice. It was very rough on you, but now we know - most of us, anyway - that you don't mean us harm."

She poured milk over bran cereal, which she carefully placed in front of Henry. "Please eat this."

He was not yet convinced that Dee's kindness was anything more than a 'good cop' approach. At any second, he thought, Lars could come bursting in with fresh ideas for inflicting pain.

"So where do we go from here? Can I go home, or will you and your peace-loving friends require more of my time?"

"We'll talk about it. You can't know about our location. If you return home, will you feel safe? People around you are dying, Henry, and we don't know who's responsible. Maybe you can convince yourself you're safe. I can't. I worry for your safety."

"As an alternative, are you offering me protection or am I being optimistic?"

"I'm offering you a chance to meet with other members of our group. I have no idea where that will lead, but the fact that you made it through Lars' rough treatment did not go unnoticed by any of us. I'm not the only one that feels we owe you a lot for what we've put you through."

"I'll think about it."

"Take your time. Rest more." Dee left the room.

As Henry contemplated the offer, he considered what he would be going back to. It would certainly include a business that was probably in a desperate situation, which would require his attention to rebuild while constantly looking over his shoulder. That could be a treacherous situation at best, but if he stayed with this group, could that even be a normal life? Of the group of Origenists, so far he had only met Dee and Lars, and of course Herbrit. He would make his decision once he understood the composition of the whole group, or what was left of it.

He prodded her with questions about how they operated. Were they always on the run? Did they live as a community? How many in the group?

As Dee tended to his returning strength, whenever he engaged her in conversation she kept it brief. She painted a picture of a small group of people who deeply believed in their cause but were trying to understand their future after losing their mentor. Despite Henry's prying, Dee make no mention of their progress about who would be the new organizer or how their agenda might change. Henry asked whether Lars the Torturer was lobbying to become the group's new leader. She bristled when he said that would be their worst possible decision. Her expression made it clear that it was not a path she wanted to see her group take.

During their frequent visits, he also tried to learn as much as he could about her personal life, including her occupation. His questions were met with polite and sometimes creative deflections, which became a source of fun banter between them. During various conversations he guessed that she worked in an animal shelter, or a spy for the federal government, or a guard in a women's prison. She laughed at most of his inquiries as she playfully encouraged him to keep guessing. He tried to prolong their visits by striking up conversations from the philosophical to the inane. She remained reserved in their conversations, but never seemed to be in a hurry to leave.

Each day she reminded him that the others were waiting to speak with him, to understand whether he would leave them seeking to destroy them, help them, or put them behind him for good. In their struggle, she continually told him, there was no deadline, only their modest goal of surviving to continue to spread their belief system under their terms, no matter how much time that would require.

As he pondered his own future, it seemed to be a decision of whether or not to commit to helping this group of damaged believers, and if so to what extent. He was confident that with some extra effort in the short term, he could resume his work as a medium. It would require many phone calls to upset customers, apologies, and perhaps a few carefully formed lies that would explain his absence, but he was confident it could be done.

His choice became clear. Rising above all other factors in his decision, Dee was the one who drew him to their cause. He would align with the Origenists because he believed in their cause but only on the outside, if they would allow it. If Lars was to be their leader, there would be no more contact. He announced that he was ready to meet with the larger group.

She brought him clothes she thought would be his size, and he insisted they would be small. When they fit him perfectly, he looked at the waist size of the pants. To his amazement, it was a size 30, which he had not worn since high school. His time in this place had taken its toll.

When the time came, Dee noticed immediately that Henry was very much on edge about the meeting.

"You have nothing to worry about Henry, we're a very peaceful group."

"Yeah, you keep telling me that."

She made no attempt to conceal her annoyance. "I can only tell you so many times how sorry I am. After a while it's up to you to forgive us."

"Let me see who I'm dealing with first."

Each was satisfied with this middle ground.

Dee led Henry down the long hallway. The house was much larger than Henry thought. His room had been in a far end of a sprawling split level home that appeared to be on a large property. No neighbors were visible through the large windows that offered a panoramic view of nearby woods and a small pond. It was a serene setting for a group that professed to be all about peace.

She led him into a large, spacious room, a combination eating and living space. The kitchen was modern and well equipped, and the living space was filled with couches surrounding a large television mounted to the wall. The Red Sox were playing at Kansas City. Soft music was playing. The fifteen people in the room all appeared to be somewhere in the range of their thirties to their mid-fifties. People held wine glasses and were relaxed, speaking quietly as he approached. Their conversations hushed as he entered the room. Their stares were a mix of anxiety and curiosity.

"Would you like a glass of wine?" Dee was smiling, but her nervousness showed.

"No thanks. Water is fine."

Dee marched to the kitchen, avoiding being the center of attention. After setting a tall glass of ice water before him, the soft music was all that could be heard. No one was sure who would speak first. Henry sat on a high stool near the kitchen, looking around at the diverse group assembled. As he gazed around the room, some smiled nervously, others avoided his eyes completely. He made no attempt to smile in return, and felt no desire to engage with anyone in the room. His cold stares as he studied everyone the room made most uncomfortable.

On the opposite end of the large room was Lars, defiant as ever. He was the only other person present carrying any sort of hostile demeanor. Henry made a point of glaring directly at him, and holding his glare. Others in the room noticed. Dee finally spoke.

"Henry, I've said this to you privately and now I'll say it in the company of my colleagues. I'm sorry for the treatment you've endured during the past few weeks, but we are under siege. Anyone who cannot be proven as a friend must be assumed to be an enemy. We know there are people who are looking to harm us. It's an undeniable fact. No one in this room wants to see further damage to our cause, nor for our message to die off, so we were hard on you. I believe without any question that you mean us no harm."

Lars crossed his arms, now staring at Dee. A woman near Lars spoke to him in a quiet voice and he shook his head, not changing his expression.

"Thanks for saying that," Henry replied. He glanced at Lars. "I know the coward in the back of the room doesn't share your opinion, but I am curious to hear from others."

There were a few awkward throats cleared, then an older man gestured to speak. Henry guessed him to be about sixty.

"My name is Richard. From what I understand, Mister Chimera, our friend Lars was quite hard on you. That makes none of us proud but as Dee has indicated, this isn't high school. All of us here are in danger, and we cannot be sure if you're a friend, an enemy, or merely a passing acquaintance. Even the latter could be very dangerous. Some of us could lose our lives because you were in the wrong place at the wrong time.

"It would appear that we now have very powerful, ruthless enemies. Each one of us has felt things change. Even getting here to meet with you was incredibly complicated. Again, we're very sorry for the suffering you've been through, but you just have to get over that. We've suffered too. Some of us feel the need to stay in hiding indefinitely. Despite all that, you're here now, we're here now, and we need to find an acceptable path forward."

Henry listened quietly, pausing to choose the right words. "What you all have been through is not right, and it's not fair, however there's one big difference between my situation and yours. I didn't join your group, and I'm not here willingly. *You kidnapped me.* I'm very sorry that you all have some angry enemies, but the biggest threat to me right now seems to be you people."

A woman spoke up. "My name is Rachel. What did you think you were getting into when you became a medium? Did you think that by getting into issues that affected human souls in various states, that you'd have immunity on through the whole process? I understand that John Donnelly stumbled into your business and stirred things up, and that led you here. I bet you wish that didn't happen but guess what? We wish it didn't happen either. But it did and here we are, so please drop the 'poor little me' bullshit. We're trying to figure out if we have a future, as a group or even as individuals. Our best mind was just murdered. He was the guy that always had the plan, always kept us going. Now he's dead, and you're one of the last people that talked with him. Perhaps you can get past your hurt feelings and just tell us the question we all want to know. When you leave here, can we trust that you won't get us all killed?"

Henry was invigorated. Instead of someone tending to his feelings or trying to tear down his resistance, here was someone that explaining plainly what was on their minds.

"Thanks for the honesty. The fact is, I'm not on your side."

There was an uneasy silence around the room.

"And I'm not on the other side, whatever that side is. I don't want any part in your battle."

There were surprised looks all around the room. Some sneered toward Lars, others turned toward the floor.

Lars finally spoke. "You became involved when Donnelly approached you, and you stayed involved when you tracked David down. The moment that man walked into your web, you were in this game. You absolutely signed up for this when you picked this profession. If you're a plumber, you'll see some shit now and then. You're a medium. Stop pretending you didn't realize things might get serious. Nobody's buying it."

"Let's say we have it your way," Henry replied. "What were you expecting, that I would join your group or die? Let me guess: that's exactly what you told these people right before I walked in. If I'm allowed to leave here and resume my life, everyone here will be at greater risk. Did I get that right?"

There were more awkward glances around the room. Lars kept his stare on Henry. Dee was the first to speak.

"It's either that you join with us, or you go away. If you go away, then have nothing to do with us. Never mention that you've heard of us. We don't exist. Otherwise, if you decide this is something you want to be a part of, you have to explain why. What can you do for us, and why do you care about our mission?"

The expressions around the room showed agreement with Dee's summary.

Henry spoke calmly. "Well, it would be easy to put this experience behind me. As for giving anything up about you, it doesn't feel like I have much of value to tell anyone.

"Look, I appreciate what you guys stand for. I believe everything you believe in, other than the way you reacted to David's death. There's no question in my mind that the teachings of Origen are important, and that Christians have been in denial for almost two thousand years. Where I'm puzzled is in trying to understand what CHANGE you guys are holding out hope for. Do you really think you can get all the Christian churches to change a foundational part of their faith? It won't happen. The Catholics can't even find a way to make women priests or allow priests to marry, after all this time. Do you think they'll ever admit, 'Oh sorry, that whole Trinity thing? We got that wrong.' What you guys seem to be suggesting won't happen for centuries at the soonest, probably not ever.

"Nothing," Dee spoke. "We expect them to do nothing. We're not looking to change their belief system, their faith, their tradition, nothing. When the Mormons came along and laid their beliefs over the church, they didn't change a thing in their doctrine, and the Mormons still exist today. That's all we're expecting, to be ignored. We're no threat to them. That's the whole point."

"That seems reasonable," Henry said quietly, "but I gather you have no idea how to make that happen."

"Exactly," Dee said. "We don't know who's after us or why they care what we think."

"Who is it you suspect the most? The Church of the Tortured Christ?"

"Yes," Dee was quick to reply. "That's who we suspect the most."

"Does everyone agree?" Henry looked around the room. No one spoke but the expressions were revealing. Some looked directly at Henry and nodded. Others, including Lars, folded their arms without revealing their suspicions.

"I gather there's some disagreement over this. Can anyone please explain who else might be behind all this? Any theories?"

"No theories." It was a young woman in her mid-thirties with strong features and a dark, attractive demeanor. "I just don't see any reason for these Evangelicals to target us. Sure they're out there, really high profile, advertising a lot and growing fast, but I'm not convinced that our presence is anything more than a blip on their radar screen. How would they even know we exist?."

"I agree." To everyone's surprise, Lars spoke up evenly and without emotion. "I've been saying for weeks, that church is too big to even notice us. It would be a waste of time and energy to come after us. Their competition is from the Catholics, the Baptists, the Mormons. We have nothing they want or need."

"Then why the hell did you come after me with such a vengeance?" Henry snapped.

"It wasn't vengeance, it was protection. I don't know if you're with that church or not, but I'm still not convinced that *some* group didn't put you up to up to infiltrating us."

Henry snorted at this but said nothing.

"Whether or not it's you that's after us, someone is," Lars said. "As you're heard clearly, we can take no chances. If you mean us no harm and have never meant to harm us, then I will apologize, but someone is after us, so the apologies can wait until later."

Henry chose a neutral tact. "So Your strategy is to hide until all this blows over?"

The woman spoke. "We haven't decided on our strategy. That's not a simple task, as you will appreciate given that our most senior member was just slaughtered."

"Yes, I understand that. So tell me, why the secrecy? You had one important member of your group murdered, and another guy was killed who was only trying to learn about your beliefs. Why go underground? Why not just go to the authorities for help? If you shine a light on what you've been through, maybe your enemies will be less likely to come after you."

Dee chose to answer. "We had no intentions of going underground, but none of us were the victims of any crime until David was killed. In recent months a few of us noticed people following us, especially around the time we'd meet. When we complained about it to the cops, they just considered us a paranoid cult. Instead of protection, we got visits from detectives asking pointed questions about crimes and other things that have nothing to do with us."

"I don't suppose the investigating officer was Detective Lacey, by chance."

Dee stared at him with surprise. "It was indeed."

"He's the one who investigated Donnelly's death, and the guy that questioned me."

Lars spoke to Henry. "Tell them what you told me, that you met Grandby's daughter."

"I met her. She seemed fine but nervous, like you guys are nervous. She told me that she reported to Lacey that she felt some people were snooping on them. It sounds like they've been on edge in that church, just like you guys."

Dee was quick to speak. "That sounds like a cover to me, like they're saying what they want the cops to hear. If somebody's spying on them, they have the money to go figure out who it is. I don't buy any part of that."

"You never quit, Dee." It was Lars, stepping forward to the center of the room. "They have no motivation to come after us. They're just bible thumpers, interested in building up their power and their base. We're the least of their concerns."

Dee appeared troubled. "I don't know. I can't explain it. There's just something about them that worries me. A lot."

Lars stifled a smile as he replied. "Then why not send your friend Henry in to see what they know? He's already met one of the top people in the church. He's in the perfect position to get in the middle of their business."

Dee turned in her chair completely toward Lars. "That's an absurd idea, and completely reckless. Haven't you already done enough to this guy? Now you're looking to get him killed?"

Lars answered quickly. "What danger would he be in? They have no knowledge that he's been with us. It would accomplish one thing, convince you guys that the Church of the Tortured Christ doesn't give a shit about us, and we shouldn't give a shit about them. What do you say, Henry? Are you up for proving your innocence?"

Henry's response was fast. "Why don't you do it? I didn't get in to meet her by magic. I stopped by her office after Donnelly's death and told her secretary I'd wait until she could see me. We had a nice conversation. Even someone like you could probably get in to see her, as long is you didn't, you know, threaten to kidnap and torture her. I bet you could manage that if you tried."

Lars ignored the pointed comment. "Well, there's one big difference, Henry. She knew who you were before you even walked in there. You told me yourself."

Dee looked at Henry. "Is that true?

"She knew who Donnelly was, and knew he had come to see me," he said. "She didn't seem to know why, so I explained that to her, and she didn't seem to have much to say about it. Considering our conversation, it would be very odd if I were to go back there pretending to be interested in their faith. I can't think of a way to make that seem normal. Again Lars, why don't you do it? They probably don't know who you are, and you don't think they're behind this anyway. It's probably more risky for me than it is for you."

Dee spoke up. "Since he's already part of our group, I suspect he has quite a bit to lose. Personally I think that anyone that goes in there is exposing himself to plenty of risk, so I'd rather that neither of you get close to them. I think this is all a very stupid discussion."

Lars spoke before anyone had a chance to agree with Dee. "Henry could easily come up with a story that makes sense. They're a church. Their mission is to expand their flock. Henry could say that he's decided there are missing pieces in his life, just like anyone else who walks in the door. You told me yourself, Henry, that Ellen Grandby Sullivan saw no problem with what you do, as long as your intentions are good. Where's the risk, exactly?"

"It makes me nauseous to say this," Henry said, "but I kind of agree. If they're hiding something, I'd be interested in knowing what. They'd have no way of knowing that I've been in touch with you."

Lars replied. "Maybe he can learn something from them that we couldn't possibly learn. I'm beginning to think this is one thing we can do that would feel like we're doing something instead of hiding."

Dee cut him off, shaking her head in disgust. "It's also possible that the church is lying and that they murdered two people. I can't believe we would seriously consider this. It's insane."

"Dee, why would they make up a story about suspicious activities? Why would they call the cops?" Henry asked his question in a voice meant for her ears, not caring if Lars heard.

"To confuse the police! If they're the ones on the attack why wouldn't they pretend they're being threatened? They could be creating conflicting signals that these cops could never sort through."

"All the more reason for one of us to burrow into their business, don't you think?"

Dee saw that she was being cornered by two people who clearly had no interest in agreeing on anything. "If it's a reason for somebody to burrow into their business, it shouldn't be somebody that I care about."

This comment caught the whole room off guard. Neither Henry nor Lars wished to be the first to speak.

Finally Richard broke the silence. "I can't think of a better way to get into their organization to learn about what they're up to. It feels as though we have ample reason to be wary of this church, and we have no other way to learn whether we're right or not. If anyone has a better idea, I'd like to hear it."

There was a pause as the group considered the possibilities. Richard continued. "So Henry would leave here pretending he knows nothing about us other than what Donnelly told him. The last few weeks did not happen. If he chooses to find out whether they're the ones after us he can do so, but that's his choice once he leaves here. We contact him, not vice versa. He has no way to reach us or find us. Is that agreeable to everyone?"

More silence. Dee looked at Richard then down.

Finally there was a voice that spoke from the perimeter of the group.

"What if he betrays us?" It was a matronly woman who looked like a librarian.

Dee stared back at the woman. "How can he betray us? He knows nothing about us other than what he sees in this room right now. Would he describe our appearance? I doubt that would help them very much. He doesn't know where he is right now, nor our names."

Lars spoke. "If he betrays us, I believe that would give us all the reason we need for retribution. That would be a gift-wrapped invitation to orchestrate his disappearance."

Dee looked down while the rest of the group was silent.

Henry spoke, turning directly to Dee.

"I'm comfortable with that arrangement. I want to know what they're up to, just like you, so I'll get in touch with them. I can't promise what I'll find out, but I promise to tell you what I learn. Put a note on my car with a number to call. Throw a rock through my window or something. I don't care. Just tell me how to get back in touch with you."

They agreed to blindfold Henry and drop him off a few blocks from his home. He insisted that Lars have no part of that arrangement, and Dee was quick to make sure his wish was granted.

Henry's path to his old life lay ahead, if it still existed.

It was twilight when Henry was brought to a quiet corner a few blocks from his home. His attendants, Richard, Rachel, and Dee, asked him to agree to keeping his blindfold on until their vehicle could no longer be heard. Henry obliged. When he made his way into his apartment, he noticed first that all his plants were dead. There was a musty smell that turned putrid when he opened the refrigerator. He cleared out the rotten food and brought it to the dumpster outside. He collected his stack of mail from behind the door then checked his email messages. Several customers had emailed him to either express concern or ask why he had abandoned them. Some were very angry, taking his absence very personally.

He meticulously built a story that would be used only for those customers who really pressed. It would be a viral infection followed by sepsis that had him unconscious for days, nearly on the brink of death. His gaunt appearance could be explained by the heavy toll taken by the infection.

With some sense of normalcy, he helped himself to some canned stew and a glass of wine. It was the first time in weeks that he felt his time was his own. He turned on some soft music to consider whether the medium business was the life he still wanted. He compared his state of mind to a veteran returning from war, unsure of his place in a setting that was distantly familiar. The idea of resuming a busy schedule of readings and clients and the intensity of communicating with spirits on the other side seemed overwhelming.

He relaxed on the couch with his wine. His eyes grew heavy and his mind was weary with uncertainty. He dozed. Deep in slumber, he felt the tug of an old friend urgently trying to reach him. They exchanged affectionate greetings, with Aisling expressing relief for his safety. Henry asked about her well-being but she avoided answering directly, only indicating that she was there for him and worried for his well-being. He asked her what prompted the unexpected visit.

"Henry, you're walking into a trap, and it's a trap that will cost you dearly if you're not aware of the forces around you. Please be prepared: it's been set by someone you are close to."

He felt lucid, awake, aware. It was as if Aisling was in the same room.

The only people he had been close to, physically anyway, for the past few weeks were the Origenists. Lars proved himself to be a betrayal waiting to happen, so there was little chance Henry would allow himself vulnerability at his hands. He felt sickened at the possibility that perhaps Dee could be the one setting him up. Aisling was vague, including what "close to" meant. She could be referring to any of his clients, or even Aisling herself. It seemed clear that no one could be ruled out as the "Judas" she warned of.

"Can you explain what's happening? How we are talking right now? I'm not asleep. Yet we're talking as if you're physically here in the room with me."

"I am with you, just not in the flesh."

Henry was startled. "Aisling, I'm a medium. You're a medium. When this happens, it means somebody has moved onto another realm. I'm fairly certain that my condition hasn't changed, so can you explain what's happening with you?"

"No, I cannot. You just need to accept that for now. Henry, I've always admired your curiosity, but you need to be patient. My condition is not important. Just please remain vigilant. The time for action is close, but for now you have important work ahead of you."

And just like that she was gone.

He decided on a very early start to his first day back, arriving at Aisling's house just after 6:30 am. He wanted to allow himself enough time to acclimate and absorb the damage from his absence.

He organized his appointments, creating lists of those clients who had given up on him, those who seemed to be holding out hope for a call back at any time, and those who just displayed their anger and sense of betrayal. He vowed to call each of them back, but it would take time. There was bound to be some attrition, but he was determined to overcome it.

He checked his calendar to try to determine which appointments, of those previously scheduled for today, might still happen. He had five appointments scheduled. Of those, two were monthly customers who probably knew nothing of his disappearance. The other three customers had already been let down by his absence. It was unlikely any of the three would show for the day's scheduled appointment without hearing from him, so he called the three. He reached two, apologizing profusely, and persuaded them to reschedule. The third call went to voicemail, and he left a similarly apologetic message.

The restoration of his business was underway. Soon he would be free to focus on more important matters.

The sessions in his first week back were cleansing and rewarding. He had a refreshed focus and determination, and the clarity of his visions was striking. The spirits he contacted spoke to him on an even level, as if they considered him a trusted peer rather than an interloper or interpreter.

Between readings, Henry used all available time to connect with clients who were affected by his absence. Nearly all were just glad to have him back. Any residual resentment passed quickly, and most were content to set appointments by his timetable.

The following Saturday, Henry enjoyed his first weekend day at home organizing his life, filling his refrigerator with fresh food, and trying to continue to piece together a normal life.

Following an early afternoon highlighted by his best nap in memory, he prepared for an afternoon service at The Church of the Tortured Christ. There was no reason to wait around to formulate a strategy. He promised the Origenists that he would try to get close to the church to learn more about them, and there was a five o'clock service that afternoon.

He timed his trip to arrive fifteen minutes early. If Reverend Sullivan noticed him that would be a positive, but he would be careful not to overplay his appearance. If he was not noticed in this visit, there would be another service the following week.

He took a seat on the left side of the semicircular auditorium, allowing himself a grand view of the pulpit area and of the entering congregation. While it was Reverend Sullivan he was most interested in seeing and meeting, he was also watching for Janice Donnelly and Joan Swenson. Joan was his first client to mention The Church several months before when she came in to connect with her father. All seemed fine during her reading, although she did have an unusual curiosity about reincarnation. He had not spoken with her since John Donnelly's funeral.

The auditorium was nearly filled to capacity at five o'clock. The perimeter lights dimmed and bright lights immersed the stage. Uplifting orchestral music played, and the Reverend Ellen Grandby Sullivan emerged from the shadows in a slow but majestic walk. She wore a flowing white robe accented with red trim. Two male acolytes followed her onto the stage in simpler black and white robes. The congregation stood, sang a rousing hymn, and applauded in rhythm as she took her place at the podium after a grand walk around the altar. The acolytes sat in the wings behind her, also clapping.

"Brothers and sisters, welcome to the Church of the Tortured Christ. We would like to extend a very special welcome to those who are here for the first time. I see a few new faces out here this evening." She looked directly in Henry's direction.

"I hope this is the beginning of a relationship that lasts to eternity." She flashed a winning, welcoming smile. The congregation let out a warm, gentle laugh in response.

The service alternated between readings from the gospels, boisterous singing of modern Christian music, and lectures from the Reverend. The theme of the evening was repentance from sin. Her primary message was that sin seemed to be everywhere in these times, but in fact mankind was surrounded by sin in biblical times too. Temptations are everywhere today and perhaps more readily available thanks to technology, but it has never been far away.

To underscore the message, her quote was from the book of Mark.

And whosoever shall not receive you, nor hear you, when ye depart thence, shake off the dust under your feet for a testimony against them. Verily I say unto you, It shall be more tolerable for Sodom and Gomorrah in the day of judgment, than for that city.

And they went out, and preached that men should repent.

And they cast out many devils, and anointed with oil many that were sick, and healed them.

And king Herod heard of him; (for his name was spread abroad) and he said, That John the Baptist was risen from the dead, and therefore mighty works do show forth themselves in him.

Others said, That it is Elias. And others said, That it is a prophet, or as one of the prophets.

But when Herod heard thereof, he said, It is John, whom I beheaded: he is risen from the dead.

The passage, she explained, was about quarreling over the propriety of marrying the wife of a dead brother, and the aftermath of John's beheading. It resulted in the well known story of Christ multiplying loaves and fishes for his congregation. He was left to believe that the reference to John the Baptist's rebirth and the topic of sin were not coincidental.

During his detainment, one of the many magazines available to him was *Psychology Today*. He had read a captivating article about "delusions of reference", which was the belief by some people, including some with bipolar and other disorders, that random and unrelated events around us have special meaning and reference in our world. Sitting here, alone among hundreds of strangers in the Church of the Tortured Christ, he wondered about his own mental stability. Perhaps a church was exactly where he needed to be at this moment.

Despite his uncertainty about the woman preacher before him, he recognized the power of her charisma. Her delivery was eloquent, and her command of biblical scripture was impressive. She orchestrated a moving service and the congregation was completely in the palm of her hand.

The service finally concluded with a modern gospel tune that was performed by an acoustic guitarist, a pianist, and a bassist, all excellent players. Many in the congregation danced without hesitation or self-doubt. When it was over the crowd applauded loudly and the Reverend blew kisses and fist pumped to the crowd as she galloped off the stage.

The congregation was slow to leave. Henry imagined this was the highlight of the week for many, some of whom hoped to have a chance to speak with the Reverend before climbing into their cars before another long week. A line of congregants was outside in the warm evening waiting for a chance to exchange quick greetings with the Reverend. Henry took his time exiting, biding his time to try to be among the last in the queue.

When his time finally came, he paused until she had a chance to fix her eyes on him only. He wanted to give her a chance to recognize him, if she could. Her fresh gaze did not suggest any recognition.

"Hello! Thank you for attending the service!"

"Why thank you, Reverend. We've met once before, in your office. My name is Henry Chimera. I dropped in unannounced one day, and you were kind enough to visit with me."

"Why yes of course! How are you, Henry? I almost didn't recognize you; you look a little different. Did you lose some weight?"

"I've been dieting. Thanks for noticing. It's a pleasure to see you again, Reverend. I really enjoyed your service."

"I'm so glad to hear that, Henry," she replied. "Is it your first time here with us?"

"Yes, actually it is. I'm sorry it's taken me so long to come." Henry was not accustomed to acting, but in this role he was to appear as a lost sheep who may have finally found his flock.

"Not important! What's important is that you're here with us now, today. I'm honored that you would choose our little congregation as your place of worship."

"It feels like I'm more ready for this than I ever have been." He looked down, self-consciously.

"We're ready for you, Henry." She looked at him as a patient parent looks at child who just came home with muddy shoes.

Henry allowed himself a chance to look directly into her eyes. "Thanks, that means a lot. I wonder if I can ask you about volunteer opportunities with the church. Is that kind of thing possible?"

"Of course it's possible! We're always looking for sincere, caring adults to help in our outreach efforts. Call the office this coming week and ask for Ronnie. He coordinates those activities for us, and does a blessed job. Would you do that for us?"

He offered a weary smile. "I will, and I can. I could use some positive distractions in my life. I'll call Ronnie this week. Thank you so much."

"It's my pleasure, Henry. God bless you. We'll see you soon."

He turned and walked toward his car. He resisted the urge to turn and look back. Instead he looked to his left toward the side entrances of the auditorium. At each door were men in dark suits looking in various directions, including his.

When Henry called, Ronnie Wilcox welcomed him in for a visit the next morning. He arrived a few minutes early, as usual. Wilcox was a short, hugging man with a kind face and wire rim glasses. He seemed perfectly suited for this kind of work. When they were settled, Ronnie did all the talking. It was obviously a speech he was accustomed to giving.

"We have outreach programs that cover the gamut around the Boston area. We organize food banks for needy families. We round up homeless people on cold nights. We have coat drives, food drives, sock drives, you name it. We even build homes for families who might be the victims of fires or floods, or who just need a home. This time of year we work with teens to plant and tend gardens as an after school activity. What kind of work appeals to you?"

"Well, all of that sounds really appealing," Henry replied. "However I'm a little limited on time and distance because I run my own business and need to be fairly close by for my customers."

"I think the best fit would be anything where I could spend most of the volunteer time here at the church. That would give me some predictability, maybe a routine. Do you have anything like that available?"

"Oh yes, but the choices are a little more limited from within the church. Most of our volunteer time is done in neighborhoods, outside grocery stores, at strip malls, that kind of thing. Probably the thing we do most from here in the church is phone banking. We'll call out to our congregation and beyond to the whole community, for donation drives of money, clothes, food, or just time."

Henry perked up at this suggestion. "That sounds really great. I've done phone work before. I think I come across as welcoming, non-threatening."

"DING, DING, DING! Sounds like we have a winner!" Ronnie Wilcox was a man who enjoyed his job. "We can always use good phone people. I probably shouldn't say this, but most of the people we have on the phones tend to be less mobile ... older, quite bluntly, and less enthusiastic than the people you normally look for to make phone calls. You'll be great!"

They agreed that Henry would start with two evenings a week, Tuesdays and Thursdays, and adjust the commitment up or down depending as he adjusted to the role. He was to show up for training the following night, a Thursday.

When he arrived, Ronnie was the one to greet him. He brought him into a simple office space with a few windows and a bland view of the main thoroughfare. There were three other volunteers in the room, each older in years. As Ronnie had warned him, they seemed low in energy but they were contributing in about the only way they could.

This evening's effort involved phone outreach to the congregation, "the family," as Ronnie called them, to collect shoes for needy children and adults. Ronnie explained that they refined the phone list from their list of several thousands congregants by zip codes, focusing on middle and upper class neighborhoods. This would mostly avoid asking for donations from people who were themselves in need.

Ronnie brought Henry through the procedure of making phone calls. He would introduce himself as a representative of the church, explain why he was calling, then go right to the heart of the matter by asking if they had any new or nearly new shoes that could be used by children and adults in need. He would arrange a pickup time by area, and let them know that a reminder call would come the day before.

Henry easily flowed into the routine, carefully collecting notes from each call. He was able to move through his list steadily and pleasantly. It was very low stress work.

From the feedback he received from Ronnie Wilcox, Henry was a natural. After a couple hours of phone calling and socializing, he requested time to stretch his legs. Ronnie was quick to oblige.

Henry walked toward the exit door, but instead took a right turn down a hallway that seemed familiar. While the auditorium in the Arlington church was impressive, the office complex that blended subtly around it was even more opulent. The carpets were rich and plush, and the wall decor and lighting were subdued, serene, and first class. Artwork was strategically placed to constantly remind visitors of the suffering of Jesus Christ and the sublime rewards waiting in heaven for those who chose to follow his path.

As he walked the halls admiring the surroundings, he noticed cameras at each corner. Sections of the building were marked in bright colors, Youth Ministry, Day Camp, Administration, and the like. He glanced at the office labeled Reverend Ellen Grandby Sullivan and tried not to pause too noticeably, mindful of cameras near each corner. Within her heavy wooden door was engraved a Celtic Cross, evidently a nod to the Irish family into which she had married. The door reminded Henry of a pathway to the Middle Ages, clearly there to be admired. Henry wondered if she would take the door with her when her work in Arlington was complete.

Henry walked with purpose, pausing only briefly to admire the stylish, evocative artwork. Although he had yet to see a single soul walking these halls, he hardly felt alone. When he began to recognize hallways already walked, he returned to the Volunteers office.

He resumed his phone calling, looking only at phone numbers and not names. He only jotted down notes after he had reached either a voicemail box or a person. When calls went to voicemail, he was instructed to leave a message only on the third try. No one was called twice on the same day for the same reason. About one-third of phone calls resulted in a person answering the phone directly, and nearly half of answered calls resulted in a donation. Some calls were more memorable than others.

"Hello, this is Joan."

"Hello Joan, this is Henry calling on behalf of The Church of the Tortured Christ. How are you this evening?"

"I'm fine. What can I do for you?"

Having connected with a human voice, Henry glanced at her full name on the sheet before him. Joan Swenson! Her voice reminded him of her near paranoia in the first time they met, as though she was never sure she should be speaking with him at all. He remembered her as a sincere customer who missed her father a great deal. When they connected, she was legitimately touched and grateful. She never fully explained how she came up with the idea to visit him.

He cursed his lack of preparation, deciding to play along with his comfortable routine in the hope that she might not recognize his voice.

"We're conducting a drive to collect new or nearly new shoes for those less fortunate than us, in particular children from disadvantaged homes and homeless men and women. Would you have any shoes that you could spare for a good cause?"

"Your voice sounds very familiar. Is that ... Henry Chimera?"

Henry played along. "Yes, this is Henry ... Oh my gosh! Joan Swenson! I wasn't paying attention to the names on my call list. How are you, Joan?"

"I'm fine. Are you really volunteering for The Church? That's really surprising."

"I am, actually," Henry replied earnestly. "I had kind of a rough stretch there for a while, and I came to one of their services last weekend. I enjoyed it so much that I offered to volunteer. This is my first night on the phones."

She said nothing.

"Joan, are you still there?"

Quietly she spoke. "Yes, I'm still here. I just find it so bizarre that you of all people are volunteering for The Church of the Tortured Christ. Are you sure that's a good fit for you, Henry?"

"Well, like I said, I just started. Why do you ask?"

"It's just that ... I learned some things about that place that I probably wasn't meant to learn."

"What kind of things?" Henry spoke in a hushed voice. He tried to sense if any volunteers were paying attention, but they seemed preoccupied with their own calls.

"I'd rather not talk about it over the phone."

Henry felt foolish placing her in that position. "I'm sorry about that, Joan. Perhaps another time." He paused.

"Yes, I'd like that."

He was relieved. "So back to the reason I called. Would you happen to have any new or nearly new shoes you could donate for people in need?"

"No, I don't think so. It was nice to hear from you again, Henry."

After hanging up, Henry discreetly entered her home number into his cell phone. When he turned to retrieve some water, he was stunned to see a figure standing directly behind him.

The Reverend Ellen Grandby Sullivan was smiling down kindly.

"Henry, it's lovely to see you again."

A Medium High

Henry nearly jumped when he saw the Reverend standing behind him, smiling warmly.

"Why Reverend, I didn't expect to see you here. It's after hours - I thought you'd be long gone. Are there any hours when you're not working?"

"I don't work banker's hours, that's for sure. Working for the Lord can be a twenty-four hour a day job."

Henry nodded and smiled, trying to avoid additional awkwardness.

"So how is your first evening of volunteer work going, Henry?"

"It's going well. I'm enjoying it. I don't have a ton of time to donate, but the fact that I can work here, close to home, makes it a lot more convenient for me. Making these calls is easy, pretty low pressure compared to calling I've had to do for other jobs. It's good to be able to honestly tell people I'm not a telemarketer."

"That's nice to hear. Our congregation is usually very quick to open their hearts when we approach them the right way. Would you like to take a little break? I just made some tea in my office." She turned and began to walk, waving him to follow.

"When we spoke the last time," she said in a hushed voice, "we talked about John Donnelly's murder. It was such a tragic thing, and to my knowledge they have yet to find the killer. Have you heard anything different?"

"No," Henry replied, almost too quickly. "I've been a little out of touch lately, and I haven't heard from the police in weeks. I hope they catch the killer soon, but it wouldn't bother me if I don't hear from Detective Lacey. He treats everyone like a suspect."

"Yes, well, I guess that's what police are supposed to do."

The Reverend Sullivan paused, as if considering just the right words. "I'm not quite sure how to ask this Henry, but as a medium were you able to offer any ... special assistance to the detective?"

"You mean like some special insight into the crime?" Henry had no intention of telling her about his vision, which would only make him sound like a suspect, but he was interested in where the conversation would go.

"With your gifts, I wondered if you know things that others could not." Her tone was that of someone who wanted to pry without it seeming like she was prying. "We've all heard the stories of psychics who help solve crimes, find missing children, that sort of thing."

"Well, I communicate with spirits that have passed. The only way I would have anything of value for the police would be if a spirit told me about it. So I didn't have anything of value to tell Lacey."

Henry chose to stop there. Donnelly did indeed visit him, and Henry did share that information with the police, but he saw no reason to share the information with the Reverend.

"I see. That's too bad. I was hoping there would be some way you could give the police an edge to help find this vicious murderer."

"Me too. I suppose it's still possible, but nothing yet." He knew she was hoping for much more. Perhaps she considered him the murderer. If that were the case, he wondered what she thought his motivation would be.

Another possibility was that she had something to hide, and she wondered what he knew that might be damaging to her in some way. This possibility seemed remote because there was nothing he could even imagine that would matter about John Donnelly to a leader in one of the fastest growing churches in the world.

A third option was that she was legitimately concerned that a killer was on the loose, and that both of them could be in danger. Even in Henry's conspiratorial frame of mind, this seemed the most plausible explanation for her curiosity.

They entered her office suite through the ornate wooden door with the Celtic cross, and she led him to her plush inner office. She offered him a seat and moved to a serving area, where a pot of hot tea was on a warmer. She poured two cups and settled into an elegant leather chair with a high back that framed her figure perfectly. She crossed her legs casually, sending the message that this meeting was just two friends talking.

"So I've been dying to ask you. Oops, I could have chosen better wording." They both chuckled, knowing what was coming. "What's it like being a medium? I've never met one, and I can't even imagine what that kind of work is like."

"You'd be surprised, Reverend. It's really rewarding."

"My friends call me Ellen. Rewarding in what way?"

"It's rewarding because the new customers don't really know what to expect, and they're usually really pleased with the outcome. I can usually tell right away whether I'll be able to help them or not."

"How can you tell that?"

"There's an energy they carry around with them," Henry explained. "I can typically pick it up when I first start talking with them. If there's potential for a strong reading, it shows in the energy that surrounds them. I've learned to recognize it before I even hear what they have to say. My mentor left me in a great situation, so I can focus on being good at my job. If my customers are not satisfied with a session, I won't take their money."

"But how can you be sure you're helping them?"

"If people came in and paid for sessions but no spirits came to connect with them, they wouldn't come back. That happens sometimes. I usually don't have to tell people when it's pointless to return. They know because the spirits let them know, either by not appearing or by telling them directly."

"The spirits tell them to go away? That seems a little harsh. Why would a spirit tell someone they love to stay away?" The Reverend's tone was polite, but now it was becoming clear why she wanted the conversation.

"It's not that they tell my clients to stay away. It's nearly always a loving exchange, but it can be a little direct. Sometimes I have to water down the strong messages they want to get across. Usually the message has to do with letting go of the past and moving ahead in life. If the message isn't getting through, or the same message needs to be delivered time and time again, the spirits can show some impatience."

"That's almost incredible." Reverend Sullivan was leaning forward in her chair, either fascinated or appalled, or perhaps both, with the picture Henry was creating.

"Which part?"

"That the spirit of someone's parent wouldn't show limitless patience with a child that went to this extent to reconnect. What's the harm? Is there an energy limit in these spirits or what?"

"No, but if the spirit has had to deliver the same message time after time, the message changes to 'didn't you hear me last time?' That kind of thing. Some people ask for advice then don't like the advice they get, so they need to be told again. Humans aren't perfect, and their imperfection can get annoying and perhaps tedious. I'm sure that's true in your line of work too."

"Yes, certainly. Very interesting parallels. Does the subject of Jesus Christ ever come up during your sessions?"

The Reverend's tea was kicking in.

"Very often, especially whenever there's a Christian in the reading. I have quite a wide variety of clients from many faiths. If a client and their associated spirits are Christian, then Christ will be a very important part of the session. Jewish clients will rely on the presence of their manifestation of God, the same way Muslims, Hindus, and all other faiths do. I don't change my approach based on religious persuasions, and they seem to respect that. God is God."

"Okay, let's pause a minute." The Reverend's tone changed. "The respect and devotion that a true Christian commits to our Lord Jesus Christ can't be compared to those other religions. I know they have many devoted followers too, but let's be realistic. True Christianity has very little in common with Islam, Hinduism, and Buddhism."

Henry was feeling his tea as well. "You mean besides the one true God that they all follow?" He smiled to the Reverend.

"Don't kid yourself, Henry. The Gods they believe in were relegated to the scrap heap during Old Testament times. As you say, there's only one true God, and it's the father that Christ Himself spoke of."

"I think most of my customers would agree with you on that last point. I certainly do."

"Well, thank God for that." Ellen Grandby Sullivan gave Henry a generous smile. "Pun intended."

Henry was quick to acknowledge her quip with a smile. "When you talk about the 'one true God' during your travels, do you have a chance to speak with people of other faiths about their views?"

"The subject doesn't come up much," she replied, "but I see such a large gap between what Buddhists consider God and what we Christians consider God. There isn't nearly as much in common with the Buddhists as with the other monotheistic religions, but even for the Jews, the Muslims, and the Hindus, who believe in many gods, they're missing a key message. Their beliefs are not based on the sacrifice of Christ our Lord. We have four written records from those who lived with Him. If you want to talk about an authoritative gateway to God, it doesn't get much closer than his son. Don't you agree, Henry?"

Henry considered a counter-point, that the four gospels emerged decades after the deaths of Matthew, Mark, Luke and John, and a century or two after Christ's life. He also resisted the urge of answering her question directly.

Instead he returned her warm smile with a question. "What's your take on reincarnation?"

This seemed to catch the Reverend off guard. "Excuse me?"

"Well, the notion of reincarnation existed in many of the early canonical teachings, but as I'm sure you know, it wasn't embraced within the New Testament Canon, probably for reasons that made a lot of sense at the time. However, at one time is was considered a fundamental part of Christian faith. So what's your opinion of reincarnation within the context of Christianity?"

Ellen Grandby Sullivan looked closely at Henry, then took a very long pause before speaking.

"I think you answered your own question. The Church did not embrace the concept in the books chosen for the canon, therefore it's not doctrine. Is there something I missed in your question?"

"Probably not." Henry was prepared to leave the discussion at that.

"However," the Reverend continued, "I'm not so naive as to believe that just because the early Church didn't include it as doctrine, that it never was valid. I don't believe that. I do believe the notion was once valid, but things change. The notion went the way of Old Testament values."

"How so? What' changed between Old and New Testament times that it would no longer be viable?"

"Is that a serious question?" The Reverend had her gazed fixed on Henry, rarely even blinking.

"Absolutely."

"Jesus Christ came. He lived, he died, he came again, then he ascended into heaven. Considering what the early church just experienced, the notion of reincarnation became obsolete in the eyes of the Church, and if it didn't have the weight of the Church behind it, it had no chance of being sustained, at least not in the second and third centuries. Irenaeus and the others had some hard decisions to make, and all the decisions they made needed support. Reincarnation was not a notion that could easily be supported after God sent his only son to save us. Also, by the late second century it was apparent that the growth of Christianity made the notion of reincarnation preposterous. Where would all these souls come from? The Church was growing so fast that there couldn't possibly be enough to inhabit all those Christian newborn bodies. Where would they come from?

"Lastly and perhaps most importantly, the Church wisely chose to preach the idea of virtue, which leads to everlasting life. It's reality, Henry. How can you talk about virtue when the basic message of reincarnation is that none of your actions will last forever? That you might screw up in THIS life, but in the next one you can make it up. How do you explain that to an eight year old who you're trying to convince to share his toys, to just be kind and sweet?"

"I'm not sure that you would want to," Henry replied.

"That's because you can't. If spiritual matters can't be explained to a child, you really need to ask yourself whether they make sense at all."

"My God, that makes perfect sense!" He hoped that his exclamation sounded sincere. The relieved look on the Reverend's face settled his worry.

"I'm glad you think so." She seemed content and satisfied as she set her tea cup aside.

Henry's tone turned serious. "I haven't had a good impression of this Origenist group. They scare the hell out of me. From the first moment John Donnelly mentioned them to me, I've had a bad feeling that hasn't gotten better."

The Reverend leaned forward. "Really? I don't know much about them, and I certainly didn't know they were a concern for anyone. What do you know about them?"

"Not very much. I gather they're back in hiding. So I guess there isn't much to talk about."

"What do you mean by that?" She halted in mid-motion, waiting for his reply.

"By what?"

"You said, 'back in hiding.' Is there some reason we should think they're retreating from their murderous ways?"

"I have no idea what they're up to." Henry's mind was whipping as control of this conversation slipped away.

She leaned toward him from her high leather chair. "Is there any doubt that they're the ones who killed Mister Donnelly?"

And what of David Herbrit, he thought. Who killed him?

"I have no idea who else could it be," Henry said diplomatically.

"Indeed," she said. She glanced at him, then off into the distance.

"Well, Henry, I've taken up far too much of your time. I hope you'll continue helping us out. We can always use smart, energetic people like you. By the way, it seems like using you only on the phones might be an under-utilization of your talents. Would an expanded role on the volunteer side be something you would consider?"

Henry hesitated before speaking. "Is there something in particular you have in mind?"

"Nothing in particular," she answered, "but I'll keep my eyes and ears open."

When Henry left, the Reverend Ellen Grandby Sullivan opened a large cabinet behind her desk that contained a bank of television monitors. They offer a comprehensive display of the church property, inside and out. She tracked Henry's progress as he said good night to Ronnie Wilcox, then walked out the front door toward the parking lot.

She picked up the phone and dialed an internal extension. "Edgar, it's clear. Can you come in here?" She hung up.

The door opened and he sat.

"So how did our first meaningful encounter go?"

"It went fine. He seems to be putting on a nice act."

"I'm not surprised. He's a devious little creep. So how long do we need to play this silly little game?"

"As long as we need to. It could be days, it could be months."

"That's not what I want to hear, Ellen."

"Well, you're going to just have to live with it. He has no idea we know what he's up to. It's a perfectly controlled situation where we hold all the cards. Right now we have to be patient."

"What choice do we have?"

"None. No choice. He's right here in front of us, and what we show him - what he sees - feeds directly into what these amateurs believe. As long as he's working with us, believing he's helping them, they'll feel like they're in control. That's what we want them to think."

"Why not give them a reason to run and hide, maybe forever? I can help make that happen in a hurry."

Her tone sharpened. "No shit, Edgar, but what does that accomplish for us right NOW, exactly?"

"It makes them go away, that's what. Forever this time. How could that be a bad thing?"

"It's a bad thing because it would undo all the work we've done to get this guy in our pocket. The plan is going exactly the way we drew it up months ago. We never talked about terminating Henry Chimera when he walked in the door. The plan was always to pull him in here because he has special gifts that could prove useful for us, then cast him out when it makes sense.

"Besides, if they run and hide, that's temporary. They'll pop out of hiding at the earliest opportunity, and continue to be a pain in our asses. One more death won't change anything. They need to be eradicated."

He exhaled slowly. "What exactly are you hoping to get out of this guy, anyway? I just don't see him as gifted or talented as you think he is."

"Insight we need to help us accomplish our mission. We need all the help we can get. These are things we're only beginning to understand, and this guy has a handle on all of this after what, six months as medium? If we can get a harness on him, it could save us months or even years in our mission. It might make the difference between success and failure."

"Maybe yes, maybe no, but how do you plan to use what he brings to our benefit?"

Edgar laughed. "Highly unlikely. The guy doesn't seem to trust anyone."

"And that would be thanks to you." She looked dryly at him.

He smiled back. "Hey, I did what I had to. I've been following the plan all along. I'm just looking forward to the part about taking out our little Mister Chimera the second he proves to be more trouble than he's worth. That part of the plan cannot change, and I reserve that task for myself."

"We'll cross that bridge."

Edgar nodded. "Hey, sometimes it looks ugly but as you're always reminding me, it's results that matter."

"Well said, Machiavelli," she smiled back, "or should I call you Lars?"

In his apartment late that evening, dozing on the couch, Henry felt the presence of a familiar visitor.

"Hello Aisling. To what do I owe the pleasure?"

"Hi Henry. You owe this pleasure to my concern for your well-being."

"Excuse me?"

"Henry, you may not realize it, but you're navigating in some very dangerous waters right now. There are some very dark forces around you."

"I think I do realize that, Aisling. I know there's a murderer, or murderers, on the loose, and that there's a decent good chance they know who I am."

"I couldn't have said it better myself."

"If I hadn't, Aisling, I'm sure you would have." They shared a laugh.

"There are some things going on that I can't explain, and I can't just sit by while they happen."

"Continue to follow your instincts, Henry. At times, they're all you'll have."

"Yes, I do know that. Aisling, there's something else I need to ask you." Silence.

"Have you passed on to the higher realm? Is that why you're able to communicate with me so easily?"

There was a pause before she spoke to him. "Yes Henry, I went to Ireland because I was ill. Rather than seeking treatment that would only delay the inevitable, I went home to die."

"I'm sorry to hear that. I hope there was no pain."

"It hurt like hell! Cancer sucks Henry, but my spirit guide was there to help me along, and ease the transition when my body had had enough."

"I'm glad to hear that. Is it true that God only gives you what you can handle?"

"Yes, I think so. In Paul's first letter to the Corinthians he says, *'There hath no temptation taken you but such as is common to man: but God is faithful, who will not suffer you to be tempted above that ye are able; but will with the temptation also make a way to escape, that ye may be able to bear it.'"*

"I'm glad to hear you're free from pain now. How are things for you on the other side?"

"Things on this side are wonderful. I'm able to reconnect with many of my soul relations. Whatever I need or want is there for the taking. It's an existence that is all about healing, restoration, and learning from lives led, in particular the last one, and there's SO much to learn. I have a great deal of work ahead of me, but it's the kind of work that is delightful to perform."

"That's wonderful to hear. It must be fantastic to be completely free from pain, fear, and worry."

"Whoa there, Henry. I wouldn't go that far."

"What do you mean?"

"I'm still very worried. In particular, I'm worried about you."

"You don't need to worry about me, Aisling. I proved in the last few weeks that physical pain won't break me down, and I'm not afraid of dying."

"That's not the issue. We both know that you've lived a tough life and that you're not afraid to die."

"Then what? Why should you be worried when I'm not?"

"For that very reason. You should be worried. This cavalier approach will not serve you well. You're capable of some great things, Henry, but you'll accomplish none of them if you're dead. Things are very, very complicated right now. I'm just beginning to understand myself, and I'm even wondering if I've done enough, or whether I'm doing enough. You might think that giving your life is the most noble thing you can do. It's romantic, it's heroic, and it's pointless. If you die too soon, it will mean you never really understood the larger factors at play. Somebody else will be left to clean up the mess. Or no one."

Henry spent the days following his first volunteer experience digesting and contemplating. He was uncertain whether his apparently successful immersion into the church was a blessing, a curse, both, or neither. He had little trust in the Reverend Ellen Grandby Sullivan, but also was not convinced she nor her church were the Big Bad Wolf the Origenists believed them to be. His general dislike was based on the reality that they had enriched themselves on the backs of their flock, many of whom were desperate for the blessings they believed could only come from the church. In the sermons he had heard, he expected to hear Reverend Sullivan and her father to encourage followers to live a holy life, and achieve blessings through the rewarding lives they lived. Instead he heard an emphasis on worshipping God through Jesus Christ in the way they prescribed. This, they maintained, was the only sure path to salvation. From the top down, starting with the Reverend's father, the church only encouraged that reliance.

Henry went online to research their growth. As a private entity their assets were not available for scrutiny, but critics guessed their total assets - cash, property, and real estate within the US - at well into the tens of billions in value around the world. Their growth was remarkable, yet it happened discreetly. They rarely built the kind of "mega-churches" that other evangelical groups preferred in decades past, instead favoring a wide network of medium-sized "Soul Cleansing Centers" that were met with less hostility in the hundreds of towns and cities in which they took up residence. To the established churches - the Catholics, the Jews, the Protestants, and the Mormons - the presence of The Church of the Tortured Christ was just another competitor in a crowded field.

Still Henry marveled at their growth during just the past decade. They were in 42 states with hundreds of locations around the country, including big cities and towns he had never heard of, and according to their website, almost as many countries around the world and growing. Their focus in the last couple years was on international growth. Where there was any form of historical Christian presence, The Church of the Tortured Christ was there.

It had been over two weeks since his miserable experience with the Origenists ended. He was glad to be conducting this gradual clandestine work with the church for their benefit, but was beginning to wonder when some signal would come. More precisely he wondered when he would hear directly from Dee, the person who fueled his motivation for helping the group.

Two weeks was probably too soon for them to risk a contact, he decided. Even during the short time since being with them, he needed to justify his reasons for being their secret agent. He made a promise to them that could possibly save them. He was not completely comfortable with the arrangement they agreed on, but he was proud that in such a short time, he had become cordial with the Reverend.

When Henry considered that he had direct access to one of the top people in this powerful and influential organization, he was bedazzled. He came to believe this had to be much more than simple coincidence, but from a power with intentions he did not understand.

He thought back to his brief conversation with Joan Swenson. She was very reluctant to talk over the phone, almost afraid of what fate may be ahead if she spoke openly. He recalled that he scribbled down her current phone number after he spoke with her, just before the Reverend approached him. The possibility that Sullivan overheard their conversation was a lingering shadow in the days since the call. With any luck the Reverend did not hear anything out of the ordinary, but Henry knew he could not afford to count on that. His mission was to learn all he could about what the church was up to, and it was apparent that he could not accomplish that without finding out what Joan had seen. However there were a few obstacles in the way.

It would be absurd for Joan Swenson to trust Henry after finding out he was volunteering for the church, particularly considering the way she found out. She trusted and confided in him at one time in the most intimate of settings. Their session was a successful one, and she seemed sincere in her appreciation for the chance to speak with her father.

At the time of the reading, he remembered her as reserved and hesitant but not necessarily distrustful of the church or of Henry. On her question whether he was sure it was "a good fit" with his role as a volunteer, something must have changed in either her opinion of Henry or her opinion of the church.

Another shadow was Henry's recent history of people dying shortly after meeting with him. The last thing he wished to do was bring harm upon someone like Joan, who he doubted had done anything to attract the fate met by Donnelly and Herbrit. She seemed to only want to remain loyal to her faith and to stay close to her family.

If Henry was to contact her, he had to find a way to assure her that her safety was paramount, but that his reasons for approaching her were important too. Compounding the difficulty, he had to find a way to explain all this without exposing the Origenists. It would be a tricky conversation.

"Hello, this is Joan."

"Hi again Joan, this is Henry Chimera."

A pause. "Hello Henry."

"Joan I'm sorry to bother you again. This time I'm calling from my own house, and I'm alone."

"Still, do you think that's a good idea?"

"I think it's important."

"I don't know what's going on lately or what's so important," she said, "but I do know things have been weird since John Donnelly died. No one around there seems to know who to trust. It's not a situation I care to be involved with."

"I completely understand that, Joan. It's just that John's death has sort of put me in the middle of a couple of serious factions, neither of whom I feel I can completely trust yet. I've been worried about my safety, quite frankly. For your sake, I don't think it's a good idea that I tell you everything I've been involved with lately, but I'd like to talk to you more about ... what you mentioned the other day to me."

"I'm not sure I should do that," she replied. "The stakes are pretty high right now."

"We should both be concerned," Henry answered, "but I've made promises to people very important to me that I would find out what's happening inside the church. These people are far more worried for their safety than you and me. They're terrified, and they're trying to figure out if it's the church they should fear or someone else. I wouldn't be contacting you if these people didn't consider themselves under attack today. I won't lie to you, there are risks involved. John Donnelly wasn't the only person who was murdered."

"My God. Who else was killed?"

"I'd rather not say, but it was someone I had gotten to know quite well. His death caused a lot of heartache, and it took its toll on me too."

"Well, I probably shouldn't do this," Joan sighed, "but I can't just do nothing."

"I feel the same way," Henry said. "I gather you'd like to meet. When and where?"

"As soon as we can, but it needs to be in a safe place. Somewhere in public."

"How about if we meet at the Somerville Place Mall? Tomorrow at two in the food court, after the lunch crowds."

Henry arrived at the mall early to watch for anyone who might have any way of knowing about their meeting. He milled around the area, occasionally ducking into stores to browse, but mostly eyeing the other mall customers to make sure there was no one who looked out of place. He saw nothing suspicious.

Finally she arrived. He subtly waved at her and they sat at a table near the rear of the dining area, where they could see anyone coming or going.

"Sorry for all this cloak and dagger stuff, Joan, but things are messed up right now."

"I understand. The truth is, I've been worried too, even before you called me. I wasn't sure what to do, and I never felt right about just sitting on what I know. So I guess your phone call was a blessing in disguise. At least I hope it was."

"Deep disguise maybe," he said. "It's hard to imagine anything about all of this is a blessing. I'm not sure who to trust in all this, if anyone. Perhaps nobody."

"So Henry, why haven't you gone to the police with whatever you know?"

"I thought long and hard about that, but the last time I spoke with the police, they made it clear that I was not beyond suspicion in John's death. I'm not sure what I can accomplish by going to them."

"That's not very encouraging," she said.

It occurred to Henry what Joan must be thinking, that if the police considered him a suspect in Donnelly's death, that there was a distinct possibility she was sitting across the table from a murderer.

"So Joan," Henry was quick to change the subject, "when I called you randomly, you were open to meeting with me so I called. Here we are. Why?"

"Well, I was in the church a couple weeks ago, on the Saturday before Easter, helping to set up for an event after the morning services. They asked me to rearrange a room that would be used for food preparation, setting up tables and that kind of thing. When I went in there I noticed there was a television with a camera hooked up. The TV's power was standby, but the camera's power was still on. Just out of curiosity I hit the Play button. What I saw was really disturbing.

"It was a man tied to a chair. He was older, an Asian man. There were two guys with their backs to the camera talking to him, yelling at him, obviously trying to get him to tell them something. I could see the man was exhausted, almost ready to pass out."

"Oh my God!" Henry managed to keep his voice from rising above the din in the food court. "Oh my God. The vision!"

It was the first time in weeks he thought about the vision he had about men with a distinctive cross interrogating the Dalai Lama. He shared the vision with both Dee and Herbrit. Shortly after the discovery, Herbrit was murdered and Henry was kidnapped.

"What vision?" Joan whispered as she looked around the food court.

"I saw men interrogating the Dalai Lama. They were wearing a distinctive platinum cross. Later we found a picture online of Ernest B. Grandby wearing the same cross. We all took the vision seriously, but it's possible that I might have seen a picture of Grandby wearing the cross before then. There's no telling whether it meant anything or not. Are you sure the scene wasn't staged," Henry asked, "or some realistic-looking TV show?"

"I don't think so." She seemed determined. "It was obviously shot in that room. The lighting wasn't great. It looked like they weren't too concerned about the picture quality. I was too nervous to turn the sound up. God only knows what would have happened if someone came in and saw me watching it."

"I don't blame you. Do you think it was the Dalai Lama?"

"I didn't think of him at the time, but he was about the same age. It's very possible."

"Joan, did you happen to notice if the men in the video were wearing a cross?"

"I can't say for sure it was a cross, but I do think they were wearing something around their necks. I looked pretty quickly and didn't notice too much detail."

Henry nodded. "Your vision seems a lot more reliable than mine. It seems that one of the fastest growing churches in the country may be behind the abduction of one of the world's most well known spiritual teachers."

Tears came to Joan's eyes, and she put her face in her hands. Finally she looked at Henry. "Is there anything you can do to stop this insanity?"

"I have no idea," Henry said, "but they can't get away with this."

In the days that followed, Henry was consumed by the possibility that The Church was behind the kidnapping of the Dalai Lama, and he labored through long hours about what to do about it. He considered an anonymous call to federal authorities that would tip them off to what he knew, but decided against the idea because a search warrant would be needed. The police would never obtain one only an anonymous tip. He needed something more tangible, such as a location where the spiritual leader might be held captive. Through each round of "what to do," a mental exercise that haunted him throughout his days and nights, he always came back to the reassurance that what he was doing now - infiltrating The Church to find out what he could - was the only thing within his power.

Henry showed up for his next volunteer session on time and wearing a smile. He had devoted time preparing for this session, determined to put on a strong, happy face and be exactly the Henry they would expect. Near the end of this Tuesday phone calling session, Ellen Grandby Sullivan showed up behind him quietly, at the same time and in the same manner that she had before.

"Hi Henry! How has your session been this evening?"

"Excellent, very positive. You have a very generous congregation. These people are more than happy to give."

"We're very blessed. I guess we're doing something right." She gave him a warm, blushing smile.

"Henry, I wonder if you might have time after your work is done to visit with me again. I had a thought I'd like to share with you."

"Sounds great," he replied. "I should be done within about twenty minutes or so."

When he finished he walked to her office then knocked gently on her door. She invited him in without standing. She had a computer on her left, and in front of her on her large desk was only a file, a notepad, and an elegant writing pen. Reading glasses were perched on her nose.

"So glad you could come in. Please have a seat."

He sat directly in front of her, his demeanor easy and open.

"Your church is a remarkable amazing place."

"We're pleased to have you. We have hundreds - probably thousands - of volunteers around the country, and now even in other countries. It's the lifeblood of our ministry. So much of our time is spent trying to figure out the best ways to use the time that's so generously donated to us. Usually the decisions make themselves, with so many talented volunteers who bless us with their presence. We have so many basic activities, like phone work, going door to door dropping off flyers, picking up clothes and household goods that are donated, that kind of thing, but in your case, it's a lot more challenging. I feel like I can't squander an opportunity to make use of your special abilities."

Henry just smiled lightly, showing his curiosity.

"The challenge," she said, crossing her fingers and leaning back in her chair, "is in trying to figure out how."

"Well," Henry offered, "I hope I'm not overselling myself. I want to be clear, my job is in helping willing clients find friends and loved ones that they miss. It only works if those spirits are willing to cooperate by making themselves available. Sometimes they're not. It's kind of an inexact science, and I don't have full control over the outcome."

"I see, that's good to know," she said. "I have an idea that might be a good fit. This is a challenging situation, but it feels like we need to try something, anything. There's a couple from our flock who lives just a few miles from here. They're lovely people, Max and Devona Geary. They've always been willing to help out at the times we need them most, despite the burden they carry."

"What burden is that?"

"They have just one daughter. Her name is Sophie, and she's eleven years old. From what they told me, Sophie was born a normal child, happy and healthy. Then when she was four, she and her mother saw a terrible accident. A car ran a red light and hit a man crossing the street in a crosswalk. The man was thrown not far from their car, and he died at the scene. Sophie saw the whole event from her car seat. She hasn't been the same since. It's as if she retreated into some kind of inner world. She doesn't speak, or really communicate with them at all. Doctors have been working with her all this time, and they tell her parents that Sophie's condition is very similar to severe autism, but that they've rarely seen such a condition brought on by trauma. There was nothing her mother could do about it, yet she carries an immense amount of guilt with her still. It's a heartbreaking situation, and I just wish there was something I could do about it."

"It's agonizing for everyone when children are involved, in my line of work too." Henry was not sure what the Reverend had in mind for this difficult situation. I completely understand that you would want to help. Anyone would, but how do you think I can help? It sounds like they're providing her with all the help they can, and I'm guessing they're using people who can do her a lot more good than I can."

"Well, that's where it gets a little complicated." She leaned forward in her chair, taking off her glasses. "Her parents are convinced she sees spirits. Out of nowhere she'll start talking in some kind of gibberish, holding a conversation with people who aren't in the room. Out of nowhere she'll act terrified, or have some kind of emotional reaction that's completely out of context.

"Her parents try to get through to her in these incidents, but it enrages Sophie. She's unable to accept help of any kind. You can imagine how her parents feel after several years of this."

"Okay, I get it," Henry said. "If she's really seeing spirits, then you think maybe I can see them too."

"Exactly. Maybe you can figure out what, or who, is influencing her to live in that other world. Maybe you can communicate with them, and try to explain the impact it's having on the family. They're stuck in quicksand, and I have no idea how to help them. No one does."

"You know, Reverend, it's possible the girl really is autistic and there are no spirits involved at all."

"I realize that," she said. "but even that conclusion would bring some level of acceptance for the Gearys because they've tried all the so-called 'explainable' treatments, to no avail. They're desperate. They just want answers."

"I would want to know too," Henry said. The most difficult reading of his career seemed inevitably ahead.

"Out of curiosity," the Reverend asked, "given your understanding of reincarnation, why would this happen? Why would a child be thrust into a situation that places so much strain on her and everyone around her? In the context of living different lives, what purpose does a life like that serve?"

"My understanding," Henry started, "is that souls can choose that kind of life perhaps as a counterbalance to another life they lived. Perhaps in her past life, Sophie was a fabulous movie star who had everything she could possibly desire - an adoring audience, wealth, and romance. Perhaps after that life, the soul decided it was time to restore some karmic balance and live a life that was filled with frustration and heartbreak, that called upon patience and determination. Souls make their own decisions about the lives they'll live. Nothing is forced upon them. The same goes for her parents. During the interim period between lives, they chose this challenge, to be the parents of a happy, normal girl, only to have it torn away with no power to change things."

"Fascinating interpretation, Henry, I have to admit." She leaned back in her chair. "Highly implausible and seemingly pointless compared to the Christian version of the rewards that await us in heaven for a life well lived, but it is fascinating."

"Well, Reverend," Henry sat upright in his chair, taking care to choose his words carefully, "we talked about this a little last time. There is the belief that reincarnation should still be part of Christianity. So maybe it's not so far-fetched."

"Well it ISN'T part of Christianity, is it Henry?" Her tone sharpened, catching Henry off guard.

"Obviously not. Sorry if I offended you."

"I shouldn't have snapped at you. My apologies. Look," the Reverend said, in a lower but firm voice, "what this family has been through is not something anyone would wish on their worst enemy, let alone would wish upon herself to restore some kind of soul balance."

"It's fine. You care deeply for your congregation. I've never done anything close to this before. I suppose it doesn't hurt to meet with them. When would you like to set up this meeting?"

"Thanks for offering to help. I'll call them tomorrow and try to arrange it for later this week."

The next day, Ellen Grandby Sullivan's Administrative Assistant called Henry to schedule a meeting for the following late afternoon. He checked his schedule and agreed.

Henry spent the evening before the encounter in the local public library, researching Autism. He pored through all the literature he could find, online and in the stacks, to learn about the brain patterns of people suffering from the condition and whether there were any references to spirit contact, even anecdotal. He found nothing on that subject but he learned more than he ever expected about the condition.

He slept that night as soundly as he ever had. If Aisling had wanted to visit him to talk about his encounter with this eleven year old, she would have found it difficult to penetrate his deep slumber.

All during the following day he could not keep his mind from the encounter that awaited. He did his best to focus on his readings for the day, and his clients did not seem to notice his distraction.

When he arrived again in the office of the Reverend, her assistant asked Henry to sit until they were ready for him. More than twenty minutes passed before the Reverend appeared.

"She knows something's up," she said, without a hello.

"How can you tell?"

"She's more agitated than usual when she's here. She's resisting everything. She obviously doesn't want to be here. Before, she never really seemed to know or care that she was here. Are you ready to give this a try?"

"Ready as I can be," Henry answered.

She led him down a hallway toward a conference room. Reverend Sullivan hesitated for several seconds before opening the door. She closed her eyes, as if praying, then looked back at Henry nervously. She opened the door and walked in. Henry followed slowly behind her.

Immediately he felt the pressure of the room. It was if he was a diver that had suddenly submerged ten feet below the surface. He followed the shape of Reverend Sullivan as she stopped and stood, and was unable to clearly focus on the other figures in the room. He strained to adjust his eyes.

"Max and Devona Geary, I'd like you to meet Henry Chimera."

Henry walked sluggishly toward them, extending his hand. "It's a pleasure to meet you both."

"Thank you for meeting with us," Max said.

Henry said nothing in return, still disoriented. He simply nodded and attempted a smile.

"And this," the Reverend said, "is Sophie. Sophie, I'd like you to meet Henry. You two have a lot in common."

Sophie was a beautiful girl with bronze skin and captivating eyes. Her mother appeared to be African American, perhaps of Caribbean ancestry. Max was a fair skinned white man with reddish hair and bright blue eyes.

Sophie had inherited a riveting confluence of reddish-black hair, lovely skin like her mother, and icy blue eyes.

Sophie's eyes lifted slowly from their fixed position on the floor in front of her. Slowly her focus moved to Henry. As she turned toward him, an intense emotion began to envelop her face. Within seconds it moved from the vacant look of a child to the fierce glare of a wary soul.

Slowly Henry acclimated to the foreign pressure in the room. When he was able to lock onto her spatially, he labored to apply his focus in her direction. Despite his difficulty keeping his eyes focused on the girl, it was far easier for his mind to see her.

There were specific features that were impossible to ignore, in particular the eyes inside her mind. They appeared limitless. It was very different from looking into the mind's eye of other living humans, or even into a normal spirit. Her eyes suggested depth, caution, and danger. Henry knew immediately that this spirit's view into his essence was utterly complete, while he was only seeing the parts of her, or this spirit, that he was allowed to see.

The other feature that was impossible to ignore was the color that surrounded her. If it was possible for the color black to be nearly blinding, this was it. There were tinges of violet and an earthy gray, but mainly it was a blackness that held a steady place around the essence of this eleven year old girl.

He knew from reading about auras that the colors represented a complex combination that included a tendency to absorb surrounding energies, a psychic connection, and self defense. This was a complex soul that was engulfed by a form of energy that Henry viewed as threatening. The spirit or spirits surrounding the girl were ready for any kind of challenge.

For what seemed like several minutes there was a sizing up process occurring between the two. If the other three people in the room were talking, neither Henry nor the girl heard what they were saying. The connection was a powerful link that would not be easily interrupted.

Henry was little more than an unwelcome distraction, an intruder at a private gathering.

"State your business," a voice spoke to him, coming from the direction of Sophie.

"I was asked to help this girl." Henry felt as though he was speaking up through an inverted well.

"Your help is not required."

Any thought of defiance did not seem to be an option. There was a strong threat of harm from the slightest misplaced communication.

"The girl's family is in misery without her. What shall I tell them?"

"What they see of her is what they are entitled to. The rest is unavailable."

Henry remained engaged with this voice, but he assumed the posture of an obedient servant. He could not forget his promise to try to help the Geary family, but he felt that he had few options available. Despite the risk, Henry's sense of obligation as a medium emboldened him. He was put in this situation to try to help, and so far he had done nothing for the girl who at the center of so much concern.

"If I can't help, they'll just find someone else."

There was no message in reply, only sensation. The sensation was like the weight of the ocean crashing down and through Henry's chest. He was paralyzed as a force more powerful than any he had ever felt bore into, through, and around every cell in his body. The sensation was the force of a tsunami striking land. He had no chance to resist against a force so powerful.

While he was completely aware of the energy that enveloped him, he had no awareness of the state of his physical body. He knew he was in a room with the child and three other adults, but he lacked any ability to comprehend what was physically happening in the room.

Instead of water pounding against him, there was a concoction consisting of nearly every negative emotion that could be experienced by living man. Fear, jealousy, terror, humiliation, physical pain, intimidation, exhaustion, greed, dishonesty, cruelty, and self-loathing. It all blended into a ghastly amnion, with Henry simmering at the center.

Around the edge of this helpless state he sensed other spirits. Many others, each of whom was in the same desperate situation as Sophie Geary. He heard their groans, their retching, their crying. All the voices were female, and each was as helpless as he and Sophie.

He began to lose his grip on the surface of this sea of despair. He began to sink, until he was fully submerged.

Then things went completely dark.

ASCENSIONS

The darkness eased. Light gradually broke through the haze. As light increased, the pain did as well. It was an intense ache that Henry imagined a migraine must feel like. He winced to ease some of the edge, then moved his fingers, hands, and arms, then gradually opened his eyes. Regaining his five senses allowed him to cope with the pain, then his other realities.

He was on the floor, exactly where he had been standing when he lost his way. He thought he had been away for hours, so he was surprised he had not been moved to a more sensible place, such as the inside of an ambulance. Devona Geary was at his elbow, with Max Geary and Ellen Grandby Sullivan just behind her.

"Can you hear me, Mister Chimera?"

"Yes." He stretched his neck and attempted to sit up straight. "How long was I out?"

The three looked at each other.

"Well," Devona answered, "just a few seconds. You were in sort of a trance, then you just kind of fainted. It's a good thing the Reverend was nearby, otherwise you might have really hurt yourself when you fell. It was very sudden."

He looked at Ellen Grandby Sullivan. She wore the same concerned look as the other two.

"Thanks for catching my fall, Reverend."

"You're welcome. Do you faint often?"

"First time," he replied in a coarse voice.

They helped him onto a chair. In the corner he noticed the form of Sophie, just as before. Her condition had not changed. Her arms were wrapped around her knees and she was lightly rocking, still in her own world.

To his surprise, she gave him the briefest of glances. It was unmistakeable. She locked eyes with him, tears newly formed. When she saw his surprised reaction, she burrowed her face down again before the others noticed.

Max Geary spoke to Henry. "So what do you do from here? What happens?"

Henry was still coming to terms with what he had just been through. The spirit that overwhelmed him and was such a dominant part of this girl's existence had left its mark on Henry. He had never before experienced a contact of any kind as intense and intimidating. The presence made it clear that it was capable of great power and would have its way. Henry was left with no appetite for challenging the ground it had staked. He tried to maintain a calm exterior, but internally he desired only to leave this room as quickly as he could.

"It already happened," Henry said. "I connected with your daughter right after I walked in."

The girl's father moved forward in his chair.

"I guess it happened really fast, but it didn't seem fast to me. I wasn't sure it would ever end."

"Well, what happened?"

"I should clarify," Henry said in a tired voice, " that I connected less with your daughter than the spirit - or spirits - that surround her."

"*Excuse me?*" The man was nearly out of his chair. "There are spirits surrounding my daughter?"

Henry considered how much to share with her parents. If he disclosed too much they would be heartbroken at the anguish she was enduring, and angry with him for being unable to do anything about it. If he disclosed too little, they would continue under the impression that she was in some sort of brain-impaired state.

He chose to soften the blow, as there was little he could say about her current state that would ease their concerns.

"Yes, but I'm not sure if they're there to protect her or not. I do know they're very powerful, and I didn't see any possible way to change Sophie's condition, or increase the level of her ... engagement here in the conscious world."

"Just like that? You're here in the room for a few seconds, you drop to the floor for a minute, then you declare there's nothing that can be done? Mister Chimera, your 'help' hasn't been too helpful." The man looked away from Henry in disgust.

Henry understood the torment pediatricians must endure when they have little hope to offer anguished parents.

"I'm sorry, Mister Geary. I'm worried that too much meddling on my part could cause more harm to your daughter than good."

Max Geary sat back in his chair, staring straight ahead.

"I don't know what I can do to help her," Henry said, "and I'm sorry that's the case. If there's some way I can help Sophie in the future I'll do it, but right now it's best that I back off."

Henry began to leave meekly, wishing he had never entered the room. Before exiting he turned to Sophie.

"Hang in there, Sophie. It's all going to be fine." She stared straight ahead with no response.

Henry was scheduled to volunteer at the church that evening, but instead told Ronnie Wilcox that he was not feeling himself.

Approaching his apartment, he felt something had changed from the time he left. He stepped back toward the street and chose a slow walk around the building. He tried to be discreet as he looked at the windows inside for any sign of movement. He scanned the area but saw nothing out of the ordinary, just the normal activities of a weekday evening.

He approached his front door quietly, then turned the key and entered quickly, thinking he might surprise someone waiting for him into quick motion. As he entered he noticed no movement, and nothing in the air suggesting the presence of another, but something caught his eye. It was a piece of paper that had been slid under the door.

"We need to talk. Meet me at the Civil War statue in Webster Park, tomorrow morning at 7:15. Looking forward to seeing you. Be safe. D."

It was a welcome end to a deflating day.

Henry arrived at the park early, seeing only the expected joggers and dog walkers. In his drive around the perimeter of the park and his slow, winding walk to the meeting spot, all seemed normal on this cool, damp morning. He only hoped that Dee would arrive alone.

She appeared on time, a slender, alluring form emerging from the distance. She was an exquisite sight. It had been a long, lonely stretch and his pulse quickened with her slow approach.

"Hi Henry." It was the first he had seen her smile since the two were spending time with Herbrit.

"It's great to see you, Dee. You came alone?"

"Yes, of course. I told the others I would try to touch base with you, but I didn't give any details. Shall we sit?"

Henry sat facing her on the bench to allow a view of all approach angles. Behind them were woods, in front of them the two trails that went past the monument. An occasional walker or jogger would stroll by. They felt secluded.

Dee turned to him. "How are you adjusting a normal life again?"

He explained about the challenges of resuming the business of being a medium, but assured her that he had picked up exactly where he had left off. She seemed relieved.

"I wasn't sure what we had done to you. I'm still coming to terms with the treatment you received from Lars."

"It was miserable," Henry replied, "but I made it and I'm here now. It usually doesn't pay to underestimate me."

"I've noticed," Dee said with a soft smile.

"You won't believe what happened to me," he said eagerly. "I was asked by the Reverend to intervene in the case of a young girl with some sort of impairment, like Autism."

"Reverend? What Reverend?"

"Oh my God, I'm getting ahead of myself. I mean Ellen herself."

"WHAT? You've already been in to meet Ellen Grandby Sullivan?"

"I have. It's kind of a long story." He explained about his decision to approach the Reverend and offer to perform volunteer work, then her interest in his unique abilities.

Dee absorbed his explanation with eyes wide open. "Wow, this is all happening so fast. Are you sure you know what you're doing?"

"So far so good. I told her that I'm there to try something different in my life, and even though she remembered right away that I'm a medium, it didn't seem to be a problem. She was just hoping I could help this little girl and her parents."

Dee quietly considered the implications as Henry described in detail his experience with Sophie Geary, including his sense of powerlessness in the presence of this entity, whatever it was.

After hearing it all, Dee sighed, leaned back on the bench, and looked into the distance. "I wonder what in hell we've gotten you into."

"I'm not doing anything against my will," Henry explained. "I made the decision to engage with the church, and I decided to try to help the girl. If it turns out that I can't get out of it easily, then it will be my fault."

"I understand that," Dee replied, "but I also want to remind you, Henry, that you're a valuable person to us. To me." She caught herself, looking down.

Henry stayed quiet.

"As fearless as you've been, you can't help if you're not around. We would go to your funeral and mourn over your death, wondering why it happened. Then it would be over. You would be of no help to anyone ever again. I don't think that's something we want. It's not something I want."

"I don't plan to be reckless," he answered softly, "but it's not in my nature to do nothing. If anyone has little to lose, it's me."

"I could say the same thing about myself," she said.

The two were silent, considering their loneliness together.

"It was a very frustrating experience," Henry continued, "not being able to help that little girl. It's impossible to get her out of my mind, but that's not all."

"What do you mean?"

"I told you I was doing some volunteer work for The Church. It was phone calling. One of the people that was on my list to call was a woman that I had met before named Joan Swenson."

He described the circumstances of how he knew her, first as a client who came in for a reading, later as an acquaintance of Janice Donnelly and a member of The Church.

"So why is that significant? It sounds like a coincidence."

"She saw something in the church that she was clearly not meant to see. She thinks it was a video of the Dalai Lama in captivity, being questioned by two men."

"Oh my God! She thinks the church is somehow involved in his disappearance?"

"I have no idea what to make of it," Henry said. "The Dalai Lama has nothing they would want or need. Maybe his disappearance clears the way for them to accomplish something, who knows what."

"What I think we're beginning to see," Dee said after several quiet seconds, "is that this church is dangerous in ways that we don't understand."

She turned to him. "Henry, you need to back off. You need to get yourself out of this situation. I don't see any further good coming from you being close to these people."

"I disagree," he said, turning from her. "In just a couple weeks, look at the progress. I learned some things about The Church that nobody else knows, and I've gotten to know one of the very top people in the church."

She put her hand on his arm, holding it firmly.

"Will that do us or anyone any good? The cops won't do anything with your information. If there's nothing we can do on our own, what good is knowing?"

"I have no answer to that." Henry stood up to leave. "But I can't just suddenly stop. Even if I wanted to, it would raise suspicions if I just up and quit. I'm moving ahead to see where this takes me, Dee. Just stay in touch with me. Please."

He stood up from the bench and offered his arm. "Shall we?"

They walked leisurely from the center of the park talking about the other Origenists, neither eager to return to their secluded, guarded lives. She assured him that Lars had been behaving himself since Henry's departure, and that there had been no further incidents or threats.

When it was time to make their good byes, each paused uncomfortably.

"I'm really glad we had a chance to talk, Henry." She looked into his eyes.

"Me too. I was worried about you." He moved slightly closer to her, unsure whether a hug would make her uncomfortable.

Without a word she threw her arms around his neck and pressed her lips to his. After his initial surprise, he returned the kiss with passion. Her scent was subtle, fresh, and full of life, and he breathed in her essence with all his senses. The moment overpowered him in a splendid embrace that ran through and over him like a warm breeze in a cold winter. Her lips moved with his as their kiss endured, neither wanting the moment to end. When their lips separated, their eyes remained closed and their lips stayed close, each extending the moment. In a haze they slowly looked into each other's eyes.

"What a nice surprise," he said, laughing softly.

She looked into his chest, shyly. "I care about you, and I don't want anything to happen to you. It was rough losing David, who was the closest thing to a father I ever had. I'd be completely lost if something happened to you.

Her words landed with unexpected weight. "No one has ever said that to me before."

"Well, now someone has. Deal with it." They laughed softly, eyes locked and unblinking.

"When will I hear from you again, Dee?"

"I don't know. Not long. I don't want anything to follow a pattern. Please watch yourself, Henry. Take nothing and no one for granted."

"You as well." They released hands and went their separate ways.

In the distance, a pair of eyes watched as they kissed, then walked in different directions. He silently waited for the right moment to move.

The middle of Henry's day was spent alternating between clients who depended on his full attention and the administrative work required to keep rebuilding his clientele. Among the clients that came to see him on this day was Will Gilkyson, the father of Rayna Gilkyson, the teenage girl who died in a single car accident. She was a spirit who had not left this realm. Each time the man had come in to visit her, she refused any direct communication. Her messages to Henry were clipped. She had no choice but to acknowledge their presence because there was no one else able or willing to communicate with in her condition, so she spoke only to Henry in messages that were brief and laden with powerful negative emotion. She was a confused and angry girl, who blamed her current condition on her father. Each time Will came in for a session, he made it clear that he would not rest until his daughter was able to do the same. Theirs was a puzzle that Henry had not yet solved.

Henry welcomed the man into his reading room, and the two settled in for what would likely be a draining session for both of them.

"I miss her, Henry, and I'm so worried about her. I've done some reading about these spirits that can't find peace, and cannot - or will not - ascend to where they're meant to be. It breaks my heart to think that my daughter is suffering. I want to get the message to her that I love her now more than ever, and that her mother and I will not rest until she's at peace."

They opened the session with the usual prayer of thanks, extending the message to any spirits listening in that their intentions were pure and selfless. They prayed for a session that would begin and end in love.

Henry closed his eyes and attempted to summon Rayna. Within moments he felt the distinctive vibrations that could only come from the troubled teen. He welcomed her, assuring her that her father was present to check on her and that, as promised, he would never abandon her.

"Your father would like to know how you are. He misses you terribly. He and your mother are very worried about you."

There was little more than a rumble that Henry could detect, barely audible even to his keen senses.

Most of the spirits Henry communicated had reached adulthood by the time they passed on. Some were selfish or childish or immature, but nearly all were adults in their last living state. Because Rayna died before reaching maturity, she required special handling.

"I think we need to lay some ground rules for this session," Henry said aloud so that both father and daughter could hear.

"During this session we will avoid the subject of blame. When we talk about blame, we're talking about the past. The past cannot be changed. In this session we will focus our collective energy on what lies ahead. I trust this is clear to everyone."

"Yes," Will Gilkyson said.

Henry detected a vibratory pattern from Rayna that was not clearly a yes or a no.

"That will be our starting point. Rayna, your father is here because he and your mother love you very much, but they remain very concerned about you. They cannot live their lives in peace knowing that you are not in peace. So please tell me, Rayna, how are you?"

The girl's message came slowly. When it was recognized by Henry it was weak and uncertain. "Scared. Alone."

"I'm very sorry to hear that Rayna, but that's why your father is here. He wants more than anything to comfort your loneliness, to ease this pain you've felt. He wants you to be where you belong."

"He can't make that happen," she said.

"You're right, he can't make that happen - by himself. It can happen if all three of us align our energies in the same direction. It's like rowing a boat. It only moves in the right direction when all are in unison. Remember Rayna, there is no changing the past. Only our actions in the present can change the future, and in the future you will be with your father and mother again. Things will be better. You must believe that."

"How?" Her hard exterior was beginning to crack.

"We need to understand what has you upset. Can you tell me exactly what's bothering you?"

She was quiet but engaged. The energy Henry sensed was that of someone who was unable to explain her emotions. He needed to calm her down. Perhaps another approach was necessary.

"Would you prefer that I keep whatever you're about to tell me private?"

"Yes," she said quietly.

"Will, she'd like to talk to me privately. I'd like to ask for your patience for a few moments."

"Of course," he said, "whatever you suggest."

Henry directed his focus to the girl. "Please talk to me. What's bothering you?"

"He's thinks I was irresponsible that night, that I wrecked his car and it was all my fault."

"He doesn't care about the car. Would you mind telling me what happened? Nobody else was there. Only you can tell us."

In a virtual whisper, she tried to explain. "It was dark. I was coming home late from work. There were no lights on the road. I looked down to see how fast I was going, and when I looked up there was a deer running right in front of me. I couldn't hit it, I just couldn't. So I turned away from it and the car went straight into the woods. I just didn't want to kill the animal. He should be proud of me instead of mad."

"He's not mad at you, Rayna. He's blaming himself for not doing more to protect you. He thinks he should never have let you drive alone at night."

"I didn't kill the deer. He and my mom always taught me to value life first, and I did. Now he won't let me leave here."

"Your Dad isn't keeping you here Rayna, and he doesn't know that you were trying to do the right thing. He'll be very proud of you when I tell him. You were a hero! You put the safety of another living creature ahead of your own. Rayna, this will be important for your parents to know, don't you think?"

"I guess," she replied. Her voice was stronger.

"I would very much like to share this with your father. Would that be okay?"

"I guess."

Henry then described the conversation to Will Gilkyson. When he was finished, the big man put his face in his hands and cried.

Henry turned his attention back to the girl. Her demeanor had changed completely. For the first time in Henry's sessions with the two, she was looking directly at her father, trying to understand the emotions around him. Sympathy and compassion emerged. What had been guarded and resentful was now caring and loving. She seemed to understand for the first time what it felt like to be a parent who lost his child. She felt his many months of pain all at once, and it was a powerful sensation for the girl's spirit.

"Tell her," Will Gilkyson said through a choked voice, "that I could not be more proud of her. I can't imagine a more perfect daughter. We're very blessed to have been with her for the time we had."

Henry replied softly. "She heard you. Finally."

After several moments in which the two seemed connected in spirit, Henry addressed her directly. "Rayna, together we accomplished something really important today."

"I know," she said. "Thank you."

"You're welcome, but there's something just as important that you need to do." Henry sensed her guardedness returning, so he continued. "This thing is necessary to allow your parents to move past their grief and to know you're safe and happy."

"What do you want me to do?"

"You need to take the next step. Find the light, and move into it. Don't be afraid. It's the only way your family can find peace. It has to be you. No one else can do this."

Will Gilkyson was following Henry's conversation through his tears. He was smiling to his daughter, encouraging her to listen.

"How do I know things will be better? I belong here." Her tone was dejected. "This is where I've been my whole life."

"This place is more familiar, that's all," said Henry. "You told me before that you're lonely. You won't ever be lonely again. If you move to the light, you will find comfort and peace. If you stay where you are, you will be alone. Rayna, do what is best."

There was a long pause. "Do you promise?"

"I promise, Rayna. I wouldn't steer you wrong. We're in the same boat, remember?"

Henry heard the giggle of a teenage girl.

"Tell Daddy I love him, and to tell Mommy I love her too."

Later that evening Henry chose his normal way to unwind after an emotional day, on the couch with a glass of wine and soft jazz playing. His meeting with Dee brought him more joy than he could have hoped for. The possibility of a future together, if there was one, did not stray far from his thoughts at any time.

The session with the Gilkyson family was draining but satisfying. There were so many positive things possible in his life that just one year before were so distant.

Still, there was the sordid mess hanging over his head with the Church of the Tortured Christ. The complexity of the situation was also never far from his thoughts. As his thoughts moved from happy to daunting, he embraced his exhaustion as sleep began to engulf him.

As quickly as he closed his eyes, he felt the presence of a familiar friend.

"Aisling, to what do I owe the pleasure?"

"I'm not of a mind to exchange pleasantries, my dear."

"I see. Well then, what's on your mind?"

"Your encounter at the church yesterday is on many minds, my dear. It's the talk of the town."

"And which town would that be?"

"Don't be smug with me, young Henry. I know you're giddy over your first kiss, but these are very serious matters indeed."

"My first kiss! As if! I've had plenty of w..."

"It's not important. We have important business to discuss."

"It's been an interesting week," Henry answered, "even terrifying at times, with a child at the center of it."

"Yes, we know all too well."

"What else do you know, Aisling? I've never been so overwhelmed by a spirit."

"It was more than a mere spirit, my boy," she replied. "We're trying to understand what it is you stumbled upon, and why. If it was just a displaced spirit, it would be visible in the tapestry. This one is completely off the grid."

"The tapestry? Can you explain?"

"Each soul is accounted for," she said, "even the ones like the Gilkyson girl you helped today who are stuck in this dimension. The hierarchy can usually identify any soul at any time, but the entity that has a hold on Sophie far exceeded the energy of a normal soul. It even exceeded the energy of some of our elders. Most alarming, it seems to be able to conceal it's true essence. This presented quite a shock to the balance, to the point where concerns have been raised about vital processes that are at risk of interruption."

Henry asked casually, "And I gather I'm in quite a bit of danger."

"To put it mildly. Henry, you've managed to bring self-preservation to advanced levels through your life. I admire you for that, however there has never been a more important time to be very careful about the decisions you make."

"Message received, but I made a promise to help the Origenists. I have no intention of backing down from that commitment."

"It's never wrong to listen to your heart, but it's always wrong to ignore your head. You have great survival instincts, Henry. Please follow them."

Aisling entered the Great Hall. The high walls were made of a luminous, sparkling crystal, the warm light coming from all directions. The room was filled with a loving glow that filled her senses, seeping into her whole being. The top of the cavernous space was especially bright and warm, where an omnipotent, unfathomably powerful energy seemed to hover. She paused for several moments, allowing the energy to surround and engulf her before she gradually moved toward the front of the hall.

In a line sat the Elders, each with distinctive symbolic markings on the large medallions they wore. The symbols were distinct, and symbolizing something - emotion, wisdom, or knowledge - that was well beyond her comprehension. Each seemed to represent a unique perspective, but together they presented a wholeness of vision that she had never experienced, or even imagined.

Their connection with Aisling was non-judgmental but completely in tune with her thoughts and emotions. It was, of course, unnecessary to explain her reason for being before them, but she conveyed gratitude for allowing her to be in their presence.

Their question to her was inviting and warm. "*What is your challenge?*"

"Our challenge is to overcome obstacles that are beyond our current abilities. We believe the risks are great, and that the journey of many souls are at risk. There are adversaries we confront who possess power we have never encountered, and may not understand."

"*What of our pledge to avoid interference?*"

"We believe that interference has already occurred, and further disruption is what we are trying to prevent. Without contravention, the tapestry may be torn. We believe ourselves to be without other options."

"*Your goals in trying to overcome these challenges?*"

"Maintain fairness for all, the same equal start that we have all enjoyed. Prevent an imbalance that would deny even the most basic opportunities for growth, for many souls."

"A noble pursuit. The assistance you desire?"

"Access to an advanced soul. One from the second sphere who could provide the guidance that we currently lack to confront this challenge."

"A highly unusual request."

"Yes, but it is one we hope you agree is essential given the circumstances."

"Unique circumstances to be sure. Do you realize the risks presented by access on the earthly plane to these highly advanced spirits?"

"I do not believe I do."

"It would be unprecedented. The portal attainment you request is highly complex. The impact of this level of intervention cannot be predicted. Your chances for success are just as uncertain. If the access is granted, what safeguards can you ensure for the resource we provide?"

"None, I'm afraid. However if we succeed, we will have prevented a grave injustice to the process we so depend upon. Maintaining the balance we have enjoyed for millennia will not come without risk. I can only promise that we will do all we can to ensure that our quest succeeds."

Aisling retreated while they communicated with each other at a level of energy beyond her comprehension. She sensed that their consultations were intensive, with wide disparities in opinion. She anxiously awaited their response. Finally they turned their attention to her.

"It will be Hildegarde. She possesses the wisdom you require."

The black Cadillac Escalade moved slowly down the secluded gravel road. It curved along through a thick forest that obscured much of the bright sunshine above the thick southern foliage.

"How can you be so convinced that this is anything more than just a very powerful, very pissed off spirit?"

"It doesn't work like that. Simple spirits don't grab onto a living human like this and not let go. They might haunt and harass a person, or a house, or even a family. Usually they're the leftover spirit of a formerly living person who's stuck on the earth, and failed to ascend for whatever reason. In an attempt to gain some sort of connection with the living, they attach themselves to people or objects associated with certain people. I think a lot of them don't even know they're dead. They're just following some of the habits they picked up in their lifetimes, like following the same routine, day after day, year after year. Or children who never leave their parents' home. Or couples who stay married for years even though there's no love left, and all there is left is unsatisfying companionship. This is different. This isn't a haunting. This is an utter, complete takeover of a living human being by a spirit."

"You said you did some research. What did you find out?"

"I contacted a university professor who I had met once at a fundraiser. I remembered he introduced himself as a professor of theology, but that most of his research had to do with theological history. I kept his card and gave him a call. I made up a story about a young staffer who had been having dreams about pagan gods. I told him that this staffer's family came from Pakistan, and she was having what she believed to be visitations from some god who she thought was trying to do her harm, even abduct her. I told him it was probably just a dream, likely the result of wavering faith, but I asked him if he could look into it.

"He contacted me within a couple days with an urgent request to meet. He was all excited about it, almost alarmed. He told me about a god he studied up on called Immat. Evidently it's a pagan god that was worshipped by people in eastern Afghanistan until about 1890, when nearly all the people in that region were converted to Islam. The region is called Kafiristan. 'Kafir' is an Arabic term that's usually translated as an unbeliever or an infidel. Anyway, before the conversion, Immat was one of several gods they worshipped for many centuries. After the conversion, Immat was left with almost nobody to follow him."

"Well," he asked, "I guess that's the nature of being a pagan god, right? Pagans believed in many gods, which is what made them pagans. Considering there aren't many left on the planet, I guess that means there are a number of jilted pagan gods somewhere out there too. What makes this one special"?

"Well, for starters, this one was considered a demonic god."

"Demonic? I didn't know there was any such thing as a demonic pagan god, other than maybe Satan."

"Pagans are pagans, and gods are gods. Pagans believed, and still believe, in all sorts of gods. Some gods don't depend on exclusive arrangements, like the current one does. Anyway, that's why the professor was so eager to talk, because I gather this is fairly unusual. Anyway, that's not even the most intriguing part of it."

"Do tell."

'Evidently this particular god was accustomed to receiving human sacrifices, to the tune of twenty or so virgin daughters every year."

"Twenty virgins per year? That is one voracious appetite. I like this god."

"I wonder if he'd like you. Probably not."

"So you think that somehow this is the pagan god that you met the other day? That seems like a stretch."

"I do. Everything seems to fall into place. The more the professor talked about this Immat, the more I was convinced he's the same one. The pure energy over those two was overwhelming. It's just how a god would behave who was accustomed to sacrifices, and hordes of people adoring him over many, many centuries. In Immat's case, those perks just stopped, almost overnight. It sounds as though he'd like things to return to the way they were."

"Starting with Sophie?"

"I suppose, although I'm not sure Sophie is the start."

"That's a somewhat horrifying thought."

"More horrifying than you and I being the first followers in his comeback tour?"

They drove in silence.

When the SUV approached a discreet dwelling, it glided off the road and into the driveway, almost completely hidden from the road.

Ellen Grandby Sullivan and Edgar approached the front door and knocked. Within seconds they heard the sounds of multiple deadbolts unlocking.

"Welcome," a man intoned with a deep voice. "Any trouble finding us?"

"No, the directions were just right." Ellen Grandby Sullivan moved quickly through the door, followed by Edgar. "Well, where is he?"

"Follow me." The man was large and menacing. He wore dress pants and a turtleneck that showed his thick arms.

Around his neck was a cross, etched silver with a garnet in the center.

The scene inside was not as she expected. He sat in a corner, tied to a chair but sleeping peacefully. His face was swollen.

"Can you update me?" She was in the shadow of this enormous and imposing man, under whose care she had entrusted one of the most revered men in the world.

"Update you? He's still alive."

She glared. He stared back blankly.

"What have you two been talking about?"

"You asked me to find out who he's met since he's been here. I have to tell you, that's not a very interesting conversation with this guy."

"Why?"

"Because he's in contact with everyone but he doesn't remember last names or places very well."

"Is he being stubborn or does he really not know?"

"I'm not sure. Probably a little of both. Look at his face. I hit hard. Look at his hands and feet. Fire doesn't feel good when it's uncomfortably close to your skin."

"You burned him?" She turned abruptly to the captor.

"Not me."

"Explain."

"Looking after this guy isn't a one man job. You paid me enough to get relief, and I did."

"I assumed you would need help" she said, backing off, "but I assumed you would take the lead in carrying out my orders."

"I have, but it's been weeks, and we've been getting nowhere. What took you so long to get here?"

"Prior commitments. You're well paid. Where's your help?"

"His turn to snooze. He's downstairs."

The pause in their conversation seemed to make the sleeping man wake. He yawned and stretched to the extend that he could, mildly interested in his new visitors.

"How have my charges been treating you?"

"I would love to tell you that it's been with nothing but brotherhood and respect," he said, smiling gently, "but that would not be truthful."

"Well, I'm sorry your stay hasn't been pleasant," she replied, "but there are important matters at hand."

"Yes, I understand." The Dalai Lama was respectful. "There always are. In every day of every life."

She stood over him as a teacher would stand over an unrepentant student.

"Your holiness, what are the important matters in your life?"

He stretched his swollen jaw before speaking. "The important matters in my life are those that should be important in all lives. Cherishing what we have been given. Nourishing our spirit so that we may nourish those around us. These are important matters to me, and I hope they are important to you as well."

She was unmoved. "But what really affects you? You travel more than most people will travel in a hundred lifetimes. During those travels I'm sure there are experiences that stand out more than others. There are people you meet, places you visit, things you see, that especially stand out. What are those places and people?"

The Dalai Lama looked at her with a nervous smile. "I try to assign special meaning to every person I meet in every location. In America, I suppose I prefer my experiences in larger cities, both the rich and poor ones."

"And why is that?" She smiled intensely, with sincere interest.

"Because there are so many people with so many diversions, most of which offer little reward. There is so much work to do there, but not much is truly fulfilling. Still, the potential is great."

She seemed energized.

"What kind of reward should they be looking for? It seems to me that people wandering in our big cities have nothing in mind ... NOTHING ... except reward."

"Yes, it is true that many are after reward, but it is short term reward they seek. I am referring to the kind of reward that can only be earned through a lifetime of commitment. This is the reward that will help them beyond this lifetime."

She smiled, pausing before continuing. "Now we're talking."

He looked at her and smiled. "What else would you like to talk about?"

"Your reference to 'this lifetime.' Can you elaborate?"

"We are each on a journey that goes beyond our current life and circumstances. The challenge that each of us faces is unique to our lifetime. We all choose our challenges in this life, then when circumstances are presented through the course of our life's journey, it is the way we address those challenges that determines how our soul moves forward."

"Now let me stop you there." She turned and walked. "Forward in what way? In my faith there is the today, and there is heaven. We believe very strongly in heaven. It's where we all want to be. I preach that we should make every move as if it's a move toward our eternal reward." She paused.

"I do as well." He smiled. "We have much in common."

"I wonder if we do."

His smile faded. "Why do you wonder? There are actions and there are repercussions. We learn from our mistakes and our understanding grows. We move forward. How do you believe our philosophies differ?"

"In my faith we treat a single life as a test. Either we pass or we fail. Either we move on into the Lord's arms or we don't. There are no 'do-overs'. Either you get it right or you don't. I'm here to make sure people get it right."

"As am I."

"See, that's the thing. It doesn't seem as if you are. Bad behavior seems to be little more than a minor inconvenience. If things don't work out this time, like if you murder five people in a robbery, HEY, you get another shot. Just try harder next time, and don't do that again! Is that how a soul advances?"

"No, that is not how a soul advances. A learned soul would never commit such an inhuman act. It is more about learning than advancing. A soul learns about itself by examining its reaction to circumstances, then increasing our wisdom to have better reactions. We try to control our emotions and reactions, but we are not all strong and mature. As a parents tell teenagers, we may not always be able to control our behavior, but we can control the circumstances with which we find ourselves."

"So you're saying that by controlling our circumstances, we can limit the challenges that might come our way? And this promotes soul advancement. Are you really saying that?"

"To some extent, yes. Christians have a wonderful saying. 'God will not give you more than you can handle.' It is a very wise expression. We have a say in the circumstances presented to us."

He looked down at the ropes confining his movement then back up to the Reverend. "We maintain some control over the events that come before us, but is it complete control? No, of course it is not."

"This sounds like gibberish. We control some circumstances but not all, and we aren't presented with anything we can't handle. Does that about sum it up? Because in that situation nobody would ever be the victim of war, or terrible crimes or plane crashes." She stood over him impatiently.

"Each of us lives through many lives. Following each life, we contemplate the things we learned, how our soul grew. The direction it still must grow. We contemplate the things that might be learned in future lives. We may consider the life we just lived, then choose to spend a lifetime as a blind man, or as a widow with children in extreme poverty, or as a child with severe autism. We may choose to live a life that ends violently, wrongly at the hands of another. Mine may end that way today. While it may be impossible to overcome these difficult challenges, how we accept and react to them are the victories that create the opportunity for your soul to learn and grow."

"An interesting philosophy, to be sure, your Holiness. Unfortunately the major religions of the world don't really see it your way."

"There are many reasons for that," he replied. "Some were lost along the way, through the centuries of these religions. In other cases it was the result of the circumstances of the time. However I assure you, the notion of the iterative nature of the soul's growth dates back many centuries."

"That's one viewpoint. Another is that Jesus Christ our Lord died for our sins. Despite the overwhelming evidence that this is what happened, others believe he survived his crucifixion and went on to have a long life and children. There are many unsupported theories out there. Thanks for another example." She turned her back on him, slowly circling the room. Edgar and the large man listened silently.

"So your Holiness, how will your soul grow from the circumstances that you find yourself in now?"

"I am certain I will learn from this experience, whether in this life or in future lives, but I cannot be sure of what those lessons are. I pray that my actions will be sincere and true. I remain open to any lessons I gain from this ... unpleasant experience."

She offered him a conciliatory smile. "It isn't pleasant for us either, and we're extremely interested in the lessons you have to teach us."

"I will tell you anything I know. I hide nothing."

"How does it happen?"

"How does what happen?"

"How does one life go into the next life? What's the process? How are things kept straight? With only a slight mistake, one soul can go into the life of a wealthy, entitled brat while another goes into the life of an impoverished third world nobody. What are the controls in place to ensure that no mistakes happen?"

"You ask difficult questions." He smiled again. "No soul is a 'nobody.' There are no dead end souls. Some souls are at the beginning of their journey, others nearing the end of the road. It is a long road."

Her countenance transformed. Rage enveloped her. She bounded to his face.

"We are not children, and we are not STUPID. I'm not interested in hearing any more about how how a soul LEARNS. I'm interested in the PROCESS. Now speak about THE PROCESS."

The Dalai Lama took a deep breath before speaking.

"Just as you have choices today about what you'll do tomorrow, we have choices in what life we find ourselves. That impaired child in the city chose those challenges because perhaps in his most recent life he chose the gift of advanced intellect. That wealthy child chose an easy path in this life, for whatever reason. Perhaps it was because the prior life was an especially difficult, challenging one. We all need a break now and then." The Dalai Lama smiled through a swollen face.

She smiled through clenched teeth. "Yes, I understand your views on that. You decide the next life you'll live. I'm interested in knowing how it happens once the choice is made. What is the process involved in assigning your soul to a child that is born in that place in time? How does it happen? What forces or spirits or THINGS intervene to make sure nothing goes badly in that process?"

"Buddhism is not concerned with these matters. Our beliefs concern enlightenment. We know that there exists a process of assigning souls to specific places and people. However, exactly how this happens will probably always remain a mystery to us."

She slapped her hand to the back of his head, clutching his long hair.

"How," she began, "can you be the leading religious figure of Tibetan Buddhism, which is KNOWN for your belief in reincarnation, yet you don't know how the process works?"

She pulled tighter with each syllable. "It seems implausible to me that you would not know this!"

The Dalai Lama grimaced, closing his eyes.

"If the process were provided for me, it may be too complex for my level of comprehension. When we consider the many thousands - millions - of souls who go through the process each year, and the important consideration that by necessity must go into these decisions, it seems well beyond our reach to understand how the process occurs with such effectiveness."

She relaxed her grip, stepping back and drawing a deep breath. "How can you be so sure it's done effectively? There are very evil people in the world. Perhaps it's not quite as flawless as you think. Have you considered that?"

"Yes, I have considered that. However we are resolute in our belief that each soul must be free to choose the next life. The process cannot happen by force, or by happenstance, or by random chance. If the soul chooses poorly, then the soul will live with the choice and humanity will live with those poor choices. We do not claim the choices are flawless, but I find it is doubtful the process could be to blame for lives that end up badly or tragically."

She cast a quick glance at the other two men in the room. They glanced back impassively.

"Your argument isn't too compelling. If it was a flawed process, I'm nowhere near convinced that you would know about it. It appears, your Holiness, that we're in search of information that you cannot possibly provide."

"I am truly sorry if I've disappointed you," he said.

"I'm sorry too," she replied, "but we'll get past the disappointment and continue on our mission."

After the three hour drive to Massachusetts, Edgar dropped the Reverend Ellen Grandby Sullivan off at her home. She walked quietly into a studio that was tastefully decorated in calm colors. It was her room for prayer and meditation.

She lit several candles and kneeled on a lavish Persian rug. She bowed her head, much as a subservient soldier would. Gradually she drifted into a trancelike state. She began to chant slowly in soft tones.

"Ispata Immat khoday. Ispata Immat khoday. Ispata Immat khoday."

She repeated the phrase several times, pausing intermittently.

After several minutes a chill came over the room. The candles began to flicker, then each rose in height and intensity. She was startled at first, then resumed her focus and submissive posture.

"You have come," she said.

The powerful entity enveloped her entire consciousness. She was completely within the power of this spirit, her body nearly paralyzed in its grasp. Its presence in the room seemed to add many pounds of pressure. She did not resist its control.

When it spoke, its message was delivered around and through her. The communication was intensively powerful, intended to be received as irrefutable, definitive.

"Explain why I was summoned."

She trembled, trying to display reverence while hoping her message was important enough to disturb this immense force.

"I seek instruction over matters important to each of us."

The being conveyed impatience, the expectation of a delivery still unmet.

"You knew what is expected when you last summoned me. Nothing has changed."

She inhaled, determined not to waver. "I remain clear on your expectations, but I request instruction on delivering this offering. I have not done this before, and I did not ask how to make the delivery to your Highness."

Immat responded quickly, brusquely. *"As all sacrifices have been delivered through the ages. An offering through the purification ritual that we discussed. You know what is to be delivered to me."*

"Yes, I see."

His expectations were a clear disappointment. Her hope was that she misunderstood his expectations in their prior communication, but his was not the case.

"I hold the Tibetan Buddhist."

Immat shot back a fast message. *"It is a beginning, but no substitute for the sacrifice I deserve."*

Her thoughts were naked before this god, who she depended upon so heavily.

The demon god instantly sensed her disappointment. *"His life serves your purposes more than mine."*

"I am hopeful it will serve both our purposes."

"Explain," the spirit declared. Its tone suggested curiosity, a slight degree less hostile.

"The assignment and selection of souls is a process that developed and changed through the millennia. It is as much a product of human history as it is celestial preference. In a time of unprecedented growth, the process is skewed to favor the few. A rebalancing is needed, with your guidance. I humbly offer to be your servant in this mission."

The spirit radiated a strong interest in her message, emboldening her to continue.

"I learned of your long, rich reign on this earth. It was magnificent, even though it occurred many centuries ago, and many are not familiar with the great power that you held."

The spirit's bitterness came as a strong chill to her senses. "If we succeed in our mission, I will help all those who are able to help me. I expect that you, Immat, wish to regain the stature that you so richly deserve."

"It is so," Immat replied without hesitation.

"Then perhaps as part of our continued association, there are ways you can assist us in our mission."

The chill in the air eased. It remained interested in her message and where it was going next.

"We seek access to ethereal levels that humans would not normally attain. In this way we can most effectively promote our beliefs by attracting souls to our faith."

The chill was back. *"Your beliefs are the reason my reign on earth ended. I would have no reason to help further."*

She steeled herself to respond, hoping to continue to keep this fallen god engaged and motivated to assist in her mission.

"Respectfully speaking, there appears to be no chance for your reign to return without some sort of compromise. It was not all Christians who challenged your authority, but rather the Christians who held power at the time. I humbly submit that the only viable way to regain some or all of your prior glory is to side with us."

"Which side?"

"The side of our Lord and Savior, Jesus Christ."

The spirit bristled, but she expected the reaction and was ready with a quick response.

"God does not close the door to those who wish to follow. A powerful spirit like yourself, whose reign predates Jesus Christ, can serve an important need in the kingdom. It is there but for the asking."

Immat was quiet, in some form of contemplation. Finally it spoke to her. *"If I can be assured of some form of acceptance in the Light, I will consider assisting your quest."*

She tried to withhold her relief and near excitement at the prospect of this fallen god helping her with access to higher portals. "This is very welcome news. We can accomplish much together."

New Clues in the Disappearance of the Dalai Lama

Police reported new developments in the disappearance of the spiritual leader of Tibetan Buddhism, the Dalai Lama, who was abducted on June 4. A letter was mailed to various news outlets, including the Washington Post, accusing the Dalai Lama of being a traitor to his country and suggesting accountability. The letter suggests Chinese interests are behind the murder, however the veracity of the letter could not be confirmed by the Post or other news outlets as of press time.

"We're investigating the source of the letter and its authenticity," said Brandon Michalewicz, FBI spokesman. "It was received by a number of news outlets, and they each appear to be from the same source."

Details of the circumstances surrounding the Dalai Lama's death are not being revealed by the FBI, and the Post has complied with FBI requests to not reveal the contents of the letter.

A spokesman for the Chinese embassy in Washington quickly and forcefully denied any involvement in the Dalai Lama's disappearance by China. Still, an international furor is sure to follow.

Before his ascension to the position of Dalai Lama, his name was Phuntsok Gyatso. Following a Tibetan uprising in 1959, the prior Dalai Lama fled to India, denouncing the People's Republic of China and forming a Tibetan government in exile. Relations have been strained between China and Tibetan loyalists through the decades, but there have been no recent public differences that would have foretold recent events.

Police have offered no additional details on the progress of their investigation into the kidnapping.

KÁRMÁN LINE

In the days that followed his failed attempt to help Sophie Geary, Henry felt utterly void of direction. He wanted greatly to do something to help Dee and her colleagues, but knew of no way to help. He had pledged to help the Origenists by ingraining himself into the church, but his efforts thus far were fruitless. He was unsure how to reengage with Ellen Grandby Sullivan, or if he should even try. Should it be an apology, combined with an offer to try again to help the girl? He doubted the girl's parents would welcome his help. They would likely consider him a failure at best, a phony at worst.

A worthy mission, he decided could be a search for the videotape Joan Swenson mentioned, however his chances seemed remote of being able to discreetly search church rooms and offices for the tape. He phoned Ronnie Wilcox, the volunteer coordinator with The Church, to reassert his commitment to helping the church through his volunteering. Ronnie accepted Henry's offer without hesitation, giving no indication that he was aware of Henry's experience with the Gearys.

While considering his current directionless state, he compared himself to spirits who were anchored to the earth, unsure how to move to the next level. He was unaccustomed to having little idea or even control over what would happen next in his life, and the feeling troubled him. He chose to concentrate on the one thing he could control, the business of being a medium. He would refocus on connecting his customers to their loved ones, and continue to hone his skill in this challenging occupation.

All the while he would keep his eyes and ears open for signs from any of the three women who seemed to hold the keys to his fate.

On occasion Henry spent time in the local library. He felt safe in the public setting, and enjoyed the solitude of researching mysticism and spiritualism in a place where he could see anyone coming and going. The book collection was impressive for a city library, and their catalog of online research databases was vast.

On one rainy evening he braved the elements to lose himself among the volumes. He was picking through the religious history section in a remote corner of the old building when he was overcome with the sense that someone was tracking his movements. He discreetly moved around the end of a row of books to see if he could detect any movement that mirrored his. He sensed a person moving slowly, several rows away. He was careful not to drastically change the cadence of his movements, but he subtly moved into a nook beyond the shelf where he could not be easily seen. He would have the advantage on anyone wishing to catch him off guard.

He waited quietly and without moving, one hand on a hunting knife he now carried at all times. He quietly opened the blade, waiting for his unwelcome visitor to slip past his nook without knowing his position.

The figure began to move slowly toward him. He froze, waiting for an opportunity to make a calculated move. His pulse pounded, but he stayed perfectly still as the figure stepped closer. A slender figure in a long coat glided quietly, attempting to track his movements.

He pounced forcefully from behind. He wrapped his left arm around the midsection to restrain the arms, and his right leg wrapped around the intruder's right leg. His knife went directly to the throat, firm enough for his subject to feel the sharp blade but short of slicing through flesh.

The figure gasped. It was a woman.

"Please Henry, it's me!"

He loosed his grip carefully.

"Dee! I nearly slit your throat! What are you doing here?"

"I needed to see you. I'm sorry. I'm sorry." Tears welled in her eyes.

"It's okay. Calm down. Let's find a quiet place to sit."

They settled into a secure area where they would not be easily seen or heard.

"I'm glad to see you Dee, but your skills in the fine art of espionage can use a little work."

"That was clumsy I know, but I wasn't sure it was you."

He moved the hair from her eyes gently. "What brings you out on a night like this?"

"I can't stop worrying about our safety. I'm out of touch with everyone and going crazy." Loneliness and isolation enveloped her expression and tone of voice. "The group hasn't met lately. I feel like I'm sitting here waiting to be the next victim."

Henry sighed, looked down, then back into her eyes.

"Sometimes waiting and watching are the only things you can do. I know it's painful, stressful. I feel it too."

"How do we know this is the right thing to do?" She snapped back, nearly crying. "Maybe now is the time when we should be on the attack ourselves!"

"Don't forget what we talked about, Dee. The group thought it might help if I got inside the church. I'm still working on that, and we've learned a lot about them. So we're not really doing nothing. To go on some kind of offensive right now against them, or anyone, would just be reckless."

"Henry, what do these people want? What is it they're after?"

"I have no idea," he sighed. "If they're really responsible for kidnapping the Dalai Lama, that must mean something big is coming. I can't think of any direct gain to be gotten from the most peaceful man on the planet, so they must need something from him. From the papers, it sounds like a sloppy attempt to implicate China, or at least people that are loyal to the Chinese, but who would gain from China looking bad? Not the Church of the Tortured Christ, from what I can figure."

"I just read about the Tibetan Buddhists," he continued. "Dalai Lamas are supposedly enlightened beings who are on this earth only because they want to be. They're delaying their own nirvana by returning for another life instead of ascending and attaining Nirvana. They choose to stay in the cycle of death and rebirth to serve man. When one Dalai Lama dies, a search takes place for his successor, and it might take a couple years to find the new incarnation. It's quite an amazing process."

"That's all fascinating," Dee said sharply, "but what's your point?"

"My point is that it seems like the church might have a sudden interest in reincarnation. The Buddhists are the most visible proponents of reincarnation, and the Dalai Lama is the most visible of the Buddhists. Either they want to learn something he knows, or by taking him out of circulation they're trying to say that not only doesn't reincarnation apply in the Christian church, but it doesn't apply anywhere. Maybe they're trying to make it obsolete as a concept."

"Either possibility is horrifying," Dee replied. "Where would they stop? There are probably a billion Buddhists in the world. Could they even do anything to change that? When we talked about this in our group, we could never agree on what they're after. Most of the group thought they're just evil, that they want to damage anyone who promotes beliefs they consider sacrilegious. The Dalai Lama would seem to be in that circle, along with Origenists, but probably also Jews, Muslims, Hindus, pagans, and on and on."

"There are plenty of people out there doing sacrilegious things," Henry said. "That doesn't seem like reason enough to put an extermination strategy into action. With all the different belief systems out there, including some people worshipping things a lot more radical than reincarnation, I wonder why anyone would single your group out."

Dee just shook her head, unsure how to make sense of it.

"What were some other theories?"

"Some think there's some sort of effort going on in the church to use reincarnation for their own purposes. Maybe they want to adopt the practice because it's part of Christian history, and they'll stop at nothing to make it their own. The pacifists in the group think nobody is out to get us, that all of this adds up to a fucked up society where murders happen for senseless reasons. We were just finally bitten by it. Still another idea is that no religious group could have anything to do with David's death. They even suggested that perhaps David was involved in something harmful to us, that maybe he was out to expose us to the world, that his death was a protective measure performed by one of our own, someone who hasn't owned up to it yet."

Henry asked, "There are some wild imaginations at work there. Which of all these theories are you siding with?"

"I tend to believe they want to exterminate us because we're undermining their belief system. That seems most in line with some of the other Christian churches. There are plenty of people out there who aren't pleased with our message. Maybe they think we won't stop at reincarnation, that maybe our next agenda items are abortion, beastiality, or devil worship. Who knows what they think?"

"What does your buddy Lars think?"

Her nostrils flared. "First off, he's not 'my buddy.' He's a colleague who shares my belief system. That's all. Second, I think he believes what I do, that whoever is out to get us is motivated by the warped opinion that our beliefs are harmful to them. I'm betting they see reincarnation as a threat to their long term viability. We've argued among ourselves many times that it's much too late for traditional Christian churches to embrace reincarnation. They've put too much into the notion of a heaven or hell that awaits us right after we die. They've spent centuries convincing their flocks that it's only behavior in this life that matters. He thinks what I think; that they would never embrace reincarnation."

Henry pondered, then quickly dismissed, the idea that Lars might be a rational human. "Dee, are you safe where you're staying?"

"How can any of us be sure?" She looked up at him with dark, soggy eyes.

"True enough. I don't want to ask where, but you have to be safe. If something happened to you ... I'm not even sure what the fight would be about anymore."

"It would be about many important things, Henry, with or without me. I'm staying with a trusted girlfriend who's not part of my group, who has no idea what kind of business I'm involved in. It's as safe a situation as I can imagine."

Her serious look turned into a shy half smile. "Still, that's very sweet of you to say." She reached her hand across the table and placed it over Henry's. He returned her grasp. Each enjoyed the warmth of the other, enjoying a rare but simple, affectionate touch. It was a welcome break from their insulated worlds.

"It's a nasty night out there. Will you be safe getting home?"

"As safe as ever, I suppose. I could tell you not to worry but you probably will anyway. Just like I worry about you." She looked into his eyes, unblinking.

"I think we both need to keep worrying. I just wonder if we worry more because we never see each other."

"Is there something you're trying to say, Henry?"

"What's the harm in us being together, watching out for each other?" Henry sat upright in his chair and spoke defiantly. "I want to be with you, Dee. Waiting for you to check in, not sure about your safety, is no way to coexist. It's maddening, for me anyway."

"For me too," she said, "and exhausting. I'm tired of hiding, of moving in the shadows. I feel like a ghost."

"Maybe you are," he said. "You know how well I get along with ghosts. Most of them, anyway."

She smiled. "I'm not a ghost."

"Well, I'm glad we cleared that up."

She maintained her serious gaze, but a tender smile showed in her eyes.

"Stay at my place tonight, Dee. It's nearby, probably closer than where you're staying. I'll give you all the privacy you want. It's the only way I'll know you're safe."

She sighed slowly, delaying her response. After a few seconds she looked into his eyes. "Why not? What else is there to lose?"

He tried to hide his relief, but failed. They both smiled and hugged.

The walk to his house took only ten minutes, but both were soaked from the driving rain. He offered her his smallest sweat pants, tee shirt, and sweat shirt. After each changed in separate rooms, they sat on the couch, glasses of red wine cupped in their laps. She asked about his family.

"I grew up an orphan. I had an older brother but he died when I was very young, in Colorado. I was told my parents died in a car accident, but I never found any proof of that. After my brother died, I was separated from my parents. I was really young. I barely remember them. I bounced from foster home to foster home, and eventually I ended up here in the East. I was with some decent families, but mostly I was in my own little world. I guess I built a wall around myself until I was older. It was only when I graduated high school and went on to college that I began to feel like I belonged in this world."

"That must be an incredibly lonely feeling."

"I suppose. I never really knew anything else growing up. What about you? Tell me about your family."

"I guess we have loneliness in common. My parents were around, but it felt like we were in each others' company because we had to be. I have two older brothers that don't really talk to each other, or to me. We're not a close family, never were really. It always seemed just cold and distant. I don't think my parents liked each other too much, so over time that spread to us."

"It sounds like my situation wasn't so bad," Henry said. "At least I had myself to rely on. In your case, it was your family. They're supposed to offer love and support, no matter what. It sounds pretty bleak."

"Bleak it was," she said. "You're gonna laugh when I tell you my last name. You'll completely understand."

"What a dope I am. I never asked you your last name."

Since meeting her, he held her and the Origenists under a cloak of secrecy. As they became closer, her identity became something to protect.

"That's so hurtful. And you said you cared for me!" She gave him a mock pout.

"I guess I just never wanted to be in a position where I knew too much about you," he said. "I suppose it was my protective instinct."

"For me or for you?"

"For both of us. Some of my recent new acquaintances haven't fared so well, and I need to change our luck."

They fell silent briefly, thinking about all they had in common.

"Well, what's so funny about your last name? Is it as bleak as 'Bleak'?"

"Pretty close. My family name describes our existence and relationships perfectly. It's Stark."

They laughed together, enjoying the irony nearly as much as the shared relief that she was no longer part of that world. Then blood rushed to his head. He froze as old memories came rushing forward. "Your name was Stark? Really? I lived with a family named Stark when I was little."

"You did?" She leaned forward on the couch.

"Were you here in Massachusetts?"

"I was!", she exclaimed.

"One of my only friends as a kid was a girl about my age named Delilah Stark. Please do NOT tell me your real first name is Delilah!"

"Yes! My name is Delilah Stark. OH MY GOD! You're the Henry that lived with us. Henry, I remember you!" She lunged into his arms, clinging to him with all her strength.

"You were my first true friend." She kept close to him. "You were the first boy I loved. Probably the first person I loved."

They spent the next three hours talking about how they passed the time when they were the closest of friends, alternately laughing and crying. They talked of the imagination games they played together and how it helped both of them cope with a world that, even at that young age, they knew would be cold. They remembered how Henry would try to convince her that she was adopted like him because she had curly blond hair while the rest of her family was dark. She remembered wanting it to be true, wanting to be more like Henry and less like her real family.

As she spoke, reminiscing about their brief but joyous time together, her eyes glowed. Henry noticed, feeling a warmth inside that he had never felt. It was a foreign emotion, one he would need to learn to know. He smiled inwardly as he assured himself that he would find a way.

"Then my father announced that we were moving. I didn't care about moving. I only cared about whether we could take you with us. When he told me no I cried for days. He insisted that we couldn't but I knew it was his choice. I never forgave him for that. I never will."

"I don't see how he could've taken me along," Henry asked. "I was a ward of the state of Massachusetts. I think you've been a little hard on him."

"He could have adopted you, Henry. I didn't really know what that meant at the time but as I grew older I knew he had options. I think he did it because he wanted me to be as close to my brothers as I was to you."

"Did that happen?"

"No," she replied. "We weren't close when we were young and we're not close now. They're not nice people."

She regained her focus through moist eyes, looking closely at Henry. "I felt so sorry for myself during that time. I felt like the unluckiest kid in the world, but I can't even imagine what that did to you. The loneliness you must have felt. It must've been twenty times what I felt."

As the words came out she burst into tears, sobbing loudly. Her arms held tightly around Henry, her face nestled into his neck. He held her, stroking the back of her head.

"It was rough on both of us, Dee. I was used to being alone before your family took me in. For me it was a return to my old life. I hated being alone again, but that's about the time I began to believe that was my fate. I found happiness in our friendship and it was taken from me. It was a mistake, not meant to be. I was meant to be alone in this world."

"Nobody is meant to be alone, Henry. Nobody."

They pondered the moment quietly. Each waited for the other to say the next important thing, that they found each other after all this time, that their separation in the past resulted in their togetherness now. Instead of words they looked into each others' eyes through tears and a smile.

They lost time, locked in an embrace on Henry's couch in this room that only knew loneliness. They brought each other the comfort of closeness that neither had felt in more than two decades.

Henry stirred, thinking of warm blankets and deep sleep. She held him tight. Her parted lips met his. Her kiss was deep, passionate, and long. They drifted into a perfect union, seeming to float above the room. The love they made was effortless, driven by pure white emotion. They found their way to his bedroom, where they spent the night merged at last.

It was daylight, a warm summer's morning in New England. The window was open a few inches, and even by seven, the heat of the day was beginning to overwhelm the mist from overnight. A slight breeze blew into the cool, dark room. The first view of his day was Dee's golden blond hair over her peaceful, resting face. Henry basked in the moment, the enchantment of the previous evening etching as a real thing, not a dream.

The tinny alarm of Henry's cell phone pulled him from a contented, restful sleep. When he found the phone, it was not a number he recognized.

"Good morning. This is Henry."

"Henry, can you talk?" It was a woman's voice.

He glanced across the room at Dee. She began to stir.

"Yes, I can talk. Who is this?"

"It's Joan Swenson."

His sleepy fog dissipated rapidly. "Joan, is everything okay?"

"I highly doubt that, Henry. The news stories about the Dalai Lama never end, but there's no way to know what they've done with him. I feel so helpless. Harm could come to one of the holiest, most peaceful people on the planet, and we're sitting by doing nothing. It's eating me up inside."

"You're not the only one," he said softly. "Somehow we need to do something. If the church is behind it, they should be held accountable."

"I agree," she said, "but that's only IF they're responsible."

"You doubt that?"

"Look Henry, I've never been involved in anything like this in my entire life. My family is from Minnesota. We owned a retail clothing store. I only came here because my husband transferred here. I don't want any part of this. I only joined the church because it gave me comfort when I needed it, after my husband left. I've never been so scared in my entire life, Henry, and quite honestly I don't know who to trust."

"I'm not sure any of us do," Henry muttered into the phone.

Dee whispered, "Who is it?"

"A friend from the church, the woman I told you about who saw the video," he said, cupping the phone.

"Who's there with you?" Joan was alarmed.

"A great friend. Someone who I trust and is helping me. Not someone you know. Joan, the unfortunate fact is that you shouldn't trust me. I'll tell you as a friend that you can trust me, but the truth is that you should trust nobody right now. You probably shouldn't even be calling me on your phone. Whether it's the church or not who's behind this, we don't know what they want or what they're willing to do to get it."

"So I'm right to be paranoid," she said, more of a statement than a question.

"At least for now," he said.

"I bet you're wondering where we go from here."

"Exactly," she said.

"Well," Henry looked in the distance, "we can either retreat or we can resume. It seems to me that resuming is less risky. Retreating - going silent - would only draw attention to both of us, probably."

"Probably," she said, sounding exhausted.

"So let's keep moving ahead. Keep doing the things you would normally do, and I'll do the same."

"Easier said than done," she said, "but I know it's what I have to do."

"Joan, I have an important question for you."

"I'm not sure I like where this is going." The woman's defenses were up as Henry was about to make a calculated gamble.

"What do you think the chances are of finding that video that you told me about?"

"Slim to none," she said in a steely voice. "I had a feeling you'd ask me that."

"Why? Do you think they know you saw the tape?"

"No, probably not. I tried to leave it exactly as I found it. I don't think anyone was nearby when I saw it."

"So," Henry asked, "why don't you think you can find it?"

"Don't you think I already looked for the thing?" She snapped at him. "I've been in that room a half dozen times since that night. There's no sign of it. It's like it never existed."

"What kind of access do you have to the church? If the camera is somewhere else in the building, how likely would you be to find it?"

"Well, I have keys," she said, "but I haven't really figured out what they open. So far I've been able to go wherever I've needed, but I'm not really sure what I have access to."

"I see." Henry pondered her reply and paused. "Let's work together, Joan. Maybe I can cover more ground than you're comfortable covering. I would need your help."

"Meaning what, exactly?" She sounded concerned again.

"Your keys. I would definitely need access to your keys."

She paused before replying. "Okay, I guess."

"My concern," Henry said, "is that this isn't isolated. I'm worried they have other things in the works that are even bigger than this."

"That's a horrifying thought," she said.

"It is indeed. Joan, protect yourself."

They talked through logistics, agreeing to work through cryptic text messages to coincide in the times they would be in the church.

Dee listened to the whole conversation in silence. After he hung up, they laid down in bed, discussing all the dangers and possible rewards of their infiltration into the complex operation that was the Church of the Tortured Christ.

"I've spent some time researching them," he said. "What you see here in Massachusetts is only the tip of the iceberg. Their headquarters are in Atlanta, but they're growing around the world. There are 'photo ops' on their web site of Reverend Grandby with presidents and heads of state from every continent. These guys are ambitious."

"I want to help," she said. "They don't know me. What if I were to go in there somehow, and see what I can find?"

"That's a terrible idea," he said. "The last thing we need is another person who's in their web. Why would you do that willingly?"

They argued, they reasoned, and they balanced the pros and the cons. In the end he agreed to consider the possibility, but privately had no intention of allowing her into the building.

They spent the rest of the morning making tender, passionate, whimsical love. They learned each other's bodies, movements, nuances, and quirks. All the time since either had been with another were erased in a tangle of pleasure. She invited his curiosity, his yearning. He wanted only to fulfill her.

Henry showered and readied himself for a challenging day. Dee was never far from him, giggling and playing as if they were children again, but hugging and nuzzling. It was a Dee he never expected to see. She had always seemed so worried about what was around the next corner. She was letting go of years of loneliness, finally with one she trusted completely.

He embraced her with a contented smile. "It's great to see you this way, Dee."

"Which way is that? Half naked and following you around your apartment while you try to leave?"

"Exactly. That's the girl I want etched in my memory." They enjoyed a deep laugh, the kind that can only be shared by lovers.

"I love feeling this way," she said quietly. "I love not worrying about things, if only for a few hours."

"There's no rule that you have to spend all your extra time thinking about your troubles, Dee. Just think about them enough to know your next move. Then go on with your life."

"It sounds so easy when you say it like that," she said, exhaling. "It seems like life is nothing but a struggle. So when I have down time, what else is there to think about?"

He squared toward her, his eyes boring into hers. "LIFE, Dee. You think about living your life. That's what normal people do."

She looked down. He exhaled. "You can't be defined by this struggle. You define what struggle looks like. It happens on your terms."

"I'll work on it," she said. She moved her hands down his chest, below his navel. They melted into the couch to make love yet again.

With Dee on his shoulder, caressing his face, Henry turned on the television to CNN. Coverage of the Dalai Lama still dominated the news. The lead story was about how his disappearance seemed to provide a trigger for the release of countless pressure points around the world. Crawlers across the bottom of the screen were describing alarming increases in tensions between opposing sides in various geographic regions, many with no apparent stake in the tensions between China and Tibet.

Japan lashed out about lingering disputes over islands that China has also laid claim to. Arabs and Israelis were losing all patience with one another in their disputes over the handling of settlers in occupied territories. North Korea was provoking their southern neighbors with missile testing that was clearly intended to frazzle nerves. Russia was making loud noise about neighboring countries who were leaning toward the West, threatening everything from trade embargoes to military action. Following pressure from the United States, South American leaders squabbled over who bore the blame for narcotics flowing north at higher levels than ever. Many world leaders were using the heightened tensions as an excuse to pull old resentments out of storage.

In a limited statement, China again denied involvement in the disappearance, and they began to aggressively suggest that Western actors were to blame, perhaps government actors. An analyst on CNN discussed the sources of the intense backlash against China, that there were anti-Chinese demonstrations in various countries demanding action from the international community. It was not clear what meaningful actions they expected, but the backlash was emotional and passionate.

"Wow, what in the world is happening? Everyone is at each other's throats. It's like this mystery gave everyone the green light to be pissed off." Henry stared at the screen, shaking his head.

"Well, it is unsettling," Dee said, lying on his shoulder. "If someone can make the most peaceful man on the planet vanish, what chance to we have for peace anywhere?"

"I guess I've been in my own little world," he said. "I didn't realize there were so many situations about to pop. I can't watch this," he said, turning off the TV. "Time to get productive."

"When will you be back?"

"I need to pick up Joan's church keys. She's headed out of town but leaving them under her mat. I have some readings during the middle of the day, easy stuff. Then I was thinking of taking care of some business later on."

"That sounds curiously vague. What kind of business?"

"Church business."

"Are you serious? Henry, these people are probably murderers. Do you really want to go right into their den right now?"

"Well, I guess there are two ways to look at it. Either I avoid them, which accomplishes nothing and may even make them suspicious, or I jump right back in and offer to help them somehow, since I wasn't much help last time. They have no idea what we suspect, so I don't think there's much of a risk right now."

"Watch yourself Henry," she said. "Text me when you're headed in there, and when you leave. We can't leave each other hanging."

"We can't." They kissed, holding it an extra few seconds. Each savored their time together, neither knowing how much remained.

Late in the afternoon, Henry pulled his car into the parking lot of the Church of the Tortured Christ. He strode with a smile to the portly receptionist with too much makeup and a permanent smile. He glanced at her name plate.

"Good morning, Cecilia! Would Reverend Sullivan happen to have a few minutes to chat?"

"It's Henry, right? I can find out for you. Make yourself comfortable."

"That's so sweet of you. I'd also love to visit with Ronnie Wilcox while I'm here. Is he in today?"

"Ronnie's out of the office at a conference, but you can leave him a message. I'll let you know if the Reverend has time for you, okay?"

She went through a door to the rear office, returning with the same cheery smile.

Before long she returned. "The Reverend can see you in just a few minutes. She's finishing a few things up before her next set of appointments."

"May I go leave Ronnie a message while I'm waiting?"

"Of course. Just don't be too long. The Reverend has some visitors coming in later, but she is finding time to see you. You remember where Ronnie's office is?"

"I do. Two minutes at the most and I'll see you back here."

He remembered Dee's words as he moved down the long empty hallway about not leaving each other hanging, so he stopped and texted her. "I'm in, should be able to see the Rev."

He checked for surveillance cameras and saw none. He moved down the hallway, and in case someone was watching he put his hands on his hips, pretending to be slightly confused about his location. He tried a door that he knew was not Ronnie's. It was open, so he flipped on the light and left the door open as he moved in purposefully.

Keeping an eye on the door and his ears open to hear any oncoming footsteps, he quietly opened all desk drawers in search of the incriminating videotape. He found nothing suspicious and moved back into the hallway within a matter of seconds, leaving the room as he found it.

He moved down the hall and found another open door. He took the same approach with this office, leaving the door open and the light on. He tried the desk and cabinet. The cabinet was open, stuffed with files. The desk was locked. He tried Joan's keys, but none worked. He moved quickly back into the hall, until he found Ronnie's office.

For good measure he tried a few drawers, finding nothing. When he finally reached for a pad to write a note to Ronnie, he heard quiet footsteps approaching the office from the hall. He pretended to not hear the approach.

"Hello Mister Chimera, lovely to see you again." It was the Reverend in the flesh.

"Reverend Sullivan! You surprised me. Sorry if I kept you waiting. I was leaving a note for Ronnie, but I got a little lost on the way." He attempted his most sheepish expression.

"What brings you back here?" She stared at him unblinking, unsmiling.

"Well, I feel like I let you down last time I was here." He stared back.

"Nonsense, Henry." She broke the stare, finally smiling. "You did what you could to help Sophie. I could never fault you for trying. Proverbs says, 'The hand of the diligent will rule, while the slothful will be put to forced labor.'"

"How is she doing?"

"Still no progress. She's in a different world, sadly." The Reverend crossed her arms and looked down.

"I'm not sure what world that is, but it isn't one that I ever want to be a part of." Henry folded his arms, looking away.

"How do you mean?" She moved to his side.

"The spirit that has a hold on Sophie is a powerful one that has no intention of letting go. I've been beating myself up wondering if there's anything I could have done to help her, but I can't think of a thing."

"You're not alone, Henry. We're all terribly frustrated. We had heard that your spiritual powers are substantial, so we thought it might be worth a try."

"My abilities were almost meaningless. I was nothing more than a gnat to that spirit."

"You're not the first person that the devil has swatted away, Henry."

She paused, waiting to see if he would react before continuing. "After your ... experience with Sophie, her parents decided to just ease her suffering and heavily medicate her. That's the state she's in today."

"I'm not so sure that's a great idea," Henry said. "Do you think you could talk them into reconsidering?"

"What in the world for? You said yourself that there's little that can be done for her."

"That's not exactly what I said, Reverend. I'm just at my limit in knowing what can be done. That's a reflection on my abilities, nothing more. Surely we can do something, but I just don't know what that is. More to the point, I'm worried the medication will weaken her resistance against this powerful spirit. She needs to maintain her defenses."

"For what purpose?" She was smiling curiously.

"Whatever this entity has in mind cannot be good. It can't be in Sophie's interest to be drugged up, along with being under its spell."

Reverend Sullivan slowly walked the room, then sat on a window sill. "What harm are you worried about, Henry?"

"I have no way of knowing. How can anyone?" Henry avoided eye contact.

"Who even knows if there's a spirit involved?" Her arms were crossed as she looked at him with a narrow smile. "You seem to think there's some sort of possession, but from what everyone else says, including countless doctors who have examined her, she has severe psychological problems. No one but you is claiming there's some sort of evil spirit involved."

"I work in the spirit realm every day, and I can promise you that a very powerful entity is involved with Sophie Geary right now. I don't know if it's the devil, or sent from the devil, but it's potent. If you're really interested in helping her, you can help shift the attention to where it belongs. Sophie's troubles won't be solved by conventional treatments. This is very different."

"Duly noted," she said. "So what brings you here today, Henry?"

Henry sighed and scratched his head as he looked at her. "Well, I certainly didn't come here to argue with you, Reverend."

She gazed at him steadily, waiting for his answer.

"I came here for the same reason I came here the first time, to offer to help in some way. If that means volunteering with Ronnie, then I'm glad to do it. If you had something else in mind, I'll do what I can. I feel like I let you down last time, and I came here to make it up to you."

"That's very kind of you. That experience with Sophie was obviously more intense than any of us expected. Besides Sophie, that was probably hardest on you. You've been nothing but helpful, Henry. You don't owe us anything."

"I believe in what you're doing," Henry lied. "How can I help?"

"Helping Ronnie is probably best for now. If there's something else I can think of, I'll contact you through Ronnie."

"Sounds great." He smiled. "I was just writing a note to Ronnie. I can spare some time here and there."

They said their goodbyes. She promised to stop in and try to say hello on occasion. When she left, he was tempted to continue looking for open doors and drawers, but he resisted the urge. He was invited back, after all.

The next day, he received a call from Ronnie Wilcox inviting him to volunteer. Henry arranged to volunteer that evening.

He arrived on time, refreshed and ready to help, and with Joan Swenson's keys in his pocket. He gathered instructions from Ronnie and launched into the phone calls as if he had never left. This time it was about reaching out to parishioners who had not responded to emails or phone calls. It was not especially pleasant work, but he knew he would be knocked down to the simplest of assignments.

His calls mostly went to answering machines or to a message that the number was no longer in service. Occasionally he would reach someone in person, in which case he would try to persuade them to regain contact with The Church. After each call he dutifully filled out the notes in the online program that tracked parishioner contacts, and changed the status accordingly.

After about two hours on the phones, approaching eight o'clock in the evening, he stood and stretched, looking around to see if anyone was paying attention. The few other volunteers in the room were either busy on the phones or taking breaks of their own, so he slipped out of the room.

As he moved deliberately down the hall, stretching and taking his time looking through the magazine articles, children's artwork, and other pieces of interest along the hallways, he was careful to take note of the position of small glass eyes that he took for video surveillance cameras. At every corner the small eyes were discreetly embedded into the ceilings. He casually studied art work on display as he subtly prowled for unlocked doors

Once inside each office, Henry was all business. He rifled through each open desk drawer looking for videotapes. He moved from one drawer to the next quickly, careful to leave each detail exactly as he found it.

As he completed each frenetic office search, he exited into the hall slowly. To any video camera in the hallway, he entered the offices casually and exited casually, as if he was simply nosey, taking a needed break from the phones.

He paid close attention to his watch, ensuring his break from the phones was not long enough to attract attention. In a few short minutes he was able to perform detailed searches on four offices. The incriminating video was nowhere to be found.

He paused in front of an especially uninteresting piece of art in the hallway as he contemplated trying for a fifth office, one that looked promising. It was in a far corner down a shorter hallway, seemingly out camera view. He wandered in that direction, turned the door knob, and found it open. The label on the door read "Special Events, Project Archives."

He entered the room and made a quick visual scan of the contents. There were several large file cabinets and a few smaller bureaus that probably held all kinds of interesting artifacts. Cabinets and shelves lined each wall, while in the center was a large table that was likely used for assembling displays, crafts, and artwork for special events. He glanced again at his watch, deciding there was too much to cover in the time he allotted for this venture.

As he turned to exit the room, he heard an unmistakable woman's voice coming from somewhere in the room. He froze quietly to listen. To his astonishment, he heard the voice of the Reverend Ellen Grandby Sullivan herself. It sounded like a phone conversation coming from another room. He quietly moved to understand where the voice was emanating from. In a far corner, above a large shelf was a ceiling vent. Henry carefully positioned himself close to the vent. He could hear her conversation clearly.

"I AM giving him whatever he asks. I DO trust him."

After a pause, "How do you suggest that I do that? Do you realize how difficult this will all be?"

"Yes Father, I know that. I know exactly what we've been talking about. He's making the transition back to that level. It's happening, just the way we hoped it would. He's beginning to remember his way around again. Little by little, he's regaining strength"

"Soon. I think she can be ready for him within a week or so, but we can't rush it."

"This is their daughter! They're not about to give her up without being 100% convinced that this will be best for her. That takes time. I'm working on it, believe me. She'll belong to him soon. This has to be done right."

"Yes, I'm very aware that you're doing your part. It's in all the papers. I'm reading about all of it. It seems flawless. What are the next steps?"

"That's amazing. How are you able to pull the strings for things like this?"

"These are important times, Father. We're doing God's work, unlike it's ever been done."

"You too. I'll talk to you soon."

"Jesus be with you too."

Then there was silence from the office above. Somehow Henry finished his shift, numb with confusion over questions to which he had no answers. So many questions.

Aisling approached Hildegarde with reverence and humility, her ethereal head bowed before this highly advanced soul. She had never encountered a spirit with the shimmering brilliance that Hildegarde possessed.

Her adjustment was difficult, similar to walking from a dark night into a room filled with blinding bright light, with a single person in the center of the room as the source of the light. In this dimension time was relative, not linear, but adjusting to Hildegarde's presence seemed to take many minutes and a great deal of energy.

Acclimating to a spirit of this high energy level was about learning to calibrate the wavelength of incoming communications as well as outgoing. Aisling compared it to the job of translator for a conversation that was moving at light speed, and in a language which she was slowly learning.

As she adjusted, her mentor in this mission waited patiently. She was a loving and caring soul who allowed Aisling all the time and missteps she required in order to become comfortable in this new position. While it was laborious, the gratification was immediate. With each step forward in her ability to communicate with Hildegarde, the more enlightened she became. Even simple queries were met with answers that broadened her understanding of life and the world around it. It was as though Hildegarde was replying to her inquiries with a vocabulary that was many, many times larger than English, and which covered vastly more than mere actions or ideas.

Hildegarde's descriptions and responses had one common theme, that love was at the center. Kindness, patience, forgiveness, trust and similar emotional responses were the glue that held all meaningful interactions between souls who were in this light, Aisling came to understand. Interaction between souls that lacked these feelings was shallow and fleeting. The variations on the word "love" particularly caught Aisling's attention. There were uses of the word that Aisling never would have considered, and subtle derivatives that Aisling increasingly came to appreciate. She also came to appreciate that she was fortunate to be learning from one of the most advanced souls who had ever walked the earth. This was an opportunity that did not come to many.

Hildegarde was born last in a family of ten children, just before the turn of the twelfth century in what is now Germany. She was a sickly child who had visions at an early age, but was reluctant to share her experiences with those around her. Her visions were incredibly vibrant, consuming her senses. Some believed these visions may have contributed to frail health throughout her life.

As the result of her early maladies and her emerging spiritual powers, her parents gave her up as an oblate to the church at the age of eight. She came under the care of the abbess of a Benedictine convent, who taught her to read and write in a pious, serene setting.

Hildegarde thrived. She became a poet and musician, as well as a prolific author on spirituality, medicine, mathematics, linguistics, nature, nutrition, health, and astronomy. Over time she became one of the church's most prolific prophets.

After once being overtaken by what she described as an "army of angels" for what she believed to be a full month, she began to document her visions with the assistance of a monk named Volmar.

Her mysticism and writings attracted the attention of Pope Eugene, who was enthralled with the powerful, sublime images she presented. At the center of her writings was the role of women in propagating and accentuating life, in a time where the entire notion of humanity was based on the male prototype. The role of women was to support men, primarily through the production of children, but Hildegarde's writings placed women at the center of humanity's spiritual existence.

Hildegarde ultimately became abbess of a monastery following the death of her mentor. Rather than remain under male rule, through a protracted process that included another debilitating illness, she ultimately was granted the power to create her own monastery. In Rubertsberg, it was the first of two monasteries for nuns she would create during her long, productive life, but it was a far more challenging, austere existence than the one to which the nuns were accustomed.

Hildegarde became a prominent voice on political issues, highly unusual for women during the Middle Ages. Europe's most powerful voices were sensitive to her criticism, and she was able to exact change on a number of issues merely by speaking out.

Through her writings she created a term that has persisted through the ages. "Viriditas" refers to the lushness and vibrancy that threads through living existence. Hildegarde used the term to link the vitality of spiritual health to the vitality of bodily health. That she lived more than eight decades after a very shaky start may be attributed to the viriditas that flowed through her frail body.

Her presence before Aisling was that of a tested, proven soul who had endured some of the most trying challenges imaginable. Aisling was grateful for the opportunity afforded to her by the Elders. From what she knew of the challenge before them, she would need all that Hildegarde had to offer. She hoped it would be enough.

Aisling's questions for Hildegarde mounted and persisted. They had moved past the challenges of basic communication and were now preparing for the pressing matters that awaited them. It was Aisling's responsibility to draw her to the place where she would be best positioned to confront the tests that awaited.

"The process of soul reassignment is a complex one. Who bears the responsibility?"

"Why the individual, of course. All of us are so imperfect. The soul must use the love of God to expand, to grow, to learn new ways to use his love to honor him."

"What are the limitations in the selection of future incarnations?"

"The selection is so vast that there are virtually no limits. One can choose nearly any kind of life to live. The selection is bounded only by the courage of the soul, the willingness to take on life missions that stretch the boundaries of what the soul believes it can accomplish."

"How is it possible for the soul to view all these possibilities? Wouldn't the sheer number be overwhelming to the soul who has many possible directions to travel?"

"Yes, most definitely, if the soul were to attempt to survey all of them. However the selection process begins with a true assessment of the current state. The soul that is bathed in the light of God will know the many directions that must be traveled. All roads cannot be traveled in a single lifetime, which is why He allows us many, many opportunities to learn and grow. For each single selection, the soul will have available to it the wisdom to make the best choice at the right time. An appropriate opportunity will always be available."

"Always?"

"Always, my dear. A life is just a canvass. Canvasses come in all shapes and sizes, nearly an unlimited number of possibilities. The tools we are given to live our lives are the paint and the brushes. The brush strokes we make are the choices we choose."

Aisling contemplated this message. To her understanding, there was a movement afoot to change the number of available canvasses. Would this indeed be a problem?

"But what if," she asked, "there was a limit of the colors available, the brushes available? What if someone were to somehow place a limit on the possible lives that were available to live?"

"I'm not sure how that is possible, my dear. Regardless of the tools that are available for a lifetime, the individual will still make choices that will determine whether the soul has moved closer to God or further away. The soul holds the key to its fate, no matter the circumstances surrounding that lifetime. Some lifetimes are of course more challenging than others, but the impact that a soul can make on humanity can know no boundaries."

"These questions I am asking you have purpose. These are the levels that are in some form of contention."

"Contention in what way?"

"I wish I knew, Hildegarde. I think that is our challenge."

"I have an idea," he said, turning toward her in his chair.

"And what would that be?"

"I get the group together. It's been a while since we've met. We'll talk about next steps. These guys have to be on the edge, down to the last one. They probably think the Origenists are done as a group. The kidnapping probably has them thinking that was the nail in the coffin for their cause. Every last one of them is probably scared to death right now."

"Well, wasn't that the plan all along?"

"Sure, but that doesn't mean they'll all go away. Our annoying little medium friend seems to be hot on Dee. Maybe I can give these guys some ideas that will expedite matters."

"By doing what?"

"By coming in for a service as a curious churchgoer."

"Are you crazy?"

"Not at all. Something's cooking. Dee has been laying low, and that cannot be sitting well with her. She's not someone who's happy sitting around doing nothing."

"Interesting," Ellen Grandby Sullivan said. "It sounds as though you've developed a certain level of ... familiarity with this woman, or is it something a little more?" She threw him a devious smile.

He glared back. "She's an adversary, nothing more."

She stood from her chair and walked slowly toward her office window, that overlooked a panoramic view of the Boston skyline in the distance.

"You think these two are a couple now?"

"Almost certainly. I'm watching them. About a week ago she moved into his place. I suspect they became tired of being scared alone, and decided to cower and hide together."

"Why risk it? Henry is back volunteering," she said. "He's like an addict who can't quit. Is it really worth blowing your cover to get her into the nest too?"

"Of the whole group, she's the one I'm worried about the most," he replied. "Now that Herbrit is gone, she's the one person who seems to have some ability to get them in motion. Besides, what cover am I really blowing? Nobody at the church knows anything about me except you. Your plan to have me volunteer as a bookkeeper will give us the perfect cover."

She turned toward him. "What if Henry sees you here, Edgar? How do I know you won't do something ridiculous?"

"That would be very uncomfortable, granted, but he has no reason to think we're not on the same team. I'll pull the group together, tell him about this idea, and Dee will fill him in. It wouldn't be a surprise. In fact, he'd probably go out of his way to avoid me at the church. He hates me, and she probably does too, but I'd be willing to wager they're crawling out of their skin to know what's going to happen next, for the, for the Dalai Lama, and in the bigger picture too.

"I know everyone in the group," he said, crossing his arms. "They won't want to stay in hiding forever. Eventually they'll want to take some action."

"Any idea what they think we're attempting to do?"

"Oh, I doubt they have any idea," he said. "That's our strong suit, that they're itching to know. I'll just try to pull some triggers and watch for how to bring them down permanently, even if it means picking them off one by one."

"If Dee is the one you're worried about," she said, "maybe you should start with that little bitch."

"It's the strangest thing," Dee said to Henry. "I have a text message from a number I don't recognize."

"What's so strange about that?"

"The message uses the same language that David used to use to pull the group together."

"What's it say?"

"It's cryptic for anyone who wouldn't know how to decipher it. It says, 'Turkey on rye, 424 Seventh St.'"

"So how do you interpret that?"

"Turkey means we'll be meeting Tuesday, and 424 is the street number for one of our members' house, so we know where to meet. Seventh Street means 7 p.m. So we're meeting at Winfred's house Tuesday at seven."

"Who do you think sent it?"

"I have no idea, but it's one of the veterans in the group. Only a few of us has access to the phone numbers for all members."

"Are you really thinking of going?"

"Henry, I have no choice. I'm doing nothing right now to help. We can't let all of this finish us as a group. We need to stay together. Our group has a mission to bring back one of the earliest and most important tenets of the church. We've seen that they'll stop at nothing to oppose that. I don't think David Herbrit, or Origen or Christ himself, for that matter, would want us to abandon our mission."

Henry paced before replying. "Dee, I just don't see the sense in risking your life over a belief that hasn't been part of church doctrine for almost fifteen centuries. I understand your mission, but it just seems your chances of bringing back this doctrine are beyond remote. Now that the stakes are so high ..."

"This is the fight we chose!" Dee said this with a rattling hand slap on the table in front of her. "Maybe reincarnation will never be part of the Christian faith again, and we'll just allow them to keep selecting which church history we care to remember. It's a hole in our faith that needs to be filled. We're not giving up just because some whack jobs splintered off, then decided to take our position as a personal challenge. Most Christian churches couldn't care less what we believe, but for some reason the Church of the Tortured Christ is the one that feels most threatened by what we're promoting. Why the hell do they care? We're not after them. They could ignore us instead of trying to kill us."

"We don't know for sure they're trying to kill anyone."

"Oh please, Henry, wake up! They have to be the ones behind all of this."

"I understand why you're so eager to take action, to do something." Henry clasped her hands, looking in her eyes. "I really do. You want to make them react instead of us being the ones backing down."

He stood and walked slowly toward the window, rubbing his eyes. "I'll stand by you, Dee. I don't doubt that this church is capable of evil things. We don't want to risk any more damage, but we can't play into their hands either."

"I'm not quitting," she said, "and I refuse to do nothing."

He exhaled in defeat and plunked down next to her. "We haven't spent much time together since we were kids, but I remember you. It was really hard to change your mind once you've decided on something."

"You have a good memory." She threw her arms around him, burying her head into his chest.

The following Tuesday, Dee arrived at the gathering a few minutes after seven. The group was already immersed in deep conversation but went silent when she stepped into the living room.

"We were hoping you'd come," Lars said. "I hope you don't mind that we started without you."

She took a seat near a corner, content to avoid being the center of attention. All eyes in the room followed her as she sat. There were almost twenty people occupying every possible space in the large living room, including the floor. There were beer bottles and glasses of wine, but the group was all business. This meeting was clearly about damage control, and Dee could see immediately that no one was sure about what to do next.

"I thought perhaps your friend Henry might be with you." Lars looked at her blankly.

"He's not interested in being part of this after the way we welcomed him."

"I see," Lars said. "That's too bad. He could be very valuable, but of course we've never been about forcing our views on anyone."

There were murmurs in the room. Dee said nothing, avoiding eye contact with Lars.

"So where do we go from here?" It was Rachel, one of the veterans in the group.

"Well, we certainly can't stay in hiding," said Richard, the older man.

"Why not? We could go public, but any one of us might die in the process. Will that help our cause?" Rachel's teary eyes reflected the somber mood.

"If we stay in hiding indefinitely," Richard said, "we may as well disband. We accomplish nothing by staying holed up. If that's our only option then we may as well admit defeat. We lost the battle, and we're not even sure who we lost to."

"Look Richard," she replied sharply, "if these people, whoever they are, are willing to kill people, perhaps even killing the Dalai Lama, they wouldn't hesitate to kill any one of us. I'm not suggesting that we stay in hiding indefinitely. I'm suggesting that we let all of this blow over. Maybe we let them think we disappeared. In the meantime we formulate a strategy that includes avoiding our own extermination."

"I'd agree with you, Rachel, but I'm not sure what possible strategy we can develop that would make a difference. We're not even sure who we're up against. We think it's the Church of the Tortured Christ, but we don't even know that for sure."

The group was silent for almost a minute. Finally a quiet voice spoke from the corner.

"I think we're pretty sure. There is some proof, but I haven't seen it myself."

"Excuse me?" All eyes to turned to Dee in the back. "What are you talking about?"

"A female associate of Henry's says she saw a video that proves the church was involved in the abduction of the Dalai Lama."

"Who was this woman?" Lars was eager for details, as was the rest of the group.

"I'd rather not say. It's someone who ... was in a position to see it."

"Of course. I understand." Lars withdrew. "Can you tell us exactly what she saw?"

"It showed the Dalai Lama tied to a chair, being questioned by thugs who were wearing the church's cross around their necks."

Lars listened patiently, making sure her description was complete before speaking. "Can you be sure it proves the church was involved? Is there any possibility it was a fake, or that it wasn't staged by someone who was trying to frame the Church? Could she identify these guys?"

"No. I suppose it's possible it was staged, but I doubt it. She saw it on a digital video camera on Church property."

"Assuming this unnamed woman is being truthful about what she saw," Richard said, "that sounds like fairly compelling evidence. Dee, how much stock do you place on her word?"

"I don't know her, but I can't think of a reason why she'd lie about it. She has no idea what to make of it. It scares the hell out of her. She believed in what the church was all about, until this."

"Would Henry lie about it?" Lars asked quietly, trying not to provoke an emotional reaction.

"Henry has no association with the church, other than the volunteer work he did before we kidnapped him. He doesn't know anything more about them than we do."

"That sounds fairly convincing," Lars said. "I didn't want to believe the church was involved, but it's hard to think otherwise after hearing that."

The room was silent for several seconds, each lost in their thoughts. Finally Lars spoke again.

"I'm with Richard." They all looked up, startled. "We can't sit idly by, doing nothing. We have to act. I have to act."

"What do you have in mind?" Rachel asked.

"Infiltrate the place. We have to get in there."

"Are you nuts?" Rachel stood up, taking a few steps toward Lars. "That's suicide. Why would you go willingly into that place?"

Dee was quiet, looking down. She considered whether to reveal that Henry had returned to active volunteer status, but decided against it.

"What would you do once you got in there?" Richard directed his question to Lars.

"I have no idea, but if they're after us I'd rather see it up close, with my own eyes. They have no idea who I am," he lied. "Maybe I go in there as someone who's quietly been attending for a while, but I want to be more involved. I don't have much money to give, but maybe I can offer my services."

Richard asked, "What type of service would you offer?"

"I'm an accountant. I noticed on their web site they were looking for some bookkeeping. I'm sure they wouldn't turn down free accounting from a working CPA."

"I suppose that can work," Rachel said. "but then what? Are we after their finances?"

"Who knows what I can find out about them if I have access to their books? Maybe I can find evidence that links them to the Dalai Lama. From there we expose them, take them down."

Lars took their silence as acceptance and continued.

"It would be more believable if I wasn't alone. I'm guessing that most of the people my age attending church are married or dating someone. I think it would raise less suspicion if I was with someone."

"Probably," Richard said.

"Dee, you're about my age." Lars looked directly at her, unblinking.

"Excuse me?" The question threw her entirely off her guard. "What the hell are you talking about?"

"It wouldn't be difficult. We could just act like a couple that began dating in the last few months. I talked you into checking out this great church that I heard about."

"Why me?"

"Because out of everyone in this group, you're the one who would be most believable as my girlfriend."

Her stare bordered on contempt. As she looked around the room at the others, she noticed that all the women in the group were older than each of them.

"It was your idea to go in there," she said. "I don't think you need a partner to make it more believable."

"I respectfully disagree." Lars wore his most sincere expression. "Men are far more trustworthy when they have a woman by their side than when they don't."

"Unfortunately I think he's right, Dee." Richard turned to look at Dee. "I have no idea if this little adventure is worthwhile, but if Lars is going to make any progress he's better off with someone believable."

Dee fought through each of the possible scenarios that might unfold. Henry was already spending time at the church. What if their paths crossed inside? It could create a dangerous situation if they weren't careful about hiding their grudges.

She shook her head, closing her eyes tightly. After a few seconds she threw her hands out, palms up.

"Fine. If everyone thinks it'll help, I'll do it. At least I won't be sitting around waiting for them to come after me, but I would only be there during church services. I'm not going in there while Lars is sniffing around."

"Thanks Dee," Richard said. "I think your appearance will help him get better access."

"Yes, thanks Dee," Lars said quietly. "I think we can learn a lot in there."

"This is insane," Henry said angrily. "You were worried about me going into the teeth of the church, now you're doing the exact same thing. And with a psycho as your sidekick! Dee, do you even realize how crazy this sounds, how dangerous this is?"

"I've been thinking about nothing else, Henry. I had to make a quick decision. Besides, there's hardly anything to this. I go attend church with the guy and pretend I'm his girlfriend. Big deal."

"It IS a big deal. It's a big deal because he's psychotic. Who knows what kind of situation he'll get you into? Who knows whether he can get either of you out of any situation he creates? Neither of us has any idea of what this guy is capable of, or what's going on inside that twisted head of his."

"I've been around him a lot more than you have, Henry. He believes strongly in the cause. Plus, he's not exactly defenseless, in case you haven't noticed."

"Oh far from it," Henry replied, still angry. "I've noticed. While I was in there tied up, I wondered if he was taking out his aggressions on me that were meant for someone else. You guys, maybe."

"Are you seriously questioning which side he's on? Do you have any idea how much time he's spent with us, how committed he is to our cause?"

"Maybe so, but you weren't on the receiving end of his 'commitment.' I won't question that he's on your side, but he's not somebody I'd want on my team. You can have him."

"I think we have a lot bigger things to worry about than Lars. He's overly protective, maybe even paranoid, but I happen to think he's more dangerous to them than to us."

They were quiet for several long seconds. Finally Henry spoke.

"It's risky for both of us to be there. I don't want the Reverend to connect you and me."

"That's true," she replied, relieved that Henry was coming around. "Also, if run into Lars at the Church, you need to act like you've never met him."

"That will be my pleasure," he said.

She smiled, clasping his hands in hers. He returned a loving gaze, but not a smile. The stakes are higher than they've ever been, he thought, saying nothing.

They were in her spacious office in the evening. Her window shades were open with the radiant Boston skyline on display. Edgar was sitting in one of four comfortable chairs that faced her desk.

"This person saw WHAT???" Ellen Grandby Sullivan bounced from her chair, nearly climbing across her desk.

Her wild look caught Edgar off guard. As she lunged partway toward him, he rocked back in the chair, nearly tipping it back.

She stopped and hovered above him, hands on hips.

"She says that someone here saw a video of the old Buddhist being roughed up by a couple of guys wearing crosses that were recognizable as ours. The men couldn't be identified, but she seems pretty convinced that it's legit."

"So who is this person that saw the video?"

"Dee wouldn't say. It has to be someone on the inside, otherwise she never would've gotten access to our inner offices, or the camera."

"Undoubtedly." Ellen Grandby Sullivan returned to her chair, breathing heavily. Her eyes darted around the room as she tried to calibrate their next move.

"We never should have shot that video in the first place," Lars said, attempting to calm her.

"It could've been useful if somebody didn't forget about the crosses."

"I already apologized about that, over and over."

"The damage from your poor decisions continues," she said, glaring at him.

"Let's figure out what to do about this, Reverend."

"Did you manage to do what we talked about?"

"Yes, it went perfectly," he said. "She's agreed to pretend to be my girlfriend while we attend a service. She wasn't thrilled about it, but some of the other members got behind my idea."

"Well, it seems we still have some cards to play." She leaned back in her chair, deliberating over Lars the Origenist.

"You need to find out who this woman is."

"She's keeping her distance with me over the way I handled Henry. She seems determined to protect her identity, even from the rest of the Origenists."

"Another missed opportunity. You had this hack medium right in your hands. That gave us nothing of value, from what I can tell."

"It had to be authentic. I had to mean business to eliminate all doubt that I was on their side. Now they see me as their guard dog. Besides, I almost managed to convince them that he was the one who killed Herbrit, and likely Donnelly."

"Well, you have a chance to make up for all this messiness. We need to find out who this woman is, and you need to keep Dee in your sights until the time is right to close the book on her. Make it happen, Edgar."

He nodded and walked quickly toward the door, not looking back as he walked out.

She walked to the door, quietly throwing the deadbolt. She closed the curtains in her office and moved through the inner office door that was discreetly behind her desk.

She lit candles that were spread neatly across the small room. She bowed and kneeled, her eyes closed. She brought herself into a meditative state before chanting.

"Ispata Immat khoday. Ispata Immat khoday. Ispata Immat khoday."

She repeated the phrase several times, pausing before each. The candles flickered, then cool, musty air began to permeate the room. A heavy presence descended. She remained in a kneeling position, eyes closed.

"You have come."

At once, the entirety of her being came under the control of this powerful being. Her nostrils stung from the dank, overpowering scent that seemed to be the signature of this spirit that had been idle for centuries.

Beyond the powerful odor, she noticed an intense irascibility. Her hope, after their last meeting, was to leverage his interest in seeking redemption from the Light, as Immat called it.

"*What progress do you bring?*"

She swallowed hard before answering.

"The progress continues, but to advance our cause I need more of your ... direct help."

"*Continue.*"

"It is vital that you do everything possible to regain your prior position. If it means that you go directly into the Light, repentant and requesting forgiveness, then it must happen. It is important for so many reasons."

An intensity flared, a pressure that seemed to pull the air from the room. The thickness increased until she gasped, unable to breathe. Only then did Immat choose to speak.

"It is them who should repent. There was awareness of my mortal needs for ages, but they chose ignorance. Then the time came when they learned to do without me, so they cast me off. My contributions meant nothing."

The God before her had come to realize that the heavens operate the same as on earth. They were aware of his proclivity toward virgins, but they may have hoped that he would eventually correct his path. When he never rehabilitated, they had had enough. Yet here he was, bitter about his treatment.

"You were a vital part of the reassignment of souls, but I suspect your behavior could no longer be tolerated, particularly someone in your position."

There was an easing of the pressure, and a pause.

"Perhaps."

In her limited dealings with this powerful but disgraced god, this was the first time she was in a position to maneuver, a chess player who had finally taken the opponent's Queen. She had the upper hand.

"If we are to work together and achieve progress for both of us, you must find a way to regain your prior stature."

"My prior stature." There was inflection on the last word. *"My stature emerged from my deeds. Never had one in my position possessed the totality of vision that I provided. The Elders knew the rareness of my mastery. They have suffered without me, and would no doubt welcome me back."*

The conversation confirmed that his was the one she had read about in obscure Christian texts. There was one who was so gifted at seeing the right opportunity for souls in transition that his skills were beyond all others. This former God who was with her now, conversing as a peer, was unequaled in the task of assigning souls to the best possible life assignment.

"As you approach them, after all this history," she began delicately, "you must convince them that your past should be forgotten. You must first believe that your past transgressions will not emerge again, and then you must convince them of your sincerity."

The pressure in the room tightened.

"I would require a sign from the Elders."

"How has your existence been since leaving that domain? Have you been content since leaving that realm?"

There was silence.

"With all respect, I suggest that your existence has not been suited to one with your gifts. It is plain to see that your current position is beneath you. We've discussed the challenge. You understand what we intend to achieve. Are you able to join us, or shall we seek alternatives?"

"*Yes,*" he replied after a pause. "*The time is now to resume my work.*"

"Wonderful! It is now necessary that you get before the Elders to explain your change of heart, and that you do so convincingly."

"*I must try.*"

"We can do great things together," she replied. "Our combined work will yield everlasting fruit. Having you back in your rightful position will be a blessing to all mankind, however it will require great discipline.

"There is one other piece of business. You must let the girl go."

The energy from Immat sprayed into her, then tapered. A change of attitude was occurring before the Reverend's eyes.

"*It will be so,*" he said.

"Thank you. With our commitment to His Lord Jesus Christ, and the plan we have in place to spread His word above all others, we will change the course of humanity."

"*I consider it a blessing that we met.*"

She sighed, offered a prayer, and left the conversation content. Another essential part of the plan fell into place perfectly.

He took his place in front of the elders, a place he never believed he would see again. They were gathered in order in the Great Hall, just as he remembered from so long ago.

The most senior of the group were toward the middle and each wore a medallion that symbolized a distinct holy virtue such as unwavering love, loyalty, compassion, and generosity. Each of the elders exuded a superior wisdom that came from its particular holy attribute, and all complemented each other. Together they formed a solid wall of the best facets of the human spirit.

Even to a former highly placed celestial being such as himself, the light and goodness were overwhelming. He had forgotten the power that was complete and omnipresent in this place, and how much he missed it. It was so long since he felt this pervasive sense of goodness.

The crystal cathedral was as glorious and overwhelming as it was the first time he entered. His awe was apparent to the elders, as they were able to sense every emotion and thought that was held by anyone before them. Despite this much higher level of cognition, they slowed their communications to a level that would make him more comfortable.

"We welcome our old friend Immat to the house of God. We hoped we would see you again one day, but were not sure that day would ever come."

"It is not possible to express my gratitude that you've welcome me back." He bowed his head, ashamed to look directly at them.

"You should know from your experience that the One True God is not a vengeful god. He takes in all who are pure in their heart and sincere in their intentions. We welcome you to the Great Hall because we believe you understand and remember this."

"Indeed I do." Immat's tension began to ease before these intimidating but kind beings. He looked up at them in an attempt to assure them of his sincerity. They returned his gaze steadily, without judgement.

"What is it that brought you back to the Light after all this time? We've thought often of you, and the many good works you performed before God and in the interest of mankind."

Immat struggled but finally formulated clear ideas to present. "For all this time I have missed the contributions I was able to make, as you were so kind to point out. I feel I have a special talent, but recent contacts with humans has led me to understand that my failures were the result of my own weakness and pride. I allowed the power of my position to corrupt me, my vanity to overtake me. As it says in Proverbs, 'When pride cometh, then cometh shame; but with the lowly is wisdom.' My undoing was that I believed my talent could not be replaced. I was wrong, so very wrong in so many ways. The machinery of the heavens and earth did not cease just because I chose to leave."

The elder beings listened patiently, allowing Immat to speak until his contrition fully apparent. Finally the elder who was associated with kinship and empathy spoke.

"We missed your talent. There are others who perform the role of surveying the life opportunities for souls about to transition back. It is a very, very challenging role, and no one has filled it as well as you, even after all this time. With so much talent in this regard, it is not surprising that pride would be your biggest challenge."

The elder of equality and judgement spoke next. "You miss the position. This is understandable. It was a very important role, widely respected with so many angels available to assist in your efforts from the second sphere. The Dominions, the Virtues, the Authorities, they all depended on your wisdom to ensure that the best life opportunities were presented for consideration by so many souls.

"Yet judgement is what failed you, and for something as terrestrial as the flesh of human virgins. For what? We discussed it often so long ago. How can you be so sure that your decision making will not fail you again?"

"I cannot be completely certain," Immat replied, looking down again. "I can only assure you that the loss of this position was far, far more devastating than any power I felt when I held it. I thought I had lost everything, not only position but all the trust that others placed in me."

"What of these people who contacted you," Judgement continued. "what do you know of their motivations, of their reasons for conjuring you from the darkness?"

"I do not know enough," Immat conceded, "but I will know soon. If their intentions are anything less than to improve the lot of man, it will be my responsibility to recognize this and to choose the correct path."

The elders spoke among themselves briefly, or what seemed so to Immat. Their conversation was at a level he could not comprehend, however he saw that each of the elders was involved. It was obvious they were discussing whether to allow him to regain his position. After an intensive series of questions, answers, and deliberations, the most senior elder addressed him.

"We believe you are sincere in your desire to contribute only positively to the future of man and to the betterment of all souls. However there remains concern among this council on whether your judgement will be completely reliable. Therefore we will allow you to resume your prior work, but there will be measures in place to ensure that your lapses will not happen again. We place in you the trust that if you sense weakness returning, you will be back before us."

Immat bowed. "I am eternally grateful. It means everything."

No words came from the elders, just a silent acknowledgement of his gratitude.

"Will you tell me what these measures will be?"

"That is not necessary. If there are no lapses, you will be entirely unaware the measures exist. Be clear, they are to protect you from any possibility of your own weakness resurfacing."

"I thank you again."

On a crisp Sunday morning, the large ebony doors of the Church of the Tortured Christ were open wide to embrace any passersby who might be curious about the warm music and inviting smell of baking bread. Parishioners were casually strolling into the stylish, angular structure, wearing bright clothes and smiles.

Inside the vestibule, the Reverend Ellen Grandby Sullivan was extending a welcoming hand to all the visitors she could reach, although there were far too many coming in for the ten o'clock service for her to greet personally. A handsome young couple approached the steps to the church cautiously, remaining behind the oncoming crowd.

"Lars, I'm not ready to meet this woman. Let's just blend in and catch the service. Maybe we meet her later."

"Why? She's out here trying to meet people. There's no second chance to make a first impression." He gently but firmly pulled her arm toward the Reverend. She resisted at first but relented when they were too close to avoid drawing attention.

He waited behind another couple chatting with the Reverend. Finally they moved ahead and Lars jutted his hand out with a wide smile.

"Reverend Sullivan? Hello, it's so great to meet you. My name is Lars Essington. This is my girlfriend, Delilah."

The Reverend matched his smile with even more charm. "Lars, it's a true pleasure to meet you. And Delilah, welcome! Is it your first time visiting our parish?"

"In fact it is," Lars replied.

"What brought you here? How did you hear about us?"

"Well, I occasionally watch your father's TV show, and when I found out we had an extension of that family of churches right here in the Boston area, I needed to see for myself."

"Why that's lovely! My father, bless his heart, is still our best recruiter, even after all these years."

"He's a very compelling orator," Lars said convincingly. "Quite a man."

"I like to think so." She smiled sweetly.

Dee remained quiet, with a closed mouth smile.

"Well, we'll let you be," he said. "I look forward to your service."

They moved into the cavernous church, looking for an open area.

"That was nauseating," Dee whispered to Lars.

"You need to work on your acting skills."

"Don't give me any shit. I smiled and acted the part of the quiet, stupid girlfriend just fine."

The Sunday affair started with triumphant music coming from a twelve piece band on a perch that overlooked the altar. They played a mix of classical and new age music, with perfect acoustics cascading chords through the brightly lit space. Dee was captivated by the experience, but careful not to display any semblance of enjoyment to her companion.

The Reverend Ellen Grandby Sullivan came onto the stage at a perfect lull in the music. Her gown was flowing and full. Somehow a breeze caught her at the perfect angle, throwing her hair up in such a way that it reminded Dee of a shampoo commercial.

She gracefully approached a carefully positioned cushion to the left of the altar, then deliberately kneeled.

"We pray. Dear Lord, what a glorious day. What a glorious week. What a glorious life you've given us. We pray that we have the wisdom to appreciate every living moment, and spend it wisely. We pray that we appreciate the things around us, the people around us, the family around us, if we are so blessed. We pray that we have resources and generosity to help those in need of our help, and the discretion to know when our help is not needed. We pray that we serve you with honor, dignity, and a trust in your plan for our souls. Amen."

On queue the entire organization, a crowd that Dee estimated at more than fifteen hundred congregants, echoed her amen in unison. Reverend Sullivan brought the large, engaged room through an event that was always upbeat, filled with prayer, music, even a puppet show for children. It was masterfully choreographed, with expert segues between segments. Dee remarked to Lars that the show was more about entertainment and keeping the audience engaged than it was about purification and cleansing.

The service ended as it began, with a rousing musical crescendo accompanied by a stunning light display around the periphery of the worship hall. It was not an easy feat, Dee noticed, given the magnificent lighting through ornate stained glass windows. The experience wound down elegantly, offering a subtle queue for congregants to exit. The Reverend was able to leave the stage without drawing attention. Few congregants left until the music had subsided into a low, slow organ standard.

"Wow," Lars said softly. "I have to admit, I'm impressed. I've heard of 'opium for the masses', but I never knew what it meant until today."

"Hmm." Dee was standing, still taking in the scene. "Impressive show. It seems like the Vatican on growth hormone, with a mix of something I can't quite figure out. Either Disneyland or Vegas. Maybe all of the above."

"Dee, I have to play the part."

"What part?" She half looked at him.

"The part of the star-struck congregant who was just blown away by the show. I'm going to approach her again, asking about volunteering."

"Won't you feel like a teenage girl at her first live concert?"

"Maybe I should," he answered without blinking.

"And I still have to act the part of your girlfriend. Fucking rapture."

"Deal with it." He stepped past her into the aisle. She followed as the dutiful girlfriend.

Outside the vast, ornate front doors, Ellen Grandby Sullivan was surrounded by congregants, all glowing and hanging on each word. Whichever lucky person that held her eye contact felt the most blessed. It was like an extension of the service for these admirers, a service that could not last long enough. Dee stayed on the fringe, hoping to remain unnoticed. Lars charged through the throng, a wiry frame moving easily through the crowd.

"Reverend?" He asked once, and the woman made immediate eye contact. Dee noticed.

At the first break she looked up to him. "It was Lars, wasn't it?"

"It is Lars! Thanks for remembering. I loved your service. It was sublime."

She nodded and smiled an obligatory smile, as if to say "Of course it was."

"Reverend, I wonder if your church is in need of professional services, gratis of course."

"Well, we always appreciate any form of generosity, if not for us then for our congregation. What kind of work do you do, Lars?"

"I'm a CPA. I can do anything from basic bookkeeping to tax preparation."

"Can you call my office this week? We have an accounting firm that Father has used since his early days with the Church, but we do try to support of our congregants who run small businesses. I would imagine some of them would LOVE to have your help. We would provide the office space, of course."

"Of course," Lars replied with a big smile. "Tax season is over so I have some time. I'll call your office this week."

"Lovely seeing you again." She whirled to a middle aged woman in front of Lars. "It's Gloria, right? Gloria, how is that grandson of yours?"

Dee and Lars approached the parking lot.

"I thought your first conversation with her was nauseating, but that was even more wretched."

"And perfectly effective. We're in."

"You're in. I'm not in. I never want to come here again."

"What in the HELL am I supposed to do, say we broke up? Dee get real. Now that she's seen you, you can't just disappear. I'm not asking you to pretend you're as enthusiastic about this place as me, but it would help if you'd just play along. If we're committed to the cause, then we hold our nose and do our job, don't we?"

Her silence was grudging acceptance.

The silver-haired man in an elegant suit, bright blue tie and expensive Italian loafers strode into the office of the Prime Minister. The two men smiled broadly as they approached one another from across the long, ornately furnished office. They met in the center and hugged.

"Old friend!" The Prime Minister beamed as he hugged his visitor.

The office of the Prime Minister of Israel, called Beit Aghion, provided in a dual role as his official residence in Jerusalem. The office was modest compared to the official homes of other world leaders, but it remained in place through the years mostly due to the desire of Israelis to remain true to their history as a modest people who avoid the trappings of good fortune. The building was built by a wealthy merchant in the years between the first and second world wars, and was used as a hospital during the Arab-Israeli war of 1948. It was a perfect fit for its current occupant.

Joram Berkovic, the popular Israeli Prime Minister, was a member of Likud, Israel's prominent right wing political party. He retained his seat through several serious challenges during his seven years in office through a fierce desire to make Israel's national defense among the most prominent in the world, and his ability to assert his desire to place the interests of Israel far ahead of others in the region. Berkovic was not afraid to rock the boat in international affairs, and he showed little hesitation in testing the boundaries of the patience of the US, which provided billions in financial aid each year.

Berkovic demonstrated an uncanny ability to connect with the voters of Israel and proponents of the Israeli state around the world, particularly in the United States and Europe. His English was heavily accented, but his ability to bring forth dramatic oratory on the world stage was unmatched. Israel's need to remain among the strongest defenses in the world was not only an urgent matter of survival, he maintained, but critical to the balance of peace in the Middle East and around the world. From the inevitable skirmishes that took place in and around the Israeli-occupied territories, Joram Berkovic managed to present a compelling, unceasing narrative that the future of the Jewish state was a whisker away from extinction. He kept the message fresh and current, and American political leadership had little choice but to support the message.

"What a wonderful surprise it was to hear from you. You were very mysterious on the phone. Is this merely a matter of being 'in the neighborhood,' or are you here for our fine Jewish cuisine? You couldn't stay away from kosher delicacies this long, correct?" The Prime Minister let out a deep, bellowing laugh.

"Well, in fact I was in the neighborhood," the dapper visitor replied, smiling coyly, "but I'm in the neighborhood because it was important to visit. This is a matter to discuss that is much too important to leave to a phone call."

"It sounds very serious." The Prime Minister lost his smile and clasped his hands before him on his desk. "So tell me Reverend Granby, what is this urgent matter?"

The senior leader of the Church of the Tortured Christ, one of the fastest growing, most influential Christian organizations in the West, paused several seconds before responding.

"You're aware of the growth of our church. We've been very blessed to grow by leaps and bounds, not only in the US, but around the globe. Our message of world tolerance and acceptance is resonating. We knew the message of Christ is one that people could connect to for centuries, but we underestimated just how anxious people were to avoid the condemnation that has been such a part of traditional churches, and the ... tackiness of many of the recent Christian churches in the U.S. People have been waiting for a church like ours, one that avoids stale traditions but which delivers a Christian message in a way that can be tolerated, embraced even. We're very different from the money-first message of our predecessors. We don't start conversations by asking for money and we don't flaunt our wealth. We give back, and we use our resources discreetly and wisely."

"Yes," the Prime Minister replied, "the growth of your church has been very impressive, and you've done so much good around the world and in your own country. But this is information we both know. I wonder where this conversation is going. You have me very curious, Ernest."

"Yes, my apologies, Joram. I mention this to underscore that the influence of the Church on the international stage has never been more prominent. We have followers in several dozen countries on each of the inhabited continents. Wherever the Roman Catholics established influence over the centuries, our popularity is booming."

The Prime Minister nodded. This information was not news.

The Reverend continued. "What you may not know is that the complexity of our mission has exceeded the growth of our flock. As our congregation has grown, the demands of the congregation have grown as well. We're increasingly involved with decisions being made in various parts of the world, whether we want to be or not, and our congregants are extremely forthcoming in keeping us apprised. We have quite a network of 'reporters.' to our pleasant surprise."

"Interesting," Berkovic replied. "I wasn't aware that your influence was quite so expansive."

"As it turns out, some of the information we receive was wholly unexpected. It's a two-edged sword, I suppose. Along with the satisfaction we derive from bringing Christ's message to places that badly need it, we also obtain information from our flock that compels us to make difficult decisions. Some of this information is highly sensitive."

"I gather," Berkovic asked, "that some of this information you've obtained is the reason for your visit?"

"Indeed it is," Granby replied solemnly.

"I further gather that this information is relevant to our national security."

"Extremely relevant, I'm afraid."

"Please continue," the Prime Minister said. His gaze was steady and stern, as if readying for bad news.

"I was surprised to learn," Grandby said, "that there are almost 3 million Christians in Syria. They represent a substantial minority to the mostly Islamic population, but that is not a small number. As we are learning these days, where there are Christians, there is a very high likelihood that some of these Christians will be followers of the Church of the Tortured Christ."

"So you have even church members in Syria? Remarkable. There are Jews there as well, but their life is not easy, from what I am told, particularly in recent days."

"I can only imagine. Our members who have been diligent and thoughtful enough to stay in touch with us have talked about the challenges of living in a country that is almost 90% Muslim. I just can't imagine the challenges of living there as a practicing Jew.

"But I digress. The urgent business that brings me here, Mister Prime Minister, is that one of our congregants works in government circles. Despite the overwhelming majority of Muslims in Syria, their government has been mostly fair regarding their employment practices. They seem quite willing to allow qualified candidates to occupy positions in government regardless of whether they are Muslim or not. That seems to be relatively rare in this part of the world, where religion and state are so closely entwined."

The Prime Minister nodded, saying nothing.

"We discovered that we have a congregant who is a technician with very specific communication skills. Evidently someone of his abilities are quite valuable, and he happened to take a contract position with the Syrian government."

"I see," said Berkovic. "This is becoming more intriguing by the second."

"Yes, well, he explained there are very substantial safeguards in place to ensure that he only gains access to information that a contractor would normally be entitled. He said the safeguards are strong, that his Syrian supervisors are very diligent about the information he can access. However exceptions are bound to happen. There was concern about a security breach with one of their internal email servers. He investigated records around who accessed the server, and it was necessary for him to view emails that were sent outside. As a matter of routine, he reviewed the contents of many, many emails. It seems there were communications that strongly indicate a plan of aggression against the Israeli state."

The Prime Minister inhaled deeply, then looked down at his folded hands. Without looking up he asked, "Could it be determined how imminent a threat this is?"

"Not specifically, no," Grandby replied. "However he said that the tone of the email suggested that the plans were not just beginning. It sounds as if they've been in the works for quite some time."

"I see," Berkovic said looking in the distance, "and could it be ascertained what the nature of this aggression would be?"

"Not entirely, however it is very worrisome. He hand-wrote some of the terminology being used, as anything he printed would be very risky. In the email there was reference to the status of acquiring '239.' He wasn't sure what it could refer to, and wasn't even certain of whether it was something to be concerned about.

"Then he did some research on his own, and he came away convinced that '239' refers to Plutonium 239, one of the primary ingredients in the production of nuclear weapons."

The Prime Minister of the nation of Israel stared at him, mouth partway open in disbelief.

"You think you have evidence Syria is planning a nuclear attack against the nation of Israel! How strongly do you believe this?"

"I have to emphasize, Joram, that his information is highly speculative. There is no way to confirm that a nuclear attack is planned," Berkovic challenged.

"However it appears clear that some form of attack is planned."

Grandby considered his response carefully before replying. "That seems very likely, but there is no sure way to know how soon."

"And there's a substance they've tried to acquire that is mentioned in this communication that is essential to their planned act of aggression."

"That does seem to be the case," Grandby replied, "yes."

Both men were silent for several seconds. Finally Berkovic spoke.

"Have you gone to the US government with this information?"

"Not yet," Grandby replied, "but I suppose I must. I thought it was most important to tell you first. I only found out about it myself late last night, and I happened to be near Athens. We changed our itinerary. I couldn't trust that any standard communication methods would suffice. I came as fast as I could."

The Prime Minister's tone changed. "I cannot adequately express my appreciation for what this means to the entire state of Israel. You are a dear friend. Thank you."

"Of course. It is my duty, one friend to another."

"You have done so much for the Jewish people already that this pains me, but I have one small favor to ask," said Berkovic.

"Yes, of course, anything."

"Can you allow us the opportunity to disclose this to the US government? We are compelled to inform them of any offensive or defensive actions planned. I would like to frame this around our continuing dialogue. They will of course insist that we consider alternative actions. However, without any understanding of the timing of this aggression by these dogs from Syria, I doubt we have any choice but to preemptively act."

Grandby looked at the Prime Minister, considering the implications of holding back information from his government that had very real consequences for a new war in the Middle East.

"It's probably better that it comes from you than me," he said. "The truth is, I don't even know who I would contact in the State Department. I've never had any contact with them before."

"Yes, well, we're in contact with them far more often than would be my preference," Berkovic replied. "They're continually concerned that we'll do something to provoke a full war in this part of the world. We can't pass gas without getting a phone call from some State Department staffer with a sensitive nose."

Grandby laughed heartily, appreciating the break in tension.

"If it puts your mind at ease," Berkovic said, "this is far from the first time we've had to worry about an attack from one of our neighbors. Sadly, plans of attack of one form or another are a routine occurrence."

Grandby was unfazed. "How often do countries obtain nuclear weapons as part of these threats?"

"Not often that we know of, but we have no way of knowing which threats are real and which are not," Berkovic replied. "We have an elaborate process in place for escalating these things through our government and through our channels in the US government too."

"I can accept the risk involved in allowing you to share this with my government," Grandby said, "but I must insist that you avoid mentioning where you obtained this information. We prefer to stay out of any international political situations. It's considered bad form for a church in the US, exempt from paying taxes, to become involved in these matters." Grandby smiled at his colleague.

"It's more than possible, Reverend Grandby. It is our preference as well."

"From your experience dealing with them," Grandby asked, "won't the US State Department expect a high level of confidence that the threat is real?"

"Of course," replied Berkovic evenly. "However it is not their citizens that are a target of Islamic lunatics. It's the citizens of the nation of Israel. I have an obligation to protect my electorate from harm, and that's what I plan to do. Out of courtesy and appreciation for their profound support through these years, I will keep the US government informed of the position we are in. However we have an understanding that Israel has a right to defend itself always. This is one of those times, and they will have to trust our judgement. Divulging the source of our information would only complicate matters. There is no reason to bring our sources into the conversation. I consider the source very credible, and that's what our partners in the US State Department must be content with."

The two men had little more to discuss. Grandby got up to leave.

"I was really dreading this discussion, but I feel as though a tremendous weight has been lifted."

"I am honored that you would trust us with this information," Berkovic replied. "I pray that you and I will have the opportunity in years to come to discuss the times in which we live, and that all turns out well for our people everywhere."

"I will pray for the same thing," Grandby said.

The two men embraced. Grandby somberly left the office of the Prime Minister, and out the front door of Beit Aghion. His limousine awaited. He stepped into the vehicle and pulled out his phone, pressing the number two, the first speed dial on his phone.

"Hi. I just left him. It went perfectly. He's motivated, and prefers to keep his sources quiet. It could not have gone better."

Descent of the Asuras

The Chinese government invested vast resources to ensure the communications heard by their citizens were consistent and on point. The Chinese public needed to believe that the social fabric in China was superior to any other, and that the rest of the world was at its core jealous of all that the People's Republic of China represented.

This controlled messaging included television, radio, print, and most difficult of all in recent years, the internet. Chinese government cybersecurity experts managed to configure a complex network of servers that combined to create an online experience that was one hundred percent Chinese. No outside news was invited without filtering, modification, or complete removal. To the average Chinese citizen with no view beyond national boundaries, the internet was dominated by China.

To accomplish this, the government relied on vast departments of government workers, carefully arranged, staffed, and managed to ensure the most consistent delivery of content. This level of orchestration involved the continuous review of content from the outside world, then determining which could be converted into language that was useful for government purposes.

The role of Translator was a highly skilled position. Not only was the Translator expected to understand the nuances of two or three languages, but each was expected to effectively convert the most prominent news into stories that made the outside world shrink in comparison to the grand People's Republic.

Behind the Translators were several waves of management reviewers. The copy that was reviewed and approved by a second level manager would never be seen by the public. It would then be read by a third level manager before going to print, online, or broadcast media. In the case of the more sensitive international topics, a fourth or even fifth-level management team would be responsible for collectively scrutinizing these stories to ensure the messaging put the Republic in the most favorable possible light.

Following the approval of messaging, responsibility shifted to an army of government workers who published stories into the proper form for consumption by eager Chinese readers. The copy approval process could take time, so to ensure messaging was delivered to a citizenry hungry for news, tremendous weight fell on the production staffs to do their job quickly. They were expected to work as long as needed on any given day to deliver approved messaging in their particular media.

With a population of nearly one and a half billion citizens, there was a craving for all forms of news. Civic affairs, politics, natural disasters, business, sports, and weather provided ample material for the traditional reader, but there were also many thousands of younger and hungrier consumers of media who required more, and were willing to go to great lengths to get it.

These hungrier information consumers knew there was a big world outside China that was moving at a different pace, and in completely different directions. These were the people the Chinese government was most concerned about as her vast media machine was put into place. The Chinese government passed into law severe restrictions on "high risk activities" by online citizens, and promptly created a force of a few thousand members of a newly formed Cyber Team, which aggressively pursued citizens who knowingly attempted to work around their veil of censorship. The Cyber Team jailed hundreds, some on the mere suspicion of violations.

The wall of information, combined with strict laws and regulations, were almost completely effective during normal times, but these were far from normal times. Religion in China was deeply rooted in Buddhism, as demonstrated by the customs, gestures, and communication styles that had developed over centuries. Yet Buddhists represented only a fraction of Chinese, about a tenth of the overall population. What they lacked in relative numbers, they compensated through their unchallenged identity. The Buddhists were always an integral part of Chinese society, quiet, spiritual, and omnipresent.

The government did not generally condone religion, but it was not hostile either. More than half her population was atheist, agnostic, or generally uninterested in formalized religion, so most citizens remained disconnected with spiritual possibilities. The typical Chinese citizen was far more concerned with inching his way forward in this life, with very little thought given to the next. This presented quite a substantial divide from Buddhists, who held loyally to their faith and were always considering their lives ahead.

The news of the abduction of the Dalai Lama was handled by the government with extreme caution. Information reviewers at the highest level were unsure how to frame the story, and were keenly aware of the likelihood that it was bound to leak through unauthorized sources to the Chinese populace. When it did, the story would spread fast.

In the West, China was being accused of either directly or indirectly orchestrating the disappearance of the de facto leader of much of the world's Buddhist population. Chinese leadership was adamant in all of its communications that China had nothing to do with the troubling situation. Their approach in Chinese media was to express outrage, then to demand his safe return followed by accountability for the parties responsible.

The messaging vaguely referred to 'envious forces' that were wrongly placing China in the crosshairs of this terrible event. They openly accused the United State of using the tragedy to make themselves appear morally superior while minimizing the violence and chaos that was a part of everyday life in the West. They avoided mention of the decades of tension between the Tibetan spiritual and China that began in the 1950s and resulted in his flight and the creation of a government in exile.

For the majority of Chinese this messaging was accepted at face value, but for a fraction of the population, the recent events were the most significant of their lifetimes. Many non-Buddhist Chinese were sympathetic with their cause, knowing Buddhism was rooted in the history of China. They were aware that Tibetan Buddhists were part of their fabric for more than six centuries, while the current political structure had only been in power for a century.

For several years, younger, technically savvy Chinese citizens had spent all of their available time collaborating across the country to learn how the government's cybersecurity operated. Over time they developed discreet ways to communicate that avoided detection by Chinese authorities. Their daring experimentation had many trials and error during recent years, but each failure resulted in newer and more inventive ways to share learnings about how the infrastructure worked. Over time there was a strong core of internet surfers who managed to devise ways to bypass the tight security layers that were in place, deftly avoiding detection by always staying two or three steps ahead of authorities. If their avenue for reaching the true worldwide web came to a close, they always had multiple alternatives.

They called themselves the PLAboys, a sardonic reference to the People's Liberation Army, or PLA, which was the military whip of the Chinese Communist Party. While these adventurers were able to freely surf the internet, absorbing a wealth of information about world events that was free from doubt about what their leadership was filtering out, they exercised great caution in sharing their knowledge. Most of the information gleaned from the outside world by the PLAboys was shared in very tight circles to avoid detection, but there were some international stories that were too important to keep close.

The disappearance of the Dalai Lama was a story that inflamed these internet mavericks. Regardless of each's belief in God or adherence to any formal religion, all agreed this information needed to be spread as far and fast as possible. They started with their most reliable method of communication, the cryptic messaging protocols they developed to maintain contact with each other. The first messages were simple, but spread quickly among the few thousand PLAboys, some of whom were not boys at all. Some of their more active members included young women who never had a realistic chance of making a difference in prominent Chinese circles, and gay men and women, who had no more effective way to exercise their independence and freedom in this place and time.

One story from CNN online that drew much of their attention quoted a Chinese dissident who offered a few guesses about why Chinese authorities might want the Dalai Lama out of circulation. His most compelling argument was that they were the only logical suspects with operatives in the western world with both the motivation and the means to conduct such a high profile operation.

The article also offered details about the letter that was sent to various news organizations in the United States by unnamed sources. The letter was not mentioned in any Chinese news reports, which immediately raised suspicion among this internet underground. The accusation in the letters was that the Dalai Lama was a traitor, and a target too dangerous to allow to roam free during these changing times.

A group message went out at four o'clock in the morning, Beijing time, to the PLAboys distribution.

"They've gone too far this time," the message said. "Copy the online article and spread it. We need to stand behind our Buddhist brothers and sisters. Use extreme caution when sharing. Be careful with public copiers , but exercise the utmost urgency. Find convenient drop points. Start with the colleges. The cutoff is Thursday midnight. Remove all evidence by then. Be safe, be strong, PLAboys."

Word spread fast. Within a few days there were hardcopy versions of the article spreading across the largest cities in China. Protestors appeared almost immediately, catching authorities off guard. At first the guards of the MPS, the Ministry of Public Security, looked the other way, instructing the protestors to move along or risk arrest. A sense of outrage, fresh and energized, was in the air.

Hour by hour, beginning in the early evening on Thursday, before the stated cutoff, the tensions began to grow. At first the density of the crowds was most noticeable around college campuses, but by Friday paper versions of the article were easily available wherever large congregations of young people were likely to assemble. Shopping malls, strip malls, arcades, coffee shops, tea rooms, and even grocery stores were abuzz with the news.

The MPS mobilized quickly. They made a point of arriving in a spectacle in areas where crowds gathered. They made no arrests immediately, under orders to get the crowds to disperse peacefully. Their efforts worked well at first, but as more flyers circulated through the day on Friday and the weekend approach, Chinese citizens began to gain courage in numbers.

By the dinner hour on Friday, crowds in the larger cities were numbering into the tens of thousands. Outraged citizens were carrying signs and chanting in unison. Buddhist Chinese were front and center as the assemblies turned to full protests, although many avoided their traditional Buddhist attire for more common garments to avoid being singled out by authorities.

Individual voices were impossible to discern among the tens of thousands of protesters in the largest Chinese cities. As daylight leaned into evening, the crowds gained fuel from the coming darkness. Small groups began peeling from the larger crowds to inflict damage on any standing structures that offered links to the People's Republic. Government office buildings were the first to feel their wrath, followed by statues encouraging devotion to dead Chinese leaders. Signs that pledged allegiance to this perfect society were up in flames all around the People's Republic.

Friday was a restless, loud night. The MPS knew that by midnight that it would take a complete turning of the tide of emotion to give it any chance to control these swelling crowds. Chinese government leaders, accustomed to a relaxing Friday night sipping Jiu and watching approved network programming, were summoned to an alert status, one that most had never experienced in their careers.

As they convened to watch video and assess the situation, senior leadership in the Chinese power structure watched quietly as the protests grew enormously before their eyes. They had been attentive students of protest movements in modern history, and likened the protests to the antiwar protests of young people in the United States during the late 1960s. They remembered the lessons of Kent State, and decided on strict orders from the generals to the troops to avoid fire at all costs. Troops were equipped with guns, but instructed not to use them unless their lives were under a direct threat. For interim threats, they were equipped with batons and tasers.

The MPS stayed on the perimeter through the night, monitoring activity but mostly remaining out of the way of protesters except to protect structures from damage. Where they were challenged, the MPS used force. There were batons on heads followed by wailing, and the most active demonstrators were regularly dragged off and driven away in Beijing, Shanghai, Guangzhou, Shenzhen, Tianjin, and many other larger cities.

While most in the crowd were content to chant and point, there were occasional sorties by smaller groups, strategically timed and covertly executed to inflict shocking damage in the most unlikely places. The protesters were careful to avoid attacking anything inhabited, but rather focused on icons that were the foundation of the People's Republic. The MPS was distracted by the gathered thousands, ignoring many landmarks and other public places that were outside the crowd zone.

As the MPS discovered each incident of vandalism and damage to public property, their patience grew thin. They escalated each report of damage, and the information was shared rapidly through Chinese government circles.

By Saturday morning, the air was filled with toxic blend of smoke, anger, and government fuel dressed in green. Many protesters from the night before never left, continuing a string of loud, hostile chanting throughout the night.

Tensions had been at the breaking point for hours when the real PLA arrived on the scene in the largest gatherings. The protesters had been doing all they could to provoke a violent reaction by the MPS, who were in turn convinced their restraint was having no effect and could not last.

The mission of the People's Liberation Army, China's muscle, was to consolidate the ruling status of the Communist Party, ensure China's sovereignty, safeguard national security from expanding national interests, and maintain world peace. In that order. They were a force of more than two million soldiers. None under the age of forty had engaged in active warfare during their lifetimes. They were ready for this spark from the outside that was ignited by the fuel that lingered within.

By ten in the morning on Saturday, protesters from the night before were back out in force, stoking the fire of an angry working class that swelled to voice their support for those who were brave enough to be in the first wave of protest against a government they were convinced had committed this abomination against their spiritual master. These late arrivals had little reason to know that they were on the front line. When the army arrived, they came in huge numbers and with nowhere to go but forward.

In most cities they arrived on two or three points from where protesters congregated, but in other places they covered all four points. That meant the citizens' exit options were limited. Unfortunately for all involved, many had no intention of exiting.

The fresh Saturday morning arrivals were invigorated the moment they blended in with the enduring protestors. They joined in the hostile mood. As the morning went on, the noise became deafening. The crowds swelled and throbbed. Army troops were on edge. The more disciplined of the army troops managed to maintain their composure, only flailing protesters at the knees and midsections while herding them outward, intending to disperse. When protesters fell, those soldiers who dropped from their ranks to ensure the safety of the protester were swarmed by young men who would flail them with whatever weapons were available to them. The other troops realized that these were not normal circumstances, and that these were not the peaceful, compliant citizens they were accustomed to.

In places where the crowds were in a full lather before the PLA arrived, troops moved into the crowds with a purpose. Their intention was to move the throngs, who were mostly surprised by the sudden arrival of thousands of these men in green, toward an exit direction. However as citizens continued to arrive, the exits became clotted. The new arrivals were often couples with their children. The timing for those families who arrived ten minutes after the army was no better than those who arrived earlier. All would make history merely by being present.

As troops pushed the crowds from the congregated areas to exits between immovable structures - buildings, bridges, and walls - those on the front of the defensive were the first to suffer. They felt the first of the batons of an angry Chinese army front line. If they maintained consciousness, they would turn to retreat toward the throng directly behind them. There would be no available exit. The troops were driven by fear and rage. The only way to get past this front line of protesters was to pound them with batons, fists, and rifle butts. Civilians went down by the score, so the advancing troops stepped over and through the fallen civilians to gain access to those still shouting.

Beyond the front wave of protesters who felt the first effects of the decision by the troops to advance, the second group to suffer early were smaller people. Children and women were pushed and squeezed until they had no control. If they fell they were trampled. If they stayed on their feet they wailed until they passed out and eventually fell. As the troops slowly herded the crowd in the intended direction, they stopped looking down at the fallen citizens, many of whom reminded them of wives, sons, and daughters. The soldiers pressed on.

The citizens first reeled, backing up at first, but then they came to realize what was happening on the front line, at the stacks of people laying still in the street behind the troops. This enraged the crowd further, so they pushed back with all their might.

PLA troops, under direct attack by the citizenry of the People's Republic of China, began to open fire. At first it was to get the crowd to stop advancing on them, but as the troops came to the understanding of how vastly they were outnumbered and how angry were the layers and layers of people coming at them, they went through their ample supplies of ammunition, retreating to the back to reload, then returned to continue firing.

This scene played out in sixteen of the largest cities in China. It was chaos on a massive scale. Before the "weekend of blood" was done, nearly a quarter of a million Chinese citizens and troops had lost their lives across the Republic. Hundreds of thousands more were maimed, and many were refused assistance by Chinese hospitals, under strict orders to treat troops, children, women, and men, in that order.

Outside China, the world was aghast at the news coming out through an unending torrent of videos that showed bloodshed on a massive scale. The world could do nothing but watch and wait. A world superpower was going through turbulence that had not been seen in over a century.

In Atlanta, Georgia, the Reverend Ernest Grandby was on the phone.

"Hard to watch indeed, but it needs to happen. Messy but necessary. Stay tuned. I love you, my daughter."

The well-dressed, attractive young couple approached the inviting doors of the Church of the Tortured Christ. The Reverend Ellen Grandby Sullivan was outside the doors surrounded by a smiling swarm of congregants. She graciously answered their questions, returning many with her own. She called each person by name, asking some about remarkably specific things going on in their lives, how an elderly aunt was feeling or whether a sick cat was back to his old grumpy self. Everyone that surrounded her felt like the only person that mattered.

"Ah fuck, here we go again," Dee said softly through smiling, clenched teeth.

"Try to behave yourself, Dee, starting now." Lars smiled to her as they approached the group, putting on the best of appearances for the Reverend and her starstruck followers. Lars stopped at the edge of the crowd, grasping Dee's arm tightly.

The Reverend glanced in their direction as she continued her conversation with the others. She offered gracious compliments in all directions as she deftly suggested that they might still find some of the best seats for the service. They took her suggestion one by one, peeling after each had received some form of personal acknowledgement.

"Lars, it's lovely to see you again. We're so grateful for your willingness to help out with our bookkeeping. What a blessing for us."

"It's my pleasure, Reverend. I'm glad to do what I can to help out."

His smiling gaze stayed with her too long, Dee thought. Don't overdo it, you fool. This woman is dangerous.

"And your friend, what was her name again?" Reverend Sullivan cast a warm smile in Dee's direction.

"My name is Dee. Delilah." Dee smiled as broadly as she could, but worried about how sincere it would appear. She offered a handshake as a hopeful distraction.

"My, what a lovely name. Delilah. It's not one I hear often, but I'm so thankful whenever I'm reminded of the stirring story in the book of Judges. It offers lessons that should never be forgotten."

Dee smiled back politely, saying nothing. They both knew Delilah was the one who betrayed Samson for money. The lesson eliminated any chance for continuing their conversation.

"Well, I hope we see more of you, Dee. Our church welcomes you. I'd encourage you to find a seat toward the left section, but slide to the right. For whatever reason, the middle of rows on the right side seem to fill up last. With only two of you, I think you'll find a perfect seat for our service. We have some rare gifts in store for you this morning."

They thanked her and moved past her as she extended her hand to the family behind them.

Just as the Reverend predicted, they found an excellent seat toward the left side of the auditorium. The sound system pulsed with a glorious resonance. It was loud enough to discourage any lingering conversation, but low enough that people could exchange general pleasantries.

Even though it was a cloudy day in Massachusetts, the lighting in the church was inspiring. What the room lacked in natural light was more than made up by subtle artificial lighting that appeared to be perfectly natural. The stage was set for a service that would inspire even the most doubtful attendees, of which Dee was one.

The room lighting dimmed and the altar lighting brightened. The music picked up, and the Reverend came bounding onto the stage in a swirl of flowing robes and brightly colored vestments that perfectly complemented the surroundings.

She shouted. "Hello team!"

The crowd rose as one. "Hi Ellen!"

They stayed on their feet, some on tip toes. Many in the crowd had never seen her in person, only online and on television, and appeared to be

the most excited. Some of the most enthusiastic attendees were rewarded
with the best seats, in a clear line with the video cameras discreetly placed at
around the auditorium.

"As we give thanks to Jesus Christ our Lord on this magnificent day that
He has given us, we bow our heads."

The Reverend kneeled on a firm pillow that was slightly out of view
from the congregation. The entire room kneeled, some in clear discomfort on
the slightly padded board that folded down before them. None showed
discomfort.

Dee noticed a young girl off to her right, staring at her. The girl had a
remarkable appearance, with icy blue eyes and curly reddish-black hair that
was immaculately braided. Her skin was a lovely shade of chestnut brown.
She was obviously sitting between her parents, a lighter skinned white man
and a lovely black woman. They were attending to her as if she were a child
much younger. Dee guessed that she had some sort of learning disability,
perhaps something on the Autism spectrum.

The girl would have been easy to notice for anyone, but the girl would
not take her eyes off Dee. Her gaze was not hostile, but it was fierce and
curious. Dee smiled to her, entranced. Her mother noticed her daughter
staring, and smiled uncomfortably in Dee's direction, trying to distract the
girl toward the front.

The service was a dizzying, impressive array of sight, sound, speech,
spirituality, and inspiration. A particularly moving classical piece would be
followed by a scripture reading that brought tears to the congregation, many
wailing in divine inspiration, palms pointed to the heavens. A woman in the
crowd was asked to rise. The Reverend talked for several minutes about her
courage in not allowing Multiple Sclerosis stand in the way of a divine plan
to bring her before the Lord. The touching exchange brought many to tears.

Reverend Sullivan even found time to ask for God's blessing and relief
in China, where if reports were to be believed, thousands were dying while
the clashes between protesters and government troops grew worse by the
day. The crowd followed her lead by closing their eyes and bowing heads,
silently praying.

Dee was impressed with the presentation, thinking of the incredible
effort it must take to produce such a display multiple times each weekend,
week after week. When it finally wrapped up with a stirring prayer followed
by triumphant music, the crowd rose in unison, applauding, raising hands to
heaven, and singing along.

"Wow, what a show," she said quietly to Lars.

"I doubt there are any like this anywhere," he replied quietly. Dee turned
away from him bitterly after she noticed a tear forming on the inside corner
of his eye. She said nothing.

The attendees were in no hurry to leave, but the music died to a quiet
ballad that played in the background, soft jazz with clarinet, percussion, and

rhythm guitar. She listened closely to the oohs and ahhs coming from the people around her.

"Stand up, Sophie. You need to get your jacket on. It's still chilly out there. Be a good girl, now."

Dee froze. She remembered Henry's vivid description of a girl, down to her reddish-black hair and icy blue eyes. This is the girl, she thought, possessed by a spirit so powerful that it nearly knocked Henry into a new profession.

"Oh my God. It's Sophie Geary," she mumbled. "She's just the way Henry described her."

"What's wrong?" Lars barely noticed the distraction.

"Nothing," Dee said, finally catching herself. "It's just that girl. She's so lovely, but just in her own world. What a tough situation for that family."

As they were leaving, Lars spoke quietly. "Shoot, I just remembered. I left my reading glasses here when I came in Wednesday night. I've been without them for the past few days. Do you mind waiting while I pick them up?"

"You've got to be kidding. I want out of this place now."

"It'll take five minutes, Dee. They're prescription glasses. I've been trying to work without them, but I've had a headache for two straight days. This will be quick."

"Fine. I'll wait by the front doors."

"I don't think that's such a great idea. This service ran long. The next one starts in thirty minutes. Just come wait in the office lobby. That way we won't lose each other. I don't want to be here any longer than I have to either."

"Lead the way," she sighed. The last hour rattled her senses. She was not in a mood to argue.

They entered the church office, dimly lit on the inside. There was a receptionist sitting a few feet past the front door.

"I'll be fast. Have a seat," Lars said as he walked away. As he passed the receptionist he gave her a silent nod. She nodded back. Within about a minute the woman rose and walked through a door to an inner office.

Dee was left alone. She picked up a Time Magazine. "Roaring Protests Rack China," the headline screamed. The cover photo showed a woman crying, horrified, pleading for help while kneeling over a small body lying in he street. She began to read the story when the outer door opened. Two men walked in toward the receptionist's desk.

"She just stepped away. She'll probably be right back."

"Thanks," said one. The other walked back toward the outer door, out of Dee's sight. She heard a click, as if the door was being locked. It startled her, and she glanced up at the man by the receptionist's desk. He looked toward the inner door, then down a hallway. When it was clear that no one was nearby, he took a seat in a chair a few feet from Dee.

The other man stepped into the waiting area and stood. Dee avoided their presence, continuing to read the magazine, but she glanced toward the outer door which was blocked. A sense of panic overcame her as she tried to think of possible escape routes from these two men, both serious looking and large. One was sitting to her left, the other standing to her right. She impatiently wondered what was taking Lars so long. She put the magazine down and looked up. Both men turned to look at her.

She decided to step outside the building, one that she had no intention of entering in the first place. She stood and began to walk around the standing man toward the door, as wide as she was able to without making it seem obvious she was avoiding him.

The standing man moved fast. Without a hint of what was coming, he lunged toward her, throwing his large arms around her midsection, lifting her from the ground. The other man rose from his chair, moving behind the two. He pulled out a thick damp cloth, then quickly, forcefully reached around both of them, placing the cloth over Dee's nose and mouth.

She struggled briefly, but within seconds her body went limp.

The two men carried her through the door behind the reception area, down a stairway and down a long hallway, then into a windowless basement room, probably meant for storage. Lars was waiting inside the room, sitting on a chair.

"Any problems?"

"None. She made it easy by getting up to leave."

"No great surprise," Edgar said, no longer bothering with the Lars facade. "Make sure she's tied up tightly, with no possibility for escape."

The men laid her on a reclining chair, fully extended. Then they tightly coiled thick nylon cord around her and the chair.

Lars pulled out his phone, pressing and holding a single button.

The Reverend Ellen Grandby Sullivan answered. "How did everything go?"

"Perfectly. She's down here now. She'll be out for a while."

"Well done. It's time for you to disappear, Edgar. Too many people saw you two together talking to me."

"Are you sure about that? Nobody here knows me from the other side."

"Let's just stick to the plan. As far as they're concerned," she continued, "you both disappeared together."

And he waited.

The mass they attended started at eight thirty, which meant they should have been on their way out by ten o'clock at the latest. It was now almost one, and Dee had not called and was not responding to his calls or texts. Things were not right.

He drove toward the Church of the Tortured Christ, which was miles away, stopping a few blocks short. He walked the neighborhood keeping his phone close to his ear. He did loops and figure eights in various directions, focusing all his energy on Delilah, keeping his senses open for a sign that might point him in any direction.

The original idea was hers. He never wanted her to take a single step into the church without him nearby. He stopped arguing because nothing would stop her from getting what she wanted, which was one of the things he loved about her.

Was it possible that she would have stayed at the church for some sort of post-service event? It seemed like a remote possibility. She would have wretched at the idea of staying on premise any longer than needed, but Ellen Grandby Sullivan could be compelling. She had a way of charming anyone. Perhaps she somehow got wind of the idea that these were Origenists before her, and she needed to toy with them.

He called her mobile phone again. This time, rather than ringing and ringing, it went straight to voicemail.

He returned home on the hope that she would be waiting for him with a story to tell, a tale of an unproductive but eye-opening afternoon spent among tortured souls.

But the apartment was as empty as when he had left it in the afternoon. There was no sign of Dee, no smell, no mental image of Dee having been there. It was as stale as a cemetery.

He remembered a crumpled business card he had saved from Detective Lacey in his desk drawer. He dialed the number listed for the detective's cell phone. It was after ten o'clock, he noticed after the phone was ringing. His knees were tapping. His ears were ringing. His hands were clenched.

It rang three times before a tired voice answered.

"This is Detective Lacey."

"Hello Detective," Henry answered. "I'm very sorry to bother you at this hour. This is Henry Chimera."

"I didn't think I'd hear from you again. What can I do for you, Henry?"

Henry blurted. "Well, that's funny, detective. I did expect to hear from you but I haven't. Not a word, and Donnelly is still dead."

"Here's the thing, Henry," Lacey began slowly. The television was audible in the background. "I wouldn't worry your pretty little head over whether I call you or not. In fact, if I DO call you, perhaps you should start to worry. You're not exactly above suspicion, my friend. Now what the fuck can I do for you?"

He filled the Detective in on the events leading up to Dee's disappearance in detail. Finally he paused, wondering if he had put the detective to sleep. He heard a grunt at the end of the line. "I'm listening. Anything else?"

Henry talked about his suspicions of the church, including the story Joan Swenson told about the video of the Dalai Lama being restrained. He did not mention her by name.

"What is wrong with you?" Lacey was angry. "You should have told someone sooner about this. There are authorities who would greatly appreciate that information. As far as your friend Dee goes, unfortunately there's nothing I can do about it until she's been missing for at least twenty-four hours. She's an adult, and she could have chosen to leave on her own."

"There's no way she would do that," Henry replied.

"Maybe not, but it does happen sometimes. When it does, it almost always surprises the shit out of whoever was left behind."

"Impossible," he replied. That group is paralyzed with fear. Dee is the only one who's motivated to act. The others are laying low. I don't even know how to reach any of them."

"Well, that's inconvenient."

"Tell me about it. What about the Dalai Lama? Doesn't this give you enough reason to dig in to what's going on at the church?"

"Sure there's interest," Lacey replied, "but number one, it's not my investigation, as you can probably guess. Number two, you don't get search warrants issued based on rumors. Unless you can convince the person who saw this video to come in and give a statement, it's just another crazy lead. When famous people are murdered, people see it on the national news and suddenly they're convinced their next door neighbor is the guy who killed him."

Henry sighed.

"If I could see that videotape, now that would be something. Or even if I could talk to the woman who saw it."

"I'll try to talk to her."

Both men were silent. Finally Henry asked, "Are there even any suspects in John Donnelly's murder?"

"The case is still open," Lacey said in a dry retort. "If you have any new information for us, we would be most appreciative."

"I wish I did. And nothing on Herbrit's death either?"

"It's not even in the state of Massachusetts, let alone my jurisdiction."

"Was Reverend Sullivan any help when you talked to her?"

"That's none of your fucking business and you know it," Lacey growled. Then he exhaled. "Sorry, Henry. Obviously the case is still open, and that doesn't look good for anyone. I called the Reverend and couldn't get through. Now that your friend is missing, maybe I have a reason to go meet her in person."

"I'd appreciate it if you would, Detective. This is more than just an instinct."

"It's not as easy as you'd think. The Dalai Lama story is too important to ignore, but it's still a second-hand account. I know you have reason to be worried about your friend. Come by the precinct to file a Missing Persons report once you haven't heard from her after a full day. I'll take your official statement, then we can look into it."

"Thanks Detective. Sorry to call you at night."

"You did the right thing." Lacey's tone was reassuring. "Henry, you might want to watch your ass."

"So everyone keeps telling me."

Late the following morning he went into the police department to file the report. He gave Lacey the details of the visit by Dee and Lars, including their real reasons for being there. Lacey patiently transcribed Henry's account.

Much to Lacey's annoyance, Henry kept Joan Swenson's name from the report, in the hope that another acquaintance would be kept from harm.

PASSAGES

Darkness and fog. Her senses were a deep murkiness that cleared slowly. She stirred uncomfortably, restricted in movement. Finally she was alert enough to crane her neck and begin moving and stretching her limbs. She believed her eyes were open, but the darkness remained.

"Where am I?" She spoke in a craggy voice, dry throated and uncomfortable. "Why can't I see anything?"

"Is there something you need?"

It was an unfamiliar male voice, deep and barely interested. From the sound, the man was across the room from her on the right.

"To be out of here, for starters. I asked you, where am I?"

"That's not information you can have right now," the voice said. "Do you need water? I can get you water."

"Yes, water, and I also have to pee. I don't want your help with that."

Her hands were bound in front, and she was unable to lift them. She heard the man step toward her. A key ring jingled, and the man fumbled with a lock and chain that bound her whole body to the chair. Her hands remained constricted. He led her out a door, down a hall, into a bathroom.

"There's a toilet straight ahead of you, about eight feet. I'll close the door but if you lock it, I'll break the door in and you'll have no privacy. Besides, there are no windows in this bathroom. You're in a basement, below ground. Take care of your business and make sure your mask is over your eyes when you come out. You have two minutes, then I come in after you."

She went in, closing the door behind her. There was no lock. She removed the mask from her eyes and turned on the light, revealing a stark bathroom with no magazines, nothing on the walls, and nothing to give any indication on her location. She guessed that she was in some hallway in the basement in the Church of the Tortured Christ, and that very few people knew she was here. Ellen Grandby Sullivan was probably one person who did know.

Her senses were coming back, although she still felt drowsy and weak. She managed to urinate clumsily with her hands bound in front of her with a tight plastic locking strip. She managed to organize her clothes and straighten out her skirt before noisily flushing the toilet and washing her hands to indicate progress. Before putting the mask back over her eyes, she scanned the room one more time. There were no clues of any kind. Obviously they were planning on her being there. She put the mask back on, flipped the light off, and stepped out.

"Well done," the man grumbled. Before leading her away, he slid his hands around her body in an impromptu pat down. When he came to her breasts he went slowly.

She inhaled then breathed out, "A fucking pig, just like I thought."

"Watch your mouth, or I'll put it to much better use."

He led her back down the hall to the same room. He sat her down in the same hard-backed chair.

"Don't you have a better chair than this? I'd like to sleep."

The man hesitated. She sensed another presence in the room.

"Yes," he said. "I suppose that's fine. Stand up." He grabbed her wrists and slowly led her across the room to a soft chair.

"That's better. Thank you."

He spent several minutes reconfiguring the chain that bound her wrist to her ankles. From the sound of it, there was plenty of chain to go around the back of this larger chair. He offered a bottle of water and held it to her mouth as she sipped.

She heard the man go and sit across the room. She relaxed, dropping her head back. Her legs were close together, and her bound wrists covering her front. With her eyes covered and no sound in the room except for the occasional shuffling of her captor in his chair, reading a magazine, she lost track of time. She eased in and out of sleep.

After an unknown time, she heard voices in the hallway. She remained still when the voices came near, trying to appear asleep. The muffled conversation from the hallway was between a man and a woman. The woman appeared to be doing most of the talking, and the conversation was animated.

It soon became apparent that the woman's voice was that of Ellen Grandby Sullivan. She seemed to be talking with someone named Edgar. Her voice seemed to rise whenever she addressed him, as if she wanted this man to go away. She had a hand on the door and her impatience was growing. The door opened a little as she was finishing the conversation.

"Just be scarce. Like NOW. I know how to reach you, so go."

"Fine!" the man's hushed voice said from the hallway.

Dee was startled. It couldn't be! He tried to mask his voice, but it could be no one else. The Reverend began to step into the room, but before closing the door, Dee let loose.

"Lars? It's you, isn't it, you traitorous piece of shit!"

"Spectacular," Sullivan said, "another unexpected problem."

"What the hell is the difference? It doesn't matter what she knows or doesn't know."

Dee was enraged. "You've been with them all along, working behind our back! You *fucker*!"

Lars stepped into the room. "Grow up, Dee. You and the other idiots have been in way over your head for months. I could have made this happen any time I wanted. You're lucky you've been free this long."

"I went against my own instincts. Henry warned me about you. Herbrit warned me about you, and still I trusted you. Lars, you're the lowest form of human life."

"My name isn't Lars, it's Edgar. You were too easy to play, Dee, once I figured you out. You're like an oyster, all rough and crusty on the outside, but soft and snotty on the inside."

"Edgar? That's your real name? I'd go with Lars. It makes you sound less like a pussy." The mask did not conceal her contemptuous snarl.

"So Reverend, and whatever the pussy's real name is, why would you come after us? We never tried to hurt you or anyone."

"You'll find out in due time," the Reverend replied.

"I have my doubts that you'll ever answer that question," Dee said defiantly, "considering your chosen occupation, professional killers. It's unlikely you're in the habit of sharing stories about your latest victims."

"You've always had a vivid imagination, Dee." Edgar's tone was condescending.

"Why am I even alive now? Is it Henry you're after?"

"We're not 'after' anyone," Ellen said. "You're in the way. If you people knew your place, perhaps you'd stop getting into situations you can't get out of."

"Reverend, this is quite a 'Christian' church you have going here. Have you sacrificed any babies lately?"

She ignored the question. "Why is she in the soft chair?"

"She asked, and I had enough chain to make sure she couldn't go anywhere." Her captor sounded sheepish.

"Move her back. She doesn't deserve to be comfortable."

Dee kept prodding. "We intentionally stayed in the shadows, and we were never a threat to you. Considering this situation I'm in right now, you don't believe any of the Christianity that you preach. You're obviously not Christians, so what are you? Some sort of pagan church that has a problem with reincarnation?"

"Oh I assure you, we're very Christian."

"Oh really Reverend?" Dee was becoming animated, a fiery waif struggling against her bound hands, a chain holding her down, and a blindfold concealing the rage in her eyes. "Here's a thought: PERHAPS YOU START ACTING LIKE CHRISTIANS! What you're doing now is anything, ANYTHING but Christian."

"Our actions have a greater purpose. The decisions we make today, no matter how offensive or difficult they might be for some to understand, are necessary for the long term survival of the Christian faith."

"How does kidnapping the Dalai Lama advance the Christian faith?" Dee's tone was mocking, sarcastic.

"WHAT?" The reverend shouted at Dee.

Dee continued to press. "I probably don't have long to live, and that doesn't really bother me too much, obviously. But surely you can educate me on how a man who has only condoned restraint, serenity, tolerance, and peace is any threat to you. Please, Reverend. I'm all ears. Talk to me about Christianity."

There was a pause of several seconds.

The Reverend turned to Edgar.

"Kill her."

Just after two o'clock the next afternoon, a Monday, Detective Oliver Lacey approached the Church of the Tortured Christ. He removed his cap before entering, straightened his tie and checked his zipper before he turned the knob. He walked slowly into the vestibule of the church's office, unsure if some customs were expected that would completely elude him. This was not a man accustomed to being anywhere near a church of any kind.

"May I help you?" The pasty receptionist, dressed as if she was ready for a Sunday service, offered Lacey an unblinking, wide smile.

Lacey offered a weak smile back, the best he could muster. "Uh yes, I'm Detective Lacey with the Waltham Police Department. I'm her to speak with Reverend Sullivan?"

"I see." The receptionist's smile turned to one of concern. "Did you have an appointment?"

"No, this is in regard to an open investigation. Reverend Ellen Grandby Sullivan is the person in charge of this church, correct?"

"Yes, of course she is," the receptionist replied. "However the Reverend Sullivan's calendar is completely full during weekdays. Right now she's on a video cast that goes all the way to Brazil!" She smiled, waiting for an awed reaction.

Lacey showed none. "Well, this is very important too, a police matter. How soon can she squeeze in five minutes to speak with me?"

She looked toward her screen without moving her neck. After a pause her eyes went back to Lacey. "I can see if she can squeeze you in before her next meeting, however I can't interrupt the Reverend when she's videocasting."

Lacey stared, unblinking.

"Please have a seat, Detective. Her next call starts in about twenty minutes. I'll see if she has any kind of break in between."

"I appreciate it." He scanned the room as he slowly moved to sit.

Two-thirty came and went. When it was nearing three, Lacey trudged back to the receptionist's desk.

"I thought you said you were gonna try to sneak me in?"

"Oh Detective, I'm under strict instructions not to interrupt the Reverend. If I find there's any open time between meetings, it's because the Reverend let me know that's the case. She can go hours, from meeting to meeting, without a break that I can see."

Lacey looked up at the ceiling, then looked at his watch. Then he looked down at her name plate bearing the name Cecilia Hargis, which he had not noticed before.

"I see, Miss ... Hargis," he started gently.

"It's Mrs.," she said, holding up a wedding band.

"Mrs. Hargis," he continued, impatiently. "If I have to spend extra time driving all the way back to the Court House to bother the Magistrate, my best friend from school, for a search warrant, when I return I will be in a very sore mood. I will make sure the time is not wasted. I'll turn this building upside down. Do you get my drift, Mrs. Hargis?"

The woman's mouth was open for several seconds before she replied. "Yes, Detective. I suppose I underestimated the seriousness of your visit."

Lacey said nothing, only stared.

The receptionist rose from her chair and disappeared behind a wall. Lacey heard a doorknob turn, then a door close. Within about a minute she returned. Lacey had not moved from his position, hovering above her desk.

"She was able to tell me that she can probably end her current call shortly. I relayed your ... sense of urgency."

After a few minutes the Reverend came turning around the corner, hand outstretched. "Hello Detective. I'm Reverend Sullivan. Please call me Ellen."

"Detective Oliver Lacey." He coldly returned her handshake then followed her into her office.

He eyed the room deliberately. "I've never seen art work and decoration like this. You have some taste."

"Well, when you've traveled as much as I have," she explained, "to the outer reaches of the globe to spread the work of our Lord Jesus Christ to those who need it most, you develop an appreciation for design that are a little outside the norm. These furnishings might look expensive, but I rarely pay much for any of the things in my office or home. I guess it's just become my hobby to look for really special pieces from local artisans. I've always believed in supporting local talent."

"I see," Lacey replied. "Makes sense, but it can't be cheap to ship this stuff halfway around the world."

She stared back at him without replying. The Reverend sat behind her desk, folding her hands. She did not offer Lacey a seat.

"What can I do for you, Detective? Cecilia said you're here on an urgent matter."

"I am," Lacey said, settling carefully into a stuffed leather chair. "There's a woman who is believed to have attended one of your services yesterday. She hasn't been seen since."

"Oh my goodness," the said as she leaned forward. "That's extremely serious. Is it someone I would know? Is it one of my regular congregants?"

"I doubt she's a regular here. Her name is Delilah Stark. She's in her early thirties, with shoulder-length blond hair, pulled straight back, and light features. She was wearing a light blue dress that was about at knee length. She would have been with a tall blondish man, about the same age."

"Do you happen to have a picture of either of them?"

"I'm sorry to say, I don't."

"What's the man's name?" See seemed legitimately concerned.

"I don't have a last name, but his first name was Lars. They were an attractive young couple, easy to notice."

"It isn't ringing a bell, Detective. However we're blessed to have somewhere around twelve to fourteen hundred congregants for a service, so it's nearly impossible to notice everyone. After all," she smiled, "my services are quite a production. There are so many things that demand my attention. Which service do you think they may have attended?"

"The ten o'clock. Tell me, Reverend, do you have security cameras here in the church?"

"We do but typically we don't position them for crowd shots."

"The tapes I'd like to see would be in the common areas - hallways, entrances, that kind of thing."

She paused, uncomfortably. "I suppose we do. I'm not exactly sure how these things work. I'll speak with our Security Director about what he can do to help you."

"What would that person's name be, Reverend?"

"Why do you need to know his name?" Her tone was cold.

"This isn't about theft or somebody spraying graffiti on the side of your building. At least one person is missing, and someone is worried about her. Besides, you said yourself, on the days you have church services, there's a lot going on. Your Security Director would be an extremely useful person for us to speak with. Is that going to be a problem?"

"His name is Stanley Lafarge," she said impatiently. "You can reach him through the front desk, but I put a lot on his plate besides just security, so I hope you won't take much of his time."

"That can be hard to predict, Ellen. I need to see all the security tapes from yesterday. If he can make that happen quickly, then I won't take much of his time."

"All of our tapes? But we rotate them around every two days. We'd need to buy all new tapes to make sure we're covered while you have our other ones."

"Well in that case, it's important that we do it today. Otherwise I'll need to take them with me, so they don't get overwritten."

"No, that won't be necessary, Detective. We'll figure it out."

"I'm sure we will. It sounds like you know more about those surveillance tapes than you thought you did," he said, smiling.

The space was vast, as spacious as his eye could see, still it was purposeful and perfect in form and function. Although the realm exceeded boundaries that could be defined by ordinary human senses, it was a place that was suited to serve vital, specific needs. In every direction were bright, glowing forms of energy. Some were brighter than others, some near, many further away.

Each orb was on a unique path. Nearly all appeared to be headed upward, although some more gradually than others. Some appeared to be moving laterally, even losing their desire to climb at all. These tended to be less shimmering, less certain in their direction and destination.

Some of the life forms congregated around each other. From a distance they appeared as a single source, but in truth they were beings who were closely linked, preferring to remain close throughout the ages. There were groups of perhaps a dozen, then some as small as two individuals, inseparable.

As each completed a repeating pattern of movement, it passed by a portal. There were many of these portals throughout this vast space. Each was similar in outer appearance, but from within each portal there was a distinctive radiance. They covered the entire spectrum of color, from darkish brown in the lower reaches, where the newer, more timid orbs dwelled, to the brightest golds, blues, and silvers toward the top of this vast cavern.

Henry was invited to peer through one of the portals. He did so instinctively, readily, feeling the comforting presence of an old friend guiding him. As his mind moved through he was offered a view outward, toward the vast space where the energies made their progress. This view was one he never could have imagined.

There was a radiance surrounding each of the forms that was clearly distinct in essence from every other. It was a positive, loving, and supporting energy, there to encourage advancement and growth. It gave these beings the power to choose their velocity and direction while not mandating either. Each orb had complete freedom of movement, but was constrained by its own perceived limitations, doubts, fears, and insecurities. Each being's ability to ascend and mature was a direct product of its ability to contend with its own limitations, while at the same time making use of the positive energies that were available to it.

The speed, pattern, and colors of these energy fields were endlessly varied. Henry instinctually knew these wave patterns were the emotions, positive, negative, or neutral, that made each being completely unique. He also felt blessed to be in this place, as he knew this portal view was meant for highly specialized beings, those who bore the heavy responsibility of assisting these glowing travelers through their journey. Their purpose was to do everything within their power to help them choose from the endless number of choices that awaited them in their next incarnation. There were billions of them to assist.

They were souls, each moving along its unique path from life to life, accumulating the experience that only lifetimes can provide. Most of them would find a way to build on their experiences to advance the wisdom they acquired through life's boundless joys, unthinkable cruelties, and everything in the massive middle.

Some moved more quickly on an upward trajectory through the seemingly endless space. Those that were oldest or most effective at using life experiences to enhance their knowledge and wisdom tended to be the brighter and bluer orbs, easy for Henry to spot. They were more in harmony with the more positive forces surrounding them while remaining able to fend off the negative forces, remaining completely aware of their limitations and tendencies while keeping their upward trajectory.

The souls who were less effective at using their accumulated experiences to improve their wisdom were just as easy to identify. These souls moved slowly, dimly through the space. Through the portal Henry could see the many obstacles they faced. He was unable to interpret these waves of energy, but he could discern positive from negative. He could see that the negative energies surrounding these souls roamed freely, nearly unchallenged, while the positive energies that were meant to combat them were tepid and weary.

These were souls who, Henry surmised, would move from life to life without notable improvement. Their recent lifetimes had not advanced their development. They were mostly stuck in a routine they had no easy way to escape. He saw in many the accumulating frustration of a challenging lifetime and how it wore some of these spirits down.

He thought of his own life near Boston, a large city that could be hard on lost souls. He saw them every day, living beneath bridges, in shelters, or wherever they landed. He guessed that death to many of these souls would come as a relief, but would they benefit from the hindsight of such a life lived? Only if they chose to learn, he realized.

Other lost souls lived an affluent existence, but they confused material gain with spiritual gain. These souls were as stuck in their current state as any, and equally unaware of their condition and how to change it. No matter what circumstances they would choose in the next life, the chances were high that they would repeat the same mistakes. He thought of many souls around the world who were less on the fringe, not homeless and not disadvantaged by wealth, but who lived isolated lives. They were just trying to get by, trying to fight through the limitations of intellect or social placement or physical appearance that hindered their growth. Through it all, most souls were trying to find an upward trajectory. That was the common thread. Even those making no progress could see that those around them were still fighting to advance.

He took his eye from the distant, endless variety of souls and their journeys, to the spirit energies that surrounded him now. He was in a portal that appeared to be somewhat lower than halfway to the top of this vast space, although it was difficult to be sure because the top of this universe was a blinding array of white, loving light. It was not evident how far along each of these souls were in their journey but they mostly appeared to be younger, in search of meaning and momentum. Most at this level of development had not gone through many life experiences, but still had some to draw from as they prepared for the next.

This level was crowded. There appeared to be more souls at this portal level than at any of those above or below. It appeared to be a key hurdle on the long journey, and many struggled to move past. The souls below eyed this as an important destination, and the ones above appeared to gain velocity the further they moved away.

The portal possessed an orange glow. It was a convergence of varying ideologies. The air was thick with tradition, which heavily affected their journey as they moved through. This, Henry believed, represented young adulthood, a gateway in which souls decided the path that would advance their journey.

Some souls were able to use their faith, including the monotheistic religions - Christianity, Judaism, Islam, or others - or even some of the less conventional religions, to enhance the impact of the life just lived. The religion itself did not seem to change how many succeeded. What mattered was the soul's ability to use the strength of each religion to assist in the journey.

Behind the portal, hovering through this portal and controlling its power, were at least three essential spirits that Henry could sense. One was an older spirit, wise in his ability to see through the portal to the endless array of souls before it. It was quiet, complex, and incredibly powerful. Henry could see that this being possessed the ability to scan the ages and the miles with ease. It had a distance, a coldness about it, but it was unique in its ability to truly see through a soul. The being's expertise was in his ability to quickly view one's progress, consider the challenges and possibilities, then contrast this progress with opportunities that might be ahead. Most importantly, the being possessed the ability to convey what a soul was capable of, where its limits were and where the limits did not exist. It could present a range of possibilities for each soul considering a new incarnation, and it could do this with clarity, evenness, and no hint of bias. As the souls who moved past him exuded reverence, awe and gratitude, Henry was able to grasp the important assistance it provided. This entity was a matchmaker of souls to lives.

"Incredible," Henry thought. "How does somebody get that job?"

The other powerful spirit Henry could sense was unquestionably female. She gave forth a mystical quality that Henry had never seen. This was a soul who made a mark on all of humanity during her time on earth. She clearly came from an ecumenical perspective, deeply rooted in Christian faiths but not bound to the restrictive conventions of conventional religion. This entity was far from new, but did appear to be new to her role in the spirit realm. Henry gathered she was finding her way, understanding how things worked. Her capacity to learn was beyond anything he could comprehend, but he was able to sense clearly that she was working hard to keep pace, absorbing information in massive quantities from the energies all around.

She and the wiser male entity were only partially familiar with each other, but both were deeply committed to the mission before them, which was to identify opportunities for souls that reached their portal. They each had a purpose, and neither purpose conflicted. The male entity was there for his sheer ability to assimilate all possibilities to allow the soul to choose. The female entity was there to provide nurturing, comfort, and a window to the heavens as each choice was made. She was there to reinforce for each soul the importance of the selection, to provide perspective on the timing of choosing one life over another, and how the choice of a life would equip the soul to contend with the infinite possibility of events that could occur in each life circumstance.

If a soul were to choose an especially easy path after one or more lives that were not especially useful for advancement, the soul could risk losing momentum and its overall sense of purpose. Conversely if the soul chose one challenging life after another, without relief, the soul could harden and grow embittered. Negative experiences compound over lifetimes, and without caution could erode the good that comes from growing through adverse circumstances.

She learned that less challenging lifetimes needed to be interspersed with more challenging lives. This came to her quickly in her new role, as a vital benefit for the souls she served. She provided the context that could be easily lost between lifetimes for souls on a long, complex journey. This connection between the past and the future was precisely how she affected humanity in her own most notable life, as Hildegarde of Bingen in the twelfth century AD.

A third soul was nearby. This one was far more out of place, far less intimidating, and far more familiar to Henry. She also provided comfort to all the souls she touched, but her vision and reach were more limited than the others.

"Hello, Henry! Letting your hair grow, I see. A valiant effort but alas, you still look like a lovable geek."

"Aisling!" Henry was elated to be with her. "I can't remember how long it's been. It's so great to see you finally. Where have you been?"

"Taking care of important business, my dear. We've had quite a transition in these parts, and I've been asked to assist."

He looked around again at the astounding scene before his eyes. "This is a sensational place."

"It certainly is, as I learn each day, but don't be too impressed. They allow the likes of me in here." She joined his sense of awe, mindful of the strong spirits nearby.

Henry warmly absorbed her charm, along with his wonder and elation at being here. A question barely formed in his mind before Aisling spoke.

"I know what you're wondering, Henry. I brought you here because it's very important that you understand how these things work, especially considering some of the forces that surround you today. Also, I brought you here because you have gifts that allowed me to bring you here. Very few souls have the vision you have that allows you to see the scene before you."

"It's wonderful," he said, "but I'm not sure there's much about this that I truly understand. I can see some of the forces surrounding these souls, how they exert influences in the way they live their lives. This way of seeing souls is something I never imagined before. You can probably use the same view to look at my life, seeing all the crazy things going on, can't you?"

"Yes, and it's very alarming" she offered. "I'm far from proficient at understanding all of this, but it's very easy to see the turbulent forces that surround you. I was permitted to bring you here because of the uniqueness of your situation. I thought it would be useful to allow you, as one so involved in such serious matters, to view this high place. The higher authorities agreed."

"Higher authorities? Do you mean God?"

"Beings close to God, without question. They're in a high place, but I can't say if it's God who permitted this. It's possible, I suppose."

Henry was stunned by the notion that he had been invited here with God's permission. He processed the thought slowly, carefully, and with pure humility.

The reunification between these two old friends was joyous, and the emotions they felt were echoed and amplified by the strong spirits in their presence. There was a pervasive sense of comfort and well-being that radiated. There were no worries in this place, at least not the worries that were familiar to him. This feeling of safety was not one he had been able to enjoy for as long as he could remember.

He felt each of these two powerful spirits seeing through him. Hildegarde's presence was reassuring and enlightening. He felt inspiration just from being nearby. She was a spirit who exuded goodness through the wisdom acquired from at least one historical lifetime.

The other spirit was immeasurably powerful in its vision and wisdom, so much so that Henry was unable to grasp the nature of its interest in him. There was an odd familiarity about it, and he felt sure the spirit recognized him. There was nothing about Henry's thoughts or experiences that this being did not know. It was unsettling, and Aisling noticed. There was no way for Aisling to speak with him privately, so she spoke directly.

"There's no reason to be concerned, Henry. You are in the presence of two spirits who have incredible influence over the choices available to souls, and an incredibly difficult job. You have nothing to fear."

"Thanks Aisling," Henry said timidly. "I just feels as though I've met the ... male spirit before."

"Oh how embarrassing," Aisling burst out. "I was so happy to see you that I complete forgot to introduce you.

"Hildegarde of Bingen lived her most prominent life in the twelfth century. She was a Christian mystic who opened a convent which really changed the course of the whole Christian church, and the role of women in particular. She became known to the pope at the time because of her incredible visions, her window into the heavens. A spiritual connection was common for prophets of the time, but Hildegarde's exceeded any. She was one of the most prominent of the Christian visionaries. The truth is, she was one of the people who made our occupation as seers for the living even possible. Thanks in part to her good works, people learned to respect us instead of fearing us."

"I'm so thrilled to meet with you," Henry addressed Hildegarde. "I'm very familiar with your work. I've read 'Scivias' from cover to cover. It inspired me."

"The pleasure is all mine," Hildegarde of Bingen said to Henry. "Something tells me you will make your mark as well, in due time."

Henry bowed his head. He felt overwhelmed by her presence.

"The other spirit that I didn't introduce you to has one of the most important roles in these high reaches. He was never a mortal, but has enormous responsibilities in helping mortal souls know what life opportunities are available. He occupied this position for ages, and has only recently returned. The heavens opened up for his return. Henry Chimera, this is Immat."

The spirit enveloped Henry, but this time in a completely non-threatening way. Both knew they had met before under much less pleasant circumstances. The powerful being seemed to be truly getting to know Henry for the first time. He still felt a profound sense of security, but he remained suspicious of this spirit's intentions.

"I am humbled to be in your presence. I pray that I am wise enough to learn from you."

"The learning should never cease. I myself have learned some very important lessons. My failure to learn would have meant that I could not resume this most important responsibility."

The spirit resonated with a deep sense of regret. "I am glad to meet you again. I owe you a profound apology for my unkindness the first time we met."

Henry's intimidation began to melt away. He easily remembered the miserable state of Sophie Geary when she was under his control. She was an eleven year old girl who was in an especially vulnerable state from early trauma in her life. Immat seized upon her condition to imprison her, probably for archaic reasons that made no sense in the present day. Although their meeting was many weeks before, he could still see the look on her face, pleading for his help. It was an image he would never forget.

"It went far beyond unkindness," Henry said evenly, "and I'm not the one you owe an apology. I was merely in your way when you controlled the girl."

Aisling and Hildegarde were silently watching this discussion. Neither allowed emotions or thoughts to influence the exchange.

"I tried to help her and you would have none of it. Why?"

The sentient spirit intensified its feelings of guilt, remorse, and regret.

"I put my needs before all else. It was wrong. It was behavior that was accepted in another time, but that was false reasoning. I will always regret it."

"I am told," Henry asked quietly, humbly, "that the girl is still in a captive state."

"Indeed she is," the elder spirit replied, "but the state you describe is the state she was in when I took her under my control. It was the result of trauma she suffered as a smaller child, and was the reason she was so vulnerable."

"There's nothing you could have done to help her regain a normal life? What about the suffering of her parents?"

"This was the path she chose. You should understand that souls are presented with alternatives in the life they are about to live. They select the path that presents the challenges they wish to pursue. This soul chose a path that included a disability from an early age. It is not my place to intervene in that."

"But you did intervene," Henry replied sharply. "Why?"

"I mistakenly reasoned that my desires could be easily accommodated by her weakened state, and that the repercussions would be minimal. If I caused her or her parents additional suffering, I allowed my weaknesses to blind me. I sought forgiveness for this unspeakable act, and I am blessed. I was forgiven."

Henry remained dissatisfied that the powerful spirit, so controlling such a short time ago, was now in a position with such an impact on so many souls. Could God be wrong about this spirit? The mere thought defied everything he thought he knew about God.

After quiet contemplation, which each of these wiser spirits invited, he reasoned that if God could forgive this man, he could as well.

There was an unspoken relief in the room as Henry found his peace.

His visit was nearing an end. Aisling approached him, escorting him back through the portal to the vastness of the hall of souls.

"These are trying times for you, Henry. You are experiencing challenges that few have confronted in their lives. The work you are doing is incredibly important. There will continue to be pain and struggle, but it is vitally important that you stay strong and hold closely to your convictions. You have great power, much of it that you have never used before. Remember that your greatest strengths are your knowledge of what is right, and the lengths you will go to defend it."

"I miss you, Aisling. I wish you were with me."

"I am with you, Henry. You know that. It feels lonely, and more lonely days are ahead, but you have to trust in your ability to decide the right course of action. It is not my place to tell you what to do, what to decide. The path is for YOU create. Only you. However you must know that I am always nearby, always watching."

INTROSPECTION

He awoke on his couch, a half empty glass of red wine on the coffee table. It was 4:14 in the morning. The first thing he noticed was that his sleep was deeper than any he had in weeks. Initially he remembered little of any dreams he might have had. Only a fog was pervasive, anchoring him to the couch. Only after rising to relieve himself and splash cold water on his face did the details start to come back to him.

Once the visions came, they came vividly. Many of the same emotions were lodged in his short term memory, and with the same intensity. He clearly saw the wonder of the hall of souls, with many millions on their unique journey. He felt the transformation of senses as he moved from the hall through the portal where dwelled the spirits who orchestrated the fate of souls.

He felt the full sense of wonder from being near Immat, Hildegarde, and Aisling in their environment, working together to keep the machinery of rebirth functioning, along with the sense of anger and confusion over Immat having regained his role in this vital place, so soon after taking personal advantage of one soul for his own purposes. He considered Immat sincere in his regret and truly appreciative of the forgiveness he was shown, but still something stirred inside Henry. There were questions that required answers, and the experience forced him to realize that the answers were his alone to find.

Wherever this journey would take him, his deepest hope was that it would bring him back to Dee. Otherwise it would be empty. He knew there were larger, far more important factors in play, but for the moment nothing was more important than the love he finally found. The cold reality confronted him that Dee might never again be available to him in this life. It would be his biggest heartbreak, and he questioned whether this would be the one to break him after a lifetime of so many others. Still, he took Aisling's words to heart, that he had to stay strong no matter what. If Dee was taken from him in this life, they would have other lifetimes together.

As daylight came, Henry knew that time was precious and there was much to accomplish. As he glanced out the window to the East, at the beginning strands of light, he saw a clear Wednesday morning ahead. There was nothing in his way but his own limitations, which he was in the best position to control.

His primary mission would be to find Dee, or at least what became of her. This goal would guide his every move. If it was too late for Dee, then his primary mission would be to find who was responsible for her fate, and to make them pay. If these goals brought him to find other answers, to right other wrongs, then he would accept those challenges completely. His path to the truth would probably require the help of the authorities, in particular Detective Lacey. It would be a wise idea to contact him, but given the slow pace of police investigations, it did not seem a high priority.

He needed to contact the Origenists. Lars was with Dee when they went into the mouth of the lion, so either Lars was part of the plan or he was also in danger. Either way, he had no choice but to find out, and the group of Origenists were the only allies he could count on.

The question would be how to contact any of the group members. He knew none of their names, and Dee had been careful during their weeks together to never reveal any personal information about them.

What if she maintained a private list of their contacts? Could it be possible that in her written records or computer records she maintained a backup list about the members? He believed it unlikely that she would have their information only in her memory or only on her cell phone, neither of which could be completely reliable.

He started with her laptop. He knew her login from her mumbling when she spelled David Herbrit's last name incorrectly, so within a few seconds he was searching her local disk for any files that may indicate contact names or numbers. He saw nothing that seemed to indicate an affiliation with the Origenists, so he decided to search based on date. He figured there would be updates to contact information when the group met, even if that information was passed discreetly. He scanned through hundreds of files, including system files that change on a daily basis, looking for any that might have a file name to tip him off. There were a few possibilities that he was able to open easily, but nothing offered promise.

After nearly an hour of tedious visual scanning, he decided to change gears and focus on her notebooks, address books, and other hard copy documents that she left around. He went through everything in writing he could find, learning much along the way about how his best friend lived her life. Behind tears, he adored her organized mind and silly notes, mostly to herself about things she needed to do to make her life easier and happier.

In a binder notebook he found a page with a picture she had drawn. It was clearly a rendering of Henry, smiling and looking down. She had probably taken a photo with her phone, and this was her freehand version. It brought forth a stream of tears that he did not try to abate. His emotions needed to be let loose over the loss, temporary he hoped, of his friend.

In thinking through the routines they shared, he was able to recall the process of the Origenists assembling. Someone in the group, always a senior member, would send a cryptic text message to the others. Embedded in the message would be the logistics for when and where to meet. He remembered it had something to do with a deli order for a sandwich, but he could not recall any details about the last contact. Still, it was a start.

He knew that Dee had taken her cell phone with her to the Church, so there was no chance he could search for details of the last contact. He had searched every place that Dee would have intentionally put info about her group, but what about unintentional places? Their last visit was only a week before.

What about the trash? To his relief, he had been so distracted with her disappearance that he became lax about emptying it. He started with the receptacle nearest to Dee's computer desk, and he meticulously went through all scraps of paper within the desk, with no luck. He sat on the bed, exasperated and searching for other answers.

The apartment in need of some organization, probably due to Dee's many recent distractions, so he moved magazines, organized mail, and separated belongings into their appropriate places. While moving a book about ancient religions, he noticed a bookmark sticking from the pages with handwriting on it. He looked at it more closely. It was clearly Dee's handwriting.

"Turkey Rye 424 - Winfred's - 7 p.m."

Joram Berkovic calmly picked up his phone. It was a Friday morning, just an hour after daybreak. "Shoshana, please connect me with General Zahav."

He waited while his secretary made the connection. The General's gruff voice came on the line. "Yes, Prime Minister, what can I do for you, sir?"

"The plans we discussed, General," the Prime Minister said slowly into the phone.

The general paused, exhaling slowly. "Yes, sir. What about them?"

"We need to execute those plans."

The general's voice rose. "Am I hearing you correctly, Mister Berkovic? This would be the largest offensive since the Gaza War. Much larger in fact, and on foreign soil."

"I trust," the Prime Minister interrupted, "that you've had your forces ready to act on my orders. I explained to you that this action was a distinct possibility."

"Yes, of course they're ready," the general answered hurriedly. "They've been on alert since we spoke. I'm just ... surprised this is really happening. Have there been new developments since we spoke a few days ago?"

"Movements have been reported to me that suggest strongly something is coming. If we don't move now, it might be too late."

"Begin immediately," the Prime Minister replied.

Within fourteen minutes, an array of F-16 fighter jets rumbled to life on the tarmac of Ramat David Airbase in Northern Israel. The jets were fully armed, manned by senior fighter pilots who had been moved to the North in the tense few days leading up to this bold decision.

One by one the jets roared into the sky toward Syrian targets to the Northeast. They bombed key targets near Damascus and beyond, all the way past Homs to near Aleppo. Their strikes were tactical and precise, focused on military installations that had been under surveillance by Israeli satellites in the prior weeks. Most targets were far from residential areas, focused on air bases and suspected weapons and missile launch facilities. The pilots had mapped out their destinations weeks before from the list of targets provided by their superiors.

Even the most careful planning could not prevent some civilian casualties. Some facilities that had been under scrutiny by Israeli military analysts were perilously close to residential communities, which of course included apartment buildings, schools, shopping areas, and office buildings. Despite this risk and their concerns, the fighter pilots were not going to miss the opportunity to succeed in their mission because of poor planning by Syrian developers, public and private, who mixed residential and commercial properties near national assets in the name of profit.

The strikes were fast, thunderous, and came to Syrians without warning. Civilians were caught completely off guard by the offensive, more tuned to the upcoming weekend on a lazy, warm Friday morning than on the remote possibility of lethal air strikes. Those close to military targets scrambled for cover, pulling in family members to the safest locations they could find. Younger Syrians who were out of immediate danger flocked to social media outlets to report the firestorm that rocked them from sleep. Word spread around the globe within minutes, and suspecting eyes immediately turned to Israel.

Syrian military forces were slow to react. By the time the Syrian Air Force was able to get retaliatory fighter craft into the air, the Kheil HaAvir pilots were taking safe routes back to Ramat. Syrian pilots who managed to get airborne brushed the border with Israel, but were unwilling to engage with the Israeli planes that by now were simply on patrol. Within twenty-five minutes of the first strikes, no Israeli planes were over Syrian soil. The attack was precise, fast, and lethally effective.

The most substantial damage was done to ground-based installations that were spread throughout key locations in the center of the nation. The first estimates of human casualties numbered in the hundreds, and most were either Syrian military personnel or others who were in proximity to targets that Israeli satellites identified as posing a meaningful threat to the safety of Israeli citizens and the state of Israel herself.

Syria had had a checkered past in the ever-present struggle between Arab nations and Israel. It was a diverse country but its politics were dominated by Arab Sunnis. Between civil wars and accusations of human rights abuses, it sided with the West while its Ba'athist leaders struggled fiercely for control. Its traditional allies throughout its rocky history remained Iran, China, Russia on the global scene, and Yemen, Lebanon, Sudan, and Iraq in the immediate region.

In the hours following the attack, language from the world's superpowers was muted. Leaders from the US, China, and Russia spoke in largely vague terms about maintaining peace in the region. Each of the analysts interviewed online and in traditional media outlets did not see the offensive coming, and focused their speculation on the reaction that would be generated by Israel's actions.

The American President asserted in a news conference just hours after the attack, very early in the morning in Washington, that Israel had a right to fight for survival, and preemptively take action against impending threats. The implication, speculated but not confirmed, was that the President was made aware of the impending offensive before the event.

Reaction from Arab media sources and the leaders of Arab countries was swift. The President of Iran was the first to speak out loudly, proclaiming the Israeli offensive as a direct, frontal attack on the Nation of Islam. He decried the "culture of aggressive decline" that was fostered by the United States and the United Nations in favor of Israel. He positioned the action as not an attack on Syria, but rather a call to arms for all Arab nations.

As volume increased over the implications of the offensive around the world, covert intelligence sources from the West were buzzing with reports of plans for immediate retaliatory action by Arab nations. While Syria herself was no match for the might of Israel's air and ground offensive, it was much more alarming when reports of impending action by Iran began to surface.

When the sun had gone down over the Middle East, the US President decided to take the unusual step of interrupting his day to have a second press conference to try to calm tensions in the Arab world. He called upon the leaders of other superpowers to come together to remind their allies in the various Arab countries to wait until all information was known before taking impulsive action.

Even though it was nearly midnight in Jerusalem when the President delivered his remarks, as if on queue, Joram Berkovic released a statement to the press explaining Israel's decision to launch the offensive.

"During the past few days, we obtained highly reliable information about an impending threat to the nation of Israel, and to the safety of our citizens. A threat of this magnitude could not be ignored, and our inquiries on the subject with Syrian leadership fell on deaf ears. In the interest of protecting the existence of the state of Israel, we chose to take action against only those targets that we viewed as most threatening, most lethal to our citizens. These targets were only a few hundred miles from our border. The threat was very real. We make no apologies for defending our right to continue to live in our homeland."

Within an hour of the press conference by the Israeli Prime Minister, the Syrian President, Nizar al-Azma, conducted his own press conference.

"Ignore the claims of the head of the Israeli snake. There was no attempt to speak with me directly about any threat, real or imagined, to Israel from Syrian sources. I have received no communication from Israel in the past several months. This attack was nothing more than an unprovoked act of war on the Syrian State and on the Nation of Islam. I call upon the support of my brothers and sisters in all Arab nations to respond quickly and lethally to this despicable attack. We will join you in this response, beginning immediately."

Western news sources expressed surprise at the tone of al-Azma comments, openly questioning the veracity of Israel's information sources.

Despite the carefully planned strikes by Israeli air forces, Syria was not left defenseless. Shortly after the brief but emotional speech by the Syrian President, ground based missiles were in the air, headed to Israel targets. Syria's strategy was to launch many missiles simultaneously, knowing that Israel possessed anti-missile defenses that were highly effective against small, isolated airstrikes. The strategy was to target a mix of civilian and military destinations.

Syrian strikes were only marginally successful against army and navy bases, missile sites, and air force bases, as Israel's tactical defenses were more effective in protecting military targets. Strikes against Israeli residential areas were far more effective and lethal. Payloads pounded high profile targets in the Israeli cities of Safed, Hahariya, and Tiberias, destroying less populous but high-profile and symbolic targets. Hundreds died in the first series of missiles that were launched simultaneously. Syria followed each volley of missiles with a second, then a third, every ten or fifteen minutes. Israeli defenses adjusted the best way they could, but were largely scrambling to react. Each round of Syrian missiles ended the lives of hundreds more unsuspecting Israeli citizens.

That was the first wave response from Syria. The second wave was a series of air strikes by the modest but determined Syrian Air Force. Syrian pilots were selective about taking on Israeli fighter planes, choosing to engage with the older F-16 Fighting Falcons instead of the newer, more effective F-16 Eagles. The Syrian strategy was to keep the Israeli air-based assets occupied while other forces were in motion.

Israel, for her part, seemed surprised at the ability of Syria to counterattack with such ferocity and determination. The first Israeli strikes were meant to include missile launch sites, but clearly they had missed many. Following Syria's backlash, Israel shifted its missile and air attacks to commercial installations. Israel had no intention of targeting Syrian residential areas, but some targets around Damascus and other cities and towns not far from the Israeli border would inevitably fall on office buildings, apartment buildings, and retail areas that were busy with activity late on a Friday morning.

Many souls were disembodied on this hostile Friday, and very many more would not be alive much longer.

Jordan and Lebanon were on edge, waiting for the appropriate time to jump into the fray based on the information available.

For the first time in memory, Israel's ability to defend herself was not the top concern on the mind of Joram Berkovic. About a thousand miles to the East, Iranian leaders were enraged by the images on their televisions and computer monitors. Action was needed, they decided, and sooner rather than later.

American warships were on the way to the Mediterranean Sea and the Arabian Sea. It was a rapid escalation that most did not expect, and one that would result in more casualties than any conflict in the millennium in this region of the world.

Several thousand miles away, in the Southeastern part of the United States of America, Ernest Grandby spoke into his phone.

"It's happening. They're at each other's throats. This will continue to escalate, and much more powerful forces are going to be very, very involved."

His daughter listened, then let out a throaty laugh. "Right you are, Father, on at least a few levels."

That was it! He remembered asking her about the cryptic code that Origenists used to summon each other to a meeting. It would initially sound like a sandwich order, but the message was to be converted to a street address for one of the members. On her note on the back of the bookmark, Dee wrote the number 424, which was instinctively followed by the person who lived there, Winfred. Had she not written his name, the message would have been completely useless to Henry in trying to reach other members of the group.

He began an online search of residents of the Greater Boston Area with the first name of Winfred. The name was unique enough that it only produced a few hundred results. He pored through each return carefully, looking for someone with a street address of 424.

He found three. One was located in Lexington, one in Dorchester, and one in West Roxbury. He wrote down each of their names, addresses, and phone numbers on a pad. He preferred to avoid suspicion with anyone who knew nothing about the Origenists, but he also wanted to leave nothing to chance. He had nothing to lose by referring to them directly with each of these candidates.

The first was Winfred Chen in Lexington. He dialed. The phone range twice, then a man with a slight Asian accent answered cautiously, not familiar with the incoming number.

"Hello, am I speaking with Mister Chen? Winfred Chen?"

"Yes. Who's calling, please?"

"My name is Henry Chimera. This isn't a sales call. I'm looking for a friend who has gone missing, and I wonder if you might know her."

"Why would I know your friend?"

"Well, you would know her only if you belong to the same ... interest group as her."

"This sounds like some sort of sneaky sales pitch. I can't help you, Mister Chimera. Please don't call this number again."

"I promise I won't call again, but just one more question. Have any Origenists tried to reach you lately?"

"Any who? This is crazy. Don't call me again." There was a click.

Henry moved on to the next name, Winfred Harding from Dorchester. The phone rang and rang. No one picked up, so he decided to leave a message.

"Hello, my name is Henry Chimera. I'm not sure if we've ever met, but I'm looking for a friend who has gone missing. Her name is Dee Stark. If you are a part of her interest group, you probably know Dee well, and you probably know who I am. Could you please call me as soon as you get this message?" He left his number.

The next candidate was Winfred Meade from West Roxbury. He found the same result, leaving a similar message.

With no other leads, Henry looked back at his search results to see if he missed any Winfreds who lived at 424. He checked Dee's note again to make sure that he had not misread any of the numbers. With nothing more to pursue from this small scrap of paper, he exhaled slowly and leaned back in his chair, staring at the ceiling.

So much was out of his control. He felt an emptiness inside, a loneliness that was from frustration and fear for another, the one person he allowed himself to love.

"This is why I've always been better off alone. I was meant to be alone when I was little, I stayed alone for more than thirty years, so maybe I need to be for as long as I live." He said the words aloud.

With no appointments on his calendar for the day by his choice, and no other great ideas about finding Dee, he searched for a logical next move. If she was still alive, it had to be possible that she was still inside the church. He considered going in by himself, but doubted he could accomplish much on his own. He had heard about a network of surveillance cameras in the building, and from his past visits as a volunteer he knew that while he might have access to some of the offices and conference rooms on the main floor, he would not be allowed to reach any of the upper or lower floors.

He saw very few options other than to go the legal route. Lacey knew almost as much about Dee's situation as Henry did, and perhaps had made some progress since Henry had last spoken with him. He dialed.

"Detective Lacey." The officer answered his phone as if he had just washed down a mouthful of coffee.

"Good morning Detective, it's Henry Chimera. I was just checking in on your progress."

"Henry, do you think I have nothing better to do than to give you status reports every couple days?"

"I suspect not, Detective, but I doubt you'd call me soon, if at all, if you found out anything. So I'm saving you the trouble. Anything new?"

"You first. Do you have any new information for me?" Lacey was on the defensive, weary from the questions he faced on a daily basis about unsolved crimes in his jurisdiction. The possibility that the highest profile death in the world might be related was undoubtedly a factor too.

Henry decided to throw the detective some information.

"I might be getting somewhere on this Origenist thing. I found a note that Dee wrote a few weeks back that gave me at least something to go on. I might be able to find one member of the group. I'm working on it."

Lacey's tone seemed to lighten. "I'd like to hear all about that. Are you available later today? I made plans for another visit to the Church. This time I'm meeting with their security guy to run through some surveillance videos. You could help me with that. Maybe you can spot your girlfriend."

"You think *maybe* I can help with that? How could you spot Dee without my help, Detective???"

"Calm down, Henry. I was going to call you later. This isn't the only thing I'm working on."

Henry continued. "Dee might still be alive. It's your case, no one else's. You know exactly where she disappeared, so you guys should be all over that place right now."

"We don't know that for sure. We don't even know if she made it onto their premises. That's what we'll find out today."

Henry was silent, fuming.

"I'll pick you up at 12:30." Lacey confirmed Henry's address, and they hung up on each other coldly.

Henry was standing in front of his apartment building when Lacey's unmarked sedan pulled up. He climbed in, not looking directly at Lacey.

"Look, Henry," Lacey began contritely, "just because you're not hearing everything doesn't mean nothing is happening. After you told me all about the Dalai Lama situation I went straight to my superiors with it. It floored them, knocked their dicks off. They're in contact with the FBI now. The Bureau is taking the information very seriously obviously. In the meantime, we've been talking about the approach with these church people. We don't have enough to get a warrant right now. There's nothing yet to tie the church to her disappearance. If they resisted showing us these surveillance videos that might have been enough, but now we have to go in there and prove that she was even on the premises. Even if we see her on camera, that still might not be enough for us to get a warrant to search the place. Anyone could have grabbed her, either on premises or after the service. We just have to see what we can see and take it from there. So what can you tell me about this progress in finding the Origenist?"

"I haven't heard back from anyone yet. I'm waiting for a call back." He filled Lacey in on Dee's note, his internet search on the first name and house number, and his subsequent phone calls.

"If I'm on the right track, this Winfred guy will probably want to talk to some of the other group members before getting back to me."

"Makes sense. Good work. I'll try to keep you posted on our progress, and I'd ask you to please do the same." Lacey exhaled and paused. "Sometimes we forget how hard this can be on people close to the victims."

Lacey glanced nervously at Henry. In a missing person case, to referring to a 'victim' could sometimes provoke a reaction. Henry did not seem to be affected.

The afternoon was hot and sunny. Even on a weekday, there were more than thirty cars in the parking lot of the Church of the Tortured Christ. Henry and the Detective walked slowly from Lacey's sedan to the ornate front door of the church office. The detective approached slowly while visually scanning the church windows, the grounds, and design of the tunnel-like structure that connected the church and the church office.

Henry was content to take a slow walk for a different reason. His emotions were turbulent. He was nervous about the experience ahead, but fearful of what might have happened to Dee in this place. Was she taken away in someone's trunk, wrapped in plastic? Or was she off in a secluded church getaway, being tortured or brainwashed? Perhaps she was, right now, in a remote corner of this labyrinth, bound and gagged, waiting for help of any kind.

"Hello Mrs. Hargus. I'm Detective Lacey from the Waltham Police Department."

"Hello again, Detective." The plump, carefully prepared woman seemed uncomfortable not smiling. "How can I help you this afternoon?"

"I'm hear to visit Stanley Lafarge. I called ahead. He should be expecting me."

"Very well, I'll notify Mister Lafarge. Would you and your guest mind signing in, please?"

They entered their names and the time into a large guestbook that was nearly filled to the back pages, then took a seat. The receptionist phoned Lafarge and seemed to get him on the first or second ring.

Within a minute a man appeared around the corner. "Detective Lacey?"

He was a tree trunk of a man, with a thick neck and limbs, and a menacing face. His hand, the size of a frying pan, was outstretched to Lacey. A pistol harness was visible under his perfectly tailored jacked, light grey with subtle dark threading, accentuated by a bright blue dress tie.

Lacey returned the handshake. "Detective Oliver Lacey from the Waltham Police Department. This is Henry Chimera." Henry scrambled to his feet, clumsily grasping the man's hand for a hurried shake.

"Right this way, gentlemen." Lafarge turned toward a door away from where Henry had been before.

"You look like a former athlete," Lacey said. "Football maybe?"

"Good guess," Lafarge said, turning his head slightly back and down toward the men. "Two years as a tight end at BC. A linebacker hit me from the side, and that was the end of all my knee ligaments and my football career."

"Tough way to finish. Mister Lafarge, I'd like to borrow your guest book. We need to scan through your guest list on Sunday, June 29th."

"Please," replied the tall oak, "call me Stan. I'm afraid the book can't leave the building. You're welcome to look through it all you like, but it has to be on premises."

"Well, then, you might want to get used to seeing me around here, Stan." Lacey smiled. Lafarge offered no response.

He led them into a large, discreet room illuminated by many monitors that were stacked in an open angle along three of the six walls in the room. Another security guard, also neatly dressed and large but more plump than Lafarge, was seated in front of the main wall of monitors. He glanced at the men nodding but not smiling. He made no attempt to engage with them.

Lafarge pointed to two seats toward the back of the room. On the table before the seats were two video players and connected monitors. The men sat before them, with Lafarge in a chair behind.

"I'm not sure how you'd like to do this. Together or separate? I have you set up for both."

"Well," replied Lacey, after rubbing his chin, "I'm depending on Henry to identify our missing woman. One monitor, please. We'd like to look first at the crowds coming in and out of each service."

"First? I thought that was all you were planning to view."

"Oh no," Lacey said. "We need to look at all your footage from Sunday. Two people haven't been heard from since that morning, and we think the last place they were seen was in this building. It wouldn't make sense to look at only the videos from people entering the church. Is that going to be a problem, Stan?"

"Not a problem. We can round up the other videos."

Lafarge left the room, then returned with a small box of cartridges. He helped them organize each video in sequence from each camera vantage point, going from shortly after six in the morning, when no one was in the building except security, to as late in the day and through the next morning. They started with the most prominent camera angle, which showed visitors entering the church vestibule from outside, then choosing where in the cavernous parish they would look for a seat. There were two full services each Sunday, one beginning crisply at eight o'clock, the second at ten. Henry told the detective that Dee attended the ten o'clock service, but Lacey was determined to have them both pore through both services and each camera angle from beginning to end.

Hundreds of congregants came through the main door for the early service. Lacey allowed the video to run through at normal speed while congregants were arriving. He stopped each time a younger looking blond woman showed on the tape.

"Is that her?"

"No."

"What about her?"

"Still no."

On they went, through the early ceremony until they were seeing everyone leave.

"There's no point slowing the tape down for this, but watch closely, Henry, in case we missed her coming in." Henry sighed. This would be a long afternoon.

Eventually people started trickling toward the church for the ten o'clock service. At about nine-forty, they could see Reverend Sullivan moving out the front door, shaking hands and hugging congregants as she gradually made her way to a position and just to the right of the entrance. To their relief, she was still visible at the top of the stairs. The doors were enormously wide, and congregants could easily get around the crowd gathered around her if they chose.

At nine fifty-three, a couple walked up the steps. Henry spotted her right away as they were approaching in the distance, while Lacey was busy poring over the people gathered around Sullivan.

"There she is." He pointed to her image on the monitor. Lacey excitedly pressed his face close for a better look.

The video image was not sharp because it was at a distance, but it was in color and in good contrast. Henry assured Lacey that the woman hanging off behind the crowd was Dee, and that the man pressing the edge of the group was Lars. Lacey paused the video.

"Did you notice anyone approach with them?"

"No," Henry said confidently. "Back it up and see for yourself. It was just the two of them walking, and Lars starts to move toward the Reverend. They said something to each other. It seems clear that Dee didn't want to stop and talk to her, but of course Lars did the dumbest thing he could have done in that situation, draw attention to themselves by approaching the Reverend."

Lacey turned from the monitor to face Henry. "I get the impression you aren't too fond of this guy."

"Uh, that would be accurate. We've had our differences. I couldn't convince him that I wasn't trying to harm their group. This guy would have put a bullet in my head if he could have. I let Dee know that I would never trust him, but she accepted the risk to go in there with him."

Henry looked down at his clasped hands. Lacey turned back to the monitor.

"Henry, let's take our time and look closely at this. If you see anyone who looks like they're focused on these two, that's the kind of thing we're looking for, or if there's any kind of coercion at all. Just unnatural movement of any kind."

Lars waited patiently for his turn to greet the Reverend. They exchanged a few words, then Lars introduced Dee to Sullivan. From Dee's body language, she was not thrilled to meet the Reverend, but she forced a smile.

They ran through the sequence of Lars and Dee entering the church over and over, with only one camera angle to consider. Tears framed Henry's face as he watched the first few times. He longed for her as he watched her every movement. He found, emerging within, a determination that he would not allow the last view of his love to be on a cold surveillance video. She had to be alive. This man next to him might be the only chance he had of seeing her again. He had made a wise choice in opening up to the detective. It was all about access, and Lacey could gain access to places Henry never could. He cooperated with Lacey as long as progress seemed possible, but he did not plan to place full trust in him or anyone.

They continued watching, noticing nothing suspicious as the couple moved through the vestibule and found a seat on the left side of the auditorium. After they moved below camera range, others moved into the church behind them. Henry tried to recognize people nearby with no success. It seemed like a random gathering of strangers.

At the close of the service they just as carefully watched as the congregants moved out. The passage was uneventful until they saw Dee and Lars moving out the front doors and down the steps. They paused, looked around, and exchanged some words. Dee was shaking her head in disagreement at something Lars was saying, but it was mild. It finished with them both walking to the left of the door, where the church office would be. They disappeared from view.

For the next several hours, Henry and Lacey pored through all available videos of the exterior and interior of church premises. A distant camera angle showed the couple moving from the front door of the church toward the office entrance. They appeared to enter the building but not to leave. They watched the front door of the church office for the duration of the videos, with no sign of Dee or Lars leaving the building.

Lacey rose to find Lafarge. Henry followed.

"Stan, next I'd like to see your available video of the church office. You do have some, correct?"

"Yeah, we have some internal video," he replied casually, "but it's the main entrance. Nothing else is open to the public, so we never installed cameras."

"I need to see what you have," Lacey answered.

This time Lafarge was gone for nearly ten minutes before returning. They advanced through video footage showing the entrance from early in the morning, both anxious for the time stamp to approach eleven, about when the later service dispersed.

The camera angle was not ideal. It was positioned above the right shoulder of Cecilia Hargus, outward through the front door and an adjacent window.

At 11:12, the couple walked through the door by themselves. Dee moved to the right of the camera toward the small waiting area. Lars said a few words to the receptionist then moved past her to left, outside the camera angle.

"What the hell do you think he was doing?" Lacey directed his question both at Henry and at Lafarge, who was now paying attention to their review of the video.

"Well, there aren't many people in the building on a Sunday around the time of our services," Lafarge said. "He probably went to use the bathroom."

"How would he know there's a bathroom back there? And why would he go into the church office instead of using the one in the church?"

"I wouldn't know about his choice of latrines, sir," Lafarge said dryly. "I've never met the man. Cecilia probably told him there's a bathroom down the hall. Perhaps he was looking for a little more privacy than dropping a deuce a few yards from where he just prayed."

"So do you recognize this guy? Ever seen him before?" Lacey stared, unblinking, toward the guard.

"I haven't seen that guy before."

Lacey looked back without blinking. "He looks familiar with the place."

Lafarge just shook his head. "I don't ever remember seeing him."

They spent the next few hours reviewing the remaining video footage of the church office entrance and the hallways of the church office. There was no footage of Lars nor Dee leaving the premises.

Lacey turned to Lafarge again. "So this couple entered the building and never left. Stan, do you think they might still be here?"

"No Detective, I don't think they might still be here. There are three other exit doors in the building, and none of them would trigger an alarm. The one on the Southwest side of the building is right next to the rest rooms, and it's right next to the lot where they probably parked. They could have left through any exit they wanted."

"Well, that's convenient," Lacey replied with a smirk. "How about you show us around the premises?"

"Sure, as long as it's on this floor." Lafarge looked dryly back at the detective.

"What's on the other floors?"

"Offices. Storage in the basement."

"Now what could the church possibly have to keep private in its offices and storage areas?"

"Well, let me think, Detective. Oh yeah, all of our financial records, all the records of donations and donors, public and private. All our tax records. All of our electronic equipment that allows the Reverend to communicate with other people around the world. All the records of abused women and children the church has supported through the years. The personal effects of the people who work here. I guess that's it. NO, you can't go roaming through this property."

"Can I speak with Reverend Sullivan about this?" Lacey was rigid, in the larger man's face. Henry stood back, impressed.

The veins were showing in Lafarge's neck, but he kept his tone even. "Reverend Sullivan is the person who explained to me what you were entitled to see before your visit."

"No problem. A search warrant is just a formality. Oh that reminds me!" Lacey snapped his fingers close to Lafarge's nose. "I'd really love to look through that guest book."

Just then Henry's mobile phone rang. He did not recognize the number, but saw it was from a local area code.

"Hello, this is Henry."

"Hello," said the man's voice. "This is Winfred Harding. I got your message. I think we need to talk."

Catalysis

The spectrum of souls needing assistance following each life was more diverse than all the billions of stars in all the galaxies in the universe. The formula for creating unique souls in the earthly plane was founded on the principles of DNA, the wonder of which was discovered by humans only in the past century. The DNA model presented limitless possibilities for ensuring the uniqueness of humans, but it also provided a foundational model for the creation of new souls as well.

Every living human represents a cauldron of genes that dates back through the generations. A single person born on earth today was combined from more than a hundred other humans who were alive at some point in the last centuries, and more than a thousand people who were alive in the past three centuries. These were the parents and grandparents, their parents and grandparents, and so on.

The design was beautiful, Immat understood. It presented him with an infinite parade of unique souls, each with distinct experiences in previous lives and limitless possibilities for future lives. He bore the responsibility of gathering future possibilities from the information each brought from lives lived before.

Following the conclusion of each life, the soul would retreat to this vast place where space and time are limitless. The being would gather to heal, to rest, and to contemplate the growth that was possible in the next life. Each lifetime was a mission that would, if approached correctly, advance the soul to a wiser, more complete state. The idea was to seek out opportunities to learn and to grow while correcting past mistakes and strengthening weaknesses.

The lives could be challenging, even brutal. Some souls would return to this place of healing in great need of repair before any thought could be given to the next earthly challenge. Many would choose a life that would be a continual struggle, surrounded by poverty, disease, bloodshed, or brutality. They would return wiser, but some would be scarred. This was the place for rest and reparation.

Some souls would choose lives that offered hardships such as a learning disability, a physical handicap, or physiological or mental condition that would make routine living especially difficult. Severe depression was a common condition that many souls bravely confronted through the ages. Living a life that required going to war, losing one or more close family members, or dying young were also very common.

Each soul went into these lifetimes knowing most of the circumstances that were ahead, but not knowing all the turns in the road. Each had to trust its ability to contend with the unexpected. The idea, after all, was to win the battle and come back more enlightened, more able to take on increasing challenges.

Other souls during other lifetimes would choose circumstances that were less trying. Either they had been through a stretch of difficult life cycles, or they were simply growing tired of the battle. There was no rule that the next life had to be more difficult than the last. It was purely up to the individual to decide, following a period of rest and reflection, where they wanted to go next.

Immat's gift, unsurpassed by all others who had ever been in this position, was to read the appetite of these beings and present the appropriate options. He was like a waiter in the largest, most diverse restaurant imaginable. When a customer arrived, ready for an enticing meal, he would be the one to decide which of many menus to offer.

There were many available, and they tended to be grouped by culture and philosophy. Souls would often arrive with recent history of living in similar regions or religious circumstances. They may have just come from a series of lives living in a Western culture, replete with all the unique complexities, or it may have been in a simpler locale in Africa or Asia where the challenge was in staying alive and healthy. Many millions of the souls who came through had experienced rigid cultures that were rooted in ancient traditions.

It was Immat's job to narrow the broader set of possibilities into a digestible menu that made a wise choice possible. And what a series of menus he had to offer! If the soul had not recently experienced a life as a Buddhist, Christian, or even as an atheist, these circumstances were there for the choosing. His options would often include life opportunities that stretched the boundaries of the soul's prior experiences, sometimes beyond a place of comfort and confidence. He was always impressed when a soul chose to make such a total departure from prior experiences.

Immat possessed the unique ability to view recent past lives, understand what the soul was seeking in the next life experience, and to provide a framework of culture or religion or region that would offer a broad list of choices to move forward. It was very rare that a soul would be dissatisfied with the choices available. In these cases, typically the soul was not quite ready to choose a new life, or was having second thoughts about the learnings it had gleaned from its most recent experiences.

When a soul was having a difficult time choosing between lives, Hildegarde was available to help. Her special class of spirit devoted its kind energy to explore the intricacies of the lives ahead. This included the events that surrounded the life and how equipped the soul was to positively affect these events.

The class of spirits that included Hildegarde were called Principalities, and their mission was to work directly with Powers to fulfill the heavenly mission that was laid out before all of these ethereal spirits. The central premise was to deliver blessings to the living world. Principalities were tasked with recognizing the difficulty these souls would experience, and to partner with each to explore the details of the lives they were considering.

It was the Principality's job to remind souls that lives change events as much as events change lives. Through this analysis, souls would be encouraged to examine their ability to not only cope with the challenges ahead, but positively change outcomes for themselves and the people around them.

One soul named Eralu, who had most recently died as a female genocide victim in Africa, came into this introspective phase wanting to again be a woman, this time a mother of many children. In the lives that were presented to her by Immat, the life settings were generally in poorer places. The challenge she sought was to influence the lives of other young people while contending with external factors that were out of her control.

Hildegarde worried about Eralu's ability to contend with specific external factors, such as a spouse who would be ill or die young, or in other life settings in which her family or religious circumstances might create stresses that would prevent her from being a strong mother. Hildegarde helped her assess the wide variety of possibilities, including the structure around her that would support her in weak moments that would happen during any lifetime. Eralu was given all the time she needed, but eventually chose an extended family in India that, while lacking in money, would likely offer solid support through the challenges that she and her husband would face while raising their children.

Principalities like Hildegarde were there to remind souls that choosing a new life is about challenging the soul to achieve greater wisdom, not to accept only those that would go smoothly. Sometimes an easy life could be chosen, but she would remind them that it could be a wasted opportunity for growth.

They were the guardians of souls between lives on earth. They were available to assist during rest and repair, which needed to be complete before each soul could seek a new life in the long journey of growth and realization.

There were many others like Hildegarde in this realm, of course, due to the immense number of souls that required this peaceful, nurturing place between lives. Like Hildegarde, these spirits had usually achieved a high level of wisdom, understanding, and accomplishment in the living realm. The many lives each had lived offered a vast array of challenges which, lifetime after lifetime, they learned to overcome. These advanced spirits understood the importance of perseverance.

They served to remind that taking on challenges that were too difficult could be counterproductive, while eroding their confidence, their zest for learning and growing, and their curiosity about what adventures lay ahead.

It was much like raising a child into adulthood. The lessons often needed to be targeted toward developing very specific skills and defenses. Development of a soul was never a straight line, but rather a twisting road that took many turns and offered many routes. Principalities like Hildegarde were available to help ensure the soul understood its limitations and areas of development, and to choose its next path with the best possible information.

Also there to help them was a vast army of angels. The angels inhabited every corner of this loving place to make the machinery move without distraction. The angels had never been human, but instead were conceived to assist the higher level beings, the Dominions, Virtues, Authorities, Archangels, Principalities, and the others, perform their duties efficiently and effectively.

In the case of Principalities, the angels would perform duties that included visiting the earthly plane to explore in detail the circumstances that a life was contemplating. Their visits were lightly referred to as "scoutings," a combination of "scouting" and "outing," that were meant to uncover any surprises that might await the ready soul, whether positive or negative.

The angels also worked tirelessly behind the scenes to ensure that each soul was able to set up its environment in a way that made repair and regeneration possible. If a soul wished to be surrounded by familiar spirits in a setting that was similar to a life they had all lived together, the angels would ensure that happened.

One could long for a setting that closely resembled the simple life she lived in Finland in the 1920s, shortly after the country's independence. The country was abuzz with a common sense of purpose that included a focus on independence, education, and growth. It was a perfect setting to recount the elements that combined to form a healthy, productive person, and by extension a healthy, productive soul. Angels would work together to ensure that every important detail was in place, which would allow the soul to study, learn, and grow in preparation for the next challenge, which might not be so accommodating.

As Hildegarde settled into her new role as mentor to these many souls in their selection of a new life, she depended on more than just Immat and the angels to perform her role well. As a new Principality, she needed other support to allow her to concentrate. She required an assistant who had experienced a wide variety of lives from which to draw. This spirit had to be special, deeply committed to helping others, but in a way that allowed souls to make their own path and express their own independence. Hildegarde forged new pathways in most of her lifetimes, some of which had never been seen before on earth, so she was most interested in finding a spirit who could, like herself, see past each individual religion, culture, and belief system.

Some spirits preferred to stay in their comfort zone, but this one needed to be fluid. This one needed to love the idea of working daily, even hourly, with the angels. Angels consisted of pure goodness and light, but they were exhausting. The instructions they received were required to be precise and concise, with no room for improvisation or ambiguity. This spirit needed patience above all, and it need to be one who could tirelessly serve the greater good.

As she assessed the various spirits who vied to be her apprentice, one made her presence rise above the others. This one had a unique sparkle, a sense of humor and exuberance that made Hildegarde's choice easy. When she was chosen, the successful candidate let out a whooping war cry that reverberated through this celestial layer. Hildegarde herself enjoyed a gratified laugh at this outpouring of joy from her new assistant. It sounded like a howl from a drunken, exuberant wolf. Clearly she had made the right choice!

Aisling had found her place in heaven.

The two spirits, mostly female in their essence and in the number of lives they had lived, fell in easily together as the specialist and the assistant. Aisling was usually tasked with researching details from past lives, which could require a great deal of time and attention. She would focus on events and influences that would likely affect decisions made during the lifetime, which could always have a rippling affect on others' choices and events.

Aisling's job was to meticulously gather and organize this information before presenting it to Hildegarde, who was very patient in communicating which information she needed and when. Having just the right information at the right time allowed her to focus all of her attention on the needs of the spirit before her. Aisling carefully watched Hildegarde as she worked, inspired by her pure attention to what was best for the spirit seeking counsel. Aisling understood why Hildegarde was so ideal for this position. Her wisdom was beyond any that Aisling knew, as was her ability to weave past lives into a stronger, more resilient future.

Hildegarde would spend time, in relative terms, with each soul assigned to her care. She would gently probe the spirit to learn about what it had learned in the time it spent in consultation and repair with the souls in their closest circle. She would then subtly shift the spirit's focus to learn each's appetite for challenges in the next life. When Hildegarde and the spirit would arrive at a sensible course for the next life, this desire would be passed along to Immat, who was in the valuable, unique position of knowing what life circumstances were available.

Immat would present the possible lifetimes to Hildegarde and the other Principalities in a kaleidoscope of rotating views. There were usually somewhere between twelve and sixteen visages presented in order of complexity, from very simple existences to the more challenging.

The range of life possibilities usually matched well with the information Hildegarde presented to Immat after conferring with the soul. On occasion the lives presented were in a particularly narrow range, varying only slightly from each other in their respective degree of difficulty. When the available choices were skewed to be more or less challenging than Hildegarde expected, or the range was just too narrow, Hildegarde had the opportunity to resubmit her request.

Immat was not especially flexible in how he would respond to these resubmissions. Hildegarde would patiently explain why she required opportunities that offered different challenges, or a wider variety. Immat would acknowledge each request, but it would rarely receive a high priority.

After some deliberation, he would typically provide a similar range back to Hildegarde, with a few additional options included in the mix. As if anticipating another response from Hildegarde, he would provide some form of explanation about the challenges around her request. Usually it was because of high demand for these life circumstances, but sometimes the explanation included an opinion about the spirit behind the request, for example that Immat did not believe the spirit could possibly handle the challenges it seemed to savor.

Hildegarde was patient in her dealings with Immat in all of these occurrences, but she wondered about the boundaries of his authority versus hers. She was right to be concerned.

Lionel Mazur was starting his day at seven in the morning in his customary way, with an array of newspapers spread across the right side of his vast desk, daily briefings from his key cabinet members on the left side, and a large cup of coffee in the center.

Mazur was a second-term US President from Michigan. The moderate Democrat was approaching his seventy-second birthday, weary from nearly seven years of trying to help his nation replace millions of American jobs that had gone overseas or were lost to the most recent recession. He campaigned and won on the promise to find a path forward for tens of millions of working age citizens who were not equipped for the higher skilled professions required in this new world economy.

He served for twenty-eight years in Michigan's Ninth Congressional District, succeeding in each election on the progress he made transitioning Michigan's labor force to be more competitive in industries that had less to do with auto manufacturing and more to do with newer technologies that he and others managed to draw to the state.

He was admired and respected by his colleagues on both sides of the aisle during his days in the US House of Representatives, and seemed a logical choice as a presidential candidate. Born of Polish and Irish parents, he was a faithful Catholic who managed to keep his religion and family out of the spotlight. He remained scandal-free after decades of public service, and he was ready for the job when his name was called. When his first term neared its end, he thought he had four strong years left.

He may have reconsidered if he knew what was heading his way in this second and last term, not the least of which were the Alzheimer's symptoms that began to be noticed by his closest advisors and assistants. It was becoming increasingly apparent to all around him that Mazur's memory was nothing like it was even a couple of years ago, and his energy level was noticeably lower. This was a tired man entering the most trying period in his presidency.

He picked up the New York Times and scanned through the top stories of the day. There were so many developments competing for space on the first page, he mused that the Times needed a larger first page.

There was a quiet knock, followed by the entrance of his Chief of Staff, Jeffrey Middleton.

"Good morning, Mid. What's the good word?"

"Good morning, Mister President. Not too many good words to offer this morning. Things seem to be blowing up all over the place. Except here, of course. Things are peaceful here."

"Well, something tells me that's about to change now that you're here," Mazur replied. "I haven't gotten to your briefing yet. Have a seat. Let's talk."

The stocky blond man with a ruddy but pleasant face and wire-rimmed glasses set his coffee cup on his boss's enormous desk and settled in with his papers perfectly organized before him.

"We can be grateful, sir. The protests over the Dalai Lama's disappearance seem to have subsided for the most part. The FBI is handling their public statements fairly well, trying to appear as open as possible about their investigation and what's known. But the fact is, they don't have much to go on. They aren't making much progress, so I don't know how long they'll be able to keep this up before people demand that they find him, dead or alive."

"Are they getting everything they need from local governments?"

"Yes sir, there are no problems with cooperation, but this hit was carried out by someone who knew what they were doing. They weren't amateurs, and they carried this off flawlessly, it seems."

"Our problems are relatively minor," he continued. "The really big problems continue to be in China. In the two weeks since the first clashes, more than half a million people have died violently. And these aren't just citizens. The PLA, their army, is taking a lot of casualties. We haven't seen this kind of uprising in China in any of our lifetimes, where citizens were confronting and damaging the PLA. It's unprecedented."

"There's still nothing we can do about it," the President added. "As awful as all this is to watch from these videos we're seeing, we cannot be seen as interfering. Half a million people? Really? Dear Jesus."

The President rubbed his eyes before looking up again. "What's next?"

"Africa is the most surprising, to me anyway," Middleton answered.

"Why is that?"

"Well, there are local skirmishes happening across the continent. It's remarkable. Suddenly we have these armed insurgent groups that are popping up in a bunch of places where we had no way of seeing it coming. Niger, Sudan, Angola, Tanzania, Nigeria, Zambia. It's amazing.

"In Zambia alone, a country of only about 15 million people, we're seeing armed rebels popping from the East to the West, seemingly out of nowhere. They're challenging a power structure that's been in place for decades. This uprising, which has kind of mysterious goals and roots, started on the perimeter of the country and seems to be moving fast toward Lusaka, which is in the center of the country.

"Still, that's not even close to the worst on the African continent. The worst bloodshed seems to be happening in Ethiopia. It's a toxic mix. In various regions the Christians seem to be trying to overtake the Sunni majorities, and they're not doing it peacefully. In the North, the Oromo ethnic region, things have absolutely exploded. The reports coming out of there are ghastly. The Christian minority has this firepower that the Sunni majority cannot contend with. In the Amhara region, sort of in the center of the country, where the country gets its language and identity, the Ethiopian Orthodox and the Jewish population seems to be trying to drive out the Islamic Sunnis. It's getting very, very ugly. Across the country there have been over 175,000 deaths in just the last few weeks. The nation is in turmoil. No one is backing down."

"What's their government and military doing about it?" The President posed the question wearily.

"They were as caught off guard by this as anyone. Besides, they've been on their heels trying to deal with rebel groups that are still upset over an election that occurred years ago. They have no ability to contend with these ethnic conflicts."

"Okay Mister Sunshine," the President said. "What else do you have for me?"

"A lot," the Chief of Staff said. "India and Pakistan are at each other's throats again. The source of this conflict is uncertain. Sound familiar? This one seems to involve some of the border land between Lahore in Pakistan and Amritsar in India, which is a heavily Sikh area. The area around Lahore is nearly entirely Muslim, and for some reason there's a movement afoot, among Shia I think, to claim land that they feel belongs to them. It includes the city of Amritsar, which is the spiritual center of the Sikh faith in India. That isn't going over well with the Indian government, and they're sending troops by the thousand to that area, ready to fight. In response to that, the Pakistani Army, largely volunteer but with more than a million soldiers, is gearing up to move toward that border region. So far casualties are in the tens of thousands, due mostly to hand to hand conflict. If the heavy artillery starts flying, this could get really ugly."

"Nasty," the President replied, "but again, out of our control. These are things we can do little about, other than calls for peace and people keeping their heads on straight. By me, I suppose."

"Yes, sir, it does appear that way. In your public comments, that's going to be a recurring theme. We have our speechwriters word-smithing now. The theme will be, 'Everyone keep your wits about you. Dial it back. These things are much more difficult to end than to begin.'"

"Great advice. Glad I thought of it." The President offered a weary smile. "What else do you have for me?"

"The Koreas," Middleton replied.

"Oh Christ, again?"

"Yes, and this one *really* seemed to come out of nowhere. Evidently South Korea - our allies, by the way - have decided it's their turn to stir up some tensions. Usually it's the North that takes umbrage at something the South says or does in the region. South Korea has decided to position some warships along the maritime border near the Yeonpyeongo Islands, which are on the South Korean side of the border. The ships are positioned in a menacing way, according to the language coming out of the North, and they are prepared to respond."

"What the hell?" Mazur's face grew red. "Haven't we been through enough trying to keep these guys from getting blistered that they would know not to provoke the North?"

"That's what makes it so strange. I assure you, our diplomats and the Secretary of State are in touch with them daily asking them to back down and keep their heads on straight."

"What are they saying in response?"

"Something about a bountiful harvest of some kind of shrimp." Middleton looked at his notes. "Penaeid shrimp, which are especially valuable to these guys."

"These guys are about to start blowing each other's heads off over shrimp?" The President was nearly yelling at his Chief of Staff.

"Not just any shrimp, sir. These include Tiger Prawn." Middleton shook his head, looking directly at his boss to ensure he understood his sarcasm.

"Fuck me," Mazur said, burying his face in his hands.

Middleton was taken aback, as the President rarely cursed. "We don't buy it, sir. According to our diplomats who are in touch with them, there has to be more going on here."

"Such as?"

"In the past the North has tried to make a power play toward these Islands, even going so far as shelling the main island back in 2010. A few people were killed and injured, you might remember, and it was a serious situation. We were all worried it would come to outright war between them.

"Well, now the South may be going tit for tat in trying to make a move toward some islands north of the border."

"Why would they do that?"

"No clue, sir. It makes no real sense, other than to stick it to the North. There has to be something else behind it. They wouldn't risk this politically, in their own country, nor in the support they get from the West, unless there was some compelling reason to provoke a response from the North. Our speech writers have that on their plate too. Their suggestion for sharp remarks directed at the South will be on your desk before lunch."

"Good. You read my mind Jeff, as always. Let Tillman know I want to talk about that situation when we get together later." Kendra Tillman was the Secretary of State, a very busy woman.

"What other stink piles would you like to talk about?"

"Well, there's a mess a-brewing in Eastern Europe, in one of the former Soviet republics, but this will not be our problem."

"What's the latest there?"

"In addition to all the problems in the North Caucasus region that the Russians have been dealing with, there have been some recent incursions in Azerbaijan. Azerbaijan is mostly Muslim, and one of the more modern Muslim countries in that part of the world. It also happens to be rich in oil and gas reserves, which of course makes it the prettiest ugly girl at the dance. Lately it appears to be attracting some attention in the form of bombings on some of the holiest Islamic sites. With Armenia nearby, a traditionally Christian country, Muslim eyes are pointed on their neighbor to the East. So far it's localized bombs that are meant to kill, maim, and provoke tensions. It's working, and we're watching it."

"Are you sure this is Russia's problem and not ours?"

"Well, no sir, not entirely," Middleton answered, "but for now it's way down there on our list of priorities."

"What else do we have to talk about?"

"There is a World War about to break out in the Middle East, but I think you know all about that."

"How could I forget it?" The President's staff had been up late into the evening trying to broker peace between Israel and Syria, with Iran and Russia making their displeasure known about Israel's unfair aggression toward their ally.

"Are we nearly done?" The President appeared on the edge of his seat, an old man in need of a toilet visit.

"Almost, sir. Our neighbors to the North are causing us some unwelcome agitation. Evidently they're threatening an embargo on Canadian beer unless we get a little more lenient on allowing them access to our premium cable channels, especially the soft-core porn ones."

The President flopped back in his chair. "Are you serious?"

"No sir. I thought you could use a little humor this morning. I'll be leaving now."

"Hello, Father." Ellen Grandby Sullivan lounged on an ornate divan in the living room of her upscale condominium in a Boston high rise. Her fingers lightly held a glass of Moscato. A large TV was tuned to CNN. The sound was muted as correspondents reported on escalating tensions and death tolls rising in some of the most unlikely places.

"Things are really heating up. These pinheads on TV are saying how there's never been a time when so much turmoil was going on simultaneously, how it's happening all it once as if by coincidence."

"It's astonishing they've noticed."

"It reminds me of the movie 'Ghostbusters' where all the evil comes poring out of the sewers."

"I remember the movie," the senior Reverend answered, "but the opposite is true here. These are good spirits chasing out the evil that's bottled up inside people. What you see happening is catalysis, a reaction that is being hastened but which would occur anyway. Instead of happening over years and even decades, they're happening all at once."

"The number of lives lost ..." Ellen was speaking as much to the large flat screen TV in front of her as she was to her father on the phone.

"It is enormous," he said, "and growing by the day. Ellen, my love, I need to remind of you of the bigger picture. Imagine the impact of these events beyond this world."

She broke from her concentration, taken in by his words. "You're right, Father. I can't imagine how all these souls can be accommodated."

"There have been times in our world's history where great numbers of lives have been lost in a short time," he said calmly, "but at the current rate, and given the broad nature of these conflicts, the ascension of souls will soon be unprecedented.

"Speaking of all this," he continued, "have you been in touch with your colleague in the upper regions?"

"Immat? Not lately. I've tried a few times but I can't reach him."

"I suppose he's adjusting to his reclaimed role. It will take time. Don't push too hard, but do keeping trying. We have an arrangement."

"Can we really count on his cooperation?"

"Absolutely. He understands that what we are doing is for the betterment of all of humanity. There's no turning back. Very soon, the number of souls requiring placement will be a torrent. Without us it will be chaos. He needs us, and he knows it."

Collaboration

Henry gasped. "Oh ... Yes, hello," he said unevenly into his phone.

Lacey and Lafarge snapped their heads in his direction.

"Is everything okay, Henry?" Lacey was looking at Henry through narrow eyes, signaling Henry not to give anything important away to the church's large security guard.

"It's fine, but I need to take this call in private," Henry said to the two men. Then he spoke into the phone, "Sir can you hold on for just a minute?"

"There's a little conference room through that door, then on the left." Lafarge pointed to the door they came in.

When he was out of range from the two other men, Henry's voice was hushed but urgent.

"Mister Harding, thanks for returning my call. Do you remember me?"

"Of course I remember you, Henry. You were Dee's friend, the one that Lars didn't trust."

"That's right. As it turns out, I'm the one you should have been trusting."

"Where is Dee? What happened to her? She hasn't responded to any contacts by me or anyone else."

"She's missing," Henry said. "She never came back from the church with Lars. I'm with the police right now at the church, looking through their surveillance tapes."

"Look Henry," Harding said, "we all felt bad about the way we treated you. When you feel like you're being hunted down, sometimes politeness goes out the window. The question I have is, how did you find me?"

Henry explained about the cryptic note he found from Dee, and his methodical way of trying until he found the Winfred who lived at a street address that began with 424.

Henry remembered him as a thoughtful, intelligent man who did not say much, but when he spoke people listened. He was African-American, probably in his late thirties. He had a slender frame and wire-rimmed glasses. During the meeting he was mostly preoccupied with making sure everyone was comfortable and that there were no unwelcome observers or eavesdroppers while he was the host.

"Impressive. I guess you were meant to be a detective. I could tell from your message hat her disappearance has you upset."

"That's right," Henry said somberly. "No sign of her leaving these premises, so far anyway. Has anyone heard from Lars?"

"Nope," he answered. "I think we should bring the group together to talk about this. Who knows, maybe he'll show up."

"I wouldn't count on that," Henry replied.

"What a piece of shit," Harding hissed. "We should've known from the way he treated you that he was hiding something. We've never treated anyone that way. It was appalling."

"It's history," Henry answered. "What is not history is that we have a great friend who is in trouble. We need to work together to somehow find her. I imagine your other members are pretty spooked now."

"Agreed," Winfred said firmly. "Rather than pull together the whole group, I'd suggest we pull together just the senior members into a small meeting, then decide where to go from there. What do you suggest?" Henry's exhaustion was audible.

"Wait for my contact. We'll meet at my house. You have the address. I need to contact the others to make sure they can make it. I'll let you know when."

When Henry returned to the church's control room, the lights were on and Lacey was carefully looking through the guest book.

"Just in time, Henry. I'm looking for a needle in a haystack with all these names. Would you mind looking through and seeing if you recognize any?"

Henry settled into the chair next to Lacey. Lafarge was standing a few feet away, his imposing presence meant to send a message to the two visitors.

Henry methodically went through the list of names. Evidently it was a custom for all visitors to sign into the guest book, as there were many hundreds of names from the morning. Henry remembered a queue behind the Reverend when he attended one of the services from a few weeks before.

He viewed name after name in the book, not recognizing any. When he turned the page to the last page for the day, the name on the top row jumped out at him.

Joan Swenson, signed in perfect cursive. Henry moved down the list as if they were all strangers.

"Nothing?" Lacey gestured as if to leave.

"Nothing. Sorry."

"Thank you for your time, Stan. We'll be back in touch soon."

When they were in the parking lot, Henry spoke discreetly to Lacey in the likely event that cameras were on them.

"I didn't want to mention it in there, but I saw a very familiar name."

"Tell me about it," Lacey replied nonchalantly.

"Her name is Joan Swenson. She was a client of mine who came in for a reading for her dad. It was uneventful, a pleasant visitation actually. Remember when I told you about a friend who had seen the video of the Dalai Lama being held captive and roughed up? It was Joan that tipped us off to that. She was also a friend of Donnelly's widow. I'm guessing she wishes she could get out of this church and never return, but she probably doesn't dare to."

Lacey listened intently to Henry while unlocking his sedan. "Have you tried to contact her lately?"

"Oh God no," Henry answered. "I didn't want to do anything to put her in harm's way."

"This is information that would have been helpful a few weeks ago, Henry." Lacey cast him a cold look. "She sounds like someone I need to speak with."

Henry easily found Winfred's house on a quiet suburban street in Dorchester. He rang the doorbell and paced, looking up and down the street for anyone who might be watching the home. He saw no one.

The door opened with a whoosh. "Hello again, Henry. I didn't introduce myself the first time we met. I'm Winfred Harding."

Harding was thin and fit with a strong hand shake. His eyes were more intense than Henry remembered. He guessed he was in the academic world, or perhaps the sciences.

Harding invited Henry in. The living room was small but inviting. He recognized each of the other three people in the room from their earlier meeting.

"This is Richard Shoemaker." He was one of the few to speak up a few weeks before. He was in his fifties, gangly with unkempt hair, the look of a professor. Henry remembered him talking about how at least some of the Origenists were continually on the run from their unknown aggressors, even to the point of changing addresses. He offered a consoling smile as he shook Henry's hand.

"I'd like you to meet Rachel Foster," Harding said as he led Henry to a woman sitting on a sofa. She was attractive in her middle years, with smooth skin and round, brown eyes. Henry also remembered her as one who had spoken up previously. He appreciated her candor in explaining how lost they felt after Herbrit was killed. She was the one, he recalled, who asked him to stop being a 'pious asshole' and focus on convincing them he would not get them all killed.

He smiled as he took her hand. "Good to meet you, Rachel, under slightly less tense circumstances." She nodded in return.

"Finally I'd like you to meet Naomi Pike." Seated next to Rachel, Naomi was an athletic-looking woman in her thirties. She had a darker complexion, her black hair in braids. Henry did not recall hearing her speak but remembered her piercing gaze.

"Nice to meet you," Naomi said with a smile. "Sorry that our first meeting sucked so much."

Henry laughed as he shook her hand gently. "Me too, but that's in the past. I'd prefer to talk about where we go from here."

Winfred invited Henry to sit, offering a drink. Henry declined.

"So can you bring us up to date on what you know?" Richard Shoemaker sat as he sipped a drink. "Dee and Lars never returned from church. That was days ago."

Henry filled in the group on his conversation with Dee before she reluctantly decided to attend, and his visit back to the church with Lacey. He described what they saw on the church's security tapes, how they both entered the church offices but neither appeared to leave. The Origenists were quiet as he spoke.

"I sincerely apologize if this offends any of you," Henry said slowly and evenly, "but it's hard for me to imagine that Dee disappeared without some cooperation by Lars."

"Look, Lars treated you poorly," Richard replied quickly, as if to chase the thought from Henry's head, "but you can't let that get in the way of facts. Lars was and is an important part of our group. He's fought for us, and he's been a primary contributor to some of the important decisions we've made recently."

"How long have you guys been together?" Henry looked in the direction of Rachel as he posed the question.

"Almost ten years. It started as an online blog with people from all over the country and even internationally, and we decided to get together in the Boston area when we realized how many of us are here."

"How long has Lars been a part of the group?"

"Maybe a couple years," Rachel said. "He was a late arrival. I think he found us online and expressed an interest. He seemed sincere, asked the right questions, and we had no reason to question his motives."

"Is that unusual? How many others have joined in the last few years?"

"Not too unusual," Richard replied. "There has been some growth in the last few years, although we play down the online presence lately. It's too dangerous. Naomi joined just before Lars did."

Henry turned toward Naomi. "What was the experience like getting in with these guys?"

"It was hard to find them," she laughed. "They were a secretive bunch. I think it was somebody on the web site from another city that told me about a group of Bostonians who get together. Once I found them, they were really welcoming, but it wasn't easy getting in."

"How did Lars find you guys?"

"The same way I did, I think," Naomi said. "He came in right after me. I assume he saw my inquiries, and followed the same trail as me."

"So Henry," Richard asked, "aside from your unpleasant experience with Lars, why are you so convinced that he isn't in trouble too?"

"I'm a medium," Henry said dryly. "Dead people tell me things."

"Seriously?" Richard looked at him doubtfully.

"No," Henry answered, smiling. "That was too easy. One thing that convinced me was his body language in the surveillance video I saw at the church. He seemed very at ease, even though both of them should have been very much on their guard. Dee looked on edge as you'd expect, like she didn't really want to be there. It appeared that Lars talked her into going into the church office because he was comfortable there.

"Then, once they were in there," Henry continued, "he disappeared down the hall. Lacey figured he was just going to the bathroom, but who does that when they're nervous about being someplace?"

Rachel spoke. "What do you know about this detective?"

"Detective Oliver Lacey of the Waltham Police Department is the guy who investigated John Donnelly's death. I contacted him about Dee's disappearance. It's taken him a while to become interested, but he seems determined to figure out what's going on. I've been keeping him informed about all this, and I'm guessing the church considers him a pain in the ass right about now. I told him that I saw Joan Swenson's name on the guest list. She was the one who told me about the Dalai Lama tape and I passed that info along to Lacey."

"I think I can speak for the group," Richard offered, "when I say that we have no interest in speaking with the police. We have nothing important to tell them. Plus we have an agreement among our group that we'll keep our private lives private, even from each other. The less we know about each other the better. I know that probably seems odd to you, Henry, but it's not about each of us. It's about our faith in the early teachings of the Christian church."

"I can respect that," Henry said, "but in times like these, it doesn't offer you much protection from forces outside your group."

"That may be," Rachel replied, "but it's the path we've chosen."

"Well, this has been a lovely visit," Henry said, standing up and stretching, "but is there anywhere to go from here? If you guys are going to continue to hide away, then I guess I'm just relying on Lacey."

"I'm not sure we have much of a choice," Richard answered. "If Lars manipulated Dee into this situation as you claim, I suppose we could call a general meeting and hope that Lars shows up, but what are the chances of that? If he did have something to do with her disappearance he would want us to believe he's in trouble too. I doubt there's anything we can do to draw him out of hiding."

Henry sat down again as the group quietly considered their options. Each of the four people in the room were in the same suspended state of mind, thinking but saying nothing. Finally there was a deep inhale that came from Naomi.

"I might have something," she said quietly.

"What is it, Naomi?" Richard asked through tired eyes.

"We dated briefly," she said. "I've been to his apartment."

In this ethereal plane, an exquisite dimension where time and space were defined in ways that would be incomprehensible to souls on earth, all the important decisions of the lifetime were meticulously examined. The entirety of a lifetime was viewed objectively, with the help of the spirit who guided the soul through the life and all the souls who made up the inner circle.

This inner circle could be thought of as the soul's closest family, although during lifetimes they were not always blood relatives. They could be best friends as children or adults, or they could be spouses. All in each of the many circles were also going through a period of examination, healing, and learning. It was the ultimate support group.

During the soul's respite period, decisions made during the last lifetime were compared with their outcomes in the great quilt that made up the soul's persistent state of being, across many lives. One seemingly inconsequential decision made while the soul was young and naive could have long lasting implications that would unfold not only in the life of the one before Hildegarde, but in the lives of other nearby souls. Sometimes these adjacent souls were in the inner circle of her subject, while other times the impacts were to souls who the subject barely knew.

Souls who were employers, deciding between prospective employees, exerted a huge influence on lives of people in their decisions to hire. The acquisition of a job, or continued rejection by employers, could completely change the direction of a person's life. A decision to pour another drink for someone who was already beyond his limit could lead to the death of an innocent victim who may have been the main caregiver for a child. If the child who was at a key juncture in life, the child's life could lose direction, just by the pouring of a single drink. A mother troubled by the mood of her daughter as she was leaving for work decides to turn around halfway to her destination. Her daughter was only minutes from packing and running away or worse, taking her life.

Too often, while in the earthly plane, the impact of decisions could not be viewed in entirety. Only in this place of comfort and reflection could the full range of decisions and actions be completely assessed, both for their positive and negative effects. The process of sorting through these decisions was painful and tedious. Not all souls had the courage to examine the most difficult decisions, and it was the spirit guide's challenge to encourage a thorough life review. The individual soul was to decide how much they wished to learn from the life just lived.

Each person that came before Hildegarde was like a new morning. The soul had been in a relaxing state of contemplation over its most recent triumphs and failures. By the time it reached her, it was ready for change. Only the individual could decide when this restorative period was complete, but by the time it met a Principality like Hildegarde, it was ready for a new roller coaster ride.

She would begin by reviewing with the soul the lessons gleaned from the rest period. Each set of lessons and learnings she read were new, unique to the soul before her. She would absorb the lessons as if they were her own, eagerly connecting these recent, often difficult experiences, to more successful, rewarding experiences in the next life.

After all, she had been through this process herself many times. Some of the choices she had made about lives to live were brilliantly appropriate. Others proved frustrating, not nearly as useful as she had hoped. No lifetime was a waste of time, she came to appreciate, but some offered more opportunities for advancement than others. It was her job to leverage her experience of a few hundred lifetimes into the best choice for her student from the array that Immat placed before them.

For the soul in the seat of decision, it was an exciting time with enormous implications. This one choice would lead to so many thousands of future decisions that could have ripple effects on so many other lives. Hildegarde expected the person to be bursting with the possibilities ahead. As she gained experience and confidence, she understood that one important aspect of her role was to encourage excitement and passion. She became a motherly guiding force, explaining the life choices while exploring all the things that could go right and wrong in each life, and the hard choices that may lay ahead for the person in that position.

On one occasion, a soul named Charu came before her. She immediately sensed a lack of enthusiasm from this spirit, who otherwise seemed completely peaceful, calm, and fully healed from past lives.

"You seem a bit tentative about the possible lifetimes before you, and I haven't even gone through all the details yet! Are you sure you are ready for this next step?"

"Oh yes," insisted Charu. "I'm ready. It's just that some of the hurdles that I'm sure are ahead of me are things that I dealt with in past lives. I entered into those circumstances with the full intention of conquering them, but it simply didn't happen."

Hildegarde knew that some of these limitations tended to be self-induced, the result of the soul's inclination to take on more challenges than it could realistically address in a single lifetime.

"I see that one of your goals is to become a better teacher and mentor," she offered. "It looks like you had some dissatisfaction with the level of patience you showed to younger people around you. I noticed that you've tended to take on life circumstances that are rather ambitious. In a recent life you were the owner of a manufacturing plant. In another you were a professor at a university in India. You don't have to be a top achiever in order to be an effective mentor and teacher. Most of the lives before you offer plenty of opportunities to share wisdom. Let's keep things simple, shall we?"

Hildegarde reviewed the life possibilities that were made available by Immat, and they worked together to choose a life that would offer the ability to focus on the achievement of others instead of Charu's. Together they agreed on a life that would lead her to the life of a language teacher in South Africa. The country would have an influx of immigrants from all around Africa during the time Charu selected and as a female language teacher in a humble setting, she would have the opportunity to teach and mentor, and to see the impacts of her work. She would not only teach language skills, but guide the immigrants as they assimilated productively into South African society.

As a newer Principality, Hildegarde appreciated the chance to work with more experienced souls like Charu, who had been through several dozen lifetimes. The collective learnings from these lives provided her with a bedrock that was useful for younger, less experienced souls. Through this process, enriched by Hildegarde's loving, supportive mentoring, each soul was completely aware of the rewards and challenges that were possible in the lifetime ahead.

Immat was a master at bringing forth challenges that made the choices meaningful, both for the soul making the decision and for Hildegarde. For each life, Hildegarde depended heavily on Aisling to perform the important research about many of the details and circumstances that would affect these lives in unique ways. There was no way to predict the many possible twists and turns that would emerge with each life, but with the range of options made available by Immat and the contrasts and variables identified by Aisling, there was no shortage of information available for the soul to make his or her choice.

The majority who came before Hildegarde were newer souls who had experienced lives in humble surroundings, often without education or a solid support structure. Many had only lived lives in developing, poorer countries where the focus was spent on food and shelter, just staying alive. The opportunities for true spiritual growth in these circumstances were most commonly experienced from choosing to live as a parent. Organized systems, such as schools, businesses, and government, were rare. The many thousands of souls who existed in these circumstances lived out their lives with little contact with anyone or anything except the many souls around them. This population growth increased rapidly during the twentieth century due to a combination of improved treatments against disease and much-improved agricultural production. World population would soon grow from just over two billion people to levels that approached ten billion in less than a century.

This growth placed an immense strain on the ability of the earth to support such huge numbers, but it also created an unprecedented need to produce souls to fill these bodies.

Aisling, new in her role, could not help but wonder about the process of creating new souls.

"What can you tell me about where souls come from?" Aisling was ever the student, eager to collect whatever knowledge she could from this wise spirit.

"Is it time for our 'birds and bees' discussion, my dear?" Hildegarde asked as a mother would address her child. They both laughed. "I'm afraid I won't have much to explain to you. The production and cultivation of souls is performed far above this level, in ways that you and I could not possibly understand."

"Do you think the action is performed by the One True God?"

Hildegarde smiled. "I am guessing 'overseen by God' is probably a more apt description. God has willing servants to perform all kinds of tasks, just like the vital task we perform. The creation of souls is a highly important one, and I suppose God Himself is very close to how this occurs."

"But how is it even possible?"

"How is what possible?"

"How is it possible to create a soul from nothing? With such a staggering demand for meaningful souls to fill, how can God ensure uniqueness and meaning for each?"

"You underestimate divine power, my naive one. Uniqueness is easy. If you need proof, look no further than how life on earth is created. DNA consists of a series of nucleotides that in turn consist of one of four nucleobases. Using just those basic building blocks, humans are able to mix their genetic structures with each other over and over to form an endless supply of unique humans. The chances of two unrelated humans having the same genetic structures is nearly impossible. The more human population grows, the more remote are the chances that any two are alike, except for identical twins of course."

"My opinion," Hildegarde suggested gently, "is that the DNA model was based on a much more complex model that is used above to produce unique souls."

Aisling considered this hunch, eyes staring widely into space.

"The challenge," she continued, "is not in producing unique souls, or unique bodies to serve as their hosts. The challenge is in keeping up, one with the other, to maintain a world where there are enough experienced, wise souls who are positioned to positively influence the less experienced souls."

"So what you're saying," Aisling tried, "is that because humans have been mating with such urgency for the past century or so, the maturity of the souls we work with here on this level is bound to be, shall we way, watered down over time."

"That's certainly one way to phrase it," Hildegarde said with a smile. "However it came about, it is our challenge to make the best of this inevitability."

"Even in the short while I've been here," Aisling said, "I've noticed that mature souls are a rare commodity indeed."

"As I said, this was inevitable. The rapid growth of the human species into the twenty-first century makes our job - yours and mine, and Immat's - incredibly vital to future life on earth."

Aisling was beginning to understand the fast-changing dynamics of matching souls to life choices, paying closer attention to the maturity of the souls who came before them. It was rare when one did not have at least a handful of lives to draw experience from. When this was not the case, the choice of life opportunities presented by Immat were nearly always in very poor, simple circumstances. The soul would have clear opportunities for growth and development, but the ceiling was low. It would be very unusual for a man choosing a life in Congo, Mozambique, Afghanistan, Malawi, or Burundi to rise very far above his humble origins because opportunities for education were weak if they existed at all, and exposure to people outside the region was rarer still.

This did not mean there was not an abundance of lives that Immat could present for the soul's choosing. The variation would be in the culture and religion, and in the family or tribal support that was available. The more appealing, easier lives were those that offered more support, often where religious or cultural disputes were less a factor.

A stark reality for many of the newer souls who came before Hildegarde was that these represented the easiest path, or a relatively easy life compared to the majority. Most children born in this era would experience conflict in one form or another during the early years and the death of someone close to them, whether by disease or conflict.

Much of Aisling's energy was spent among these people, researching their cultures and environments, and most importantly the factors that would directly influence the specific lives that were being considered. Through her research she became expert at the most obscure living circumstances, such as a Hutu child growing up in rural Burundi, thrust into a life of harvesting coffee beans for a meager existence. An easier life would be one where this person or her mother were relatively healthy at birth. In these fortunate circumstances, the child might have an opportunity to grow to full adulthood, passing acquired wisdom to offspring.

Aisling's job was to dwell in the vicinity of expectant women as their children were nearing entry into the world. She could gather an immense amount of information about earthly surroundings in just a little time, in relative terms. Her mission was to understand potential dangers as well as opportunities. She would gather meticulous notes about circumstances this life would present, including the presence of a strong male figure, the cultural constraints that might exist, the place of women in the local society and family, the influence of the religious structure on the family, and the dynamics of religions or tribes that co-existed nearby.

Being a spirit from a higher realm meant that Aisling had the benefit of knowing things that even the prospective family might not know, such as whether the mother or other close spirits would be inflicted with HIV or other infectious diseases, how likely the mother was to give the child up for adoption, and even the likelihood that the pregnancy would be carried to full term.

Fears for the budding human were not limited to disease and poor nutrition. The threat of religious conflict was always present in some poorer countries without a stable government. A less structured society could subject females to a host of moral crimes in some harsher societies, including sex slavery.

There were favorable opportunities to consider as well. Some countries would see an increase in average income from their citizens through undeveloped or undiscovered natural resources. Others would benefit from a period of peace and political stability that could affect entire regions for a generation or more.

When a birth seemed viable and likely, Aisling would take detailed notes about the worldly circumstances above to Hildegarde and Immat. There the two considered the fit, whether the maturity of the soul was ready for the environment it was about to encounter. Their decisions were meant to always result in the right balance of challenge and ability to succeed. A life challenge that was too much for the soul's progression was not necessarily a failure if the soul advanced in its journey.

When a more mature soul came before Hildegarde, one who had lived at least three or four dozen lives, the life opportunities provided by Immat would predictably be richer, offering a more varied set of circumstances and challenges. A more mature soul was more capable of fully digesting all the advantages and disadvantages, as well as the distractions that could stand in the way of the original purposes that made the life appealing.

When Hildegarde and Aisling were new in their roles and in working with Immat, the array of lives for a mature soul would usually be dotted across cultures and countries. Each offered unique merits and challenges, but the variation was wide. Perhaps it was a matter of Immat becoming accustomed to the larger world and the many millions more lives to contend with, but it made the process more difficult.

Such variation in life options meant more detail for Aisling to uncover about varied cultures and regions, many of which had little in common. The experiences helped her grow and become more effective for each new research assignment. For Hildegarde, it meant covering a spectrum of each of these unique circumstances and presenting them in such a way that her customer could digest the possibilities. For the expecting human, more varied lives made the challenge of mapping lessons learned to new life possibilities far more difficult and time consuming.

A narrower range of lives made all of their jobs easier. As Immat settled into his position, he learned to make the process easier on all of them by refining these arrays of lives. Aisling was the first to notice because she had the busiest travel schedule. Moving between lives in the Middle East for subtleties at a very local level was far easier than bouncing from the Middle East to the middle of America to a mid-sized city in China, and then to ten or twelve locales that were just as diverse. The concentration of prospective lives in one area of the world allowed her to become more focused and proficient with those regions and cultures. For a given prospective soul for which Aisling was sent on a scouting mission, there would typically be eight or ten expectant mothers in one part of the world, and perhaps three or four that were mildly scattered elsewhere.

This array of about two-thirds of life opportunities that had much in common, plus another third that varied was about the right mix, Hildegarde and Aisling agreed. Hildegarde communicated this to Immat, although she did so while wondering whether he really cared what they thought. She received an acknowledgement from him this time, not verbally but in the form of dry consent.

"That," Hildegarde mentioned lightly to Aisling, "was the richest, most fulfilling conversation I've had with him in weeks."

"He is indeed a man of few words," Aisling replied, "but it does appear he's paying attention to our efforts."

Their period of settling in to their new roles was complete. They had found the right balance in their important work. The other Principalities and apprentices used the approach set forth by Hildegarde and Aisling in their work with Immat as a working model across this ethereal plane. Hildegarde and Aisling were commended by their guiding spirits for their innovative approach in working with Immat, the stodgy but valuable spirit that he was.

These halcyon days were not to last long. Their chemistry would soon be tested in ways that none of the three could imagine.

STEALTH

The rumpled detective emerged from his unmarked dark sedan, threw his cigarette to the curb, and exhaled deliberately while staring at the small house. It was near evening on a quiet street in Newton, just past the time when most of the neighborhood's working middle class would be finishing dinner.

He shuffled toward the front door, rechecked the address against a small book he kept in his coat, and rang the doorbell. After an uncomfortable wait, the door cracked open.

"Hello Ma'am. I'm Detective Oliver Lacey from the Waltham Police Department. Are you Miss Swenson?" He held out his badge.

"Mrs. Swenson," she said quietly.

"Can I speak with you, Mrs. Swenson?"

"What about?" She made no motion suggesting he was welcome to enter.

"I think we have a few things to talk about, Ma'am," he said firmly through the screen door, "starting with a death I'm investigating. A friend of yours I think, John Donnelly."

"Yes," she said clumsily, moving to open the door, "I suppose." She opened the door. As Lacey entered she turned toward the kitchen, removing an apron.

Her home was warm with a floral theme throughout. The home was Catholic-themed, with pictures of the Virgin Mary and images of Christ on the cross throughout.

"You're a Catholic. I was raised Catholic too," Lacey tried. "It's encouraging that the Church of the Tortured Christ accepted you anyway."

She coldly asked him to sit.

"Mrs. Swenson, is your husband at home? Should I be speaking with him as well?"

"My husband has been gone for years," she replied quietly. "It didn't work out."

"Sorry." Lacey allowed a proper pause before getting directly to the reason for his visit. "What was your connection to John Donnelly? How did you know him?"

"I know his wife through our church," she replied. "We became friends through some fundraising and after-service events. We just had a lot in common."

"Such as?"

"Well, our interest in the Church for one. As you pointed out, we both used to attend Catholic churches, and for various reasons we sort of drifted away. Then we found ourselves at the CTC, which offered some excitement, and more acceptance I guess. They weren't as judgmental about your past. They seemed more concerned with what's ahead."

"I'd like to talk a little more about what you two had in common." Lacey softened his tone. "Was your interest in mediums a part of that?"

She exhaled at first, looking down, embarrassed. Then she smiled and looked directly at the detective.

"Yes, that was definitely part of it, but Janice and I came up with that on our own. The church had nothing to do with that. She and John devised some kooky idea about trying to work through a medium to make sure their coming child would be especially gifted."

"And that's why he went to see Henry Chimera?"

"Yes, exactly. John made up some lie about learning his family's medical history. Obviously he didn't think the idea through very well. If he saw a legitimate medium, which Henry certainly appears to be, the medium would probably see through his lie and call him on it."

"Is that what happened?"

Her tone shifted. "I think so. They became friendly after that, so I think the truth about John's little scheme came out."

"So why do you think he was murdered, Mrs. Swenson?"

"I don't know anything about that, Detective. I ask myself that question all the time, and I don't have any answers."

"Do you think anyone at the Church would have a reason to want him dead?"

"No reason I can come up with. I can't imagine anyone at the Church putting that kind of harm on another person." She looked down at her hands with a distraught stare.

"I'd like to change the subject, and this one isn't pleasant either." Lacey shifted in his chair, moving to directly face her. Henry explained to me that you came upon a video of the Dalai Lama in a chair, being brutalized. Is that correct?"

Her head snapped up to look at him. After a pause she answered. "Yes, unfortunately."

"Please tell me about it. Every detail is important."

"I was just going through rooms looking for something and I came upon a video camera set up on a tripod. Out of curiosity I hit the play button, and I saw an image of a couple of big men surrounding this man who looked like the Dalai Lama."

"Why in the world wouldn't you come to the authorities with that information? You do realize the man is missing, correct?"

"I didn't know for sure it was the Dalai Lama. I thought it might be some sort of dramatization they might have made."

"For what possible purpose, Joan?" Lacey's tone was sharp as he leaned in.

"I'm not sure," she replied defiantly. "Maybe to draw modern comparisons to Christ's suffering?"

"Well, did you ask anyone at the Church about it?"

"Of course not. I wasn't even supposed to be there to see that. It wasn't my business. Besides, if I asked them about it, they might have chased me out of there."

"Who else did you tell about the video beside Henry? Janice Donnelly or any other acquaintances at the church?"

"No one. Not even Janice."

Lacey showed open doubt as he continued. "I find it a little implausible, Mrs. Swenson, that you would hold something like that back from the person who was your best friend in the church."

"I didn't want to put her in an even more difficult position. She's preparing to have a child, and she's still mourning the death of her husband. She needs the church right now."

"But you shared it with a medium who you had just recently met?" Lacey gave her an exaggerated, doubtful stare.

Joan Swenson looked back fiercely at Lacey as she answered. "Look Detective, when my husband left me, I chose to distance myself from the friends in my old church that I had built up over a number of years. I have aging parents and no one else I'm close with in my family. Henry is the one person I've met who can see things that others can't and who avoids judgment about the things people tell him. Of all people, he's the one who really understands that you can't get away with big lies for very long. You can fool the people around you, but the forces around us who might influence our ideas and actions, they're not easily deceived. Anyone who ignores the unseen is a fool. John Donnelly learned that."

"Do you think that was one of the reasons he was murdered?"

"Maybe," she answered slowly and thoughtfully. "I really don't know the answer to that question, Detective, but I suppose it's possible."

Lacey's phone rang. He stood quickly. "Excuse me Mrs. Swenson, I'd better take this." He turned his back on her as he walked into her dining room.

"Lacey," he answered into the phone in a deep, quiet voice. "What's up?"

"We have a 910 just off Main that you should know about," the male voice said.

"So? You don't have anyone else who can respond to a B and E?"

"This ain't your normal burglary. I think you know this guy."

The three drove west in Henry's small sedan, from Boston through the Back Bay area out Brighton Avenue as it crossed the Charles River and turned into North Beacon Street. It was nearly dusk on a cool May evening. Naomi Pike was in the front seat providing directions. Winfred Harding was in the back. They passed a cemetery, and as they approached Newton Street, Naomi spoke.

"This is it. Take a left."

Henry turned into a residential area with some single family homes, but mostly small apartment buildings. He drove slowly, allowing Naomi a chance to gain her bearings.

"Turn left here." Henry veered onto Barton Street.

"That's it!" She pointed to a multilevel apartment building on the right.

Henry drove slowly past the building as they inspected it from the street. There were a handful of cars in the lot on the side, and about half the windows were illuminated. It appeared large enough to accommodate about six apartments, but about half the building was dark. Henry parked about a block away, out of sight from the building.

They walked slowly toward the building, allowing darkness to fully descend on their approach. As they came near enough to see the building's details, Naomi stepped forward.

"His apartment is on the left, second floor. I think he had half the floor."

"It's dark," Winfred said.

"Not only that," Henry said, "but the one below it is dark."

"What's your point?" Winfred asked as if he had his own ideas about their approach.

"See that fire ladder heading up the side? It wouldn't be difficult to at least see if one of the side windows is open."

"You cannot be serious," Naomi protested. "Busting into his apartment is not what we talked about."

"Well, we didn't really go into detail about what would happen if he wasn't here," Henry replied calmly. "I wasn't really worried about that. I was more worried about what would happen if he was here."

"I'm up for it," Winfred said. "I mean, we could find the building manager, if he lives on premises, but he might not. Besides, what would we ask him? 'Is the guy in 2A here?' Obviously not. Then we're done for the night?"

"Exactly," Henry said, "plus if he does live here, he certainly wouldn't let us into Lars' apartment."

"We could at least find out his last name," Naomi replied sharply.

"That's worth the trip out here? To find out his last name? The cops can do that, but the cops may or may not be able to get inside. We can." Henry was rigid as he looked at the building, gearing for a mission.

"I understand your concern, Naomi. You should stay down here on the ground, close to the window. Be ready to signal us if we need to get out of there."

Henry moved toward shadows in a path toward the foot of the fire escape that led to Lars' window. Winfred and Naomi followed. He put both hands on the ladder, testing it for its ability to support their weight. He turned to Winfred.

"I think it's strong enough for at least one person going up, but I'm not sure about two. How about if I climb up to see if I can get the window open. If I can get inside, you can follow me up." Winfred nodded.

Henry slowly climbed the ladder, attempting to avoid any sound that would draw attention to his incursion. Winfred held the ladder in place from the bottom.

As he neared the top, one window was directly to his right. There was a short ledge about three feet below the window, meant for temporary footing in the event of a fire. The ledge moved under the ladder to another window a few feet to the left. It appeared Henry would have two windows to try.

He carefully moved himself in place to try the nearest. With one hand on the ladder and both feet on the ledge, his right hand was free to exert leverage on the window. If this window opened and was not securely locked, he had a reasonable chance of getting in. These were probably not the original windows. That gave him some hope that the window was not warped permanently into place.

He gave it an initial shove upwards, but there was no movement. He ran his fingers along the top to make sure it was not painted shut, but it appeared to be a functioning window that was just securely locked.

"No luck," he whispered below to the two accomplices watching his maneuvering.

The second window was far enough away from the ladder that he would not be able to maintain a grip for leverage. He would be scaling the wall laterally, but only for about five feet.

He moved across the ladder and to the left. As he shuffled along the ledge, he made sure that his footing was evenly balanced between both feet. He was able to lean in toward the building and move his feet side to side. The exterior of the house was wood frame, which allowed him to exert upward pressure with his hands. This created a vice effect, and allowed him to confidently use one hand to work on the window.

With his left hand he grabbed the middle of the window while reestablishing his position for an upward push. With one hand anchored on a horizontal wood plank and two feet firmly on the ledge, he gave the window a shove. It moved open a few inches. It wasn't locked! He calmly moved toward the center of the window, with his fingers under the window and inside the apartment. He turned each hand sideways, exerting even pressure on both sides of the window. It slid open easily, and he opened it up wide enough to crawl inside.

First he moved his head inside the apartment, all senses peaked. It smelled musty, and there was no movement. It was dark, but streetlights offered some visibility. He climbed in.

The apartment was barely furnished, with only a few tables, a small couch, and two hard-backed chairs. He paused and stayed still to ensure he was not missing someone hiding, but the stillness and musky smell was a sure sign there was no one else in apartment. He walked toward the window nearest to the ladder. The wooden floors creaked quietly as he walked. He unlatched the window and slid it open easily.

As he stuck his head out to give them the okay to rise, he saw Naomi halfway up the ladder. "I thought you'd be our lookout," he whispered.

"I'm already an accomplice," she said back. "Too late."

When all three were in the apartment, they began to look around in the dark. They opened curtains to allow streetlight in while they rummaged through drawers, on flat surfaces, under beds, around appliances, and in closets. They were careful to step softly, but the wooden floors creaked with many of their steps. Henry dismissed this as worth the risk, especially considering that the apartment underneath was empty.

"It's like he planned to leave," Naomi finally said.

"There are no plants here," Henry answered. "No food in the fridge. No clothes. Did it look like this when you were here?"

"There was a little more here. It looked lived in, at least."

"It's probably a furnished apartment," Henry said, "and this is probably what it looked like before he moved in."

Henry took a small pen-sized flashlight from his shirt pocket. Shielding the glare from the windows, he began to look behind furniture for anything that might be left behind. He scoured along the floor boards, under the desk, under the bed, and behind and under the couch, not finding anything.

Then he moved to the kitchen. He noticed that the refrigerator was wedged tightly between cut Formica counter tops, leaving only a quarter inch on each side of the appliance. He used his light to look on the floor on each side. He saw a small scrap of paper just an inch or two from the front corner of the refrigerator. He slide the thin light between the surfaces and pulled it out. There was writing on one side.

"Well, this appears to have been a pointless mission," Winfred said from the dining room.

"Not necessarily," Henry replied. Naomi and Winfred walked to his side. Henry shined a light on it, looking closely. "Bosom Bay - 7/14 - ES, JD, JS."

"Any idea what that means?" Winfred directed the question to Naomi.

"A meeting place and time, and who he's meeting," Henry said. "I assume ES is Ellen Grandby Sullivan. So I think we have something."

"And the rest?"

Henry jumped in. "We'll try to figure it out later. Let's get out of here."

They started to move toward the window. "I think we can make a reasonable conclusion that Lars was part of Dee's disappearance," Henry said. "He's in with the church."

"Shouldn't we go to the cops with this?" Naomi directed the question to Henry.

"I'm not sure how much they'd do with it, considering they seem to have done nothing with the info we gave them on the Dalai Lama video."

Winfred had one leg out the window when the door flew open. There were flashlights in their faces and voices shouting.

"Get down on the floor! Hands on your head!"

Henry and Naomi dropped to the floor in compliance. Winfred, in an awkward position halfway out the window, first raised his hands then rolled to the floor next to Henry, who was already on his knees with his arms up.

"It looks like they came to us," Henry muttered into the floor.

There were two uniformed police followed by a small bald man, the building manager. He flipped on a light switch, which exposed and humiliated the three as nothing more than burglars caught in the act.

"Names." The first officer shined a light in each of their faces, still blinding, as they gave their first and last names.

"Let me see some identification, first from you."

Henry reached into his pocket and pulled a driver's license from his wallet, then handed it to him.

"I left my purse in the car," Naomi explained.

"My wallet is out there too," Winfred followed.

"What the hell are you three doing in here?" The second cop stepped in front of them.

"We were just leaving, actually." Henry was hoping to lighten the mood.

"Well, I guess you didn't leave soon enough, did you?"

Henry looked at the badge of the officer. "Murkowski" and "Waltham Police" were the inscriptions.

"We were looking for a former occupant of this apartment," Henry said.

"For what purpose?"

"We think he's involved in the disappearance of a mutual friend."

"So you're interfering with an active investigation, the second policeman said. "Did you think that a missing person should be reported to the police, and that the police would investigate the crime? Since, you know, that is the JOB of police, to investigate crimes and all."

"Look, I'm embarrassed by this," Henry said meekly, "but my colleagues and I have been the subjects of some recent threats lately, and there's only so long that you can wait for an investigation to play out. At some point you decide you're a target waiting to become a victim, and you get tired of sitting around. I admit, this was a dumb idea that did nothing but expose the three of us. But if you were in our position, you would have done the same thing."

"I highly doubt that," said Murkowski. "If you feel your life is in danger, you can ask for help. By breaking into someone's apartment you're asking for trouble, and now you have it."

"I understand that what we did is considered 'breaking in' to the apartment," Henry said, " but the window was open. We didn't damage the window." He looked directly at the Building Manager.

"From your badge, Officer, I gather we're in Waltham?"

"Correct," replied Murkowski.

"It so happens that Oliver Lacey is the detective investigating her disappearance, and I know he works here in Waltham. Can I ask you to give him a call? He knows me."

"Lacey? Oh, this just gets better and better. Stay put."

Murkowski pulled out a mobile phone and found a stored number. The detective answered.

"We have a 910 just off Main that you should know about," Murkowski said.

After a pause, he replied into the phone. "This isn't your normal burglary. This guys says he knows you. Henry Chimera. He says he's been talking to you about a disappearance?"

Murkowski ended the call and turned to Henry. "If you're thinking Lacey is coming to save you guys, prepare to be disappointed. He sounds pissed."

The three sat in silence while they waited for Lacey. Murkowski took a seat at the table with the building manager, completing paperwork. The second officer stood between the three suspects and the door.

Within fifteen minutes Lacey arrived. He glared at Henry. "Decided to take things into your own hands, I see."

"Not exactly, Detective. We just wanted to learn what we could about this guy. We meant no harm."

"Yeah, I hear that a lot, usually from idiots who just did harm."

Murkowski filled the detective in on the events of the evening.

Lacey looked toward Henry. "Your friends here, they're part of this group you've been telling me about?"

Henry avoided eye contact with Naomi and Winfred. "Yes, they're concerned about her too, and anxious to know exactly what Lars' involvement was. It's not just me, Detective. These guys feel like someone is trying to exterminate them."

"I understand that, Henry, but here's the thing. If you're going to continue to do stupid things like this, why exactly would I try to help you and your friends? At some point it becomes obvious that you're the one I should be keeping an eye on."

"I thought I could find something out about Lars that you wouldn't be able to, Detective. It was dumb."

Henry turned toward the building manager standing in the next room. "We meant no harm, sir. I hope you might consider forgetting this whole thing."

Lacey ignored Henry's gesture. "So did you find anything in this little amateur sleuth operation of yours?"

"We did, actually." Henry reached into his pocket to pull out the scrap of paper. "I found this under the fridge." Naomi and Winfred stared at Henry, saying nothing. Henry handed it to Lacey.

"Looks like plans for a rendezvous. I assume 'EGS' is Reverend Sullivan. Any idea who the others are?"

"Not at the moment," Henry replied. "Maybe JD is Janice Donnelly?"

"Maybe," Lacey replied. "You know what's unfortunate, Henry? What's unfortunate is that it'll be really hard for me to take any action with this scrap of paper."

"Why the hell is that? Because we got it by coming in through the window?"

"Exactly. You say you found it in here but who's to say you didn't plant it?"

"You've got to be kidding me, Detective." Henry stared at him, disbelieving. "We did you a favor by finding it. We have information we didn't have before that might tell us where Dee is. Why the hell would we plant it?"

"I'm sure some attorney or my boss could come up with some reason why, and I wouldn't be able to say with complete certainty exactly what your motivations are. Maybe because you're hiding something yourself, and this is your way of deflecting attention. Did your friends here see you find the paper?"

He stared at Naomi and Winfred. Each looked at each other, saying nothing.

"See, Henry? Even your friends don't know if you planted it.

"From this little stunt, it's obvious we're not really working together, isn't it? As far as doing me a favor, a *favor* would have been coming to me with this information so that we had a chance to find this, but you didn't do that, did you Henry?"

Henry took on a defiant tone. "My friends here have preferred to remain a little under the radar, Detective, as I explained. I'm sure you can appreciate when people feel like they're being targeted with little protection."

"Well, they won't exactly be under the radar with an arrest on their record, will they?"

The three looked at each other, then all looked back down toward the floor in unison.

Lacey walked over to the building manager, putting out his hand. "Detective Oliver Lacey."

"Irving Richards," said the man awkwardly, returning Lacey's handshake.

"Can I speak with you out here?"

They moved out into the hallway, Murkowski following, closing the door behind them.

The three sat silently for several moments, staring down. Finally Henry whispered to the other two, out of range of the police.

"Even if we pay, we found something that matters."

The door opened. Lacey and the Building Manager stepped into the room.

"Well, it might be your lucky day. Mr. Richards has generously agreed to avoid pressing charges, on one stipulation. If you ever come within 500 yards of this property, we'll nail you with being 'Peeping Toms,' which in the Commonwealth of Massachusetts means you would have to register as sex offenders. Are we clear that you'll never see this street or this building again?"

The three nodded in unison. "Very clear. Thank you Mr. Richards," Winfred said.

"Mr. Richards, how long ago did the last occupant of this apartment move out?"

"Just last week," the man replied.

"Was it sudden? Did you know he was leaving?"

"He gave me a couple weeks' notice. He was on a month to month lease, so he did what I asked him to."

"What kind of tenant was he?"

"Edgar was quiet, respectful. He paid the rent on time and never caused me any trouble."

"Did he leave a forwarding address?"

Henry loudly interrupted. "Excuse me, but did you say Edgar?"

"Yes, that's the name of the guy who lived here," Richards replied sharply. "Who were you looking for?"

"Oh for Christ's sake," Lacey said disgustedly. "Are you telling me you guys broke into the wrong place?"

"That's not possible," Naomi exclaimed. "The man who lived here's name was Lars. I've been in his apartment before. What did he look like?"

"Tall," the building manager answered. "Light hair, athletic build."

"A black earring in one ear?"

"Yeah, that sounds like the same guy," Richards said.

Lacey turned to Richards. "What was the name on the lease?"

"Edgar Grandby."

Henry stared at the man in disbelief. "*Grandby?*"

"You heard me," Richards said.

Henry's head whipped around to his two accomplices. "Our boy Lars is related to the Reverend herself!"

He turned to Lacey. "Is this enough 'probable cause' for you to search the church, Detective?"

"No doubt about it," Lacey replied.

THE MACHINERY OF LIFE

The province of Guizhou is nestled in the southern lands of the People's Republic of China. A hilly province with a subtropical climate, highly valued for its rich forests and accommodating wetlands, for centuries Guizhou has been the recipient of countless incursions by the dynasty of the times. Its proximity to the South China Sea to the Southeast and the border lands of what are now Laos, Myanmar, and Vietnam to the Southwest made it an appealing occupation zone for passing hordes.

The transitive history of Guizhou resulted in a local dialect that can be difficult to understand. Consequently, many outsiders consider its people less refined than neighboring provinces, although this reputation was mostly forced upon them. It is the home of more than thirty-five million living souls, and holds the distinction of being one of the poorest, least productive provinces in China. Its chief agricultural products are rice, corn, grain, coal and timber.

One of the larger cities in Guizhou is Liupanshui, with a population of about three million. Along with industrial and chemical plants, an important but modest source of income for its residents was in the tourist trade. Many locals made a living from hawking products from craftsmen in outlying areas to the many passersby on its busy streets.

In such a city, rich with cultural diversity, including many distinctive nationalities and folk cultures, it was rare when one child would stand out. Li Xia was such a child. From her earliest days, her mother described her as radiant and perceptive, with the profound ability to absorb her surroundings. Her waking hours provided energy that was easily missed when it was gone.

Her father would travel the local regions gathering unique trinkets and curiosities, while her mother would spend her days with her only child on a busy thoroughfare in the city, selling these wares to the business people, factory workers, and service workers who passed by. Li Xia and her mother, Liu Yang, were a common sight for the thousands who walked by on a weekly basis. Regular customers, who would chirp friendly greetings to the child, appreciated the wide variety of items for sale on their table. The selection was due to the industriousness and creativity of Wang Jie, their father and husband, who searched the countryside to find sale items that would stand out from the rest.

The small family made a tidy living, and the parents were deeply committed to the development of their extremely gifted child. They envisioned a day when the rest of the country, and indeed the world, would appreciate the rarest of gifts that God had bestowed upon them. They would not be the only ones to have great plans for this child.

Shortly after learning Miao, her native language, fluently by the age of two, she quickly moved on to absorbing the languages, mannerisms, and discourse habits of many others as well. She was in a unique position to do so, as she would witness with her own eyes and ears the mechanics of communication that were so broadly used by the diverse population who passed by their table daily. When she wasn't napping in the special carriage that doubled as a cargo hauler to and from the thoroughfare, she was alert and absorbing her surroundings.

As Li Xia approached her fourth birthday, Liu Yang spoke with her husband about enrolling the child into one of the more desirable schools in the province. It would be a great sacrifice for the family, not only monetarily but as a disruption to their day. After much discussion, the parents decided that a gifted flower like this must be given the best possible care.

Once in school, Li Xia's teachers noticed wisdom they had never seen in a child so young. It was not uncommon to have a child every few years that absorbed lessons much faster than the others. Li Xia was surely this, however her teachers were astounded at how quickly she could bring routine facts about history, language, or mathematics to a higher level. She had a knack for not only remembering the information presented, but for bringing the information to a higher level of understanding.

If her teachers explained the turbulent history that Guizhou had experienced through the centuries, Li Xia formed the conclusion that the province's location, as a stopover point between many more populous lands, was a key contributor to her people's current diversity. This explained the many cultures and languages they were so fortunate to call their own.

If her teachers explained the importance of coal and chemical production in the same lesson as their production of grains and corn, Li Xia would form wonderfully sound arguments on the importance of balancing the diverse industries in a way that would protect the province's inhabitants.

If her teachers explained the violent clashes between rioters and the PLA which was audible in the distance, Li Xia would press the teachers to learn what they were fighting about. Because the answers were filtered to avoid upsetting the other children, none seemed to satisfy her curiosity.

Throughout the city and eventually the province, word spread about Li Xia. On occasion her mother noticed that her table was the only one that received more refined visitors, but only in the hours that Li Xia was by her side. Some of these visitors seemed more interested in the girl than the items that were for sale. This made Liu Yang proud, but it is, after all, a mother's job to worry. She would allow the girl to engage with these strangers briefly, allowing them to see only glimpses of her brilliance and charm.

In the higher domain, the learning process was running smoothly. Hildegarde and Aisling felt the presence of eyes from higher places watching their progress as they learned and gained experience. As always, the scrutiny was loving and supportive, nonjudgmental, yet clearly the oversight was present.

Over time the great attention from above that was drawn to this new working arrangement was subsiding considerably. All depended on Immat, who had become very consistent in his delivery of life options for the souls who came before the Principalities. Hildegarde would regularly interact with her peers in the same role, learning from their experiences and sharing hers. Her level of confidence in his delivery grew with each soul who passed through.

Most of the life options received by Aisling from Immat were close enough together in region and culture that she could easily manage the research required for the soul to make a meaningful, informed choice. As had been the recent trend, many life options were narrowed into a specific region, culture, religion, or "class," as it was called. Other life options could be outliers that were slightly outside the primary class presented. Aisling found these outliers to be annoying and distracting at first, but more recently interesting and challenging because they provided some contrast for comparison soul. As long as the outliers remained a smaller fraction of the life scenarios or the prospect, they were manageable.

Aisling's knowledge of various regions, cultures, and religions was also growing massively. Hildegarde noticed, and complemented her frequently, on her deftness in understanding subtle differences in classes, and how they varied from category to category. These distinctions could be subtle but very meaningful to the soul who was pondering how to spend the next eighty or so years.

They even noticed a difference in Immat's demeanor. He was evolving in his role like a giant hermit crab, they teased, moving from shell to larger shell as he gained the social skills needed to peek outside his comfort zone now and then. In time he even began to give them helpful hints about the life classes he would present.

"Each offers a chance to travel, but in very different ways."

"Every one of these gives the choice of being a parent or not."

"Each allows the chance to become mechanically proficient."

During this time in the twenty-first century, mortals would typically die at the rate of about 100,000 per day, given the time's mix of natural life spans across countries. The formula adjusted upward constantly by exponential growth of the human population. Only occasionally were there spikes or troughs that represented periods of war or disease, but in the long run the growth would always resume.

Hildegarde and Aisling only worried about one soul at a time. They were more concerned with sequence and order rather than elapsed time, which had little meaning in this dimension. The number of souls entering versus exiting were watched by some in the heavens, but Hildegarde and Aisling could not say who these spirits were. Whoever they were, they had the burden of worrying about these numbers in order to benefit those choosing from among future lives.

This number of deaths per earthly day factored directly into the number of souls requiring a new life in a subsequent day. The powers above Immat, Hildegarde, and Aisling slowed the process down considerably during their apprenticeship, cycling it up gradually as they became more proficient. Whatever the pace, they managed to turn the process into an efficient and orderly selection of lives by souls ready for the next plunge.

Recently, they noticed, the numbers were changing. The number of life opportunities presented by Immat was no different, but the number of souls needing to find a new home body were increasing. This meant that their workload was increasing as well.

Hildegarde and Aisling initially attributed this increase to a continuation of their training period, but Aisling astutely pointed out that there were conflicts underlying nearly all the circumstances she discovered, especially in more developing societies. The increasing conflict on earth, resulting in the premature death of many thousands, was having a clear affect on pressures coming to bear on the delivery mechanism in the upper reaches.

As the pace picked up, the three spirits devoted their energies to their roles completely, and in increasingly efficient ways. Aisling observed that Immat was not alone in his work. In his delivery of life opportunities to Aisling, she noticed for the first time that there were countless angels transporting these profiles into her queue. They were always focused and positive, doing their busy work with joyous determination. They worried little about communication, focusing only on their function, so she gathered they were never part of the cycle of birth and rebirth. They were created to be angels devoted to a specific purpose, and this was where they happily remained.

While reviewing the learnings from recently passed lives, Aisling made a habit of comparing prior experiences to the possible lifetimes that awaited each. She was especially interested in the movements from one life to the next that were particularly in contrast with one another, as in the case of a soul who moved from a wealthy, privileged existence to a stark impoverished one, or vice versa.

She noticed that Immat tended to queue up lives that offered some continuity with the prior existence. As they moved from one life to the next, males tended to want to be males and females to be females, although this certainly was not a rule. Regions seemed to attract repeat performances by souls, and often the choice would be only a few towns or miles away from the most recent life.

Religion was another important factor in the life that was chosen. Souls tended to stay within religious environments most familiar, but that was not always the case. Immat offered opportunities to jump across the religious divide in the arrays presented. Some of the challenges were very appealing. A soul who seemed most comfortable and familiar with Christian lives might have six or eight varied, new Christian lives to choose from. Each would offer a reasonable amount of predictability, but they would be offered along with one or more Muslim lives in a reasonably comfortable setting. There would be other choices in the array as well, mostly among the more common - Buddhism, Hinduism, Judaism, Sikhism, Jainism, Shintoism - but also some that were prevalent in less common religions of the world too.

A sizable number of the lives recently lived, and the life scenarios under consideration, were for non-religious existences. The experience and contemplation over these lives was always exhilarating. Hildegarde noticed that many souls would consider a life of strict religion as a burden, while others would consider it a blessing. Some souls who had lived an agnostic or atheist life would want to try one of the less stringent religions, although few would jump to a more formal religious existence, fearing the stark change and how they would react to it.

At the end of one long day, as Hildegarde and Aisling were relaxing and reflecting on their experiences, Hildegarde offered an interesting question.

"Have you noticed," she asked, "the tendency for more experienced souls to choose more religious lives, and for the newer souls to be a little more adventurous in their next life choice?"

"I suppose so," Aisling answered. "Although what I've noticed is that more experienced Christian souls seem less inclined to stray from Christian paths forward. They seem more likely to stay in their comfort zone than the others."

"Perhaps," Hildegarde replied, "but what you may not have noticed is that the wiser, more experienced souls that come our way tend to have more attractive options to choose from. Whether there's a trend toward Christianity, I haven't really paid much mind."

Aisling looked at her curiously. "I haven't noted a correlation in the appeal of lives that are offered to older souls versus younger, but I have traveled through some very appealing Christian classes. I even thought of extending my stay." She winked.

"You've been so busy uncovering all the important details of each individual life," Hildegarde replied patiently, "but it has me a little concerned. I'm seeing more Christian life choices for the more experienced souls. I noticed it recently for one of my more advanced charges. The choices were rather easily divided between the appealing and the not so appealing. There were about a half dozen marvelous life opportunities that offered a wide variety of challenges across the globe, all in a Christian setting. The other five or six choices were rather stark, with little opportunity for growth. This example stands out from the others, but I have noticed it in others as well.

"I hesitated mentioning this to Immat until I was sure," she continued, "but now I've seen this trend continue. I encourage you to observe for yourself. If I'm mistaken, I'll drop it completely."

"I'll watch for it," Aisling said cautiously.

✧ ✧ ✧ ✧ ✧ ✧ ✧ ✧ ✧ ✧ ✧ ✧ ✧

At nine-fifteen on a sweltering June morning in Eastern Massachusetts, five cars hurried into the parking lot of the Church of the Tortured Christ. Three were shiny, identical black Dodge Chargers with "US Government" plates. The fourth was a dark unmarked, older sedan with Massachusetts plates, and the last a squad car with "Waltham Police" in dark letters over a white horizontal stripe.

A total of twelve men emerged from the vehicles, spread across the front of the complex in a show of force. Two men in dark suits moved to the outer perimeter of the lot while the other ten strode inside. Some were carrying thick cases with handles.

"My name is Agent Thurber and I'm with the FBI. We have a warrant to search this property. Is Ellen Grandby Sullivan on the premises?"

The eyes of Cecilia Hargis, the receptionist, were a pair of white, staring moons. She was speechless, alone in the tastefully decorated waiting area that was her little lot in heaven before these intimidating men filled up the space.

Thurber softened his tone. "Ma'am, this is routine police business. We're in the middle of a criminal investigation, and we'll get our work done in the next hour or so and be out of your hair. We'll be able to conduct our business whether or not the Reverend is here." He held an official looking document in the air, about eighteen inches from her nose.

He paused for several seconds, allowing her to focus on the document and pretend to comprehend.

"Now, is the Reverend here this morning?"

The woman cleared her throat. "No sir, sorry, she's not in today."

"Are you expecting her?"

"No. She's traveling."

"Traveling where?"

"She didn't say. She asked me to clear her calendar for this week. Something about urgent personal business."

The agent ordered Cecilia to have the church's head of security, Stanley Lafarge, meet them with a full set of keys. As they were waiting for Lafarge, Oliver Lacey stepped forward.

"Hello Mrs. Hargis. Remember me?"

"Yes, Detective," she said nervously. "It's nice to see you again." Her eyes shifted nervously between Lacey and the imposing FBI agent.

"When did the Reverend last leave the building?"

"Two days ago. At the end of the day."

"Did she seem to be in a hurry? Was she packed for a business trip?"

"No, not at all. Just a few personal things. She told me about the trip earlier in the afternoon, so I was able to move her appointments around. She seemed fine, totally at peace with her travels."

"If she was planning to have any meetings, TV appearances, or any church business," he continued, "she would do that through you, correct?"

"Definitely. This is much-deserved time off for the Reverend. You have no idea how much of her heart and soul she puts into this church."

"Yes, I'm sure." Lacey smiled politely.

For the next seventy-five minutes the men combed through the church, paying closest attention to the areas that were hidden from the public. Lafarge eagerly complied with all of their orders, including opening up the office of the Reverend Sullivan and the rooms behind her office where she performed prayers, meditation, and anything else she wished to do in such a private setting.

Their briefcases opened up to reveal a full spectrum of lab testing equipment, ideal for collecting and storing samples. The men each wore white gloves and collected samples throughout the building in an orderly, efficient way. Thurber instructed Lafarge to keep all doors unlocked as he allowed his team free reign to move through the building methodically.

They used swabs and gauze pads in combination with clear liquids to pick up samples from some surfaces, razor blades and tape from others. When they moved to the rooms in the bottom floor of the building, they combed carefully across all horizontal surfaces, collecting any solid materials they could identify, including hair, fibers, food particles.

Thurber explained to Lafarge that they would need to take all media that was capable of capturing video or audio images. That included not only the surveillance tapes from the church and the office, but also any video cameras. Lafarge objected briefly, but Thurber made it clear that violating the terms of a warrant would mean time behind bars. The men carefully removed several cameras, along with boxes containing video cartridges. The material filled each of the large trunks of their cars, and even part of their back seats.

When they were finished, Thurber thanked both Stanley Lafarge and Cecilia Hargis, coldly without shaking their hands. They left the church in nearly the same condition as they found it, with just a bit more space inside.

Lacey followed them to the lot. "How long will it take to go through all this?"

"A good solid week," Thurber replied, "and that's with this being high priority."

"So where from here?"

"For comparison we need to gather some of Miss Stark's personal effects. You said her boyfriend can help with that?"

"Follow me," Lacey said, moving toward his car. "We'll try his apartment first. Maybe he's got a late morning."

"Lacey," Agent Thurber said. "We appreciate you keeping this quiet. No press is a very good thing."

"Keeping secrets is no problem around here," Lacey replied.

Thurber instructed two of his cars to go back to their offices, while he climbed in the third with another agent. Lacey left the lot as Thurber and the squad car followed him toward Henry's house.

As they approached Henry's front door, Lacey turned back to Thurber. "His car is here so we should be in luck. If you don't mind, Agent Thurber, I'd like to handle the introductions. I don't want you to scare Henry into hiding."

Thurber nodded. Lacey knocked. The door opened after a few seconds.

"To what do I owe the pleasure, Detective?" Henry appeared surprised, hair askew and coffee cup in hand. He was wearing an oriental bath robe.

"Good morning, Henry. May we come in?"

"Well, that depends. Who is 'we'?"

"This is Agent Thurber from the FBI. He and his men just finished sweeping down the church."

"Any sign of Dee?" Henry's face changed from wry to anxious.

"No visible sign," Lacey said, "but you'd be amazed at how thoroughly they swept the place. They had a forensics team cover it from top to bottom. If she left a stand of hair, they found it, but it'll take time to sort through, and that's why we're here. They need something from Dee to compare it to."

Henry invited them in.

"Mr. Chimera," Thurber said evenly to Henry. "Do we have your permission to search your place?"

"What are you after, exactly?" Henry asked suspiciously.

"Primarily DNA samples, like from a hair brush she might have used.

"That's no problem," Henry said. "Is that all?"

"Any other signs that might lead us to her whereabouts."

"I doubt you'll find any clues about that since she didn't expect to be abducted," Henry said, "but have at it."

Thurber meticulously looked through the pockets of her clothes and through her dresser in search of any scraps that might help their investigation while the second agent collected samples from Dee's personal items. Henry and Lacey watched from a distance.

Henry excused himself to change into something more presentable.

When they finished poking through the apartment, Thurber turned to Henry.

"You'll be here if we need you, Mr. Chimera? No travel plans?"

"I should be here," Henry said without elaboration.

"Henry, it's really important that you stay in touch with us," Lacey said in a fatherly tone. "I'd prefer to focus on finding your friend and not be distracted with keeping tabs on you. Don't make our jobs harder, Henry."

As the men were ready to leave, Henry spoke out.

"Detective, what about the scrap of paper I showed you?"

"What about it?" Lacey's eyes stayed fixed on Henry.

"It seems important, don't you think?"

"What's he talking about?" Thurber cast a heavy look toward Lacey, who reached for his wallet and pulled out a small scrap of paper.

Lacey read as Thurber looked over his shoulder, "'Bosom Bay - 7/14 - Meet EGS, JD, JS.' That's Ellen Grandby Sullivan for sure, but who are the others?"

"I've been wondering that myself," Henry said. "The only JS I can think of is Joan Swenson, and the only JD I could think of at first was John Donnelly."

"I'm quite certain he's dead," Lacey replied.

"That is true, Detective," Henry replied, "but his wife Janice is alive and well."

A TILTED ARRAY

On this large lake, a vacation destination for generations, there was a discreet cove, barely visible from mid-water. Just off the cove, behind a thin strand of trees no more than a hundred feet from the shore, was a subdued but elegant compound. The house was originally intended as a faraway retreat for wealthy families in the 1930s and was large enough to accommodate extended kin on those rare occasions in which the owners felt so inclined to share their seclusion. A family that owned such a property was not to entertain often.

Finding the house required detailed directions from the nearest road. Even the boathouse was discreetly hidden from water's view. The paint was an emerald green, and the boat within was a deep brown. Passersby would need to know the property existed before they would think to find it along this vast, largely uninhabited shoreline.

The home was tastefully decorated with fine Italian furniture, accents, and art that spanned centuries. No detail was ignored when the inside was modernized, as it had been very recently. The kitchen was a sprawling affair, designed to allow the hard work to be done toward the back, but for more fun, collaborative meals to be prepared near the living space.

The bedrooms, four large and six small, offered great privacy. Each of the large bedrooms was en suite, along with ample closet and dresser space. Two of the larger bedrooms were toward the front, the rest arrayed through connected corridors and passages away from the shared living space.

On this lazy June morning, Ellen Grandby Sullivan was the jewel in the room, comfortably sprawled across a sofa positioned for a perfect view eastward through the trees, overlooking the lake.

"It's the perfect location for such an adventure. When we heard about it, we had to see it. When we saw it, we had to have it."

"How in the world would you ever 'hear about' a place like this?" Janice Donnelly was lying just as comfortably on an opposing couch, in easy reach of a cup of herbal tea.

"That's why we pay realtors, my dear." The Reverend laughed. "Although this one was more of a location scout than a realtor. We gave him explicit instructions to find a place by the water that was secluded, not easily available by any means of transportation. This is not a place that we wanted to visit on weekends. Our specific purpose required just the right property.

"I think," she continued lazily, "that he nailed it."

"It's lovely. I've never seen such a place." Joan Swenson was sipping coffee from a table across the room.

Her eyes were transfixed through the trees to the sunlight and the water. Her forward position suggested that she wanted to be out above the water, in a more comforting place than where she was now.

"I'd encourage you both to find some inner peace here. Our mission is one of the highest order, one that's never been attempted. We'll need complete focus and dedication from each one of us. So many things have to go perfectly for this to succeed."

"How soon," Janice Donnelly asked, "do you think we can hope for this transition to occur?"

"Within a few short days." Edgar stared expressionless out toward the water. "The plan is in motion now. I expect to get confirmation of her availability at any time. Just be patient and keep yourself well."

"And how are our guests faring?" Ellen posed the question to her brother with feigned concern.

"I guess you could say they're resting comfortably," he replied blankly, "but it's strong sedation. When they start stirring we let them go to the bathroom. Then back to sleep they go."

"I still don't agree with you bringing Dee here," the Reverend replied. "We all know there are no long term plans for her."

"Yes, well," Edgar looked uncomfortably out the window, avoiding Joan Swenson's stare, "consider her our insurance policy. I expect everything to go exactly as we've planned, but if it doesn't then we have another card to play.'"

"I suppose," Ellen said. Her peaceful smile was replaced with a disapproving look to the distance.

"It's not for us to make her uncomfortable in any way," Janice Donnelly said. "We're here on a holy mission. We can't choose when we're holy and when we're unholy."

"It's under control," Edgar replied. "You have my word that I will not place any undue suffering on either of them at any time. That's the very reason I'm keeping them sedated, to avoid any unnecessary suffering."

The room fell silent.

After several minutes Ellen spoke. "It's nearly time for our morning prayer. Janice, are you feeling well enough to join us?"

"I think so," she said brightly. "Things seem to be settling down now that the second trimester is behind me."

"That's delightful to hear," Ellen replied. "Shall we?"

In one country after another, clashes were occurring that pitted one large faction against another, usually along religious lines. In the Middle East, China, and Africa, the blood shed was most apparent, although it was even boiling over in places like Brazil, Indonesia, Eastern Europe, and even the Southeastern United States. The trend was that the ruling religious, economic, or social class would force social change they felt was long overdue. The subordinate classes would rebel and violence would erupt. Fuses had been lit across the globe, and the explosions were free. As events roiled, web sites and newspaper headlines were filled with one conflict after another. Consumers of these stories became numb to the impact as they continued day after day, week after week.

The number of deaths around the world during normal times, most due to natural causes, numbered about 100,000 per day. During these extreme times it was not unusual for this number to come close to 200,000 or even 250,000 per day. Very few people paid attention to birth rates compared to death rates, but those who did noticed that the world's population boom was subsiding substantially, at least for the time being.

In the higher reaches, these changes were noticed by all who had a role in the welcoming, assimilation, and continuation of souls traveling on their journey. Because of all the turmoil, the souls restarting the cycle into a new life were newer and younger. As was always true, newer souls who had just left the earth required more time to refresh, heal, and learn. Their most recent mission was not complete, so many left the earth with more questions than answers.

The capacity for the heavens to accommodate souls was unlimited, which meant that each soul had all the time it needed to prepare for its next turn. Recently, however, the volume of souls pouring into the bottom of the funnel, where Immat, Hildegarde, and Aisling performed their important duties, was more compressed than at any time they could remember.

While the volumes increased they deftly adjusted the pace with which they were able to work, not allowing the faster pace interfere with their progress. The sequence was becoming routine. Immat presented an array of life choices for the incoming soul. Aisling would perform her research with boundless energy and precision. She would next present it to Hildegarde to wire into the selection processes. The cadence of their work was a joy to watch, which many angels and other spirits chose to do. Hildegarde would look back on prior lives as a wise grandmother looks at the lives of the children and grandchildren she made possible. Meanwhile Aisling would look ahead, eagerly pulling information from the surroundings of the life arrays.

When they came together, past and future, to a decision point for the prospective soul, it created an exciting choice that overwhelmed many newer souls. Hildegarde would patiently explain, again and again if necessary, how important it was for them to stay on the path of their long range goals.

The consistency of the lives they received from Immat was quite another matter. Under normal circumstances, before this recent increase in volume, they would welcome perhaps one in four souls who had lived less than twenty lives. At about fifteen lives, Hildegarde noticed, a soul went from being a puppy, bouncing through each new experience with wonder and energy, into an existence of more focused learning. Such a life had probably been conceived in the late middle ages, so through the prior seven or eight centuries they saw the world move from a lean, harsh reality into a place that burst at the seams with new opportunities. Just a few centuries before, a soul that reached its fortieth birthday had lived a long life.

The older souls who passed through may have lived during the time of Muhammed or Christ, or in many interesting cases, in Old Testament times. Recently the number of wise, veteran souls was approaching half what they had grown accustomed to. For every wise soul who was on the stretch run of their journey after seventy, eighty, or even more than a hundred lives, Hildegarde and Aisling would see many more who had been through five or ten lifetimes.

The newer souls had so many experiences still before them that they could not afford to be selective. An array of lives presented by Immat could be so starkly different from one another, as researched by Aisling, that Hildegarde needed only to help remind them of their highest priorities.

Still, the trend they had seen from Immat continued.

"Aisling, see if you notice something strange," Hildegarde quietly said during one brief pause in their busy work. "The next 'salty old soul' who comes through the gate will be offered a series of Christian-based lives. There will be a handful, a couple maybe, that are in a more sheltered setting that offers the soul no perspective on what growth means. If the soul is older and toward the end of a long path, the best choices for growth will be in Christian settings. However that won't be the case for newer souls. They won't get the more appealing choices."

"I think you're imagining things. It's a bet," Aisling replied playfully.

The next spirit to come through their celestial gate, with his life opportunities floating above and around him, was a spirit named Billot. He was approaching his seventieth life and was conceived around the time of Christ, although none of his experiences crossed paths with Christ or his immediate followers. He had lived in a variety of settings in his later lives, mostly in structured societies in Europe and the Middle East.

As Aisling gathered in the 'bubbles', as she called the orbs from Immat that represented the life possibilities, she did a quiet count.

"One, two, three ..." then she went silent. "Okay, there are nine Christian lives here, spanning very rich to very poor. There are two others that would place him in small villages in India, one in a South American tribe, and another in a village in rural Cambodia."

"Each of them offers unique challenges," Hildegarde said, now loud enough for Billot to hear. "Rising from a privileged existence into an enlightened state can be even more difficult than rising from a sparse existence to a slightly higher place, only a modest gain over the course of a lifetime."

Billot stared in quiet contemplation at the possibilities before him. He barely noticed the two spirits who would help him with his choice.

Lowering her voice, she turned to Aisling. "Nine Christian choices, two non-Christian. Less than thirty percent of the world is Christian. Could that be chance?"

Aisling shook her head. "That is odd indeed."

At ten o'clock on an early summer morning in Revere, Massachusetts, a group of anxious friends bound by a common concern were gathered. Coffee cups were spread around the apartment. A half full box of Dunkin' Donuts was open on the kitchen counter.

"Could it be a code name for some place that's not a bay at all?" Naomi Pike was leaning forward on Henry's couch. A notepad was on her lap and a pen in her hand. Disjointed notes were scrawled in blue ink on the pad.

On the largest wall in Henry's apartment was a whiteboard, which looked nearly as chaotic as Naomi's pad. Names were connected by arrows to large question marks placed before locations in small print.

Wales? Hudson? San Fran? Australia? New Zealand? Fiction?

Henry was sitting on a stool next to the whiteboard. Richard Shoemaker was on the couch next to Naomi, and Winfred Harding was positioned at the dining room table staring at a tablet computer.

"Maybe," Winfred said, tapping and scrolling on his tablet, "it has to be a place that's familiar to him and whoever told him about the meeting. I do think it has to be on water somewhere."

"Well, have we at least decided what the initials mean?" Henry was staring at the upper right portion of the large board, where initials were separated from names by equal signs.

"With as much confidence as we can," Shoemaker replied, "yes. Without inside information about the people who work in the church, this is the best we can conclude for right now. 'EGS' has to be the Reverend, without question. The other two initials must be people, and since we know that Janice Donnelly and Joan Swenson are acquainted, it's our most logical conclusion for right now. In that church with a few thousand people, even if we had a list of names, we could come up with others with the same initials. There's no sense wasting our attention on long shots."

Henry walked slowly to the board. "The three have the church in common. Joan and Janice were at John's funeral together. The part that's not clear to me is how much Janice Donnelly really cares about the Church of the Tortured Christ. John originally scheduled a session with me based on some ridiculous story he made up about Parkinson's disease in his family, and it turned out they were really just trying to get an inside opinion on what kind of soul would be inhabiting their unborn child, as if I have some sort of inside knowledge about that kind of thing. His deception was revealed by a relative of his who appeared to us in the session. She showed up to tell him to knock it off. It was kind of funny at the time, really. He was embarrassed and after that we became friends."

"There really aren't many options for Bosom Bay," Winfred said, flipping through search results. "I see a place off the coast of Wales that separates the mainland from Anglesey Island. I see a place they call 'Abraham's Bosom,' which is a bay off the southern tip of Australia, off New

South Wales. I see 'Bosom Bay' referenced in some fiction works, actually quite a few."

"New Zealand seems out of the question," Henry replied, "and would they really have flown across the water to England? It sure seems doubtful they could have done that with one or more hostages in tow. Dee wouldn't have gone willingly, that's for sure."

"We have to be realistic." Naomi gazed steadily at Henry as she spoke. "If they went across the ocean, they don't have any hostages with them. If our only option is a flight to one of these places, I suppose we might find them. But then does it just become a mission of retribution? What can we really hope to accomplish in that situation, other than a nasty showdown?"

Henry looked down toward the ground in response, contemplating.

"Huh. Interesting." Winfred was scrolling and tapping.

"What's that?" Henry looked up.

"I found a reference to a place that isn't called Bosom Bay any more. Not since the nineteenth century."

"Where is it?"

"It's called Huletts Landing now. I found it after about seven pages of results. It's on the East side of Lake George, New York."

The three huddled behind Winfred, looking at his tablet.

"It looks remote, that's for sure." He scrolled through the entry for Huletts Landing, which explained that the area was settled after the Revolutionary War by a Huguenot family named Hawley. Generations of the Hawley family lived on the property until one enterprising family member opened the property for business through the creation of a steamship landing and a post office.

"Here it is, almost 150 years after that effort, and the place still looks like a pain in the ass to try to reach. Look at the donkey path you need to drive on - I assume - to get there." Winfred clicked on the geographic map view, showing the lush foliage and winding roads that veered off route 22.

"There's still a post office and a marina there," Shoemaker said. "I can see why they called it Bosom Bay. The area above Huletts Landing looks like a couple of breasts."

"Saggy eighteenth century breasts, maybe," Henry offered.

"Yes, Henry," Naomi said, "perhaps if they were more attractive boobs they would have kept calling them bosoms."

"Not in the eighteenth century," Shoemaker said. "They probably changed it because the name was bad for the family business. The very idea of topless Upstate New Yorkers! Can you imagine?"

"They look more like testicles anyway," Henry said. "I bet they didn't think of that. 'Droopy Balls Bay' would've really gotten the steamships rolling in."

The group enjoyed a much-needed laugh.

"Well, it looks remote," Henry said. "Winfred, can you scroll up the shoreline north of there?"

They scanned along the shoreline.

"There are some impressive-looking properties up there," Winfred said. "Remote, that's for sure."

"And a lot of them," Henry replied. "We'd have to figure out which one could possibly be one we're after."

"That seems very daunting," Naomi said absently. "If the church is renting one of those places, how could we possibly find out who they're renting from? Landlords are hard to reach, and they'd protect the privacy of their tenants. If they want to avoid a lawsuit, anyway."

"I rather doubt this would be a rental property," Shoemaker offered. "If the church is involved, they're an owner, not a tenant. They have more money than some small governments."

"I think you're right," Henry said, "and I'm guessing they would've bought this property fairly recently, at least within the past year or two."

"Why do you think that?"

"Because of their growth, and their success. I doubt they would've bought this property just to own it. It's too remote to be a getaway for the Reverend."

"It says here," Winfred said, "the nearest airport is in Burlington, Vermont. About an hour away."

"I'm with Henry," Shoemaker said. "This is a 'purpose property.' If indeed our friends are up there, it's because the Church bought it with seclusion as the intent. They don't want to be found."

"I have an idea," Henry said. "We can spend some time and effort talking to realtors, which can be hit or miss, or we can contact the local county government to find out which properties were bought in the last couple years. It's public information. The only question is how accessible it is online."

Henry moved across the room to his desktop computer.

He typed in a search for *Washington County NY assessor's office* and easily found a listing of towns under a heading marked Tentative Assessment, with a link on each town name that opened a PDF file.

"Town of Hubbard, correct?" His question was directed to Winfred.

"That's the one."

"Thank you Washington County," Henry declared.

The three gathered behind him.

"Look at this. It gives all the properties and their assessed values, the exact town or township, and the owner's name. Beautiful. The only thing it doesn't give is their phone number."

"That's a lot of properties," Naomi said. "This could take a while."

"Maybe not," Henry replied. "These are all Hubbard properties, but it breaks that down into smaller groups. See? There are a few for Hawleys Landing. We can scan down through the list for the more expensive ones in that little area. I'll just paste those into a file, and we'll start there."

As he went down the list, most of the properties were in the range of three to six hundred thousand dollars in value.

"Three hundred thousand bucks doesn't seem like a lot for lakefront property, even it is hard to reach," he explained. "I'm seeing some for more, but under 'Class' they look like commercial properties."

He scrolled while the others watched.

"Whoa." He stopped, moving his face closer to the screen. "Here's one that's classified as a 'seasonal residence with improvements', and it's assessed at more than three million bucks."

"Who's listed as the owner?" Shoemaker moved in closer to see.

"Well, look at this," Henry said. "The owner is listed as '*His Blood Limited, Atlanta, Georgia*'."

"Isn't that where Ernest Grandby is based?"

"It is indeed," Henry said.

"Who's up for a road trip?"

Business was good so far for Liu Yang. The mild weather in Liupanshui had brought many out to stroll on the streets in the middle of their day. She was set up in the normal place, her table, chair and cart perfectly situated to the greet passing visitors. A tarp covered her table, and kept the bright light from her eyes.

Her husband, Wang Jie, had recently delivered a cache of intricately carved animals with bright colors and faces with remarkable detail. These happy creatures were the stars of her table.

Early in the afternoon, Li Xia joined her mother after school.

"Hello my dear. What did you learn today?"

"Hello Mommy. Did you know that football has been played in China for more than one thousand years?"

"I did not know that, sweetie. That is a very interesting fact!" Liu Yang organized her affairs nervously, looking into the distance as a rumbling sound of shouting and chanting sounded as if it was coming closer.

The little girl settled into her routine. She took off her coat, pulled a book from her bag, and sat in the cart behind her mother.

On the campus of Liupanshui Normal University, a movement was well underway. Hundreds of students and ordinary citizens had gotten word of the unrest spreading through the People's Republic. It began with the news of the disappearance of the Dalai Lama during a visit to the United States. Under suspicion were people loyal to the government of the People's Republic.

Some of those gathered on this warm day spoke outwardly of their suspicions that the government itself was to blame. After all, they reasoned, this government had spent decades suppressing the ideas and independence of its own people. Why would they allow a lone voice to spread its message across the globe about the power within? The very idea would undermine their agenda.

The rhetoric went from agitated to angry to fierce within minutes. The few hundred gathered at this quiet campus began to march along Minghu Road toward the main town. As they marched, their chanting grew louder. Fueled by young people with mobile devices connected to social media, they drew energy from each other as they moved in unison toward the Modern Capital.

A few hundred became a few thousand. An agitated crowd became a hostile mob. By the time they arrived at the People's Square, they were loud and combative. One young man would start a chant about how the people's voice would not be ignored. The others would join in loudly, aggressively. When one chant died down, another would emerge. A different young man would speak up about how the unwelcome sacrifice of the most sacred religious leaders were only the latest abomination perpetuated by those in charge. Who would be next? The angry words became a chant.

As the chants ran their course, young men growing increasingly impatient would look around, inviting anyone to challenge their will.

The MPS, China's version of the city police, were in force around the perimeter, waiting for events to become violent. They were several hundred strong, each carrying riot shields and batons. Many of the young men under the dark helmets were the same age as those in the center of the shouting. A few looked for familiar faces, hopeful for the chance to defuse the tension.

A lone figure settled into position on a rooftop two blocks from the chaos. He had a clear view in all directions. From this position he could take in all important activity, essential for calibrating his next, most important move.

This was no coincidence. He had planned this day for weeks, taking care of every detail in preparation for one attempt, a mission he was paid generously to accomplish.

He moved his AR-50 to shoulder height, gaining a comfortable hold with his tripod on a ledge in front of him to bear most of the gun's weight. He carefully adjusted the scope, measuring his aim down to the fraction of an inch on his target from a distance of four hundred yards.

His focus was locked. His target was still. He squeezed.

The bullet tore through the chest of Li Xia in an instant. The sound of the burst was lost in the roar of the crowd.

A man was lazily sifting through the contents of Liu Yang's table as a sudden movement caught his eye. The little girl behind this sales woman fell straight back from her perch, arms outstretched from the impact, flat on the ground. Her eyes were wide open, staring straight above.

The man's mouth opened in silent alarm. Liu Yang looked at him, then glanced curiously back at her daughter. Her horrified look and long shriek went unnoticed by the crowd and police.

RESTORATION

The long black Lincoln Town Car cruised at the speed limit north on route 4, past the town of Hudson Falls toward Fort Ann. Along the scenic, rural road, an occasional clearing would illuminate the thickness of the forest. Small stores, farmhouses, and barns appeared just often enough to seem out of place.

Two men in dark glasses and suits were in the front seat of the limousine. Their front pockets showed the outline of a shoulder harness supporting a handgun.

"Years of preparation," Ernest Grandby said from the back, "all leading up to this time."

The venerable Reverend was reclining comfortably in the back. A textured tie adorned his striped green oxford shirt. A blue sport coat was draped lazily next to him on the seat. His gray hair was brushed back casually, a contrast from the more formal, slicked-back appearance that so many millions were accustomed to seeing on television. The seventy-two year old stared out the window as the rural countryside passed. He was in a contemplative mood.

"It has taken you to many places, I gather." The words came from a man sitting across from Grandby was also in his older years, Asian with a single gray ponytail adorned with intricate red beads. He wore a slight goatee, gray in contrast to his deep brown skin. His appearance gave him an authoritative, spiritual presence. His clothes were a blend of East and West.

"Too many to count," Grandby said. "As you know very well, the church has been blessed with great influence across the globe."

"I am aware. I am also aware that many millions revere you, Reverend Grandby."

"Well, perhaps," Grandby replied, politely brushing off the suggestion, "but it's the message that resonates. We're building a new face of the Christian church. The old conventions have been dying for centuries. Our message has gained popularity because over a billion Christians around the world maintain their faith, but they've grown tired of the messenger. They need a new vehicle. What brings you and I together on this day, on this journey, is a critical next step in filling that need. I know you're not a Christian, Indazita, but this mission you have agreed to help with will bring the world together in one of the most important ways imaginable. You're from Burma, correct?"

"Yes," his guest replied. "It's officially been called 'Myanmar' since 1989, but many around the globe still refer to our country as Burma, and her people as Burmese."

Grandby nodded patiently. "I have friends in high places in your country," Grandby replied casually. "They have warmly embraced our message."

The mystic smiled and nodded.

"Where we have exerted our influence most aggressively," Grandby continued, "is in those countries that seem to have a lingering debate over which theology will prevail. The friction in many of these countries was harmful to their growth, both spiritually and economically. Their citizens have suffered greatly, in some cases over centuries."

"And you have," Indazita replied, pausing for the right words, "been available to bring these tensions to the surface."

"I would phrase that differently, but yes. We've taken action based on the reality that many good souls have been enslaved in circumstances that are not of their choosing. Tussling between the shifting spiritual influences has bound them to miserable lives. I spent years working with the Jews in building their trust. Then, when a threat to Israel emerged in Syria, one of our faithful happened to be positioned to discover it. I alerted the Prime Minister and he took the appropriate action. By the time this is over, it will rise to be a great conflict that will put to rest many old tensions. We are in the unique and fortunate position to set them free.

"In Africa, there are so many millions of souls living under a curtain of oppression. Across that vast continent we've done our most satisfying work. Our emissaries have been active in so many countries, with great success. Places like Zambia and Ethiopia are in the process of a great purge that will cull the herd, to the betterment of mankind. Angola. Sudan. Tanzania. Niger, I can go on. We had no *idea* how much bitterness was festering in those places, or how many people were living under a veil of fear. So many hopeless creatures trying to scrape out an existence. For what? Do these souls have any chance at living a meaningful life? My associates are setting them free! Hundreds of soldiers for the one true God are working diligently, every day, to bring bad intentions into daylight, for all to see and for all of this business to be settled for eternity.

"Things are just starting to heat up between India and Pakistan, and North and South Korea. I have very high expectations for tensions to go far beyond the boiling point in those two places. Over half a million Chinese have passed from this life and are ready and waiting for a better chance in the next."

"All because one confused man visiting the States went missing," replied Indizita.

"His was the easiest mission of all," Grandby said. "The Dalai Lama has been nothing more or less than an inconvenience. When people thought of reincarnation, they thought of him. No more."

"Just as we calculated, Buddhists around the world are blaming it on China. They've gone on a rampage, and it appears they have no intention of stopping anytime soon. The images on television are amazing. The bastard Chinese are pulling their hair out trying to end it. No matter how many young boys in military uniforms they send out to disperse the crowds, they're met with two and three times as many protesters who are beyond frustrated with their life under this regime. They feel hopeless and are perfectly content to move on to the next life! How great is that? How many of those souls will be better off in a life that includes a devotion to God the Father?"

The response was without emotion. "Very many indeed, but one in particular."

"Yes," Grandby said, exhaling and looking out the window. "The little girls' death was an unfortunate necessity." He paused, closing his eyes.

Then his tone brightened. He looked at his guest with a confident smile. "But we move on! The time is near when I can make amends for that very sad event. The world will be a better place, and it will be because of our determination. Many souls will find their proper home, in the arms of Jesus Christ, our Lord and Savior."

Interstate 93 moves North from the Boston area and gradually bends to the Northeast. Ponds and lakes dot the landscape, which becomes increasingly rural as the road crosses into New Hampshire, where it bends toward the state's largest city.

"A few miles past Manchester, when we get near Concord, 93 and 89 will split. We'll want to take I-89 to the Northeast toward Vermont." A large atlas was spread across Winfred Harding's lap.

Richard Shoemaker was behind the wheel of an older Range Rover II. Henry was in the passenger seat, Harding and Naomi Pike in the back. The rear area of the small SUV overflowed with bags, mostly black equipment cases mixed in with some small backpacks.

It was 10:30 on Thursday morning. The group timed their exit from the Boston area to avoid the worst of the morning rush hour. Drops of rain were starting to form on the windshield.

"Does anyone know if this storm is supposed to move inland?" Shoemaker wore a weatherproof baseball-style cap. A light all-weather jacket was across his lap.

"It's big enough that it'll probably soak everything from the coast to the Great Lakes within a day or two," Winfred replied. "This is just the start of it. It'll move inland today."

"Perfect timing," Naomi Pike mumbled. "So can someone please explain to me again why we're taking the law into our own hands?"

There was silence in the car for a few seconds. Finally Henry spoke.

"It's impossible to know who to trust. Lacey is a local cop who is a suspicious of the church, but little more. I've been completely honest with the guy. He knows just about everything I know, but he doesn't feel like he has the cause to act. This is despite the fact that Donnelly was killed just outside Waltham, Lacey's town. If Lacey wanted to take action by now, he would've taken it. I don't trust him."

"Are you suggesting that Lacey is in the church's pocket?" This time it was Winfred.

"No," Henry said impatiently, "but I'm not assuming he's someone we should trust either. After Donnelly, Herbrit was next. It was way out of his jurisdiction and he couldn't investigate, but I assumed he filled in the FBI about how the two might be connected, especially given the information I gave him about what Joan Swenson saw."

"And now Dee is missing. And the Dalai Lama."

The car was silent for a few moments.

"I'm not so sure it was the right thing to do," Henry said, "telling Lacey about the slip of paper and Bosom Bay, but I didn't want to be accused of withholding information. Now I'm having my doubts."

"Couldn't we just contact the FBI directly and go around Lacey?", Naomi asked.

"And tell them what? That we think Lacey is working with the church, who is somehow behind the disappearance of a holy man from a different faith? They'll think we're lunatics."

"They would be correct," Richard offered. "We're geared up as if we're going on a Navy Seal mission in hostile territory, yet we have very little intelligence to go on, such as the layout of this property we're about to approach, or where on the property the hostages, if there are any, might be."

"What do you suggest, Shoemaker? That we sit around and wait for the authorities to crack the case? It's been weeks, and it's yielded nothing. There's nothing new being reported about either investigation. It's as if the local cops are convinced Dee just ran away, and the feds are resigned to the idea that there's nothing they can do about the Dalai Lama's abduction without stoking up tensions with China. That's the last thing they want with all the chaos going on around the globe, so they're not acting. Even though he's dead, there's still a *missing person*, for Christ's sake!"

"We don't know if they're not doing anything," Winfred said. "With such a high profile incident, they're not going to be leaking information to the press."

"That may be so," Henry said, "but I provided Joan's story about the video with Lacey. Either he didn't share it with the feds, which is bad, or he shared it with the feds and they're doing nothing with it, which is worse."

"We're on your side, Henry, which is why we're taking action. We can do things they can't, or perhaps won't," Shoemaker said, "and we can do them faster, without having to worry about checking in with the local authorities."

"We can also get arrested for doing those things," Naomi replied. I think it's reasonable to assume that these people that we're about to go spy on are armed. Probably heavily armed."

"Once we get there," Henry said, "if there's no opportunity for a move that will help find Dee, we should back off. If we can't reasonably do anything ourselves, we'll call in the authorities. I have the number of the nearest FBI office in Albany in my phone."

"We came prepared, and we have a strong crew," Shoemaker said. "Naomi, you have all of your camera equipment, right?"

"Yeah, my best telephoto lenses are on board, but here's the thing. I mostly do portraits. Long range viewing comes in handy for nature photography but that's only a hobby, not something I make a living at."

"It'll help to see what we're working with," Henry said. "Richard, you're a former military guy. You're armed, and you know all about approaching a target."

"I was a reservist for three years before I was called into active duty in the first Iraq War. I was stationed mostly in Kuwait, but that was after we had already chased the Iraqis out. I've never experienced hand to hand combat, so don't get some inflated sense of security. While you guys are playing G.I. Joe, I'll be at the bar."

"I'm sure you'll be a brilliant strategist and point man. We're counting on you! I'll join you at the bar later. Winfred," Henry said, turning to the back, "thank goodness you're here with us. With your knowledge of electronics, you'll fill the role of our resident Angus MacGyver. If we need electronic wizardry, you're the guy we can count on."

"Yes, Henry," Harding replied dryly, "if anyone needs a design for a printed circuit board, I'm your man."

"Excellent!" Henry's voice reached a falsetto as he pumped a fist in the air. "We have just the right crew to pull this off!"

The team enjoyed a much-needed laugh.

"Let me guess your superhero strength, Henry," Winston asked. "Is it fantasy-based delusion?"

"No superpowers," Henry said as he glanced across the countryside under a darkening sky, "but I might have some tricks up my sleeve. I'm not sure how useful they'll be, but if there's a way to get Dee out of there alive, I plan to find it."

The spirit Sau rose from its earthly vessel, initially confused and alone. Behind was a chaotic scene, one of conflict and violence, heartbreak and loss. The life was cut short by a single fatal blow, leaving a sadness behind that was powerful enough to reverberate through the living world and well beyond. The small vessel that had carried this immense life force was broken beyond repair. Returning was not a possibility. It was the life force of Li Xia, a mere child of six brought down by a purposeful bullet on a busy street in Liupanshui.

This soul had been through hundreds of lives and had continued to rise in stature, one of the rarest and most valuable kind. He had chosen to return for another life, that of a Chinese girl in a small industrial city, because there was important unfinished business. These circumstances were selected in spite of the turmoil that would be present, believing he would at least have the opportunity to correct one flaw that remained from his many prior lives.

Sau looked back at the tormented scene he was leaving behind. A mother shrieking uncontrollably over the small body that laid gently on the grass, arms stretched upward. Strangers scrambled nearby, trying to comfort Liu Yang, the shrieking mother, as others sought help. The soul's ascension was heavy with sadness. Ahead was the familiar light, the white tunnel that would return the spirit to familiar surroundings, a place it had left a few short earthly years before. As Sau rose to be enveloped by the loving, welcoming light, peace returned, mixed with a sadness that would remain.

Through the transitional tunnel Sau traveled. Across the distance, the healing power of the destination became stronger. His familiarity with this place of healing and repair made the journey easier. Unlike newer souls who would forget that the destination ahead was the true Home, Sau had the benefit of having made this journey many times before. The last one seemed like yesterday. Such a pity, he thought.

As the tunnel widened, ahead were stars. Stars that were cast in a backdrop of white, loving light. Such a sight would confuse a newer soul, but Sau knew these were the countless souls at rest and repair. Each soul that was on the earth, living a life that would bring wisdom and experience, also maintained a presence in these heavenly surroundings. A soul would never leave this place unless it was to ascend to a higher calling. Its essence stayed, even during the many lives it would live among other souls in mortal bodies.

As Sau advanced, he came closer to a cluster of stars that were his celestial family. They reached out with hearts that surrounded and embraced him. "Hello, old friend. Normally I would say how long it's been, but it really hasn't been very long."

Telan was a frequent companion of Sau's along their life journeys, often a sibling, parent, or child. Telan was not as experienced as Sau, but had benefited greatly by being around a spirit of such profound wisdom.

"Not as long as I expected or hoped, but we cannot control everything," Sau said. "This sadness will not leave me soon."

"Welcome home," Telan replied kindly. "As always, this where you can decide what to keep and what to leave behind."

Sau moved easily back into the familiar circle of souls. He was welcomed by all as a teacher who was sorely missed. While his essence remained in place in his celestial home, his attention was still almost completely on the life of Li Xia. Although his spirit had moved from the child, part of his energy remained with her family. In a life with such a traumatic, abrupt loss of a young life, the wound among the immediate family and the departing spirit was immense. Their energies could not be easily separated, and Sau found it very difficult to leave them in such pain. Part of his energy remained to nurture and comfort them in their sorrow.

Like a mortal having two conversations at the same time, he could only attend to one effectively.

Soon, realizing there was a limit to the comfort he could provide to those he had to leave behind, he eased back into his home place, surrounded by his closest friends. He went around to each member of the group, asking them about their latest experiences. Most were in living circumstances currently, so they could only report on how their current missions were coming along. Their answers were distracted by their current challenges, so Sau needed to rely on their respective spirit guides, where they were being used, to help communicate.

Each soul had a spirit guide assigned, but the extent to which the soul and its spirit guide worked together varied in each case. Newer souls tended to rely more on their guides, older souls less so. Spirit guides offered many important things to a soul, including guidance during the darker times.

Sau offered encouragement to help each soul through whatever waters it was currently navigating. Souls currently inhabiting a life were not always able to accept his advice, partly because of distraction, but also as a function of its maturity. Some were like human teenagers, not open to advice because no one could possibly know the challenges they faced. More mature souls would find themselves on an island, cut off from the advice of their closest companions, even though the advice was there for them all along.

There were several friends in the circle who, like Sau and Telan, were not currently on a life mission. These were the most attentive and focused of the group. They used their time of restoration to view from a distance the lives being lived by their friends. Sau engaged with them casually, critically, and comically as they wormed their way through life's mysteries. They labored through early years, dating, drug and alcohol abuse, pregnancies, the burden of raising children and caring for aging parents, and the challenge of growing old, which always came too soon.

One of the souls in this restive state was named Alfan, a soul that tended to be more female in temperament. Like Sau, Alfan had recently come from a life that was too short. She was a mother in Western Canada who had developed a rapidly lethal form of cancer. Her three children were in their late teens when she died, and her abrupt departure left her with many conflicting emotions about whether she had lived as full a life as possible in her time on earth. She was also angry that she did not see her early demise coming, which would have allowed her to better prepare for her family's loss.

"The feeling of regret needs to be temporary," Sau explained patiently. "It's a wasted emotion unless converted into something useful. Besides, I don't see that you have anything to regret. Would you have raised your children any differently if you knew you wouldn't make it to your fortieth birthday?"

"I would have done more with them. I wouldn't have spent so much time at work. I worried a lot, but about the wrong things. My family was important, not my clothes, my job, or my money."

"You chose a life where your husband wasn't a wealthy man, which meant you had to work. Your children saw how much you worked and cared, and they learned and grew from it. If you look closely you can see that the things you are learning from now, they are too. Their memories of you will include the choices you made given your circumstances, but they will be warm, loving memories."

Alfan considered the advice from her wise old friend, and the two embraced. "It's so great to have you back."

She paused, wanting to shift the conversation but not wanting to do so awkwardly. "I'm so sorry about your short mission with Li Xia. We were all heartbroken as it happened."

"Some things are just out of our control," he said. There is evil in the world and it always tests our faith in our own mission."

"You couldn't see this coming? This was supposed to be a very special life."

"It was a special life," he said. "It just didn't last as long as I would've like and no, I didn't know it would be so short."

"Aren't you curious who was behind it?" As she asked, Telan and the other spirits hovered in the background, quietly awaiting his reply.

"I would rather not know. If there were dark forces that targeted this little girl, they got what they wanted. So now they must live with the consequences. As for me, I have unfinished business. My work is not complete. The life I lived with Li Xia was a happy one, filled with support, nurturing, and attention. I would have rather grown from a brilliant girl into a brilliant woman who could make real, meaningful change. I believe that within this little girl there could be an amazing woman who might have transformed China."

Telan spoke up. "Perhaps in your next life, the early dangers may not have to be so present as they were in this one."

"I suppose you're right. The lure of changing the culture was perhaps unrealistic."

Telan was eager to make a point. "This was a risk you were aware of when you chose, and it can serve as a lesson as you move forward. Sau, do you recall the weakness you sought to address in this life? It may have played a slight role in your selection of this life in this setting."

"Please explain." Sau was defensive. Clearly his memory was affected by his latest experience.

"Several lives ago, when you emerged as a leader in the province of Bengal, you ascended the right way. You became the leader of millions by your fairness, your commitment to the greater good. Your people were suffering, and you gained their trust by promising to change the way the world viewed them, and in turn how they would respond to a rapidly modernizing world. Do you remember that?"

"Of course I remember."

"It was an important lifetime, a valuable lifetime, but one where the promise was not fulfilled. Can you recall the primary reason that we all agreed the promise was not fulfilled."

Sau thought before responding. "I am beginning to recall, yes."

"It was a very challenging time and place to be a leader of so many souls who were in such a state of need. The problem you could not overcome was that once you obtained this high status in your country, you became obsessed with maintaining the office. To make the changes you sincerely intended to make, it was necessary to hold onto your power. None of us in your circle disputed that, but what we agreed, after much prayer and discussion, was that you needed to do both at once. You needed to fight for the right to hold the office while beginning the process of helping your people. You thought that one had to follow the other, and together we decided this was the wrong approach."

Sau was silent, looking down in contemplation and recollection.

"Your weakness, my dear friend Sau, was that you allowed your position to overshadow your mission. When you were here last, before your brief life as Li Xia, you vowed you would not make the same mistake again. This is the weakness that forced you to return to a life on earth. This is the weakness you must correct before ascending to the place you belong."

Sau nodded.

"As we discussed, the temptations that come with great power are intoxicating," Telan continued. "It takes incredible courage, and an unbending commitment to the power of good, to overcome this sense of power and to stay committed. In your next choice of a life, you must recognize your tendencies."

In the short time that followed, Sau made the most of his return to his celestial home. He studied the great scriptures from each of the great religions, the great minds from all the ages of man. He scanned the lives being lived by souls not only inside his circle, but of notable lives on the outside. He watched as souls made mistakes and adjusted or failed to adjust, and the consequences of each.

He observed the conflicts raging around the planet, watching as enormous forces in various geographic regions challenged the might of one another toward goals that seemed to usually be based in unfounded fear. There were many premature deaths, just like Li Xia's, that would produce a flood of souls in the celestial regions. These many souls were now streaming into this place, trying to get resettled and trying make sense of their short lives to prepare for the next.

There was no need for an extended restoration period following his life as Li Xia. The brief time was not especially taxing, and the death was completely pain-free. The difficulty, and the burden he carried to this region, was the pain experienced by his mother and father. They were two souls who were not in his circle, which was part of his decision. The abrupt death of the girl caused his parents great pain, which he was able to help with the assistance of their spirit guides, and which was lessened only by the power of prayer.

His prayers paid. Within days of the death of Li Xia, Liu Yang announced to her husband through tears that she was expecting another child. Wang Jie hugged his wife. The two cried in each others arms for the rest of the evening.

Sau was finally ready to move on.

SPIN THE WHEEL

Under normal circumstances, Aisling would hear the distinctive, beating wings of approaching angels. They would usually descend in unison, trying to time their arrival to avoid any form of bias toward one life circumstance or another.

These carrier angels came directly from Immat's sanctuary. Aisling had never been to the place where Immat dwelled, but imagined that it was an enormous room with dynamic whiteboards, each changing and rotating, offering him ideas as fast as he could process them. All she knew was that the life options she received from him, through these angels, were as varied as there were places, languages, and religions. Each of the ten or twelve or fifteen typically fell into similar categories with a few outliers that would allow the soul ready to see contrasts, to break from the recent past if desired.

Each of the angels carried a scroll that represented one life option. The scrolls would give Aisling the basic information about the life, including the parents' names, the geographic location, the exact time of birth, which could be during almost any era, and a series of symbols that she was trained to translate easily into a combined portrait of the religion, culture, and political environment in which the soul would be born.

Aisling's assignment was to visit each of these life options and, using her powers of intuition and psychic ability, gain an understanding of the circumstances surrounding this impending birth. It was most important for the soul to see all possible detail about the lives available for the choosing. The ultimate choice rested with the soul, but the details that made the choice possible were provided by Aisling. The simple Venn-like diagram that he handed down was the road map; it was her job to fill in the topography.

In the time that she had grown familiar with the job, Aisling grew to admire the way they were consistent in their cadence as they approached her. No matter how many angels, they were always carefully spread apart, like jet planes in an air show. She playfully called them Blue Angels but none seemed to get the reference, so she stopped trying.

"Not the sharpest thorns on the bush, are ya now?" She knew that all angels had a purpose, and this was theirs.

The sound of the oncoming beating wings was different this time.

"My, my, we're in a rush this time!"

She greeted them as she always did, welcoming them while sincerely eager to see what possibilities they brought.

She opened the packages as a parent would on Christmas Day, one by one from each of her children. She "ooh'd" and "ah'd" her way through the life options, offering her curiosities and wonders about each of the locales and the time periods that each life would be lived.

Each pregnancy was occurring in the twenty-first century or beyond. Eight were located in Eastern Europe and in some of the former Russian states. Each appeared to offer a variety of challenges but all with profound opportunities to spread spiritual wisdom around to adjoining lives. Political struggles were still the order of the day during this time, along with the religious traditions that thrived for centuries in each geographic area. Each of the lives would be framed by these realities.

Two of the scrolls described lives in India in the middle of the twenty-second century, after the country had overcome its problems balancing population with resources, and in the years following an especially bitter and costly war with Pakistan that spanned many decades.

The opportunity for growth in these Indian lives seemed appealing, but neither seemed to be the reasons for the angels' excitement. Still she treated each one as a special opportunity for the prospective spirit, whoever it was, and she was dedicated to finding all she could about each.

She opened up a package containing the scroll of a life that took place in the northeastern United States. This child would grow up fatherless, but with great expectations surrounding his arrival. The opportunity was curious in the energies that surrounded it, some very dark and some very light. This would be an eventful life. As always she tried to avoid judgment, but quietly she was planning to look a little more closely at this one.

There was the life of a girl in New Zealand who would grow to be the mother of two children requiring special needs. There was the life of an exceptionally smart boy in Montevideo, Uruguay who would face special challenges in the acceptance of his sexual orientation.

Aisling thanked each angel personally, with sincere assurance that she would give her utmost attention to all the details surrounding the life. She wished them blessings on their return to Immat's level, and told each how much she looked forward to their return. Then her difficult work began.

The travel, assimilation, and analysis required for each was substantial. From her prior journeys, she found that traveling ahead then working back in time allowed her to retain her sense of historical context on a global scale. For a thorough investigation of any single life, Aisling needed to travel, observe, understand, and record. On her return she was required to present this myriad of details for each life to the waiting soul.

She first mapped out a strategy for investigating each situation. She decided to move to the lives in India first as they required a jump ahead in time, hence a little more planning and calibration. Next she would visit the lives in the European and former Russian states, followed by the American child then the Uruguayan, and finally the life in the southern hemisphere.

The energy that surrounds an expectant mother is among the most powerful and important that exists on earth. The process of infusing life into a conceived child is an exhausting process, and one that is immensely prone to error. To cut corners in any single life might mean cheating the awaiting parents, along with the thousands of people that will be affected by that life, for good or for bad.

At conception, a perfectly unique set of genes are combined and passed to a child. The genetic mix dates back many generations, containing trait variations the child will carry through its development. Still, it is only the start of the process. So much more is required.

The inherited traits that form a human embryo can also be accentuated or suppressed by the mother's delivery system. During the nine months of the child's development in the womb, nutrients flow from the mother in a complex process that includes the food she eats, the air she breathes, the water she drinks, and all forms of spiritual energy she encounters.

The time between conception and birth is far, far from a straight line. The embryo is a miraculous sponge, staggering in complexity but utterly dependent on three things: what the human mother delivers, what mother earth delivers, and what the heavens deliver. In each of the three, many energies flow around and into the developing human long before birth.

It was Aisling's job to worry about the last.

During her research she first studied the temperament of the mother as she prepared for birth. Would the child be surrounded by the excitement that a new life brings, or be a new addition to an already large family, just another mouth to feed? Would the child learn loving behavior from her family, or would she be left to find out what love means on her own? Would formal religion play a part in the child's life, or would expectations be formed in other ways? Would birth defects be treated as an opportunity for growth, or as a 'curse from the gods' that will result in isolation?

To gather all of these factors, Aisling needed to decipher the nuances of each culture, of which there were many thousands. It was not necessary for her to learn each language, however it was her job to scan communications between the parents, their families, and other acquaintances to discern their meaning within the context of the social, religious, and cultural factors the child would face.

She found it very valuable to observe the spirits that surrounded the expectant mother. Much as family tended to gather around their love ones during key stages of life such as births, weddings, and deaths, spirits tended to congregate nearby before birth. However, just as some humans in these important circumstances helped to create a loving, supportive environment in preparation for the arrival, others were merely in the way. This made Aisling's job even more challenging.

Aisling was ideally suited, from her time as a medium on earth, to read the intentions of the spirits and to recognize the good from the bad from the indifferent. She was advanced in her ability to scan through the energies that surrounded the child, which would come to bear on the pending life. When her research was complete, she took great pride in presenting a holistic view to the anxious spirit in the higher realm and to Hildegarde, the mentoring mother figure.

As she meticulously gathered all of these factors, she would carefully build a spectrum for presentation to the eager soul. The spectrum would contain a panorama of detail about all the important genetic, physical, environmental, and spiritual factors that would be useful during the selection process. Each of the spectrums would compete against each other for the attention of the soul choosing a life. Aisling knew that some would naturally be more appealing than others on the surface, but a deeper look at the details around the life might create some interesting dilemmas for the spirit in waiting. A certain obstacle or opportunity buried in Aisling's notes might trigger a memory of an opportunity that was missed in a past life.

The choices made by her patrons were predictably unpredictable. When she was first on the job, she and Hildegarde would playfully guess what life the soul would choose, but she was wrong most of the time. Finally she stopped trying, deciding it was wasted energy that might unduly influence how she assembled and presented her spectrums.

She delved into the Indian lives first, examining the regions and the cultures around each. The first life to examine was off the southeastern coast of India, in the large city of Chennapattanam, usually shortened to Chennai. With more than seven million residents in the middle of the twenty-second century, the city had grown to be a hub for culture and advanced information technology. This life would be one of a girl growing among the city's elite. Tangible comforts would not be a challenge, but finding acceptance and human comfort would be. In a society where arranged marriages were still the norm, being a wealthy Hindu girl in an unshapely, unattractive body would be a burden through childhood and into what was bound to be an unhappy marriage, or perhaps several.

The next subject of Aisling's research was that of a very poor boy growing up in the Pilkhana slum of Kolkata, also known as Calcutta, in West Bengal. The boy would be the sixth of eight children to be born to a very close Muslim family. The father would not be part of the boy's upbringing for long, as an industrial accident would claim his life while the child was young. Five of his seven siblings would be female, so the expectations were that he as a male child would take an early leadership role in helping his family survive. The pressures to meet expectations, while avoiding negative influences, would be enormous.

Aisling examined the realities of each of these existences that were at the extreme ends of Indian society, each of which carried unique and challenging burdens. Positive spiritual influences were available in each life, but unhelpful, troubled souls hovered nearby, casting a pall over much of the good this soul would generate. A younger, newer soul would want nothing to do with these challenges. Aisling made copious notes to that effect.

Her work in India complete, Aisling next focused her attention on the budding lives in another place and time. A young boy would be born in Bishkek, the capital city of Kyrgyzstan, in the fall of 2079. Kyrgyzstan was a mountainous country bordered by several other former Russian countries, along with China to the East. The country had a long history of religious and political conflict. This boy would be born to a small family of Roman Catholics, a fierce minority in this isolated region. The boy would be large and athletic, just like his hockey-playing father but as fate would have it, he would prefer the company of men. His lifelong struggle would be in finding acceptance and a productive place in such an unforgiving circumstance.

Aisling noticed that the spiritual energies surrounding this life were exceptionally positive. There was an abundance of spirits of long lost relatives, who seemed to be making up for difficult lives on earth by coming together in the afterlife. The earthly life for this young man would not be easy, but the spiritual support would be strong.

She next moved to the female life of a child born in the mid-21st century to an educated couple in Donetsk in Ukraine. The father would be a professor of medicine, prominent in his field but neglectful of his family, while the mother would be a former model who was drug-addicted and unfaithful in the years following the girl's birth. This child would be blessed with great intellect and beauty, but with a wholly dysfunctional family life. In her early years, the girl would be tempted by the people that flocked around female beauty, and her challenge would be to forge a meaningful path from such a crumbled foundation.

Aisling observed that the spiritual forces around this girl were tumultuous, among the least settled she had ever seen. The challenge, to pull great gifts from a tangled existence into something meaningful, would be arduous. Immat was not making this an appealing option for any pending soul who wanted an easy ride, but just the right soul might relish the challenge.

Aisling shifted her attention to a boy who would arrive in Poland in the twenty-first century with very poor social skills. He would be the first of four sons born to working class parents who had neither the patience nor the inclination to learn about Aspergers or other disorders on the autism spectrum. He would be forced to watch, with little defense, as his siblings surpassed him in development and life successes. Along the way he would have the opportunity to change lives, but it would be a monumental test of the soul's patience.

Aisling paid special attention to a girl born to a prostitute in France. The girl would grow up an outcast, unable to run from the dark cloud that followed her. Aisling expended immense effort looking for opportunities for spiritual growth in this life, and did her very best work to illustrate the opportunities and challenges this life would face.

She examined the physical, genetic, and spiritual forces around a boy who was one in a multiple birth, a triplet born to a coal mining family in the Czech Republic. The opportunities for this boy were vast, but the challenges, like each of the other lives, could be daunting.

In one of her more difficult assignments, Aisling examined the emerging life of a lovely girl born in Smolensk, in Western Russia. This child would be cursed to be part of a family that looked the other way as her extended family took opportunities to sexually abuse her. The hardships the girl would face would be enough to shatter a newer soul, and the spiritual forces to help her would be few. Her advantage in life would be a connection to the spirit world, which in itself could be quite a burden for many. As always, Aisling did her very best to explore the positive as well as the negative in her portfolio.

At about this time in her journey, Aisling felt her mental energy running low. She had examined eight pending births with only three to go. As she looked ahead in her assignment book, none seemed quite as grinding as the ones she had just scrutinized. She executed each task carefully and thoroughly, trying to leave no small detail undiscovered. As always on such an assignment, the journey was exhausting. It was as if she was on a long journey during her recent living years, but with seven or eight senses open instead of five. She reminded herself that the hardest work was complete. Only three lives remained.

The most interesting of the lives ahead appeared to be the boy that was to be born in the United States. She decided do take an unusual approach and jump out of her planned sequence to save this most intriguing life for last. S

he zoomed south and east, into the lower hemisphere, to enjoy the beauty of the Indian Ocean and the vast desert of West-Central Australia on her way to Wellington, New Zealand.

There she dug her energy into the factors surrounding a girl that would be born to traditional Jewish parents. Her early life would be wrapped in the comfort of a nurturing faith. Her challenges would come in early adulthood, as each of her two children would have some form of birth defect. Her first son would be born with Down Syndrome. Knowing the second child could also carry the gene, she and her caring husband would hesitate in attempting a second birth for seven years. The second child, a girl, would not possess the Down gene, but the parents would not find this child without complexity either. The pregnancy would be difficult, complications at birth restricting blood flow, so their second child would be born blind. After a carefree youth, this budding soul would have decades in duty as a mother, with both of her offspring requiring special care through their lives and hers.

Aisling next turned her attention to the small South American country of Uruguay, where the wife of an ambitious young politician awaited the birth of the first of her three children. Her husband's career was on the rise when this boy would be born in the early twenty-first century. By the time he reached maturity, his father would be a strong candidate for a move into the Presidential Palace. All of this would signify a happy, high profile life, except for the undeniable truth that this young man would be gay. His father was a devout Roman Catholic, and his son's presence on campaigns and in the limelight could be a source of embarrassment if his sexual orientation became public. This child would be forced to live a life outside the inner circle of the family in his early years, and he would be forced to make some difficult decisions throughout life.

From these outlying adventures, Aisling next shifted to the last of her research subjects, the one she had been waiting for, a boy that would be born to a woman in Boston in the early twenty-first century.

In her most recent incarnation, Aisling had spent many happy years in the area around Boston near the time of this coming birth. Still, from the time she accepted the scrolls from the carrier angels, there was something very familiar about this coming life. The forces and energies around it continuously reminded her of some of the spirits she encountered as a medium, just before this time.

The expectant mother's husband had been senselessly murdered just a few months before. She found great comfort in a large church congregation she had recently joined, and the church was now at the center of her life. This was a woman who was raised in a large Catholic, northeastern family, rooted in the old ways. Families like hers kept their family secrets safely tucked away from the wandering eyes and wagging tongues of neighbors and family members they preferred to keep at a distance. They went through life leaving nothing to chance. Life to her family was an exhausting endeavor of straightening out curvy roads, of minimizing risk and maximizing reward. This most unexpected turn, the inexplicable death of her husband that had just followed their joyous announcement, represented a cruel twist in her life that she never could see coming.

At first, this woman came to the church as a favor to a friend, but then she had a chance meeting and a long, intimate discussion with one of the leaders of the church, a flamboyant, expressive Reverend, a woman whose date of birth, including the year, was exactly the same as hers. This Reverend would never have children, she proclaimed, so she took a special interest in the woman's exciting news.

When news of the death of the father-to-be reached the Reverend, her outpouring of grief and support was exactly what the mother needed and craved. Her world had been shattered and the Reverend, with all her resources and generosity, made the transition to widowhood much easier. Her child would be born of this Church.

Despite Aisling's familiarity with the surrounding geography and energies, she found her approach to this assignment difficult to bring into focus. At first she attributed it to her own weariness from having traveled so many miles, having examined so many distinct life circumstances in each place. For this life, she found it difficult to distinguish light energies from dark energies. It was as if the details surrounding the birth were shrouded by forces too complex for her senses to process.

As a living medium she was skilled at helping the people around her by connecting them to souls who cared about them but were no longer in their presence. It was a skill she had developed over many lifetimes that made her a perfect fit for this role. However with this coming child, so near in place and time to her most recent past life, her ability to interpret the collection of energies was almost completely ineffective.

The energies around the birth of this male child were very strong, this much she knew. There was pain and passion and the desire for good swirling around, but there was also an overwhelming energy that suggested a desire to change the course of history through this birth. This life was the narrow end of a funnel, a vortex, where many competing energies were moving around and through each other, jostling for position to brace for a coming battle. Fueling these energies, like dry kindling on a new fire, were violent events, many by living humans who would be close to this child.

There were great expectations around this birth. The boy would be born into a highly charged environment where his learning would be scrutinized, monitored, and influenced by nearby spirits not currently dwelling in human bodies.

There were the normal spirits excited for the delivery, including some proud New Englanders from the mother's side, the Schultz's, and from the father's side, the Livingstons. Their pride showed clearly, but there was also a hovering level of concern. These were not worries about the health of the child, nor the stability or health of the single mother anxiously awaiting the boy's arrival. This was a different kind of worry, directed at other nearby spirits.

Aisling could feel their presence, and they felt hers. They knew precisely why she was here, but she could not say the same about them. She was unable to read their intentions, nor the reasons for their heightened interest in this coming birth.

The child's mother would be capable of providing love and care, and the extended family that was alive was stable, kind and benevolent. The mother's mother was alive, living nearby, and was also available for any support required. Together with the support offered by the Reverend, this child's needs would be more than amply met.

The challenge with this life, Aisling began to understand, were different from all the other spectrums under her watch. There were no physical obstacles to overcome, no dysfunctional family situations that would be a persistent test, nor any traditional religious constraints to work through.

The impact of this life on the world could be tremendous, but the challenges far more complex. Aisling was able to envision a profound life, one that was lived in the limelight, perhaps a President, a Pope, or another leader of many. Alternately, the life could be lived below the surface, as a business or technical mastermind who will change the course of human events through his vision, and the will to bring that vision to reality.

Aisling froze when she hosted a vision of a third possibility. This child could be at the center of one of the greatest injustices ever to befall the human world, and maybe even beyond. There was a link, faded and barely recognizable, between the coming birth of this child and many thousands of deaths that had inexplicably surged around the world in recent months.

She attempted to focus her remaining energy on what could possibly link the arrival of an eight pound boy to the violent, wrongful deaths of so many, but her intuition was not enough to penetrate the complexity of this pending life. So she went back to her normal assignment, collecting detailed observations, converting them into notes for later discussion and analysis in the higher realm. In her analysis, which was the very reason she was in this place, she would be left to observe and transcribe. She hoped her assessment would give this budding life the same fair treatment she had given the others. She would rely on the wisdom and comfort of her mentor, Hildegarde, who would bring a fresh view to this complex coming life.

Before concluding her assessment of this fascinating life, one detail worth exploring more deeply was the violent death of the father. The spirits she had surveyed so far, both living human and non, had seemed to accept the death of this baby's father as something that could not be reversed. Their adjustment seemed healthy, but on the father's side there was bitterness. The father's presence was here, but it was shielded, protected almost, from an array of spirits who formed a paternal front line.

In the midst of familiarity with this group of souls, the name Livingston kept her attention. She had met them recently, not in some distant past life. The name Annabelle Livingston seemed most familiar. As she continued to survey the nearby spirits, carefully sensing their expectations and emotions about the important event that was to come, this was a warm, accepting environment for a child to enter the world. The wounds of the unexpected death of the father were easy to read, so the arrival of this boy would be a welcome, happy diversion.

Then she saw him. Lurking behind the Livingstons and other close spirits was the soul of a man who was badly wounded and very afraid. The family was clearly trying to protect him from the energies that swirled nearby to allow him to heal and rejuvenate, but the soul of this man wanted no part.

Since his death about six months prior, this soul had not ascended. He remained vigilant, close to his wife and the burgeoning mass of life that would be his son. Although he meant well, his presence was not helpful or useful to the development of the boy. Still, it did explain the strong showing by the Livingston family and the extended family Aisling had not met before, the Donnelly's.

John Donnelly was the father of this child.

Suddenly the memories came rushing back to Aisling. Just a few months before the time she was to leave the earth, John Donnelly had come into her parlor with a lie about trying to find out about the likelihood of illness on his wife's side, and whether their coming child would be affected in any way.

The moment was memorable to Aisling for several reasons. She recognized the spirit of Annabelle Livingston because Annabelle appeared during his reading to scold John about his deceit, and to insist that he change his path. The more important reason was that Annabelle delivered the message to her dear friend and understudy, Henry Chimera. This was the moment she realized Henry possessed sensory powers that exceeded her own. It was also when she realized that she could relinquish her business to Henry and go home to Ireland to pass to the next life.

She focused her full attention on Donnelly. He sensed her stare and showed just a hint of the same familiarity as he glanced in her direction. He had been watching, which allowed Aisling to see clearly through to his pain. Donnelly was in a very bad state.

A violent, unexpected murder was enough to put any soul into a state of despair, but most people who were living a reasonably happy life, free from addictions or cycles of violence or depression, were able to move up to the higher realm to begin the process of regeneration. Other less fortunate spirits would remain anchored to the earth, sometimes because of their confusion about whether they were alive or dead. In their state of disorientation, these spirits would cling to the people, places, and things that were most familiar, afraid to look to the Light.

This was not the case for John Donnelly. He stayed anchored to this realm because he legitimately feared for the beloved wife he left behind and the son he would never meet on earth.

His murder was not random and it was not done by a stranger. The ones who put him here were using his family as a tool that would change the course of human existence on earth for all of eternity.

FROM BOTH SIDES

The clouds were low, layered, and moving as Richard Shoemaker's Range Rover hummed northward along Route 9N, one lane in both directions, with hotels and a few restaurants on large lots. The road snaked up the West side of Lake George, where highway 87 - the Adirondack Northway - dumps travelers off at touristy Lake George Village.

"It looks like Bolton Landing is a fair-sized town for this county," Henry said.

"I just saw a sign. It's coming up in about three miles," Shoemaker replied. "What's the name of this rental place?"

"Holmquist Marina and Rentals," Henry said. It should be lake side, on the right. I called ahead."

After a couple minutes Winfred spoke from the back of the SUV. "I think I just saw a sign. It's in yellow, just after the gas station."

Shoemaker pulled in and parked. "So I meant to ask, Henry. What exactly do you know about boats?"

"Not anything," he said. "Well, I know they're only supposed to have one hole, and that's on top where you climb in. Why, are you a boat guy?"

Shoemaker shook his head. "When I was in the Army near water, I was always a passenger."

"Typical," Naomi said from the back seat. "The woman has to take over, otherwise the men will be in a fetal position within a couple hours, grunting, farting, and swatting at flies."

The conversations during the drive were focused around the various scenarios they might face when they reached their destination, including all the possibilities for approaching the house to retrieve Dee. There was no decision on whether they would approach the lake house from the boat or from the small road. They wanted to make their approach discreet, and agreed their vantage from the boat would be useful in observing the property and making their decision, with the help of binoculars.

"We had boats all the time I was growing up, mostly around Plymouth Harbor." Naomi accentuated 'harbor' in her thick Boston dialect, probably for effect.

"Sounds good," Henry said. "You can help us pick one out."

As they sorted through their gear in the truck, the reality set in that they needed to decide which tools would be necessary. Winfred asked what they had all been avoiding.

"Are we getting ready for an approach right now, or are we just getting in this boat to plan a mission for tomorrow morning, after we've gotten some sleep? Is this a mission to observe, or will it be a full confrontation?"

"The latter," Henry said without hesitation. "If we see an opportunity to hit the place, we should do it."

"Hold on, Henry," Shoemaker said. "We have no strategy whatsoever. We barely know the layout of this place. We could be headed into a very dangerous situation."

Henry turned sharply toward him. "Look Richard, if I see Dee in there, I'm not going to want to wait twelve hours in some crap motel while we figure out how to attack the place and get her out of there."

"Agreed," Shoemaker replied calmly. "If we see her in danger we should move to get her out of there, but that's not likely. Like we talked about on the way here, our priority today is to observe this place, learn the layout, and develop some logistics. Whether Dee is here or she's not here, we probably won't see her through a window from a boat on the lake, two hundred yards from the house."

He paused to pick through his gear to ease the anxiety the group was clearly feeling. "We might be able to learn how many entrances there are, which direction the road approaches from, how close they are to neighbors, whether there's cover near the house, that kind of thing. We couldn't see that level of detail from the online satellite images because of all the trees, so I suspect we'll see a lot more from the lake."

"Fine, but I think we should gear up as if we're going in, just in case." Henry said this as he looked into the eyes of each of the three.

"You definitely should do that, as we all should. Naomi, you're bringing your cameras and lenses, correct?"

She nodded.

"Keep them protected," Shoemaker warned, "we might get a little wet. The clouds look nasty and the water is choppy."

Each member of the group loaded a separate pack with their essentials. They put on the life jackets and boarded the sixteen foot powerboat.

Naomi navigated through The Narrows, a collection of islands that formed a gateway to the large northeastern stretch of the lake.

"Huletts Landing looks like about four or five miles past the Narrows," Henry shouted over the wind and waves.

Naomi kept the boat's speed slow and steady to avoid too much bouncing on the turbulent water. As they moved north the headwinds seemed stronger, punctuated by an occasional strong gust from the East or the West. Light rain from above mixed with spray from below to form a steady mist. There were few other boats on the lake, even fewer that were moving. Their approach would be noticed. It would be necessary to move very slowly as they approach the lake house.

After about ten minutes they noticed a busy area behind a few islands.

"That's Huletts Landing," Henry said above the engine, waves, and wind. "The compound is less than a mile to the North. Look for the green boathouse. It looked big from the satellite image."

She cut down the engine to a crawl. From the shore they would look like adventurous fishermen, out for a try at large bass and trout on a wet day.

As they moved past the bays of Huletts Landing, the wind seemed to come from all directions. Lake water mixed with rain to form a sheet. Even in the remaining daylight, a view of the shore was blurry. Straight ahead the clouds were in a swirl. It was as though the origin of this weather front was above their target, directly where they were moving.

Henry felt a bolt and a bright white light. He was suddenly transfixed, unable to move or look around at the others. All his senses locked onto the energies churning in the clouds above this house. The white and gray streaks of mist took on new shapes, new detail that came to life as he stared, amazed. There was a slow rumbling that formed into separate strands of energy, very distinct from one another. These were spiritual energies, moving above him, jostling as if to compete for position. They sized each other up, looking for a foothold, gathering strength. They moved around and through one another with ferocity, creating a thousand points of friction. Their movements generated the rumbling vibration felt by each of these mortal souls in the small vessel.

The energies were not all the same. Some were lighter, feathered but sleek and strong. Others were rippled, dark gray and textured, undulating and sliding. They moved around, between, and through each other as if preparing for a coming showdown.

Henry detected the very faint sense of familiar energies, spirits living and non-living that he had known very recently. Whomever they were, they recognized his presence. For a brief moment he was in among the twisting, turning creatures, moving for his own position. Some gushed with relief that he had arrived. Others made it clear he was not welcome.

His focus expanded beyond the chaotic scene before him back to the other three living souls in the boat, each staring at him, eyes wide.

He stared back solemnly. "This is the place."

"Another long journey comes to an end," Hildegarde said to her dear friend.

"And a wild one it was," Aisling replied. "This one should be fascinating."

Aisling had spent her recent days devoting immeasurable energy researching the details around an array of eleven lives. She then forged these factors, physical, geographic, religious, spiritual, into one spectrum for each life. They were prepared with meticulous care and great pride, with a special emphasis on thoroughness. One small detail could make a life more or less attractive than all the others in the eyes of the eager client. Each soul had its own experiences, the things it cherished or despised about previous lives. For example, Aisling could have no way of knowing whether a soul had no desire to be Caucasian again, or to have a large family nearby, or to live in an area that experienced earthquakes.

Meanwhile Hildegarde devoted all of her attention to become acquainted with the soul who was about to make a choice. An angel would arrive to tell Hildegarde that a soul was nearly ready to move to her level, and would soon need her assistance.

Rather than simply waiting for the soul to arrive, Hildegarde would travel to meet the soul in its circle. She felt it was important to get a sense of the other souls surrounding her subject, including their conversations about what should be next for this life and the agreements and disagreements this close group of friends shared.

The process of choosing a life was grueling. With so many complexities and options, it was common for a soul to forget some of the important lessons that were learned among its circle of friends. The lure of an easy life, or of riches, fame, or beauty could be tempting, especially when compared to more difficult lives. Hildegarde's role was to help the soul stay true on its path, or at least not forget it too soon. Understanding how overwhelming the process could be, Hildegarde would try to keep these goals at the forefront as she accompanied the soul from its circle of friends to her level.

The two considered it their sacred duty to preserve all the work that went into gathering, analyzing, and presenting the life options to the soul in waiting. They had made a recent pact that they would come to each of these sacred, vital ceremonies with a fresh perspective. They would save all of their conversations for when the subject spirit was present, and avoid sharing private opinions about the path the soul would choose. In this way, they agreed, there would be no hint of bias toward one life or another.

After all her hard work, Aisling was finally ready to meet the soul who would have to choose between these lives. At first glance she was instantly struck by its deep blue hue. This was a soul who was very seasoned.

"Wonderful," Aisling said. "This one has been through this many times. It's a good thing. This will not be an easy choice."

Hildegarde smiled toward her subject. "Sau, I'd like you to meet Aisling. She's here to present you with your options for your next life."

The three became acquainted. Sau explained that his restorative period was fairly easy given his relatively brief time on earth as Li Xia, the six year old Chinese girl who was murdered in the streets of her hometown.

"It was a short life," he explained. "Free from worry or stress of any kind. I was a gifted child and my parents had such great expectations for me. The most difficult thing was leaving them. They were so heartbroken. It was especially rough on my mother. I died right next to her. I still don't understand why it happened."

Rather than talking about the circumstances of the tragedy, they focused on the things that were intended but not accomplished in that short life. Sau explained that with the help of his friends, he was reminded that his challenge was to make a difference in the world without allowing his office or his position to corrupt his mission. He spoke to Hildegarde and Aisling about the steps he would take to ensure this would not happen again.

Aisling was impressed. Sau would not shy away from any challenge.

"Each one of the lives in this array will be very meaningful, but in very different ways. There isn't one of them that will leave you wishing you had an opportunity to accomplish more, assuming of course that you're able to live a complete life." She paused after this point. The girl's early death was obviously not foreseen by Sau when he was last in the position to choose.

"Immat must have known that such a veteran soul was coming along," Hildegarde said, changing the subject to the future. "There are some exciting options available for you. The ritual before us is the most fulfilling, exciting part of my job. I always feel like I'm the one doing the choosing."

One by one, Aisling placed all the spectrums in front of Sau. As she presented, she was careful to keep her emotions out of each description and explain only what was known with certainty. For each morsel of information, she carefully presented the facts in a way that fulfilled three basic requirements. Was it factually correct? Was it free from bias? Was it useful? If a detail about a life passed these three basic checks, it would make it onto the spectrum. Across the eleven lives there were hundreds, perhaps even a few thousand of these tidbits.

With each life Aisling went into great detail about her first impressions of the energies surrounding the expectant mother and whether those impressions changed as she studied more closely. She dove into the culture, the family influences, the religions in the region and in the family, and any environmental factors that would likely exert an influence on how the life would play out. With her charm on full display, she went through each of the lives in colorful detail, all the while maintaining the dignity and solemnity of the ritual.

Many angels were nearby as Aisling went through her presentation. Sau's circle of souls, the group that knew him best through the millennia, were there to observe. Spirits who happened to be in this realm had an open invitation to observe these important events, but to stay in the background to avoid distraction.

The process was solemn and structured. The subject would review each candidate in great detail, be allowed to ask enough questions to completely satisfy his curiosity, and then narrow down his choices to the lives that seemed most appropriate for his objectives.

Finally, after what seemed like many hours, Aisling finished her formal presentation. Hildegarde stepped to the front.

"Aisling, that was a magnificent presentation. You did your job beautifully, with just the right mix of compassion, insight, and careful research. In our many efforts, through all the many souls we've placed with lives, I cannot recall an array that was so diverse, so challenging. Bravo, my dear!

A chorus of cheers went up in this high spiritual realm, echoing from the crystalline chamber walls. Hildegarde led the applause, and Aisling blushed and bowed. Sau joined in the spirit of the moment, smiling and clapping in appreciation. Even Immat's positive presence was felt, pleased with the process of discovery that Aisling displayed.

When the room quieted, Hildegarde spoke again.

"As is customary, it is time for you to narrow down these lives to just a handful. The lives that you can safely rule out will be made available for other souls to consider. Which are your finalists?"

"The one that seemed first to jump off the spectrum," Sau began, "is the American life near Boston. The possibilities for making an impact seem the highest in this life."

The feeling of contentedness filled the room. No one seemed surprised by the first selection.

"The challenges I see are the energies that surround this birth and, from what I can tell, all the years of its life. It would be very difficult to make the most of such a life, with so many strong living and nonliving forces at play."

Aisling and Hildegarde shared a meaningful glance, and a shared thought. Sau was duly aware of the strong energies at play in this life.

"Still," Sau continued, "I have to consider this one a finalist because of the impact, the influence, and the potential it offers."

"A wise choice, I think." Hildegarde said this as she scanned the spirits huddled in the periphery. This pronouncement brought contended murmurs from the crowd.

"What other spectrum caught your attention?"

"For a variety of reasons, I was really drawn to the life of the girl born to parents in Ukraine. This one intrigues me greatly. The father is a university professor, while the mother is a disgrace, but a beautiful disgrace. This girl will inherit her father's intellect and the beauty of her mother, but the child will grow in the absence of a true role model. What a challenge! Living this life would be quite a test of character. I have confidence it would emerge in a loving, productive, and compassionate way, but what a test!

"Complicating matters further, there are dark forces near the girl that Aisling so adeptly pointed out. Ukraine could be at the center of some very important events during this time, and this girl will have some extremely difficult choices to make in her lifetime. So I would like this life to be considered a finalist as well," Sau concluded.

"Very good," Hildegarde said. "Two strong lives to choose from so far, and each seems to align with your desire to make a difference on a national or even international scale. Your goals are high, and I commend you for that. However, I might remind you that changing the world that is immediately around you can have just as strong an impact as changing events in the world at large. A strong leader who changes the direction of a small village can make a positive difference that will last for generations. When done correctly, this can be greater than all the changes made by a head of state, or the leader of a large organization.

"Which others caught your attention?"

Sau smiled. "Your advice is timely, Hildegarde. One that seems to show great promise but on a smaller scale is the girl born to traditional Jewish parents in New Zealand. While the impact in such a life would be so very local, the challenge of coming through an early life of such strong faith, then having two children with birth defects that would require care throughout the life, well, it seems like the most sacred of lives I could live."

The hush in the room persisted.

Hildegarde brought the energy up with her voice. "Ah! A stark contrast from the other lives. I think you are being true to your path in each of the choices you've made, and this one would be a very blessed life indeed. The pressure to stay healthy and available for needful children would be high. It would not be a life that would afford much travel, or carefree later years."

She looked down at her lectern. "You've made three choices. I would encourage you to consider no more than one or two more."

"My last choice," Sau replied, "might surprise you. It's probably the most appealing of all so far. It's the boy with social challenges growing up in Poland. I think they call his condition Asberger Syndrome, which is a form of Autism, but that label belies so much beneath the surface. As Aisling pointed out in her analysis, there have been many people with similar conditions who managed to make a great contribution. What they lack in social skill, they sometimes can offset by concentrating on a skill or talent that will make a world of difference. That could be anything of my choosing. Even without the support of my parents, who would be disappointed by my condition through the life, I think I could do wonderful things. Sometimes the underdog rules the day. I find this life very challenging, perhaps the most challenging of all."

"You've made some very strong choices, Sau," Hildegarde said. "Are you certain your selection process is complete?"

"I am certain," Sau replied firmly. "These were the four lives that clearly stood above the rest."

"Very well." Hildegarde turned toward the many spirits who were assembled to watch the process of selection.

"As you have heard, Sau has made his selection of finalists for the life he will choose. Normally during the remainder of this ceremony we invite all to observe, all to watch. This is allowed for souls who are in the growth stages of their journey, those with much remaining in their path toward enlightenment."

Her smile faded and her faced turned solemn. "However, Sau has reached the level of Master. He is continuing his journey through lifetimes by his own choice. Because of his highly advanced status, his choice has profound consequences. Whatever life he chooses will carry blessings from many realms. This decision must be made in the most prayerful way, free from influence of any kind. As such, it is necessary to restrict observation of the final selection process to a very small group, which includes only the Principality, myself, and my Apprentice, Aisling. Our Power in this process,

Immat, is also free to observe. Everyone else must leave the chamber as the final decision is made."

As she went silent, hands on the lectern, there was an orderly, disappointed procession through the gates and out of the chamber.

When the last angel and all other spirits left the room, only Hildegarde, Aisling, and Sau remained. Immat's presence was felt as well.

"Well, it's just us three," Hildegarde said, smiling. "Sau, for the final selection you may take all the time you require. Your choice will have profound consequences, not only for you in your continuing journey, but for all the people who are blessed by your presence.

"It is essential that you think back to what your mission was when you first came here, before you became aware of the specifics of each life. You studied it intensively in your soul circle, but Aisling has not had the benefit of hearing it directly from you. Please summarize, if you would be so kind."

"Of course. I believe humankind has been moving, through the twenty-first century, toward a state of isolation. Attention is directed inwardly, at the self, when it should be directed at the good of all of humankind. My mission is to encourage those around me to be more involved with the struggles of their brothers and sisters. This is the essence of life, and too many are forgetting this basic truth.

"My struggle in recent incarnations has been in retaining a full focus on my mission and to not permit myself to be distracted by maintaining my platform. In my last full life, the circumstances were in place to make a wonderful difference in the lives of so many, but I worried too much about things that might prevent me from fulfilling my mission. At first it may appear that I am after glory, or some other attention directed to my human persona. I am not. I am interested in making the most significant difference I can to the widest possible audience.

"Hildegarde's advice is invaluable. I must think small as well as large in my next incarnation. I suspect this will be my last before I ascend into a higher realm to take on weightier responsibilities in the grand order. Some would have me be thought of as 'The New Messiah' in my next life, but of course I am not and it is not my goal. However, if I am blessed enough to receive that kind of attention, I would embrace it as an opportunity to change human existence for the better. Regardless of faith or circumstance, these people need to be awoken to the reason they are in living bodies. So many have lost their way."

Aisling watched in rapt attention. When Sau was finished, she smiled and nodded, a tear forming.

Finally she spoke. "It is indeed a weighty responsibility you are taking on. I don't envy the choice before you."

Sau replied, "My intention was to fulfill this through the life of Li Xia, however things became so tumultuous that I suppose the mission was doomed from the start. In this next life I choose, I hope there will be more factors that are within my control."

"Very well," Hildegarde intoned. "With that I think we have come full circle. It is time for Sau to begin his deliberations. Are you ready to begin?"

Sau nodded. Hildegarde led him into a chapel-like structure called Surveyor Hall. Its walls consisted of ornate glass that was in motion, with images from all major religions depicted in a stunning montage. Within the hall, Hildegarde led him to a small enclosure, private and serene, bathed in a gentle, holy light. It was the place where all souls who came through her chamber made their final selection.

In this private enclosure the soul could alter the mood in any way he or she wished to create the perfect setting for pure contemplation. If it wanted orchestral music, it would enjoy the finest created in the heavens and on earth. If it wanted to be surrounded by pictures of the sand-swept Sahara or sweeping mountain ranges of Alaska for inspiration, they were available in an instant. Complete silence and total darkness was also an option.

When the door to the chamber closed, Hildegarde's and Aisling's work was complete. From outside the booth, they could only observe. No further influence was possible unless the soul emerged with questions.

The meaning of the moment, another job well done, came upon each of them. They exhaled and embraced when the door closed.

Sau's prayer would determine which direction the heavenly winds would blow.

It was certain they would be fierce.

"My friends and family, I would like to introduce you to Indazita. He has graciously agreed to join us to help perform this most holy of ceremonies."

Ernest Grandby was standing proudly just inside the front door of the spacious lake house, a panoramic view of a raging Lake George showed through a large window behind him. The storm was churning well above the lake but seemed to be moving downward by the second. Dusk was approaching as the wind and rain intensified.

Also behind him near the doorway stood two unsmiling men in dark suits. Their hands were clasped before them, as sentries at the door. Now and then one would look out the window, on the watch for intruders.

In front of Grandby sat a visibly uncomfortable Janice Donnelly, bearing the weight of a growing child in her womb. Joan Swenson sat beside her on the sofa.

"Welcome, Indazita! I am so honored that you were able to make the trip." Ellen Grandby Sullivan strode confidently from the back, holding out her hand. She wore a sweeping summer dress with a light green print, as if she had just stepped from the pages of a magazine. Her hair, nails, makeup, and dress were perfect.

"This is an event that has taken so much effort by so many people over months and months. The time is finally here!"

The Burmese man accepted her hand smiling and nodding but saying nothing.

Ellen moved to her father, hugging him without disturbing her presentation. "Father. It's been too long."

"Well worth the wait," he answered, taking in her radiance. "You just grow lovelier by the year."

His daughter smiled and nodded comfortably.

Grandby walked across the room to the two ladies on the couch. They blushed as he kissed their hands.

"You look ravishing," he said to Janice. "The promise of motherhood suits you well. Ms. Swenson, I thank you for being available to support your friend through this transition."

Joan smiled nervously below the imposing man and his mysterious assistant. She avoided looking at either of them directly.

Grandby pulled a chair next to Janice.

"Are you ready for what's about to happen, Janice?"

"I think so, yes." She smiled, trembling slightly.

"The path you have chosen for your child is the holiest, most sacred you could imagine. His life will make a more profound difference in the world than anyone alive today, probably more profound than anyone who has been alive for generations."

"My God," Janice said. "That's almost too much to think about."

"Then don't," Grandby replied, smiling. "Just know that when it goes according to plan, you will have played a central role in making the world a better place."

Janice looked back at him, eyes wide, then stared into the distance in contemplation. The magnitude of what she had agreed to was jarring, but she tried to display courage as all eyes in the room were fixed upon her.

"Are we doing this tonight?" A deep male voice came from a hallway adjoining the large room.

"My son." Ernest stood, hands on hips, as Edgar Grandby slowly walked toward his father. They embraced.

"It's been a long journey, Edgar. You've done everything we've asked of you."

Slight tears formed on Edgar's face as he spoke quietly to his father. "It has indeed. It's good to be home."

"The family is together again. We're changing the world," the elder reverend whispered in his son's ear.

Then he turned to the others in the room and spoke in a louder voice. "We're changing the world. Everyone here must remember how far we've come, how much hard work and time went into getting us to the point where we can meet here for this sacred event.

"But our work is not complete. We still need all hearts and minds focused on the task at hand. In answer to your question, Edgar," Ernest said, turning back to his son, "I don't see a reason to wait. We can start tonight."

"Agreed," Ellen replied, "but first let's eat. We've been holding dinner for your arrival."

"That sounds wonderful. I'm famished," Ernest answered.

He wrapped his arm around his daughter's arm and walked her to the kitchen. "Is your friend above ready for what we are about to do?"

"He has no choice. Immat knows that the time has come to return our favor."

Clouds and Water

As darkness descended on Lake George, the storm grew in intensity. Winds swirled in all directions, and the rain began to pelt the four souls struggling for balance inside the sixteen foot fishing boat. Every few seconds a bolt of lightning would turn their struggle into a chaotic daylight scene of waves, spray and a distant view of the trees surrounding a few structures on the shoreline just a couple hundred feet away. It took each several seconds to adjust their eyes between the darkness and the alternating blinding flashes and pure darkness that followed. The head of this storm was swirling directly above.

Naomi Pike was at the wheel, keeping momentum moving ahead through the waves. Henry was in the front passenger seat. Shoemaker and Winfred were in the rear, holding onto equipment with arms and legs.

"What are we doing out here?" Naomi shouted above the crashing waves and swirling winds.

"We're saving a friend," Henry shouted back.

"This is insane," Winfred yelled from the back. "We should not be on the water."

"I agree," Shoemaker replied. "Besides, they might see us through the windows when the sky lights up. Unless we're turning back, we should head for land."

Henry nodded then said to Naomi, "Let's take it up the lake just a little. I don't want to make landfall on their property."

Naomi piloted the boat north, then found a stretch of shoreline that was clear to land safely. Henry jumped out with a rope, securing it to a tree. The group gathered their gear from the boat and walked carefully away from the shore through the thick trees. The lightning and rain continued raging above, but from within the canopy of trees they were no longer taking a direct hit from the wind and water.

"That was hairy," Winfred said. "Any place is safer than in that boat."

"What do we do from here?" Naomi posed the question to no one in particular.

"We came all this way for a reason," Henry said. "If Dee is in there, we need to get her out."

They walked slowly in the general direction of the large lake house. It was completely dark, except for a flash that every few seconds illuminated the entire area. The lightning allowed them to gain their bearings and avoid the uneven, sloping terrain they were navigating.

Finally they spotted lights through the trees.

"If we can find a good vantage point," Shoemaker offered, "I'll string up some plastic. That will at least give us a chance to keep our binoculars dry while we see what's going on in there.

They slowly approached the house, using each lightning strike to survey the area and to stake out the house. There were two cars and a dark van parked in a driveway on the far side.

The largest windows faced the lake, with a large clearing separating the house from the shoreline. Finding a place to set up that was hidden from view of the large windows was essential. They chose a spot that was inside the woods but which offered an angled view of the main living space. Those inside would find it nearly impossible to spot them.

Shoemaker set up a dark plastic tarp between trees, and both he and Naomi dug into their packs for binoculars. No one was visible inside the house from the plate glass windows and the few small windows on the side.

Henry was impatient. "Can you make out anything? I just see walls from here."

Naomi and Richard stopped their work and turned to the house. "Nothing yet, but I wouldn't expect to see anyone," he said. "The lights are on. They're probably sitting around talking."

They watched for several minutes. Finally a figure came walking from the rear of the house past the side windows toward one of the large windows facing the lake.

Henry was the first to notice. "Is that Reverend Sullivan?"

"It is indeed," Shoemaker said. Ellen Grandby Sullivan stood staring out at the darkness and swirling winds, occasionally lit up by lightning. She stayed at the window for several minutes. It appeared she was waiting for someone or something.

"I can't tell who else is in the room with her," Naomi said, "but with all those cars here, she's obviously not alone in the house."

After a few moments, Ellen moved away from the window.

Suddenly Henry noticed a different light in the distance.

"A car is coming," he said. All four instinctively crouched, not knowing what direction the car lights would point.

As the car neared the house, it took a place very close to the front door. The headlights blazed over the lake but never turned in their direction. When they went dead, Naomi and Shoemaker peered through their lenses.

"It's a limo," Shoemaker said. "It looks like four men but there's no light out there. I can't make out any detail."

The men walked around the corner of the house to the main entrance, which was visible at an angle through the window. Ellen Grandby Sullivan rushed to hug the first man through the front door.

"Holy shit!"

Henry asked Shoemaker in a hushed tone, "What is it, Richard?"

Naomi cut him off, looking through her lenses. "None other than the Honorable Reverend Ernest Grandby!"

"Isn't that sweet?" Winfred's tone was heavy with sarcasm. "The Right Reverend drove all the way up here to visit with his daughter."

"Who are the other guys?"

Naomi handed the binoculars to Richard Shoemaker.

"It's quiet a rugged crew, from what I can tell," Shoemaker answered. "I see a couple of bodyguard types. Those guys mean business. Then there's some kind of Asian-looking dude with them. He doesn't look like part of the family." He handed the glasses to Henry.

"A family reunion, I guess. With bodyguards." He looked back toward the others. "I need to see who else is in that room."

"Whatever you're thinking, Henry, it's probably a bad idea." Naomi's voice was filled with alarm.

"I'll be discreet. There are a couple trees between here and the boat house. I'll stop at each one and stay close to the ground."

"Just take it slow. Fast movements always draw attention, even from inside on a night like this," Shoemaker said evenly. "Henry, I have a small pen light here. If I see anyone coming toward the door, I'll shine it in your direction. Focus on the house, but make sure you can see it if I warn you."

"Got it." Henry looped Shoemaker's binoculars around his neck then tucked them under his waterproof jacket. He patted his side for comfort, to make sure his blade was safely hanging from his belt.

"I won't make a move toward the house," he said, trying to reassure his partners. "I'm just going to take a look, promise."

He waited until the next clap of thunder that followed a bolt of lightning, then moved slowly and low toward the first tree, about forty feet away. He waited a few moments to make sure his movement was not noticed, then he pulled the glasses from under his coat. The view offered little more than what he saw under the tarp, so he tucked the glasses away and prepared for another move.

The next tree was another thirty feet away and the boathouse a short distance beyond that. He waited for the right moment, then moved carefully behind the second, larger tree. There was no movement from the house, and he glanced back toward the tarp. He saw no light.

This tree was on a slight rise, thus offered a much better view of the living room. His angle was behind Grandby and his Eastern companion. Grandby appeared to be speaking to the gathering, although Henry could only see part of the space. Occasionally one of the two guards would peer out the window, but seeing nothing outside they would turn back to the discussion in the room.

Henry stood straight up to get a better view. As expected he saw Grandby's daughter, Ellen Grandby Sullivan, standing and listening to her father.

To his amazement he saw two familiar women on the couch. His former customer and friend, Joan Swenson, and a very pregnant Janice Donnelly!

He recalled the last time he saw these two together, at the funeral for John Donnelly. While he remembered their friendship and had guessed that the initials on the scrap of paper may have been theirs, seeing the two of them were here among the Grandby clan was startling.

While he had never spent much time in conversation with Janice Donnelly, thus had never formed much of an impression, he considered Joan Swenson a genuine, well-meaning person. Their first meeting was when she came in for a reading to connect with her father. Henry sensed no bad intent, but he remembered that she was very Christian and unsure whether she should be there. Connecting with her father gave both of them a sense of relief and closure, he recalled.

She later confided in Henry about the video she saw that showed brutal treatment received by a man who looked very much like the Dalai Lama. Most importantly, she found the video on Church property! What could she possibly have seen or heard to make her forget the damning evidence she saw with her own eyes? Was it all a lie, meant to fool Henry, Dee, or everyone? If she fabricated the story about finding the video, what benefit could that possibly provide? He assumed the group was gathered here for some important event, but how could that story have made a difference?

These thoughts raced through his mind as he absently kept watch on the events in the living room of the lake house. Suddenly he saw a new figure appear from the back of the room, this one tall and athletic. Henry lifted the binoculars to focus.

It was Lars! More accurately it was Edgar Grandby, the traitor Origenist. He knew he should not be surprised by his appearance with his family, but the sight of the man made Henry want to sprint into the house. He clenched his jaw with rage while reminding himself that he could do nothing without the help of his friends.

Edgar walked toward the front of the room, to his father. They embraced, saying a few words into each other's ear. Henry looked back toward the tarp. His team was barely visible, and no light appeared from under the tarp. He could make out the image of Naomi's lenses fixed on him. He gave her a thumbs up then pointed down to the ground as if to say, I'm staying right here. At least for now.

"By God's grace we are united here at this table," Ernest Grandby said, eyes closed tightly and fingers clasped before him.

Outside the thunder and lightning were intense. The lights in the lake house flickered after each blinding flash and clap of thunder.

To his right was his daughter, Ellen Grandby Sullivan. To his left was his son, Edgar Grandby. Joan Swenson sat next to Ellen, and across from her sat Janice Donnelly. Indazita sat on the far side of Joan. It was his request to be near the expectant mother, and she did not object.

Edgar's two bodyguards, identified only as William and Jason, sat quietly at the far end of the large table, several seats separating them from the rest. Joan Swenson looked again at these two men. She felt certain she had seen them before, but was unable to find the context.

"The circumstances that have brought us here together for sustenance before such a holy event could only have happened in the light of our Lord and Savior, Jesus Christ. So many things came together over so many years, with the help of so many soldiers working in your name. We thank you, Lord, for the bread before us, and the divine light shining on us that has made this holy night possible. Amen."

"Amen," the table said in unison. The group unclasped their hands and started to feast on an aromatic meal of prime rib, baked potatoes, green beans, and fresh salad.

"Who do we have to thank for such a feast," Ernest asked.

"It was a group effort," Ellen replied. "We planned it on the trip up then stopped by one of the local grocery stores. Joan and Janice and I had a lovely afternoon in the kitchen, preparing for your arrival."

"You put Janice to work in her condition?" Ernest directed his mock outrage to his daughter.

"I didn't do much," Janice said. "I cut up a few green beans, and mostly relaxed on the couch."

"Ellen has been filling us in on many of these events you referred to in your prayer, Reverend Grandby," she continued. "What an incredibly ambitious undertaking."

"Please, call me Ernest. That goes for everyone." He looked at Joan Swenson as he said this. She smiled then looked back at her dinner.

"It's true. Without question, this is the most difficult thing I've ever attempted. It's a mission we've talked about for several years, since the popularity of the church began spreading. When it became apparent that our message was resonating so widely across the globe, we knew that we had an opportunity to do something monumental. No single religion or church or even government in the modern era has had the power and the ability to accomplish what we are about to.

"In some ways our timing was perfect," the patriarch explained in the smooth baritone that so many found so distinct and familiar. "Around the world, those who are open to the message of Christ have not let their faith waiver. The Catholic Church, who carried the torch of Christ for many centuries, has had so many problems to contend with in recent years. They've let many millions of people down, but just because the Catholics have been fallible doesn't mean people have lost their faith in Christ.

"Strangely enough, the other religions have not benefited from the failings of the Catholics. The world's other major religions, Islam, Hindu, Judaism, Buddhism, they've largely held the same numbers, at least regarding their percentage of world population.

"So former Catholic Christians have not abandoned their faith, but many came to us. I think we've filled that void nicely, not only in the US but around the world. We project that within the next two decades, by the time this young one reaches maturity, we may have as many as one billion followers. We could, and almost certainly should, surpass the Catholic Church along the way."

The senior Grandby leaned back in his chair. "We can never know God's plan completely. So many things can change in time. It is my sincere hope, Janice, that your son grows into the role that we have planned for him, that Immat helped us fulfill."

An enormous clap of thunder occurred just above the house. Everyone at the table trembled briefly, except Ellen and her father.

Grandby continued. "I believe we are doing all we can to make that hope become a reality. If God has a different plan for him, then at the very least he will always be the one who led the way. He will always be the first."

"The first? I'm not sure I follow what this all means." Janice Donnelly posed her question through tired eyes to the senior Grandby.

"Ah, I gather Ellen didn't explain how much went into this night, and how much it has meant to our vision."

"I explained things in general terms," Ellen replied. "I wanted to leave the rest to you."

"Wonderful," he said through a wide grin. "This is a life passion for me, and I don't often get the opportunity to talk about it in detail.

"I mentioned how the other religions have largely stayed along their current pace, and how the Catholics have fallen off the aggressive pace they set over many centuries, largely from their own neglect. But it isn't only the Catholics. Many from the Protestant faiths have also grown tired of the stale old version of Christianity. The message we are shaping will be very different."

"Different how?" Joan Swenson spoke up unexpectedly. Grandby rewarded her question with a winsome grin.

"The traditional version of Christianity is mostly based on threes. The Catholics, most prominently preach about the Trinity, which consists of Father, the Son, and the Holy Spirit. The Holy Spirit is the great mystery to many. People understand who God is, for the most part. They understand which of his messengers they choose to follow, and for Christians this is of course Jesus Christ, our Lord. But this Holy Spirit is beyond the grasp of many. Even the most devout traditional Christians have a hard time explaining its meaning.

"Another threesome that Christians rely heavily upon is the notion of life on this earth, heaven, and hell. According to tradition, your life here on earth will send you to heaven if you're good, hell if you're bad.

"The new version of Christianity we will put forth will turn that upside down. We know the original flock, the ones who were the generation or two after the life of Christ, took the cycle of birth and rebirth for granted. For them it was not what traditional Christianity would have you believe, that you live your life, then you go before a tribunal that examines the totality of your life to give you a simple thumbs up or thumbs down.

"Humanity has evolved beyond that notion. The Third Wave of Christianity will build upon the invaluable lessons of the Old Testament, and it will depend mightily on the life of Christ as documented faithfully in the New Testament.

"As we know from the New Testament, the Book of Revelation chronicles the end of humankind, the Apocalypse. The Messiah will come again, and he will judge the totality of the work we've done here on earth.

"While I am in concordance with this traditional belief, I am not content to wait out the return of the Messiah. I do not see us winning the battle against evil. I see a world with over seven billion souls in it, and only about two billion are considered Christian. This is not a path toward victory for the Word of Christ. This will be a grand stalemate at best.

"Something new is needed, and that is to turn back the clock to the original notion of reincarnation. We are the new leaders of Christianity, and we plan to return the meaning of life to what it was in the days that Jesus walked the earth."

Joan was upright in her chair, almost defiant. "Won't this shatter the faith of all the Christians who believed in Jesus' death on the cross?"

"I don't believe so, my dear. Jesus did die on the cross that day, and he died for our sins. Nothing is different. We believe we can reframe a message that beautifully accommodates Christ's ascension and return. There are many ways to interpret that single instance of rebirth.

"Between the first and third centuries following Christ's life, there was much debate about which writings to adapt. There is an entire collection of books, called the Antilegomena, whose message was discarded during the process of closing the New Testament Canon.

"The decisions they made were extremely difficult, and many of the books of the New Testament were adapted even though they held little in common with the books of the Old Testament. It took a great deal of courage to adapt those books into a more modern version of God's word that became the New Testament.

"We believe that these decisions made by our greatest minds served us well for nearly two millennia, but this group-think needs a substantial revision as we head into a third. If anyone requires proof, he or she needs to only look at the emergence of our biggest enemy in the West. Some call it 'humanism,' which is really code for things like atheism and agnosticism. The atheists staunchly claim they can live a good and decent life without acknowledging the presence of God. Agnosticism is even worse. Their message may as well be, 'I'm too lazy to go find faith on my own. Somebody has to prove it to me.'

"I see this emergence of atheism and agnosticism as a symptom, not the problem itself. If we put a more realistic, palatable message before these cynics, I think they will come back to Christianity, which is where they belong."

"How exactly, does my son play into this?" Janice Donnelly surprised the dinner table with her question, which she asked evenly but quietly.

"Integrally," Ernest Grandby said. "We have to start this process sometime, and it has to be now. We cannot leave the process of rebirth to chance. My understanding, Janice, is that you and your husband generated this idea of 'Soul Math,' which you so cleverly termed it. It is so relevant and so vital that it cannot be ignored.

"You see, we came to the same conclusions before you and your husband. We've been talking about this phenomena for quite some time."

"What phenomena?" Joan Swenson's eyes were riveted on the charismatic man.

"Within a few years we'll see annual birth rate climb to nearly one hundred million per year. Can you imagine that? With all those new souls finding homes in remote stretches across the globe, how in the world can many of them be what we consider 'old souls?' The souls that occupy these many millions of new bodies will be watered-down replacements.

"You can't build a potent army to spread the New Christianity without making sure you have the right ones leading it. Janice, your son will be the first of the New Apostles. I won't be on this earth long enough in this life to see his work through to completion, but I most certainly give him the best possible chance to be its great leader. We can create the circumstances for the best and brightest of this generation to guide the Christian faith in future generations.

"Today's ensoulment is just the first of what we hope will be many millions in the coming years. Wise souls being directed into Christian families and away from the flawed religions, the ones who would have Christ's message forgotten. This is what we've been working so hard for."

Janice Donnelly leaned forward. "How can you orchestrate which soul will enter my son?"

"Again," Grandby said, "a combination of factors. Critical in that process are the gifts brought by my daughter Ellen. Even as a small child, we knew she had certain gifts that would make many amazing things possible. We channeled her energies into loving the Lord, and in recent years she has been able to reach into the heavens to speak with spirits, very highly placed spirits.

"There is one spirit in particular she has been speaking with. This one, called Immat, has a very important position in the process of ensoulment."

Everyone at the table turned to look at Ellen.

"It's not a gift that I asked for," Ellen said humbly, "but it's a gift that I've learned to treasure, and to use wisely."

"These are powerful gifts," Grandby said. "We were very reluctant to use them at all, but the opportunity became available and we chose to act, so tonight we have high confidence that we can ensure your son will possess a very advanced, enlightened soul."

The elder reverend paused and shared a wide smile. "After all, isn't that what any parent would want?"

Janice Donnelly paused before speaking, appearing to be in a fog. "These events that you talk about. Did any of them have anything to do with the death of my husband?"

There was silence at the table. Finally Grandby spoke. "I wish it weren't true but we do suspect there was some sort of connection, yes."

"Why do you think that, Reverend?"

"There's no way to know for sure," Ellen spoke out before her father had a chance to respond. "What we do know is that your husband talked openly about this problem with Soul Math shortly before he was killed."

Janice's head snapped toward Ellen. "Who? How do you know that?"

"After John's death, I received a visit from Detective Lacey, the lead investigator in the case."

Janice nodded.

"Lacey told me that John had been in to see Henry Chimera, the new psychic, and that he was talking with Henry about this very same subject."

"Lacey told you about his discussion with Henry?"

"He did," Ellen replied. "but he only mentioned it in passing. I don't know why Henry would care about a thing like that, but evidently he did. Quite a bit. Lacey also said that Henry provided some details about John's killing that only a legitimate psychic could know. My understanding is that Henry has been a psychic for a very short time. I suspect Detective Lacey is leaning toward a different explanation."

"Which is what?" Tears were rolling down Janice's cheek.

"That Henry was there when your husband was murdered. Our guess is that the top suspect in your husband's death is Henry Chimera. I can't say why he would do such a thing, but this idea of reincarnation and the direction of souls is profound. Perhaps Henry dreamed up a way to use it for his own benefit."

Janice looked down at the table. "I wonder what Henry could possibly do with information like that."

"He's a very convincing character," Ellen answered. "We've even had him in as a volunteer at the Church. He did some fine work for us, although he wasn't around long."

Joan Swenson, who was listening attentively to this exchange, suddenly spoke out. "How did the death of the Dalai Lama fit in with all of this?"

The elder Reverend Grandby raised a hand to speak.

"I can't say that it 'fit in' at all," Grandby answered. "I can say that it was a very unfortunate event that provoked very strong emotions across the globe. The premature death of such an important spiritual figure is difficult to understand, but perhaps in the end we will all find a way to make something positive come from it."

"Will my son receive the soul of the Dalai Lama?" Janice asked quietly.

"No, I don't think so," Grandby replied. "It was a consideration. We simply put all of our energy into securing the wisest possible soul for your son."

"I would never want to feel that someone died just to give my son an advantage," Janice said coldly.

"I would feel the same way," Ellen said. "Besides, the Tibetan Buddhists have a very elaborate process for locating the reincarnated soul of the Dalai Lama. We would never interfere with that and besides, I highly doubt we could."

Ernest Grandby leaned forward in his chair.

"As unfortunate as his death was, it did serve an important purpose for our cause. It generated a tidal wave of opposition to the Chinese government. That opposition led to these protests, nearly a civil war that is still occurring in many of the large cities in China. It is sad and unfortunate that so many tens of thousands are dying in the streets, but it means that of those many dead, there will be older souls available for the campaign we are embarking upon.

"Things are in a state of disorder around the globe. There are conflicts raging everywhere, from the Middle East to Africa to Europe, and of course through much of Asia.

"As difficult as they are to read about, these will be advantages for the New Christianity."

Lightening his tone, Grandby spoke again. "Well then, are we ready to change the world?"

Sau chose to be surrounded by a cool blue light. The sound of angels singing in soothing, calming chords filled the chamber. He was in the perfect position to choose his next life, the life that would likely be his final mortal visit before ascending higher into the heavens.

Before him were spread the four spectrums he had chosen from the number that Aisling had so carefully assembled. Two girls and two boys, each with very different starting points in life, each providing a varied existence within different cultures, and each with family settings that varied greatly from one another.

He could choose to be a boy in Poland with a condition that would likely prevent him from ever being accepted socially, but who could help the world around him in so many other ways. This life would be one that could provide the perfect opportunity to do something profound in the arts or the sciences. Children with Autism growing up in the middle of the twenty-first century were often given extensive support and care, which allowed them to roam and explore the depths of their potential. Could this person grow up to find a cure for Autism, or some of the more lethal forms of cancer that remained? It was a tempting existence.

The Jewish woman in New Zealand would have so many difficult family responsibilities, but she would have a chance to make such a profound difference on a smaller scale. Sau considered the souls who would be her children, one blind and one with Down Syndrome. How could souls choose these existences without the support of a strong mother? It would take a very special soul to accept such a life.

The girl who would grow to be a beautiful woman in Ukraine would be challenged early in life and possibly rewarded later, but this was far from certain. She would grow through a troubled childhood with parents who considered her nurturing a lower priority. She would battle dark forces in an uncertain political environment, with little in the way of faith to support her. Would Sau's potential be realized with so little support around?

The life of the boy to be born to the widow in New England seemed the easiest path. This child's future was being orchestrated by what could be the largest, most influential Christian church in the world, perhaps even more popular than the Catholic Church. The expectations for this life would be high, but the rewards could be vast. The test in this life would be to maintain balance, perspective, and decency while positively using the attention that would be lavished upon it.

Sau examined each of the lives in detail. He calmly considered the positive implications for each existence, while giving fair treatment to the negatives as well.

As he contemplated his choices, he began to feel a tugging, a pulling toward one life in particular. He experienced doubt over his ability to block out external influence. As his decision process moved forward, his choice was becoming no choice at all.

The answer was clear. There was only one life before him: that of the Donnelly boy.

FROM WITHIN

Something was different this time.

For each of the hundreds, even thousands of souls for whom Hildegarde and Aisling had by now placed into new lives, they were able to observe the selection process clearly. Every impression and impact experienced by the subject during the analysis was always clearly visible. This time, because of the lofty, senior status of Sau, the survey was a private affair. If higher spirits were watching, they did not make themselves visible.

In every other case, Hildegarde would return to Surveyor Hall with her subject from its closest, most intimate circle of souls. The subject would be rested and refreshed, ready to convert lessons learned from its most recent lives into a new beginning, a new chance to learn and grow. Hildegarde and her subject soul anxiously awaited the choice of lives that Immat had identified, and which Aisling had researched. They were ready for challenges, opportunities, and experience to come together in the next life.

Aisling would meet them in the Hall at the appointed time, weary from an ambitious travel schedule that often included exotic or isolated locations across the globe. The process of researching all the details of each life Immat handed her, leaving no important detail undiscovered, was exhausting but rewarding. Her mission was to give each subject the clearest possible picture of each life that was available, and to leave little to fate or random chance.

Typically they would enjoy the survey among a group of interested spirits, who were grateful for the opportunity to enjoy the process in their company. Despite their disappointment with their limited insight into Sau's process, they were pleased to even be present. They proudly watched as Sau entered the chamber, like proud parents watching a child go off to college. The process was as fun for Hildegarde and Aisling as it was rewarding.

The door closed as it always had, and they exhaled, hugged, and celebrated another diligent effort that was coming to completion. The moment the chamber door closed, reality set in that they had done all they possibly could to ensure a successful next life for this subject.

They watched as Sau reviewed the lives, methodically and carefully. They would wince as some important detail was glossed over, then smile proudly as the subject would dwell on a nuance that could mean a great deal as a particular life played out.

From their prior experiences with veteran souls, they expected some visibility into Sau's thought process as he cycled through the lives. There was none. They could see him through the chamber but it was as though their sensory abilities were completely blocked.

"I do not understand," Aisling said to her friend and mentor, worry in her voice.

"I'm afraid I don't either, my dear."

Hildegarde typically had little direct contact with Immat. He did not interfere in the process of introspection she would conduct with her subjects, and she would only question the array of lives presented if they proved to be too limited or ambitious for the subject before her. That was a very rare occasion, and when it did occur she usually struggled with how to summon him. On these occasions she relied on Aisling, for she interacted directly with Immat as each array of lives was received.

"Aisling, perhaps you could summon Immat to find out if this irregularity should be of any concern."

"Of course," she replied.

This would require Aisling to retreat into a mode of consciousness that was finely tuned to communicate with Immat, a higher being than either of them. It was a channel that had been bestowed onto her by Immat, and which required extensive practice to refine. The opportunity to communicate with Immat in this way was available to Hildegarde as well, but she preferred to rely on her friend. This allowed her to direct her full energies to the soul subject before her, and those in her queue for upcoming surveys.

Aisling excused herself from Surveyor Hall to complete the process. It required all of her concentration, and virtual isolation from any distraction.

She focused with all her mind and heart toward a visitation with Immat. She felt fully alive, all of her energy clicking in unison as she envisioned Immat's level. In a rush of dizzying speed and energy, she rushed to the door where she knew he dwelled. Outside the door she summoned him. She felt his presence on the other side.

There was no response.

She tried again, but again Immat did not respond to her call. She examined her approach for contacting him, making sure she was forgetting nothing. Her approach was true and correct. She tried yet again, but no success.

She became alarmed at the possibility something was subverting the process she and Hildegarde had worked so hard to maintain at the highest possible level of fidelity.

She considered returning to the level that she and Hildegarde occupied, but decided it would require too much effort to return, and perhaps it would be too late. If something was interfering with Immat, it could be interfering with Sau as well. This was the most important soul they had ever placed and time was of the essence.

Aisling decided to do something she had never considered doing before, and was not sure was even possible. She would try to get through Immat's door without his permission. This was a desperate situation, she decided, and it was worth the risk asking for forgiveness later if her judgement was seriously in error now.

With every shred of energy left, she focused on the obstacle before her, getting past the gateway to Immat's lair. She summoned psychic strength from within that she did not know existed. With each burst of energy and strength that came her way, she pushed and groaned and thrust ahead. She heaved with all her might through the door, refusing to back down.

Finally she was able to view the scene before her, on the other side.

Immat was there, but unable to see or respond to her calls. He was locked in a form of communication that Aisling had never seen before or dreamed about. It was ornate and twisted and complex beyond her ability to perceive.

His head, or the celestial equivalent of his head, was enmeshed in a complex, turbulent ring. Around the ring were serpents and angels in the early stages of a battle. The opposing energies were beyond her comprehension. They were enormous combative forces, gathering strength for a clash that would be triumphant for the victor and very deadly for the loser.

Aisling's focus held firm. She was barely inside the door, struggling to take in the scene that was so completely engulfing Immat, himself an extraordinarily powerful spirit.

While the many thousands of angels and serpents and other spirits that Aisling did not recognize were escalating their fierce dance around one another, Immat's attentions were locked on two separate but related scenes, clearly visible in a bubble before him.

One was a scene by a lake. Inside a house next to the lake were several ordinary mortals, one of whom was the focus of many energies hovering around the scene, a pregnant woman with a healthy boy in her womb.

Also within the house were mortals who were anything but ordinary. A father and a daughter, each with immense power and might on the terrestrial plane. These people had been the beneficiaries of much personal gain that rose from the power of prayer from many millions of other mortals. These two were wealthy and wise on the earthly plane, and obviously advanced souls as well. Their orbital hue suggested questionable intentions, including the strong suggestion of corruption that can only be made possible by massive power and influence

In the second scene before Immat was Sau. Immat had Sau in his grasp.

This was not meant to be! The selection process was, by definition, designed to be free of external influence of any kind, yet Immat was clearly interfering with this holy process. Aisling could see clearly that from Sau's position in the chamber within Surveyor Hall, he was not the master of the critical decision before him.

Aisling boiled as she saw a linkage forming between the two scenes. The scene above Immat quickly coalesced into a full battle scene, with lines clearly formed between serpents and dragons anchored firmly against warriors and powerful angels of the heavens.

This menacing dance that was moving into a ferocious battle was over the birth of a small child. So much energy, light and dark, around a single birth, Aisling thought. When she had investigated the coming birth of this child, she knew there were familiar energies and great challenges ahead, but she had no inkling of the spiritual energies that would invest so much into the events around the birth of this boy to Janice Donnelly.

She was about to retreat back to her own level to seek wisdom from Hildegarde when she noticed other souls surrounding the lake house. One in particular shined brightly. It was a very familiar aura indeed.

She gasped, "Henry! What in heaven's name are you doing there?"

He could not hear her, of course, nor sense her presence. She was seeing his dilemma as if she were viewing it through a telescope. She felt desperate to help but obviously could not from this place, with all her energy devoted to just observing Immat.

She remembered that her great friend had been experiencing difficult times recently. A new found love was taken from him. She stopped by occasionally, often without his realizing, to make sure that his path was true. Each time he seemed firmly in control of the situation before him. She had warned him time after time to be careful of what lay ahead, and if he was not listening to her advice by now then he probably never would.

Now she felt a wave of fear and regret that she had not been to check on him in his recent weeks. Her recent assignments had consumed her full attention, but she reminded herself that there should always be time to check on the ones who were left behind. Things must have taken a very serious turn if he was in this situation, far from the place she left him.

From all she could perceive, all she could grasp, there was nothing that could be done to prevent this scene from unfolding. She tried summoning Immat, screaming primally in an attempt to cut through his haze, but to no avail.

She examined the scene all around him. If there were higher spirits monitoring his activity, she could not see them. She looked through his lair, above and all around. He was on his own. This was a situation he had helped to create. He obviously went to great lengths to be sure there would be no interference in his activities and Aisling knew no way to change it.

In a desperate desire to protect her friend, an unlikely thought came. Perhaps she was looking in the wrong direction! Maybe the answer was not in any of the heavenly realms at all.

She retreated. Simply by releasing her focus on this high place, she found herself immediately near her familiar domain. She entered the chamber. Hildegarde was there as she left her, more worried than before.

"What did you find out? What's happening, my dear?"

"There is a conflict raging over Sau. Immat has created a situation where there is no choice being made. He will end up as the Donnelly child, and many spirits are in a conflict over this happening."

Hildegarde was stunned. "Is Immat behind this, or is he being manipulated by other powers?"

"There was no way to know for sure whether anyone else is behind this," Aisling said. "I couldn't get his attention. He is locked in a rapt state between Sau and the Donnelly widow. This appears to be the destination for Sau, regardless of the merit of the other lives."

"This is a disaster," Hildegarde said. "An abomination. A subversion of the whole process that we and so many others work so hard to uphold."

"I wonder if that is true," Aisling said. Hildegarde stared back at her, appalled. "Bear with me, Hildy. Sau is a strong spirit, the most veteran we have yet to come across. Despite the dark energies that surround this process right now, are we abandoning our faith that he would make the right choices?"

"A reasonable question," Hildegarde explained patiently but with some urgency. "However Sau's past weakness has been to allow the pressures of his office to eclipse the overall mission. This has been his weakness, in fact it's the primary reason he continues to cycle through lives on earth. It is a substantial road block to his complete enlightenment. He must overcome it."

"Why do you think he won't?"

"Because, my dear," Hildegarde said, "if what you say is true, that Immat and perhaps other forces are changing the process to divert aged, wiser souls to one side or another, there will no longer be any real choice by our subjects at all. You and I have spoken of this before, Aisling. Do you recall?"

Aisling stared. "Yes, of course."

"We noticed that more veteran souls were being offered more appealing, interesting and challenging lives in Christian settings, while newer souls were only being offered a relatively narrow selection. We brought this to his attention, but God only knows if he cared about what we saw, or if he even heard us."

"Oh my," Aisling gasped.

"If Sau, a spirit with incredible strength and wisdom, is put into position as the head of this new Christian church, and he's surrounded by only the wisest and most veteran of souls, his test would be no test at all. He would never remember his mission. He would be working within a false framework to begin with, and the deck would be stacked.

"This cannot happen," Hildegarde said.

"I need to go down there," Aisling said with pure determination.

"Aisling, interfering in something like this is strictly forbidden. We need to find another way."

"Interference is already happening. This is our test, Hildy. Just because we're no longer cycling through earthly lives doesn't mean we should stop righting wrongs.

"Plus," Aisling said through flaring eyes, "my friend is in trouble."

From Henry's perch outside the lake house, he had little in the way of protection from the elements. The rain was pelting down at a three-quarters angle, which made it difficult to avoid water seeping under his rain gear as he kept vigil.

The thunder was steady and unrelenting, almost in cadence as the powerful energies above churned. Every few seconds a flash of lightning would illuminate the area all around the house and across the lake. Henry kept low behind a tree that was on a berm between the house and the lake. He was careful to avoid changing the outline of his shape if anyone were to feel the need to look out the window.

From this vantage he maintained a clear view of the living room, along with part of a door that probably led to the bedrooms in the rear of the house furthest from the water. If Dee were to emerge from one of the rear rooms, he would notice her immediately.

Suddenly an entirely different force enveloped all his senses. At first he thought a bolt of lightning had struck nearby, but he still had his senses. He was unable to move, under the hold of something firm and powerful, yet at the same time gentle and loving. If it was lightning, he was dead where he crouched.

"Hello, old friend." It was familiar, female voice that he grew to trust above all else. "What kind of quandary have you gotten yourself into this time?"

"Aisling! You're the last person I expected to see."

"Not surprising, and I might be the only one who wants to see you here."

"If you came to tell me again that I'm in danger, I'm afraid that's not news to me."

"I am not," she said. "You are, of course, in a great deal of danger, but I'm certain you already know that."

"I'm here to save my friend," he replied. "It's something I have to do. If it means sacrificing my life, then I'm prepared to do that."

"A noble cause indeed. I wish you only success, but I am here to ask a favor, the most important I have ever asked of you."

"You know that I owe you everything, Aisling," he said, "but I came here with a purpose, and I can't put anything in front of that."

"You can and must accomplish both," she said. "If you save your friend, you can also save a lot more."

"It's all I'm after. There's nothing more important to me."

"Well, there needs to be. After all this time of searching, wandering, wondering, you were meant to be in this place at this time."

Henry was uncertain how to react, so he said nothing.

"These people came here to perform an ensoulment process for the Donnelly child. The soul they have chosen is Sau, the wisest, most advanced soul who has ever come through our realm. He was chosen by them because his prior life was terminated by their agents. They murdered a little girl on the other side of the world so that this event could happen. Tens of thousands of other lives have been lost so that we can be here today.

"If they succeed, the path of soul selection will forever be changed. That would be catastrophic. We cannot allow it. You cannot allow it"

"You came to ME for help with that? Shouldn't I be asking for your help?"

No sooner did he allow these words to come before he noticed a sadness in Aisling that he had never seen. Henry had never noticed anything resembling desperation from his great friend, but it was clear she desperately needed him.

"Henry, you're the only one in position to make a difference. There is a great battle occurring in the upper realm, and the outcome is very, very much in doubt. Your strength, and the fact that you are here now, could preserve the order of soul selection.

"I should not be here speaking with you now. I've violated a sacred oath by interfering, and I did this because I am powerless to help. Spiritual forces who are immensely more powerful than me are powerless to help. I cannot tell you what to do, Henry, but I can remind you that you've advanced to this place in your soul's development by always knowing right from wrong, and by choosing the right path."

Henry was silent, the reality of the moment submerging through the many obstacles he still saw awaiting.

"You have experience with Immat," she continued. "I do as well. He is at the center of this. Your adversaries inside have formed an arrangement with him, and that arrangement was forged in blood and violence. It's a corrupt alliance, Henry, and you and your friends are the only ones in position to stop it."

Henry closed his eyes in prayer, retreating to look for strength and guidance. When he opened his eyes, the grip Aisling held on him had eased. There was no sign of her.

He was back in a crouched position looking through the large picture window of the lake house. The group appeared to be finishing dinner. They were stirring at the table, appearing to talk about what they would be doing for the rest of the evening. Henry checked his watch. It was only nine-thirty.

He scanned the property all around for any sign of someone watching through the window or who had slipped outside. When he was satisfied it was safe, he moved slowly along the ground until he was safely back with his team.

He filled the group in on what he saw.

"I don't think it makes sense to go in there," Shoemaker said finally. "It will be violent. I don't see a sign of impending danger to Dee or to anyone."

"There's something else," Henry said. The three fell silent, each staring at him.

"I had a visit from a soul that I would trust with my life. I guess you could call her my "Medium High," since she was a medium when she was alive, and she became my medium in the afterlife.

"Her name is Aisling. Before she died she trained me as a medium, and I've been in steady contact with her in the months since she died. She explained why these people are here. It's not a social visit."

He went on to explain what Aisling shared about the ensoulment process that was about to occur.

"It looks like they plan to do it tonight. We have no time."

Winfred was the first to speak. "Look Henry, I've gone along with this because we're a group who believes in our cause, but what you're saying cannot be real. You have to be imagining this."

"I'm not imagining anything," Henry snapped. "I told you guys about an experience I had with a spirit called Immat. Immat is a demonic spirit from many centuries ago, from what is now Afghanistan. The legend said that he would carry off twenty virgin daughters every year, and I experienced his wrath when he had a young girl under his power who I was asked to help. It turns out that was a lie, and the lie happened inside the Church of the Tortured Christ. He threw me around like a rag doll. He was the most powerful, angry spirit I've ever encountered, and there have been hundreds, perhaps thousands I've met."

Shoemaker spoke out. "Why would Sullivan have done that to you? What was the purpose of bringing you into that situation?"

"To size me up. They wanted to know what I'm capable of."

No one in the group spoke, each drawn into their own thoughts.

"I know what you're thinking. I failed that test, but I learned a few things about him in the process. I had never seen that kind of energy before."

"Somehow he convinced those in the realms above that he was reformed, and now he's working with Grandby and his daughter to forever alter the way souls are selected. He's about to stack the deck so that this 'new Christianity' will be able to cherry-pick only the wisest, most veteran souls. They have to be stopped."

"I don't understand," Naomi spoke quietly, "how this ceremony changes everything about reincarnation. Nothing changes. It's one soul."

"It's one soul that was hand-selected for this assignment," Henry said. "It's the wisest soul that Aisling or Hildegarde have ever seen, and they've seen many, many more than me."

"Hildegarde?" Shoemaker said just above the trumpeting of the rain. "Hildegarde of Bingen? The Christian mystic from the Middle Ages?"

"The very same," Henry said. "She's been Aisling's mentor, and she's no slouch in these matters herself."

Winfred exhaled loudly. "Look guys, these people have Dee in there. I'm sure of it. They killed David Herbrit. They killed Donnelly, and they probably set off a chain of violence by killing the Dalai Lama. That single murder cost many tens of thousands more lives, not only in China but other countries too. They've been working toward this for years, but it's a process that will completely undo everything the Origenists have stood for. If we leave here tonight without accepting this challenge, we may just as well drive back to Boston and forget we ever met each other. There will no longer be any purpose in what we're doing."

The four fell silent, each sinking into their thoughts.

"I can't think of any reason that Ernest Grandby would be on the shores of Lake George right now to meet with this collection of people," Naomi finally said.

"We came here to try to get our friend back," Shoemaker said. "If the rest of that turns out to be true, then it reinforces that we came here for a reason."

They each looked at Winfred.

"You guys are nuts," he said, "but I'm in."

"The power of our Lord and Savior Jesus Christ brings us together on this stormy night, fitting weather for such an important transition that has been years in the making. We pray for your blessings, Oh Lord, and we pray that the path we have built, stone by stone, will last for all the remaining generations until the final day of judgement."

They were assembled in a spacious den in a rear corner of the house, plush with lavish couches and stuffed chairs. In the center sat Janice Donnelly. She was flanked by Joan Swenson on one side and Ellen Grandby Sullivan on the other. The Reverend Grandby sat upright in a large red couch in front of Janice, with their Burmese transitional guide Indazita to his right. Edgar Grandby, the distant but ever-vigilant son, sat next to a fireplace near the wall in a position where everyone in the room was in his sight. The two guards stood away from the group near the entry to the front room. From their position they could see the door and several windows in various rooms, although their attentions were locked on this curious ceremony.

"Our path has been a difficult one," Grandby continued, scanning the room as he spoke.

Ellen swelled with pride as her father set the stage. Each person in the room, even the guards, felt that he was speaking directly to each of them. Though his seventy-seven years showed, the power of his oratory remained strong in any setting.

"Many fine souls have contributed to our movement to form a New Christian Church, which after tonight will become the name that replaces the 'Church of the Tortured Christ.' It will be the gold standard for Christian churches, a truly universal church that will lead a more rational, modern path toward the return of our Lord.

"The New Christian Church will assert our moral imperative to reclaim the cycle of birth, death, and rebirth in the name of our Lord. The New Christian Church will reject all impostors who would use the sacred event of rebirth for their own selfish gain. In the New Christian Church, ensoulment will become the most profound of the sacraments. All others will become secondary, recast to support and define each Christian incarnation.

"Many sacrifices occurred to bring us to this place, some tragic but all necessary for the enduring holiness that will be bestowed upon us. To those who gave their lives, willingly or unwillingly toward this end, we express our profound gratitude. In future lives, as your soul becomes wiser and more experienced in the complex ways of the world, we invite you to join us in the New Christian Church as we move forward on our mission.

"To those souls who left this earth with great wisdom, we pray that you will join our mission."

He cast a serene, fatherly smile around the room. Indazita, Edgar, Ellen, and the guards beamed back. Janice Donnelly offered a weary smile, and Joan Swenson kept her head bowed, eyes clenched.

"Amen," Grandby said. The group repeated the word in unison.

"Indazita, I invite you to begin the first of many holy and solemn ceremonies to come."

The intricately dressed man moved to a small table that sat in front of Janice Donnelly. He lit three candles, then closed his eyes and began chanting in broken English.

"We reach on high for the chosen soul for this holy child. We invoke the spirit who presents this soul to this mother and child. We pray." He bowed, then he looked at Ellen and smiled.

On this queue Ellen knelt on the floor next to Indazita, cast her eyes up through the ceiling, and spoke.

"Immat we beseech you to present the soul that will occupy and honor this child, make his life a full and holy life, and to fulfill the gift promised in the Book of Malachi. 'Behold, I will send you Elijah the prophet before the coming of the great and dreadful day of the Lord. And he shall turn the heart of the fathers to the children, and the heart of the children to their fathers, lest I come and smite the earth with a curse.'"

As she finished, a clap of lightning struck nearby, illuminating each window. The lights flickered in the house, and dulled momentarily. There was a distinct pop, then all lights in the house went dark.

The group was stunned. No one spoke.

Then there was a flickering light, visible in the front room through the entry way. Jason, the larger of the two guards, hurried through the doorway.

"Holy shit, something's on fire!" He yelled. Both men went running to the front door. Everyone in the room followed.

"Take this," Shoemaker said to Henry.

"What the hell is that?" Henry stared back at him.

"It's a handgun, Chuck Norris. Jesus."

"I don't use guns," Henry replied defiantly. "I can do the job with my knife and my other God-given skills. If I didn't think so, I wouldn't have signed up for this."

"Henry, I'm quite certain the other guys have guns. If you have any hope of coming out of there alive with Dee, you might want to try to make it a fair fight. I bet the guns those two gorillas have are better than this one, but at least it's something. I've had it since I was in the Middle East. It's served me well. Take it, Goddammit."

Shoemaker had been a contractor for the United States government in both the first and second Iraq wars, seeing action in both conflicts. His physical skills were no longer what they once were, but his tactical skills were strong. The group understood this about him, and all were ready to take his advice, even Henry.

The storm was showing no signs of letting up, and it did not appear to be moving from this epicenter. Shoemaker saw this as an advantage for the Origenists.

"Those guys won't think anyone is crazy enough to be out here. The element of surprise is our amigo. Naomi, will your surveillance cameras work, even in this rain?"

"Yeah, they resist water really well. If we can get them mounted in the right positions, they'll zoom in through the windows and I should have a decent picture of what's going on in there. As long as Winfred can get them in place, we should be able to see what's happening."

Winfred offered to return to the spot Henry had found to peer into the living room.

"I'm headed in that direction anyway. Let's test the remote audio system before we get this party started. I've never actually used it before." He began peeling equipment and wires from a small compartment in his pack.

"It would have been nice to know we had a remote audio system. Hand signals aren't nearly as efficient," Henry said matter-of-factly.

"Well, here's the thing about that," Winfred said. "I forgot I packed it. I bought it a couple years ago and just threw it in the pack. Sorry, Henry. Besides, it sounds like you had your own audio uplink going on with your spirit friend."

They tested the system with each of the three men wearing an earpiece equipped with a microphone. Winfred instructed Naomi on how to manage the system, in particular the sound levels.

The plan was for Naomi to remain in the trees away from danger, communicating what she viewed through the small video receivers that were set up to be safe from the blowing rain. Winfred would create a distraction, then position himself on the far side of the house in the woods near the driveway. Shoemaker would stay in a neutral zone ready to help any of the others. His reaction would depend on how things progressed.

Shoemaker pulled a map of the house from his pack. Using Winfred's sketching skills, they converted a satellite outline of the house into logical sections. Shoemaker reminded each member of the group of the numbered quadrants they had agreed to use for reference. All seemed to have them committed to memory.

"This might take some improvisation you guys, some fast thinking." He was speaking mostly to Henry. "Make sure you know where you are at all times, and always know where the rest of us are in case you need help.

"We think there are nine people in that house, the two reverends, our traitor friend formerly known as Lars, the two guards, the curious Asian dude, and three women who we hope will not resist us - Joan, Janice, and Dee. Do not forget that there might be others in the house we don't know about.

"Keep your communications concise. Don't speak any louder or longer than you need to, then focus on the situation in front of you."

As Henry moved into position, but tuned in as the team strategist spoke.

"Henry, be careful. We prepared for this, so now it all comes down to timing. Wait for just the right moment, then make your move. I'll be nearby."

Henry nodded, and he was off.

"Well, folks, it's been great but I have some work to do." Winfred pulled a small pouch out of his pack, and moved along the lake behind the berm to the woods near the driveway.

After about five minutes Henry spoke first through the audio system. "I'm in the tree that looks in through the kitchen. I have the camera secured. Naomi, I just turned the power on."

"Roger," she said. "It takes a few seconds Henry. There it is. Good image but move it slightly to the left. Perfect. Right there. Tighten it down please."

Henry tightened a vice that connected the camera firmly in place onto the tree. The lens was pointed through the window, and he ensured it would not move. Naomi would have a steady image to view what was happening inside the house while Henry was free to roam. If there was some activity he needed to be aware of, Naomi would relay it to him through his earpiece.

"I'm going silent, moving in position behind the house," Henry said. "Time to look for our friend. I'll speak again when I have an update, or before I made any moves. Henry out."

"Roger," Naomi said calmly. "Winfred, you're up next. Speak when you're ready. No rush."

"Almost in position," Winfred said.

"Okay, I've got my camera mounted too. It should be looking over the living room. I don't see a soul in there. Wait, I can see one of the henchmen through a doorway toward the rear. They must be in some sort of sitting room. Naomi, how's the view?"

"Too high. Move it down just a tick. Great, keep it there. Lock it down."

"That's job one. I need about ten minutes for job two, assuming I don't see anyone out here. Winfred out."

"Fine, take your time," Naomi said. "Nobody moves until we get the green light. The next voice you hear should be Winfred. Home base out."

In less than a minute, Winfred's voice came through again.

"The decoy is set. Henry, I'm going to time this to the next big lightning strike. When it goes, you'll hear from me. Give it a few seconds after that. Naomi will be the one to tell you when you can penetrate. Winfred out."

The four waited. The rain continued to pelt, and the thunder was nearly steady. The lightning was less frequent and seemed to be happening in every direction but especially above the lake house.

Within a few seconds there was a clap of lightning that hit with a booming eruption. Winfred hit a button in his rain proof jacket. A small explosion followed beneath Ernest Grandby's Lincoln Town Car. A blown tire began to ignite, and this was followed by larger flames from inside the car.

"We have takeoff," Winfred said. "Somebody in there has to notice this."

FLASH

The waiting after the clap of lightning and Winfred's mini-explosion was torture for Henry. From his position behind the house, he was unable to see through any windows in the rear, and he had no intention of moving near the windows of the den areas where the group was likely congregated. No lights were on in the section of house before him, apparently four bedrooms to choose from. He knew his choice had to be one of the two in the middle, which would give him the best odds of being no more than one room away from the woman he loved.

That was if she was there at all. None of their team saw any proof that the Grandby family was holding any hostages in this grand house on the shores of Lake George, in the Adirondack Mountains of New York State.

In the darkness, despite his efforts, doubts entered his mind. Why would they even have brought her here? For what purpose? By the time they decided to convene here, about two hundred miles from Boston, wouldn't they have already decided to either set her free or ...

There was an explosion from the front of the house, then Naomi's voice erupted through his ear piece. "They're on the move. Henry, this is your moment. No turning back. Home base out."

He rushed to the window that was closest to the ground toward the center of the house. He pulled masking tape from his coat, pealing one layer after another until it covered most of the glass. Then he threw a sharp elbow into the glass, shattering two of the windows. The tape was effective, as only a few pieces of glass fell quietly onto the carpet inside the bedroom. Breaking glass would not be heard above the thunder, nor the distraction of a flaming car just a few feet from the front porch.

He peered into the small hole he created. There was no movement. With his gloved hands he reached in, pulling one handful of glass at a time until he was able to find the window clasp. He unlocked it, slid the window up, and climbed into the room. With both hands on the carpet, he was quickly inside.

His first thought was that there was no human scent in the room. There was a double bed on a far wall, slightly illuminated from the open door to the hallway. The bed was empty.

Suddenly he heard footsteps from the front of the house. They were moving across the hardwood floor in his direction.

"Henry," his ear piece hummed. "There's someone coming. Protect yourself!"

He instinctively reached for what looked to be a small sculpture that was displayed on a dresser. To his relief it had some weight. The steps moved closer, into the hallway and onto carpet as they approached. From the weight of the steps it was probably a male, and not a small one. He flattened against a wall that was behind the door that led into the room. The unseen visitor stopped as it passed the open door where Henry hid.

The window! Whoever was in the hall feels the wet breeze coming from the window!

After a hesitation, the man continued to the next bedroom, opening the door. Then all was quiet. Henry guessed that the intruder knew the window was broken, but not in the more important bedroom. Perhaps he would assume the glass broke from a branch that the wind knocked into the window.

He heard a creak in the floorboards as the man was on the verge of entering the dark room where Henry waited. He felt he had the advantage of position on this unwelcome visitor, who would be distracted by what might be waiting outside the window.

Henry froze in place, right arm stretched across his body, allowing his guest to move first. The man took a step forward and looked in Henry's direction. He showed no sign of seeing him, then looked toward the other, more spacious side of the room.

With all his weight, Henry swung the statue toward the tall man's head. With a sickening thump the man's head snapped to the side. He crumpled to the carpet, unmoving. Henry moved over the man and looked down.

Henry whispered with a smile, "My old friend Lars! Or is it Edgar? I can't tell you how long I've wanted to give you that long overdue gift."

He pulled Edgar by his shirt further into the room, away from the doorway in case someone else happened by. As he stepped over Edgar and slowly into the hallway, he listened for approaching footsteps and heard none. As a precaution to conceal Edgar and the open window, he closed the door behind him.

To reach the bedroom next door he needed to cross an entry way that led to the main room. He listened again for approaching steps but heard nothing. He peaked around the corner, and just at that moment a woman was walking across the main room. In the flickering light cast into the main room by the burning limousine, she noticed his movement.

Joan Swenson glanced at him, expecting Edgar. When she saw a smaller man in a dark, wet rain slicker, her eyes grew wide and she stopped in her tracks. Henry heard steps behind her, the sound of the others coming into the main house from the excitement off the porch. He slowly put one finger to his lips, the universal sign for quiet.

Joan's expression changed as she finally recognized him. She looked behind her at the others entering the large room, about twenty feet away.

Henry kept his finger to his mouth. She nodded quietly and turned her back on him toward the bathroom, closing the door. He could hear no change in the cadence of footsteps nor voices, so his presence was still undiscovered by all but Joan.

He moved swiftly down the hall to the next door, which was the subject of Edgar's attention. There was a dead bolt on the outside. He slowly unlocked it then he grasped the handle firmly, turning the knob. There was darkness inside. He quietly closed the door, ensuring it would stay closed. There was no lock on the inside.

He fumbled in the dark for a light switch. Finally finding one, he flipped up the switch. On the bed, under a down comforter, was Dee.

He leaped across the room to touch her face, to smell her.

"Dee, it's Henry!" He whispered directly into her ear. "Can you hear me? Dee!"

There was no response. She was breathing heavily, more heavily than he remembered, but she was breathing. He pulled off her blanket. She wore baggy cotton pajamas. Her hands and feet were bound by a nylon yellow rope.

Animals, he thought. Kidnap her, drug her, then tie her up like a criminal. You'll pay for this.

He pulled his knife from a leather belt holster and carefully began to cut apart the rope. Her skin was red and swollen beneath the rope. She had been in this position for too long.

He paused, hearing noise from the other room. He patted his coat the for reassurance that Shoemaker had insisted upon.

The reality of the situation set in: an unconscious hostage, her kidnappers in the hall, and Henry by himself, with only two hands to carry her to safety while defending her, if needed. It was vital to contact his team. He flipped the switch to transmit.

"This is Henry. I'm in. I clocked Edgar, and I've found Dee! She's passed out and I'm cutting her loose."

"Henry, the others are coming back in the house. Thank God you're okay. Can you get her out of there?"

"Not sure," Henry replied.

"It's Richard. I'm on my way. Meet you at the window. I saw the light from the bedroom. Open the window, Henry. Be there in a few seconds, out."

He bounded to the window, unlocked it and slid it up to its widest position.

"Guys," Winfred said, "one of the guards is moving toward you. The big one is still out here by the car scratching his nuts. Watch out guys, he's on the way."

Henry lifted Dee's limp body. So light, he thought. She should not be this light.

By the time he reached the window Shoemaker was there, hands outstretched.

He froze. There was a hand on the door. Grandby's guard was outside in the hall.

Did he even realize Dee was here? Had he noticed Edgar, unconscious in the next room?

The hand released from the door. There was a pause.

Henry began to hand Dee through the window to Shoemaker, when the shattering sound of wood splintering filled the room. The door came flying across the bed behind him. He turned back to see a large man with a shaved head and a cheap suit, gun pointed in their direction.

Henry instinctively moved in front of Dee to protect her. Gunpowder erupted in the room. The sound was deafening. Henry felt a bullet slice through his shirt and jacket. He let go his grip on Dee, trusting Richard to pull her out the window to safety.

When he looked to his friend for confirmation before confronting his attacker, he saw only blank eyes. A bullet hole was in Richard Shoemakers's forehead above his right eye. His head rolled back and Shoemaker dropped to the ground just outside the window. Dee fell limply, folded over the window ledge.

Henry fell to the ground spinning. While falling he reached his right hand into his coat and wrapped his hand around the grip of the gun.

The guard was quickly changing his attention between the window and Henry's form rolling onto the floor. The guard was unsure where return fire might come from, and he was hesitating to avoiding hitting Dee.

Henry used the man's momentary confusion to land squarely on his side, point, and fire.

The power of the handgun surprised Henry. It kicked back intensely. Richard had understated the power of this piece, just as Henry had understated his willingness to use it.

The bullet pierced the man's chest. His confusion turned to shock, then a wince, then a stare. He slumped to his back, arms limp.

Immediately following the blasts, Henry's ears rang. After a few seconds he again heard rolling thunder outside, more distant, and the sound of screaming coming from the main room in the house.

"Henry, what's going on?" Naomi's voice was panicked as it cackled into his ear.

"Shoemaker is down," he replied. "He can't help us. I need to drop Dee out the window. Somebody come take her!"

"Henry," Winfred said loudly, "the other guard heard the shots. He's coming in through the front door. I'll come around and pick up Dee. Get her out of there fast and get yourself out of there!"

Henry carefully picked Dee up from her position, folded over the window sill. One arm was under her thighs and one under her chest. He lifted her out the window, and seeing Shoemaker crumpled on the ground, carefully dropped her a few feet, down on top of their fallen friend. Her head landed on a soft part of his stomach and she rolled gently over on her back.

"She's out," he whispered into the device, "but I have to stay. This thing can't happen."

Henry carefully walked near the doorway, turned off the light switch, then backed into the room.

As the larger guard came running into the living room, gun drawn, he slowed down, unsure where the shots came from. Calmly he positioned himself to the right of the doorway that led from the living room to the den.

Inside he heard sobbing from a woman, and a consoling voice from Ellen Grandby Sullivan.

The man walked carefully toward the hallway and glanced around the corner into the den. Grandby was holding Janice Donnelly's head in his arms. He was whispering to her. The guard made himself visible to the Reverend by stepping slightly further into the doorway. From this angle he could also see Ellen and Joan. Ellen was stone-faced. Joan had tears streaming down, but her face was otherwise unemotional.

Grandby pointed to the back room. He fiercely mouthed the word "Go!", trying to avoid alarming Janice further.

The guard slowly crept toward the corner bedroom, out of sight from the adjoining hallway. He peered slowly around the corner and saw his partner sprawled in the hallway, blood streaking down his white shirt and puddling on the carpet. The door was splintered off its hinges and the room was dark.

He approached the doorway from the left side. If someone was waiting for him, it would be from the far left or far right. He saw the hallway light switch. He took an angle that would expose the right side of the bedroom when he turned on the light.

With the gun pointed to the corner he flipped on the hallway switch. The bright light exposed his partner fully, dead with his eyes open. Most of the bedroom was brightly lit and there was no one waiting in the corner straight ahead on the right. With his pistol ready to fire, he angled slowly toward the center of the doorway. On the bed there was no movement, just a still figure. He moved slowly to his right, and he noticed a wide open window, rain sweeping into the room. He moved to his right to see to the left, behind the door. He moved in quickly, ready to fire. There was no one in the corner.

He turned his attention to the window and crouched to approach it. From his jacket he pulled out a high power, compact LED flashlight. Without putting his head in a line of fire from anyone outside the window, he shined the flashlight outside in a sweeping motion. There was no reaction outside, no sudden movement. He slowly peered out the window. He looked first below the window, flashlight in his left hand and gun in his right. He saw two figures, side by side. The thin blond woman next to an older man with a bullet in his forehead.

The scene made no sense. Did the two fire and kill each other simultaneously? But the woman ...

Henry leaped from the bed, sweeping the blanket away with one arm. The guard made a quarter turn, but his gun hit the side of the window.

Henry plunged the knife under the man's chin, through his mouth and into his brain. The struggle was brief. Blood covered Henry's arm. The man went limp.

Adrenaline was rushing through Henry's entire body. He had never seen one person die, let alone three.

Snapping his head to the hallway, he heard nothing but the blowing wind and rain. Almost unbelievably, their plan was still intact. The tragic exception was Richard's death, but Henry could not indulge himself with regret.

He thought of Aisling's words. Important work remained.

"Psst Henry." It was Winfred, outside the window. "All okay?"

"Still in the game," he replied. "I got the other guard. Take her to Naomi. Quickly please."

"Get out now!" Winfred was furious.

"This job is not finished. We're almost there, buddy. Get my girl to safety."

He remained still, ears alert, while considering his approach toward the remaining Grandbys. Suddenly a piercing, agonizing pain engulfed his left arm. Henry howled in pain and looked down. A thin, long knife with an ornately carved pearl handle jutted from his bicep. Indazita was in the hall, angry that his shot missed its mark.

Indazita pulled another knife from his belt, this one shorter but wider than the first. He began to rush toward Henry.

Henry's knife was still in his hand, sticky yet slippery from drying blood. His left arm was useless, the knife still protruding outward. He released his grip on the knife in his right hand, crouching as he faced Indazita. From his belt he pulled the revolver. He pointed it at the smaller man, whose eyes widened as he continued his charge.

With the knife less than a yard from his face, Henry pulled the trigger. The man's throat opened up in a dark red torrent. He spun and fell, stunned. On the ground he reached for his throat, gurgled and writhed. In a few seconds he stopped moving.

Henry sat on the bed gasping. He inhaled deeply and with one motion, pulled the knife from his arm. He wiped it off on a bed sheet and tucked it in his coat. He did the same with this own knife, slick with blood.

With his gun securely in hand, he moved to the hallway. He looked into the adjoining bedroom where Edgar was still on the floor, not moving. He slowly moved into the living room, watching carefully for any sign of movement. He heard sobbing and whispering to his left.

This must be where they were planning the ceremony.

Carefully, fighting pain and exhaustion, he approached the doorway so as not to be seen or heard. He listened. It was Grandby's voice, speaking calmly and soothingly. He heard sobbing.

With his gun leading the way, he stepped into the doorway. He saw Grandby holding Janice, with Ellen and Joan nearby.

"So what's it gonna be? Your guards are dead. Your lame little Samurai is dead. Edgar is out. Dee is safely out of this hell house."

Ellen Grandby Sullivan pulled on the back of Joan's collar. A long shiny knife appeared at her throat.

"Drop the gun, Henry, or she bleeds to death a little at a time, right in front of your eyes."

From within Surveyor Hall, Aisling and Hildegarde impatiently watched as Sau sat in the booth, showing no sign that he was in a state of deliberation. From their vantage he was impassive, unthinking, unresponsive.

The two were far from unoccupied, however. Aisling connected Hildegarde to the war raging on the shores of Lake George. The two maintained a dual existence between the two scenes. They were prohibited from physically interfering in such a vital series of events, and Aisling had already pushed the boundaries by encouraging Henry to intervene in the ceremony. Henry was her understudy and events were in his hands. Hildegarde agreed, her sadness and alarm apparent.

They watched wordlessly as Henry rose to the occasion to cut down one attacker after another. Despite her determination to remain dignified during the battle, Aisling pumped her fist each time Henry eliminated a threat. They cried when Shoemaker died, and shared the same vow to take a very personal interest in his next life choice.

With each conquest by Henry on the earthly plane, in the ornate house at the edge of the meandering mountain lake, the struggle in the ethereal plane began to wane. The scaled reptilian combatants fell one after another, and those that remained in the battle began to retreat into a defensive posture. The fight was far from complete, but the various legions of paragons, led by the fierce archangels and followed in stride and gesture by warring angels, were surrounding their wayward combatants.

The end seemed near. Hildegarde exhaled.

"Aisling, I think we need to pay a visit to our friend Immat. This has gone on long enough."

"Well, I managed to do it once but it wasn't easy," Aisling said. "I hope you don't need my help in ..."

Before Aisling could finish, Hildegarde waved them both directionally across a vast space. In an instant they were outside Immat's door.

"Really?" Aisling was not pleased. "Do we get hernias in our level? Because that's what almost happened to me getting here the first time."

"Yes, well, sorry about that, my dear. I felt you needed the practice."

Aisling shook her head and smiled.

Hildegarde pounded on the door. "Immat, we need to talk." She entered Immat's space, sweeping in Aisling behind her.

This commanding spirit, experienced across many centuries and through countless lifetimes and conflicts, was broken. He leaned over the expansive view of the conflicts raging below him, and he cried.

"Old man," Hildegarde said gently, "did you really believe this could work? Were the greedy desires of this group of phony Christians really so compelling, so convincing, that you could not say no?"

He lifted a weary head. "Their argument was strong and my judgement was weak. I sought to prove that I could make up for past mistakes with one sequence of events that would be driven by the powerful religious figures of this time.

"All of that death," he said through a weak voice, "for what? They made enemies of friends across the globe. They destroyed countless lives, and I did nothing to stop it."

"This time you meant well, but it seems the one lesson you have not yet learned is the most important one. The end does not justify any means." Hildegarde spoke the words compassionately. "The journey is *about* the means."

Immat bowed, prostrate with grief.

"It is not my place to judge," she continued, "but the Elders explained there were safeguards in place to prevent your weaknesses from recurring. Did you forget?"

Immat was surprised. "You knew about that?"

"Yes," she smiled. "Immat, you are looking at two of them. We could have helped you but you chose to make your own path, without the advice of others. There has been so much needless suffering borne by our brothers and sisters on the ground."

"Why did you not stop me?"

"The decisions were yours to make. Just as we are not permitted to interfere with the choices on the earthly plane, I was not permitted to interfere with yours. We only became aware of them because of Aisling's connection with the one at the center of this conflict."

He nodded and looked at the scene unfolding near the lake and in the battle still raging above it.

"What is to become of me?"

"That is for the Elders to decide," Hildegarde said. "For now you need to release your grasp."

"I have no control over them," he said. "Our plan has failed. I never controlled their actions. I just offered my services."

"Then you can call off your minions. These energies need to cease."

He nodded and turned to the scene below. He focused his energies on the serpents and other forms of spirits who were in a mighty struggle above the house.

In Old Persian, he commanded his servants to retreat and return. The battle stopped. The rain, thunder, and electricity that hovered above this portion of the long northern lake moved up and away.

"We wish you well in your future labors, whatever they may be. It is never too late to be reborn, but your time here is complete."

Immat vanished.

The thunder became a low, soothing murmur. The lightning rose into the sky, no longer flashing downward, but outward. The winds calmed.

Drawing strength from encroaching peace outside the window, Henry was calm as he pointed his gun between the eyes of Ellen Grandby Sullivan.

"Ellen, it's over. We can all walk out of here without anyone else getting hurt. Put the knife down."

"I will not," she answered defiantly. The knife pressed deeper into Joan Swenson's throat.

"Ellen, I don't want to kill anyone else. I've ended the lives of the two guards and your Asian midwife. If this continues, you or your father will die tonight, perhaps both of you." He waved the gun toward Ernest.

Ernest Grandby grabbed Janice Donnelly by the shoulders, thrusting her in front of him.

Henry trained the gun back on Ellen. "This is going nowhere. It's over."

"Oh really?" Ellen smiled at him. "It's over when the Grandbys SAY it's over."

Joan Swenson's face contorted. "Watch out, Henry!"

Henry felt a thump on the side of his head. It whipped sideways, taking his body with it. Through the pain of his pierced arm, his pistol flew into the corner of the den.

He fell to the ground dazed, but kept his vision enough to see Edgar raising a long piece of firewood down toward his face. He kicked his right leg as if it was a punch, catching Edgar in the stomach. The wind escaped Edgar's lungs and he hunched back and to the side, dropping to one knee. Henry popped to his feet and charged his full body weight into Edgar. The two were locked in a struggle on the floor of the living room.

Joan Swenson was quick to capitalize on the confusion of the moment. She pushed Ellen's arm away, then with both hands grabbed the hand holding the knife. She bit down on Ellen's forearm, forcing her to drop the knife. Ellen climbed on her back, trying to drag Joan away from the knife, but Joan was able to get a hand on it. With a single sweeping motion, she swung the knife around behind her toward the chest of Ellen.

"OWWW!" Ellen shrieked, "You stabbed my tit!"

"You have plenty of money to buy another one." Joan stood over her, knife held high. Ellen Grandby Sullivan laid on the ground, flailing in pain.

"Drop it, young lady." Ernest Grandby was holding Henry's gun. He had it pointed at Joan Swenson.

Joan noticed something unexpected, a large read dot on the side of Grandby's head.

From the other room he heard a voice. "Hey Reverend!"

Grandby looked toward the living room. Suddenly the red dot turned into a cluster of laser dots pointed directly toward the man's eyes. Grandby arched back and covered his eyes, blinded by the beams.

Winfred Harding was pointing a device directly at Grandby. "Learn some Braille, bitch!"

Joan picked up the gun and ran into the living room where Edgar was getting the best of the struggle with Henry. Blood was gushing from the wound in his arm and his eye was swelling quickly. Edgar was raising a fireplace poker, in preparation for a finishing blow.

The gun blast tore off one side of Edgar's face just below the cheekbone. He fell back, writhing in agony but unable to summon more than a loud, painful groan.

Within minutes, local police and county sheriffs filled the house. After ensuring that all threats were under control, they began to systematically interview all survivors. A Washington County Sheriff's deputy approached Joan Swenson.

"Are you Joan?" She nodded.

"Sorry we didn't get here sooner, but thanks for staying in touch with Detective Lacey. That'll make it a lot easier to keep these people in custody, since we know that Federal charges are waiting for them back in Boston."

Henry managed to call across the room to Winfred.

"Really, buddy? Lasers?"

"Hey man, you go with what you know."

After answering all the investigators' questions, each of the Grandbys was led away in custody in separate police ambulances.

In the crush of authorities combing through the scene, Henry found Dee on the porch, wrapped in blankets. She was conscious but groggy. A female detective was completing her interview.

Henry turned to the detective. "Can we be alone for a few moments?" The detective nodded and left them.

"I always knew you'd find me," she said. "I never lost hope."

"That's my girl," he answered, wrapping his arms around her. "If it wasn't going to be in this life, it would be in another."

"Maybe," she said, "but I'd rather be your wife than your sister. Or your brother."

EPILOGUE

The media ravenously attacked the story of the fall of the leaders of the famed Church of the Tortured Christ, the most successful Evangelical Christian organization in the past two decades. In the immediate aftermath, the hungry public was eager to learn details around their fall. Every media outlet offered multiple angles on the story, from the church's humble origins to its rapid ascent across the US and well beyond.

The Grandby family, and many who worked directly for them, were widely blamed for violence and discontent in many regions through their covert influence on elections, insurgencies, and assassinations. When they fell, it was as though a grip had been released on politicians everywhere. Stories of their payoffs, bribes, and brutish tactics were shocking to the many millions who held them above suspicion for so many years.

And then there were the heroes of the "Showdown in the Adirondacks." News networks and web sites probed high and low to learn about the unlikely heroes who brought the church to its knees, and their supposed metaphysical tools. The term 'Origenist' was rarely mentioned without accompanying descriptions that included shadowy and secretive, depicting them as a splinter group from traditional Christianity. Curiosity about their beliefs moved in waves across the online world, with web sites popping up by the day that explored the history of reincarnation in the Christian faith.

Henry Chimera, as the one person with a view into the church, the Origenists, and even into the heavenly reaches, was a target in high demand from all media outlets. Eventually he was forced to hire a security firm, allowing time to piece his life back together with Dee during her recovery.

Over time more dignified requests for interviews were presented, so Henry enlisted the help of a media agency to determine which time demands should be accommodated. A strategy was developed that would not avoid the attention, but instead selectively capitalize on the high demand to build credibility for both himself and for the Origenist's belief system.

He deflected the attention about his psychic skills at first, but gradually came to understand that misinformation was rampant about his profession, If he could build a profitable career in a dignified, honest way, there was no reason to resist. He invested time on higher profile interviews to reach the widest possible audience, including more respected television talk shows and National Public Radio. He made it a goal to grant half his interview time to smaller media outlets, broadcast and online, that would benefit from the boost brought by his interview. His agency sought to balance his exposure while keeping public interest high.

For stories about the Origenists and their unique belief system within the larger context of Christianity, Henry enlisted the help of Winfred Harding and Naomi Pike as his spokespersons. The absence of David Herbrit and Richard Shoemaker was difficult for all to come to terms with, but Winfred and Naomi eagerly took on the challenge. Both mainstream and Christian media outlets clamored for their views of the world, and they explained it patiently and with great passion.

As the media clamored for information, Joan Swenson and Janice Donnelly became largely reclusive. When they granted interviews, it was together with a media representative closely controlling the conversation. The two shared a luxury condominium in downtown Boston that offered privacy while they concentrated on the healthy delivery of Janice's son, free from negative influences of any kind.

Over time, Janice came to terms with the truth, that the people she trusted in the aftermath of her husband's death were the ones responsible. In her grief she turned to her church, but in the end it was the same church who seduced her after murdering her husband.

Joan Swenson remained thankful that instead of running from these dangerous people as she was inclined to do, she stayed close by to be a living angel for Janice Donnelly and her unborn son.

International outrage over the murder of the Dalai Lama was fierce. The international community eagerly watched as the US justice system took on the task of ensuring fair, efficient, and speedy trials that were planned for Edgar Grandby, Ellen Grandby Sullivan, and Ernest Grandby, in that order. The trials were not televised, but the press congregated outside the courtrooms, breathlessly reporting every new development.

In a jury trial at the Massachusetts District Court in Boston that stretched just beyond two weeks, a disfigured, bandaged Edgar Grandby was convicted of First Degree Murder and Conspiracy charges in the disappearance and death of John Donnelly and of the Dalai Lama. The jury deliberated less than two hours. He was sentenced to two life sentences without the possibility of parole at the federal penitentiary in Canaan, Pennsylvania.

The prosecutor chose a jury trial for Ellen Grandby Sullivan on Conspiracy charges for her involvement in the two deaths. She was cleared in the death of John Donnelly due to a lack of direct evidence, however she was convicted of First Degree Murder in the death of the Dalai Lama. She was sentenced to life without the possibility of parole at the US Penitentiary in Hazelton, West Virginia. Her jury required almost two full days to arrive at their decision.

Ernest Grandby waived a jury trial, and in a Bench decision he was convicted on fourteen separate Conspiracy charges, but was cleared of a Manslaughter charge in the death of the Tibetan holy man. The presiding judge chose to apply the maximum sentence for each Conspiracy charge for a total of 280 years, which was to be served at a federal prison in Allenwood, Pennsylvania.

The most common talk show pun was a cheap one that involved speculation over whether the many life terms of the Grandby clan would be served over the course of multiple lifetimes.

The Church of the Tortured Christ ceased operations as a worldwide entity. Its domestic and international assets were valued by an independent auditor hired by the US Justice Department, and they were sold separately in a process that required more than two years to complete.

The assets received in the sales totaled more than four billion dollars. An elaborate claim process was developed to reimburse church members who could prove their contributions. The remainder was parsed among secular charitable organizations whose focus was on poverty relief.

The turmoil wrought by Immat over the selection process was mostly limited in scope to his own future. He was given the opportunity to become a soul like so many other souls, searching for his pathway to the truth through a series of lifetimes on earth. He found a circle of supportive souls and restarted his journey as all did, by studying his past and learning from his most recent successes and failures.

Sau was unfazed by the bizarre series of events that knocked Immat from his perch. Following events on the terrestrial plane, he determined that a life as the Donnelly boy would offer little in the way of soul development.

He chose a life as an Autistic boy growing up in Poland in the middle of the twenty-first century. His timing was fortunate in that children with Autism spectrum disorders would be viewed differently than in past generations. In all societies in recent years, the potential contribution of such children was considered to be extremely limited, however during this time European psychologists began to question this assumption. As a result of their work, specialized schools emerged that began with the premise that each such child had the potential of possessing one or more specialized gifts that might prove highly valuable. In the right setting these gifts could be not only be uncovered, but nurtured to great effect through careful education.

The human incarnation of the spirit Sau, this imperfect boy in Poland, would develop into a world-renowned expert on the structure and function of the human brain. His work would forever change human understanding of this vital organ, and would have a profound effect in the treatment for many forms of brain abnormalities, including depression, Post-Traumatic Stress Disorders, seizures, and even blindness.

The soul who assumed the life of the Donnelly boy would live his eighteenth life, this one his first as an advantaged American. His life would be a relatively easy one, but he would be exposed to a world view that he would not have seen in so many other lives on earth. It would serve him well in his many future lives.

Yangsi, the process for finding the reincarnated soul of the Dalai Lama, would take the High Lamas across Tibet on a long, sad journey. Ultimately the signs would lead them to a four year old boy living in the mountain township of Biru. The boy was extraordinarily gifted and appeared to have all the makings of a Lama who would be a great spiritual leader in the Gelug school of Tibetan Buddhism for many generations to come.

As a direct result of the profound courage shown by Hildegarde and Aisling in their struggle for the fate of souls, Hildegarde was promoted into Immat's position as a Power. She would be responsible for assessing the available life scenarios for souls ready to reincarnate, which required a careful, balanced touch to ensure each soul had full control over its destiny, where the risk of regression was limited.

Hildegarde relished the challenge, promising to implement a transparent process that promoted learning and growing at all levels, including her own.

Aisling was rewarded for her bravery through a promotion into Hildegarde's role as a Principality. She would be responsible for accepting the array of lives selected by her understudy, who was yet to be found, and consulting with the waiting soul to choose just the right life option for the development needed.

During her acceptance speech to those gathered in celebration, she wondered openly about her replacement.

"My preference would be my dear friend Henry, but his lingering life presents somewhat of an obstacle. Perhaps he'll become a TV medium! That should shorten his life because then *everyone* will want him dead!"

Hildegarde smiled and some angels laughed wildly, but the other high spirits in attendance did not appear amused.

Following the fall of one of the most new and powerful churches in the world, the result of their quest to gain control of the dizzying notion of rebirth, Christian churches around the globe began to reexamine their long-held beliefs on reincarnation. Debates over the place for reincarnation in the Christian world began slowly but did not quiet even after many months.

A new, progressive pope, the first leader of the Catholic Church from Africa, announced the formation of a Third Vatican Council. The reasons given for the Council were to bring church teachings closer to the perceived intentions that Christ himself spoke of, particularly in the areas of redemption, forgiveness, humility, and simplicity. The church was clearly looking to go back to its roots by revisiting many of the reasons for the popularity of Christianity in the first few centuries following Christ's death. In doing so, they reasoned, they could move the church closer to New Testament principles that were so attractive to the developing Christian flock.

While the pope nor his staff never openly mentioned reincarnation as a key agenda item in Vatican III, it was widely assumed to be a cornerstone concept that they could not afford to ignore. The challenge of the council would be to reconcile current notions of reincarnation with the church's traditional standing on the Holy Trinity. They were fully aware that this work would take decades.

Several weeks after the news of the fall of the Grandby clan, there was a knock on Henry's door. A rumpled detective stood at the door with an elderly couple on the sidewalk behind him. He spoke forcefully to the security agent who answered the door.

"I'm Detective Oliver Lacey from the Waltham Police Department. I'm here to see Henry. He knows me. Tell him Lacey has some people out here who would really like to meet him. Tell him I said it's worth his time."

The guard nodded. "Please wait here."

Within a few seconds Henry emerged, offering a handshake. "Hello Detective. I didn't think I'd ever see you again."

"You probably wouldn't have, at least for a while. Looks like you've had your hands full, being a celebrity and all."

Henry smiled. "So Detective, you've been in touch with Joan Swenson this whole time."

"Thanks to her. Keeping tabs on you guys has been a lot more difficult."

"None of us were sure who to trust," Henry said. "I kept expecting you to throw me behind bars."

"I knew you didn't commit any crimes. The problem was, we had nothing on Donnelly's murder. You were all I had, and you didn't give me much to go on."

"There were times over the past few weeks when I thought jail would be the safest place for me. But I chose another strategy, and it all worked out the way I planned it."

Lacey waved to the couple to join him. "There are some people here who'd like to meet you, Henry."

The guard stepped aside as the three visitors followed Henry into the parlor where Aisling and Henry had changed so many lives.

He invited the three to sit. Dee emerged behind Henry in the doorway, curious about their visitors.

Lacey smiled. "Henry, I'd like you to meet Lucas and Hannah Chimera."

Henry's eyes opened wide as he processed the words.

"Did you say *Chimera?*"

"I did," Lacey said. "Lucas and Hannah believe they're your parents."

The man and woman had tears in their eyes as they tried to smile.

"How can that be? I was told you died years ago!" Henry's expression showed doubt and anxiousness.

The older man spoke. "Some powerful people wanted us to go away, so we did. They didn't give us a choice. It was a matter of leaving the country without you or going to prison. Keeping you was not an option for us. They assured us they'd find you a proper home. We've lived in grief our whole lives. I only hope you can forgive us."

Hannah Chimera, with tears flowing, spoke in a shaky voice. "We've missed you so much, Henry."

Henry moved to them, hugging both. They stayed, hugging in tears, for minutes.

Lacey excused himself and left the house quietly.

The couple explained how they had fallen into the habit of dealing marijuana in the years before the birth of their children, but stopped before the children came. In a tragedy that tore apart their world, their older son Freddy was killed by a hit and run driver. Hannah heard the sickening sound from her kitchen, then ran out to find her son's lifeless body on the side of the road. She called 911. While she and her husband were racked with grief, they were appalled when the Sheriffs turned on them. They did so only after it was clear Hannah could not describe the car that hit their son. Their investigation went from questions about the hit and run to their past involvement in dealing pot in northern El Paso County.

Evidently the Sheriff's Office was aware that Lucas was a low-level pot dealer, and even had tried to set him up for an arrest on more than one occasion, but the attempts failed. Lucas suspected the authorities were after him, so he completely stopped the illegal side business. At the time of Freddy's death, the Sheriffs probably believed Lucas was still a drug dealer. Rather than take the chance that the grieving parents might ask for a full investigation into the boy's death, they obtained a warrant to search the Chimera property.

In all the years since their children were born, the one decision that cost them the most was to hold onto a small supply of marijuana as an insurance policy if they ever ran into hard times and needed cash. The police brought in drug-trained dogs who easily found about a half pound of marijuana wrapped tightly in plastic in their basement.

The sheriff's office presented the family with a heart-wrenching choice: go to prison or leave the country. Making their decision even more agonizing, Sheriff Mahon personally delivered the news that their son Henry would not be allowed to leave the country. In a matter of days, they would go from a happy family of four to a childless couple forced out of their country of birth.

They chose to allow Henry, still shy of his second birthday, to live freely in the United States without them. Sheriff Mahon personally guaranteed that he would find a safe, loving home for their son. It would be with his sister in Massachusetts, who merely wanted a playmate for her daughter Delilah.

The Chimeras held out hope that by choosing to move to Mexico, they might still have a chance to return to the United States to find their son. They made a life in the port city of Manzanillo in the state of Colima. Lucas built a business as a seafood distributor to some of the larger cities in Mexico. Over time he was able to establish distribution to cities in the southeastern US, which allowed him the chance to travel legally into the US as a Mexican citizen. During these trips he would quietly try to locate his son.

Using the information that was available on the web and an occasional trip to Colorado, he was still never able to find any trace of Henry. He had vanished, and years ago the couple had come to accept the fact that they would likely never see their surviving son again.

Then the dramatic news of the fall of the Church of the Tortured Christ splashed across the airwaves. Hannah immediately saw the name of the hero at the center of the story. Henry's decision to change his name from Stark to Chimera only a few months before was a blessing for all.

Over the next few hours Henry filled his family in on his upbringing, the various foster parents he endured, and the odd set of events that brought him back to his earliest and fondest memory, Delilah. The older couple alternated between tears of joy and sadness as he told them his life's story. He assured them that his upbringing was fine, that he learned to live with his circumstances and how to survive no matter what challenges his way.

Henry vowed to keep the Chimera family together. He would use his credibility and leverage to help his parents reestablish their residency within the US. It might mean legal actions to have documents unsealed, and perhaps even suing the city of Colorado Springs or El Paso County, but Henry was prepared to take whatever actions were necessary to restore his parents' status as legal US citizens.

The funeral for Richard Shoemaker was painful for the Origenists, and it was made worse by the attention they received from the outside world. The members were not accustomed to being in public with one another, and initially avoided eye contact or conversation of any kind. As the service moved along and the Catholic priest, a long time friend of the Shoemakers, lightened the mood with some stories of his own about Richard's upbringing, a sense of togetherness came in to this house of God.

Following the service, Henry noticed that Delilah was more quiet than the others. Holding her hand while asking if she was okay, she said quietly that she didn't know how to talk to her friends when they were not in hiding.

"Would you mind if I pull them together? I think your friends really need each other right now."

"How? Where?" She had a look of near panic.

"Let's invite them to Aisling's house this afternoon. I'll pick up some beer and wine, and maybe we can order some pizza."

"I doubt you'll get anyone to come. None of us are used to that kind of gathering."

"Well, you all should get used to it. There's no one to hide from any more, plus it's only a few miles from here. If we don't round them up now, it's going to be really hard to see them together again."

He forced her to point out the members, then one by one Henry went around to each, selling them on the importance of staying together. One by one they agreed to come over.

By the time the wine was uncorked and the beers flowed, there were more than thirty people in the house, including spouses and some children.

"It would be a shame to lose such an important collection of people," Henry said loud enough for all to hear. "I know you've all been through some terrible losses recently, but you've come so far! You won the battle, and it was against a fierce, powerful opponent."

"Thanks for the help on that, Henry." Winfred Harding raised a glass in Henry's direction. The others joined in.

Henry nodded and continued.

"The hard work is behind you, where you had to live in secret. Now it's time to do your work in the daylight. People care about what you think. You guys need to get together regularly, just like this. How about the first Saturday of every month, in the afternoon? I'll put together the first agenda and we can rotate. We need a path forward, including a mission statement. Let's talk about how we bring new members on board. You guys are in the papers, and everyone wants to know what you stand for. Capitalize on it!"

"You sound like you're lobbying for office as the new organizer, Henry." Winfred smiled as he ribbed his friend.

"I'm happy to organize, but I don't deserve to be your leader. I'll put together an agenda for our first official meeting in the open."

Henry found a sheet of paper and asked each to write down their contact information. He promised to share it by email before their next meeting.

When their guests were gone and the house returned to its peaceful, majestic state, Dee clasped Henry's hands.

"Thanks for keeping us together Henry. You're the only one who could have made that happen."

With his thumb he wiped a tear from her eye. She smiled, the first smile he had seen from her in weeks.

Through a literary agent, a large New York publishing house contacted Henry with a generous offer for a book deal. The offer included near total freedom in how he chose to write the book, and he chose to co-author it with Dee. The deal also including a choice of authors to perform the actual writing, with Henry and Dee having the first cut at editing. On the cover of their book they insisted on including their surrogate author. Despite the publishers' reluctance, they managed to include her name along with theirs but with a title for what she truly was: the Ghostwriter.

The book was an enormous success, and money would not be a concern for Henry and Dee for the rest of their lives.

Dee and Henry married in a joyous, memorable ceremony on Martha's Vineyard exactly six months after she was freed from her captors. His father, Lucas, was his Best Man, and Hannah embraced Dee with her whole heart as they worked through the details of the wedding. The two became like school girls in preparing for a great celebration.

The Chimeras used the occasion to bring family together who had not seen each other in decades. Nearly all the Origenists attended. Henry invited a collection of friends from his days working for others. Even his bosses from *Finders Keepers*, Ryan and Shelly Keefe, attended. They teased him about finally using his experience at the dating service to find his own soul mate.

When they were finally alone in their honeymoon suite, a quiet cottage that would give them a perfect view of the sunrise, Henry snuck behind Dee and buried her in his arms, surprising her.

"Do you think it's okay for us to live a normal, peaceful life?"

"You mean like with a house, kids, a minivan, and all of that?"

"I'm not sure about all that," he said, "but at least a life where you and I can wake up every morning, make love, and do whatever we want without worrying about who's watching."

"I could get used to that I think," she said with a sigh.

About the Author

Bernard Buckley was born in 1959 in Glens Falls, New York. He moved to Colorado in 1977, where he met Teresa (Terre) Picillo at the University of Colorado in Boulder. They married in Orange, New Jersey in 1983, then were blessed with three children, Benjamin, Kyle, and Carlin and, as of this publication, three wonderful grandchildren.

Bernard has spent decades working for financial services firms, mostly in technical project delivery roles.

Over the years, Bernard and Terre have fostered many, many animals through Terre's long time affiliation with the magnificent Dumb Friends League.

Bernard now lives in Highlands Ranch, Colorado, where he can be found spending time with his family at every opportunity, working at his day job, writing, playing "fetch" with his tripod mastiff, skiing, biking, hiking, playing softball (just win, Taco Stop!) and playing tennis.

Medium High is his first novel. His web site is www.BernardBuckley.US.